ROAN

THE TALES OF CONOR ARCHER
Volume 1

by

E. R. BARR

TELEMACHUS PRESS

This book is a work of fiction. Names, characters, places and incidents are either the product of the author's imagination or are used fictitiously. Any resemblance to actual persons, living or dead, or to actual events or locales is entirely coincidental.

Cover designed by Telemachus Press, LLC
Cover art:
Copyright © Thinkstockphoto/101159968/Hemera
Copyright © Thinkstockphoto/113145880/iStockPhoto
Copyright © GettyImages/Thinkstockphoto/87766077
Copyright © Thinkstockphoto/931162221/iStockPhoto
Copyright © E.R. Barr/Labrador Retriever
Published by Telemachus Press, LLC

http://www.telemachuspress.com

Visit the author website:
http://www.erbarr.com

ISBN: 978-1-937387-65-5 (eBook)
ISBN: 978-1-937387-66-2 (Paperback)

Version 2012.10.01

Printed in the United States of America

10 9 8 7 6 5 4 3 2 1

REVIEWS

E.R. Barr's novel holds one's attention as he weaves his tale like an Irish bard of old. As his story unfolds, it becomes more convincing because of his obvious familiarity with the setting in which the adventure takes place. He describes the river and its environs with such vivid and yet foreboding detail. Barr's knowledge of religious tradition and ritual adds to the authenticity of his story which turns out to be not just a mystery but a venture into the murky world of fantasy and ancient myths.

William Schwartz

ROAN is a riveting Celtic mystery set in modern times that seamlessly blends Celtic legends with present Wisconsin topography.

Michael Kurz

As Conor Archer tries to uncover his ancestor's secrets, E. R. Barr creates a splendid and fascinating story where Irish lore and Conor's world become inseparable. Barr creates a suspenseful tale that you will not want to put down.

Renee Lynn Johnson

What a tale! The characters pull you into the story from the first page. It's an amalgam of present day and Celtic mythology. I could not put it down. Way cool!

David Berger

This story has something to capture the hearts and imaginations of all--a classic tale of Light versus Dark, fought amidst an eclectic backdrop of old world lore and new age technologies. Our hero suffers the usual trials all people struggle with as he grows into his own, but his courage must be greater, for there is a frightening yet remarkable transformation he must embrace if he is to survive. The adventures, characters, and moral undertones in this book combine for a thoroughly enjoyable, exciting experience!

Mary Beth Hampton

TABLE OF CONTENTS

Prologue	i
At the *DerryAir*	1
At Buckingham Fountain	10
At Death's Door	14
Going Home	19
A Gathering Crowd	23
Of Monasteries and Medicine	28
Dreams and Visions	31
At the *DewDrop Inn*	36
The Healing	41
Piasa Restless	48
Whispers in the Dark	51
The Sons of Cate	55
A Chance at Friendship	61
A Walk in the Dark	64
Aunt Emily	68
Oz	74
Planning a Funeral	84
Of Lies and Misdirection	89
Dr. Nicholas Drake	92
The Smell of Starlight	95
Out and About	101
Ashes to Ashes, Dust to Dust	107
The Forsaken	113
An Irish Wake	117

Drake and the Devil   121

Buried Dreams   126

Trouble's Story   130

The Hunt   136

At the Crossroads   148

DIOGENE Rises   155

More than a Friend   159

Hatred in the Heart   163

Summer into Fall   170

Underwater Panther   176

Beyond Dreams   179

October Country—The Fight   186

October Country—The Song   199

October Country—The Story   205

The Living Memory   216

Jason Goes Fishing   220

What Conor Found Out   232

A Fateful Afternoon   242

The Wisdom of Jace   247

The Unmasking of a Riddle   253

A Lesson Unlearned   260

An Unexpected Passenger   265

Sight Amidst Blindness   269

Confession—Good for the Soul   272

Night Visions   277

The Plot   280

The Harvest   284

Decisions   289

Conor's Angst 292

Discovery 297

A Vision in the Water 300

Cate and Drake 308

Dort Martin Gets a Conscience 311

Threats 315

Conor and Emily 318

The Harvest Continues 325

Hangin' from the Old Oak Tree 330

The Flight of the Swans 339

Fear 345

The Closing of the Web 349

The Plan Moves Ahead 353

Father and Son 357

The Worm Uncoils 366

The Abbot and Drake 372

Rise, Men of the West 375

Soul Searching 382

Panic 386

A Rift Among Friends 389

In the Belly of the Beast 393

Break In 399

Escape from DIOGENE 405

What Dort Did 409

The Pooka 417

Flight to the Crossroads 426

The Jace Race 429

To the Crossroads   436

Hangin' on the Crossroads Tree   440

Jace to the Rescue   444

Aunt Emily's Ride   449

A Meeting of Worlds   451

The Passing   459

Conor on the Hangin' Tree   464

The Fight at the Crossroads   472

The Flight of the Morrigan   482

The Battle at the River   484

The Raising of the *Gwennan Gorn*   491

At Last to Fly   498

The Battle Begins   503

Chaos on Shore   506

Piasa's Lair   509

From the River to the Sea   516

Home to the Sea   526

An Evil Strike   530

Where the Waters Flow   534

Places to Go   537

Epilogue   540

Sources   543

About the Author   545

ACKNOWLEDGMENTS

Thanks Mom and Dad for giving me a love of story.

Thanks to my brothers and sisters for their encouragement.

*Thanks to the wonderful folks at Telemachus Press for their expertise
in editing and publishing a novel.*

*Thanks to the One for creating the magical place that marks the junction of the
Wisconsin and Mississippi rivers—a land of wonders waiting to reveal itself ...
down by the river where the waters flow.*

WHEN ANGELS FELL,
SOME FELL ON THE LAND
SOME ON THE SEA.
THE FORMER ARE CALLED THE
TUATHA DE DANAAN—
THE PEOPLE OF THE HOLLOW HILLS;
AND THE LATTER ARE
THE ROAN—
THE PEOPLE OF THE SEALS.

ANONYMOUS FROM THE ORKNEY ISLANDS

ROAN

THE TALES OF CONOR ARCHER
Volume 1

THE BALLAD OF WILLIE ARCHER

Oh, as I was a-walking down by yon mill-town,
The fair and lovely mountains they did me surround;
I spied a pretty fair maid and to me she looked grand.
She was plucking wild roses on the banks of the Bann.

Well, I walked up to this fair maid, and to her I did say,
"Since Nature has found us, to me come this day.
Since Nature has found us, won't you give me your hand,
And we will walk together on the banks of the Bann."

Now it being a summer's evening and a fine quiet place,
I knew by the blushes that appeared on her face.
Her feet they fell from her on a sweet bed of sand,
And she fell into my arms by the banks of the Bann.

She said, "Young man, you have wronged me;
Won't you tell me your name?
So that when the child is born I might call him the same."
"My name is Willie Archer and you must understand
That my home and habitation lie close to the Bann.

"For I cannot marry you, for apprenticed I'm bound
To the spinning and the weaving in Rathfriland town,
But when my time is over I will give you my hand
And we will walk together on the banks of the Bann."

So come all you pretty fair maids and take warning by me—
Don't go out a-courting at one, two, or three,
No don't go out a-courting so late if you can
Or you'll meet with Willie Archer on the banks of the Bann.

Old Irish Ballad

PROLOGUE

"JUDAS PRIEST!" SWORE Walter Johnson, "Damn brandy's goin' to be the death of me yet!" Wrenching a hook out of the fleshy part of his palm, he spat into the darkening twilight. He heard the gob hit the river, reached for his bottle, poured just a tad on his bleeding hand and took another deep drink.

"The mist," he muttered, "comin' in fast." He watched the fog creep from White Creek into the main channel of the Wisconsin River. At night, the mist often collected around the river bottoms, sloughs, and 600 foot bluffs that made up this section of the great United States. This night was no different. The fog never rose from the great rivers. It always started in the backwaters and small creeks that fed them. As the mist crawled over the banks of the tiny tributaries, it made its way down to the rivers Wisconsin and Mississippi, just like it was doing this evening.

Walter knew this was going to be a very foggy night. He imagined the ranger at Wyalusing State Park just south of Prairie du Chien, where the rivers ran together, had already radioed over to Iowa's Pike's Peak State Park [named by Zebulon Pike who paused on his way west and figured he wouldn't get another chance to name any hill so high] and claimed that by midnight the tips of the bluffs would be the only feature the stars would reveal.

Dipping his fingers into the bait pot, Walter grabbed another moldy cheese ball and stuck the hook through it, correctly this time. Just love fishin' for the Great Cat, he mused. Lots of big catfish in the river, but not one worth catching except the silver beauty he had stalked since he was a kid. Must be over a hundred and seventy pounds by now. Its silver skin shimmered luminescent in his dreams. Like the mystical fish from the old country, Walter was sure the Great Cat would bequeath him wisdom, but more importantly, would give him status with the folk in Tinker's Grove.

i

Catch the Cat, he thought, and they won't think me a loser no more. He was obsessed. Thus, the fishing trip in the fog.

He figured he had about fifteen more minutes before he had to get off the river. Shouldn't really be here though, it being the entrance to White Creek and all. Everybody stayed away from this place. Haunted, holy, whatever one wanted to call it, most folks stayed away. Unexplainable things sometimes happened here. Bad things.

Not that he was afraid, mind you. Grandma Swift Deer, his foster-mama in the absence of his real mother, God rest both, told him that memories as old as the hills clung to the land and water around here. Earth and good old H2O were not ordinary in this part of the country. The water and the land—they remembered. Not like people do with thoughts that dart about like fireflies on a hot summer night. No sir. The memories were etched into the very landscape by Mother Nature, a sculptor with the patience of time. Each raindrop, every track of an animal or human, even a sliding pebble making its way to the river made its mark, and the place remembered. The southwest corner of Wisconsin and the northwest parcel of Illinois had a memory that stretched back farther than any of the lands in the northern United States. Walter remembered that from geography class oh so many years ago. This part of the earth had never felt the last of the numbing glaciers that crept across the northern states so long ago, wiping out the accumulated landscape of centuries like a stroke flattens the face of its victim.

"Walter, you hear me now," said the old Indian woman in Walter's mind. In fact, he could almost hear her voice whispering through the mist. "This land and the waters around it hold secrets, and us poor humans that walk and swim barely know the stories they can tell, or the mysteries they still hide."

He chuckled for a moment, wistfully, remembering Grandma Swift Deer, last Winnebago Indian in the tri-state area. Yep, thought Walter, she died when he was just eighteen. Sure do remember her, sitting on her porch in Tinker's Grove, signing postcards of her in her pretty bead worked costume. Man, she looked ancient of days. But she always had an ear to listen and wisdom to dispense.

Why that time she gave him some change to walk across the street to Mike Delahanty's service station, where the best soda pop in town could be found, she had some choice words for him. She didn't like him going over there; rather he had gone to the Burke Hotel. She thought it had a better clientele. He didn't think the same. Just a bunch of old toothless railroad men sipping coffee—Walt the kid felt really out of place there.

Spitting in the river again, he remembered. Couldn't have been more than ten or eleven, but more than he hated the Burke or loved the service station's ice cold Coke in bottles, he loved the rattle snakes that Delahanty kept in a wire cage right in the same garage where the cars were fixed. Always had six or seven Timber Rattlers hissing and striking and rattling. Cool stuff. He remembered the mingled smell of oil and gas and musty reptile along with the fear smell of the mice Delahanty had in a cage—lunch for the pets. Used to watch the help throw a mouse in, see it get bit and roll in pain, and then get snarfed down by the biggest rattler. There was the day he reached in and picked up one of the smaller snakes. Whipped out his knife and cut off the rattle. Old Mike never saw. But the snake—why it looked at him with green eyes, if you can believe it, green eyes! And he knew, even at that young age, what the rattler hissed. "Going to get you for that Walter Johnson. Going to get you for that." Heard the hiss in his heart, and it stayed there, in the dark places of his soul, waiting to haunt his dreams.

Grandma Swift Deer knew something had happened. Maybe she heard him jiggling the rattle across the street in one hand, soda pop in the other. Whatever, her eyes, her piercing black eyes, pinned him and drew him across the street where he sat down, mortified, at her feet on the porch stoop. That's when she told him one scary, bad ass story. That old lady could tell stories, right? Last of her tribe, she told what the land remembered and told what her ancestors said to her—how an evil manitou formed the Wisconsin River. Its names were many: Underwater Panther, Great Serpent; the Indians and the blackrobes who came to convert them called it "Piasa," the Devourer of Souls. Elemental evil. Evil with no purpose but to feed. The Indians called it that because it stole their children and their squaws when they walked too close to the river in the twilight. The black-robes, Jesuit priests mostly, saw it seldom, but when they caught its wake in the river, they flung holy water out from their canoes begging protection from all that was holy. The Indians called the thing bad medicine; the priests just knew that whatever swam there was mud ugly evil. "That's why you don't mess with its children, Walter." She had held out her hand, grubby with encrusted dirt. Shyly, with remorse, he had placed the severed rattle in her hand. She buried the rattle in a pot of geraniums next to her. Only time he thought of it before this night was the next time he visited her. The geraniums were dead; he was too scared to look for the rattle.

Taking another drink from Wisconsin's worst, but most easily available, brandy, Walter wondered why in the world he was thinking on all of this, meaning Piasa, granddaddy of snakes and vermin and all things that go bump in the night. The original bogeyman, at least to the Indians. He remembered a school trip taking him to see the pictures of Piasa the Indians drew long ago on the rocks overlooking the river. The beast had the head of a bear but its fanged face morphed from animal to human and you never really knew what you were looking at (so Walter had heard from the lips of Grandma Swift Deer herself), and on its head were horns that would put an elk to shame. Piasa's body wore the scales of a fish and though its legs were like those of a bear, they had no paws; instead, they bore the talons of some great bird of prey. Web-like wings clung to its back, but Piasa's home was the water and darkness for it feared the air and light. Walter remembered most especially the snake's tail with a bony spear point at the end. That horrific picture tormented his childhood dreams and even now caused a chill to rise swiftly up his back.

"Dammit, Walter, you keep drinkin' and you'll be forgettin'."

"Grandma?" said Walter running his free hand over his grizzled face. He laughed to himself. Mist playing tricks with his ears. He knew what she meant though. He didn't want to forget that the evil manitou first lived in the great forests up near what Grandma Swift Deer had called the Big Lake, 'Superior' by the whites. There came a day when Piasa wished to go to the sea. As it crawled across the land through the dark night of a new moon, it carved the Wisconsin River. Its huge tail splashed water over large areas that became the lakes and ponds that dot the central part of the state. Lesser manitous fled its advance, and carved smaller grooves in the ground that became the tributary creeks and streams that flowed into the Wisconsin River. In turn, the Wisconsin poured into the Mississippi which ended its long journey in the vast Gulf to the south. But the Winnebago Indians never said what became of Piasa. On certain evenings when the fog came, it was as if the manitou rose out of the water and snaked its body through the hills and bluffs. When the fog came, the night belonged to the mist and to a time thought long past.

Walter shivered again. Too late to be out tonight. Grandma Swift Deer was dead, Delahanty's was long gone as were the snakes, and the Burke Hotel was a shadow of its former self now that the railroad had vanished. Old memories just scare up ghosts, and he didn't need none of that tonight. He saw that part of the mist had made its way out of White Creek and into the Wisconsin toward the village of Tinker's Grove. The river made a little cul-de-sac here. On its north side, White Creek. South, where the fog now headed, there was a patch of sand where a stand of willows wept by the banks of the river. What little breeze there was still gently caressed the long willow fronds, their bright green-yellow leaves glowing in what was left of the twilight. Bleary eyed with a head as foggy as the night, Walter reeled in an empty line and put his earlier catch of catfish in the boat. The Great Cat had bedded down early for the evening. Like the wisdom it supposedly carried, it was elusive.

Time for another drink. He swirled the brandy around his mouth as if it was a fine, aged wine and listened for a moment to the willows whispering in the night breeze. Always sounded like they were talking. What was it the old Indian woman used to sing to him—some old Winnebago song about how the trees could talk?

> *The trees in the spring,*
> *Long to meet, long to meet.*
> *Gazing at each other,*
> *Wishing to touch, hoping to touch.*
>
> *And along comes wind,*
> *Blowing softly, blowing mild,*
> *And the trees in the forest,*
> *Bow their heads, lift their heads.*
>
> *The trees are in love,*
> *Hear them whisper, hear them laugh,*
> *The joy that they have,*
> *Makes them sing, makes them sing.*
>
> *But then comes the autumn,*
> *With its cold, with its pain,*
> *And the love of the trees,*
> *Leaves again, leaves again,*
> *to come again.*

Beautiful, he thought, looking at the two willows in the vanguard of the grove silhouetted in front of the advancing mist. The largest one stood in the middle of a mound of earth eight feet above the flood plain, and the smaller just off to the side. Walter had been here before; the Indian mound was in the shape of an owl. Could never figure out why those long dead natives built their graves in the shape of animals. Whenever he asked, Grandma Swift Deer just shook her head. He laughed. At least no damn scientist was smarter than him on this; no one knew.

With tendrils of mist creeping forward across the water, the trees had a faint golden glow to them. Like two crowns on a cushioned pillow, thought Walter. His eyes weren't that old and he swore he could see the largest willow bend its branches and twine them around the top of the smaller tree.

And by God, if it didn't sound like they were singing, just like in the song! Walter swigged another mouthful of brandy, shook his head and laughed again as the first strands of mist began to reach him. Time for this old man to go rolling home.

Suddenly, he heard a large splash out in the channel. If he'd been down Wyalusing way, he'd swear a rock just tumbled off the bluff into the river. But here, a little north and west, the Wisconsin River had not carved out such large bluffs. Here the bluffs were set back a bit from the water, and hilly land gently rolled down the flood plain to the water's edge. Perplexed, Walter thought it was an awfully large splash; but fog does funny things with sounds.

Then he saw it swimming. Big and monstrous, a hundred yards away from him. With the thickening fog, he couldn't see that clearly, but whatever it was headed toward the banks of the willow grove. Not very far from where he was.

A huge tail snaked out over the water and thumped the shore. Back and forth it raked. A screeching of wood under pressure, and then a thunderous snapping again and again. The thing was twisting and shredding the willows—except the two that Walter saw still glowing with an unearthly light, still untouched by the mist. A bellowing shriek split the night air, a frustrated cry of rage.

Normally not an easily frightened man, Walter was all for waiting to see the outcome of this strange sight. Until he saw the face. Whatever roared reared up in the water and turned toward him, green eyes glowing brightly. He could have sworn those eyes flickered in recognition.

Walter remembered reading in *Field and Stream* about a man torn apart by a grizzly bear. The man survived but said looking at the face of that bear as it came toward him was like looking into hell. Walter thought that hell might be preferable to this vision of a monstrous head that vaguely resembled a bear with horns. As the face came closer, Walter thought he saw scales on its neck. The mist was tangling all over Walter's boat by now, and still he was paralyzed with fear. He thought he heard the willows singing, and threw himself out of the boat, swam till his heart felt near to burst, then threw himself onto the bank, just as something heavy smashed into his boat and pulled it into the mist. Walter screamed and aimed himself to where the willows sang. Something moist and large crawled out upon the bank and followed him. He forgot he was screaming as he turned around and beheld the thing that pursued him. It towered over him, batlike wings framing a fanged snout. Morphing, the beast-like face took on the appearance of the old Indian woman as it opened a mouth full of rotten teeth and spoke, *"Mine is the life that is yours."*

Backing away on all fours, he saw the thing's tail rise and smash down towards him. He threw himself further up the bank and suddenly found himself out of the mist and onto the mound beneath the two remaining willows. The mist was a sick, luminescent grey around him, and he heard the singing of the trees. Shrieks of rage came out of the fog, but nothing broke into the clearing. Walter hugged the trunk of the smaller tree and sobbed. Nobody will ever believe me, he thought. Nobody will ever believe me.

AT THE *DERRYAIR*

HE JUMPED FROM the bus at the corner of Michigan and Monroe. Too slow, not going to make it to work on time. Gripping his tin whistle like a runner's baton, Conor Archer darted through the pedestrian traffic of downtown Chicago. Five blocks to go; three minutes to do it in. Music at the *DerryAir* was waiting.

Conor could see the bar from blocks away, one of those "authentic" Irish pubs beloved by Irish Americans and Celtic wannabes. Just enough Guinness on tap and enough lacquer on the tables to create the illusion of Ireland. Of course it helped that the bartenders and service staff were all Irish imports. Soft brogues could always be heard above the din of the crowd. A little bawdy like all haunters of the Magnificent Mile liked, but nothing too out of the ordinary.

Except Conor shouldn't be there. Too young by several years. But he got away with it for two reasons. He looked older; dark eyes, dark as the depths of Lake Michigan, beneath a mop of thick black hair. That helped but not as much as Fintan Carr's blessing. Fintan was the owner of the *DerryAir* and heard Conor playing on the street the year before for dimes, nickels, quarters and the occasional buck. He knew talent, so he asked the kid to play with the off-night band. When *Dun Aengus* wasn't performing, Fintan cobbled together a group called *Selchie* and had Conor play the tin whistle.

Still, he shouldn't be there—especially not tonight. Not on the day his mother was dying. They shared a flat on the South Side, near St. William's. As with most kids from a single parent family, Conor was fiercely protective of his mother.

Man, he hated cancer. Sapped her beauty faster than a sponge sucked up water. Finola had been a looker once; Conor kept a picture of her as a young woman in his bedroom, just to remind him that the wasted wreck on the hospital bed in the living room had not always suffered, had not always hurt.

As Conor understood it, his mother came from a little County Kerry town twenty years before, a single girl from Ireland without a penny or friend to her name. Came to the big city, and met a man there. Willie Archer was his name. She told him she had distant relatives in a little town named Tinker's Grove, Wisconsin, in the southwest part of that state. They went to visit. She was welcomed; Willie was not. And on an autumn day, he disappeared. When Conor was born a few months later, his mother took him to Chicago. She never returned to the little town in Wisconsin. The embarrassment was too much back then. Different times. Now she was dying.

"You're late, lad," growled Fintan from back of the bar.

"Sorry, man," said Conor, forcing a smile to his face. "Won't happen again."

Fintan glared at him. "Damn right it won't. You play tonight, then come see me tomorrow, and we'll see if there's a job waiting for you. You're a good lad, just not very reliable."

Conor slouched past him, not overly worried. Fintan could be brusque but he'd proven his worth to the bar owner over the past year. Without even thinking, he reached up and touched the plaque that hung over the entrance to the main bar. On it was written:

I ask and ask, but no one ever tells me,
What place we go when I meet Celtic music
And we are left a little while alone.

When he performed, Conor knew where he went—it was his little heaven on earth, just for a little while. People liked to hear him play. Off nights on Sunday weren't as empty as they used to be at the old *DerryAir*. Conor went over to the stage where the other members of *Selchie* were already tuning their instruments. It was the usual Celtic band with the expected assortment of instruments—fiddles, accordion, flute, a bodhrán, guitar, tin whistle. He didn't know his mates well, but that was not unusual. For years, he'd play in sessions in café bars or some of the downtown university hangouts that would tolerate young talent with whomever showed up on an evening. Didn't matter who played. It was the music that counted. It kept him focused and took him away from the problems of the day.

"Don't pay any attention to Finn," said Cecy, Fintan's wife. Third wife to be exact. Just entering her forties, she had a soft spot for Conor. She hadn't paid much attention to him when he first started showing up around the bar, but when he once mentioned to Fintan he had to go home early because his mother was sick, Cecy overheard. Fintan opened his mouth, no doubt to make a caustic reply, but his wife butted in. "Leave that tongue

silent, do you hear?" said Cecy, flipping her bleached blond hair towards
her husband. "The boy is just trying to take care of his family responsibilities. You leave him go." Since that time she'd always stuck up for him.
"How's your Mom tonight?"

Conor looked away. Guilt and grief crossed his face. Guilt that he left
his mother with the helpers from Hospice. Grief because she'd been the
only one that ever really cared for him and already he missed her. She'd
been dying for a while, but the fast approaching moment still sent shivers of
horror through him. "You're going to go play in the band tonight. I'm not
quite ready to say goodbye to you or this life yet," she smiled her weak
smile. "But when I'm gone you must go back, Conor. Go back home, to
where you belong, with folk of your own kind. You've got family there. But
enough of that—go play and enjoy yourself." That's what his mother said
to him not more than an hour ago.

Breaking into his thoughts, Cecy gave Conor a swift hug. "If you need
to get out of here early, just let me know. I'll make it right with Finn."

"Thanks," he said, grateful for an ally. "She's not doing so good, so if
it's okay, I will."

Conor and his mother had always been on the fringes of society. He
had little formal schooling though his mother had taught him much at
home. Things being what they were, he spent a lot of time alone. His
mother's impending death would put an end to that. A high school age boy
alone in a big city would soon attract attention. Unless he decided to
become one of the nameless homeless, the lost and forgotten. He couldn't
keep the apartment. He knew few people and had fewer friends. Conor was
seriously considering his mother's suggestion.

A tear coursed down his cheek, and he quickly wiped it away when the
fiddler said, "Conor, my man, you're so quiet tonight. Get that adrenalin
going. It's a small crowd but they'll be wanting some life in our music."

The young woman who supplied the voice for the group ruffled
Conor's hair and said, "Leave him alone. Can't you tell he's sad?"

"Yeah," said Accordion Player, "like his dog died or something."

"So did you, Conor? Did you lose your best friend?" asked Fiddler.
Voice and Accordion Player chuckled with him.

"Something like that," mumbled Conor. He didn't know why he didn't
tell them. They never knew her and he couldn't stand them fawning over
him just before he played, as they surely would if he spoke the truth. "Let's
just get playing," he said.

The sets began and the evening passed swiftly. The music calmed
Conor, his fingers flying over the tin whistle in a familiar caress. It was
during the third set, about ten thirty in the evening, when Conor noticed

him. The crowd wasn't large, maybe thirty or forty, plenty of tables up front. But the man sat in a side booth, face in shadow.

The people were into the tunes—clapping, shouting rather than singing the refrains, pounding their glasses of Guinness on the table with the beat of the bodhrán. But the man in shadow never moved. Conor's whistle lilted above the pipes and drum during the song 'The Wild Rover,' doing a free fugue rendition of his own. Yet, he stared at the stranger. He couldn't be sure—it was too dark where the man sat—but Conor thought the guy was staring back at him. An almost disembodied hand gripped the Guinness and lifted it to a near invisible mouth. As Conor and the band brought the slightly tipsy crowd to their feet with a flourish on the folk tune, the stranger drank. The boy could see the man wore leather pants and a leather jacket with metal clasps and rings—a biker to be sure.

"Conor," said Fiddler, "your choice. What do you want to play?"

The boy barely heard him, but clearly saw the hand of the shadowed stranger tip the glass towards Conor. "'Willie Archer'," said Conor, in a whisper. "You know—the one that goes with the tune, 'The Banks of the Bann'."

"Want to hear about your long dead relative, huh?" smiled Voice.

The song was obscure but told the usual Irish tale of a rogue wooing and wronging a woman and the inevitable child—the down payment of a hoped for, but swiftly lost, love. What was it they said, thought Conor, about Ireland? Oh, yeah—the place where all the women are beautiful and all the songs are sad. But he wanted to play it—for the stranger. Unseen eyes had sent a request, and Conor always tried to please the audience, even if the occasional requestor seemed a little spooky.

"You start, lad," said Accordion Player. "Forget the whistle till the end—you sing."

"Me?" said Conor. "I only play this. You know that!"

"First time for everything," leered Fiddler. "Your voice lost its virginity some time ago."

And so it had. Conor had sung for the band before. Just not this tune; but he was not about to lose face from this challenge. He managed a grin and said. "Let's go for it."

He stood at the mike. For the rest of his life, he would remember the moment. He thought he heard a distant church bell toll eleven o'clock. "Ladies and gents," he said, still grinning, fine white teeth shining under his raven hair and black eyes. "Here's a tune you haven't heard before, about a lady who goes out walking by the river and meets a handsome man she doesn't know but who smiles her into a terrible situation. There's a moral here ladies, namely, do you know who's buying you a drink tonight?"

The crowd laughed, and the band played. Conor's tenor voice sang clear and clean as he took the part of Willie Archer, lecherous rogue who seduces a young maiden down by the river. It was a story song to listen to, a cheerful tune with a mournful message.

As he sang, he stared in curiosity when the stranger stood. Conor could see him more clearly now, a powerfully built man. He wasn't tall but energy streamed out of him as he grabbed a passing bar maid and began to dance. She didn't object, and Conor couldn't figure out why. Caught up in a dare from the band, he had tried to steal a kiss from her a few weeks ago, but she had just smiled sadly and said, "When you're a little older, perhaps."

In fact, no one seemed to notice that the peculiar couple was dancing to the song, weaving between the tables. As the lyrics came to an end, the band picked up the tempo and began to reprise and extemporize on the main theme, breaking in to a reel. Conor grabbed his tin whistle and joined the impromptu improvisation.

The couple did not stop dancing. Faster and faster they whirled, two bodies in another world, noticed, it seemed only by Conor. He could see that the bar maid had a vacant look in her eyes, which, if they were focused at all, seemed fixed to the face of the stranger. Not a table did they hit, or a patron did they touch. The patrons and bar decor faded into the background. All that seemed to exist were the twirling stranger and captured bar maid. Magical dancing, thought Conor. And then, the music suddenly stopped—the tune was done.

The stranger unceremoniously dropped the bar maid into an empty chair, her chest heaving from the effort and her face looking mightily confused. Close to the band, the man stepped lightly towards Conor. The band members, used to admirers coming up to talk, took no more notice of him once they saw it was Conor he wanted.

"Ah lad," said the stranger. "That was lovely. Lovely and grand. You sang it and played it as I first learned it. Could I have a drink from your glass, if you don't mind?"

Bemused, Conor said, "It's just sparkling water."

Grabbing it, the stranger said, "Oh, I think not." He took a drink. "The water of life, it is. Have some." Thrusting the glass back into Conor's hand, he waited while Conor stared at it. "Drink!" he said, widening his eyes at Conor.

Beginning to dislike the bullying nature of the stranger, nonetheless Conor lifted the glass to his lips and drank. Stinging and burning Conor's mouth, the liquid almost made it down his throat before the boy, choking, spat it out on the floor. "This isn't water!" stammered the boy.

"Certainly it is," laughed the stranger. "Just not the kind you are used to."

"Look," said Conor quickly glancing around, "If Fintan, I mean Mr. Carr, sees this, I'm done for sure."

"Come on, lad, don't get squeamish on me. The boss is no where around. Drink!"

Conor, hoping to get rid of him, did as the stranger asked. He drank and felt his throat on fire.

Conor managed a small grin. "Never had this stuff before."

The stranger laughed, "Well now that's the truth, Conor, at least never in this world."

There was a buzzing in Conor's ears. "How did you know my name?"

"Just do, is all. Now give me that glass. You're right—far too young to be drinking all that." The stranger took the drink and downed it in one swallow. He ran his tongue over his lips, smacked them, eyes closed in pleasure. Then his gaze snapped open. Conor saw yellow sparks dancing in his eyes, almost lighting up his clean shaven face. "Want to see the world where this was made, little man? Follow me."

Conor managed to spit out a "Where're we going?"

But the stranger only touched the top of the doorway to the bar as he answered, "Who knows where we go when we listen to Celtic music?" And he laughed at his own wit, dragging Conor out the door.

Conor felt like he was moving through a fog. He'd had liquor before, a glass of Guinness here or there from some patron. Never cared for it though. Never affected him much either. But whatever he had sipped at the stranger's order must have been powerful stuff indeed. Conor didn't stumble, but he could tell things weren't very clear. It just felt like he was in a mist.

He could barely see the stranger ahead of him. And what was with those golden sparkles in the stranger's eyes? And exactly why was he following this guy? That's what the boy wondered. He was seventeen, big and broad shouldered for his age. With his olive colored skin, he definitely looked older and felt he could protect himself; but this was new territory. Still, he really didn't want to go back to the apartment just yet. He really didn't want to think about his mother. And there came the tears again, dammit. Wiping his sleeve across his eyes, Conor redoubled his efforts to keep up with the stranger.

After exiting the bar and walking north up Michigan Avenue, sparsely populated this warm August night, they reached the Tribune building.

"Let's take a walk down by the river, Conor," said the stranger. Without arguing, Conor nodded his head. Didn't feel like arguing or putting up a fight at all. Out the door and up the sidewalk, they walked in silence toward the Chicago River. This part of the river had a walkway, recently renovated into a boulevard where pedestrians could stroll and tourists, waiting for the ubiquitous Chicago Skyline/Lake Michigan boat trips, could board. Conor and the stranger walked down the steps toward the riverwalk, the dark muddy waters black against the streetlights.

Under the bridge, they paused. "Here it is, lad," said the stranger. "Water—not very good mind you, but water none the less." The biker leaned against a lamppost. The languid river slipped soundlessly by.

Conor could barely stammer. "What do you want? Why did you have me follow?"

"So I could talk to you, lad, that's why. So I could talk to you alone."

Probably, a pervert, muttered Conor under his breath.

"No, lad, not that. The ladies take too much of my attention. But I needed to talk to you, you see. Know why?"

It was hard for Conor to speak. His tongue felt thick. Though he saw the man clearly enough, everything around the edges was blurred. "No, why?"

"Why, you're one of the 'dark ones' lad," said the man coming close to him, breathing so hard that Conor smelled the Guinness clinging to him.

"'Dark ones'?" asked Conor.

"'Dark ones'," said the man. "Of the People, you know."

"Don't have a clue about what you mean."

"'Course you don't," said the stranger circling around Conor. "That's why I'm here. I always like it best near water."

"What the hell are you talking about?" asked Conor, by now afraid even though his brain was fogged.

"Gentle down, pup," said the man putting his hands on the boy's shoulders. "I'm not here to harm you, at least not much." He smiled, tiny pointed teeth gleaming in the street lamplight.

"What did you put into my drink?" said Conor.

"Nothing—it was just the drink, the *uisge*, the water of life, you know."

"No, I don't, and I'm asking you again, what did you put into my drink?"

"Ah, laddie, you would not understand if I told you. Just trust me that it won't hurt you a bit."

"So what do you want?" said Conor, slurring his voice more than he wished.

"Just your hand, lad, just your hand. I want to look at your hand to see if you're truly one of the 'dark ones.'"

"What's a 'dark one?'"

"Shush. Just give me your hand, your right hand."

Conor did not want to, but, almost unbidden, he felt his hand rise until the man grasped it in his own. He raised Conor's hand to the streetlight and spread his own fingers over the fingers of Conor. "A perfect hand, Conor, my lad," he said. "Except for that slight webbing between your fingers, just like mine."

Good thing it was dark, because Conor blushed. He had always been embarrassed with the slight deformation of his hands. Almost unnoticeable, but to a seventeen year old boy, the defect shone forth like the brilliant sun.

"There's nothing wrong with my hands. They play the tin whistle just fine."

"'Course they do, course they do," bobbed the man. "Didn't mean no offense. It's just that all the People have that mark. Like you; like me. Bet you don't have no problem swimming." The stranger's eyes glinted gold again as he laughed. "Let me take a more careful look." And the man pulled Conor's right hand close to his own face. He stared at it in silence for what seemed almost a minute and then looked at Conor, smiled that even, small pointed teeth smile, and said, "Yes, I believe you'll do just fine; you'll be a fine Roan bull."

And then he bit. Bit into the flesh between Conor's thumb and index finger. Bit long and bit hard. Conor screamed in pain. "Ah, man, what the hell are you doing?" He tried to pull his hand away but the freak just snaked his head along with Conor's flailing arm. Suddenly, the man let go and stood there smiling, red blood filming his sharp teeth. Conor moaned again, "Son of a bitch; you've wrecked my hand! Why? What are you doing?"

"Welcoming you, Conor," smiled the stranger. "Welcoming a brother."

Conor was bent over in pain. Blood was streaming off his hand. He shifted his eyes left and right. All alone; no one near. He was badly hurt, flesh torn, and who knew what else the stranger would try. No point in running. It would just mean turning his back on the guy.

But the man backed away, towards the edge of the walkway overlooking the river. He put his palms up and said, "No worries, boy. I won't do anything more. Seems like I've done just enough. Here," said the man, tossing a flask at the boy, "some more of that *uisge* you liked. Pour it on your hand and take a drink—it will make you feel better."

Conor grabbed for the flask with his left hand but it dropped to the ground and skittered away. Keeping his eyes on the man, Conor felt for it and touched the cool metal beneath his good hand. Silver. A silver flask. Too expensive to lose.

He pulled the cork out with his teeth and poured some of the liquid over the bite. It did take away some of the pain, though the bleeding didn't stop. He took a swig from the flask for good measure. The rest of the hurt eased away.

"Didn't I tell you, Conor, that the water is wonderful?" The man was balancing on the edge of the walk doing a passing imitation of Gene Kelly in 'Singing in the Rain'. "Oh yes, and my question before—Would you like to see a bit of the world where that drink came from?"

"Get out of here," snapped Conor. "Get away from me." He shook his hand and blood spattered on the ground. "You're a freak. I don't know why I ever followed you down here."

"Because your mother is dying, Conor, and your grief has clouded your judgement, that's why. And because you drank a draught from another world."

"What are you talking about? And how do you know about my mother? I'm sick of your mystery," said the boy.

"Welcome to my world, lad; welcome to the family."

Now it was true that Conor's hand still hurt, and his head was still foggy from the drink—powerful acting stuff it was. But he was sure that as the man stopped on the edge of the walk, his gold-flecked eyes, glinting with light, began to sparkle even more, and his smile became larger with longer teeth and the black leather coat and pants began to slick down, melting together. "See you, Conor. Get yourself back to where you belong. Be on the bus by tomorrow or you won't know who you are or where you are going." And with that the man executed an impossible back flip, eight feet high, and slipped like a knife into the Chicago River. He was gone.

AT BUCKINGHAM FOUNTAIN

TAKING A HANDKERCHIEF from his jeans' pocket, Conor wrapped the bleeding hand as best he could. It started hurting like hell again, and he sure wasn't going back to the bar. How would he explain all this? Cecy would fuss, and Fintan would bitch about the time he was wasting. Fortunately, Conor had stuck his tin whistle in his pocket, and already had his jacket on. Going back would simply raise questions in the already pissed off mind of Fintan Carr.

Conor climbed up the steps from the river back onto Michigan Avenue and headed south. He walked for a bit, past a rapidly thinning pedestrian crowd. Walking after midnight. Normally cool, but now, kind of frightening.

The fog in his head was not clearing, but his vision seemed changed and sharpened. He saw a rat skitter into an alley, and heard the sleepy coo of pigeons in the trees that lined the avenue. Never paid much attention to that stuff before. Yet, his mind could barely process what had happened. Already his hand was swelling, blood sopping through the handkerchief. He thought he should get to a clinic to get it looked at but he needed to get home and check on his mother. Hospice stayed late, but not much later than this.

Detouring into Millennium Park, he stepped onto the deserted concourse. Why he was aimlessly walking, he couldn't figure. Ought to grab the bus, or maybe splurge for a cab. That's what he was thinking but still his legs moved him ahead. Getting back on Michigan Avenue at the Art Institute, he kept going until he was parallel with Grant Park. At the Congress Hotel, he took a left towards the lake. He saw Buckingham Fountain, still lighted, still sparkling, and he thought he'd walk over and sit for a moment.

The beautiful round fountain, huge with its spouting water horses and lights which cast the water in different colors, was a peaceful place. The

barrier, three foot high wrought iron, was meant to discourage not prohibit. Glancing around, he saw no one, particularly no police.

Hot, he was hellishly hot. Stepping over the barrier he sat by the side of the water. He didn't bother taking his shoes and socks off; he stuck in his feet and plunged his wounded hand into the pool. The cooling water eased the growing pain somewhat. Then, he realized someone else was walking towards the fountain. A woman, tall and thin, bone-white her skin, black her single piece flowing dress. Made bold, perhaps, by his own flaunting of the barrier, she stepped over as well and sat near him. She didn't look at him but had her arms stretched up and behind her, unfastening a clip on her hair. He heard the snick as the clip let go, and watched as over a yard of lustrous red hair fell in front of her face and dangled in the water.

She began to wash her hair. Conor knew the strange folk that sometimes haunted the park. He'd seen them often, but he'd never seen her. The length of her hair fascinated him. She used no soap, just rinsed and rinsed the hair. Not able to clearly see her face, still he knew she was beautiful. Her pale white arms gleamed in the moonlight. She looked like a marble statue come to life. The woman bent her head close to the water. For a moment she didn't move. Then she began to hum a strange keening tune— no melody, just a sad and lonely sound. Her head began to sway in circles, counter clockwise, faster and faster, until with a flip, she tossed her hair behind her, into the air, where it fell down her back with a wet slap and clung to her thin dress. She looked at Conor with dark eyes, wide and liquid, as if to soak up as much light as possible.

She didn't say a word and the silence grew so uncomfortable that Conor lamely said, "Why are you washing your hair in the fountain?"

The woman smiled briefly like she was preparing to tell a secret but let it bubble back into the recesses of her heart. She only said, "And why are you soaking your hand, young man, putting your blood into this fountain?"

Conor jerked his hand out. Sure enough dark clouds of blood were slowly dissipating in the fountain's pool. "I'm sorry," he stammered. "It's just that I hurt it and the water felt cool."

"Let me see it," said the woman, walking toward him.

Why he didn't move, he could never say. Two strange people in one night was odd to say the least. But as she moved toward him, he gazed at her face. She had seemed a young woman bent over the fountain, but now, as she came closer, he could see the care worn lines on a face that had known both suffering and pleasure. "Let me see your hand," she said.

He stretched his arm out to her. Sitting by him, she held the bandaged hand. Gently, she unwrapped the bloody handkerchief and looked at the wound. Blood welled in the hand that cupped his, and began to drip again

into the water of the fountain. Conor heard her gasp slightly, and then she looked at him and said, "To heal this hurt is within my power but not within my authority. To do so will turn you from your destiny. Such pain to come." Tears began to stream down her face.

Weird, thought Conor, but he didn't say that. He was strangely moved by her care. And he didn't remove his hand from her grasp. "It's okay; I'll just go to the clinic or something tomorrow."

"You'll be dead by tomorrow," said the matron. "There's no medicine in any clinic or pharmacy that will fix this. The fool!" she muttered to herself. "He didn't have to do it this way. This way is too sudden, too … elemental."

"You know the man who did this to me?" asked Conor.

"I know of him, and what he tried to do to you."

This time Conor jerked his hand away. "What's happening to me? What did he do, and how do you know of it?"

"Did he give you something to drink?"

"Yes, here in this silver flask." She took it from him, twisted off the top and sniffed.

"Good. Listen to me carefully. Take a sip every hour or so, and like as not, it will keep you
alive … for awhile."

"Please," said Conor. "You seem to know something about this freak who did this to me. Tell me about him. Is he evil; is he dangerous?"

She laughed a cold laugh. "He changes things. He moves things along. But evil? No, he is no friend of the dark powers, though he traffics with them. Dangerous? Definitely. I will not say more—not yet. But here," she said, moving closer to him and grasping his hand once more. "I can do one thing to help you and perhaps save you for a little while longer. The stranger you met made you drink a draught from another place, another time, another world. As that will help you through this trial, so shall this." And with that she tore off a piece of her dress and bandaged his hand. "This will staunch the flow of blood and slow the change."

"What change?" asked Conor. Even as he asked he marveled at how she wrapped the cloth around his hand. It seemed to mold into his skin, and she fastened the end of the bandage with the clip from her hair. Conor could see it was enameled and had the picture of a crow or raven on it. The clip rested on his palm.

"Change? Ah, you will know soon enough. But what I have done here is only temporary. You are in danger." Conor looked around him and the woman croaked a laugh. "Not from outside, but what's inside you now." She looked on him with compassion. "Conor, Conor, to go through this on this night of all nights. How terrible for you; how dark your road. But hear

me well, you have little time now. What he has done to you is too sudden, too swift. You cannot handle it on your own. Get yourself to where the willows weep, and lay your body down. Do you hear me lad? Get yourself to where the willows weep, and lay your body down."

The fog around Conor's consciousness had not diminished but a sense of dread began to creep upon him. So strange, so incredibly weird, got to get away, he thought. But as the woman let go of his hand, Conor noticed how rough were her fingers now; no gentle touch here. And he saw grey in her red hair.

"Go now, child," she said and smiled. But no even white teeth were there as her mouth opened. Only gaps and blackened stumps. As she turned toward the water, her back bent, and she shuffled to the edge of the fountain, whispering. "I must rinse my hair again, and wash the guilt away." Thin age-blotched arms reached up and pushed her hair up over her head and down in front of her. She washed and wrung her hair; like blood, the red of her locks rinsed away. White was the color of the hair that fell over her face and floated in the fountain. And as she lifted up her head, she peered at Conor through wispy strands, water streaming over her wrinkled face, and she wailed, "Death stalks you Conor Archer, and even now visits the one you love most." She lifted up her stringy arm, and pointed with a long-nailed index finger. "Get you gone," she hissed. "Before it is too late." And as he looked on in horror, the aged crone collapsed into the fountain and dissolved in the mist and spray. All that was left was the dress she wore.

"Mom," whispered Conor. Running like he never ran before, his wet shoes squished on the pavement. The farther he ran from Grant Park, the clearer his head became. He saw a couple of cabs in front of the old Congress Hotel. He grabbed one and gave the driver his address.

The cabbie was a Pakistani and said in his broken English, "You look like you seen a ghost, man."

"I think I did," muttered Conor, "I think I did." But the bandage was real, as was the clasp that bound it tight. He looked at the picture of the raven and touched the enameled image. Immediately, the woman's voice came into his mind saying, not in the screech of the old crone, but in the soothing voice of the woman who had held his hand, "You have little time. Get yourself to where the willows weep, and lay your body down."

Whatever that meant, thought Conor. More pressing was the last image he had of that woman—her wailing about death. Hoping against hope, he urged the cabbie to speed it up. He had to check out things at home.

AT DEATH'S DOOR

THEY HAD A small two-bedroom apartment on the south side—Conor and his mother. The cab dropped him off not fifteen minutes after his strange encounter with the woman at the fountain. Running up the stairs of the three floor apartment building, he plunged through the door. Hospice was still there.

A nurse looked up, "Thank God you're here, Conor. She's not doing well." And, indeed, as Conor approached the hospital bed, set up in the sparsely furnished living room, he could see the pale face of Finola Archer. Her chest barely moved.

"Is she ..." said Conor.

"She's not likely to pass this night, but soon, soon. Father Morgan stopped by, prayed and anointed her again. He told her in that soft voice of his that she was all ready to cross over ... God and the angels were waiting for her now." The nurse had been there all evening. She looked tired. "I've bathed her, given her meds, and made her as comfortable as I can. If you don't mind, I think I'll go home. I'll be back early tomorrow morning." She passed a worn hand through her salt and pepper hair. She didn't even notice his bandaged hand.

"Thanks, you've done so much—go home and get some sleep. I can take it from here." Conor was grateful to Hospice. They didn't always send the same nurse, but the caregivers had all been great. Couldn't cure his mother but sure made it seem like there was some stability and routine in their lives.

"You get some sleep, too, Conor. I put a little soup for both you and her in the fridge. Why not heat some up now for yourself, before you go to bed?"

Conor nodded his thanks as he led her to the door. The sound of the door shutting made his mother moan. Finola Archer opened her eyes and smiled thinly.

"Home so soon? I thought you'd play till two or so."

"Nope, had to come home and see how my favorite girl was." He bent down to kiss her and smoothed her dark hair.

"What happened to your hand, Conor?" said his mother grasping the bandaged hand.

Conor winced, "Nothing Mom, just a little cut from work. Let me get you some water." Finola didn't say anything else about the wound. The cancer in her bones had wasted her flesh away. Stringy muscle knotted together her frail frame, parchment skin spread thin over her skull. She had been beautiful once, not even long ago. But the past year had been devastating. She was thirty-seven going on seventy-three. Most days now she was in a morphine stupor, but tonight her eyes were bright and alert.

"Conor, bring the water here and sit by me for awhile." The boy did as he was told. Gently he moved his mother's legs so he could sit on the bed. He was strong and well-built for his age, and the hospital bed sagged a bit under his weight. "You've grown into a man," smiled Finola. "'Tis for the best. You have your father's build, but my looks, thank the Lord and his Blessed Mother." Finola laughed lightly and then began coughing.

"Hey, Mom, drink this," said Conor, lifting the glass to her dry lips. For a moment, the faces of mother and son were together and the resemblance was striking. Sharply chiseled nose, dark hair, piercing black eyes— their fine features almost matched each other. His father had bequeathed his genetic background in the solid frame of his son. Conor had his mother's brilliant smile but, whereas his mother had once been beautiful, Conor was just coming into manhood; strength flowed through his face. And, had he only known it, the women who bar hopped and waited on tables at the *DerryAir* thought him quite good looking, if a trifle young for them.

Conor smoothed his mother's long hair over her forehead. She had a fever again. Finola spoke, "I may have been dozing but I heard what the nurse said. You mustn't worry, Conor. It's my time and we've known it was coming."

"Don't talk like that, Mom," said the boy, tears starting in his eyes.

"None, of that," she whispered, brushing a tear from his eye with the back caress of her hand. "There will be time for that later. We need to talk about your future, about when I'm gone." She took the cup from his good hand and set it down. Absently she reached for his right hand and felt the bandage. "Let me see this," and she lifted up the hand to the light and inspected the bandage. Suddenly, she sucked in her breath through her teeth as she caught a glimpse of the clip that kept the wrap together. "Who wrapped this hand?" Her voice was frightened. She snapped her eyes onto Conor's gaze. "What has happened to you this evening?"

He never could keep much from her. She had home schooled him all these years and knew him better than most mothers knew their sons. And so he told her, just the outline, but it didn't matter. Her eyes told him she was busy filling in the gaps. "I know her," she said, "and I know this cloth. Much as I hate her and what she stands for, she never lies, though she weaves the truth in a fog."

"Who is she?" said Conor, now truly frightened. "And how do you know her?" But his mother was silent, lost in a reverie from the past.

Finola seemed to be talking to herself and Conor bent to listen. "Morrie, Morrie, what have you done? Monster that you are, you betrayed me, gave me a life of fear and hiding, and now you touch my son, you dare to dabble in the life of my boy?" Her closed eyes flashed open, her gaze seeking Conor, "If she said you are in danger, then you are. If that wound from that man—and who he is I fear I already know—if that wound is as bad as she says, you must do what she demands."

"Mom, she told me to go and lay down by some tree—what the hell could that mean?"

"Not just any tree, Conor, the willow tree. Quick, go into the desk there and get the letter that's on top of the pile of papers." Conor hesitated. "Now!" said his mother "before I cannot speak anymore." As he moved to the old roll-top desk, Finola went on, her breathing labored. "Look up your Aunt Emily. She's been writing me all these years. Last week, she told me to tell you to come home to her after I'm gone. There's a letter she sent to you in the drawer of the desk." Finding it quickly, Conor brought it over.

"I didn't even know I had an Aunt Emily."

"It was for the best," said Finola.

His mother started gasping and he picked her head up and held her higher so she could breathe as she opened the letter. "She wanted it given to you when the time came. I guess that's about now." Setting the letter on the bed, he held her closer; she squeezed him tightly. He felt a renewed strength in her as she began to rock him back and forth. So amazed was he, that he let her hold him like she did when he was younger. Her voice was soft but strong as she sang,

Thou art no seal-cub round-headed and blue,
No fledgling of sea-gull greyish in hue,
*   Sleep my pretty one, Mother loves true,*
Thou are no otter-whelp coated and wry,
Nor the lean cow's little calf standing by,
*   O sleep, my pretty one, do not cry.*

When she had done, she whispered in his ear, "Over the weeks we said everything we needed. What's happened to you tonight is important, and it is not given to me to tell you more. You are in danger, but there will be those who will help you. How I wish I could be there for you, but my time is at an end. Conor, my son, my loving only son, take my body with you and keep my spirit in your heart. Do not be afraid—you'll never be alone."

And then she died. Right there, in his arms. She died with her eyes wide open and a gentle smile on her face.

In silence, he held her, for a long time. Sometime later, he felt a hand on his shoulder. He turned and looked into the face of the man from the bar. "Hello Conor," he smiled. "Keeping company with the dead, are you?"

Face bleak, Conor looked at the man and said, "She, she just died."

He pushed the boy aside and looked down at the body of Finola. He grasped her nightgown at her throat and made a fist. He was wearing those leather half gloves that bikers wear. Slowly he brought her up to his face, her head lolling backwards. Like an animal he sniffed her. Then he dropped her back on the bed. "You're right," he sighed. "Dead as dead can be."

A molten anger boiled up inside Conor. "You pig," he choked in rage. "Leave your filthy hands off my Mom." And he made an attempt to throw the man away from the bed. But the stranger was immovable. He smiled his tight smile with the small, pointed teeth.

He grasped Conor's wrist, the one with the hurt hand, and began to laugh. "Ah, you saw the witch woman. Such a nuisance she is. No matter, it will all still happen, just a bit more slowly." His index finger traced the spots where his teeth had earlier pierced Conor. "Nice bandage, nice brooch. Looks like you may have found a new girlfriend, lad." And the man began to laugh.

"Get out, you son of a bitch," said Conor. "Get out before I call 911." The man held his hands up in mock surrender. "No need to get surly, lad. I'm going. I just needed to see that she is dead, is all. Cancer, 'tis a terrible thing. And her being so pretty once, and all. Should've seen her when she was younger. A fetching lass, she was."

"Who are you?" said Conor, fear beginning again to knot his stomach. "And how do you know my mother?"

"We met once long ago. She spurned me, she did. Loved another. This is as close to her as I've ever been able to get since. Up you go lad," he said, as he lifted Conor to his feet. "Now I've got only you. Maybe you'll listen better than she did." And with that he strode past the boy and walked out of the apartment.

Conor shakily moved to the door and shut it. As he turned, he saw the letter that had fallen to the floor. Bending to pick it up he unfolded the paper. It was a handwritten note, single page that read:

Dear Conor,

If you are reading this, you now know that your mother is dying or has already passed. And there you are in that little apartment, all alone. If I was there, I would hold you tight, like I did when you were just a child, though you don't remember. When you are finished there, bring your mother and come home to me. There is a place for you here in Tinker's Grove. This is where you belong, where you were meant to be. Your mother wants this and so do I.

Love,

Aunt Emily

It was his only link to family. But first he had to take care of his mother. He called Sweeney's Funeral Home and told the on-call clerk what had happened. He and his mother had made arrangements some time before. He had every intention to take her back to Tinker's Grove. The undertakers knew what to do. They'd make sure she arrived safely; he'd take the bus. Before they arrived, he smoothed her hair one last time and kissed her on the cheek. But it wasn't the same. The hands that touched him, the arms that held him, the face that smiled at him—all were slack and limp. Whatever made up his mother was gone from this body. Only an empty shell remained. He waited till they came and took her, packed a few things, and then, as dawn was breaking, shut the empty apartment and took the city bus to Union Station.

GOING HOME

HE KNEW HE had a fever as he got off at Union Station, the dawn's grimy grey light just now stealing through the city. His hand was throbbing and his brow was sweaty. Starving, he found a McDonald's and snarfed a quick breakfast. Felt better. Got his ticket on the Greyhound for Dubuque where he could catch another bus to Tinker's Grove, Wisconsin. Hadn't been there since he was a child and had no memories of it. His mother hadn't been in the habit of talking much about it either. Must not have been a very happy place for her. Funny thing though. Virtually none of her family, supposedly present there, ever called or wrote. The Aunt Emily of the letter had never written before, to his knowledge, never sent a Christmas gift, never called, yet his mother said she was in contact with her for years.

When he was younger, Conor had tried to get his mother to tell him about his roots, but all she would say is that they were Travelers originally. Conor had looked that up once and saw they were the gypsy people of Ireland, the ones who used to be called tinkers—at least that was one of the printable names. Other than some vague stories about the old country, Finola had not given her son much background at all.

As a kid, Conor made up his own heritage. His family members were dispossessed nobles in Ireland, traveling the back roads, helping the poor. He was a pretty good storyteller and could even make his mother laugh with his tales. Yet, he was always a little sad that she wouldn't tell more. One day, not so many years before, he lifted his head up from his supper plate and said to her, "Mom, why are you so secretive about where we came from and who we are?" Without missing a beat, she put down her fork and pointed at his chest and said, rather severely, "Listen here, it's what's inside you that makes you who you are, not some dead ancestor. You're your own man, Conor, never forget that. You and I made it all these many years didn't we?"

And they had. Finola had worked in the dry cleaning store down the street for minimum wage. They got a social security check and she must have had some trust fund somewhere. They weren't well off, but they weren't dirt poor either. Conor's playing tin whistle on the streets for money was his idea, not her's. He just wanted to do something to help out.

These were his thoughts as he finished his breakfast and then climbed on board the bus that would take him to Dubuque. Not many folks going west on a Monday morning. Seats were half full. He hoped he could sleep. And indeed he did, at first. The bus wound its way around downtown Chicago and out to the Interstate. Through the suburbs it hummed. When Conor finally opened his eyes again, he found they had just passed Rockford and were on U.S. 20. As he looked out the window, sun striking the bright green corn fields, a biker passed by the bus. A familiar face looked up at him and the man's hand gave him a mock salute. The jerk from the bar. Conor watched as the man disappeared in front of the bus, speeding far ahead through beautiful farmland.

Conor had never traveled through northwest Illinois. Past Freeport, gently rolling hills began as the bus reached the only unglaciated portion of Illinois. In fact, northwest Illinois really belongs with southwest Wisconsin. Old land, very old land, untouched by the past glaciers and retaining its original form. As the passengers approached Galena, the hills rose up, hiding glens and valleys as the highway rolled toward the Mississippi.

Hardly anyone lived in these parts now. Once, Galena had been considered for the capital of Illinois. Ulysses S. Grant had come from there and 100,000 people welcomed him back from the Civil War. The whole area had been full of lead mines; most of the lead for the bullets in the Civil War came from these parts. But now the mines were closed. Every once in a while a farmer would fall into an old mine shaft when he was out hunting in his fields. Beautiful area, returning to pristine condition, and that's what Conor woke to.

Not that he could appreciate it much. He was feeling poorly. Sweat was pouring off his brow and he was grateful he had gotten a super-sized Coke at McDonald's. The cloth around his hand was tight; he could definitely tell there was some swelling.

Remembering the silver flask in his pocket, he took a swig of the strong drink. It helped some. Lessened the pain. As the bus pulled into the Dubuque terminal, Conor began to think he would be lucky to make it to Tinker's Grove. He couldn't see very clearly, and the driver of his transfer bus gave him a stern look as he boarded. "They'll be no drinking or drugs on this bus, son."

"No sir, of course not. Just not feeling well today," said Conor. He was thinking he should have changed his blue jeans which were pretty dirty and at least put on a clean shirt. He was still wearing last night's clothes, including the non-descript green polo shirt he always wore when he played at the bar. Probably smelled. His fever wouldn't help that one bit. Very few people on this bus. As a matter of fact, Conor couldn't figure out how the company made any money going to the podunk towns of southern Wisconsin. Prairie du Chien, on the Mississippi was the largest in the area at 5500 souls. But he wasn't going all the way to Prairie.

The bus left the Dubuque terminal, crossed the Mississippi again back into Wisconsin, driving up along the river past Potosi and through Cassville. Conor wiped his sweaty head, drops of liquid dripping off his hair. Sweet Jesus, he was sick. Cold too. He started shivering. Once he looked out the window and above the hills caught a glimpse of a white barn owl in the bright August sky. Sick as he was, he knew beauty when he saw it. Slumped in his coach chair, he stretched out his hand as if to touch the bird. "You are magnificent," he whispered. He had only seen them in the Lincoln Park Zoo. To see one soaring—it was like glimpsing through a window into heaven.

And then the bird fell. At least that's what it looked like to Conor. But instead, he saw it was plummeting in a dive. Closer it came, and as it leveled, it looked like it would hit the bus. In the last instant, it swerved, but its path took it past Conor's window. The yellow eye of the owl pierced him as the bird uttered a loud cry, clearly heard by all the passengers. People gasped as the white bird flew along side the bus; even the driver braked a moment.

"Imagine," said one passenger, "in the daylight, of all things!"

"Something strange here," said another, "that kind of owl should be brown this time of year."

Conor felt himself sliding into a mist of delirium, the glowing eye of the owl the only light in his fevered darkness. What the passengers heard as the owl's cry, Conor heard as a shout in his mind, "Follow!"

His gaze followed the owl as it soared above the hills. Funny, he thought, how he managed to see it, always ahead of him, never far away. The bird circled in the brilliant blue sky, and the darkness in Conor's mind blew away. "Look down," Conor thought it said. He did. Below him a river wound through the countryside. A rising in the earth, a mound of grass, covered dirt in the shape of an owl, caught his attention. On it two willows grew. *"By the willows on the hollow hill, healing waits for you, and we wait as well. Go there and lay your body down."* That's what he heard in his mind, as the owl tightened his circle around Conor. White wings enfolded him and he drifted.

The bus took Highway 35 at Bloomington and headed north, turning right on Highway 60 just after crossing the Wisconsin River. Almost home, but Conor was oblivious. His body was uncontrollably shivering now, clothes completely wet with sweat.

"Tinker's Grove," said the driver over the intercom. The bus came to a stop at Mary's Mobil—the typical combination convenience store and gas station. It stood on the ashes of the old Delahanty service station, burnt to the ground these many years ago. Mary's was the only fuel station in the entire town. "Tinker's Grove," said the driver again. He knew he had a passenger for that destination, that smelly kid from Chicago. Why the hell didn't he get up? Groaning, the beefy driver heaved himself up from his seat and walked towards the back of the bus. He saw the kid hunched over the seat and sneered at him. "Get up. We're at your stop. Come on, I got other passengers to think about." But the boy never moved. A twinge of concern hit the conscience of the man. He saw the kid was soaked with sweat. This was no hangover. Geez, what if it was something catching? Never mind, he thought, he had some of that hand sanitizer stuff in the front. He'd take a bath in that if he had to, but the kid had to get off the bus; the other passengers were getting restless.

The driver lifted the boy and half carried him down the aisle and off the steps. Opening the luggage compartment, he threw Conor's duffle on the ground as the boy stared vacantly towards the bag. He did mutter a thanks to the driver and stood until the bus drove off. Bending to pick up his bag, he only managed to fall forward, collapsing on the ground. Rolling over on his back, he stared in to the sky until it was blocked out by a dark brown face. A pink tongue lolled down and began to lick him. He reached out his bandaged hand and touched the head of a chocolate Lab. The dog bent his face down to Conor. "Help me," said the boy. "I'm all alone." The biggest brown eyes he had ever seen stared into his. He could swear there was a tear in one of them. And then the dog lifted back his head and howled the most mournful sound Conor had ever heard. Loss and grief, pain and sorrow, unspoken with words but understood by every living thing. And as the dog raised another mournful wail, Conor remembered the face of his mother, saw himself closing her eyes for the last time, felt her hand upon his cheek until it fell limp on the bed. And he wept.

The dog continued to howl until people looked out of the stores. The attendant at the Mobil station ran out. So did Dickie Bergin, proprietor of the *DewDrop Inn*, the only local bar. But it was Jim Warren, the bank president, just locking the bank who took charge. He dashed over as fast as his 60 plus year old legs would take him. He bent down and lifted up the boy's head. "Son," he said, "son, where are you from?" Conor opened his eyes and asked, "Is this Tinker's Grove?"

"Indeed it is," said the banker.

"My name is Conor Archer, and I've come home."

A GATHERING CROWD

JIM WARREN, THE banker, lifted up Conor's head. The boy was unconscious. Mr. Warren turned to the convenience store attendant, a high school girl named Beth. "Get some water will you—cold if you have it." Without a word, Beth ran back into the store. "And will somebody call the monastery and get the ambulance down here?" One of the bystanders followed Beth in to make that phone call. "And you, Troubles," he said looking at the dog, "stop that howling." The dog stopped a wail in mid howl, snapped his jaws shut and looked at the banker. "Well, go on now; go get the Abbot down here." Like a shot the dog was off up the road that led to the monastery.

Beth brought a glass of water and a wet wash cloth. She was a Michaels' girl, one half of a pair of twins, the other being named Jason, Jace for short. Gently, Mr. Warren smoothed Conor's fevered brow and head with the cool cloth and wet the boy's lips with the water glass. The crowd continued to gather.

"Who is he, Jim?" shouted someone. "Looks like a drifter, gang banger, bum maybe," said another. But the banker shut the growing questions down with a glare. "He's sick, he's hurt, but most important, he says he's the Archer boy, come home to us at last." That shut the crowd up, but only for a moment.

"You know what that means," shouted someone in the growing mass of people.

The grey haired ones in the crowd nodded their heads sagely. A mother or two gripped the hands of their tiny children just a little tighter. But nobody left, Archer boy or not. He looked pretty harmless all collapsed and sick on the ground, and he had to be cared for. That was their way. While all that commotion was happening, Beth had gone back into the store to fetch her brother who was sucking down cokes with his football pals, their afternoon practice done for the day.

"Hey, Mr. Warren," said Jace, "let me help you with him." And together they lifted Conor up and set him on one of the picnic tables that served for open air 'dining' at the store. Jace was big, no doubt about it. Mr. Warren didn't have to do much; the football center carried most of the load.

"Let me through, let me through," said a high pitched voice from the back of the crowd. Like a knife through a devil's food cake, she parted that crowd. An old woman, a tiny, old woman with a blackthorn cane, but spry none the less, appeared at the front of the gathered group of townspeople.

"Emily, no, please," said Mr. Warren standing up and blocking her view of the boy.

"Stand aside, Jim Warren, or I'll knock your bald banker's head clear into the next county. I want to see my nephew."

"He's feeling poorly, Emily," said the banker, "and I've called ahead. The brothers from the abbey are bringing the ambulance."

"Out of my way," she snapped and rapped the banker's shins with her blackthorn cane. He hopped out of the old woman's way, and even Jace, twice her size, looked cowed by her. Conor was moaning on the table, and Emily took to nursing him with the cold compress.

"This crowd your idea, Jim?" snapped the old woman to the banker.

"No, Emily, you know it's not. It's just not everyday the bus drops off a sick young one. And now that they know who it is, the crowd will just get bigger."

"Well, get rid of them, will you?" said Emily. "Can't have these rubber neckers getting in the way of the boy's oxygen. He's not going anywhere; they can come and gawk at him in the monastery infirmary tomorrow if they want. Now shoo them away."

"Yes, ma'am," said Mr. Warren, smiling inside. Old Emily O'Rourke was like a fountain of youth. Her sharp tongue could take fifty years off a man and make him quiver like a kid under that woman's scolding.

"Now folks," he began to the crowd. "The boy needs medical attention, and he's not going anywhere under his own power for awhile. Time enough for questions later, you hear me?"

"But he's the Archer boy, Jim."

"Look here, Dickie Bergin. I don't know what you'll be saying across your bar later tonight, but I don't care if he's Crazy Eddie Gehn come back to haunt us all—right now he's just a sick kid in need of a little help." The crowd laughed at that. Eddie Gehn was the local serial killer; over half a century ago he had served as the inspiration for one of Alfred Hitchcock's thrillers. Whatever or whoever Conor Archer was, he didn't look like he could hurt a barge fly.

"I'm just saying, Jim, that we ought to be careful here." Dickie could throw gossip around like the cow dung it was, and probably had to since he owned the local bar, the *DewDrop Inn*. Any info he could snag here would be grist for the chatter at his establishment for the rest of the day and into the night.

"Well, don't be saying anything, Dickie," said Jim. "Let's just take care of business here and be done with it." A siren started up above the town, the sound of the ambulance pulling out of the monastery garage. "Now you folks get on going about your business. No death, no blood here. Just a sick kid."

People genuinely liked Jim Warren, an honest man and a good banker. Sometimes that combination was hard to find, so his stock was high amongst the townspeople. Their curiosity was piqued but the man had a point. Nothing much more would be happening here. Ever so slowly, the crowd began to disperse.

"What about these two?" said Emily looking at Beth and Jace, lurking close to the table where Conor lay. Though they were twins they couldn't be more different. Both were startlingly blond, blue-eyed and good looking, but there the similarities ended. Beth was small, Jace was huge; just right for the football player he was. His sister was the outgoing one, laughing and smiling all the time. Jace was the shy one, except on the field where he gave the word "monster" a concrete appearance. Any aggression he had, he used on the field. Off it, he was just a teddy bear.

"Miss O'Rourke, let us stay," said Beth. "If he wakes up, it'd be good to have someone his age to relate to. He doesn't know anybody here."

"You mean somebody not as old as me," said Emily, a smile breaking across her severe features for the first time.

"Yeah," said Jace nervously laughing, "sorta like that."

The siren from the approaching ambulance drowned out the response Jim Warren was making, and when the doors opened a couple of black-robed brothers, the dog, and a white-haired, bearded, older monk stepped out.

"Father Abbot," said Jim, "how'd you and the dog make it to the ambulance so fast—I just sent Troubles up the hill to get you?"

The Abbot laughed, "That's his name isn't it—Troubles—wherever trouble is, he's there, even if it has to be two places at once. Emily," he acknowledged the old woman with a tip of his head and smiled at the twins. Then he looked at the table where the brothers were already attending the unconscious Conor. He walked over and the humor in his eyes faded to concern. "And so the lad has come home. Now it begins."

"What begins, Father Abbot?" asked Beth.

"Why everything, lass, everything."

Any outsider would see this whole scene as cryptic and strange. Monks running an ambulance service, a medieval monastery overlooking the town. But that would be because outsiders just didn't know Tinker's Grove, a truly unique little river town.

It's not so strange, really, having an abbey near by a town in southwest Wisconsin. The town is Tinker's Grove, after all. The old library held the old histories and newspaper articles. Settled in 1845 by a bunch of Tinkers—Travelers they called themselves. Gypsies they were; wandering folks of the back roads and by-ways of Ireland. For a while, they camped by the ocean shore. But even they starved when the land turned bad; they didn't know enough about the sea to harvest adequate food from it. They hopped a boat bound for America, forced onto it most likely by a nervous English landlord during the Potato Famine. Once here, they traveled across country till they found this place, a huge meadow surrounded by a forest of oaks overshadowed by a towering bluff, near the confluence of the Wisconsin and Mississippi Rivers.

Strangely, they did something Travelers never did—they settled permanently. Their priest came with them and he had connections with an abbey back in Ireland. Benedictines came—monks they were. Not many, but enough to start the abbey on the bluff overlooking the town. The abbey built a beautiful church that doubled as the town's parish. Some might think such a place was formal and fearsome, but it wasn't. The abbey held the town together; the monks ran a fine farm to support themselves. Some of the monks even taught in the local school and they ran a medical clinic and a small infirmary up at the abbey. There were just some Tinker traditions the people did not let go of and one of them was clannishness. The community stuck closely together. The people knew the monks well, and the abbey knew the secrets of the town.

"He's stable Father Abbot," said one of the monk EMTs. "We can move him now and have Brother Luke have a look at him."

"Fine, then, be on your way," said the Abbot. "I'll walk up later."

As the ambulance left, the Abbot turned to Emily. "When he gets better, you can come and take him to your home. I presume that you wouldn't have it any other way."

"Absolutely," said Emily. "He's my kin and I promised Finola I'd take care of him if anything happened to her, and it obviously has. A funeral home from Chicago called me not more than an hour ago and told me they were transferring her body here tomorrow. She passed away last night."

"You mean that boy lost his mother—last night? What's he doing traveling by himself and why is he so sick?" Beth's mouth stayed open with disbelief. "I mean, were he and his mother all alone in Chicago? He had to take care of all that burial stuff by himself?" Jace put his hand on Beth's shoulder. She was working herself up into one of her righteous rages.

Emily spoke softly, almost to herself. "I knew she was ill, terminally so, but I thought she had more time. That was so like Finola, keeping those things to herself." She turned to Beth and Jace. "I'm Conor's only living relative, so of course he'll come stay with me. Jim, you have to open up that bank again and sit down with me. I'm Finola's power of attorney and there's things we have to do before her body comes here. There's nothing I can do for the moment with Conor." She looked at the Abbot. "I know he's in good hands with Brother Luke. Call me though if things get worse. Otherwise, I'll be with Jim here and see what we can do about poor Finola."

And with that she took Jim Warren's arm and walked him across the street back to the bank he had locked up for the day. The Abbot looked at Beth and Jace in the now empty lot. "Taking a powerful interest in a stranger aren't the both of you?"

"He's going to need some friends," said Jace. "Guess he can start with us two."

"Doing anything now?" said the Abbot.

"Nope," said Beth. "Angie can look after the store, and if you don't mind how Jace smells now that he's done with football practice, we can walk you up to the abbey."

"Fine," said the Abbot. "Come on, Troubles, let's take Conor's new friends to see him." And the four took the road up the hill towards the abbey.

OF MONASTERIES AND MEDICINE

WHEN CONOR'S EYES opened again, he expected to see a dog drooling over him, but he was lying on a soft bed staring up at a human face, albeit dressed in the black robe of a Benedictine monk.

"Hey, Conor," said the face, "I'm Brother Luke and I'm the doctor here at the monastery. Going to take a look at you and see what's wrong."

"Oh, great," whispered Conor, "leeches and blood-letting and everything."

"You bet," laughed the monk, "but after that, we might give you some of that modern stuff just to make you feel like we're practicing real medicine. Hey, don't worry. I got my medical degree at Loyola. I haven't bled anybody for years. Now shut up and let me take your temperature."

The banter didn't disguise the concern in the doctor's eyes. Brother Luke was worried about the high fever and he knew that its source was in the bandaged hand. But every time he tried to touch the hand, Conor nearly leapt in pain. The hand was swelling and the visible finger tips were turning purple. The dark cloth seemed dry. It was the brooch, the raven brooch on the palm of Conor's hand holding tight the bandage that made Brother Luke hesitate. Whoever did this did it well.

"Conor, I know you don't feel like talking but can you tell me who wrapped this hand for you, and how did you get your wound?"

Just as he asked the question, the Abbot, Jace and Beth, and Troubles walked in.

"I'll not have the dog in here," said Brother Luke. Troubles woofed once in indignation and moved back to the doorway and lay down.

"How is he?" asked the Abbot.

"Just getting to that," said Brother Luke.

"I was bit," said Conor softly, "by a crazy man at the bar where I play the tin whistle. And a woman, crazy too, I think, wrapped my hand at Buckingham Fountain. She said I would be dead by midnight tonight, if I didn't get myself to where the willows weep and lay my body down."

Looking up at them, confusion in his eyes, he said, "Any of you have a clue what she meant?"

Brother Luke shook his head in disapproval and handed a silver flask to the Abbot. "I found this in his pocket. If he's been drinking it no wonder he's talking like this."

The Abbot opened the flask and smelled it. A memory of long ago came flooding into his mind. "I know what this is," he said. "Give him what is left, and give it to him now."

Brother Luke looked indignant. "I'll not give him alcohol in his condition. It will just make him worse."

"It's not just alcohol—it's something more."

"Well, at least let me unwrap this hand—what do you make of this brooch that's clasping the bandage together?"

The Abbot gently took Conor's hand. "A woman, you say, Conor, a woman did this for you?"

Conor whispered, "Yeah, as she was washing her hair at Buckingham Fountain."

The Abbot paled. "Brother Luke, obviously we have to release the pressure in his hand, but save the bandage, we must use it again."

"It'll be filthy!" said the monk, indignant at such a violation of hygiene.

"I doubt it will," said the Abbot. "Let's do the hand."

And the doctor took a metal basin, laid Conor's hand gently over it and unclasped the brooch. Conor bit his lip as his body arched in pain. Slowly, Brother Luke unwrapped the hand. He placed the bandage on the tray—it was perfectly dry and clean. If only the hand was. It looked terrible, swollen, purple. Teeth marks were clearly visible between the thumb and index finger.

Beth stifled a gasp at the ravaged hand but said, "Look at his fingers, there's webbing between them!"

"A common enough birth defect, especially around here," muttered the doctor. "Not quite important here and now."

Brother Luke gently probed the hand, but when he came to press gently on the fleshy part whatever clotting there was gave way, and a rush of blood and green pus flowed out. A terrible stench filled the room, and Conor uttered a loud cry. The monk held the hand over the basin while the Abbot held Conor's shoulders firmly and urged him gently to be still. "I know it hurts, lad," said the Abbot, "but without it draining, it will only get worse. Now Brother Luke, cleanse that hand and wrap it exactly as it was back in that bandage."

"But it's not sanitary!"

"I'm only going to tell you this once. He is beyond our help. You can make him more comfortable, but it is only temporary."

"Well then," said Brother Luke, "we'll have to get him to the hospital."

"Brother Luke," said the Abbot, "you are the best doctor in the area. If you can't help him, no one can, and believe me, no medical doctor on this earth can help this boy now."

"How can you be so sure, Father Abbot? You know I give you obedience in all things, but medicine is my field, not yours. Don't ask me to compromise treatment because of some babbled command by a crazy woman from the Windy City."

"I'm not asking you to violate your oath to the medical profession or me. I'm just asking for time. Give him an antibiotic and give me time, that's all I'm insisting on."

"Then what are we going to do?" said the monk.

"We're going to do exactly as he told us. We're going to take him to where the willows weep, and we are going to lay his body down. Now give him some of that drink in that flask. We'll let him rest a few hours, and when evening comes, he goes down by the river."

DREAMS AND VISIONS

"NO!" SCREAMED CONOR, awakening in a cold sweat. Lying on the bed in the monastery clinic infirmary, he sat upright. Someone had taken his clothes. The same bandage was on his right hand, but it was clear his hand, and the rest of his body, had been sponged clean. Looking toward the window, he could see the sun setting behind one of the bluffs opposite the monastery. With a sigh, he flopped back on his pillow. Just then, a wet nose jabbed into his face and a wet tongue lapped with concern. "It's okay, boy—just a bad dream I had." Conor ruffled the fur of Troubles, the chocolate Lab, who hadn't heeded Brother Luke's admonition to stay only at the doorway of the infirmary. Conor looked into the dog's eyes. "You're the first one I saw here in Tinker's Grove, so you get to know what I was dreaming about." In the August evening light, the Labrador's eyes glimmered with intensity.

"Sending me thoughts?" smiled Conor. "Okay, I'll tell you. In my dream, she's out there—this woman—by a fence post, standing on top of freshly fallen snow, wearing just a nightgown. I see a bedroom window not far behind her. She has walked from there, I think. She's not alone. She's carrying a new born child. A white owl, big—very big—lands on the post. She stretches out her hand and touches the owl's feathers. And then, the dream fades for a moment, and when I see again, she's running, running from something in the dark—a figure dressed in rags. A voice cries out in the distance: 'Finola, where are you? Finola, where have you gone?' And then the wind, and then the snow, and then the sounds of men shouting in the night. There's blood in the snow, down by the river. 'We cannot find her!' they shout. And I hear a scream on the wind—of triumph and then of rage. Kind of weird and freaky, don't you think, old dog, 'specially since Finola was my Mom's name?"

Conor turned away from the window and looked into the dog's eyes. "Doesn't make much sense, does it?" Putting his arms around the neck of the Lab, Conor buried his face in the dog's fur. After a moment, Troubles pulled back and licked Conor's face, but absently; he gazed ahead, through the window, and for a moment, the eyes of the dog met the gaze of a white owl perched on the fence post outside the monastery window. A message passed between them, in the language only the wild things know.

They found them there, Conor collapsed back upon the bed and Troubles with his head on the boy's chest. The Abbot, Beth, Jace, and Brother Luke had eaten a light dinner in the guest house dining room.

"I told you, dog, not here, never here in my infirmary!" said Brother Luke, tempering the harshness of his tone with a follow up smile to the dog. Troubles' tail waved back and forth slowly. The monk placed his hand on Conor's brow and frowned.

"Father Abbot," he said, "no matter that you think, I can't do anything more for him. His fever is rising. If you are still convinced in this mad plan to take him down by the river, at least let me come. Just in case. Just in case he needs some real medicine."

"Of course," said the Abbot. "And Beth and Jace, I'll expect you to help as well. We're not going far but we can only drive the truck so close. He'll have to be carried and we'll need a litter."

"Exactly where are we going?" asked Beth. She didn't worry about Jace's strength—he could carry anything anywhere, but herself wandering around the back sloughs of the Wisconsin river in sticky mud was another matter altogether.

"There is a place," said the Abbot, "still on monastery lands down by the river. A little hill is there and on it grow two willows, one large, one smaller. The Native Americans, the Sauk/Fox and Winnebago, held it as a holy place and indeed it is. Old burial mounds, they say, built by the Mound Builders, an even more ancient Native American race. I think that's the place Conor means."

"I don't know about that," whispered Conor, opening his eyes. But I figured out what the woman at the fountain was saying. I know it's part of an old song my mother used to sing, some old folk tune from around here jazzed up by some Chicago music guy in the 1920's. The song goes like this. And in a soft voice, weakened by his sickness, he began to sing:

There's a place I know,
Down by the River,
There's a place I know,
Down by the River,
There's a place I know,
Down by the River,
Down by the River,
Where the water flows.

My time is almost over,
My days are almost done,
What I've been has passed to memory,
Where I've run now matters none.
Take me to the light that fireflies keep,
Take me to the place where the willows weep,
And lay my body down, O Lord,
And lay my body down.

O take me there,
Down by the River,
O take me there,
Down by the River,
O take me there,
Down by the River,
Down by the River
Where the water flows.

"Geez, man," said Jace. "You've got a great voice. That's a cool song. You were right, a little bit of blues and folk mixed together."

Conor smiled a weak smile but they could tell the effort cost him. His eyes burned bright again with fever. "Brother Luke," he said, "I don't know if that antibiotic is working. Too many things about this are crazy. Am I dying or what?" he said.

Brother Luke turned his eyes fiercely on the boy. "Not if I can help it! Please, Father Abbot, let me get him to the hospital. It's a fever. We need different medicine to heal him and if necessary, surgery will fix that hand and cut out the infection."

Now the Abbot was a tall man, just on the cusp between middle age and elderly with a close cropped white beard. His usually kind eyes now flared with anger. "Listen to me, Brother Luke, and I'll not tell you again. What ails this boy is beyond the power of your medicine. Not all medicine, mind you, just the kind you practice." He softened his tone, "Don't get me wrong. You are a fine doctor. You mended Jace's arm last year when he broke it in football. You've tended each of the townspeople in their own particular illnesses, birthed their babies and stitched up their children's cuts. But this is beyond you. We must do as he was told, or we will lose him. And time is wasting."

"I'll do as you say out of obedience," hissed Brother Luke, anger reddening his face. "But if anything happens to this boy, it will be on your head."

The Abbot nodded and ordered Jace and Brother Luke to lift the boy out of bed and dress him back in his own clothes. He took Beth out to get the truck, Troubles following behind. When they returned, Conor was dressed but slumped, unconscious again, between the doctor and Jace. They carried him out of the infirmary on a stretcher towards the truck.

"Put him in the back. Beth and I have already spread a couple of bales of straw for bedding. We don't have far to go." The Abbot stepped behind the wheel of the truck with Brother Luke in the passenger seat. Beth and Jace rode with Conor in the back, the dog sticking tight to the side of the injured Conor.

Although the setting sun was partially blocked by the bluffs on the north side of the Wisconsin River, shafts of light still reflected on breaks between the hills. Sunset was close. But the Abbot was right. They hadn't far to go. They headed down a dirt road that wound its way switchback down the bluff the monastery was perched on. At its base the road ran straight towards a boat landing, but the Abbot turned left onto a path through a field. He drove about five hundred yards and then stopped.

"We walk from here. Not too far though." The Abbot smiled. "Good exercise but not too terribly exhausting." They placed Conor on the stretcher, Jace and Brother Luke taking the rear of the litter while the Abbot and Beth took the front. Carefully they wound their way through a meadow of grass and scrub. The Abbot angled for the river and as they got closer the ground got wetter. Troubles trotted ahead out of sight. They broke through the marshy land onto a much drier patch of ground and stopped. There, before them, not more than one hundred yards away, by the sandy banks of the river, stood a mound raised eight feet above the highest water line. It was in the shape of an owl. It was easy to tell its shape because the small willow trees around it, and near the river bank, had been flattened by something, some even ripped out by the roots. But the mound was left untouched. On the top of the mound stood a huge weeping willow tree. Not far from it stood one half its size. Grass grew on the little hill along with a beautiful orange flower known to the locals as Indian Paintbrushes. A shaft of setting sunlight briefly illuminated the place. The willow leaves glowed golden and the flowers fired a brilliant orange. But only for a moment. The sun fell behind the bluff, and the long summer twilight began.

"That was beautiful," said Beth. "Why have I never been here before?"

"Not many know of this place," said Brother Luke. "I've only been here once before."

"Someone or something visited recently," said the Abbot. "Those fallen trees still have fresh leaves on them."

"Whatever." said Beth "A favor's been done for us. The mound is much easier to see this way."

Jace whistled for the dog and then yelled out his name. "Where has that dog got to?" And then he saw him, sitting between the two trees, silently staring at them.

"This is a holy place, ancient and hallowed," said the Abbot. "When the monastery was built here, the first Abbot allowed monks to visit it and sometimes villagers. Many saw it once, but few came again. Fewer still come now. You'll see why. But I knew it had to be the place Conor was speaking of."

At the mention of his name, the boy moaned.

"He's getting worse, burning up again," said Brother Luke. "Whatever you plan to do, do it now."

AT THE *DEWDROP INN*

"I TELL YOU, I saw it!" said Walter Johnson, the unbuttoned long sleeves of his raggedy shirt trailing on the bar. He gestured with a beer bottle at Dickie Bergin who was wiping down the counter. His voice was loud and slurred after four beers. Twilight was falling outside and the bar was beginning to fill up. The place was nothing special. Like most southwest Wisconsin pubs, the *DewDrop Inn* had a generous bar space with stools, some nearby tables, a pool table, dart board and then off to the side a dining area—always open for business but most populated at the usual Friday night fish fry.

One of the newcomers walking through the door was Biker Man, who somehow had managed to find himself in Tinker's Grove. His muscled body was dressed in black leather pants and jacket. He snapped his head toward the bar as Walter Johnson said again for the umpteenth time, "I don't give a damn what you think Dickie, the Wisconsin River monster was real! Who'd a thought it? Our own little personal Loch Ness Monster!"

Biker Man sat down on the stool next to Walter. "Beer here," he said to Dickie. Everybody was staring at him. Walter, they knew, and had gotten used to his somewhat inebriated ravings when he deigned to visit the establishment, which was at least twice a day. But Tinker's Grove was a clannish place and strangers, while tolerated, weren't welcomed, especially strangers all dressed in leather. Walter looked at him with bleary eyes.

"Say," said Walter, "You're not from around here."

"Nope," said the man, "But your story about a river monster intrigues me. Tell me more."

Well, that was all Walter needed. He put his face up close to the stranger and breathed into him, "Shoulda seen it last night. Out of the water it came for me. Face like a bear with horns, tail like a scorpion, bat-like wings. Smashed my boat; nearly killed me." Walter looked defiantly at the stranger. "If you're just like everyone else, you won't believe me either."

"Can't say as I do; can't say as I don't," said Biker Man, smiling with his pointed white teeth. "Were you as drunk then as you are now?" Dickie snickered and some of the other patrons who heard grinned a little behind their drinks.

"Don't you laugh at me," said Walter sliding to his feet. Even then, his thin frame barely was tall enough to look the seated stranger in the eye. "Don't you patronize me. What did you say your name was?"

"I didn't, and I won't. You wouldn't remember it anyway."

Walter poked a thin finger into the biker's chest. "I don't like strangers, and I don't like you. Dickie, you ought to screen your customers better. This here's a number one class jerk."

The biker stood up and put his face close to Walter's. "Listen to me you sniveling snot nosed drunk. I think you were almost killed last night and you ought to thank whatever God you believe in that Piasa let you live."

Walter's mouth went slack. "Piasa? You know its name. How ..."

"Pizza?" said another bar stool occupant. "Is that what you're saying with that pissant Irish brogue?" The patrons began to laugh out loud.

"Pie-ah-saw, you fool," snapped the biker, giving the speaker a vicious look that shut him the hell up. "The Devourer of Souls, that's what the Indians and missionaries called it. Looks like you got to meet it face to face, Walter. What I want to know is why it let you live. Most folks who see it never see anything else."

Unfriendly as he was, the biker was the first person to take seriously Walter's story and the old man warmed to the attention eagerly. "Well, that's simple to say but harder to understand. It happened near where White Creek empties into the Wisconsin just where the monastery property begins. There was this mound down there, biggest one in the area, one of those Indian mounds, and it was all I could see because the fog was everywhere else. I beached my boat, ran to it and there I stayed. Thought I was a goner for sure. That thing didn't come up on the mound, and after a while it went away."

The biker didn't respond. Suddenly he turned to Dickie Bergin behind the bar and said, "Buy this man a beer and bring me another—over there, at the corner table." And with that, the biker turned his back on Walter.

Walter made to follow but decided he was just getting warmed up and turned to the man who had spoken before. "Let me tell you again what I saw." As fast as he was out of earshot, the biker was of no more interest to the ferret-like fisherman.

To anyone who was watching, the biker was troubled. His brow was furrowed, and he had drawn into himself. Dickie Bergin saw it right away when he brought over the beer. "Where you staying?" he asked.

"Not that its any of your business," said the biker, "but I'm staying at the Burke Hotel up the street. Kind of a run down place."

"Has been since the railroad left. Going to be around here long?" asked Dickie.

"Longer than you'll be alive if you don't let me alone."

With that, Dickie beat a hasty retreat to the bar, casting a concerned glance frequently to the table. Best keep the guy happy he thought. He's big enough to cause trouble and ornery enough to try.

The clack of a cue ball against a stripe caught the biker's attention, and he turned to the pool table. A young man with a day's growth of beard was swizzling a toothpick in his mouth and concentrating on his next shot. He sighted the cue and ended up looking past the ball into the biker's face. Sucking in his breath, the pool player snapped the toothpick in half with his tongue. "Jarrod," he said to the flat faced friend next to him. "Take my place, will you?" Handing his cue to Jarrod, the man walked over to the biker.

"Name's Gordon," he said stretching out his hand to the biker.

"And I'm supposed to be impressed now?" said the biker refusing the hand and ignoring the face.

Gordon smirked and said, "You're Rory, aren't you? My Ma said you'd be a tough ass."

The only sign of surprise the biker showed was to lift his eyes slightly to look directly at Gordon. "And who might your sainted mother be?" he asked.

"Caithness McNabb. She—we, me and my brothers, own much of the land around here."

"Ah, so it's Cate who's your mother. Well, if you're representative of the litter she's whelped, then she's come down a peg or two since I met her last." Rory took a gulp from his beer and turned his head away.

"You'll not be talking about me or my mother that way, you prick." Gordon went to grab the biker's shoulder, but Rory was faster. He snatched the younger man's hand in mid air, twisted it hard and smacked it on the table. Gordon fell to his knees in pain.

"There now," said Rory and smiled thinly. "Nothing hasty, lad. Besides, I meant no harm. Sit with me and tell me how darling Cate is doing. I knew her long ago, when she was young. But tell me now, how did she ever know I was coming?" Rory laughed as Gordon pulled himself into a chair.

As soon as Gordon got some color back into his face and had taken a drink of his own beer, he said, "She told me to tell you that the river told her you were coming. She's like that, you know, sometimes saying mystical crap like that."

"I'll just bet the river told her," mused Rory. "What's she been doing? Dabbling in the darker arts? Who would have thought it? Cate's the town's own little medium." Almost to himself, he said, "And where did she get that fetching talent?" Noticing Gordon staring at him, he said, "Tell me about her, and about the family. You'll not be leaving till I hear it all." And with another laugh, Rory sat back in his chair expectantly and waited for Gordon to begin.

To hear Gordon tell it, Caithness McNabb was a modern success story. She married John twenty-five years before, but left him dead in his grave before ten years of marriage were done. She inherited his vast farming estate. One thing about Cate, she could improve upon perfection. The family was already well off but she made it truly wealthy. John had given her three boys: Gordon, the eldest, then Rafe and lastly, Fergal. She worked them hard and never let them rest on their riches.

"Hell," said Gordon and laughed, "but she worked us in grand style. One day we had to pick up manure in the pasture and the help had already gone to another one of our properties. We thought we got out of it, but Ma was persistent to say the least. She told us to take the Cadillac out into the field and move that shit. First time I ever drove and I was fourteen. We shoveled that manure right into the trunk and hauled it away. Took me and my brothers almost the whole day. By the time we got done, the help was back and she made them clean up the Caddie. I remember she was laughing and telling us what great boys we were."

Rory smiled his thin smile again, "There's my Cate, protective and indulgent. But Gordon, the help you talked about. That'd be the Wallins family, wouldn't it? You know, the ones she fired not so long after that incident for—what was the reason again?"

"How do you know about that?" asked Gordon. The biker didn't answer. "Well, no matter. They got fired because they couldn't pay their rent. Spent their money foolishly, Ma said."

"Ah," said Rory, nodding sagely. "She would know about things like that. Did I tell you I met their youngest in Chicago not so long ago? It's true. She's a hooker now with a drug problem. Quite a good one when she's not strung out, so I hear. Look's like Mr. Wallin didn't make it very well when he moved his family to the big city."

"So you're implying my mother was at fault." Gordon stood up to take offense.

"If it didn't offend your manhood, I'd say you've some of the drama queen in you, just like your mother, Gordon McNabb. Now, tell me why Cate was looking for me, and how you'd know to find me here."

Gordon smirked again. "That's easy. She said, 'Look for Rory Nalan in the bar—because he's most at home there. He'll stink with the leather he's wearing and he'll have a beer in his hand. If his mouth isn't full of alcohol, it will be packed tight with attitude.' So I guess that's you. And she told me to tell you she's glad you're back. How'd she say it, 'You always bring a change in the weather; stuff happens with you.'"

"Well, Gordon, you tell dearest Cate, your precious mother, that it will be grand to see her again. And tell her that Conor Archer is back, will you, and", he patted the young man's cheek, as he got up from the table, "let her know that the 'dark ones' are coming into their own." Rory turned away from the young man and motioned to Dickie Bergin to get him another beer.

THE HEALING

THE FOUR TOOK the unconscious Conor on the litter towards the old Indian mound. "Lay him on the ground next to Troubles," said the Abbot.

"Why not just make the dog move?" muttered Brother Luke.

"Because Troubles has brought friends, I think," said the Abbot. "And because I don't know exactly what's happening; let's do it the dog's way." Out of the corner of his eye, he caught the small willow where an owl perched halfway up the tree. Swivelling to a cry overhead, he pivoted to where a bald eagle settled on the sturdy upper branches of an oak not far from the burial mound. Over by the fallen willows a family of racoons gathered, while on the riverbank stood two otters peering above the grass to take in the scene. Beth and Jace saw these things too and, looking deeper into the woods, noticed silhouettes of deer, woodchuck and badger in the dusk.

"What's going on?" asked Jace. "Why are they all here?"

"I told you this was holy ground, and not just to humans," said the Abbot. "They are here because of what is about to happen. They are here because of Conor."

"Honestly, Father Abbot, this is too much," said Brother Luke. "He's just a boy who hasn't been back to his home town in a few years, and a sick one at that. Warm as it is down here, the boy would be better in the hospital where he could get some decent medical attention. Holy ground is well and good, but going druid on us isn't in keeping with who you are."

Beth broke the tension as she laughed. "Going druid? What do you mean by that?"

"He means," said the Abbot with a sad smile, "that we would be better off with things familiar, like a hospital bed for the boy and a few moments of prayer in the church for the health of his body and soul." Turning to Brother Luke, the Abbot said, "And that is all true. But the Lord who is so present to us in the Sacrament is here tonight, in this holy place, and look, his congregation is gathered." The eyes of the assembled animals gleamed through leaves and amid the trees. "Leave the boy on this bed of grass. Troubles will watch over him." The dog uttered a soft woof of agreement. "We cannot stay here," continued the Abbot. "A little ways away is the closest we will be permitted. Follow me."

And without another word, the Abbot led the little band off the mound across the clearing to a small hill thirty yards away. "Now we wait," he said, and sat his body down on the ground.

"Well," grumbled Brother Luke, "at least we haven't been eaten alive by the mosquitoes."

"We should have been," said Jace. "In fact, we should be mighty uncomfortable now, but instead, it's just a beautiful evening. Look! The stars are coming out."

There was no wind. Conor lay still with a white sheet stretched up to his neck. Troubles sat sentinel over him, every once in awhile bending down to sniff and lick the face of the boy. For a while all was quiet. But then Beth began to hum the song that Conor had sung in the infirmary. She asked the Abbot, "Was that song written about this place?"

The Abbot was silent for a long while. "Yes, but it was written long, long ago. And it was sung differently then. The words were ... more archaic. More people knew it, too. In the old days, on All Hallow's Eve, there would be evening prayer in the Abbey. The old Abbot would gather the townspeople in the church and all the monks would enter from the choir in the front and flow down the side aisles. Each would have a candle. There would be incense, and singing, old Celtic songs that even the towns-folk knew, and then the monks would lead a candlelight procession down to this spot, singing that song. It was a pilgrimage to this holy place. Every Halloween. It was joyful, and the candles were brighter than the stars. So they say. The last time it was done was in the 1920's. There was a fellow, an African-American I think, who was stopping through the town on All Hallow's Eve. He heard the song and set it to his own music with his ver-sion of the words. For a while it was a hit in the nightclubs of Chicago, and even New Orleans, I believe. Its popularity died out during World War II. Nobody really remembers it, except Conor, and me I guess. Maybe he learned it somewhere in the city as he was growing up."

"Father Abbot," said Beth. "Why is this place holy?"

The Abbot said, "That would be a story for another time, I think. For tonight, just take my word. It is the holiest place for miles around all excepting the Abbey Church."

They fell silent as the first fireflies gleamed. A good night for them. Warm and still. Jace noticed them first deep in the woods and gradually they began to flash in the meadow and above the fallen willows. He had never seen so many. They were like the candles of the monks the Abbot had spoken of, the candles of the long ago pilgrimage. And they were beautiful. Not much outside of a complicated football play or an especially exciting video game awed Jace, but this—this was another world. He heard Beth utter a soft gasp and even Brother Luke could be heard exclaiming under his breath. The night was alive with light, and in the glow, there was music.

Beth heard it first: a soft, haunting song in an ancient tongue, and out of the corner of her eye she could see figures walking among the trees, only they disappeared if she struck them dead on with her gaze. Just out of reach of sight, barely on the edge of hearing. Old words from a forgotten time, beyond understanding but powerful. She could tell the others were experiencing the same, now. They turned their heads, trying to grasp the source, and then from out of the woods, where the shadowy figures sang, came a soft clear voice, a man's. *"Oh take me there, down by the river, down by the river where the waters flow."* African-American, full of soul. *"Take me to the light that fireflies keep, Take me to the place where the willows weep, And lay my body down, O Lord, and lay my body down."* It's like time folding in on itself, thought Beth. Things from years past that happened here coming together on this night.

The cowled figures singing in the deeper shadows of the woods gently moved their robed arms, seeming to send the shining fireflies streaming towards the mound. Many now flickered above the Indian paintbrushes. The two willow trees gleamed as if Christmas lights decorated them. From the river, the mist began to rise, a gentle fog that hung wispy over the ground, capturing the light from the stars and the fireflies, giving them a halo in the dewy air.

The animals moved. Tentatively at first. Like an ancient sphinx, Troubles watched over the boy, but seemed to nod his head as the smaller animals approached. All touched their noses to Conor's face, he heedless of their attention. Even the deer approached and nuzzled him. The dog looked to the trees and the owl and eagle flew down to the mound. First the owl peered down at the boy's unconscious body. Then the eagle approached and unfolded its wings over Conor. Only for a moment, and then with a soft cry, it launched itself back to its high perch on the oak. The owl too, but silently, resumed its place on the small willow. The other animals stayed in a circle around the body.

The Abbot said, "There! Look there, under the largest willow tree." The mist swirled as if an unfelt breeze had caught it and a frenetic activity of fireflies could be seen. Faster and faster they whirled until the mist itself began to glow. It floated from the willow towards Conor, a column of light and swirling fog. And, as the light moved closer to Conor, a figure coalesced inside the mist. More substantial than the night air but not really solid, it was human in form.

Jace had never seen a ghost before, and he didn't think he was seeing one now. Whatever this was, it had life and purpose. Jace was surprised to feel awe, not fear.

Beth turned to the Abbot, "You said this was a holy place. Is that, is that—"

"No, it is not," said the Abbot. "But whoever it is, he is good. Do you feel any fear, any dread?" The twins and Brother Luke shook their heads.

"Then be at peace; the boy is in good hands."

The figure was recognizable as a human male. Portions of a face, a noble countenance, crowned with a circlet of gold, could be seen here and there as the fireflies lit facial features that were at once defined, but then dissolved into the mist. He reached out his arms to the boy, bending over him. In a moment the fog covered Conor and he, himself, was illuminated within the mist. The figure bent over the boy, cradling him; the mist enveloped Troubles as well. To those who watched, it seemed whatever held Conor reached into the earth and held the boy so close to the mound that they became one with the very soil. It was then that the other animals closed up the circle upon the mound. They stood around the glowing light, while other fireflies danced amid the woods and meadow; long dead monks chanted, and a soulful voice kept singing, under a night of shining stars, down by the river where the waters flowed.

To Jace, it seemed wonderful, a time he did not want to end. But then, the figure stood and turned toward them, beckoning. Jace watched the Abbot get up and begin to walk towards the mound. He held his arms out to the glowing mist, and whoever was inside took his hands. The Abbot continued to walk forward until he too entered the mist. Jace could see the two of them together for a moment and then, he never knew how it happened, only that the mist just evaporated away. The fireflies were still there with their gentle lights brightly flashing, but the presence was gone. He heard the Abbot speak. "You can come forward now."

Jace, Beth and Brother Luke walked slowly toward the mound, past deer who looked not at them but towards the middle of the mound where Conor lay. So close that the three could reach out hands and touch them. They had to pick their way through the smaller animals, as still as lawn ornaments, all focused on the center of the mound. Finally, they broke in to the middle of that circle and found the Abbot bending over Conor. The boy's eyes were open, staring sightlessly into the starlit sky. Conor was whispering over and over, "I went down beneath the roots of the mountains, to the peoples of the past."

"He's quoting from the prophet Jonah," said the Abbot.

Jace bent down and picked up the silver flask that had fallen by Conor's side. "Hey, there's still a little of whatever stuff was in here. Maybe it would bring him around." Brother Luke nodded, and Jace unstoppered the flask and dribbled the last few drops past Conor's lips. Immediately, the boy started coughing and his eyes focused.

"How's the hand?" said Brother Luke.

"It's feeling a lot better," said Conor, holding up his arm. "As a matter of fact, I'm feeling a lot better." The Abbot silently unwound the bandage. Troubles came forward and sniffed. He woofed in approval.

"Let me see that," said Brother Luke, pointing a flashlight directly at Conor. He examined the hand in silence. "The scars are there, but the infection is gone." Touching the forehead of the boy, he pronounced, "Fever's gone too."

"Where am I?" asked Conor.

"Hey, man," said Jace, "you're where the willows weep, and we're just done laying your body down." He smiled down at Conor, lost in his confusion.

Beth pushed her brother aside, "The Abbot knew where to take you, Conor. Wish you could have seen it happen to you. It was amazing!" She told him quickly about the burial mound he was lying on.

Conor was already looking around and he started when he saw all the animals. "What are they doing here?"

"We don't know, Conor," said the Abbot gently. "We were hoping you might be able to shed a bit of light on that. What do you remember?"

Conor sat up. The eyes of the humans looked at him expectantly, but he saw that the animals stared at him as well. "This is weird. I ... I'm not sure what happened. I remember being carried by you. You put me down and left. My head was swimming and I saw these sparkling lights ..."

"Those would've been the fireflies, tens of thousands of them Conor!" Beth's eyes were still wide with wonder.

Conor held out his hand and a few of the insects landed on it blinking yellow in the night. "Then he came to me."

"Who?" said Beth, "who did you see?"

"I don't know his name, and it was so bright that I could barely see his face, but his voice was—powerful—I had to do what he said. 'Come with me,' he said. And he took my hand and lifted me up."

"Conor," said Jace, "you never left here."

"Oh, but I did!" said Conor leaning forward with an energy neither of the twins had seen in him before. "He lifted me up and took me under the earth. I mean this hill opened up. And down I walked with him. And it wasn't dark, it was all light, and I saw people there, drinking and eating, people in his hall, his hall of light, with tables and benches. And some of the people there seemed to know me; they called me by name, 'Conor' they said, 'Finola's boy.'" For a moment Conor was silent, lost in remembering.

"And then what?" asked Jace. "Then what happened, Conor?"

"He took my hand and poured some liquid on it and made me drink from a cup. A woman's voice spoke, a voice I should know but could not place. 'You must help him,' she said, 'for he is my heart and yours.' 'Indeed, he is,' said the man, giving me the cup. 'This will restore the balance, will help heal his soul,' he said. And I asked him what he meant, and he just smiled and took me back. Back to here." Conor turned to the Abbot and said, "Who was he; who was that man? And what was that place?"

The Abbot took Conor's hand and said, "He is old and has been here long before us and even before some of the Native American tribes who used to dwell here. I have met him a few times in my long life. If he did not tell you his name, then I must not either. Be at peace; he is good, and you have nothing to fear from him. And the place you were, you said it yourself as you awoke; you went down into the earth, to the peoples of the past."

Suddenly, the owl hooted lowly, Troubles howled, and the eagle called loudly in the night. The other animals shifted restlessly as a fetid breeze swept from the river through the clearing. Even the fireflies seemed more agitated. They began to move to the river, congregating, swirling, moving as a mass.

"Something's out in the water," said Conor.

"I can't see a thing," said Brother Luke.

"No, Conor's right," said the Abbot.

The water roiled for a moment, with a turbulence like the wake of a speedboat, and Conor found himself backing up till he came up against the large willow tree. He cried out, "My God, it's hideous!"

"What is?" said Jace, "I can't see anything."

A voice spoke among them, "Do not fear. There is evil in the water, but it can not touch us here." They turned and saw the luminous figure walking toward them until he stopped by Conor and placed his hand on his shoulder. None could later say exactly what the figure looked like. Noble surely, dressed in clothes of another time and place, young and strong, clearly. But almost insubstantial, as if only the light from the dancing fire-flies gave him substance. With a wave of his hand, he sent a mass of the luminous insects out over the water. Whatever had been there was gone.

Conor looked up at the stranger. "I saw it. What was that thing?"

It seemed as if the figure smiled a sad smile. "Your enemy, lad, and all of ours. Friends of this boy, good it is for you to come and stand by his side in his hour of need. For he is important to the land, and in the days and months ahead will have need of friends and companions. He knows not who or what he is, and his heart is heavy, now that he walks alone in the world. You must be there to give him strength for what is to come. The Devourer will seek him; the one who watches us from the waters. And in the way of evil, it will find him somewhere and somehow. It wears many disguises, but death is its heart and its goal. Before he comes into his own, this boy will suffer much."

The figure looked down at Conor and took the boy's chin gently in his palm. He looked deeply into Conor's eyes and grim-faced, stepped back. Raising his hand, he spoke:

Three times pierced,
Three times wounded,
Thrice to bring the king to birth,
Once, comes the Otherworld,
Twice, the pains of Change,
Thrice pierced, a Kingdom gained.
So says the crow that flies above,
So says the barrow prince hidden in the mound,
So says he who walks the twilight bound.

He turned, looking at them all. "The land is in peril, all of you are in danger, the whole world shifts as the old ones awake. Take care of him. He will find his allies among the creatures of the wild, but few of humankind will take to him. He is the bridge between the old and the new, between what was and what is yet to be." Reaching out a luminous hand, the stranger touched Conor's cheek. "Look for the mountain behind the mountain, look for the sea beneath the sea, look for the sky above the sky, then you will know who you are my son, then you will know who you are."

"And who are you?" asked Conor. "What is your name?"

But the figure was gone, dissolved in a sparkle of fireflies dimming into the night.

PIASA RESTLESS

IN THE DARK of the night, it swam down the river. It knew speed was of the essence. Fast as it moved, Piasa, the Devourer of Souls, barely waked the water. Even the denizens of that liquid environment were not sure what happened when it passed them by. The snapping turtle felt briefly the cold of winter, the walleye, the chill of an autumn day; the catfish felt frost in the depths of the river mud. But that was only for a moment, for Piasa was fast, fast. And it raced down the river toward Conor Archer and his friends.

It saw the burial mound, just as it turned the bend by White Creek. It saw the flattened trees of last night's work, and it briefly felt pleasure at the wanton destruction. But then, it saw the mound and the glowing light upon it and the cluster of humans there. But what enraged it most were the animals, its animals, for did not Piasa rule creation in this part of the world? Had it not placed fear in the hearts of creatures so that no animal would congregate with another species, no wild animal seek the companionship of a human, no animal dare approach that burial mound where its only opposition had ever existed these past centuries?

Piasa was older than the humans and the country they inhabited, and its evil was like a virus reaching out through the land to touch the hearts of humans and all living things. Tonight was something new in its experience. For many centuries, few had troubled its domain. But for the last several hundred years, long in human terms, but a blink in Piasa's existence, the human invasion had grown and The Devourer of Souls sought to use them for its own purposes. Like the animal creatures, humans were surprisingly easy to manipulate. It did not take much; it could infiltrate a human's consciousness like the river mist. And since Piasa could take several forms indeed, sometimes it was the river mist slipping its tendrils into farm homes and town houses. A touch of jealousy here, revenge there, greed in this place or that, and the humans stayed divided just enough not to threaten it or its designs.

But this, this gathering in this place at this time disturbed Piasa. Those who lived underneath the mound stirred, especially his old foe. They had not emerged for many years. It was more annoyed than worried. Always, the mounds were the source of problems. It remembered those who first built them.

Long ago. It remembered how they built their mounds on bluffs and even dared build some down by the water as a challenge to its power, as if their dead chieftains buried there were overlords of land and water. They thought to keep Piasa penned in; to keep its reach limited to the murky depths. Fools! It remembered the day they massed along the banks—almost all of them swarming like barge fly bait along the river that long ago day— challenging pridefully, daring Piasa to come to them.

It had accepted the demand. To their sorrow. Glimpses of pleasure sparked from its memory. Talons grabbing the little daughter of the chief, the smile fading from his face and screams erupting from his mouth as Piasa rose from the river and crushed the life from the little girl. Its tail raking the bank and slaughtering the people gathered there. Screams of pain, tributaries of blood running freely into the river. A feast of flesh, satiated. The mound builders were destroyed, devoured by its rage and hunger, riven from the face of the earth within moments and for many years the land was empty of humans. Then came the new usurpers, centuries ago for humans but merely yesterday for Piasa. Led by the shining one in a craft that sailed against the flow of the river, Piasa felt the magic that flowed from them. Enemies surely, but kindred somehow. The evil that pulsed inside the Devourer had a memory of them. Powerful they were and dangerous. When it did challenge them, they pushed back. Unlike the mound builders, these people who lived within the mounds themselves, these mound dwellers were not so easily defeated. They could not dethrone Piasa, but they could deny it the land. Thus an understood truce took hold. Only twice was it strained. When native peoples returned to the land and when the white man came in force. The mound dwellers, these people of the hollow hills were not adverse to some contact with the human immigrants, but Piasa could not allow an alliance. It feared what might come from such a thing. For the first and last time, it called out in the night mist to the shining one and asked for a meeting. The leader of the mound dwellers appeared one evening at the junction of White Creek and the Wisconsin River, and there the amendment was made. No mound dweller could consort with humans. And the pact was kept, for the most part. Piasa knew of the occasional fleeting encounter and did not mind, for it too sometimes touched the hearts of men, but despite these misdemeanors a fragile peace was maintained, a balance. The shining one surely knew of Piasa's forays into the land, spreading night terror among the creatures, making sure they knew that true allegiance was owed to it and it alone. Still balance was kept. All in all things worked well.

Until the shining one fell in love with a woman. Piasa could not tolerate that. It remembered the cold night when it had snatched the woman and her child, only to face the wrath of the leader of the mound dwellers. All was nearly lost to both the dwellers and the demon. But war did not come. The truce held. It would be long, as humans count time, before Piasa saw woman and child again.

But now, this tiny pack of humans and animals of the forest and meadow were focused on some boy lying upon the ground. That boy troubled him even more than the others. The shining one was there, close to the newcomer. That was the problem. To Piasa's senses, the boy seemed part of two worlds. His legs and arms seemed to flow into the mound as if he was a part of the earth. He reminded the demon of the past. Piasa could sense he had the sight that could easily spy its presence out in the water if he would only look.

And look he did. On a moment, the boy turned his head towards the river, staring in questioning silence. Then the spread of horror on his face, a yell of terror, and suddenly everything that walked that mound turned and followed the boy's gaze.

Unafraid that it had been spotted, Piasa knew that not all could see it lurking in the river. The other boy and girl stared blankly into the night. The young monk peered this way and that, but his old foe, wreathed in firefly light could see, as could the Abbot. Piasa's ancient enemy sent a wave of light towards its presence.

Piasa was amused. Water was its abode. Were they fools? It was darkness and wrapped the night around itself as a cloak. But this was not the time. Those enveloped in light, Piasa had faced before and they were formidable but not invincible. But the boy was a new factor. As the fireflies approached, illuminating the river in a gentle light, Piasa decided to leave. It had faced opposition before. Though confident of its power, it had no desire to battle with those on the mound this night. Besides, there were mysteries here. Their defense of the boy seemed too great, too concerted to be simply the protection of a loved one. The boy held secrets and Piasa would not be able to bleed them out of him tonight. The boy had allies, but Piasa was not without creatures to aid him. As it turned silently into the water and sunk into the depths of the river, disappearing from view, it pondered options. There was one who might discover the boy's secret. Piasa had a claim on her, a debt she owed. It had blessed her with much over the years in return for her worship. She would do its work.

WHISPERS IN THE DARK

CAITHNESS MCNABB LOVED to walk down by the river at night. Always had. The sounds intrigued her. The slap of a bass as it entered the water after leaping for an insect. The hum of mosquitoes. The croaking of the bullfrogs. And tonight, a visual show to go with the audio portion. The fireflies were gorgeous. So late this year, so beautiful. She pushed a strand of raven hair off her face.

Cate was a handsome woman. That's what they said at the *DewDrop Inn* and all the other taverns in the area. Never told her to her face, though she knew. She heard. She had been quite a catch for old John McNabb. Sired him three sons on her terms. All three times she let him touch her, she got pregnant. Otherwise, only his money intrigued her, and his land. He loved her deeply and doted on her, but it was never reciprocated. Beautiful as an ice queen and just as warm. To tell the truth, most folks suspected he died of a broken heart. She never shed a tear at his funeral.

But she loved the night, down by the river. At night, the one she really loved was often there. Her lawn sloped down to the water's edge. She had a boat dock built, and a gazebo placed there, too, with fine chairs and a picnic table, to grace the scene. Stopping by one of those benches this evening she sat herself down.

She never actually saw it—her lover that is. She just knew when it was there, out there in the river, treading water, looking at her. Cate even knew when it wished to communicate with her. Like the mist creeping off the water, she could feel it touching her mind. Half heard words and suggestions would come unbidden into her thoughts as she spent those nights down by the river. And she liked what she heard.

Like the time the notion got put in her head to do away with old John, her ever so loving husband. "Done what he had to do," the thought came to her. "No more use for him." And because it was clear to her that the thought had floated out of the river like a will-o-the-wisp, she gave it credence.

"Who's out there?" she had spoken into the darkness over the river that one night long ago. "Show yourself." But only an echo of laughter whispered against her ears. Still, she thought, the idea wasn't a bad one. She was in John's will; he had given her sons; his doting presence was wearing on her.

So she killed him. Over time, and not without once or twice regretting it. But the slow acting poison that had come from one of the tiny plants that grew forgotten in the back water sloughs of the river bottom did the trick. One day, John's heart just gave out. The coroner didn't even put much effort into the autopsy.

Cate had been walking down by the river one evening not long before, near sunset, wondering how to dispose of John when she sensed that presence again, out in the river. No words this time, but she felt the need to walk the paths along the river that darted in and out of the back water areas and she found that tiny plant, and just knew, just knew that it should be used as an herb on John's salad. And it was for several weeks. He got weaker, but never went to the doctor and finally at dinner, after twenty-eight days of herbal additives on the dinner salad, he simply slid off the side of his chair. It was over; heart stopped.

Cate looked stunning at the funeral. Black dress, picked out from the top Chicago stores, and a veil covering her face. All the guests at the funeral luncheon at her place had looked out the picture windows of that huge home, windows with a vista down the vast lawn towards the river, and saw her by herself walking down by the river. The mourning widow, bereft and forlorn, walking aimlessly by the rolling waters, garnered just a bit of sympathy from the guests.

Actually, Cate was quite pleased with herself. Financially set for life, she could turn her full attention on the three young boys. Strapping lads, she thought, and dozens of potential suitors just biding time to woo her and offer their services at making those boys into men.

"I will help you," came the thought. She turned toward the river. Never in the day, she mused to herself. Whatever was out there had never spoken to her in the day. "It is important," she felt it say. "Young pups should have guidance. I will help."

At least those were the thoughts Cate believed it sent her. And she found herself laughing and then said, "Get in line; John's potential successors are already circling like turkey vultures. They're ready to raise those boys just for the chance to have me."

Suddenly a warm breeze spun around her, and she felt the warm humid air from the river lift her dress and caress her thigh. For a moment, a warm thrill rushed through her. "Do not dismiss me. No one, no thing, cares as much as me for you right now."

She believed that thought, and was intrigued. From that moment on, Cate was oblivious to those who pined for her company and dismissive of those who outright courted her. It took awhile for the men to finally leave her alone. But they did as they began to feel like old John felt, stabbed in the heart by the ice queen. Cate however was content. Walking down by the river made her feel so comforted. She just loved it down there, with it.

Just like she loved it this evening. She held out her hand towards the river. "I know you are there," she whispered. "Come to me." Only the night before, she had said the same words. She knew it was out there, for last night it had sent her pictures; images had come to her mind of a dark man—one she had known long ago. He was coming back, and she wondered why.

On this night, she felt its presence more strongly. Tendrils of mist floated to her off the river, drifting over her body as she sat in the gazebo. Damp and cold on this warm summer evening, that's what the mist felt like. She could tell something was wrong. This elemental force that had protected her, guided her, rewarded her, in return for her steadfast fidelity was definitely agitated this evening.

Cate saw the river mist entwine around her and then she felt its probing touch. Reptilian almost in its concentration, Piasa entered her. Long ago it had revealed its name to her, and tonight she felt devoured. Wherever that damp touched her, she sensed it. She had learned its power lay in water and through that medium it could transmit thoughts, energy, indeed its very presence. Normally, when Piasa took her like this, she was overwhelmed with its elemental force. Something like affection would touch her own emotional center, and Piasa could thrill her with pleasure. But not tonight. Tonight she felt only urgent need, and anger. Something or some event had disturbed it greatly.

It had helped her very much over the years. Why, she was never sure. The money from her now dead husband was substantial but often the decision of what to do with it was as much Piasa's as hers. Not that it really knew anything of money. The thing in the river couldn't balance a checkbook but it surely understood what motivated greed. When troubled or confused, she would come down to the water's edge. Always it would be there, stalking her or simply knowing her need; she was never quite sure. She would pour out her dilemma in words and it would answer. Not with concrete plans but with inspirations of cunning, ruthlessness, power and stealth. She knew it molded her into an efficient capital enterprise. Anything she touched turned to gold. She bought up land, squeezed out competitors, invested heavily in stocks and real estate, and succeeded mightily. Even the locals barely suspected how rich she truly was. Because she was cunning, she made herself a pillar of the community giving to local charities and even endowing the monastery with a generous bequest each year. But it taught her also to be ruthless, so most people were quite afraid of her. Cate lamented that fact once and cast her loneliness across the waters. But it laughed at her grief, gentle in its own way, and got her laughing with it. All it took was a little nudge to remind her that power healed all isolation. She could have people whenever she wished. Cate was no fool, however. All things come with a price and she suspected that more would be required of her one day.

Or one night, she thought. This night perhaps. Wrapped in mist, she paid close attention to the urgent longings of the beast. It was trying to tell her something but in its haste, she was missing much. A perceived threat, perhaps. A demand to investigate, maybe. A command to take care of the problem. That much she knew, but the details escaped her. It was never good with details. They were kindred spirits but definitely of different species. Some things could only be guessed at.

She touched the mist around her. "Don't worry," she spoke out loud. "Whatever it is, I'll see to it. We've done well together. The least I could do is return the favor. But someday, somehow, you'll have to come out of the river and let me see you as you are. Oh, I know, it will be something difficult for me to see. But no matter. Nothing daunts me now. Nothing scares me now." She smiled a little smile. "Not even you."

And she brushed herself free of the entangling mist and made to walk away. A scudding cloud suddenly hid the moon from view and she heard something ascend from the river. A hundred yards out, she could see a dark thing rising high from the water. It was like a black hole. She saw a swirling strand of mist curl swiftly like a whip and lash out at her. It didn't hurt when it touched, but again she felt its mind, waiting for a more concrete response.

"Patience." She smiled at her dark lover. "I said I'll take care of it. And I'll let you know what I find out."

THE SONS OF CATE

GORDON MCNABB LEFT the *DewDrop Inn* without resuming his pool game, his hand still aching from where Rory had smacked it on the table. What an asshole, he thought. His mother was right. The biker goon was an unpredictable mystery. He walked past Dickie Bergin who was speculating on the Conor Archer boy who had arrived, sick, that afternoon. Gordon heard something about old legends and weird prophecies, but when Dickie yelled at him, "Whatcha think about the Archer boy?" Gordon waved him off. He had a more pressing problem to worry over.

"Go look for a stranger," said Cate earlier in the evening. "He'll look tough and he'll be cocky. If it's who I think it is, he'll answer to the name of 'Rory Nalan'. At least that's how I knew him long ago. Ask him his business."

"Is he a long lost relative, a jilted lover, or what?" asked Gordon.

A smile of memory came to Cate's lips. "He was fun once upon a time. Tell him I'm glad he's back."

So he had kept his eyes open that evening and spotted Rory. All Gordon got out of it was a sore hand and an instant dislike of the new stranger in town. Just like Cate to sic him on a dirty dog that had a good bite. Ma ought to do her own dirty work, he was thinking. He was tired of being her gofer all the time.

Grousing about his spoiled evening, Gordon drove back to the house. All the lights were on, but Cate was nowhere to be found. Gotta be down by the river again, he thought. Talking to the mist. He had often followed his mother as she went her evening walks down by the banks of the Wisconsin. He caught her talking by herself lots of times. Only she didn't act like she was talking all alone. She'd speak, then cock her head to listen. She'd laugh or giggle and then add a phrase, like she was having some kind of conversation with an invisible stranger only she could hear. Gordon found it fascinating. Even more so, recently, because she'd come back from these walks with new ideas she'd tell the boys—ideas that worked, plans that made money and made their family a power in the river valley.

Last year, she'd come back from an autumn walk with the idea to start a biotech company in Tinker's Grove.

"Technology, particularly reproductive technology, is where it's at these days, boys," she told Gordon and Rafe and Fergal. Fergal was the youngest at 20. He could care less about biotech and vanished into the living room before the conversation really got started. Rafe was curious, but if he couldn't see it, touch it or taste it, then it just couldn't hold his interest long either. The middle of the three boys, he took off as well. Cate never seemed to notice, probably because she had the undivided attention of Gordon. He smelled money anywhere, even if it was just in an idea. He had just finished up his degree in accounting at the University of Wisconsin-Madison and passed his CPA.

"You thinking about genetic engineering, Ma?" he asked. "I mean cloning and stuff like that?"

"You bet," said Cate, blue eyes flashing. "I'll go for anything that will wake up this backwater town and bring it into the new millennium."

"But why biotech? Isn't that a little high end for this part of the country?"

"Won't be once I'm done making it work. Besides, I've been thinking that this little town of ours might just have some real possibilities that will make anyone in biotech interested."

That piqued Gordon's interest for sure. "What's so special about Tinker's Grove? Besides the fact that we're about as backward as the Amish—yeah, call us Amish with a brogue."

Cate laughed. "Oh, you'll see; trust me on this one."

She always had a plan, thought Gordon. And, in fact, the biotech company was sure to become a reality. Over the past year, Cate had contacted several of the best, and one in particular, DIOGENE, seemed interested. What Cate had promised them, Gordon didn't know, but he'd find out sooner rather than later, he supposed.

Not only Cate was missing from the house; his siblings were gone as well. Rafe was out drinking and carousing, no doubt, and Fergal was probably with his former high school buddies who were fast on their way to losing their youth and hopes in this backwater town with no money and no future. Gordon just couldn't get it. Even Prairie du Chien, the nearest "large" city of 5500 people had seen its best days two hundred years ago when the fur trade was at its peak. Jesus, even presidential candidates never made it to southwest Wisconsin. Poor and beautiful, that's what this area was. But Cate had made it work to her advantage. Somehow, she martialed whatever wealth was here and made it her own. So she could talk to whomever or whatever she wanted down by the river. Gordon was sure that's where she was now. Nice night.

Sure enough, as he walked down the long lawn toward the boat dock and gazebo, he could see her shadowy figure swinging in the gazebo's swing. "Hey Ma," he said. "Been talking to yourself out here again?"

She gave her eldest son a small smile of welcome. She knew he'd seen her talking down by the river, but he didn't know and didn't understand what she was doing. Soon though, soon he would have to know. But not tonight. "Gordy, I thought you were down at the bar, waiting for Rory Nalan to show up."

"Was," said Gordon, "and he did. Just like you said. How did you know he'd be in town?"

She smiled her secret smile again. "His name's been hanging on the mist—just heard it whispered around."

Gordon saw her look out over the river. He said, "What a jerk though, all decked out in biker gear with an attitude to boot. Didn't much like me, nor I him. Gotta say it, Ma, I think he fancies you. What's the story between you two?"

Cate smiled again. "Not now, dear. Tell me what he said; tell me why he's here."

Gordon talked, repeating the conversation he'd had with Rory. Nothing much surprised Cate, except what Rory had said at the end. "Conor Archer?" she asked. "You're sure he said that name? Why did he bring him up?"

"I thought you'd know. Rory acted like you would know."

Cate sat in silence for a while. "There's an old story in the town, but it's way old. It tells of a Conor Archer who was just a baby when his mother, Finola her name was, took him away. But that was long ago."

"How long?" asked Gordon.

"Too long for it to be this Conor Archer. Why it had to be sometime over a century and a half ago, though, now that I recollect, a child with that name passed through this town in the arms of its floozy mother seventeen years ago. Maybe that's the one he meant."

"Well, why would either of the Conors be so special? Why would Rory want you to remember some old story from centuries past, or some drifter's kid decades ago?"

Cate didn't answer right away. But she felt a stirring in the depths of the river and turned her gaze again toward the water. It spoke to her again; at least she thought it did. "Look, find, discover—now!" Its need was urgent and Cate felt herself being forced to stand up from the swing. "Come on Gordy. I think I can answer you, but we've got to go to the attic." Leaving a bemused Gordon McNabb standing slack-jawed, she strode up the lawn and went into the house. He had no choice but to follow her.

She knew where she had to look. By the time Gordon reached the attic, she had already found what she was searching for, a large scrapbook stuffed with clippings. "Come on down to the kitchen table. There's something you should know tonight."

Gordon got himself a beer and poured a glass of wine for his mother as they sat at the kitchen table, scrapbook open before them. "So tell me, Gordy, how much do you know about Tinker's Grove?"

"What do you mean? Other than it's just like any other small town in this area."

"Oh, but it's not. You notice anything strange about your neighbors here?"

"Nope, can't say as I do, Ma. They seem like just folks to me."

"Granted, we've never been part of the town so the old ones wouldn't have confided in you, but you must have heard the stories. How are we ever going to build an empire together—you, me and the other boys—if you don't start getting smarter? What about the birth defects in the Grove?"

"What birth defects?" asked Gordon. "Everybody seems pretty normal to me."

"That's the problem with tolerance," said Cate. "People begin to overlook what's right in front of their faces. I noticed the mutations some time ago. In fact, it was those mutations that interested DIOGENE in locating their biotech company here. Haven't you ever noticed that our little town seems to have more than its fair share of people with webbed hands, webbed feet? Like we were sitting on a toxic waste dump or something."

"Yeah, but Ma, the defect is so small. I mean the few who have it aren't disfigured or anything—it's just a slight webbing between their fingers."

"And toes," said Cate. "Their freakishness encompasses all their digits. Besides, minor or not, only one type of person in this town has that defect. Men and women, boys and girls with black hair and black eyes."

"So? What difference does that make?"

Cate found the newspaper clipping from the 1960's. The headline read: *High Rate Of Birth Defects Not Traced To Thalidomide.* "It was the height of drug induced birth defects and this little article in the Prairie du Chien *Gazette* caught my eye one day when I was paging through your father's old scrapbook. The reporter who wrote the story said the townspeople of Tinker's Grove themselves proved the worry false when they told doctors and health officials at the time that the defect had long been known throughout generations of townspeople. Just the kids with black hair and eyes."

"So what?" said Gordon. "The town's got some minor freaks, that's all."

"It's an interesting mutation, at least to DIOGENE, and it's never been reported so specifically in any other population. What I didn't tell the corporate folks from the biotech company, and I only tell you now so you'll see its importance, is that this defect is tied into an old story, a story that has the name of Conor Archer attached to it.

"I don't have all the facts, but you know that this town was founded by Tinkers from Ireland, gypsies of a sort that never settled anywhere, but decided to settle here. Why? I wonder. Anyway, interspersed with this population of Tinkers were people with black hair, black eyes, and webbing between fingers and toes. The locals called them the 'dark ones.' They were always subtly honored and protected, so it is said, but never given outward deference or notice because, well, because they seemed to be hiding in the population of this town. The monastery itself cast an umbrella of protection around them. Something happened though, over a century and a half ago and it involved a child named Conor Archer and his mother Finola. Finola was a beauty in the town, but she and her child, the story tells, were 'dark ones.' They left town on a sudden. Whatever happened, it was big enough to be remembered. The legend said this Conor kid would come back. I think the details have been forgotten, but I heard about it twenty-five years ago—from Rory. After he told the tale, I mocked it, so far-fetched it seemed, and he slapped me."

"Slapped you?" said Gordon. "Why'd you let him do that?"

"Because I liked him, even when he was rough. He was mysterious, and he said to me, 'Never treat that story lightly, lass. He is coming back, and when he does, things will change.' And sure enough, seventeen years ago a woman named Finola and a baby, Conor Archer, were spotted in town. Only for a brief time and then they left. Related in some way to that old Emily O'Rourke up in Madoc's Glen. Just thought it was a strange coincidence but when a seventeen year old Conor Archer showed up this afternoon, it got me thinking again. Nothing about them or the 'dark ones' in the library. Years ago, after Rory told me the tale, I scoured the town's records stored there for hints. I was hoping there would be more to that story in this old scrapbook that my dear, departed husband, your father, always kept on the town."

But there wasn't. She looked in vain for anything more on the legend. She only found a brief note from her husband mentioning the Conor story, but no details were given. Yet, at the end of the note, he had scribbled a cryptic line, almost the same one that Rory had told her long ago, "when Conor returns, the 'dark ones' will rise; things will surely change."

Cate looked up at her son. "Tomorrow, you're going back into town and find out about this newly arrived Conor Archer. I want to know everything. And if you see Rory, tell him to come see me, as soon as possible."

Gordon nodded. He knew enough not to mess with his mother once she had settled on a plan of action. If she wanted to know about Conor, he'd gather the information, even if he had to beat it out of the little prick himself.

A CHANCE AT FRIENDSHIP

BROTHER LUKE UNLOCKED the infirmary door. "Father Abbot, the boy's staying here for the night at least until noon tomorrow."

Even the Abbot knew enough not to fight the doctor this time. "Of course, Brother. Beth and Jace, put him on the bed, and then you best get home. Your parents will be wondering where you are."

"Sure, Father Abbot," said Jace, "but let us stay just till Conor gets settled."

"Alright, but only for awhile." The Abbot smiled at the two hoisting a stumbling Conor onto the bed.

"Tell you what," said Brother Luke, a trace of compassion warming his voice, "step out in the hallway with Father Abbot and let me get Conor fixed up for the night, then you can come back for a few moments."

He hustled them out of the infirmary and when the three were alone again, Jace said, "Father Abbot, what happened down there? I've never … well, never seen anything like that."

Beth echoed her brother. "It was magic wasn't it? Nothing like this is ever supposed to happen."

The Abbot said, "Look, you two, it wasn't magic, but it was magical if you catch the difference. So many things, wondrous things, are just under the noses of people but they can't sense them. They think the world is only what they can see with two eyes. You saw more deeply tonight, that's all."

"We wouldn't have seen it without Conor being there," said Jace. "They were there for him."

"The boy is definitely special," said the Abbot. "He's going to need friends, and I'm afraid he won't make many."

Beth said, "Why is that? He seems nice enough"

"And so he is," said the Abbot. "But you saw his hands."

"They got a little bit of webbing between the fingers. So what? There's a few others in town with the same," said Jace. "You aren't prejudiced are you?"

"No, not at all," said the Abbot. "You know me better than that. It's going to take more than a little syndactyly to make me think someone is less than human. It's just that the legend of Conor Archer, the one the people were whispering about down at the station after the boy arrived, refers to that Conor being one of the 'dark ones.'"

Beth laughed, "Come on, that legend is way old and no one is going to seriously mistake this Conor for the Conor of the legend."

"Don't be too sure," said the Abbot. "This is a small town with a long memory. Not much happens here but when it does, the event has a life of its own. At the very least, people are going to talk about the boy."

"One of the 'dark ones,' you say," said Jace, "and I suppose that will make him mysterious and scary to everyone who's heard the stories."

"Even in the old legends we were told as kids," said Beth, "they don't really say what the 'dark ones' actually are. Why is that? Those that could pass as 'dark ones' in the town today aren't treated in any special way, don't act differently, and certainly aren't scary."

The Abbot smiled. "Legends like an air of mystery. Telling the secret would be spoiling the atmosphere. But Beth and Jace hear me out. There will be talk. Conor will need friends he can trust. You shared something with him tonight, something that was truly mysterious; something we are going to have to figure out. Be his friends."

Just then, a cold wet nose pushed Jace's hand. "How'd you get back in here, Troubles?" He patted the dog's head. The door to the infirmary opened and Brother Luke beckoned them in.

Conor was awake but in bed, his newly healed hand resting on his chest. "Thanks for your help, you guys. Kind of a strange day … and night, at least for me." He smiled a weak smile.

The Abbot laid his hand on Conor's head and blessed him, "May the Cross of Christ be above your head, the holy angels at your side, and Mary Mild holding your hand until the light of day."

"Hey my mother used to bless me just like that with those same words," said Conor.

"Of course she did," said the Abbot. "She was a Tinker wasn't she, an Irish lass through and through? And why shouldn't I do the same in her honor and for you?"

A tear slid down the cheek of the boy. With a swift flick of his finger, the Abbot snatched the tear away. "Of course you miss her, especially now that the sickness is gone and you have time to remember. When her body comes, we'll bury her in the parish graveyard, where she'll rest in peace." Looking at Beth and Jace, he said, "Don't be staying too long." And with that, he and Brother Luke left them alone.

They were silent for a moment and then Conor said, "I know you must think I'm really weird with all that happened today. I wish I could explain but I can't."

"Of course you're weird," said Jace and laughed. "You're Conor Archer, a man out of legend, come back to haunt us all." He told Conor of what the people were saying, and Conor turned from them staring at the ceiling.

"Conor," said Beth, "don't listen to this hulking brother of mine. What happened was amazing, and, if you like, we'd like to figure it out with you. That is if you don't mind."

Conor looked at them. "I've not had many friends, especially not my own age. Probably won't be very good at this. I don't talk about myself very much."

"That's okay," said Jace. "If you get too quiet, I'll just beat an answer out of you."

Conor laughed. "I'm not that much smaller than you. I might fight back."

Jace grinned, his blue eyes laughing along. "You can try, but mysteri ous or not, I'll whup your ass till you spill your guts about what's bothering you."

And as the three of them laughed, Troubles wedged in between and plopped his front legs on the bed and laid his head on Conor's chest. "Okay," said Conor, "I'll have three friends to watch over me."

Beth and Jace left soon after, but the dog stayed behind. In the silence of the infirmary, Conor looked at the dog and said, "You and me, again Troubles. I don't know about you, but I think a bunch of mojo is about to come down around my head. Not much I can do about it, nor you either." He ruffled the head of the dog and closed his eyes. Even though the boy slept in moments, the dog didn't raise his head from the boy's chest for a long time, and when he did, he lay down by the side of the bed, eyes open, ears sharply listening. Nothing else was going to disturb Conor for the rest of the evening.

A WALK IN THE DARK

THE SHADOWY OUTLINE of the Abbey loomed over Beth and Jace as they walked down the bricked driveway. It had been paved that way when the Abbey was first built halfway through the nineteenth century. A lot of monks with a fair amount of penance to work off had lovingly set those bricks in the ground.

"What do you make of it all, Jace?" Beth glanced at her brother.

"Don't know. Way strange though. Got to tell you, Beth, I like the guy. He's a loner, without anyone now, except his Aunt Emily, and, unlike Conor, she's just plain weird, living out there in Madoc's Glen—there in the woods. I'm thinking Conor's going to need somebody by his side."

"We already told Abbot Malachy we'd be there, and I for one will help Conor fit in."

"No, you got me wrong," said Jace. "I mean he needs somebody who will stand by him and watch his back, not just look at him with mouth open and cow eyes blinking at him."

Beth punched him in the arm. "I didn't look at him that way."

"Did," said Jace laughing.

The road from the Abbey led down the bluff, back towards the town. Pasture and patches of woodland lay on either side. Just the normal sounds of night. A small creek tumbled down the hill on the west side of the road. About a quarter mile from the Abbey, Jace grabbed Beth's hand and stopped.

"You hear that? Someone's behind us, I think, walking in the creek."

Beth looked back but even in the starlight, all she could see were shadows. Yet, she too heard the splashing of running feet in the water. "Let's see who it is," she said. "Things can't get much stranger than they already are."

A little girl's giggle broke the silence. "I'm here," said a voice, right across from where Jace and Beth stood. Both jumped, and Beth let out a little shriek. "I'm here," said the voice again, "over by the water." The two of them looked to where the creek was running. There under an oak, they saw a form, someone standing there. "Come closer," softly said the voice.

Not knowing why, they took a step or two closer and it was then the figure stepped out from the shadow of the oak. It was standing in the middle of the stream, wearing a hooded cloak.

"Kind of warm tonight to be wearing that heavy thing, don't you think?" said Jace. "And kind of late to be wading in the water."

"I like the water," said the figure as it pulled back the hood of the cloak.

Beth and Jace could see it was a girl, years younger than them. "Are you following us?" said Beth.

"Following the boy."

"Me?" said Jace. "Why me?"

"No," said the girl. "I'm following the boy, the Archer lad."

"Well, he's not with us, obviously. We left him resting in the Abbey infirmary."

"Yes," said the girl turning her head looking up the road towards the Abbey. "But I can't go there."

"Why not?" said Beth. "Just knock on the door and ask for Brother Luke. He's the doctor there."

"My kind is seldom welcome there."

"Your kind?" said Jace. "What do you mean?"

The girl stepped out of the creek and walked up the bank to the road. When she got to the top, she shook her hair and flung her head back staring straight up at the stars. It seemed like starlight glinted on her red hair, but when she slowly lowered her head to look at them again, the starlight stayed white on her flowing hair. Thin, ratty and bedraggled it looked now. As her eyes met their's they gasped.

"What?" she said. "The wrinkles on my face disturb you?"

"But you were just a girl," gasped Beth. "Now, you're ... What are you?"

Jason shoved Beth behind him. "You know, I've seen enough bizarre things this evening. And don't come closer, whatever you are."

The thing that was a girl and now an elderly crone just cackled and strode forward, reached up and cupped Jace's chin in her bony hand. He slapped it away as fast as he could react.

"I like your spunk, boy," she rasped. "Long time ago, you and I would have led armies." She sighed. "But that was many ages ago, and the ways of war are different now. But never the less, that boy will need your strength and your protection. And I'm telling you, lad," she poked him the chest with a bony finger, "you had better protect him, from himself and others. He is here because of me, because of what I did long ago. Time was, I could have protected him myself, but my time has faded, at least for now. He is my hope though. Perhaps he can change it all."

"What do you know of the prophecy?" said Beth. "Something's been foretold about Conor."

"Prophecy?" said the crone. "I should say I know it. I made it." She stepped back a bit, hopping like a crow, and fell to her knees in the middle of the road. A keening sound came out of her. Her head began to sway from side to side, and her mouth hung open. Beth and Jace could see her rotting teeth. When she looked at them, milk white eyes stared at them, and she hissed, "I'm the cause of why he is here. My meddling, long ago. A chain of events, so sad. And even I do not know the end.

"Much suffering is before him. And you two, because of what you saw tonight and because I found you, your fates are entwined with his; and I only forsee sadness for the both of you. You cannot run away. I weave the loom of death and life. The web has you, and nothing can change the path of your destiny now. You heard it from he who dwells in the hollow hill, but I foretold long ago that the boy would be pierced. Three times at the moment of his greatest sadnesses. The first has already happened. The one who could heal him did, but that healing will not stop the change. Already he is different. You saw that tonight didn't you? The beasts of the field and the birds of the air know it. What will happen I cannot say, but the world turns on what he does. Chosen he is, by powers greater and far older than mine."

"Are you his enemy?" said Jace. "Do you want to hurt him?"

"No, idiot!" hissed the woman, coming to herself once again. "Brawn is your strength, I see, not your brains. Why would I hurt him? He exists because of me." She stood and walked again towards Jace. "My how you will bleed for him. And yet I wonder, will you stand true? A better chance if you had someone to sponsor you; perhaps you could be my champion." She cackled and turned from him.

Reaching around Jace, she took Beth's hand. She drew Beth to herself, and traced a finger on the girl's cheek. Beth shivered in the dark. "Poor little lass. He will love you, but it will be … ah, I should say no more. Sorrows enough has this day." She shuffled back to the edge of the road. "For myself, I am glad that he has both of you. To walk the ages alone is a terrible thing." She smacked her withered lips against her rotten teeth. "We will meet again, I think, friends of Conor Archer, though never again in such peaceful times." With that she jumped into the creek. Jace ran to the bank and saw her underneath the oak. A girl's giggle wafted up to them and running splashes disappeared down the hill where the falling water gathered speed.

"You know, Beth," said Jace looking into the shadows. "We should have brought the car tonight."

AUNT EMILY

NOT MANY HOURS later, as the sun began to peek above the bluffs overlooking the river, another old woman was walking the same road as Beth and Jace the night before. Emily O'Rourke had been up long before dawn. Wearing her usual jeans, flannel shirt, and straw hat with a daisy in it, Emily moved leisurely, just the tap of her old blackthorn cane keeping pace with her step. The early morning was her favorite time. Mist on the meadow, sleepy birds chirping for the first time, deer grazing; so much to see and hear in the morning. But not this morning. This morning she was on a mission to see her nephew. The Abbot had phoned her the night before and told her what had happened down at the Indian mound.

"So he made an appearance," she sniffed.

"Indeed, he did," said the Abbot, "and it's been years since we talked. He hasn't changed an iota."

A secret smile crossed Emily's lips. "God bless the old rogue for saving the boy. It's been long since I've seen him as well. No matter, I guess. He's feckless, mercurial and totally undependable. I'm the only family Conor has now that will be raising him."

"He's not much of a boy anymore, Emily, and what's left of his raising is not your task alone. I'll be helping you."

"I know, I know," she said. "It's as we planned. Has the change started yet?"

"Oh yes," said the Abbot. "That was clear to me tonight. The animals showed me that. You should have seen it; they couldn't help but cluster around him. And when I looked in on him just a moment ago in the infirmary, both he and the dog lifted their heads in unison, nostrils flaring. There's a bit of the wild wakening in him already. They looked at me, but the boy didn't even recognize me. He was seeing something else. I think the dog was too. And did you ever notice, Emily, about Troubles? He has old eyes, but his have depths I've never seen before. And when Conor looked at me just minutes ago, his eyes looked old as well. Flecks of gold in them, too. Just for a moment, I saw. You know what that means. And then the two of them laid down their heads together and fell fast asleep again."

Emily clicked her tongue. "Will we be able to help? Will he be able to control it?"

"I don't know. You know how it usually goes. The others who are like him, they either repress it and don't deal with it, or they go mad, like Oz. Don't worry, Emily, we'll make sure he is well trained; we'll make sure this time we will succeed. He is Conor Archer after all."

"I know, Malachy. But we swore to protect them—all of them. And through the years we've failed every time."

"That's not true," said the Abbot. "We have protected them from the outside world, kept them safe, like we promised. And they know that, at least while they are young. But we can't protect them from themselves. None have chosen acceptance of what they are and that is something we cannot force. At puberty, every one of them has either chosen to blend in with the village, forgetting who they were, or, not being able to understand, have chosen madness. What's different with Conor is that the change is late. It should have happened years ago, and Rory's interference has jump-started something that has been delayed."

"You're sure it was Rory? He's definitely back?"

"Absolutely. I saw him outside the hotel as we were taking Conor to the infirmary. He smiled his pointy little smile to me and held up his right hand, wiggling it—and I can tell you he wasn't waving a hello to me."

"You think Conor's wound was his work?"

"Look," said Father Abbot. "Rory's a feral creature and dangerous. Always has been. The fact that he's back is no coincidence. Conor's story and description of the stranger who accosted him matches perfectly."

"Then we'll have to move fast and carefully," said Emily. "He can't stop us again."

"Perhaps not," said the Abbot. "But he will surely try."

That conversation of the night before was what Emily was thinking on as she walked the road up to the monastery, her blackthorn cane clicking strongly and confidently on the asphalt. Beautiful morning she thought, and it couldn't be too soon before she got a good look at her nephew.

Since the infirmary serviced the town, it had its own entrance separate from the monastic enclosure. Emily didn't ring. No point to it. Brother Luke was at Morning Prayer with the rest of the monks anyway, and she sure wasn't going to wait. Through the vestibule and straight into the infirmary she walked and was treated to the backside of Conor as he was drying off from his shower. Troubles woofed once and the boy turned his head and yelped as he saw the old woman laughing at him.

He jumped over the mattress, grabbing at some clean underwear the monks had laid out for him at the foot of the bed and then pulling on his jeans, freshly laundered overnight. "Lady, geeze, you scared the hell out of me!" Hopping on one leg trying to get his other into his jeans, Conor felt a tug. Troubles obviously thought it was time to play. No tug of war could last long while Conor was on one leg and he collapsed on the bed, half in and out of his pants, the dog worrying one half of the pair of jeans. Conor started to laugh. "This is one, way-weird place."

Emily laughed along with him. Catching her breath, she said, "I've seen so many backsides in my life; one more isn't going to matter much. It's good to see you Conor, all of you. I'm your Aunt Emily, great aunt really, and I've come to take you home."

Conor was still blushing as he tucked his green polo shirt in. He slicked back his short, wet hair and took in the old woman. He saw a thin, wiry older version of his mother. Her hair was steel grey, face wrinkled, but she looked—she looked so much like Finola.

Emily was thinking much the same. How like his mother he is, the face, the hair, the fine hands, only the eyes and the strength of his body betray his father's influence. She stepped toward him, suddenly tentative. "Oh Conor, it's a sad time you've come home to. I'm so sorry." And she took him in her arms and held him close. His body quivered as she held him and she knew there was more of the boy in him than his looks showed. He might be on the edge of manhood, but right now, he was an orphan in this world. She pushed back a little to look at his face and saw the sorrow there.

"Em ... Aunt Emily," he said. "I'm all alone, and I really miss her."

"There now," said Emily reasserting her strength. "Your mother was a grand lady, braver than you know. We had many a talk in our letters back and forth about you. I know more about you than you think, and she wanted me to take you in should it ever be necessary. And it is. Your mother's body comes back home today, and we will give her the funeral she deserves. It'll be done right and proper. But first we have to get some food in you."

"No," said Brother Luke stepping into the room, "first we take a look at that hand." He smiled at the two of them, and took Conor's right hand. "Amazing," said the monk, "look how clean that wound looks. Just the two puncture marks left. I tell you that hand was mangled when we unwrapped it yesterday afternoon and gangrenous, too. And I assume since you're here, Emily, the Abbot has already filled you in on what happened last evening. I can't describe it, and I don't know how much of it was truly real, but I can't deny the facts. Conor lay down upon that mound full of poison and fever, a dying man, I think, and he's back with us today, whole and sound."

"Well," clucked Emily, "you're mystified, Brother Luke, because your frame of reference is bounded by modern medicine, technology and medical books. There's much in these woods and bluffs and in the river running through them that heal and hurt and help in ways that are hard to fit in to today's way of thinking; but that does not make them less real. Open your eyes and mind just a bit and you'll be even a greater physician than you already are."

Brother Luke smiled affectionately at the old woman. He'd known her well ever since he came to the monastery and talked with her often about her experience in using the local plants and herbs in her own folk remedies. "I admit, I don't know everything. And it's curious, since you were being healed last night Conor, that, whoever or whatever healed you didn't bother to fix the webbing in your hand." He held Conor's hand open and to the light. "This webbing ever hurt your motion or inhibit you in any way?"

"Nope," said Conor. "I play my music just fine and never have had a problem. You got to admit, there's not that much webbing there. Few even notice, though I swim faster than anyone I ever met on Chicago's beaches. I've got it between my toes too." He flashed a brilliant smile, trying to cover up his natural embarrassment.

"Well, you have the same genetic anomaly that shows up in the village population now and then. Slightly webbed hands and feet, and every person with them also has black hair and dark eyes. Did you know there's others like you here?" asked the monk.

Conor shook his head. "Why is that?"

"Don't know," said Brother Luke. "I've looked at the monastery records for the past one hundred and fifty years. The anomaly seems random. We've had monks with it, grocers, mail men, teachers, mothers, whatever. Over the years a story has made the rounds and is accepted as fact, though I doubt it, that the anomaly has been with the people of this town from the beginning and before, and that those with it must be protected by the village. Seems that even though no one talks about it much, the practice is followed. No one with this genetic abnormality ever wants to leave the town. They always stay. Course, most everybody stays anyway. Now where's that bandage and clip you had covering your wound yesterday, Conor? There's something about those things."

"And you'll not be looking at them today," said Emily, spying them on a chair and snatching them up. "These are Conor's given to him and with him they'll stay. He may be needing them yet."

The monk sighed, "As you wish. Come on now to the guest dining room. I'm sure both of you are hungry."

"Starving!" said Conor, "and so's Troubles here." The dog woofed in agreement.

"I'm sure we'll find something for this mooch as well," said Brother Luke.

Forty-five minutes and a full stomach later, Conor was walking down the road with Aunt Emily. "Hey, Aunt Emily," said Conor, "exactly where are we going and how come we have to walk?"

"We're going home; it's not that far; and the walk will do you good." She clipped her speech in rhythm with the clicking of her blackthorn cane.

"Yeah, but shouldn't we be doing something for my Mom—funeral stuff and the like?"

"All in good time, Conor. Her body doesn't arrive till this afternoon and then we'll go to the funeral home and make arrangements. The Abbot would like to have the funeral Mass if that's okay with you."

"Sure, I guess. He seems like a good guy."

Emily cocked her head towards him. "Since you're alive today because of his foresight, I should say so."

"So you know about what happened last night?"

"Conor, you're going to find out there's not much Emily O'Rourke doesn't know around here. And while that's good news for most folks, I imagine you'll soon find it a pain in your backside after you've been living with me for a while. For instance, I know you play a mean tin whistle, and I know it's in your back pocket so play me something while we walk."

Conor smiled and reached for the instrument. "What would you like to hear? Anything special?"

"Surprise me lad."

Conor was about to play, when he lifted up his head and said, "Hey, I wonder where Troubles is? He's a pretty cool dog. Wish he was here."

Immediately from up the Abbey way a dog's bark could be heard. Conor looked surprised. "It's as if he heard me."

Emily looked at him and tapped his foot with her cane. "Don't know what you thought happened last night, but, in case you didn't notice, you seem to have a knack for drawing animals to you."

Conor paled a moment. "I don't really remember that much about last night, Aunt Emily."

She rapped his leg with her cane. "Didn't I tell you there's not much I don't know? And one thing I do is that reality, no matter how strange, always has to be faced. You saw the animals didn't you?"

"Yeah," said Conor in a soft voice. "I saw the animals. They were in a circle about me, just before he came for me."

Emily stopped and faced Conor. "Him we'll talk about later, but you can't deny what you saw, so don't."

"No ma'am," he said, and turned to the sound of four running paws rapidly approaching. Troubles appeared, coming around the corner at breakneck speed, and yipped a welcome at the boy.

Conor, between Lab jumps on his shoulders, asked Aunt Emily, "How did he know I wanted him?"

Emily turned and started walking rapidly down the hill. "Good question, Conor, and one I'm afraid you'll have to answer for yourself very soon."

Conor stood for a moment watching his great aunt walk ahead of him. She was pretty small, even for an old lady, but really spry. Besides, he kind of liked the way she took charge. Not that he needed anyone to babysit him, but it might not be bad to have someone he could lean on a bit—with all the strange stuff going on.

He took out his tin whistle and began to play, softly at first. Emily stopped and turned, listening. He walked toward her, switching into a brighter reel. She smiled and clicked her heels in a little Irish step and laughed as Troubles pranced around her. Even Conor had to stop for a moment and laugh at the sight. "All right, Aunt Emily," he said, "show me where I'm staying and then let me take a tour of the massive metropolis of Tinker's Grove."

OZ

EMILY'S HOUSE WAS set back on Abbey Road a quarter mile on a cul-de-sac called Madoc's Glen. It sat back and at the foot of the bluff on top of which the monastery presided over the town. Madoc's Glen comprised roughly twenty acres of woodland and small meadow that stretched northeast along the side of the bluff. Conor guessed that if he kept walking that direction he'd eventually end up wherever he was taken the night before. Where the house was, the river was a good quarter of a mile away with some of the town in between. But the Wisconsin made a little jog to the north just past the town limits, bringing it much closer to the bluff. Aunt Emily's home was just at the end of the flood plain. Unusual for this part of the country, her house was made of stone, two story and big.

"Why did you name your property Madoc's Glen? What's it mean?" Conor stopped for a moment, peering at the old sign.

"Well, boy, if you looked a little closer, you'd see that this place was established in 1840-quite a while ago. Named, I believe, for someone the first settlers knew. I'm just the inheritor of the property." She pointed up at the house with her blackthorn cane. "See that window on the right side of the second level? That's your's, and the room behind it as well, that looks over the woodland. Nobody's used it in years, but I've kept it as the major guestroom. You'll find it old lady fashioned, I think, but fix it up however you want."

Conor was about to speak when a car pulled into the driveway and Beth hopped out. Jace was a little slower extricating himself from the driver's side. "Or," said Emily, "take these two inside and have them act as your interior decorators. The house has only had me in it for years. It needs a little fixin' up."

"Hey," said Conor to Beth, "how do you like my new place?" He gave her a small, shy grin.

"If you can take your eyes off her for a second, you'll see I'm here too," said Jace.

"What? Oh, yeah," said Conor, tapping Jace on the shoulder with his tin whistle. "Sorry about that. Good to see you guys. Aunt Emily here was just showing me where I'll be staying. Want to see?"

Emily was right. The house was fine for a spinster, even an independent one like Emily O'Rourke, but in desperate need of being updated. Beth took things in hand after looking over Conor's spartan room. "Well, Conor, we have to make this look at least as bad as Jace's room back home. We'll head up to Prairie this weekend to get most of the stuff you'll need, but no reason why we can't start now. Jace, let's take him on a tour of the town and we'll stop at Martin's and see what Dort's got that will start shaping up this room."

"I don't know," said Conor, reneging on his earlier desire to see the town. "I've got to go with my aunt down to the funeral home later. They're bringing ... they're bringing my mom's body back from Chicago. We got funeral stuff to do."

"That's this afternoon," said Jace.

"There's no disrespect in trying to take your mind off the past two days, Conor," said Beth. "Come on, you need a break."

"Don't have any money."

Jace and Beth looked at each other. "You'll owe us. Besides, you owe us already for last night."

Conor gave that shy smile again and nodded.

Going downstairs and heading for the front door, Jace said, "Thanks Miss O'Rourke. Nice old place you got here, but we think Conor's room needs a few things. We're stealing him from you for awhile."

"No problem," said Emily. "By the way, it's Aunt Emily to you; I don't stand on protocol. Come back by noon and I'll feed the lot of you. Make sure that dog goes with you; don't want him nosing around here, tripping me up."

Five minutes brought them to the middle of what passed for the business district of Tinker's Grove. Jace parked the car across from the *DewDrop Inn*. Troubles was the first to exit and made his way down the sidewalk, investigating the doorways. Not many people were on Main Street this early in the morning, but the three were startled when Dickie Bergin, owner and bartender of the *DewDrop Inn*, burst out of the front entrance hustling Walter Johnson out of his establishment.

"Your story was crazy last night Walt, when you were three sheets to the wind, and it doesn't wear any better this morning."

"Come on, Dickie, give me a beer and let me show you on the map where it happened."

"Go home and sober up, Walt. Come back tonight if you're able, and maybe you can show me then."

The swinging saloon doors snapped shut and Walter looked across the street, staring slack faced at the three.

"Morning, Walt," said Beth.

Walt jumped at her voice and looked again as if he was just seeing them. He crossed the street, sidling side to side on bowed legs. "You folks startled me there, sneaking up and all that."

"Sorry, didn't mean to," said Jace. "What was all that about with Dickie?"

Walt ran a nervous hand through his greying hair. A day's growth of whiskers gave him a haggard look. "Aw, you wouldn't believe me neither, if I told you."

"When have I ever not believed you, Walt?" said Jace. "Heck, if it's a fish story you're going to tell, you know I'll believe you. You and my Dad were the first to take me fishing and you taught me everything there is to catching catfish on the river, so tell away."

Leaning against the blue Ford and whispering conspiratorially, though with a slight moonshine slur, Walt cocked his head towards Conor, "First tell me who this young lad is."

Conor stuck out his hand, "Name's Conor Archer."

"Well now," said Walt, "ain't that something. You're the boy that came in yesterday on the bus. Someone was asking about you last night. Biker fellow."

Conor grew pale, but before he could say anything, Walt went on. "Guy all in leather. Nasty fellow. Told him what I saw; believed me I think, but didn't give me no respect. And Dickie Bergin was talkin' about you, too, to everyone at the bar. Anyway, I'll tell you what I seen, down by the river. Something out of legend. Grandma Swift Deer, she was kind of my foster mother when I was a youngin'; used to scare my friends and me with the story on nights when wind and rain and thunder put us all on edge. She was better than a horror movie." Walt cackled at his own wit. "'Spooks in the night, dragons in the water,' she'd say. 'Gather round me kids; I'm telling you a story.'"

"Walt," said Jace, more impatiently then he wanted, "what did you see the other night?"

Just then, out of the corner of his eye, Conor caught sight of the strangest thing. Beth saw Conor turn his head to look down the street and saw what he saw. "It's just Oz Murphy," she said. "He's a little special."

And indeed he was. Every town has one, that one person just a little bit strange, that slightly daft individual the town protects and mocks at the same time. In older days, he would have been called the village idiot, but in Tinker's Grove, they just called him Oz.

He was big and barrel chested. His black hair, uncombed and unwashed, hung slack over his brow and ears. Oz was in his early twenties and lived in a world by himself. Everyone said he was okay as a kid, but when he hit thirteen he changed as his voice changed. Withdrew from folks and maybe even a bit from reality. It only got worse. Once in a while, he'd join the rest of the world, but most times he listened to the voices that came from the ear buds in his ears. The cord wasn't plugged into an MP3 player or anything, but that didn't matter to Oz. He could be heard humming to himself and the tune was whatever song was beamed into his brain from the frequency the unplugged earphones received. Sometimes, he'd pick up the plug and speak into it, having a conversation with whatever disembodied voice spoke in his ears.

That's what he was doing now as he walked up the street. Eyes half closed, lips moving, head doing a Stevie Wonder impersonation going side to side.

Even Walt had shut up for a moment to watch the advent of Oz. Jace said to Conor, "Once, when I was twelve, I was with my friends and we gathered around Oz, sat him down, and took off the earphones. It was as if you took a battery out of a toy robot. Oz froze, went stiff, became as still as a mannequin. We all shouted at him, waved our hands in front of his staring black eyes, pulled his hair, but there was no response. I made them stop. Guess I was embarrassed for him and for what we were doing. I put the ear buds back into his ears. Right away, he started humming a tuneless, soulless song. It's as if we were never there and didn't do anything to him. He just got up and walked on."

Just like he was walking today. It looked as if Oz would walk right by them. But suddenly he stopped both—his conversation into the plug and his walking. For a moment, Oz stared straight ahead. Then he slowly turned his thick neck towards Conor. His black eyes flickered with gold specks, that's what Beth, Conor, and Jace agreed on later, and the big man lifted up a huge hand and laid it on Conor's cheek.

Cold, felt Conor, unbelievable cold and wet—dark! Couldn't breathe. And deep. Pressure crushing his chest. Down he went into the depths. Faces, faces he saw, with huge black eyes coming in and out of his vision. He opened his mouth to scream but the water came rushing in, choking, choking.

By the time Jace could pull Conor away from Oz, he was doubled over gasping for air. "Conor, Conor, breathe man!" Jace hit him on his back a couple of times and suddenly, Conor's gasping had effect and air rushed into his lungs. As he straightened up, he saw Oz smiling at him. He could have sworn that Oz mouthed the word, 'Welcome.'

"Crazy," said Walter.

Oz must have heard because he snapped his head around, looked at Walter and hissed with a fierce malevolence, "Piasa, Walter. Piasa's going to get some Walter." Just a whispered hiss, and then Oz began a tuneless hum and moved on.

Beth helped her brother prop Conor up on the hood of the car. "Maybe too much has happened; maybe we should just take him home."

Conor shook his head, looked puzzled and asked Walt, "What did he say? What did Oz say? What's a pie-ah-saw? And tell me more about the biker guy in the bar last night. Do you know his name?" But Walt wasn't listening. He'd backed completely against the trunk of the car, a little spittle dancing on his lips as he watched Oz walk away.

"Gotta go, kids, gotta go." Looking like he'd been backhanded by the ham-sized fist of Oz, Walt staggered down the street in the opposite direction of Oz Murphy.

"You sure you're okay, Conor?" asked Jace.

"Really, I am. It's just that when Oz touched me I seemed to be someplace else, underwater and drowning. Real strange, I know, but not much stranger than what happened at the Indian mound."

"Or what happened last night on the way home," said Beth.

"What?" asked Conor.

So they told him about the girl, woman, hag, whatever she was. But they didn't tell him everything. Jace and Beth instinctively knew that Conor needed friends, not nursemaids. Talk of prophecies and guardians went unreported. No matter, what was said was enough to make Conor pale again. "She's here too?"

"You know her?" said Jace. Hurriedly, Conor told him of the encounter at Buckingham Fountain. "What do you mean, 'too?' This got something to do with the biker guy Walt was talking about, calls himself Rory?"

"Yeah," said Conor. "A biker guy, all in leather, like Walt said, followed me from Chicago. Looks like he's here as well."

"Just not as spooky as everything else that happened," said Jace.

"Don't rush to judgement," said Conor. "He's not anymore ordinary than that woman you talked to last night on the road after putting me to bed."

"Bikers come through here all the time," said Beth.

"Bet not one who has a thing about taking a chunk out of a person's hand," said Conor.

"He bit you? That's how you got hurt?" Beth stared at him incredulously.

"Outside the bar where I worked. He spiked my drink when I wasn't looking and led me outside."

"Pervert," said Jace.

"Don't think so," answered Conor. "Never felt threatened that way. Scared the hell out of me just the same, though. Thought he was going to kill me after he bit me, but he dove in the river."

"Sounds like he's stalking you." said Jace.

"Maybe. All I know is that since the other night, when my Mom died, things have gotten way weird. And now I've brought all the strangeness here."

Jace laughed. "That's okay. It's summer in Tinker's Grove. Way weird is so much better than boring."

"You guys are taking this awfully calmly," said Conor. "Ghosts and hands that get healed and girls that turn into whatever."

"We watch a lot of movies," said Jace. "Seriously though, you don't know much about Tinker's Grove, do you? That's okay, why should you? But like all sleepy river towns in this part of the state, we have a history, more than most really. Everyone, mostly everyone I guess, who lives here, is descended from the original settlers—Tinkers they were, 'Travelers' they called themselves, from Ireland. And that's strange in itself. From what I hear, these Tinkers or Travelers—gypsies really—never settle down but these did over a century and a half ago. They must have come over during the Potato Famine. And they brought strangers with them—people who shouldn't have been traveling with them. Dark they were. Black hair, black eyes, almost olive skin. Last night, after the Abbot mentioned them, I got to thinking what my father told us when we were young. There's a story that the Tinkers were protecting them—it had something to do with the birth defect the strangers had. Webbed feet and hands."

Jace paused and looked at Conor. "Just like you. But nobody ever bothered them here. They intermarried with one another; and kids with black hair and black eyes and webbing on their feet and hands would appear now and then. I guess the town protected them because all of them grew up here and died here over the years. Very few moved away. Some of the townspeople over the recent years have moved to the cities but not the black haired folks, the 'dark ones' we call them. Don't know why. But you did, Conor. You haven't been here, at least since you were a baby, and now you've come back. That, in itself, makes you very interesting." Jace smiled, "And promises lots of fun."

"What about the Abbey?" asked Conor. "What's the deal with that, out here in the middle of nowhere?"

Beth took over. "A priest who traveled with the Tinkers sent for the monks shortly after this town was built. They came and they built *Stella Maris* Abbey, that's Latin for 'Star of the Sea', on the bluff overlooking the town. It's kind of cool really. Most of the town goes to church there on Sunday and most of the town gets buried there in the parish part of the

Abbey graveyard." She touched Conor's arm. "Your Mom's grave will be there, Conor. It's a beautiful place, on the bluff overlooking the river. Anyway, the Abbey's a big draw for tourism in these parts. The monks run a great farm and their bread, jelly, honey and other produce are sent far and wide."

"So how does all this history make it easy for you and your brother to deal with what happened this past day or two?"

Beth said, "We've been raised on songs and stories, Conor. Apparently, just like your mother did for you. And those tales and that music told us of what happened to the early inhabitants of this town and what they brought with them from the old country. Like the Morrigan."

"The what?" asked Conor.

"The Morrigan. The being that feasts on the battle dead from war, and washes her hair in a stream or river like the banshee. She can foretell your death and sometimes appears as a girl, or a beautiful woman, or an old hag. I guess I didn't expect to see her last night for real."

"You don't know that for sure," said Jace.

"My mother, just before she died, called her Morrie, like she knew this Morrigan," said Conor.

"If she spent any time here in Tinker's Grove," said Beth, "then she certainly had to have heard about her."

"But they were just stories," said Jace.

"When you see something like that in reality," said Beth, "you make the connection. Looks like legends are coming to life." She looked piercingly at Conor.

"When I was lying on the ground yesterday, just after the bus left— Troubles was licking my face. I looked up and saw the crowd around me and I heard them, the people. They were whispering, wondering about me. And I think I told them my name, and the faces—they looked scared, like they knew who I was."

Beth said, "Since the Conor Archer of legend lived over a century and a half ago and disappeared, they were just a little startled."

"But I was born here; that's what my mother always told me."

"You must have been," said Jace, "but you couldn't have stayed long. Nobody seems to remember the newer Conor Archer."

A 'woof' down the street caught their attention and they looked to see Troubles standing before what used to be the old dimestore, but now was renamed Martin's Gift and Craft Emporium. The imposing name was meant to attract the tourists visiting the Abbey who might stop for a bit of shopping in the business district of Tinker's Grove.

"That's where we want to be," said Beth. "And don't pay much attention to Dort Martin—she's the nosiest person in town and is bound to ask way too many questions. But she's got stuff we need for your room."

Conor had seen lots of specialty stores in Chicago, but he thought this one the strangest he had ever been in. The front had been cleaned up and held all sorts of knick knacks and tourist trash that didn't interest Conor in the least. But neither Beth nor Jace gave any of that a glance. They headed for the back of the store where it was like walking into another time and place. Clutter was the rule here. Old comic books, quilts, greeting cards, toys and even board games, whatever wasn't sold in the store simply went on a higher shelf. Dort Martin had board games near the top of her fifteen foot ceilings that were over fifty years old. There was even a glass apothecary counter in which Conor could see aspirin bottles, tubes of lineament, and antacids that were stocked there decades ago.

"Why does she keep all of this?" asked Conor.

"Because junk one day is treasure the next," said a voice behind them. Dort Martin hovered in the aisle. Jace's huge hulk mostly obscured her, but her pencil thin grating voice could pass through any solid object. "What can I do you for?"

Beth explained they were just looking. But ever watchful Dort, mindful that unobserved customers were potential thieves, followed them everywhere. Beth found a stool for Conor's room, he could sit on it and play his tin whistle, a poster of the Abbey lit up at night during the Tinker's Grove October Country Fair—even Conor thought it positively medieval—and a hunter's quilt with sporting dogs romping.

Beth frowned, "We'll get more stuff tomorrow, but this is a start. Got to make your house a home. Are you bringing anything from your place in Chicago?"

"I don't know. We didn't have much," said Conor. "Most of my music is in my head, and I don't read much either. Don't know how to get it here anyway. Maybe Aunt Emily will know."

"Heard your mother died, Conor," said Dort who had processed to memory every word said in the store since they arrived. "What was her name again?"

"Finola," said Conor. "Finola Archer."

"I'm not recollecting her at the moment, and I've been here a right long time. You sure she's from around here?"

Conor flared, "Look, this is my home town. My mother said we came from here."

Dort's pinched face didn't register the anger. "I would have been a young woman when your mother was born. My old woman's memory just isn't what it used to be. Of course, there's the Finola Archer of a century and half ago, but she couldn't be your mother, could she? Maybe a distant relation?"

"Mrs. Martin," said Jace. "Could we check out please?"

"I'll thank you for not interrupting me, Jason Michaels. So your mother will be buried from the Abbey?"

"Guess so," mumbled Conor. Turning back to the woman, Conor said, "You sure my mother didn't grow up here?"

"Just what I said. As I'm remembering now, there was a Finola Archer who passed through here seventeen or so years ago—that's about how old you are isn't it?—but she was ... well, she had a child with her, a baby really, during the brief time she was here. Not married, and not really one of us, if you know what I mean. She didn't stay long. Went to Chicago I think. Didn't you say you were from Chicago, Conor?"

"Mrs. Martin," said Beth, exasperated. "How much do we owe you for all this?"

She rung up the price and as Jace paid, Dort said, "Conor, don't mind my questions; it's just that we don't get new folks here that often. People say you'll be staying with Emily O'Rourke—that true?"

Conor nodded.

"How nice for you. Course, she's a strange bird. As I'm thinking about it a little more, she may have had something to do with that Archer girl those seventeen years back. What goes around comes around, that's what I always say. Memory that is. Well, I'm sorry for your loss. If the funeral is up at the Abbey, I'll like as not see you there. Here, some candy for all of you. It's on the house."

As they went to the door, Jace whispered to Conor. "Have the dog sniff it; it's probably years old. She gives nothing good away for free."

Conor took a piece of the candy and tossed it to Troubles. He let it drop without giving it a second sniff. "Great store," said Conor. "We've got a name in Chicago for that lady though, and it rhymes with 'itch.'"

As they walked to the car, they saw Oz coming their way again, making his second pass around downtown. Oz must have seen them. He stopped where he was and waited for them to pass by. His eyes were closed though and he still kept humming his tuneless song. As they walked by, he reached out and grabbed Conor's wounded hand. Nothing happened. No visions, no drowning sensation. Oz raised the hand up to his nose and sniffed the wound. Conor was so taken aback that he didn't even move. Oz, without opening his eyes gently lowered the hand and then with his finger, touched the wound and traced a path up Conor's wrist, winding up the forearm. And then he stopped, his own finger fixed in the air. Conor moved away.

"Leave him be, Conor," said Jace. "We'll take you back now. He'll be okay." He whistled for the dog, and they left Oz there, humming to himself, finger catching the morning breeze.

PLANNING A FUNERAL

JACE AND BETH stayed for lunch. Good thing thought Jace because Emily O'Rourke was a damn fine cook. While they were gone, she had time to manufacture some fried chicken, potato salad, beans and, to top it all, fresh peach cobbler.

"Don't mind my brother, Miss O'Rourke," said Beth. "Even outside of football season, he eats enough for a team."

"That's how I've kept you slim all these years, Beth," said Jace, snatching a biscuit off her plate.

Emily beamed. It had been a while but she saw she still had the knack. Except Conor was just picking at his plate. She reached over and smoothed his hair, "Not hungry?" she asked.

Conor looked up. "Appetite's just not there, Aunt Emily. We're going to the funeral home right after this?"

"Sure," she said, "Wendell Tooms is expecting us. He's the undertaker around here."

"And furniture salesman," said Beth. Conor looked puzzled.

"We still do things the old way," said Emily. "Time was that the furniture makers were also the undertakers. Caskets needed building just like tables and chairs. Toom's Furniture Store and Funeral Home are housed in the same place. In fact, lots of shopping goes on while folks wait to see the deceased."

"Seriously? That's where we're going to wake Mom?" said Conor with a look of disbelief.

"Actually," said Emily, "I was hoping we could have the visitation in the Abbey church. Folks are doing that more and more. A little more formal than the funeral home, but I must say that down at Tooms I always feel a bit uncomfortable sitting on a sofa that has a price tag on it and a sticker saying, 'SALE, SALE, SALE!' while I wait to see the deceased and the family."

They made short work of dinner and the dishes. Jace and Beth took off and Emily shooed Troubles up toward the Abbey and started off with Conor walking back into town to see Wendell Tooms.

"You walk everywhere?" asked Conor. He was tired already and the thought of hoofing it to town on a hot day didn't strike his fancy. Still, he didn't much like the idea of being outwalked by an elderly woman either.

"Transportation was sparser when I was younger and I just got used to walking, rain or shine, snow or wind. It's what I do and it won't hurt you either. Might even wake you up a bit."

The meeting with Tooms wasn't as bad as Conor thought it would be. When he shook Conor's hand there was no pasty 'fish' grip. The man had a strong handshake. Maybe he still built the caskets. His smile was genuine even if his expressions of sympathy were a little generic and automatic. Conor was informed that his mother's body had been delivered before noon and they were already 'fixing her up' as Mr. Tooms was wont to say.

Reaching into the little bag she had brought, Aunt Emily pulled out a dress; something a younger woman would like. Where she got it Conor didn't know, but he thought it would look good on his mother—along with shoes and a beautiful gold Celtic necklace. Finely filigreed Celtic knotwork—would make her look like a princess.

Conor only had to look once at the room where the visitations were held to know that the Abbey church was the better idea. Of course, it helped when Mr. Tooms left the room and Aunt Emily sat on a discounted couch with the price tag of an old Thomas Kincaid painting above her, dangling over her left eye. For a moment, they forgot their sadness, both bursting out laughing. Neither could imagine honoring Finola in a room like that.

When Mr. Tooms returned they set tomorrow as the time for visitation at the Abbey church, pending the Abbot's approval, since it was Tuesday already. A funeral Mass would be said, too, hopefully by the Abbot on Thursday morning. Pursing her lips at a rather distasteful job well done, Aunt Emily motioned for Conor that it was time to leave.

By the time Conor got back to the house with Aunt Emily he was beat, but he wanted to get the lay of the land. Putting off a chance to close his eyes when Emily went inside, he went out back. There in Madoc's Glen the sultry summer afternoon was quiet and calm; only the buzzing of a fly here or there disturbed the stillness. The sun was hot, warm enough to dampen any chirping from the birds. Conor spied a small red barn not far from the house just at the end of the lawn, shaded here and there by oaks. Curious he opened the sliding wood door. It was a little cooler inside, and he was surprised to find a few fresh bales of straw in a corner. Not a bad place just to sit for a moment. Conor saw one of the bales was loose so he spread out the straw and sat down on it, leaning against the others.

He closed his eyes, only for a few seconds he thought. No dreams this time, but when he woke, he could tell from the sun shining through the slats of the barn wall that some time had passed. Besides, things looked different. The sun seemed brighter, the wood on the barn walls gnarlier; everything seemed more real. He smelled the straw and his mouth began to water. Nostrils flared, catching the whiff of dung from some small animal that had crawled into the barn and spent the previous night. His ears tingled as he heard the rustling of tiny mice paws skittering throughout the barn. Dust motes shimmered in the sunlit heat.

Everything's too ... too present, thought Conor. His breathing sounded like some huge blower on an industrial furnace or air conditioner. Conscious of that, he slowed himself down, quieting the noise. His hand was itching, the one that had been healed. He held it up to the light. Where the wound once was, a black strip about three inches long had appeared, winding its way up Conor's wrist. He gasped. Blood poisoning! But then he touched the ribbon of black and found it leathery and hard. This was on the surface of his skin. He looked more closely and saw it was part of his hand, smoothly linked to the rest of his flesh. He looked at his other hand. Nothing. Hurriedly, he stripped off his shoes and socks to check his feet. Just the slight webbing between his toes, nothing else. He quieted his booming breathing again.

Nostrils flared once more as he caught another odor, a smell of someone approaching, stealthy, wishing not to be seen. How in the hell do I know this stuff he thought. He wasn't afraid, surprisingly, so he didn't hide. Instead, he leaned back against the bale of straw and nibbled on a strand, waiting for whatever was coming to show itself.

A shadow darkened the doorway, and Conor matched the odor of leather to the figure standing. "You!" he said.

"Conor, my lad," said the biker. "It's good to see you again. Are you well?"

"No thanks to you," Conor said, spitting out the strand of straw. "You tried to kill me."

"Not me," said Rory. "You're too important. Just had to hurry things up a bit. I've been waiting too long to take more time."

"You've done something to me. Whoever that was in that Indian mound healed my hand, but whatever poison was in that bite is still doing its work."

"Shush now," smiled Rory, "it wasn't poison. Just a catalyst really. To help you become who you are supposed to be. Mind if I come closer?"

"What's with the politeness? Two days ago you were biting chunks out of my flesh."

Rory stood before the boy. "You really don't know what's going on do you? They haven't told you. Those devious bastards."

"Who and what?" asked Conor.

"Why the sainted Abbot of course and his co-conspirator, your supposed Aunt Emily. They know what's happening to you."

Conor held up his hand, showing Rory the dark streak. "What is this? Can you tell me what's happening?"

"Ah, sure and surely I can," said Rory. Like some primate he dropped to his haunches, hands on the floor of the barn, head stuck out to take a better look. "You're stepping sideways, lad."

Conor smoothly got to his knees and leaned forward face to face with Rory. "And what's that supposed to mean?"

"It's another world, you fool," said Rory. "You're not like them, you know."

"Like who?" asked Conor.

"Like people. In fact, that little streak on your hand and wrist tells me you're not human at all, at least not anymore. And that," said Rory with an insolent smile, "is a very good thing."

Without thinking Conor closed his fist and swung. Right on Rory's chin he planted the blow and Rory flew backwards and landed on his back, face staring at the ceiling. Conor fell on top of Rory and rolled off moaning, not from the pain of the blow, but because when he punched Rory, pain exploded from his healed wound and traveled up his arm. Clutching his shoulder, Conor looked at his arm and saw the dark streak had snaked up to his bicep. His head felt like it would explode and through it all he could hear Rory laughing.

"Great shot; and I can't say as I didn't have it coming, but look at you, just look at you. Changing right there before my eyes. Let me see that arm lad." And Rory began to crawl like some appendaged snake. Conor backed himself up against the bales of straw. He didn't want that thing touching him again. Just as Rory reached to grasp Conor a blackthorn cane smacked down between them.

"Next twitch you make, Rory Nalan, I'll whack this through your midsection, and that would hurt even you." Emily kicked Rory in the ribs. "Now move back and pray I don't beat you like the pig you are."

Rory took his time but sidled back a few feet and sat up looking at the fierce old woman. "Time hasn't changed you, Emily O'Rourke. But I'm a little troubled you haven't told the boy. Look at him there. If he was a little younger, he'd be just like a pock-marked adolescent child all a-trembly with puberty. At least when that occurs kids know what's happening to them. He doesn't. Don't you think you should tell him?"

"Shut your face you conniving menace," snarled Emily. "Haven't you damaged him enough? And with his mother to bury to boot. Have you no shame; have you not one shred of compassion in you?"

Rory's black eyes blazed flecks of gold looking like the shimmering dust motes in the afternoon sunlight. "I don't have time, woman, and you know that. He's the best chance in a thousand years we've had and I'm not going to squander the opportunity, you hear? It's his destiny."

"He's a boy, Rory, and one who's just lost his mother."

"He's not a boy nor a man and you know that." Rory smiled an evil smile, "Did you know that I looked into Finola's face just after she died? I smelled her death, and it was wonderful."

Conor lifted up his throbbing head to see Aunt Emily swing her blackthorn cane. The rough and knobbed staff struck Rory right across the face and shot him backwards several feet. "Never speak of her like that again! She was a good woman and your hatred for her because she rejected you has got to stop. You were unfit for her then, just like you are unfit to be in the company of my nephew. Now get you gone!" And she struck him again across his face. He scrambled upright. She made to hit him once more but he grabbed the cane.

"Enough. Your being old won't protect you from me."

Emily raised her free hand and hit him across his mouth. "Don't you speak to me like that. Righteous anger is all the power I need to tame the likes of you, Rory Nalan. Now out! Out of this barn. And take care around Conor. Bring him no harm."

For the first time, hurt shown in Rory's eyes and his voice spoke softly. "I am many things, Emily O'Rourke, but one thing you should know more than any other—Conor Archer's life is more precious than anyone else's, more precious than yours, and more precious than mine."

Rory turned and strode out the barn door. Emily bent down and helped Conor to his feet. "It was a good punch you gave him, Conor, but you need to throw your weight into it next time. Looks like we'll have to practice." And she helped him across the lawn into the house.

OF LIES AND MISDIRECTION

EMILY MADE TO open the screen door but Conor leaned his newly healed hand against it. His headache had given him the sweats and perspiration was pouring off his face.

"What is this, Aunt Emily?" asked Conor looking at the leathery streak winding its way up his arm. "What's happening to me?"

"We'll have Brother Luke take a look at it, but as far as I'm concerned, there's nothing wrong with you, Conor, and it's silly to be dealing with this while you're grieving your mother."

"Rory said you knew; he said you and Father Abbot know what was happening to me."

"Oh, pish-pash," clucked the old woman. "That beast lies through his smart-mouthed smile."

Conor's fist pounded the door. "Stop it, will you? I'm feeling like hell again, and that stupid fever's back I think, and I'm not … I'm just not in the mood to be lied to or put off. Now tell me what's going on."

Emily leaned on her cane and pursed her lips. "You may be far bigger than me, Conor Archer, and I'll allow you, this once, to talk back to me in that tone of voice, but make no mistake. I know many things and I've never been forced to tell them, and it isn't going to happen now either. You can pound the door and throw fits and what not, but anything I have to say to you I shall say in my own good time. You understand?"

Conor hung his head and was silent. Softly he said, "Understood. I'm sorry. Just not feeling well, I guess." He paused again and then gritted his teeth. "But I still think I have the right to know."

"To know what?" said Aunt Emily. "What's going to happen to you tomorrow? Where you'll be next week? Whether a flu bug is going to bite you or you'll someday come down with cancer like your mother? You think you have the right to know all that? Well you don't. Whatever I know isn't going to help you in the next few days, so I'll take my sweet time thinking about whether I'll tell you at all. But now I'm all for feeling a little sorry for you because you are indeed looking mighty poorly. So get yourself up to your bed and I'll be up in a minute with some cool wet cloths for your head and some ice cold lemonade. Now, are you going to let me in?"

Conor stepped back and Emily stormed into her own house. He followed and detoured up the steps to his room. Stripping off his shirt, he was so damn hot, he threw his shoes and socks in a corner and flopped on the bed. Emily had been here too, fixing things up, already putting on the new bedspread Beth had picked out earlier. Conor noticed his whistling stool, that's what Beth called it, set by the window looking out at the back yard and woods. He thought she was pretty fine, for a rural girl. Didn't have that attitude that the city girls affected. Direct, no nonsense, pleased with herself and her looks. I like that, he thought. And he closed his eyes for just a moment.

Something cold and wet touched his forehead and he opened one eye to see Aunt Emily bending over him placing a washcloth on his brow. "You're burning up again," she said.

"Well, I wouldn't be if you had something civilized, like air conditioning, here."

Emily smiled. "Never had it, never will." She noticed Conor absently stroking the leathery line on his right forearm. She sat on the side of his bed. Gently she placed her free hand over his and stilled his motion. "Stop that now. It will be alright."

"What's happening to me?" he asked. "My mother never said anything about this sort of stuff. Bad enough she died, but now I'm turning into a freak."

"Nonsense!" said the old woman, wringing out the washcloth and dipping it again in ice cold water. "You'll not be a freak, Conor; but I can't deny you're changing."

"But into what?"

"Does it really matter? You know you are not dying; you can feel it. Sick you might be, but not dying, not anymore. You're changing. To live is to change. That's what I always say. And to be perfect is to have changed often. And I think," she said with a smile, "that you are well on your way to being perfect."

"You're not going to tell me are you?"

"Conor, if I had met you when you were twelve and told you that I saw in you a grand musician and gave you a tin whistle and told you to play, what would you have done?"

"I would have thrown it away; I just hated to be told what to do."

"And what if I tell you now what you really are? Would you believe me? Would you accept?"

"What do you mean?"

"Look into yourself, boy. What's different about you since earlier in the week?"

"I don't know," said Conor, and hesitated. "Everything seems more real, I guess. I already know about the animals; they pay attention to me. I can hear the slightest sound; I can see into stuff, into things, sort of see what they really are."

"Ah," sighed Emily, "you can smell the starlight."

"What did you say?" said Conor looking at her in surprise.

"I said you can smell the starlight."

"My mother used to say something like that. It was the one thing she said she didn't like about the city. She said, 'With all these buildings and these neon signs, I just can't smell the starlight.' She said that. She really did."

"And so she should. She was from here, Conor. It's a saying we have around these parts, about people who see and hear things more clearly than others."

"I miss her," he said. "Did you really know her well, Aunt Emily?"

"So close, she was like a sister to me, at least while she was here. And I can tell you she loved you, lad. You were the most important thing in her universe."

"Why didn't she stay here? Why does everybody just solemnly nod their heads knowingly when they hear the name Finola Archer like there's some big story behind her?"

"Perhaps because there is," said Emily. "And perhaps when you're feeling better, I'll tell you a bit of it. Now, drink some of that lemonade I brought you and shut your eyes for a while and let that cold compress and ice cold drink cool you off and slake that fever. And maybe this evening, when you look up at the heavens, you'll be able to smell the starlight. That's when you'll know you truly are alive." She walked out and shut the bedroom door.

"Yeah," said Conor under his breath, "but will I still be human?"

DR. NICHOLAS DRAKE

GORDON MCNABB HAD a hard time of it, trying to discover a little more information about Conor Archer. By the time he arrived downtown—he truly was a late sleeper—Conor, Beth and Jace had already left. McNabb had to content himself with Dickie Bergin's rendition of the odd behavior; it was even more than the usual. The stories of Oz with Walter Johnson and Conor did not offer much info, but just enough to say that this Conor boy deserved more looking into.

He made it back to the house around four in the afternoon. Pulling into the drive, he saw his mother talking to a tall man dressed in black. As he got out of the car, she waved at him and the man turned around. Nothing bland or muted about him. He dressed to be noticed and moved to be remembered. Tall, he wore a black, tailored, three-piece suit even in the heat, a style which emphasized his immaculately coifed silver hair. Sweeping off his suitcoat and holding out his hand in a grand gesture, starched French cuffs winking gold where the light caught his cufflinks, his bloodless lips turned up a cold smile, he said, "You must be Gordon. Your mother has told me all about you. I'm Dr. Nicholas Drake, president of DIOGENE."

"Gordon," said Cate, "Dr. Drake is here to finish signing some papers for the transfer of the land, though we weren't expecting you till tomorrow." Bestowing her guest with a dazzling smile, she said, "It will be a little while before my lawyer can get here. Won't you come in and sit down." Cate gracefully turned and walked into the house. It was hard for Gordon not to notice the good doctor's eyes narrowing in appreciation of Caitlin's swaying hips.

"As I was telling your mother," said Drake, gently rolling a little Scotch around his glass, "we at DIOGENE are anxious to get started. We're a small gentech company and genetic research is all the rage now. But I accepted your mother's offer because of the unique possibilities this community offers for the type of work we do."

"And what type is that, Doctor, if I may ask?" Gordon inquired. He was all ready to hear about the improvement of the human species, but he knew down deep, doctor or not, Drake was a man and greed motivated most men.

"Why, the improvement of the human species of course," Drake responded. He quickly saw the cynical shift of eyes away from him.

"Don't be rude, dear," said Cate driving daggers into Gordon's heart with her own gaze.

"It's true," said Drake earnestly. "I think we can find something here that might help improve the human condition. And of course we have to make money or we wouldn't be able to do research, but I'm not in it to be a millionaire. I'm already that. I want to make a difference, that's all."

"What," questioned Gordon, "makes us such a prime choice for your research?"

Drake look puzzled and said to Cate, "I thought you said he knew. I thought you said he would be eager to help."

Cate laughed and helped herself to the open bottle of Scotch on the table. As she poured, she said, "He does know; he just hasn't put two and two together yet."

"Well, put it together for me Doctor," said Gordon, "since, in my mother's eyes, I'm being a little dense."

"It's simple, really," said Drake flicking a wrist so that the cufflink sparkled again in the afternoon light. "My company's research deals with interspecies improvements. Not like H.G. Wells', Island of Dr. Moreau; nothing so crude. Crossbreeding humans and animals can't be done, but … but" said Drake pausing for effect, "isolating the genetic markers of certain qualities in animals and grafting them into human embryos and vice versa might just benefit humanity."

"Make a super human or a super cow?" snickered Gordon.

"If you like," sniffed Drake, "but I prefer to call it enhancing the human condition. I'm not talking about boys with bat ears and girls with legs like a gazelle or cattle with baby faces. I'm talking about attributes more than I am talking about physical characteristics, though I am sure those will be present, too. Take Tinker's Grove own genetic uniqueness; namely, the webbed hands and feet that seem to pop up with every dark haired, dark eyed boy and girl. That isn't seen anywhere on earth."

"What makes you think that particular genetic anomaly has anything to do with animal genes interacting with human ones?"

Cate smiled and looked at the doctor. "I told you he was bright even if he sometimes can't see the forest for the trees." She took a drink of her Scotch. "It's like this, Gordon. The genetic anomaly is too regular, and the behaviors elicited by those who have them are too similar, for this to be a random accident."

"What behaviors?"

"You tell me. You've lived here long enough to notice."

Gordon thought for a moment and shrugged his shoulders. "They're okay, the 'dark ones', I guess. When I was a kid, the ones who played with us seemed to have a way with animals, always finding and healing the bird with a broken wing, adopting the orphaned racoon, you know that sort of thing. All of the 'dark ones' I knew loved water and swam well. We teased them about having otter in their blood. And some of them went kind of nuts when they got into high school. Drinking, even more than me," laughed Gordon, "and taking great risks. A few died. Oz is still crazy. But the others sort of grew out of it. But it's a funny thing. They never leave here. The 'dark ones' always stay."

"Exactly," said Drake. "And while it may not look like there's any connection with my desire to try to enhance the human genome with certain animal attributes, the legend about the 'dark ones,' at least what I know of it, is intriguing. The earliest settlers brought them from Ireland, protected them, so it is said, and I wonder why. I have my own ideas; I know my Celtic lore, and I'll keep my own counsel now. But I think there's a connection, and so too does dear Cate here." Drake put his hand on Cate's knee.

"That's exactly why I want you and your company here," said Cate, standing up so smoothly that Drake did not even feel the shiver of revulsion that rippled through her body as his hand slid off her leg. "Let's find out about our community birth defect, or anomaly, as you call it. Maybe it will be useful to your research. But whatever, you will bring jobs to this town and that means civilization, something Tinker's Grove desperately needs. And while it will bring you money, it will bring needed capital into this community and make us start growing. Yes, Dr. Drake" said Cate, "DIOGENE and Caithness McNabb Enterprises will make a fine partnership. Don't you agree, Gordy?"

Gordon McNabb looked at the two of them, his raven haired mother, ice cold to the bone, and Dr. Nicholas Drake, a suave serpent if there ever was one. Maybe the Age of the Reptiles wasn't over, he thought. Maybe it was just beginning.

THE SMELL OF STARLIGHT

SHE LET HIM sleep through supper. Emily had looked in on him as the sun was setting, touching his cheek and forehead, finding them cooler than before. Tracing the leathery strip on his skin, holding his wounded hand, miraculously healed so it seemed. Still he did not wake. She wondered if she had been right in being deliberately evasive with him. But no, had she talked candidly, he would have shook with fright. No one deserves to know that truth all at once. Besides, his body would do most of the teaching, if he accepted it. Then she thought of Oz, and what could happen. Could Conor lose his mind too? No. Should have happened if it was going to. How he got this far without his abilities manifesting themselves or him going as whiffly as Oz was just a source of amazement to Emily. Any of the 'dark ones' in town that were Conor's age, and there were only a few, had long ago ceased to think of themselves as different. They just had black hair and eyes and a little webbing on their hands and feet. They were busy trying to find a niche in the Grove. They didn't even wonder why they never wanted to leave. But not Conor. He was changing and he knew it. He was becoming. All at the wrong time and to what effect? She left him sleeping and went to bed.

It was after midnight when he awoke. His arm was itching again. But he wasn't sweating and he could feel the wet mist from the river snaking its first near invisible strands up through the woods, across the lawn, just brushing the upstairs window. Getting out of bed, he padded barefoot over to one of the windows and looked out on the lawn and the road. New moon again tonight. That meant the stars were brilliant. The last of the fireflies for the evening were just finishing up twinkling, looking for a mate. The rising mist was covering their faint glow. Not a fog really, just a vapor in which everything was slightly blurred. Except the sky—full of piercing stars.

He drew in a deep breath wondering if Aunt Emily was right. Could he really smell the starlight? His nostrils flared and he looked deep into the heavens. So bright they were. Like spirits flickering in the night. Conor remembered a poem his mother used to read to him. He didn't really understand it, but he loved the line about the stars, like firefolk sitting in the air. They did seem alive.

He pulled his whistling stool over and grabbed his instrument and began to play the music from one of his favorite movies, "The Last of the Mohicans." Great Celtic theme, melancholy but powerful. And as he played he looked skyward, his eyes, beacons of the mind, searching that wild frontier, like his music, looking for a forgotten faded light. He smelled it as much as he felt it, those haunting rhythms ruling the dance of the universe, the rich freshness of light from space. He loved it when he thought in poetry. What a rush. He played more loudly and wildly and he thought, even though he wondered if he was just imagining it, that he could feel the starshine touch him and smell the energy in that universal light. And his music softened as he noticed the starshadow, the gaps between the light. They were empty and dark, bereft of life and hope. He turned his theme to a minor key and smelt the scent of decay and hollowness. He pushed his music out again, searching once more for the light. All he perceived now was the greyness of the mist, and, strangely, a little girl's laughter echoing below out on the road. And then he saw.

Out of the night it appeared, ghostly at first but darkening in the mist as it got closer. No light fell on it. Even the stars could not illuminate it. But Conor knew what it was: a coffin, floating in the mist, slowly moving up the road, and on top of it something that looked feline and large. Black as the night, he thought. No, as black as a black hole, a dead star in the sky. The cat looked up at him as he sat shirtless at the window. He stopped playing. The red eyes of that black cat pierced him with malice and she hissed at him, loudly and defiantly. Silently, he watched until the coffin drifted into the mist out of his sight. He shook his head; death clinging to his nostrils.

"Not a pretty sight, lad, was it?" spoke a voice below his window. Rory stepped out from the house just far enough for Conor to see him looking up.

"That was your mother there in that coffin. Imagine, that wicked she-devil hissing on top of that casket, driving your mother's body like a horse-less hearse. Now what do you think of that?" He looked up at Conor with his gold flecked eyes reflecting the starshine and he winked.

Conor could smell him. Like a feral dog, Rory reeked. And that insufferable smile. "Well, Conor, going to just sit there watching that bag of bones that was your mother? God knows where she's being taken."

All he knew was that it happened fast. Off the whistling stool and out the window he launched himself. Two stories up and he wasn't even afraid of the leap. He felt it in his gut, that visceral urge to wrap his hands around

Rory's neck and snap the biker's bones. Or better yet, just set his jaws to rip out Rory's carotid artery. Never had such hate consumed him. For a moment, he was amazed. He wasn't falling out of the window in some uncontrolled suicide spin. Like the owl of the other day, he was plummeting towards its prey. And in his eye, the face of Rory, a surprised look on his features; did that ever gratify Conor! His face came closer until the bodies crashed together onto the lawn.

Rory outweighed Conor, but rage motivated the boy. He threw punches and kicks; he fought like a wild animal and Rory reciprocated. Both foamed at the mouth as each sought to gain advantage.

"Notice anything new, lad?" panted Rory. "Notice that you touched me without burning, without getting sick? It's happening, it is! Let it flow through you. Run with me. Run with me through the woods, and feel what you are becoming."

But all Conor wanted to do was kill him, and for a moment he thought he had the biker in a death grip. Rory laughed and wriggled free and took off into the woods. Conor could do no less than follow him.

Rory was on all fours, low to the ground. Swift he was and Conor didn't even think. Down he went like a wolf, loping through the woods. He felt his body stretch and speed was his. He was gaining on Rory. Through thickets and among the trees they raced. Ripping into his skin, thorn bushes tore at Conor, but he didn't care. In the night, he saw clearly, and the blood smell in his nostrils simply increased his rage and speed.

Bursting out into a little meadow, Conor leapt upon Rory. He caught him from behind, throwing him to the ground. But the effort of the chase had washed the strength from the boy. Rory easily threw him off and pinned Conor in the tall grass. The biker leered over him. "That was good, lad, oh so good. No human could do what you just did. You liked the hunt didn't you?" Conor howled with rage.

"Wonderful!" said Rory. "If I let you go, you'd put your hands around my throat so fast, but that wouldn't be enough would it? You want to rip it out, don't you? You want to taste my blood."

"No!" gasped Conor. "Never! I'm not like you."

"But you are! I've made you so. Perhaps I should hurry the process up even more." Rory smiled with his pointed white teeth. He smelled like a beast, but he hadn't even broken a sweat. Conor could see that now. And fear crept up his spine again.

"Maybe that's what I'll do," continued Rory. "I liked so much what I did with your one hand, let me have the other. Come on, man, just a little piece of your flesh, just a little bit of your blood." Rory licked his lips, laughing as he jerked Conor to his feet.

Conor's lungs were still heaving. He was seriously worried that Rory would carry out his threat. Wondering whether he had actually called Troubles with his mind earlier in the day, in desperation, he tried once more. He lifted his head. Unerringly he turned toward the Abbey's direction. Under his breath he muttered, but with his mind he shouted, "Troubles, come here!" A distant bark answered his thought.

"Oh that was grand!" said Rory clapping his hands. "You've already learned that little trick. But not in enough time, I'm afraid. Just give me your good hand. It only hurts but a moment." Rory reached for him.

With a new wave of rage washing over him, Conor leapt into Rory rather than lurching backward. He fought for his life now, trying to get any purchase on Rory and hold him or hurt him. Rory danced away. Clearly, he had been toying with Conor before. Eluding Conor's blows, he ducked in now and then to land one on Conor's face, then his midsection. Conor doubled over in pain and Rory tackled him. An arm stretched around Conor's throat and began to squeeze.

"Got you lad. Now you're mine. And I'm thinking on the fact of why I should go for the good hand when I've got the neck right here. Here's the deal. I won't kill you. Can't do that and don't want to. But if I do you in the neck, ah, well, the change will happen instantaneously, it being a major vessel I'd lance. My spit to your blood. Great combination. And then you'll be mine. And you'll do what you're told. And you'll take your proper place. I wonder if humanity knows what's coming." Rory laughed, head thrown back to the sky. He kept his mouth open as he lowered his head to the side of Conor's neck.

Just as Conor felt the brush of teeth, he heard the pounding of paws and saw a figure launch itself from the edge of the woods into the meadow. Rory never saw the dog coming. It barreled into the biker, bowling him over and pinning him to the ground.

Exhausted, Conor rolled to his feet and saw Troubles, hackles raised, teeth bared, about to rip into Rory's throat. It was then that Rory laughed and did the strangest thing. He turned his head to Conor, smiled and said, "Nice jousting and jesting with you lad. We'll finish our talk another time. The dog's a nice touch. There's hope for you yet." And like water poured on dry ground, Rory's body simply dissolved into the earth. Even Troubles was confused for a moment and sniffed the spot where Rory had been.

"Geez, like the Wicked Witch of the West," said Conor, and he threw his arms around the dog. "Got here in the nick of time to save me from that blood sucking asshole."

The creaking of hinges caught Conor's attention and as he lifted his eyes from his dog, he saw the coffin across the meadow sitting in the grass. The lid was up and a pale luminescence shown all around it. Moving slowly to the casket, Conor peered inside. He saw his mother as she always should have looked. Beautiful to behold. The dress that Aunt Emily had brought fit her nicely and the gold necklace sat simply on her neck. Her dark hair flowed over her shoulders but a golden circlet bound her hair to her forehead. In her hands was placed a silver rosary. She looks like a queen, thought Conor, falling to his knees and weeping.

He felt hands on his shoulder and someone kneeling beside him. It wasn't Rory, the touch was too gentle. "She truly is beautiful," said the voice. "As she once was and always should have been." Conor turned and looked into the face of a beautiful young woman. She was the one with lustrous red hair that he had seen at Buckingham Fountain only a few days before.

"But she's dead," said Conor and sobs wracked his body.

"Aye, it's true, and sadder our world is for it," said the woman. "Here, let me hold you." And she took him in her arms and pressed his head to her breast. His body shook with grief. For a long time, she held him tight to herself. He pulled away then, and looked at her.

"Who are you? And why have you done this with my mother's body?"

"I am the Morrigan," she said, smoothing the hair on his brow. "Terrible to love." She kissed him on the mouth and held her lips there for a moment. "Formidable in battle." She drew the nail of her index finger along his cheek and a thin line of blood, Conor's blood, rose to the surface. "And fierce in loyalty." She cupped her hand on Conor's chin and forced him to look into her eyes.

"Hear me well, Conor Archer," said the Morrigan. "I took your mother tonight. The man, who sought to make her presentable for her burial, did rather well, but I had to leave him sleeping. I did the rest, for me and my kind need to honor her before her body is honored by the One. She has had much in common with us, and her sacrifice is noted and held sacred.

"I will watch over her tonight, for I have much to say to her, much to atone for. Seldom does the Morrigan feel regret, but she does tonight Conor Archer—for her reticence, lack of action, inattention and her meddling. It is I who have brought your mother to this time. Never again will I sleep silent while events swirl around me. You are here to make sure of that. So let us be, and get you home to your bed. She is beyond you now, and your grief is keeping her from her rest."

Conor swayed on his knees. His vision contracting, all he could see was the Morrigan's beautiful face. "Do you know what I am?" he heard himself saying.

"The future," she said gently in reply. And he heard her call the dog over to her and he saw her touch Troubles who seemed to lengthen and grow in size. Effortlessly she picked the boy up and laid him face down on the dog's back. She cut a strand of hair from her head and used it to bind Conor's hands to the dog. "Now get you to his home, dog," she said. "And guard him carefully. And if Rory Nalan stops you, do not hesitate this time. Slash his throat and let the dirt drink his filthy blood."

OUT AND ABOUT

EMILY KNOCKED BUT there was no answer. She sighed and pushed away a wisp of white hair. Trying not to wake him, she opened the door slowly and stood in amazement. Then, one hand on her hip, she addressed Conor as he lay on the floor covered in dirt, blood and grass stains. "I'd expect this from an eight year old, but not from someone who is almost an adult. At least you had the good sense not to dirty the fresh linen."

No response. She noticed his hands, his dirty hands were bound together and she sucked in a quick breath. "Do you know anything about this?" she said to Troubles who was lying beside the boy. The dog whined and turned away to stare at a fly crawling on the wall. She bent down and examined the binding around Conor's wrists. "I think, my boy, that you've been consorting with women well above your station and beyond your ability to handle." She knew now how Conor had ended up on the floor. "Dog, you should have told me immediately when you came in last night. But I thank you anyway for bringing him home safely."

Conor groaned and opened his eyes. "Aunt Emily, what am I doing on the floor?"

"Was hoping you could tell me. Obviously, you've had a busy night. And whose hair might this be?" she asked, holding his bound hands up to his sight.

"It was the woman at the fountain. She calls herself the Morrigan."

"A little old for you, isn't she, Conor?"

"Only sometimes, Aunt Emily, only sometimes. Can you cut me loose?"

"No, because this lock of hair may be valuable. There's an easy way to get this off." Next to a little crucifix on a wall shelf was a small clear bottle. "Holy Water, Conor. Does wonders for those things created before the coming of the Redeemer that bind and compel people." She wet her fingers and touched the strand of hair. Immediately, the hair loosened, and Conor's hands were free. She twined the hair around the raven brooch and wrapped it in the cloth that had served as Conor's bandage.

"The Morrigan stole my mother's body," Conor said jumping to his feet. "We've got to get it back."

"Shush now," said Emily. "That's already been taken care of, it seems, and this little scene before me tells me how Finola's casket managed by itself to move from the funeral home to the door of the Abbey Church last night. Caused quite a stir up at the monastery."

"She brought it there?" Conor said in disbelief.

"Of course she did. The Morrigan isn't truly evil. 'Course she's not exactly good either. She's from another time and place where many of her actions would now be perceived as harsh and strange, but she's not evil. Her morality is capricious which makes her dangerous and capable of great disaster. She knew your mother, Conor, and believes she was responsible for what has happened to Finola. The mystery is why she is abroad now in this time and place so visibly." Emily touched the cut on Conor's cheek. "You've awakened something in this land, Conor, and the old ones are stirring."

"Rory was back," said Conor. "That's how I ended up outside. I threw myself out of this window I was so mad at him, and I should have died, but I didn't. I chased him, fought him, and, Aunt Emily, something happened to me. I was like an animal—stronger, faster, than I've ever been. I remember running, not on two feet but on all fours, like a beast. Look at me! Whatever happened last night, I didn't behave as a human being." Despair struck his face and his eyes mirrored the fear he felt in his heart.

"Conor, Conor," said Aunt Emily holding him tight. "Whatever is changing in you, remember your humanity. Nothing can take that from you. You're Finola's son, and indeed that makes you special but it also makes you human."

"Maybe," said Conor, "but I've seen things these past few days that tell me not everything that walks on two legs is human. What about that being at the Indian mound, the one who healed me? He's not human—how could he be? Rory, the Morrigan—what else is Tinker's Grove going to show me? Not to mention, Oz, good old crazy Oz, whose huge, meaty, webbed hand sent me to the bottom of the ocean. At least that's what it felt like; at least that's what I saw. And there were things down there. Faces with big eyes. And they weren't surprised to see me. Just why is that, Aunt Emily?"

"Seems to me," said Emily hitching herself up to a standing position, "that rather than figuring out who all those others are, you ought to be looking into yourself. Know yourself and you'll see into another's soul. That's what I always say. Now get yourself a shower and come down to breakfast. You're free to do anything you want this morning. Visitation is in church this afternoon, and, I'm sorry about it, but you'll have to be there for the whole thing, greeting the folks who come."

"Who'll come and see my Mom? No one even knew her."

"That may be true, but some folks are remembering a young woman with a newborn child who passed through here seventeen years ago. That'd be curious enough, but they wonder too about the fact that both she and you bear the same names as the Conor and Finola of old, who walked these streets when they were freshly claimed from the wilderness. Besides, we're clannish here in Tinker's Grove, but we are sympathetic too. Death touches us all and those that come to see your mother will, for the most part, genuinely express their sorrow. Think of it as their way of welcoming you to town."

After a shower and breakfast, Conor stepped outside. Already, the early morning air was hot. He hoofed it down the road into town. Took him about 20 minutes but he needed the time for thinking. He felt pretty good. All his cuts, even the one on his face, the one the Morrigan gave him, seemed to have washed away along with the dirt and grime. Like the morning before, not much was happening downtown, so he took a right down at the corner of Martin's Gift and Craft Emporium and headed up a residential street. It circled the other way around Monastery Bluff and ended at the high school. Conor could see a morning football practice had been scheduled. He quickly spotted Jace. Biggest player on the team, huffing and grunting his way through some blocking practice. Conor liked him—direct, approachable, Jace seemed to be the real deal. A few other spectators were watching the team and though they took time to notice Conor, they did not approach.

Conor felt uncharacteristically shy. He was a stranger in this strange town, and at that moment, believed he didn't belong anywhere. A shadow cast itself in front of him; he turned and saw a tall young man, a little scruffy looking in jeans and t-shirt.

"Morning," said the man, flicking his cigarette away, smiling and offering his hand. Conor took it. "Name's Gordon McNabb. Call me Gordy, everyone else does. You must be that Conor Archer people are talking about."

"Yeah, that's me. You folks must not have many strangers visit if you can pick one out this easily."

"We don't," said Gordon with a laugh. "But I can tell you're from the city anyway."

"How's that?" said Conor, puzzled.

"Well, for one thing, you're jumpy as a rabbit—nearly made you hop a foot or two when I came up behind you. Cities do that I hear. And, you're kind of suspicious."

"What do you mean?"

"Well, of me for instance. Got your arms crossed, eyes narrowed, sort of sizing me up. Don't trust me?"

"No, it's not that. City people don't approach you usually unless they have real business with you."

"Maybe I have business with you," said Gordon. "First off, I want to say how sorry I am to hear that your mother died. Understand the Abbot's going to have the funeral."

"Think so," said Conor wondering why this stranger was so interested in him. Despite being self-conscious over the tag of 'city boy,' Conor felt his wariness growing with this man.

"If there's anything me and my family can do for you, just let us know."

"Thanks for offering but I think my aunt and I are okay."

"That'd be Emily O'Rourke, right?" said Gordon. Conor nodded. "She's a fine woman, that one. One of the stalwarts of the community. My mother and she don't get along, but I've always liked her."

"Why the problem?" asked Conor.

"Oh, my mother—that's Caithness McNabb—wanted your aunt's land and Emily told her no. No one gets away with telling Cate no. She tends to get what she wants. Cate even offered her three times what the land was worth. Emily just said no, Madoc's Glen just wasn't for sale. Pissed my mother off real good. We own a lot of the land around here. I like to think we benefit the community, too. McNabb Enterprises, that's the company my family runs, gave the money to build this high school several years back. Should've seen the old one. Would make a slum look like an urban renewal project." Catching Conor's cocked eyebrow, Gordon smirked, "I've lived in the city too. Anyway, the place was a dump, so we junked it and built a new one. Like it?"

"I don't have much experience with schools. Never went to them," said Conor.

"Didn't do so well in them myself," said Gordon. "Got by, got a degree, became my mother's CPA."

"Set for life," smiled Conor.

"Just about. How come you're up here?"

"Curious, I guess. I know one of the players, Jason Michaels. Helped me out the other day when I was sick."

"Heard about that," said Gordon. "Came off the bus with a fever, but what exactly was it you had?"

"Don't know, really. Brother Luke helped me out though and Jace and his sister, Beth, got me through it and managed to settle me at Aunt

Emily's." Conor noticed Gordon staring at his hand with the dark stripe winding up his arm. "Problem?" asked Conor.

"Not to be prying, but we've got a few others in town with hands like your's."

Conor blushed. "You know, I never paid much attention to them until I got here. Everybody seems interested in them. Haven't you ever seen a little birth defect before?"

Gordon slapped him on the back. "No problem, but you gotta understand. We've never met anyone like you outside of our little community. Folks like you sort of stay in the area all their life. Your coming caused quite a stir, being an outsider and all."

"But why?" asked Conor. "I'm originally from here."

"So the rumors say," said Gordon, "and it's just kind of interesting how you got to Chicago in the first place and stayed away from us. And some of us, even me, I guess, are wondering what it means that you are back. Some folks say you're a man out of legend. Others, like me, I might add, just say you're something new in town worth knowing." Gordon shook Conor's hand. "So, welcome to Tinker's Grove. Hope I get to see you again real soon. Enjoy the practice." But he didn't let go. He stared a good long time at the strange marking on Conor's arm. "Tattoo?"

But Conor had enough of being an exhibit. He pulled his hand away. "See you, Gordy." Still looking at the arm, Gordon backed away a bit and then turned with a little wave and walked out to the parking lot. Conor couldn't really say that he liked Gordon McNabb. He had seen people like him at the pub where he had played. Friendly on the surface but really wanting information, for good or ill. They were not always unlikeable, but they were always untrustworthy. He thought Gordon was an awful lot like them. As a matter of fact, Conor was feeling like he'd just been sized up by a pit bull looking for a snack.

"Conor, my man!" shouted Jace as he plunged up the hill. Other team members were hitting the showers; practice was over.

Conor smiled, "Great blocking! Now that I've seen you on the field, I'll have to give you a bit more respect."

"Should be out there with us," said Jace.

"But then I'd have to be in school. No thanks."

"You're not enrolling here?" asked Jace.

"Never went to public school. Was home schooled by my Mom. Not bad really. From what I hear, I got as much or more than most."

"Yeah, but no football," said Jace. "And it must be hard to meet girls."

Conor cocked a smile thinking of his time at the *DerryAir* spent at tables with college girls who worked there; they had found him ruggedly cute and bent his ear now and then with their chatter. "Football, I missed out on, but women, well Jace, I think I can hold my own there."

Jace laughed and turned toward the locker room. He turned on a moment and looking more seriously at Conor said, "I'll see you later at the visitation. Thanks for coming to watch practice. Didn't have to do that, after all you've been through."

"Wanted to."

"Oh, and I think Beth will be coming with me too."

Conor visibly brightened.

Jace smiled. "Thought that would pick you up a bit." He left Conor standing outside the highschool.

Hot August day, possible friend—maybe even possible girl friend. Conor thought he had a few good things going to offset this very sad day.

ASHES TO ASHES, DUST TO DUST

FUNNY THING ABOUT the death of a loved one. Time gets compressed and you just don't know where it all goes to. Conor roamed the town and headed back to his aunt's, ate a quick lunch, sat back out in the barn again for awhile and before he knew it, Aunt Emily was calling him in to get ready to go up to the Abbey for visitation. He dreaded this. Never been to one before. Didn't know how to act. Had to meet all those people Aunt Emily said were coming.

Jim Warren, the banker, picked them up in his Lincoln, black and sleek like a limo—almost, thought Conor. At least they wouldn't have to walk. Warren was cool, thought Conor, for an older guy. Just nodded to Conor, shook his hand and said, "I'm driving you and your aunt, if that's okay. Thought you could use a little company."

While Conor was out and about, Emily had been busy and, from somewhere, scrounged up a pair of dress pants, shirt and tie that almost fit Conor. He looked pretty good in them, he thought. Emily had even picked up a pair of dress shoes from the town's shoe store. Snug, but okay for a couple of hours, he thought.

Emily herself was in a black dress, decidedly more feminine than yesterday's attire. She'd fixed her hair too and ditched the straw hat. The blackthorn cane, though, was still in her hand.

"Let's go," she said.

Walking in to the cool and quiet Abbey Church, Conor liked it immediately. Unlike the old churches in Chicago, bedecked with rococo art and stunning stained glass, this was much simpler. He touched the cut stone walls and stared at the tall gothic windows with clear glass that made the countryside beyond a frame for the simplicity and grandeur of the church. Ancient, massive oak beams crisscrossed the sixty-five foot high roof. The monks had their choir stalls up front, but there was plenty of room for pews, a few niches for saint's shrines, and a big basin at the entrance with running water bubbling into a pool beneath that served as the baptistry and holy water font for parishioners. Up front in the sanctuary, a marble altar and ambo presided and behind them a beautiful gold tabernacle with a Presence Light burning beside it proclaimed another reality.

Conor automatically genuflected and made the Sign of the Cross. Then he saw the open casket up front, just this side of the sanctuary. The large Easter Candle burned high by the side of the casket. She would have loved this, thought Conor. Simple, beautiful. He noticed a large icon of the Virgin Mary just off to the side of the casket. Inhaling deeply, he smelled and tasted holiness. For the first time since he got to town, peace descended upon him.

No one else was in church. He, Jim Warren and Emily walked to the front and looked down on Finola Archer. She was as he remembered her from the night before.

"My God," said Jim. "She's as young and beautiful as she was seventeen years ago!"

Conor said nothing but chalked him up as another who knew much more than he was telling.

"Wendell Tooms ought to get a medal for the job he's done," continued Warren.

"Don't think he had much to do with it," said Conor.

Emily gave him a sharp look.

"I mean, my Mom was always beautiful, even when she was sick."

Conor saw Abbot Malachy come out of the sacristy. The monk walked over to Emily and kissed her on both cheeks. "A sad day isn't it?"

"Truly, it is," said Emily, "though I am happy she's at peace. Listen. I know you bent every rule to have her body here up near the sanctuary. Thank you for that."

"She deserves the honor, even if most won't know what we are honoring her for." He turned to the boy. "Want to say a prayer, Conor?" The Abbot didn't even wait for an answer. He began a series of prayers that even Conor knew by heart. For awhile they prayed and then the Abbot motioned them to a few chairs set near the casket. "Sit for a while," he said, "until the people come."

"If they come," said Conor.

Not long after, the church doors opened, and Beth, Jace and their parents came in, followed by a trickle of other mourners. Conor was happy to see them and meet their parents who seemed okay. But a brief hello was all he got, because the line was moving. More were coming.

The passing crowd quickly became a blur to Conor. Emily was helpful, murmuring a name here and there into Conor's ear as people came forward. Nobody said much. A few expressions of sympathy, but it was clear people were here either for the spectacle, for curiosity or just to be polite. Every once in a while a black haired, black eyed man or woman shook Conor's hand and he found it strange. They looked him straight in his face, said all the right things, but as they shook his hand, their other hand absently traced the dark mark on Conor's wrist and arm. Awfully creepy, thought Conor, and yet, few noticed what was happening. He didn't want to be impolite, so he let the strange behavior go. Even that was forgotten when a tall raven haired woman with ice blue eyes swam into his vision.

He heard Aunt Emily say, "Conor, I want to introduce you to Caithness McNabb. And, I'm sorry, Cate, I don't know the gentleman with you."

Cate's smile, deep as a slime of algae on a pond, traveled briefly over her face. "Emily, Conor, this is Dr. Nicholas Drake, president of DIOGENE, a company that's relocating here to Tinker's Grove."

"Ah," said Emily, "the man who wanted my land."

"Not anymore, Emily," said Cate, cutting in quickly. "I sold him several acres to the southwest of town along the river." She turned a shoulder to Emily and sized up Conor. "My son, Gordon, says he met you this morning. He tells me you are quite recovered from your sickness of the day before."

"Yes, ma'am," said Conor

"I truly am sorry about the death of your mother. I believe I met her years ago when she passed through this town. In fact, she had a child with her which could only have been you." Cate's smile turned momentarily warm. "I hope we can renew that early friendship."

"And I hope we can begin one," said Dr. Drake offering his hand to Conor.

Conor was sure tired of shaking hands and mouthing polite nothings, but he took the man's hand nonetheless. Drake was a man hard to ignore.

"Oh, my," said Drake, looking closely at Conor's hand. "I've never seen anything like this." Drake moved his body to block the people waiting in line from seeing what he was doing. "Pardon me Conor, but … your skin … this band going up your wrist and forearm. Most unusual. You'll have to let me have a look at it."

"It just appeared yesterday," said Conor, not knowing why he told this stranger anything.

"Yesterday, oh my. Perhaps it has something to do with the sickness you recently had."

Aunt Emily stepped up by Conor's side. "No need to worry, Dr. Drake. Brother Luke, a fine doctor from the monastery here, has matters well in hand."

"I'm sure he does, but you must understand, I specialize in genetics and for something like this to appear so swiftly, and frankly, look so healthy, means our Conor here has an interesting genetic map. Couldn't hurt to look a little deeper lad and see what's causing it. Tell you what, I'll be up and running in just a few weeks. My office downtown is almost ready, and construction for the company buildings has started today. What do you say? Might be fun to see what's causing all this." Drake beamed an affable smile and even Conor had to smile back.

"Well, let me think about it."

"Of course, of course. After you recover from all of this. I join my sympathies with Cate at the death of your mother. It will be hard, but you have family and soon, I hope you will agree, you will have many friends here in town to help you through this."

Cate, who had been watching all of this with amusement, turned to Emily and said, "Didn't I tell you he would be an asset to this town?" She entwined her arm around Drake's. "Dr. Drake and his company will bring not only jobs to this community, but a real compassion for the people here. You wait and see."

Emily matched Cate's icy smile with one of her own. "Always willing to give someone a chance, especially someone who obviously has the best interests of our community at heart. Dr. Drake, it was a pleasure. Cate, good to see you again." With that, Emily moved those guests along.

Conor couldn't help thinking that everybody seemed to know more about him than he did himself. Frankly, that just irritated him beyond belief. He had always been a private person, sharing little with anyone. He wasn't an introvert, just guarded with his interior life. He could joke and laugh with anyone; working at the pub had taught him that. But he didn't like folks thinking they actually knew him. He stepped away from the line and went over to where Beth and Jace were standing.

"Want a drink of water?" inquired Beth, offering him a small cup.

"Thanks," said Conor. "Did you see that guy I was just talking to?"

"Yeah," said Jace, "and the woman too. Caithness McNabb hasn't had a man on her arm for years and not for the lack of the men of the town trying. She must be taken with this guy."

"He's running the new company that's coming into Tinker's Grove," said Conor, "some genetic research company."

"He's elegant," said Beth.

"Elegant," snorted Jace. "That'll make him loved around here. And popular no doubt, with all our 'elegant' farmers, bartenders, and farm implement dealers."

"He'll be popular if he brings money to the place," said Conor. "I walked around town a lot today and, except for the high school, things are looking kind of worn out once you get off the main street. Could use a little bit of extra money."

"Anyway," continued Conor, "that's not what creeps me out about him. He saw this." Conor showed them his arm.

"Where'd you get that mark?" asked Beth.

"Just started yesterday afternoon, after my little run in with Rory." Conor only mentioned having met Rory in the barn; the little chase later that night through the woods still seemed too strange for him to share.

"Why didn't you tell me this morning?" asked Jace.

"You were busy with your football stuff," said Conor, and started laughing. "Didn't think you'd be able to comprehend it after bashing your head against all those blockers."

"So anyway," said Beth, "what did this Dr. Drake say?"

"Wants to examine me."

"In a sort of Dr. Frankenstein way?" asked Jace.

"I don't know, but it sure seems that people are awful interested in me."

"Hey, your aunt is waving you back," said Beth. "Why don't you come down to Visser's Café after this is over? A bunch of us will be there just hanging out."

"Okay," said Conor. "Catch you then."

For three solid hours people came, more than Conor ever thought possible. He was bushed by eight p.m. when the last person said goodbye to him and Aunt Emily. Jim Warren had stayed as well, but though the monks had been in and out of the church for the past three hours, none seemed visible now. There were still a couple of dozen people praying in the pews.

"Aren't the monks supposed to have Evening Prayer or something?" asked Conor.

"Vespers dear," said Aunt Emily. "They delayed it for an hour, in honor of your mother, but here they come now to sing the Office of the Dead for Finola. Take a seat."

As he found a place in the pews, Conor heard the monks' chanting soar to the rafters as they sang from Isaiah, *"Once I said, 'In the noontime of life I must depart! To the gates of the nether world I shall be consigned for the rest of my years.'"* Tired as he was, Conor thought it beautiful because it was all for her, for his mother. *"I said, 'I shall see the Lord no more in the land of the living … you have folded up my life, like a weaver who severs the last thread.'" (Is 38:10-14)*

Zoning in the music, Conor lost track of time. When the monks had filed out, blessed by the Abbot, Malachy came down to them and said, "Her body will lie here tonight with the Easter Candle burning until after the funeral tomorrow. We'll do our usual prayers throughout the night and morning, Conor, but her name will be on the tongue of every monk, every hour of prayer."

"Thanks," said Conor.

"Let's go home," said Aunt Emily.

"If it's alright," said Conor, "I'm going to stay here for a while and walk back later."

"Suit yourself," said Emily, "but don't be too late." She walked away with Jim Warren.

The Abbot looked at Conor. "I'll be around for a while if you need me."

"There were a lot of people here tonight."

"In their own way, they wanted to let you know that stranger though you are, you are welcome here and they honestly wanted to help your mother rest in peace."

Conor didn't say anything for a moment. The church was now empty of people, except for them. Looking up at the Abbot, he said, "Mind if I stay for a while? I just want to be alone with her for a little bit."

"Understood."

In the gathering twilight, Conor kept vigil alone for a few minutes. He looked at the tabernacle, glimmering in the light from the Presence Candle. He thought out loud, "Couldn't you have healed her? She was all I had. Couldn't you at least have eased her pain?" Though no one answered him verbally, he felt the peacefulness of the place pressing upon him but, this time, he shrugged off its effect. He took out his tin whistle and began to play "Deirdre's Lament," a song of sorrow for the long lost flower of the Celtic race. Absently, he thought the Abbey Church of Stella Maris had great acoustics. He didn't play for the long dead Irish princess; he played for her, his mother, there in the church. It was all he could do. It was all he could give.

THE FORSAKEN

OUT OF THE corner of his eye, he saw movement outside the church windows. As if he was being watched or listened to. Exiting the church, he walked around to where he thought he had seen someone. Twilight was dimming and the stars were brightening in the warm sky. There was a field in front of him, grazing ground, and a fairly large stand of aspen. The soft breeze there made their leaves rustle with a little quaking sound.

Something or someone was in the stand of trees. When he looked directly, he saw nothing, but his peripheral vision was constantly picking up movement.

"They heard you play," said the Abbot who had walked up silently behind him.

"Who are 'they'?" asked Conor still trying to peer through the gathering gloom.

"Play again," said the Abbot. "See what happens."

Conor played again, the same tune as in the church. The movement on the edge of his vision grew more frenetic. "Geez, do you think they like it, or do they want me to stop?"

"Oh, they like it well enough," said the Abbot.

"How can you tell?"

"Because they're still here. I can see them clearly."

"And I can't because …" asked Conor.

"In order to see them, you'll have to step sideways," said the Abbot.

Conor sighed. "Rory said the same thing to me yesterday."

"Did he now?"

"He did. And it didn't make any more sense then than it does now."

In the dimming light, Conor could barely see the Abbot smile. "A few nights ago," said Malachy, "you were told by someone to see the mountain behind the mountain. It's the same as stepping sideways. Just a metaphorical way of telling you that reality isn't always what you first see. Sometimes it is deeper. You have expectations of what the world should look like, right?" Conor nodded. "The world works thus and so and anything that doesn't quite fit is either forgotten by you or ignored. Right?" Conor nodded again.

"Well," said the Abbot, "what's out there in the quaking aspens is as real as you or me, but you are not prepared to see it. You don't think they exist, and so it is easier for them to hide from you. But you can see if you want. You know you are changing. Already your ordinary senses are picking up things you never smelled, heard, or saw before. Let go a bit of your conventional thinking, and look a little more deeply around you."

Conor did. He began to play again and as the music piped, he looked deep into the aspen stand. And then the darkness grew brighter. Just like last night, he thought; the starlight illuminated the night and even cast shadows. He could see through the dark and what he saw were human figures, standing midst the aspens looking at him and listening to his music. Tall they were and almost insubstantial. In fact, they seemed to change, shift before his eyes. He could see their faces, dark eyes and hair. But they never stayed the same. As he watched, the same figure would morph into something or someone else. Together, they looked like a herd of deer, or a crowd of strangers. It all depended on the angle. It was hard to see and yet that was how it seemed to Conor. He saw the Morrigan among them, and caught a glimpse of Rory prowling in among the crowd.

"Who are they?" said Conor.

As if he had heard, out from the trees stepped Oz, only his gaze was direct and intelligent. No ear buds around his head this time. The strangers clustered behind him. "Who are we, you ask?" he said to Conor. Sorrow covered Oz's face. "We are the Lost. We are the Forsaken. We are the People who Forgot to Remember." For a moment he stood looking at Conor, his hands stretched out in pleading. Then his face went slack again, and someone came up from behind and placed his ear buds in his ears and gave him the unplugged cord. Head down, Oz turned and shuffled back into the trees, into the crowd or herd or whatever they were. They almost disappeared on Conor; but he found if he looked closely he could see them among the trees still, standing and waiting.

"What does it mean, what Oz said?" asked Conor.

"They think themselves damned," said the Abbot. "These, too, are 'dark ones' of a kind, though, with the exception of Oz, they were never born in this village. They've been here longer than the Grove has been, haunting us all, I suppose you might say. These ancients seemed similar to an old legend we brought over with us when our ancestors came here from Ireland." The Abbot closed his eyes and recited.

"Once, as you know, there was war in heaven. But what most do not remember is that some lesser beings sided with Lucifer and his angels.

When St. Michael of the heavenly host drove the rebels from those super-natural heights, they fell along with the fallen angels. Only unlike Satan and those of his kind, these beings were not bound in hell. They fell to earth, some on the land where they became what the Celts called the *Tuatha de Danaan*, the People of the Hollow Hills, for that was where they made their home. (Later, more credulous people would categorize them as faeries.) Those that fell into the sea became the People of the Roan, creatures of the water who could abide on land as well. Shapeshifters they were, selchies, men on the land, seals in the sea. That's what the legends say."

"Then," said Conor, "they aren't human?"

"They think not," said the Abbot, "and who is to say where the truth lies? They wish to honor your mother but cannot come inside the church for, as I said, they think of themselves as the unredeemed. You've seen their kin in the town, but those 'dark ones' are truly lost. Born of a forbidden tryst, they have continued to propagate, few though they may be. They have forgotten so much that they don't even know who they are. They are nearly indistinguishable from the other townspeople. And who is to say that's such a bad thing."

"Am I like them? Am I one of them?" asked Conor. "Rory seems to think so. In fact, he's made it his life's work to change me into one of them." As he said his name, Rory appeared briefly in the front of the hiding crowd, looked blankly at Conor, and then disappeared again.

"I do not know, Conor, exactly what you are. You are like them, the 'dark ones' in the town and the ancients in the Indian mound. And in some ways not, I think. In some way you are different, but kin with them."

A sob wracked Conor's body. "Then I'm not human, either? I'm damned like them?"

The Abbot grasped the boy's arm. "Enough of that. I said they thought themselves damned. That doesn't mean it's the truth, does it? Fool of a boy. Just like you have to step sideways to see what's real in the world, you have to look deeply even into legends to find the truth. You were in church tonight. Did you feel rejected, unsaved, fit for the lowest reaches of hell? No! You are yourself Conor, and everything I've seen is human to the core. Finola, that good hearted soul, would never have birthed something damned. But you have something about you, and you are changing. What that means I have some idea, but one thing I am sure of—no change, no person, and nothing on this earth can take away the humanity that One has given you. You are your mother's flesh and blood."

Conor walked closer to the stand of quaking aspens. To the silent fig-ures standing there he said, "I don't know who you are, or what you want of me, but thank you for coming to see my mother tonight, even if you felt you couldn't go in." He held up his tin whistle. "For you," he said, and began to play a soft little reel. A sigh stronger than the night breeze rose from the trees and the figures began to drift away. Conor played them home, wherever that truly was.

AN IRISH WAKE

NO MOON, JUST starlight, lit Conor's way into town. He could see quite well and the sounds of the night were strangely comforting. He knew where Visser's Café was, just at the edge of the business district. Conor never felt strange walking into the *DerryAir* or anywhere else in Chicago, but damn if he didn't get more nervous as he approached this place. He could see through the window that Beth and Jace were there; that was cool. But others he didn't know were there as well, people of his own age. That never happened in Chicago, not in the circles he traveled in. So he was nervous. Damn.

When he walked in, he found the usual diner's counter and a row of booths along the wall. It had been redecorated circa '50's style. Beth and Jace and a couple of their friends were sitting and eating pizza. Jace saw him enter and immediately called out for him to come over. Everybody looked and Conor felt himself blushing. There weren't many in there, ten, maybe fifteen. A guy not much older than Conor was cooking at the grill and taking orders at the same time. Not a busy Thursday night at Visser's. Conor met everybody there, but none of the names computed and he quickly forgot who was who. They were laughing, including him in the jokes, making him feel, well, like he was home.

So it was a surprise to him when the guy behind the grill came out and shut the shades on the window, turned over the "Closed" sign, dimmed the lights a bit, and shouted, "Visser's is officially closed; those who stay are visitors now not patrons." A few left but most stayed. Conor noticed a change in the café. Quieter, more subdued.

Conor looked at the cook. Medium height, blond- red hair, kind of stocky. Jace had called him Fergal, he remembered. Fergal McNabb. Conor figured he must be related to Cate of the ice blue eyes. He smiled to himself. Not much like his mother. This guy wasn't suave and chic; he was a party animal.

"What do you have in mind, Fergal?" asked Jace.

"Well, I was thinking that we haven't welcomed our new guest into town, and it's hard to do it on this night when Conor here is grieving and all, but we're the Grove and if we all were older we'd be at somebody's house toasting the dead and having a good old Irish wake. And, if you don't mind Conor, I thought we could do that here." And with that he stepped behind the counter and pulled out two bottles of scotch.

"Single malt," said Fergal.

Appreciative whistles from the crowd. "The good Cate had a few extra bottles that I don't think she'd miss."

"Not miss two bottles of Glenlivet?" said Conor. "Your mom has great taste if this is just her ordinary stuff."

Fergal was pouring and handing glasses around. "Got to drink fast before old man Visser comes by. He always stops two hours after closing time to see if things are locked up tight. Never before that though."

Everybody took a glass except Jace and another; Declan was his name, maybe, thought Conor. They begged off because of athletics. Beth declined saying the stuff tasted like cattle piss.

"You tasted this year's brew?" laughed another girl.

"Besides," said another boy, "this is McNabb cattle piss and we all know her highness' cows pee only the best Scotch."

Fergal thrust a well-filled glass into Conor's hand. "Look, everybody knows here that I like a good party, but that's not why I'm doing this. I didn't know your mother, none of us did, but it's got to be tough losing her so we'll drink to her memory. You know how to do it?"

"'Course," said Conor. "We toasted all the time in the bar in Chicago where I played."

"Ah," said Fergal, "a professional drinker." Fergal held his glass high—the others did the same. "To Finola Archer, may she rest in peace and walk in glory. *Slainte!*" All the other young people there, imitating what they saw their parents do at earlier wakes, shouted *Slainte!* And drank their whiskey.

It burned Conor's throat but it felt good. Fergal poured him another. "And there ought to be music," said Fergal. He popped a disc into the cafe's sound system. Conor recognized the band. He had heard them play at Taste of Chicago earlier in the summer. The jokes began again and as the liquor loosened their tongues, the laughter grew louder.

He got to thinking he was feeling a lot better. It was good not to be alone and not to have to deal with all the sadness. He was really appreciative of them all for trying to make him feel welcome and help him forget a bit. Downing two glasses of Scotch, he even allowed Fergal to stick the bottle in his hand, but once his head starting swimming he knew he needed to stop; an old great aunt would never let him live it down if he had a hangover the day of the funeral.

"Gotta go," said Conor. "But thanks, you guys, for doing this. Sang a lot of songs about Irish wakes, but never been to one before. I think maybe my Mom would have liked it."

Everyone in the café nodded quietly and toasted Conor. He walked outside and Fergal followed. "Hey, I'll give you a ride home."

"Actually," said Jace, "let me. I haven't been drinking."

"Well neither have I," said Fergal, "excepting that one drink for his Ma."

Conor's vision was spinning, and a grin crawled across his face. "It's okay," he slurred slightly, "Jace, it's okay. It's not far and if Fergal wants to give me a ride, who am I to deny him?"

Jace frowned. "All right then. But Ferg, get him home safe, and get him home now."

Beth had come out to join them. Conor looked at her and said, "Really, I'll be fine. G'nite." And he stumbled toward the car Fergal pointed to.

True to Jace's direction, Fergal drove Conor right to his house. But he shut off the car and looked at Conor. "Hey, man, you've still got the bottle in your hand."

Conor looked down and laughed. "Guess you're right. Shame to let it go to waste." And he drank deep and handed it to Fergal who drank as well.

Fergal said, "You know what I'm thinking? I'm thinking that you're not so bad of a guy, Conor Archer. Kind of fun if you ask me. Want to tear up a little bit of the countryside?"

Conor thought a moment, and through a foggy haze was able to mutter, "No, think not. Got a big day tomorrow. Got to get some sleep." He opened the car door.

"Suit yourself," said Fergal with a laugh. "But you and I need to have some fun, I think. I'll be back for you some night, and we'll ride. Sound okay to you?"

Conor smiled, "You bet. And thanks again for the wake—it was cool."

He watched Fergal drive off and then walked inside the house. Emily was standing at the steps in her robe.

"Sorry I'm late," he said. "But they wanted a wake down at the café, so we gave my mother one. Think it was the thing to do. But Fergal wanted to party some more; I said I couldn't—big day tomorrow."

Emily walked up to him, took the empty bottle of Scotch from his hand and sniffed it. "Conor, my boy, you have a ways to go on the growing up scale. The Scotch smells like a million bucks but you stink like a drunk."

She flipped the bottle into the waste basket in the hall, and left him standing there looking at her in amazement.

DRAKE AND THE DEVIL

A CAR PULLED out of a side street after Fergal drove off with Conor.

"See," said Cate to Dr. Nicholas Drake, "even Fergal, that underachieving son of mine, has his uses. This was his night to cook at the café, and I had him float the idea among the young ones to host a little Irish wake for the Archer boy. Don't know if it was sympathy or the chance to drink a bit that got them there but no matter. It worked."

"What good does it do?" asked Drake. "After what I saw tonight, Conor's a better specimen than the other rejects of his ilk that infest this town. How does this get us closer to him?" He put a hand on Cate's thigh.

She braked the car and looked at him disdainfully. "We're not in public here, and here is where reality lies, and reality says very clearly that if you touch me again all deals are off. Understood?"

Drake snapped his hand back. "Clearly, Cate. But the point is the same. So what if Fergal drinks with the Archer lad?"

"Access, doctor. He's just lost his mother; knows virtually no one and needs someone he can trust. He's got a strange sickness and a new band of skin growing on his arm. We've drawn attention to his webbed hands and feet; he's not going to want to feel different. Fergal, whatever his faults, knows how to make someone fit in. That trust will come in handy."

"Maybe, but I want Archer examined. I want to know how he is changing. None of the others like him show such possibilities."

Cate said nothing more until she reached her house. "You know what you need, doctor? A quiet walk down by the river. It's a nice night and the walk is lighted. Go on down and I'll fix your guest room."

As Drake wandered off, Cate watched him go. A fool, but a necessary fool. He would bring capital into the town's economy and that would ultimately enrich her coffers. And he was a gifted geneticist. Perhaps he could unlock the secrets of this town and maybe the answers would gain her even

more power. Knowledge was power she thought. Yes, she mused, a walk
down by the river would do him good. Who knows what he might run into?

"Ah, Cate," said a voice, "you are a mischievous bitch." Rory stepped
up on the porch and bowed.

Cate laughed, genuinely pleased to see the biker. "Why Rory, you
haven't changed in nearly twenty years."

"You've only grown lovelier, Cate, my lass. But sending the good
doctor down to the river is a dangerous gamble."

"Perhaps, but he'll have to sooner or later. Everybody comes to the
river eventually. Some are saved; some are drowned."

"And some are consumed," said Rory. "Your friendship, relationship
or whatever you have with Piasa clouds your judgement sometimes, Cate."

"Jealous, Rory?"

The biker came closer to Cate and took her hands. "I must admit,
that's why I left you the first time. I don't much like sharing a good woman
with a snake, or bear, or panther, or whatever it chooses to look like. You
had to choose Cate, and you chose it. Over me. Ah, lass," said Rory,
clutching his heart, "it still hurts here; really it does."

Both Cate and Rory burst out laughing. "You never loved me, Rory. I
was just an outlet for your needs."

"A mighty fine one I might add," said Rory with a laugh. "Ah, but we
were good, weren't we?"

"Yes, we were," said Cate with a wistful smile. Then she stared directly
at Rory. "I'm thinking it was you responsible for whatever ailed Conor
Archer when he came to this town."

"You'd be thinking right," said Rory. "And what business of it is
your's?"

"You've got something up your leathers, Rory, and I want to know
what it is. Why is the boy so important to you?"

"Do you think I'd be telling the likes of you, you faithless woman?
You murdered your withered husband, rolled in the hay with me—several
times mind you while you were married—and you've done your own modern version of raping and pillaging the farms and homesteads around here
till you're the major landowner. You're a woman of voracious appetites.
You want me to trust you?"

"I'm not that stupid, Rory. And trust is a virtue you've only heard
about and never practiced. I'm suggesting an alliance. You want Conor for
some reason. So do I. Let's work together. Perhaps each of us can get from
Conor what we need."

"What would that be?" asked Rory.

"That same as what you want him for," smiled Cate. "For power." And she leaned forward and planted a kiss on his forehead, patted his cheek, turned and walked inside the house.

"Feckless bitch," said Rory and disappeared into the night.

Drake heard everything. He knew that Cate thought him an old horny fool. "At least she loves me for my mind," he said and stifled a laugh. He had only walked a few dozen yards toward the river when he heard Rory speak so he had decided to eavesdrop. He thought he had done his homework on Cate. Ruthless, he knew. Morally ambiguous, surely. A murderer— now that was new information which surely would come in handy one day.

But before he could process that thought, he had a more pressing problem. She wanted him to go down by the river. Why? Drake had read up on the town of Tinker's Grove and the surrounding area. He had studied the types of peoples who inhabited the area now and in the past and he had learned the lore of each of those peoples. He knew about the ghosts that whispered through the streets of Oberon, an abandoned farming town up in the hills above Tinker's Grove. He had heard the tales of the dead fur traders that walked the snowy woods around the area of Wyalusing. He even had researched Piasa, the Manitou that had carved out the Wisconsin River. No ghosts out tonight. No snow either, so no were-trappers. Maybe it's a good night to do a little fishing.

Drake followed the lighted path to the river. He laughed again as he saw the placid river. Such a tease, the Wisconsin is, he thought. Looks smooth and shallow and safe. But it's not. Rip currents, deep holes, shifting sand bars—all conspired to make the Wisconsin a dangerous place for the unsuspecting. Despite what Cate thought, Drake was no fool. He knew what dwelt in the water.

Drake breathed science and medicine. Yet, he was neither a secularist nor skeptic. He knew that even science couldn't answer all questions. His study of the mythology of the area was not simply a pasttime. Drake had quite an open mind. He might inhale the dictums of science and medicine but he consumed power and wealth. He freely grazed on any field that would give him that kind of forage. Consequently he was open to the possibility of other realities and what those realities could give him. He was the last in a long line that thought that way.

Quietly, he stood looking at the river. He could barely see the water, so dimly lit by star light. I know you are there, he thought, and I'm a match for you, I think.

Without taking off his Gucci shoes and socks, without a care for the expensive suit he was wearing, Drake stepped into the river. Not far, just up to his knees. He laughed as he held out his arms. He laughed and laughed.

"Come to me!" he cried. "Come to me!" he shouted again. "Come to me Devourer of Souls!"

And it came.

Rushing through the water. Drake first thought it was a motor boat; the wake rippled white in the dark night. But there was no sound of an engine. It stopped ten yards out in the river from Drake. He couldn't see it. Whatever it looked like remained hidden from the doctor. But he could sense its presence, its malevolence, as it waited underneath the water. Like some kind of aquatic panther it crouched beneath the ripples of its dying wake. Drake saw fish skitter on the surface to get out of its way.

"You know me," he whispered. "You've known my family forever. Long have we served you, and well. See, I carry the token you gave my ancestors."

Suspended around his neck by an impossibly thin, filigreed silver chain was an exquisite dagger. No hilt; instead, a unified thing of carved power. Bone and wood, entwined with one another for the blade. Bone and wood, entwined with one another for the handle. White was the bone, black was the wood. A blood red ruby, like a malevolent eye, offset handle from blade, visible from both sides. He held it up to the dark waters.

"Yes," said Drake, "I know you who dwell at the roots of the World Tree, feed off it, poisoning its life. Why are you here? When word reached me that you were more than a savage's myth, I came. Whatever service you need, I will provide. As we have always done, my lord."

A cold voice crept into the doctor's heart. He found it hard to put it into words. A picture of an ancient land floated into his mind. Druids by standing stones. A figure on a stone table. The very knife he held, held by another. Of them? came the questioning feeling.

"Yes," whispered Drake. "I am of them."

Another picture in his mind. The Wisconsin River, White Creek, a hidden cave with skulls. "Mine," came the unhuman voice.

"Your lair," said Drake.

Rapid visions of an Indian burial mound, a raven haired prince, the 'dark ones' from the town.

"I am here for them," said Drake, "to find out what they mean, to use them. And ..." he paused and slowly began to smile, "and have them serve you, as food or slaves." He began to laugh.

The Devourer of Souls was bemused. The dagger it knew from ages old. Its kind always bound human servants with the blade from the roots of the world—dragon's bone, Tree of Life. Such a talisman had great power. Its bearer must not be taken lightly. Nor must he be given too free a rein. Piasa stretched out its mind to Drake. It would take a trick from the alligator snapping turtle which kept its mouth open for hours as its tongue mimicked fish bait. Nothing could resist that turtle's call. An easy meal. Piasa thought the same. It opened its mouth too, and spoke into the mind of Drake.

For the good doctor, it was like a rush of adrenaline followed by the peaceful calm of a pain killer. It felt good. But Drake was a disciplined man. He knew what Piasa intended. He stretched out his arms again. "Thanks for the freebie. But I'm not so easily tamed. We'll meet again, when my lab gets running. We have the same goal, you and I. The manipulation of humans, the domination of man. You've not yet succeeded in your long lifespan. Let me help you."

Piasa was impressed. The human had taken the bait and thrown out a challenge as well. So be it. It had learned patience through the ages. Piasa would see how this played out. Not without a final show however, just to remind Drake who was in charge.

Drake saw it rise from the river. The wings remained folded this time but the head snaked toward him. He couldn't help himself as he screamed. He was looking into his own face but it had horns and the body was morphing into various shapes of panther, bear and vulture. Piasa's tale snaked up over itself like a scorpion and came smashing down not five feet from where Drake stood.

And then it was gone. Drake was on his knees, waist deep in the water, soaking wet, breathless. Good, oh very good, he thought. He knew his message had gotten through, or he'd be dead. But, clearly, Piasa was not to be trifled with.

Rory saw all this happen. Never one to miss out on the fun, he followed Drake after his talk with Cate. Webs woven into webs. The dagger he knew well. He'd run across such a few times in his long lifespan, but this one he knew personally. Humans, he thought, as he spat on the ground. Always devious, always betrayers. Cate might have underestimated Drake. This doctor was definitely not a fool.

BURIED DREAMS

"I CAN DO it, and I want to," said a defiant Conor to Abbot Malachy the Friday morning of the funeral. Conor had walked the journey to the Abbey alone and early just to speak to the Abbot.

"It's never a good idea for the grieved to speak or sing," said the skeptical priest. "The emotion of the day can make any voice quaver or break."

"Except mine," said Conor with his jaw set.

The Abbot looked at him in silence for a while and then said, "All right, but if you falter, Brother Gerald will break in early with the pipes. He'll lead the congregation out to the grave side."

"Thanks. It's the last thing anyway, and I promise you I won't disappoint you. My mother would want this, and ... it's my final gift to her."

The funeral went off without a hitch. Conor didn't expect many people to come, but he was surprised. The Abbey Church was two thirds full. Later, he found out nearly every household in the surrounding area was represented by at least one person.

Conor's thoughts wandered through much of the Funeral Mass. He wasn't bored; far from it. It was simply that every word spoken triggered a memory and pictures of the past segued into his mind. As if from far away, he heard the Abbot speaking of Finola, how he had known her as a young girl, how she had come home to the Grove at last, to the people that should claim her as their own. But the priest really didn't say much about her life. He said that everyone gathered knew he could say much more but now was not the time. "Let's let her be at peace today."

The usual stuff, Conor thought, about rising from the dead, how they would all pray she was in a better place, of how the Christ always loved her. Conor's fugue was interrupted by the piercing stare of the Abbot as the monk looked away from the casket and fixed Conor with his gaze, saying,

"Here lies the body that bore you."

Conor remembered his mother across a sunlit breakfast table one morning. "Ah, Conor," she said, "you were born on the first day of spring, and the day before I birthed you I picked flowers for you—little crocuses popping through the snow."

"Here are the hands that held you."

A fall when he was six; his mother bending over him lifting him high and holding him till the hurt was gone.

"Here is the silent voice that once sang you songs of promise and told you stories of the peoples from the past."

"It's called a tin whistle, Conor; let it play the songs in your heart."

"Here lies an image of God, a piece of Christ, a vein of gold, formed by her Creator, but her soul is gone, gone she is from us, and our hearts will grieve at the sight of her grave."

A vision of her wasted self on one of the last good days came into his mind. "When I'm gone and the days become sad, get out of the city and find a field of flowers if it is spring or summer, autumn leaves if the weather has turned and run through them calling my name, and I will hear and lift your heart."

"Let angels carry her to the Lord, away from death that can only separate and not destroy; let hope carry us through the dark unto the dawn." The Abbot walked away from the ambo as the Mass moved on.

Funny thing about religion, Conor thought. When you needed it, it could really work. At the consecration, Conor looked at the host and chalice; bread and wine become his God—at least that's what his mother had always said and the priests had always thundered. He hadn't really doubted it, but hadn't thought about it much either. Amazed, he found his soul filled with peace. As the sunbeams gleamed through the east windows, he became fascinated with the rays that filtered through the crystal. As if the light itself was moving with presences he could sense but barely see. The shimmering beams coalesced around the casket and Conor blinked three times to see if it was really real—translucent hands reaching down to embrace Finola's body in benediction. Couldn't blink them away. As if the light shaped itself into something enfolding and protecting. And from the Presence on the altar, a radiating peace that struck the heart of Conor Archer as he looked at the raised host and chalice, a peace that took away his grief.

So he was ready, at the end of Mass, when the body of his mother had been incensed and blessed, when Abbot Malachy said, "Let us go in peace and take the body of our sister to her place of rest." Conor stood up and walked into the monastic enclosure to where the body lay. With his back to the people and eyes focused on his mother's casket he opened his mouth to sing. He used the tune that most folks knew as 'Danny Boy' but he sang different words to the tune, the ancient words of the Church's final farewell:

May choirs of angels lead you into paradise,
And may the martyrs come to welcome you,
To bring you home into the holy city,
So you may dwell in new Jerusalem.
May holy angels be there at your welcoming,
With all the saints who go before you there,
That you may know the peace and joy of paradise;
That you may enter into everlasting rest.

Clear and strong rang his tenor voice throughout the church. Beth told him later, that every person she looked at was crying. At the time, though, Conor thought only of his mother, lying quietly in her casket, as he sang her to her grave.

When he was done, Brother Gerald stepped forward and played the uilleann pipes. The smaller cousin of the bagpipe wasn't quite so imposing in a closed space and the piper piped the Abbot and Conor, the monks and the people, out of the church and over to the graveyard. It was a beautiful morning and a lone monk, spade in hand, marked the grave near the highest point of the cemetery.

Aunt Emily and Jim Warren had joined Conor in the procession to the grave site.

"Beautiful!" said Emily quietly, squeezing Conor's arm.

"Hope it makes up for last night," said Conor with a shy smile.

"Can't stay mad at you long, lad. Just like I could never stay mad at your mother."

"Fantastic music, Conor! Don't know how you had the stamina to do it," said Mr. Warren.

The monks lowered her body into the ground with Wendell Tombs looking officiously over the proceedings. He was happy. The monks had offered to dig the grave and serve as pall bearers so no extra hands to hire today.

The Abbot said the burial prayers and invited the congregation back to the Abbey for lunch. Of course, most people would stay. They had all baked and cooked and now was the time for talk and shrewd, judicious comparisons over who baked the best cherry pie.

Conor, Aunt Emily, Jim Warren, Beth and Jace stayed behind in the cemetery after the grave was filled.

"Peaceful up here," said Conor.

"She's got a good view," said Jace surveying the river valley. "Hey look, we can see the place where the Indian mound is." And sure enough, there was White Creek bending into the Wisconsin and just down from it, closer to the Abbey, the area where the burial mound was.

Conor easily could see the two willows that topped the mound.

"Hard to say, goodbye," said Conor. Beth squeezed his hand.

"Always hard to leave a loved one," said Aunt Emily. "To say goodbye is to die a little, I think."

Jim Warren motioned for them all to follow him back to the Abbey.

"Come on, Finola wouldn't want us to get too sentimental. She's saying to us right now, 'Get some food in you; can't grieve me proper if you're all starving to death.'"

Later, when lunch was over and people had left, Conor said goodbye to his friends and family and walked once more up to the cemetery. The grave was as he left it. Roses still strewn around where people had dropped them on the grave. But wait. Something strange caught Conor's eye. There in the midst of the pink and white roses, the color orange gleamed. A single sprig of orange. Indian Paintbrushes, thought Conor. He'd seen them only in one place—the Indian mound. Someone had been at the grave. No footprints. No path through the weeds. But Conor knew. Someone had come to say a private goodbye.

After he left, there was movement in the tree line down the hill. Out walked Troubles followed by a man dressed in clothes of years gone by, brown trousers, old flannel shirt, soft deerskin boots, a yellow neckerchief around his throat. His black hair was long.

"Following me won't bring your young friend any answers. He hasn't quite learned the language of the wild things—though the call stirs in his belly."

Troubles woofed in disappointed agreement.

"None the less, it is good you have chosen to watch over him. I cannot be everywhere and peril hovers over him like a storm cloud."

The man came up to the grave. He looked down on it with a sad smile on his face. "I had forgotten. One was not enough. She always liked a small bouquet." And he placed several more orange flowers next to the one already there.

Troubles watched him go, and where he walked, no footprints followed.

TROUBLES' STORY

IT WAS MONDAY morning, the third day after the funeral, and Conor opened the front door of Aunt Emily's house.

"You again," he said to the dog sitting on the porch facing him, just like the chocolate Lab had done the previous three mornings. "You know I'd like to let you in, but Aunt Emily has decided the house is not the place for you. Besides you belong up at the Abbey, with all those holy guys."

"Who are you talking to, Conor?" said a voice from the kitchen.

"Just Troubles here on the porch," said Conor.

"Don't know what's gotten into that dog. Spends more time here than up at the Abbey."

"Maybe he wants to adopt me," said Conor.

"You're mine, not his," said Emily in a clipped voice. "I'll not be having any animal, even one as handsome as this, get in the way of my responsibilities." Emily appeared at the doorway and reached down to pet the dog who promptly licked her hand. "Don't try and kiss up to me, and don't you look at me with your sad Lab eyes. I've known you too long. You're up to something."

Troubles spun around and yipped, eyes dancing.

"I think he wants me to go with him," said Conor.

"Not till breakfast dishes are done."

With that, Troubles took hold of Conor's pant leg and tugged. Emily smiled. "All right, get on with you and go with him. Last time he did that I had to look at the better side of you."

Conor blushed at the memory and took off at a run with the dog by his side.

The dog seemed to have nothing else in mind but getting Conor up to the Abbey, but when they got there the dog passed around back and headed for one of the barns that dotted the Abbey property. Inside, Conor found the Abbot dressed in a t-shirt and blue jeans, tending an ailing calf.

"Glad Troubles found you Conor. I sent him looking for you. This calf here was a late one and just hasn't got herself feeling right. Can't seem to make up her mind whether to really commit to living or not. Anyway, called you here, Conor, because this dog of the Abbey's is down at your house every day now, all day."

"I know, Father Abbot, and I'm sorry about that, but every time I tell him to go home, he just laughs at me."

Malachy laughed himself. "I know what you mean. He does have a stubborn streak but that's not the problem here. He seems to want to watch over you and I'm inclined to let him do it on a permanent basis."

"What?" asked Conor.

"I'm asking you if you want to take Troubles under your wing."

Conor was speechless. He'd never had a pet and really liked the dog.

"Actually, I don't think you have much choice. Troubles tends to make his own decisions in these matters. I suppose I ought to tell you how he got his name."

"I kind of wondered what that was all about."

"It's like this," said the Abbot. "It was a summer's day, seven years back, and I was down by the river near the Indian mound. It's peaceful down there and I'm the only one from the Abbey that walks those paths so it's my little place of solitude. Well, who should I see stomping towards the river bank on the opposite side but Rafe McNabb. He's the middle of Caithness McNabb's boys, always full of anger and attitude. I was going to hail him but I noticed he had something in his hand—a burlap bag. As he swung it around and around, I gazed in horror. Something alive was moving in that bag and Rafe was laughing. I tell you, Conor, you have to steer clear of that clan. Touched with darkness, each one of them. Not very charitable to say, but it's the truth. Anyway, Rafe swung that bag around and around and let it fly. As it arced over the river this dark little object flew out of the opening and fell into the water. It was a pup, and a feisty one at that. It had no intention of drowning. It couldn't have been more than eight weeks old. Poking its head up, with one look at the murdering wretch who tried to end his life, it turned toward my shore, its little lab tail smacking the water as it did so.

"Rafe hadn't even waited to see the bag hit the water so he didn't know what had happened. He'd already left the scene by the time I got to the river bank. The pup, brave though it was, was in great trouble. The Wisconsin is a tricky river, and a current had come and kept the pup from making any progress. I saw it go under once, twice. By that time, I had my Benedictine habit off and was standing there in my civies. And, stupid me, I jumped in to save that rascal. All I had was its last location and when I got there I dove. Found him right away. Limp as a fish. Got him to the bank and blew in his nostrils. Never thought I'd do CPR on a dog, but nothing doing. The little fella was still as pond water. So I took him over to the Indian mound. Laid him on it—little wet bedraggled thing—and called up the same person that came to you the other night."

Conor gaped. "Him? You can do that?"

"Yes, now hush. I'm telling the story and I don't want any interruptions. The one who came to you sat down beside me and that forlorn little body of a pup. 'Course, he didn't look like he did the other night, all splendid and magnificent. He was in his usual down home gear; don't look at me like that, I have seen him now and then over the years. As I was saying, he wore old fashioned trousers, flannel shirt, just like he'd be doing if he lived in Tinker's Grove a hundred and fifty years ago. (I thought I looked a little silly in my underwear so I quickly donned my habit—got to have dignity as an Abbot you know.)

"'Malachy,' he said, 'must be important for you to call me in broad daylight here on top of the hollow hill.'

"'It is,' I said and pointed to the puppy. 'The creature's hold on life is almost gone and I know you can do something about that.'

"'So can you,' said the dweller of the hollow hill.

"'True,' said I. 'But if you touch that creature he will enter your world and that I think is an important thing, for I rescued this little one fleeing from darkness, crossing this river. He had set course whether for me or for your dwelling I do not know, but I sense he will be crucial for the future, for you and for the one who is to come. He needs to have a foot in your world, I believe. Otherwise, his life is fleeting and you and I know the world is turning. She who weaves the loom of death and life waits to pluck this one's thread or put it in the pattern. I think the choice is yours.'

"'You know,' he said to me, 'for a Christian you have much of the pagan in you. What do you care about her?'

"'I'm not pagan,' I assured him. 'She whom your kind once called a goddess does have real power granted to her by the One and since she exists I pay attention to her.'

"As I sat on the mound, I watched that odd man stroke the wet fur of the still puppy.

"'You think, it's important?' he asked.

"'Yes, for I foresee this creature to be his guardian.'

"'The boy is still but a child.'

"'But when he grows to manhood, there will come a time when he will need a friend. He will have few.'

"The man was silent for a few moments and then said, 'As you wish, priest.' He lifted up the puppy whose half open eyes showed no signs of life. He breathed into its nostrils, just like I had done and then said in a soft, sing-song voice:

'Live little one,
Alive, alive-o;
In the Otherworld run,
Alive, alive-o;
Flee the one who kills,
Alive, alive-o;
Live the life of the hollow hills,
Alive, alive-o;
Flee the waters of death,
Alive, alive-o;
Taste life from earth's breath,
Alive, alive-o.'

"Just as you disappeared for a moment not so long ago, so did the tiny creature … only a bit more dramatically. The man thrust the puppy into the earth, and it was as if he pushed the already bedraggled thing into water again—that's how easily the dog disappeared. Out of sight only a few moments. Then, his arms up to his elbows in the mound's earth, he swept the pup out of the hill, blew into its face and a tiny pink tongue licked him. He gave the puppy, swiftly reviving, back to me.

"'Here he is, Malachy,' he said, 'though I don't know what good he'll do. I trust your judgement.'

"'And well you should,' said I.

"'What will you name the creature?' he asked.

"'Troubles,' I said. 'For I think he will be the bearer and receiver of calamity and challenge.' He said nothing else in response to me. He got up, and walked into the woods. I was left with a wriggling bundle of wet and dirty dog. Trouble's has been with me and the Abbey since, until you came."

"I don't want to take the dog from you," said Conor.

"You aren't taking; he's choosing. That is something entirely different."

"Why did you ask that stranger, whoever he is, to help you?"

The Abbot was silent for a while, hand resting on the young calf's back. "Look, Conor. In the past week your whole world has changed. You've seen things few have ever sensed. Whatever is your fate, you're going to need all the help you can get."

"You're not going to tell me his name this time either, are you?" asked Conor.

"No. That's for him to decide. But he made this dog live. And this dog has chosen you. Loyalty and faithfulness are in short supply these days. I'd take them wherever I could get them, either from man or beast."

Conor looked at the Abbot for a moment and then said, "Could you have made that puppy live, if you had wanted?"

The Abbot said nothing for a long while and then, turning back to the sick calf, he said, "Conor, there's no way that puppy was going to be allowed to die. Even then, Troubles had too much life in him. Know why? Because even as a pup, I believe that dog knew you were coming."

Conor watched the Abbot stroke the young calf and whisper into its ear, amazed that one man should spend so much affection on a mere beast.

"It's going to be okay, Father Abbot, isn't it?"

"I've done what I can; the rest is up to this little one and the good Lord who created it." Already the calf was starting to frisk about and kick up its hind legs.

Troubles had listened to all this patiently. But human talk was awfully long and frankly boring. He chose this time to pad over to Conor and sit in front of him. Conor looked at him and knelt down.

"Ok, I suppose it's time for the Lassie thing."

The Abbot grunted. "What do you mean?"

"You know, Lassie, faithful Collie, rescuer of Timmy. I watched the reruns on TV. You'd be surprised how much time on my hands I had in Chicago. Anyway, this is where the dog is supposed to put his paw in my hand, lick my face and then we're bonded." Conor laughed. "The Lassie thing."

But that's not what happened. Suddenly, Troubles leapt right at Conor and knocked him down. Snarling jaws opened and in a split second those same jaws went around the boy's throat, and they began to squeeze. Conor was so shocked he didn't even move. But the pressure stopped as the dog released and stood looking down on him. Conor stared into dark brown eyes, golden flecks moving there, shaping pictures, and he saw—a cruel boy killing a litter of puppies with a two by four, all except one. The pup's mother knocked unconscious lying by the bodies of his brothers and sisters. Harsh hands lifting him and thrusting him into a sack. The smell of the river. The sound of the current. The rushing of air and disorientation as the killer swung him around and let him fly. A brief moment and he was out of the bag, soaring across the water and then the cold touch of wet. Had never swam before but instinct clicked in. Starting for shore but seeing the cruel boy made him turn and head for the other side. Struggling. A glimpse of a human rushing into the water, then darkness. A hand lifting him up and thrusting him into the earth. And light. Lots of shining light. And noble creatures touching him, smiling at him. "Take care of the boy," they said.

"Guard him well." And then a man looking at him and breathing into his nostrils and whispering, "Take care of my son, my only son."

Conor gasped. He wasn't exactly seeing dog memories, it was more as if he was feeling them and the feelings conjured the pictures. But the words he heard and the pictures he saw made him gasp. The dog bent down and growled a low growl, and Conor knew it for a warning; what he had seen could not be spoken of, at least not now. He reached up and grabbed the dog's collar and pulled the dog's face close to his own and stared deep into his eyes. There was no malice there, just a wild devotion, a canine concern, and a waiting. The dog was waiting for him to do something. For a moment, the memory of the other night, running in the woods with Rory came to him, and he knew. He flipped the dog over on its back. No resistance. He straddled the dog, opened his mouth wide. His lips quivered as he put his jaws on the dog's neck and squeezed. Troubles did not move. Slowly, Conor raised his face and looked again at Troubles. A low rumble sounded deep in Conor's throat, startling him back to himself. What the hell did I just do, he thought, and, damn, if that dog didn't pick that exact moment to lick his face and smile at him.

"Dog breath, ugh," said Conor getting to his feet.

The Abbot was standing by the calf looking at the scene with a raised eyebrow. "Kind of primitive don't you think?"

The dog and the boy looked at the Abbot, and as Conor turned back to Troubles the dog raised his paw.

"Nope," said Conor. "Just the Lassie thing."

THE HUNT

THE NEXT EVENING, Jace came over to visit Conor. It was a warm night, late summer still keeping a languid grip on the land. He had grabbed a quick shower and a bite to eat after football practice. Looking positively massive in his grey Tinker's Grove Athletic Shirt #659 and black shorts, he found Conor sitting on the porch, dog at his side.

"Came to hang with you, man," said Jace.

"Cool. Aunt Emily had me working on my studies for most of the day."

"Wish you'd reconsider coming to school. It's just started, and you know you'd be welcome."

Conor bit his lip in concentration. "Not so sure about that. I mean everybody's been decent and all, but they have that look about them, like I'm some sort of lab specimen, unique and possibly dangerous."

Punching him in the shoulder as he sat down, Jace said, "Look at the paranoid boy. You know, my sister would probably like it a lot if you came to school. I think she finds you ... interesting."

Conor smiled, "Yeah, I think she does too. She going with anybody?"

"Not that I know of, and believe me I'd know. Anyone who goes out with her has to pass the brother approval test—not many have."

"Think I might have a chance?"

"Maybe, just."

Conor laughed. "Still not enough to get me into that school. Jace, I've never gone. Home schooled all my life. I'd be a fish out of water. This would be my last year anyway. Besides, Aunt Emily has a few extra subjects she's making me take this year, like Celtic Myth and Legend, Tinkers and Travelers—the story of the Irish gypsies in Ireland and America, and Wisconsin in the 19th century. Sounds fascinating huh?"

"Whatever," said Jace, "but you can't stay isolated from folks."

"I know, and I want to fit in, but I'm a city boy in a country town. I only know how to get along in streets and alleys. All this open space—well it's just different. My friends in Chicago weren't people who'd come to my place just to hang out. I'd meet them at the *DerryAir*, that bar I worked at, or at some café where we all hung out, or I just knew the folks who worked the shops and streets. We accepted each other as we were and didn't pry much. Here people look into your soul. It's like they want to know everything."

"You mean like Dort Martin and Dickie Bergin?"

"Them and everybody. They measure me by my name and not by who I am. 'Oh yes,' they say, 'you're the Archer boy.' And they don't say anything else but the wheels are turning behind their eyes. I don't think they're thinking about me but instead they're thinking about what I'm going to do and mean to them."

"So staying out of school is going to help you how?" asked Jace.

"Probably won't, but face it Jace, anyone who hangs with me for more than a day realizes that strange things happen when I'm around."

"You're exaggerating—so a few Ripleys happened to you. It makes you interesting."

"I don't know," said Conor, "Want to hear something strange? Yesterday, the Abbot said Troubles could come live with me. I was pumped, and what I should have done is pet the dog and take him out for a run. Bonding and all. Know what I did? I flipped the dog on his back, and put my jaws around Troubles' neck like I was going to rip out his jugular."

"Seriously?" asked Jace, mouth gaping.

"It's true. 'Course, that was after Troubles had done the same thing to me."

Jace sat forward. "You're kidding?"

"Nope. And you know what the strangest part of it all was? I knew it was the right thing to do. The dog even seemed to be expecting it. For a moment, I felt like an animal, Jace. I reacted like an animal would. I'm changing. It's not stopping. I want to be just like everybody else, but I'm not. I'm thinking that maybe I never will be again." He sat quiet for a moment and then told Jace about the other night when he went chasing in the woods after Rory.

Jace could see a look of horror cross Conor's face as he verbalized what happened with the floating casket, the dive out the window, the fight in the woods with Rory and the meeting with the Morrigan.

"There's something dark and inhuman deep inside me. I've never seen such strangeness before and the shadowy things that seem to live in these woods and around this community are more like me than I really care to admit. I don't think I'm very safe to be around."

Conor had slumped into his chair and Troubles sat up in concern. The boy looked so forlorn that even Jace's features softened. He reached out to touch his friend's shoulder but halted the gesture in mid-air.

"I don't know what to say, Conor. Yeah, you're right. Weirdness has followed you around for a week or so. But you look okay and act fine to me. So some crazy crap has happened to you. I just figure that if we wait long enough, things will clear up and make some sense. Want you to think about something, though. Whether you go to school or let your great aunt teach you here, why don't you at least make room for Beth and me? You're all right by us and, frankly, kind of exciting to be around." The football player smiled a huge smile.

Conor was touched. Truth to tell, his friends in Chicago only knew parts of him. The up side of this place was that there was more time and fewer people so he could actually let someone get to know him a little bit.

"Tell you what," said Conor. "I'm not bending on the school thing, but my life would be kind of bleak if you guys never came around."

"Deal then," said Jace. "Study with Aunt Emily; play with us. Learn from her and then teach us Weirdness 101. Bet we both can pass your test." Jace stood up. "Gotta go. Coach is having us watch films of last week's scrimmage up at school."

Conor said goodbye and watched him drive away. The sun was setting and the night insects were just tuning up. A terrible sense of loneliness washed over him. I am a freak he thought. Jace just doesn't know it yet.

Emily had gone out earlier to see a friend in town, and Conor's mood darkened with the deepening twilight. He was about to go inside when he heard a car squealing down the narrow road of the cul-de-sac. A dark blue Jaguar pulled up to the house, Fergal McNabb behind the wheel.

"Hey Conor!"

"Hey Fergal, cool car!"

"Swiped it from Rafe for the evening—it's really his but what he doesn't know won't hurt him. Remember, I told you I'd be back for you. Said we'd go riding in the night."

"Thanks, but no thanks. Not feeling up to it."

"That's why I'm here," said Fergal. "Nothing like a ride in a Jag convertible to cheer you up. Come on. Some of my friends are meeting us up at the gravel quarry. We'll all go. Back before midnight."

Troubles whined. Conor ignored him. He was tired of being isolated, and Fergal genuinely seemed to want him to go. Hell with it, thought Conor. "All right, all right, you convinced me." Then he hopped in to the finest piece of road gear he had ever seen, leaving behind a barking Labrador.

They drove to Muddy Hollow Crossroads, a four-way stop that sent travelers west to the farms and hills above Prairie du Chien, north to Richland Center, east to Boscobel, and south down to Wyalusing. It was north they wanted, and up the bluff they went to a gravel quarry not far away. As with most abandoned quarries, the pit had filled with water making a huge pond. Conor saw that several cars and about ten people were there—Fergal's friends. They were clustered around a bonfire, drinking.

Fergal introduced Conor to them and Conor recognized a few from the café the week before. Most were older than him; all were drinking from bottles in brown paper bags. Bottles were thrust into the hands of Conor and Fergal.

"What's this?" said Conor.

"Taste it, it's great," said Fergal taking a huge gulp.

Conor did the same, and as he swallowed he tried to talk and ended up coughing. "Where did you get this stuff?" he asked Fergal.

"Guy named Rory down at the hotel saw us coming out here and said, 'Boys, I've got something that will make your night rock.' And he gave us these. What's the problem?"

"Besides, the man's a biker," said someone in the shadows. "How bad can it be?"

Fergal's friends had been drinking for a while, and Fergal himself was quickly making up for lost time. "Yeah," he said, "I wonder what this is called."

"*Uisge*," said Conor. "In English, it's called the 'water of life.'" Nobody was listening to him; but they were laughing, gathering around him, making him feel welcome, and damn, but that felt good. And though he knew he shouldn't, he did, and he drank.

The familiar warm feeling coursed through him and his already heightened senses went into overdrive. Suddenly the night was brighter. Faces in shadows stood out clearly now, and the air itself was intoxicating. Conor wondered if the others knew they were stepping sideways into a deeper world.

He thought about it only briefly. After all, *uisge* was the water of life and he felt greatly alive. He liked belonging and, when he got thinking about it, he was all for a wild evening. Didn't take long for that to happen. It was Fergal who saw it first, down by the water.

"My God! Will you look at that!" he said. It hadn't been there before, at least no one had noticed it. But it was there now. A white buck—the rarest kind—14 point antler rack with a 22 inch spread, at least. Standing there in the shallows, gazing serenely at the group. Beautiful! Its presence shocked the group into silence.

From out of the shadows walked Rory Nalan. "Fine animal isn't it, lads? Not seen in your woods before I'll wager. Grand evening for a bit of the holy water as well, wouldn't you say?" Rory laughed, grabbing a bottle from one of Fergal's friends and drinking.

Conor saw the biker wasn't alone. Small things leapt around him, vaguely human in form but with indistinct features. Even Conor's heightened senses couldn't pierce the shadow around them. Nobody else but the biker seemed to notice them. Rory turned to the leaping swarm. "Yes, I know my darlings, you want the deer. You're hungry I know. That's why I thought ahead to provide you with some vessels to give you hands to grab and teeth to slash. They've drunk enough and now they're ready." With a feral grin on his face, Rory looked at the group of young men, mouths open, still transfixed at the sight of the white buck. "Take them," he said to the scampering things around him.

Like a swarm of ants the shadowy creatures were upon the group. Conor felt one crawling on him and threw it off, but it soon became clear to him that something different was happening to the others. As he tossed off the vermin clambering on him, he caught sight of one climbing up an oblivious Fergal. His gaping mouth was open and like a slippery eel, the shadowy form slid in. Conor nearly vomited at the sight, but Fergal seemed unharmed. Not even choking. Same with everyone else. In a moment, they all turned as one to Conor.

"Conor," said Fergal, a mischievous gleam in his eye, "time to hunt. Let's get this buck." The others yelped their own agreement.

To Conor it still seemed like Fergal but there was a strange light in his eyes not there before. The voice was Fergal's but the need came from someone or something else.

"Better go with him, Conor," said Rory. "New friends have to stick together. You'll like the ride; you'll love the Hunt."

Conor watched Rory walk to his bike parked at the far end of the quarry and start up the engine. Must have been here before anyone began this party, thought Conor. He drew them here for a reason, and if Conor had to guess, it was not going to be a good one and it was bound to involve him. Speeding over to the group, Rory shouted over the engine's roar, "Lads, yonder stag won't be giving up without a chase. It's challenging us now." As if in answer, the buck leapt from the water and bounded up the road into the dark.

"What have you done to them?" yelled Conor.

"Given them the hunting instinct, a killer's lust," said Rory. Already Fergal and his friends were jumping into their cars. "Better join them, Conor. Friends stick together."

Conor ran to the Jag. He wasn't about to let Fergal drive in this state.

"All right lads, listen up," said Rory. "Into the night we go, after the buck. The rules are simple. First one to bring him down gets all the meat. Follow me." And Rory laughed as he donned a horned helmet.

Turning back to Rory, Conor looked in awe. Maybe in the daylight, it would have looked ridiculous, but there before the fire, the horned helmet on Rory's head transformed him into something from another world. Shadows rippled behind him like a dark tapestry billowing in the wind. Eyes shining and pointed teeth glinting white, he nearly howled at his hunters, "Follow me now into the dark, into the night, after the white stag." And he roared off. Cars squealed their tires and out of the quarry went the hunt.

"Fergal, you can't. You're not right," said Conor.

Fergal looked at him with a fierce intensity. "I'm fine, and I want you to come." He grasped Conor's arm and wouldn't let go. "I need you to come. You're my friend; we're buds in this."

Conor felt the energy flow into him from Fergal's arm. It was as if his body was sparkling, alive with electricity. Definitely a rush and he found himself agreeing, reluctantly, to go. He jumped in the Jag, forgetting to change places with Fergal as they sped off to follow his friends. The McNabb boy hunched over the wheel, laughing softly to himself, whispering, "Feel the air; feel the night; feel the freedom; alive again."

Whoever was sitting beside him was not simply Fergal. "What are you?" asked Conor.

Fergal smiled and said, "I'm Fergal your friend, and," he giggled, "something more, something that hasn't been out in a while." And the Fergal thing turned back to the wheel and chased the others.

For what seemed like an hour, they drove the countryside and Conor didn't even see the stag. That appeared to be forgotten. It was all about the rush of the chase. Conor kept his head but he knew that he was dancing on the edge of something wild. Just a little step more and he'd let go and allow the moment to take him. The speed of the cars, the wild laughter of the boys as they followed Rory seemed to Conor the only purpose. And always Rory at the head, leading them down the highway and off on tiny access roads. Spinning in the dirt and swiping the brush on the narrow ways. Rory ran them counterclockwise around the old oak that stood in the middle of Muddy Hollow Crossroads, and then he led them up the hill again.

They found themselves back at the gravel quarry, and spilled out of their cars. They gathered as a group around the fire, Rory with them, all of them laughing and slapping each other's backs. Again, Conor thought in any other time and place, Rory would have looked ridiculous—a biker in leather with a horned helmet on his head. But here, before the fire, he looked like an ancient god come to gather his worshipers for some horrific sacrifice.

Conor backed away from the group toward the water. Feeling the wet leaking into his shoes, he quickly bent down and stripped them off. The moment his bare feet touched the water, he knew he wasn't the only warm blooded creature in the pool. Sensing a heart beat not far distant, he looked down the beach and saw, not fifty yards away, the white buck, still as a statue, staring at him. It pawed the water and bowed to Conor in greeting.

Conor risked a look to the bonfire and could see Rory, hands upraised, firing up his congregation. Red as blood they looked, and Conor sensed a hunger in them rising. He turned back to the buck. "Run!" he whispered. "O God, please run before they kill you!" He couldn't bear to see such beauty blighted by that bloodthirsty crowd. He knew only moments remained before they would be noticed.

The white stag stepped toward him, and Conor heard a voice on the wind. It wasn't words really, he thought, but he understood the meaning of the feeling.

> *All that is beautiful fades away;*
> *Time and evil,*
> *Robbed and destroyed.*
> *My moment is now;*
> *To dark I descend;*
> *Watch and learn,*
> *Little one.*
> *Creature of many names,*
> *Restore the bond,*
> *Repair the breach,*
> *Renew the trust,*
> *Let my beauty live again.*

"No, don't do this," said Conor, pleading to the animal standing before him. "You can still leave. You can still save yourself."

A whisper in his heart, "And if I do, all will be lost. You must see; you must learn."

The buck turned to the fire and bellowed. Conor shook the fog out of his head. He didn't even know deer could make such a sound. No matter, the members of the little coven by the blaze turned their heads with one accord and looked down by the water and saw the stag, standing peacefully in the shallows.

As one they screamed and charged the buck. It never moved. Paralyzed with shock, Conor watched the group attack the deer, punching, kicking, screaming, biting. Stripped of their humanity, they looked, thought Conor, like creatures from hell. He saw Fergal mount the buck's back and grasp the rack of antlers. The stag turned once more towards Conor and looked. The liquid dark eyes of the deer gazed peacefully at him.

With more strength than Fergal's body should have been able to muster, he twisted his arms and snapped the creature's neck. It dropped into the water like a stone, and the crowd swarmed over it, hands ripping flesh, teeth sinking into warm meat.

"No!" screamed Conor at the top of his lungs. In despair he rushed over to Rory. "Stop them, stop them!" said Conor to the horned leader of the Hunt. "You know this is wrong. Why are you doing this?"

"Always a sacrifice on the night of the Wild Hunt. You're lucky it wasn't a human. Used to be, you know. Those were the days! 'Tis a pity you don't understand. I did it to make a point," said Rory. He turned to the mob and after he made a series of clicks and whistles, they all looked up as one and stared at him, mouths open, sharp pointed teeth dripping blood. "Back, lads," he said. "Back to the fire." They crawled, blood spattered and gore stained. The buck was now a wasted mass of flesh and bone floating in the quarry pool. As they gathered around the blaze, Rory clicked and whistled again. Each of the young men collapsed to the ground. Out of their mouths wriggled the shadowy things, quickly scampering back to Rory. "Away with you," he said. "You've all had your little bit of fun. Back to where you came from." They whirled away into the night.

The gravel quarry was left silent, unconscious bodies scattered around the dying bonfire.

"No worries, Conor. Your friends are just fine, a little dirty but all right. And before you ask, the shadows were things that once lived."

"Human?"

"No, but stronger, older and very dead. They walk the other world hungering for bodies so they can feel, touch, breathe again. I thought I'd give them that chance if only for a brief moment."

"Why?" said Conor. "Tell me why."

Rory walked over to Fergal and poked at him with his boot. "Look at them, Conor. Husks of flesh; weak things without a real purpose. Look how the shadows took them so easily." He looked at Conor. "Notice they couldn't take you. Because you are different. You are not human. You are like me and the shadows, part of the damned."

"You stripped away their humanity," said Conor, enraged.

"Small loss; look how easily they gave it away."

"Fergal was trying to be my friend; all of them were."

"And that's the point. I couldn't let that happen without you seeing how pathetic they are and how much more powerful you are."

"The price was the death of that beautiful creature?"

"The contrast was necessary. Throw your lot in with these humans and all that is beautiful will indeed pass away."

"I don't want what you are offering," said Conor.

"You don't get that choice. You are what I'm offering whether you like it or not."

"No, I'm not. You're a vengeful thing, a creature of the night. A cold and callous thing. What have you offered me that could be in the least bit attractive? Every time you appear, bad things happen to me. Whatever change is occurring is making me less human, separating me more from people who care about me."

"In my mind, that's a good thing. You can be such an ungrateful ass."

Conor felt his rage leave him. "Ungrateful? I learned music from my mother, met people who love and care for me, seen incredible beauty here in the Grove. In this world, with these people. I don't want to be what I am becoming, because whatever it is, it's dark and frightening—like you. Leave me alone. I'm not going with you. I'm not like you. I'm staying here with them, to make sure they're okay." Conor turned away from Rory and walked toward his companions.

"That's fine; do that." said Rory. "But as the fire dies, look closely at them. You're not blood spattered or gore stained. You're not passed out by the fire from drinking the waters of the Otherworld and feasting on raw venison. You're standing. I'm standing. You're strong. I'm strong. The powers of the earth are flowing through you and you are just beginning to learn. And that's how it should be, with the humans at our feet, fearing us, worshiping us. That's how it once was, and how it can be again."

"Listen to yourself," said Conor. "You're delusional. If you were so great, so powerful you wouldn't be dressed up as a biker freak. Whatever you are you're less than what you think. And the more you walk away from humanity, the more of a monster you become."

Rory leapt the twelve feet between them and stood face to face with Conor. "You've listened too much to that Abbot. Malachy may have offered you hope, but it's a false one. Your mother may walk with her Christ in glory, but don't forget you are your father's son. And he's as damned as me, and you are as hellbound as him."

Conor thought of what he had sensed in Troubles' mind. The man who had given his dog life said he was Conor's father. Hard to believe, but during this week of strange things just one more piece to the complicated puzzle. "You knew my father?" he said.

"Knew him? I still know him. I'm your father's brother. Guess that makes us kin, huh, Conor? Feel free to call me uncle. Has a nice ring to it, don't you think? Uncle Rory. And here's my own dear nephew spewing his hate for his own flesh and blood—'You're a monster, Uncle Rory. You're crazy, Uncle Rory. You're evil, Uncle Rory.' Ought to be a bit more respectful to your relatives, Conor. After all, we're all family. Like it or not, you're going to be like me."

Conor felt his legs shaking, but somewhere he found strength to speak. "I don't know if what you say is true or not, but I know this. Whatever you are, I will not be, and tonight, I choose to be with my friends. Now if you're not going to help them, get the hell out of here!" Conor bent down to tend Fergal.

"As you wish," said Rory softly. "But I will be back, and you will see it my way."

Rory went to his bike and started it again. Before he roared off into the dark, he looked at Conor checking over the group of fallen bodies. He whispered into the night, "I know who I am and what I've done. I know there's no redemption for me, but you are like your father, Conor, and as noble as he is, you are better, far better. You just haven't realized it yet."

Conor lifted his head as Rory left the gravel quarry. The silence descended swiftly. Conor could see that neither Fergal nor his friends were harmed. He took off his shirt, dipped it in the water and began to wash the blood and grime off the faces and hands of each of them. Why he did it he couldn't say. Perhaps it was because they looked so used and violated, lying there in the gore. Rinsing out his shirt as best he could, he built up the fire and walked down to the carnage in the pond. Tendrils of mist hung over the stag's body, vaguely moving in the slight night breeze.

You spoke to me he thought. You spoke to me of beauty and the passing of time, the corruption of evil. I don't know what it all means.

Just then the carcass began to quiver, sending ripples through the water. Conor gasped in horror as the stag, or the ruined remnant of it, struggled to rise to its feet. Like some battered Pinocchio, it writhed as if it was jerked by invisible puppet strings. Weaving unsteadily, it stood on three legs, empty sockets staring at Conor, remains of a mouth sagging open, entrails dragging into the water.

A cold reptilian chill touched Conor's mind. "No beauty lasts," it whispered. "Only decay and death are forever, here in my domain. Where I am, there you must be; for you are of the damned, and the world we walk together is death."

"Piasa!" breathed Conor.

"Long is my reach, great is my strength. Do not forget it, Conor Archer."

An antler fell off the stag into the water, startling Conor out of his thoughts. The carcass swayed, and then, on the echo of cold laughter, it collapsed back into the pond.

Conor sank to his knees in the quarry pool, despair and sadness enveloping him. A beautiful, rare creature destroyed, ten potential friends possessed by things out of legend lying unconscious, and a demon who spoke out of the wreck of the noble stag. Conor walked back to Fergal. He looked at them all. Who knew what they would remember. But he watched over them through the long night until dawn broke.

As the sky lightened, Conor put the last of the logs on the fire. He didn't really need it to keep warm—the night had been heavy with heat and humidity. His shirt was still wet and he could see in the dim light blood stains that still hadn't rinsed out. He walked down to the pond and tried to wash the shirt clean one more time.

"Conor, what are you doing?" Fergal stood behind him rubbing his eyes.

"Just washing out my shirt—got dirt all over it last night."

"Where's the buck?" asked Fergal.

So much for hoped-for amnesia, thought Conor. "It's floating in the water, in the shallows over there."

"Holy shit!" said Fergal. "The thing's been mauled and half eaten." Fergal's cries brought the others around the body of the deer.

"We did this," said one. "I remember. We chased it, caught it, killed it. Fergal, you broke its neck. Rode its back and snapped its neck with your bare hands."

"And we ate it," said another. "Raw."

Conor saw them bend over and retch at the memory, and with the difficulty their stomachs were having digesting the raw meat.

"We all did," said Fergal. "And I'm not sure why. All of us except Conor here. He stood back. I saw him in the fire's light."

"Yeah," said another. "Him and that biker dude just watched."

"Why was that Conor?" asked Fergal, his voice taking on a suspicious cast.

Conor stood up to face them. "I don't know," he said quietly. "What happened last night was so strange. All I know is that I couldn't help kill that creature."

But they weren't listening. Some stood staring at him; even the retching ones stopped long enough to look. When he noticed their gaze he looked down at himself and gasped. The black ribbon snaking up his arm had traveled further circling his neck, at least as best as he could see, and like a bull whip snapping, reaching across his heart, outlining each of his ribs on the left side of his chest. He had been careful to cover his arms since Gordon had shown interest in the strange marking, but now, shirtless in the dawning light, no one could miss the tattooing on his body.

Shaking their heads, the boys remembered exactly what happened. It wouldn't have been so bad if they all could have been ashamed and embarrassed together, but Conor's presence wouldn't permit that.

"You just watched us do all that?" said Fergal. "Like you're better than us? You with the duck feet and queer hands? And what's with that stripe on you? I was wrong to think you should be part of us. You're a freak. Come on guys, let's go." They turned to their cars.

"Fergal, can you at least give me a ride home?" said Conor flipping the wet shirt over his neck, trying to hide as much of the marking as he could.

Fergal never answered. Like the others, he got in his car, and drove away, leaving Conor standing alone in the gravel quarry under a rising sun.

AT THE CROSSROADS

AS CONOR WALKED down the hill from the quarry, he thought of what could have been. Could of had some friends, he thought. Sort of liked Fergal and his buddies. They were fun. But that was done. He could see it in their eyes, hear it in their voices. Couldn't blame them really. Couldn't expect them to understand. Gosh guys, I'm changing. Really Fergal I can't help it that my webbed hands and feet aren't the only strange things on my body. Of course, you guys, snacking on raw deer after you've killed just about the coolest animal you've ever seen isn't so normal either, is it, you dumb shits. Guess he could blame them.

Thoughts like these occupied the downhill stomp, because the farther he went the madder he got. He threw his shirt in the bushes. The water had done little to wash the metallic smell of blood out of the fabric. He kept a hold of his shoes, just didn't feel like wearing them.

He saw Muddy Hollow Crossroads up ahead and as he got closer he could hear singing. A fine clear voice singing,

> O take me there,
> Down by the river,
> O take me there,
> Down by the river,
> O take me there,
> Down by the river,
> Down by the river
> Where the waters flow.

The huge oak that grew in the middle of the crossroads cast a dark shadow all around it, but even so Conor could see there was a figure, sitting under the tree. The singing was coming from him. As he walked closer, Conor guessed from the voice that the man was African-American. Vaguely, Conor saw that the stranger was dressed in old working boots, corduroy trousers, cotton shirt and suspenders. Maybe even a little grey in his hair. He didn't seem to see Conor until Conor was almost upon him.

"Who's there?" said the stranger, jumping up and looking around. "Who goes there?"

"Just me, sir." said Conor.

"Don't you 'just me' now. Show yourself."

"I'm right here. Can't you see me, or are you blind?" Conor stopped and stood just outside the shade, the morning sun shining fully on him.

"Blind? Good Lord in heaven, no. But it's near midnight and not even the sharpest eyed crow could see much on this starry, starry night."

Conor looked at the man. It was clear he simply couldn't see Conor standing not ten feet in front of him.

"I hate to tell you this, but it's nearly eight o'clock in the morning. It's not night."

The man was silent for a moment. "Well, maybe not in your world, but it is in mine. Oh, I knew I shouldn't have stopped underneath this oak."

"What do you mean?" asked Conor.

"Crossroads, son. Crossroads. Don't you know anything about them?"

"Can't say as I do," said Conor.

"Well, you sound pretty young. Maybe too young to know such things. Crossroads are thin places where time works different and people see things."

"What sort of things?"

"Things that were or might be. I'm thinking you might be one of them things. Come closer."

Conor stepped just to the boundary of the shade and heard the man suck in his breath.

"See you now," he said. "Not real clearly here in the starlight, but I can see you. Dark you are, as dark as me, and tall with eyes bigger than any man should have, eyes with gold flecks in them."

Conor had to smile; he was the same height as this man. But as he smiled the man let out a yelp.

"Whatever you are, don't bite me. Those teeth look like they could do a lot of damage."

"Get a grip mister; I'm a human being like you. Can't you really see me?"

The stranger was silent for a moment. "It's been a night of strange things for me. Stopped by the Abbey back yonder. Forgot it was All Hallow's Eve. They was having a prayer service or something and I joined in. Went down by the river, down near something they call an Indian mound. Having some kind of religious service, outside and all. Real beautiful those monks with candles singing their song."

Conor sucked in his breath. He remembered some of what Beth had told him about his first night in Tinker's Grove, down by the river. "Can you tell me what year it is?" he asked the stranger.

"Well now," said the singer. "1925 is almost over."

Conor felt his knees buckle and he sat down in the dust. "It's a long time since then for me."

"Ah," said the stranger. "The future then. I'm looking at the future."

"Why are you here?" asked Conor.

"Like I was telling you, son. What I saw was beautiful tonight so I took some of what I heard and was trying to put it to music and words just now. What do you think?"

Conor found himself smiling in the midst of all the strangeness. "I think it might be a hit."

"Really?" smiled the man. "Looks like Malachy was right."

"You know Malachy?"

"Well," said the man, "that's what the Abbot called hisself. He told me that if I saw or heard anything strange tonight I shouldn't be afraid. Guess I'm glad he said that. Hope he was right."

Conor's mind was reeling. Couldn't be the same Malachy. That would make the Abbot over a century old. "What else did he tell you?"

"Nothing. Just told me to keep my eyes open and see beneath the surface of things. Now let me look at you more closely." The man moved toward Conor, but Conor could tell he was seeing something different than what was before him.

"I'm standing in the sunlight on a warm August morning," said Conor. "And as weird as this is, I'm glad I met you. What are you seeing?"

"Well as I said, it's night from where I stand, but I see your outline. Here let me touch you." The man reached out to take Conor's hand as Conor did the same and the two touched where shadow and light met. Conor felt the man pull away just for a second but then grip his hand in a firm handshake. "Got to admit," said the man. "It feels like a paw, your hand does, but you talk normal enough."

"Then I am a freak," muttered Conor.

"You mean like someone in a carnival side show?" asked the man.

"Something like that," said Conor. "Whatever you're seeing is not how I look to people around here. I seem normal, but I know I'm changing. I've got these webbed hands and feet—syndactyly, they call it, and that didn't seem that bad till I started changing. Maybe I truly am what you are seeing—just an animal."

The man put his hand up to his chin and thought for a long while. "Well, here's how I see it. From my vantage point, I'm not seen as the most human of persons either. My skin is black, like yours. People are suspicious of me wherever I go. Excepting this town and the Abbey. They treated me real good. Here in 1925, we black folks have to stick with our own kind, or else we get hurt. I've been called an animal too. But I'm not. Guess I don't think you are either. It's what's here that counts." Reaching into the sunlight, the man smacked Conor's chest. "In other parts of the country, like as not, I'd be hanging from a branch of an oak like this. Strange fruit, they'd call me, hanging dead from the old oak tree. Put there by things that thought they were human but their hearts were long gone."

"You really can't see me, can you?"

"Not clearly. You look black as the ace of spades, but you're talking like a white boy. Like I said, this here is a crossroads and strange things always happen."

"I'm sorry it's dark where you are."

"It's only the night that's dark here. My eyes are full of light. I've seen much that is wonderful tonight, but you take the prize. Something different, something new, for all of us I think."

Conor looked at the stranger. "Mind if I ask you a favor? I played in a band in Chicago. We knew your song. Didn't sing it much since we usually did Irish stuff, but now and then, we did with a little Celtic flair. Can I sing it with you?"

Conor saw the man's smiling teeth. "Sure you can, though I haven't quite got all the verses done."

Conor laughed, "I'm the future, and I already know what you wrote and sang. I'll help you with them. Maybe we'll sing a little."

And so they did.

That's how Aunt Emily and Troubles found Conor. They'd been walking for quite a while that morning, Troubles dragging the old woman along, up towards the crossroads.

"Can't figure out why you didn't go with him," said Aunt Emily to the dog. "He's yours to protect and watch over, so says the boy, so says the Abbot."

The dog looked back at her quizzically. "Yes, I know," she said, her voice clipping along with the click of her blackthorn cane, "you can't understand me, except when it's convenient to you. Oh my ..." she said, her voice trailing to a silence.

They stopped stone-cold still when Emily saw Conor sitting in the dust of the road just beyond the shade of the old oak. She heard him singing along with the man in the shade. Even though he was in shadow, she recognized the stranger right off.

"Conor, stop!" she cried. She could see him standing up, ready to move into the shadow. When he heard her voice, he hesitated. "Wait for me!" said Emily.

As Emily came up to Conor, the stranger said to her, "I know you, I think. But, pardon me for saying ma'am, but you've aged a mite since I saw you this past morning. Don't you remember? You gave me a right tasty breakfast and sent me on up to the Abbey."

Emily tsked, "I'm sure you have me mistaken for someone else. Come away from here, Conor."

"But I want to see him, shake his hand. Emily, he's from 1925. Whoever is in the shade there is from the past!"

"And there you cannot go," said Emily. "Conor, if you cross into that shadow, I may not be able to get you back. You do not know how to do this yet."

"Oh ma'am, I'm so sorry," said the stranger. "See I don't see him as the boy he obviously is. Starlit it may be, but it's still a dark night. Though I see you right clearly. Strange."

"Indeed it is sir," she said. "More than meets the eye."

"Well, now," he said. "You all take care." Turning to Conor, he said, "Right fine singing there. A good duo we make. Too bad we couldn't shake up Chicago a little."

"Yeah," said Conor. "Before you go though, just one thing. What you see of me, tell the truth now, is it horrible?"

"Land sakes, no!" said the man. "Different yes, horrible never. Sure you took me by surprise; but when you talked, when I heard you sing, when I really looked at you, I saw something—someone—who makes this night the most wondrous I've ever had. And let me tell you, New Orleans, which is where I'm from, has given me many a wondrous night."

His laugh had a clear fresh sound. "Heard her call you 'Conor.' Taps Jeffords is my name, but you probably already knew that since you already knew my song. Earlier tonight when I was with those monks and we were down by the river, by that Indian mound, I saw someone else. He was like you Conor. Same heart. Didn't belong to this time or place. But I saw him. He was in the crowd of people, but they paid no mind to him. Turned and looked at me, he did, just me. I don't know why I'm telling you this, but I think he would want you to know that I saw you. Do you know who he might be?"

"I've met him, once."

"Whoever he is, I think he's just like you." The man fell silent for a moment and then said, "By the way, since you're from the future and all, do I make a name for myself? Time is passing me by, and I was just wondering."

Conor took a breath to speak, but Emily put her hand on his arm. "Mr. Jeffords, you've seen a lot tonight. It's best not to know the future. Knowing that takes away all hope."

The man laughed. "Oh I knew it was you, lady, old though you be now. You talked in your wise woman ways this morning, just like that."

"Shush now," said Emily, giving him a warm smile, "and be on your way. God go with you Mr. Jeffords."

"And with you Miss Emily, Conor." The man turned and walked behind the oak. His footsteps faded fast.

Conor darted around the shade to the other side but there was no sign of him.

He came back to Emily and said, voice rising, "Why wouldn't you let me go in that shadow?"

"Now that you know what the Second Sight is, you ought to know the rules by which it functions. You can see the past or the future, Conor, in the thin places on this earth. At crossroads, on thresholds lining the doorways of homes, at dawn or dusk, where water and land meet. But seeing only. If you choose to enter what you actually see, you will be lost and will find it difficult to come back."

"You mean like this?" said Conor anger in his voice, and he jumped into the shade of the oak. Troubles barked, but not in distress. His tongue hung out and he seemed to be laughing.

Emily smiled. "The moment's gone, Conor. That's how the Sight is. It comes and goes." Conor stepped back into the sunlight. Emily's eyes narrowed. She saw the mark on Conor's body sliding up his right arm, around his neck and curving around his heart. "I see Rory's been with you again."

"How'd you know?" asked Conor.

"Every time he's with you, he makes you touch the Otherworld, the Deeper World, I should say. And every time that happens, you change more."

"Make him stop," said Conor.

"I can't. He runs to his own agenda and neither I, nor Troubles, nor the Abbot, nor even he who lives beneath the mound can protect you completely from him. We can help, but Rory is your own demon, Conor, and only you will be able to exorcize him."

"Then make this stop," he said, pointing to the ribbon enveloping his upper body.

"I won't. Though I don't like the swiftness, you are what you were born to be. Pretending that this is not happening or fighting it will not help you."

One knee in the dust, despair in his voice, Conor said, "It's killing me, you know. Driving people away who might have been my friends, making folks think I'm not human."

Aunt Emily came up behind him and put her arms around his neck and hugged him close to her breast. "Tell me what happened last night. Tell me why you didn't come home." And he did. When he was finished, she said, "Those who think noble thoughts never walk alone. What I mean is you know good from evil Conor, you know what is beautiful and true. When I hear you sing or play music, your voice is clear and your music pure. Keep to the good and you'll keep your humanity. Rory, I'm afraid, plays to your dark side, and the more you walk in the darkness, the more frightening your life will become. Understand?"

Conor shook his head in affirmation. "Is that some more of, what was it Mr. Jeffords said, your 'old wise woman ways?'" Conor gave her a tentative smile, stood up and dusted himself off. Troubles came up and sniffed him, turning away.

Emily laughed. "Yes it was, and just look at that dog; even he can't stand the smell of you this morning. Put on your shoes, and let's go home."

"Aunt Emily," said Conor, "Mr. Jeffords really did know you, didn't he?"

Aunt Emily said nothing, just the quickening tap of her cane on the road gave any indication she had heard.

"Aunt Emily," said Conor. "You're not just old, are you?"

"Don't know why you're saying that, Conor." She looked at him over her shoulder. "Though I'll admit, I might be a few years older than the wrinkles on my face would allow."

DIOGENE RISES

BRAND-SPANKING NEW, that's what the new health clinic looked like next to the other rundown buildings in downtown Tinker's Grove. Dr. Nicholas Drake was very proud of himself. He hadn't built the building; the veterinarian from whom he purchased the place had gone deep into debt the year before to put the structure up. Just didn't work out. Which was quite ironic in Drake's mind. After all, if what he dreamed actually could be turned into reality, it would be quite a joke that a former animal hospital and boarding center would now be a place to help humans discover their true relationship with other creatures.

Just to the south of town, the DIOGENE plant and research facility was already under construction. Drake had accelerated his timetable so that much of the facility would be operating within two months. In the interim, thought Drake, getting the health clinic up and running was just great in gaining the confidence of the town. There would be a little diplomacy with the Abbey, but he was confident he could handle any hurt feelings. The monastery had done a good job over the years providing health care to the citizens, but Drake's state of the art clinic—free health care provided, no insurance taken—would be a boon to this area. Besides that, he would have excellent access to all citizens, particularly to those the residents called the 'dark ones.'

The expected problem with the Abbey seemed likely to never arise. Brother Luke was only too happy to have someone share the responsibilities of taking care of the health needs of the area. He had even offered to sub for Drake whenever Drake's other duties took him away from the clinic. Drake was surprised. He had expected the usual jealous attitude from a fellow medical professional.

"It's like this, Dr. Drake," said Brother Luke. "The Abbey exists for the people and we began health care for them long ago when no one else would. Your coming only enhances their options. You're higher tech than we are so maybe you'll catch some things we wouldn't be able to. Just glad to have you around. I'm sure you'll bring needed changes around here."

If only you knew, thought Drake. This Brother Luke, so naïve and trusting, was not like all the other citizens of the town whose smiles hid the knowledge they kept in their hearts.

The history of the town, as Drake knew it, seemed written to hide a secret. Whoever or whatever the 'dark ones' were, Drake bet they were originally outsiders to the community. Reference was made in early letters to the strangers that accompanied this rather different bunch of Tinkers who decided to settle in this area. And though intermarriage occurred, every now and then, a couple would give birth to a 'dark one' exactly like the strangers that accompanied the first settlers. Why would that be?

The genetic abnormalities present in the Grove really weren't extreme. Other areas of the world manifested even more unique oddities. However, coupled with the psychological peculiarities the 'dark ones' manifested, especially at puberty, the genetic possibilities in this community became quite intriguing.

What gene kicked off an obvious psychological and hormonal shift that, if not consciously agreed to, created a type of amnesia and a stopping of a transformative process? Clearly to Drake that was what was happening. Most of the so called 'dark ones' simply rejected the animal affinities they were beginning to manifest at puberty. When they did that, they promptly forgot they ever possessed such abilities. Drake had already heard anecdotal evidence of their uncanny ability to understand animals of all kinds. He had also heard whispers of these adolescents mimicking certain animal behaviors and to some extent duplicating species-specific skills.

Drake remembered Cate telling him of Declan Walsh, now sixteen, who at age twelve had been observed playing with a brace of otters, sliding down one of the banks on White Creek on his stomach, swimming with amazing speed, and even catching fish, bringing them up from the depths onto the bank. Cate told him Declan has no recollection of that event and whenever it was brought up to him his face went blank and he moved away or began another topic of conversation, as if he didn't even hear the question or the story. Quite normal now, Declan seemed a nice young man growing up with no apparent psychological difficulties. Drake had gathered several of these types of tales.

But, thought Drake, not all was sweetness and light. Sometimes, things went wrong at puberty, like with Oz Murphy. He had only seen Oz at a distance, but it was clear he was damaged goods. Rumor had it there were a few others like him, up in the hills surrounding the Grove, seldom seen, seldom heard from. Sometimes the amnesia switch didn't work as the young person moved into his or her teen years. When that happened, the adolescent went strange or even mad. Whatever could be happening on the genetic level? That's what so puzzled and excited Drake. If he could isolate the gene or genes that caused this abnormality, he might be able to determine if the 'dark ones' were indeed some sort of hybrid human capable of accepting some gene crossover from animal species, or whether they were something more.

Then there was the Archer boy, the wild card, just arrived to throw everything off balance. Apparently from Tinker's Grove, apparently one of the 'dark ones,' but well past puberty, not insane, and undergoing some sort of transformation right this very moment. Not for the first time did Drake regret the late entry of DIOGENE ino this phenomenal riddle. How he would love to get that boy into his lab and run some tests. He was the only one who seemed to be coming through the change unscathed, memory intact, and was still, what should Drake call it, evolving.

Drake was nothing if not organized and patient. No use dithering about what he had no control over, at least at this time. The health clinic would be a boon for this community and over the fall and winter, with free sports examinations, free vaccinations, and even a free physical thrown in, Drake was sure he could survey almost the entire population and get some answers. Probably would even be able to see Conor and begin some preliminary lab work. Blood work on all the residents would allow him to begin some genetic mapping.

All this could be done thanks to Cate. Drake was wealthy, but Caithness McNabb was far wealthier and Drake knew it couldn't be just from real estate or farming. He wondered how she made her money. But he didn't wonder much. As long as the gravy train kept flowing. He could build his plant, find some answers, develop a genetic human modifier serum and sell it—and be incomparably richer than his beautiful benefactor. Drake knew he was an excellent scientist, but knowledge didn't buy the toys he liked. Knowledge plus wealth meant fabulous power. That's what really motivated him.

Of course there would have to be experiments. And there would be casualties. Drake was not averse to making mistakes in the pursuit of progress and human evolution. If a few died, then so be it. Genetic research in the past decade was fast approaching a seminal moment when those engaged in such study would publicly call for human testing, regardless of the cost, even if it meant the death of some subjects. And society would accept it. There were always people ready to volunteer to be medical subjects, and given the fickleness of the economy, always some who would accept large cash payments to themselves or, in the event of an unforseen tragedy, their heirs. The benefits far outweighed the moral scruples of some. Already, the advances in genetic research had put humanity on the fast track for cures to heart disease and cancer. Parkinson's was nearly a thing of the past. Couldn't argue with success. So society swallowed hard and accepted the cost of progress.

That's what Drake was counting on. He had done his preliminary research well. Tinker's Grove was a backwater town, isolated even more by its own history. Whatever went wrong here, and some things were bound to, would only leak out as rumor. Government interference and medical oversight were sure to be perfunctory.

When the DIOGENE facility south of town was completed, he could begin in earnest; but for now, gathering information seemed the best activity. He donned his white lab coat, lifted his phone and used the internal intercom to page the clinic's head nurse.

"I'm ready," he said. "Let's make sure the football team is in tip-top shape for their first game."

In a few moments the nurse was back. "Your first patient, Doctor."

Silver hair gleaming, bright smile on his face, Drake reached out to shake the hand of the boy coming through the door. "Declan," he said. "Declan Walsh, I believe." Glancing at his chart, he looked up, "We're starting something new with the opening of this clinic. A blood test to check for any hidden viruses or other problems. We'll get you out of here as soon as we can."

Drake smiled all the way as he led Declan to the lab.

MORE THAN A FRIEND

BETH WAS PACING on Emily's porch when she looked up and saw the old woman, Conor, and the dog walking down the road. Conor was shuffling along, looking bone tired. But he still looked drop dead great thought Beth, just for a moment before pushing that thought aside. The marks on his arm, neck and chest quickly drew her attention. Oh Conor, she thought, it's like your body is tattooing itself.

"Hey, I've been waiting for all of you. I knocked, no one answered. I thought there might be trouble. Fergal and his buddies stopped by the station, bought some munchies, and I heard them talking about Conor."

"What'd they say?" he asked.

"Nothing very complimentary. Were you with them last night?"

"Yeah, friends at dusk; enemies in the morning."

"But why?"

"Enough for now," said Emily. "Conor get cleaned up. Beth and I will cook us all some breakfast."

Conor suddenly realized that Beth was looking at him, frankly appraising him in an appreciative manner. Shirtless and embarrassed, he ran his hands through his hair sending up quarry and road dust. "I'll be back down in just a bit," he said, disappearing into the house.

Emily, never one to miss a thing, turned to Beth and said, "He's a good looking lad, isn't he?"

"Yeah, I mean, yes he is," she said embarrassed at looking so obvious.

"He's more than what he seems," said Emily. "Just remember that if you choose to get to know him better."

"So he's definitely one of the 'dark ones?'" asked Beth.

"I hate that name," said Aunt Emily, walking into the kitchen. She slammed open a cupboard and took out a frying pan. "Get me some eggs and bacon, please."

"Besides the strange rule we all follow not referring to people by that name, what's really wrong with calling him that, or any of the others for that matter?" asked Beth, looking in the fridge.

"Used to be, in the old days, names told you something about people. Now we use them to create suspicion, separate those we don't like from those we do."

"But the town's founders called the special folks in our community the 'dark ones.' Why was their way okay and ours not?"

"Because when they called the people among them the 'dark ones,' they knew what they were talking about; they knew who those people really were."

"And who are they, Miss O'Rourke?"

The old woman smiled and patted Beth on the cheek. "Call me Aunt Emily, since it looks like you'll be around here now and then."

Beth could tell she was getting the brush off. "You're avoiding the question."

"Am I now dear? Make the toast, will you? That's a good girl. You'll have to have Conor tell you about his interesting night and morning. Here he comes now."

Conor pounded down the steps, a quick shower having done wonders for him. Still barefoot, he had changed into shorts and a t-shirt. Beth noted he didn't seem the least bit embarrassed about those webbed feet or hands like he did the day before.

"Sit you down, the both of you," said Emily. "I'm sure you've got much to talk about."

They did. Beth made Conor tell her the whole story. For Conor, it made it less strange to talk about it all. Maybe the heaviness in his chest wasn't quite so bad since Beth was the one doing the listening.

"Why would Rory lead you all on a chase for this mysterious white buck?" she asked.

Emily couldn't help chiming in. "Haven't you ever heard of the Wild Hunt?"

Both of them looked at her blankly.

"The Wild Hunt is ancient—it's a male obsession; supposedly, the horned god Cernunos would take his companions and scour the country-side with wild abandon—lots of drinking, male bonding, that sort of thing."

Conor gaped, "Rory is Cernunos?"

"Hardly," said Emily, "but his little re-enactment was meant to take you and your once upon a time friends into the Otherworld. Sad to say, Conor, it is all about you. He could care less about Fergal and crew except to make sure they would not befriend you. Every time you touch the deeper world, you change a bit more, and that's what he wants, all of you for himself."

"I hate him," said Conor. "All he does is screw up my life."

"I hate him too and I've never even met him," said Beth. "But what about that man you saw under the oak? Surely, he ties in with whatever dwells in that Indian mound. And what about this Second Sight stuff?"

"Taps Jeffords wrote that song that I sang, that you heard down at the mound that night with the monks singing, and I didn't have the heart to tell him when he asked about what would happen to him. Hell, I didn't even know till then how he died, but I could have told him he would be dead before two years were out. He died in the summer of 1926, pretty famous for his time."

"It was good of you not to tell him," said Emily.

"Ah, you were pinching my arm so's I wouldn't."

"He didn't need to know; his life was already full and he was happy. Such knowledge would only have darkened his last months."

Conor turned to Beth. "That's my Aunt Emily, enforcer of the knowledge of the past and future."

"Don't joke with the gifts you are being given Conor Archer," she said. "People who have the Sight find it a terrible burden—as you will soon enough, because just like with that nice man under the tree this morning, sometimes you cannot share what you see and cannot stop what you know will happen. Pray you don't experience that gift too often."

For a moment, all three were quiet but then Beth said, "Fergal and his friends won't let this go. They'll tell whomever they see."

"Like I told Jace yesterday—he was trying to get me to register for my senior year at school—people are going to look at me strange. I just don't want to go through that."

"Well, neither of us is going to let you isolate yourself here. And none of our friends better treat you differently or there will be hell to pay."

Conor paused in the middle of a mouthful of eggs and bacon. She was so cool when she got hot and bothered, he thought. Her blues eyes flashed and she shook her blond head in defiance.

"I mean it, Conor. You're not going to become some hermit." She pushed herself away from the table. "Thanks Aunt Emily, I've got to go and get back to the station. Mary Epps is covering for me, but she gets owly if she has to run the place by herself for too long."

Conor walked her out to the porch. "Hey, thanks for listening."

"My pleasure," she said. She started to walk away, but came back to him.

"What?" he asked, a smile on his face.

"This," she said, and kissed him full on the mouth.

She looked at him and laughed, astonishment written all over his face. Then she leaned closer and whispered to him, "Next time, maybe you can let me have a better look at where that mark has traveled to across your chest." Her finger touched him lightly on the neck and trailed down. She laughed again and was gone.

He stared up the road long after her car disappeared and Emily came out on the steps.

"She's a good girl, Conor," said Emily.

"That she is. Sort of makes staying here worth all the pain."

HATRED IN THE HEART

RAFE MCNABB FOUND his family down at the gazebo by the river the evening after the Wild Hunt. Striding down the long lawn he could see that his mother, ever the hostess, had laid out a spread worthy of a gourmet feast. Frankly, he couldn't care less about it at the moment. They were all there, Cate and Gordy, and Fergal, sipping wine and eating little hors d'oeuvres that the kitchen help had made, Cate being beyond that sort of thing now. He heard them laughing and it only enraged him more.

"Fergal!" he shouted, throwing open the screen door and going face to face with his younger brother. Rafe was a husky man of twenty-three years, wiry red hair and a face that grew a thousand freckles in the summer sun. "What the hell did you do to my Jag? I let you have it one night and you dented the front, not to mention it's got mud all over it, like you were driving it through the countryside."

Fergal was used to his brother's rages and he giggled. "Guess I kind of was," he answered.

The fact that the sniveling little coward didn't lie about it stopped Rafe in his tracks. He wasn't used to this kind of honesty from his brother.

"Before you get all over his case, you ought to let him tell you what happened," said his mother.

"All right then," said Rafe to his younger brother, "before I whup your ass and throw you in the river, explain it to me."

Fergal did. His memory of the night before was still pretty crystal clear. "I was only trying to do a good turn, Rafe, like Mom wanted. I picked up the Archer kid to take him for a ride, and my buddies and I were partying a little up at the quarry." He looked over at Cate. "We were drinking stuff your former boyfriend gave us."

Cate knew Fergal better than his own brother did. She stepped up to him and slapped his face. "Don't you speak like that to me. You know nothing of Rory, and even less about my own personal life. You're the fool who didn't even know what he was drinking."

Fergal rubbed his cheek but still smiled, "So I didn't really know what it was. It was something to party with, and it had a great kick. Rory led us everywhere, for hours it seemed, chasing this magnificent white buck. It was …" and Fergal's voice trailed off as he stared into the twilight.

"It was what?" asked Gordon. He had heard the basic version but Fergal was inserting a few details he had left out before.

"It was a rush. I'd never felt like that before, so hungry, so violent. It was like something got into me. Released the real me. I wanted to rip the throat out of that deer. I would have chased it for hours. Man, it was like I was possessed!"

"Was Conor with you?" asked Cate.

"Yeah, with me in body but not in spirit. Pretty standoffish, tried to talk me out of it. But all of the rest of us were into it." Fergal's eyes shone and a bit of spittle bubbled on his lips. "Rafe, you should have seen it. We got back to the quarry, found the buck there and we attacked it, smashed it with our bare fists and teeth. I broke its white neck and, though I'm kind of ashamed to say it, we dug in and ate, kind of like those reality TV shows on some island. We were like animals, and it was really radical." Fergal paused again, thinking about what he said. "When we were done, we must have passed out by the fire. Woke in the morning, felt terrible, and there was Conor super-caring and all, wiping blood and gore off of us like we were helpless or something. Guess it would have been okay, but he was using his shirt and he's got some birthmark or something snaking up his arm and around his chest and it was moving like a river around his upper body. Stranger than that magical deer. And his eyes! Flecked with gold, shining in the morning light. He looked inhuman."

Gordon stopped him, "Wait a sec. That ribbon of colored skin was only halfway up his arm a couple of days ago."

"Well, now it's not," said Fergal. "It was freakish, and frankly spooked us."

"More than eating a deer—raw?" asked Rafe, intrigued by his brother's attitude.

Fergal got a little defensive. "It was weirder than that. About the deer thing. I know I shouldn't feel it, but it just felt right what we did. Conor looked at us like we had done something horrible." Turning to his mother he said, "Look, Mom, I tried to like him like you asked me to. But he's a condescending prick. We left him there and took off, and I don't care if I never see the freak again."

Cate looked at him. "How do you feel now?"

"Fine, I'm fine; slept this afternoon and feel myself again," he said, looking at the other three. Seeing Rafe's smirk he snarled at his brother, "Don't you go high and mighty on me. I'll admit killing a deer the way we did is kind of primal but it ranks right up there with some of your exploits with the animal world. You're never shy about killing things, are you Rafe?"

"Nope, I kind of like it when the things I hunt suffer. I wasn't judging you little brother; I just didn't think you had it in you. But you're not taking the Jag ever again. Nobody muddies up my beauty."

"So now you don't like him either, Fergal?" asked Gordon.

"Who, you mean Conor?" he asked.

"Yeah, he was pretty standoffish to me, too, the other day."

"Why don't we just go beat the crap out of him?" suggested Rafe, always the one for physical action.

"No," said Cate. "Conor Archer is a new wrinkle in my plans, so I want him watched, and I want all the other 'dark ones' watched as well. There's something about them all. Hopefully we can use them to our advantage, but if not, if they pose a threat, then we'll have to deal with whatever happens, doing whatever we have to do. Moving too soon will tip our hand."

"What hand?" said Fergal. "Why am I always the last to know these things?"

"Because you're too into yourself instead of your family; I hate to say it," said Cate.

Gordon looked at both Rafe and Fergal. "Mom thinks the 'dark ones' are one of the keys to the future wealth, power and prosperity of the McNabb Family Enterprises. That's why she brought Dr. Drake here. That's why DIOGENE is building a plant. And if Drake can isolate the genes that make them tick, go weird or whatever, maybe, just maybe, such a medical breakthrough will make us a ton of cash and gain us a whole lot of influence."

"Fine," said Fergal, "Still doesn't keep us from beating the boy to a pulp."

"Or just getting him out of town," said Gordon.

"He has friends," said Cate.

"The Michaels twins, and of course Emily O'Rourke and Abbot Malachy," said Gordon. "Those last two are powerful in town and crossing them directly would bring us too much attention."

"Who said anything about involving them; just slap the kid around a bit," said Fergal.

"Beating up the new kid in the Grove would bring that same unwanted attention you idiot." Gordon cuffed his brother up the side of his head.

"And the dog," said Rafe. "Don't forget he's got the dog."

"So what?" said Fergal. "It's just the Abbey dog."

"My dog," said Rafe. "One I thought I killed years ago. You remember Scylla and her puppies. Mom was tired of them always yapping and yipping and told me to take care of it. I did."

Cate ran her fingers through her middle son's hair, "Sweet Rafe, you always were dependable. That was a little extreme though, the way you did it, don't you think?"

Rafe grumbled, "Got the job done. At least I thought I did until that last puppy, the one I threw into the river, pops up at the Abbey and those monks adopt the damn thing. Now it's walking around with the Archer kid, seven years later, and I've got half a mind to finish what I started."

Cate snapped at him, "Just like Gordon said, Rafe—leave it for now. We've got to bide our time, get a bit more information. We'll all have to keep an eye on Conor now that Fergal no longer wants to make friends with him."

"Just keep me away from the son of a bitch," said Fergal.

Cate continued, "Fine, but work with Dr. Drake to take up a census of all the so-called 'dark ones' in the area. We need to know what and who we are dealing with."

"What about me?" asked Rafe. "Anything else you want me to do?"

Cate patted his cheek, "Nothing yet, dear. But when this situation descends into anarchy, as it will, then I'll need you. We'll put your exceptional talents to work then. Now, boys, eat up and drink; this is a special night."

"The wine is good, Mom," said Gordon. "I didn't know we had anything like this in our cellar."

"We don't," said Cate with a smile. "Rory gave it to me, so I thought we could share it together. Taste familiar, Fergal?" She laughed and they laughed with her. "Drink up and eat. I think it will help you get ready to meet someone you should have met long ago. Let me go and fetch our guest."

Cate walked out of the gazebo, turned and locked the door.

"What are you doing?" said Gordon.

"Just making sure you don't go anywhere till our guest comes."

"You can't hold us here against our will," said Rafe with a laugh.

"Sure I can," she said, "because you're my good boys and you always do what I say. You're more than interested in who you will meet. Curiosity will keep you here; the lock is just a little incentive. Drink, and wait. It won't be long."

She walked down to the river. "Now," she said in to the darkening eve, "Now is the time." The mist began to rise as the last shreds of daylight faded. "Teach them, but do not hurt them. They drank the drink that Rory gave me." She felt the unease of the presence in the water. "I know you hate him, but trust me in this. His motives fit mine and yours for now, so let's use him. You can get rid of him later if you want." The unease she had felt was lifted from her. "Remember, I love my boys, so do no harm to any of them, or you will have me to answer to."

A breeze lifted her black hair. She looked fearlessly out over the water. "I mean it. Too much is at stake and you and I have come too far to ruin this relationship."

Piasa was impressed, though it knew she could ultimately do it no harm. But it liked the fearlessness in her, like the wolves that used to prowl the bluffs above its river. Piasa knew she could do its will in places where its power was weak. It would heed her warning. Riding on the mist from the river, it passed her and caressed her mind. "Do not fear. They will be bound to me but not in thrall. They will give me service of their own accord." On the tendrils of fog, it approached the gazebo.

"So who's the special guest?" asked Rafe.

Gordon was happy that the candlelight did not cast much illumination so they could not see how pale he had become. There was real fear in his gut. "We're going to meet that thing … that thing that Ma talks to in the river."

Rafe and Fergal were not exactly deep men, but even they knew what Gordon was talking about. They preferred not to think about their mother's propensity to talk to herself down by the river, but both had seen strange things happen when she did. One night, Rafe had come in late just after he saw Cate enter the house. He followed her in silently and she was talking to herself. Shreds of mist clung to her and drifted with her up the stairs, swirling about her, caressing her. Impossible, thought Rafe, but it happened. Fergal once saw her laughing down by the river to herself. She plunged in the water and something pushed her around the width of the river like those killer whales moved the swimmers in SeaWorld. She just kept laughing and talking. Fergal never mentioned that to her.

As soon as Gordon told them what was coming, they all drank the last of Rory's vintage. "She made us drink this," said Gordon. "Whatever's going to happen, she thinks this will make it easier."

"Like it did last night," muttered Fergal. Rafe said nothing; he feared little. Let it come, he thought; maybe it will be surprised.

They sat in their chairs, each lost in his own thoughts as the first bits of mist slipped through the screen windows of the gazebo. The candles wicked out and they were left in silvery darkness.

Gordon felt it first, the mist on the back of his neck. A tentative probing, a whispering in his mind telling him not to be afraid. He heard a chanting deep in his being and he knew what it said,

Mine is the eldest of the she-wolf's three,
mine is he whom I bind to me,
water and mist to blood and bone,
mine is the eldest of the she-wolf's three.

Gordon felt a crushing pressure around his chest and the tiny sharp poke to his neck. Visions of wealth and power filled his mind, what he had always thought of all his life. Better than making out with any girl; it was what he wanted and he knew that his mother's consort could give it to him. Let the Devourer eat his soul, he thought; the bargain was worth the price.

Rafe felt it too, the mist on the back of his neck. He heard the chant, the same as Gordon except the words were changed,

Mine is the middle of the she-wolf's three ...

but the rest of the chant was the same. He didn't mind the pressure and he welcomed the pain that came from the little poke to the neck. For all the while that was happening, visions of violence and degradation filled his thoughts, violence he could cause, degrading things he could do. He thrilled to the words, "water to mist, blood to bone" for they promised intimacy with violence and with that presence that now embraced him. Promises to enhance his abilities to cause pain made him laugh out loud. He truly didn't mind being eaten by one who could give him such pleasure.

Fergal was scared to death. When the mist wrapped its tendrils around him and squeezed him tight, he squeaked with fright. He whimpered when the tiniest of pinpricks nicked the flesh of his neck. He shook as he heard the voice in his mind,

Mine is the youngest of the she-wolf's three ...

But then, the fear went away, like magic.

Mine is he whom I bind to me.

It was as if he was being embraced and caressed and his thoughts were filled with power and fame. "No need to be the third," said the voice, "no need to be the weakest. Being devoured by me is strength for you to supplant your brothers if necessary. I take you to give you power over them."

No one had ever told Fergal that, and he wanted the reality badly, and he couldn't believe that he said to the presence in his soul, "Eat me then, and give me what I want."

A noise like a thunderclap startled the three out of their reverie. They looked at each other, too stunned to speak, but clearly seeing that each of them was drenched, as if they had been swallowed by a huge wave. Water dripped off of them, pools puddled on the floor before them. Gordon lit the candles again. As he did so, the other two saw the drop of blood on his neck and their hands instinctively touched their own. They looked to see a fresh drop of blood on a finger, not muted or diluted by the water.

"Whoa!" said Fergal, "too cool. Is this what happens to Mom when she talks with it?"

"No, you fool," said Gordon.

"Gordon's right," said Rafe. "I think if dear old Cate could float a mattress out on the river she'd sleep with the thing but what happened to us is different. It's like we're blood brothers."

"More than that, I think," said Gordon. "It fed on us, like a parasite, but like a parasite it gave us something in return didn't it? I bet it promised each of us different things. Right?" The other two didn't say a word.

"No matter," said Gordon. "Keep your secrets and I'll keep mine. But never forget. It needs us as much as we are bound to it." Gordon paused for a moment, and when he spoke his voice was very soft. "Otherwise, I think we would not be here. Devourer of Souls it may be, but if it ate our souls, it gave them back to us." Gordon added a thought but didn't speak it out loud—let's just hope it doesn't want them back again.

They saw their mother coming up from the river, a snap to her step. She unlocked the door and said, "So how goes it with my boys? Did you enjoy meeting our special guest?"

"Fascinating," said Gordon.

"Bitchin'," said Rafe.

"Awesome," said Fergal.

"Glad to hear it," said Cate turning to the table. "Now, how about some nice lemon meringue pie?"

SUMMER INTO FALL

FINALLY SOMETHING UNIQUE happened. Nothing. Conor couldn't believe it. August drifted into September and a sense of normalcy set in. Emily set a hard pace, but Conor liked the discipline she brought to his studies, and he liked the extra stuff she was adding, like the Celtic things his mother had talked about but seldom explained. He was enjoying watching his friend Jace play football in what was turning out to be a successful season for Tinker's Grove. And he had begun to date Beth— nothing serious yet, just some time down at the café and a few movies here and there. Had to let her drive though since he didn't have his license. That was one thing that would have to be remedied.

Even Rory let him alone. Word had it that he had left town for a while, though he was keeping a room at the Burke Hotel. Conor had no doubt that he'd be back. So Conor ate, slept, studied, had a little fun and enjoyed living a more normal life.

Got himself checked out at the clinic. Took Dr. Drake up on his invitation to investigate the ribbon of dark skin snaking across his body. That was some afternoon. Drake clucked and hemmed and hawed and had the nurse draw some blood and examined the webbing on Conor's hands and feet and spent a lot of time inspecting the curious skin phenomena that Conor was now manifesting.

"Tell me now," he said to Conor sitting on the examining table, "does it hurt at all? Does it feel separate from you? Is it as sensitive as other parts of your skin?"

Conor dutifully answered, "Doesn't hurt; feels like part of my skin; much more sensitive than the rest of my body."

"In what way?" asked Drake, taking copious notes.

"Heat and cold, pressure, wet and dry. It's intense, like there are more messages in those sensations than I can decipher right now."

"Well, we'll need a sample of that skin."

Which turned out to be harder than it seemed. The new skin was tough, and a scalpel could barely make a dent in it. Never the less, Drake got enough off that he felt would be sufficient when looked at under a microscope.

"You're a normal male for your age, Conor," he said as he finished the exam. "Whatever is happening to your skin is not damaging your health. Of course, we'll need to get the blood tests back to say that conclusively, but I wouldn't worry."

"Is this ribbon going to widen; is it going to cover more of my body?" he asked.

"Can't say for sure, son, but the good news is that there seems to be nothing to worry about."

Conor left less than convinced, but Drake was secretly ecstatic. There was enough DNA in the blood samples and skin samples to tell him what he needed to know. And he needed to know all of it immediately. So he closed up shop early that day and spent the rest of the time in his small lab. Further tests would have to await the completion of the DIOGENE complex.

Not too many days later, Conor was comparing notes with Jace down at the convenience store about the doctor's exam.

"You mean he kept you in there 45 minutes?" asked Jace. "I was in and out of there in ten. Guess you got to have webbed hands and feet to make a difference to the Doc. Declan was telling me that Dr. Drake kept him a long time too. Same with all the others who are like you, Conor. I mean, it's nice to have a clinic and all, and Drake seems really competent, but I just get the feeling …"

"That he's treating me and those like me like new bugs from the tropics, collecting us like specimens."

"Something like that," said Jace, biting his lip. "Well, if it's anything sinister, he'll tip his hand sooner rather than later. Can't do much till then."

"Like we'd do anything," laughed Conor.

"Don't laugh," said Jace seriously. "Sometimes you got to take a stand on some things that really matter."

"Like what?"

"Like friends who might be in trouble. Like a bunch of people I've grown up with who seem to be singled out for special attention by outsiders."

"Geez, Jace," said Conor, "you sound positively militant and all protective of us webbed ones."

Jace forced a laugh. "Mock me if you want, but I say all this stuff that's been happening needs to be looked at a lot closer."

"Been quiet lately."

"You just watch. It's only a lull. You may be the one who's changing into God knows what or who, but what I'm feeling now seems true to me. I'm right on in being a little worried and a little protective."

"You and Troubles ought to open an agency. That dog follows me around so close that I think you must be giving him secret orders."

"We've had our chats," said Jace and smiled.

They were having a coke and Beth was serving the counter. She joined in the conversation. "Have you filled Conor in about the October Country Irish Fest?"

"He hasn't said a word," said Conor, "but I know it's coming up soon."

"That it is," said Beth, "and you've got to play at it. There are all sorts of craft booths, and the usual carnival, but the cool things are the stages. We actually bring in music, some modern stuff, but also Irish traditional. It's the one time of the year that our population triples and we bring in money to the community in a big time way."

"How would I arrange things to play, with whom and when?" asked Conor.

Jace said, "Believe it or not Conor, you're not the only one who has musical talent in this town. We just hide our gifts a bit more."

Conor blushed. "I'm sure; I just didn't know how I'd hook up with anyone."

"Already did that for you," said Beth. "Well, really just made some inquiries. But Jim Warren plays a mean accordion, the Abbot can get a crowd foot stomping with the playing of the fiddle, Brother Gerald you've already heard on the uilean pipes, and ..." she paused for dramatic effect, "my brother can play a bodhran and other such percussion instruments."

Jason laughed. "Can't sing but I can keep time so they give me the noisemakers."

"All of them have played the last few years together at the festival so I think you'd be a great addition."

"Was going to ask you," said Jace.

"Don't want to intrude," said Conor cautiously.

"Look," said Beth, "I know you've had a hard time fitting in here, but if you played, at least to the community at large it would look like you're trying to make this your home. Plus, you have a voice, and that little band never did any singing so maybe you could help them improve their repertoire a little."

"So what do you say?" asked Jace.

"Sure if it's okay with the rest."

"Already asked them; they're fine and looking forward to you at our practices which start, by the way, tomorrow and almost every night for the next four weeks."

That's how Conor's days and nights got even more regular. Aunt Emily was pleased. Troubles slept more. All was right with the world.

***

Practice with the little Irish group was kind of fun thought Conor. Met at seven in the evening, quit at nine. Gathered down at Jim Warren's house which was right in town, just up the hill from where the bank was. Jim had moved the dining room table to the side and the band practiced in the middle of the room.

Conor had to admit they were pretty good. Brother Gerald was the funniest though. Never talked much, but when he played the uilean pipes he must have thought he was a Scotsman blowing into that instrument's bigger cousin, the bag pipes. Even though the smaller version pumped air by using a person's elbow movements, Brother Gerald blew air out of his mouth anyway, and his eyes bugged as if he were playing Gaelic airs by the shores of Loch Lomond.

"We need a girl," said Conor the night after he began.

"What?" said Jim.

"A girl, who can play something of course," said Conor.

"Whatever for?" questioned the Abbot.

"Because it would balance the band and give people something else to watch besides five guys and their instruments."

They were silent for a while.

"We're that bad?" asked Brother Gerald.

"No, it's not that," said Conor. "Actually, we're pretty good, but if we're going to entertain, we've got to do it the right way. And it would help if she could sing."

"Nora Martin," said Jim. "Dort Martin's granddaughter. Conor, I see by your face you've met Dort. Don't worry, even though she lives with her grandmother, Nora's much quieter and not the busy body type. Your age, too. I've heard her play the keyboard and I've heard her sing in high school plays and at church occasionally. Not bad. Give her a ring right now Conor and ask her."

He did. And with Jace and the older men listening, Conor explained to a rather surprised Nora Martin what they wanted. The phone went silent for a moment, and then Nora said, "I'll come. I know some of what they do. Thanks for asking."

She was there the next night and set up her keyboard in the dining room. She didn't lie. She knew their stuff. And she could sing. What's more, she was a 'dark one.' Long straight black hair, black eyes, and the tiniest of webbing on the fingers, which didn't bother her playing in the least.

"Told you," said Conor to the group after they'd done a particularly effective version of 'The Leaving of Liverpool.' Her voice was clear and fresh, and despite her seemingly shy demeanor, when she sang, she sang with strength mixed with a bit of cockiness. "They'll flock to our stage. Won't be able to keep them away."

"Well," said the Abbot, "Nora here definitely classes up the place. Even if they don't like our music, we'll dazzle them with our looks, at least you will Nora." They all laughed.

***

When he wasn't practicing or studying or doing chores around Aunt Emily's property—she did tend to keep him busy—Conor was fishing. Never had done that before and he was beginning to like it. Gave him more time to be with Jace and get to know that guy better. Jace was a superb fisherman. He knew the river well and the sloughs that snaked through the river bottom.

"Walter Johnson taught me all his," said Jace as he and Conor were fishing the river one Saturday afternoon. "Catfish is his specialty and I think I'm the only one that he ever taught all his secrets to."

"Must have taken a while to learn them," said Conor. "A fishing tip here, a quart of brandy there, a day to sober up."

Jace laughed. "Yeah, I know, Walter can drink a lot. Seems to be happening more now. Have to admit, he taught me how to handle a boat pretty well too since most of the time I had to pilot when he was a little under the weather."

They had parked the car upriver and were drifting down with the current. White Creek was just ahead of them. Jace pointed, "That's Walter's favorite spot, right where the creek runs into the river. Got a lot of catfish in this area." They stopped for a while and sure enough, Conor got himself a five pounder. "Now you have to have me over for supper," said Jace, "providing that's okay with your Aunt Emily." Conor smiled. Even Jace was beginning to talk of the old woman as if she was family. Emily had grown fond of the twins and enjoyed it when they came over, often offering them dinner. She was a good enough cook that they seldom refused.

"How's about we check out the fishing up in White Creek?" asked Conor.

"Can't," said Jace. "Nobody goes up there, not Walter, not me, not no one."

"How come?"

"Simple. Rule's been around as long as there has been a town. The creek's off limits. It's a backwater slough at first—you can see deadfall trees and branches blocking the entrance—up farther marshy and muddy, so they say, and way overgrown with cottonwood and bass trees. Just a mess and something else, I think. No one ever says, but stuff happened there once, bad stuff, evil I guess, and no one goes there."

"Come on, Jace. Never?" Conor was all for obeying rules but ones that lasted for centuries seemed a bit extreme.

"Never. And don't you go thinking about seeing what's there either. Please." Jason's voice took on a tone of pleading.

"Hey, okay. I was just curious is all."

They drifted further southwest and saw ahead of them the Indian burial mound, the willow trees silent sentinels set back a bit from the river.

Jace said, "I was with Walter a couple of weeks ago when we drifted past here. Since whatever happened in August, he's a different man. Still drinks, but something's changed. When we got to the mound, he threw down the anchor and just looked. I mean his face was awestruck. I asked him what was wrong and he said that nothing was the matter. 'It's just beautiful,' he said, 'and whatever is there saved my life.'"

Conor looked at the mound, "Seems it did the same for me."

Jace leaned back in the boat and looked up at the sky. "You know, Conor, before you got here, football was just about the only exciting thing going on in my life. Since you've come, life's gotten much more interesting. Sort of glad you are around."

Conor guessed Jason Michaels didn't much talk like this very often, so he leaned back in the boat and looked up at the blue sky as well. "Where I come from, my life was pretty exciting; it's just that no one much cares about you in the city. Here, you and Beth, the Abbot and Aunt Emily, even Jim Warren, you care about what I think and do and say. That's kind of cool. Never had anyone take me fishing either. Guess I'm sort of glad you're around, too."

Conor looked back at the mound as they drifted by. A breeze seemed to catch the willows and their branches lifted in the wind as if they were greeting the two young men. Strange, thought Conor, no wind touched the surrounding trees. Conor leaned back again in the boat. Not bad. A warm September day, fishing with a good friend, pretty peaceful. Maybe things were indeed getting back to normal.

UNDERWATER PANTHER

THAT LAST SATURDAY in September, when the boys went fishing, that was the day Piasa decided on its strategy. It had always been patient. In the days when the first Native Americans discovered its presence, it would go many months before snatching an unsuspecting child or squaw. It went for the weak mostly, not because it doubted its strength but it liked the sense of foreboding mystery it caused the tribes. Around the fires at night, disguised as the mist of the evening, it heard the name it liked the best—Underwater Panther, and so to these people it appeared like that to them, when it chose to let them see itself.

It didn't simply need the captives for food; rather, it liked to collect them and cause fear among the humans—that was the worship it craved. Of course, it didn't need that homage either. Over the years, it had snuffed out the lives of every human being within its reach, gradually letting them build their populations up again. Piasa was, in fact, a kind of plague, rushing out among the living every few generations to remind them that it still held the decision over their lives.

The strange boy who had appeared two months ago on the Indian mound still puzzled and intrigued Piasa. It now knew that Cate and the doctor considered him an asset, not a threat, and Piasa was content to see if that was so. At first, it had thought its ancient enemy was rising again to give it battle, using this human as an instrument, but it had not seen any threat to its existence.

There was the doctor's offer of assistance. How did he put it, "the manipulation of humans, the domination of man." Piasa liked that idea as well since it preferred to use humans to do its bidding on land. Its link with the Otherworld lay in the water. Away from it, Piasa had difficulty manifesting itself, which had always angered it. The doctor's suggestion that it had failed to dominate humanity gave it a strange emotion that it knew humans would tag as humiliation. So much to learn from them. Still, the doctor promised to satisfy its ancient longings. There could be no domination without feeding, and it had been a while since Piasa had fed on real fear.

Yet, it was content to watch the boat drifting down past White Creek. It listened to the boys talk and thought how easy it would be to take them. A painted turtle swept by, unaware of the monster's presence. A chilling of the water was all the shelled creature noticed and it simply sped up its pace. Like so many things, Piasa was not simply a creature of the visible world. It manifested itself there but it dwelled within existence at a deeper level. Like an iceberg whose shining ice shelf is only a fraction of its mass, like that same iceberg whose total reality had most of itself living invisibly, but just as concretely, below the water line, Piasa dwelt in the visible world. If a living thing was only looking at what it could see or taste or feel, it would likely pass Piasa by—just the barest reflections hinting of an even more vibrant living being—that's how good Piasa was at concealment. It knew that the darker of the two boys could sense it if he tried, but even that one had his senses tuned to the sky and to his friend. The other possessed no such talent and Piasa dismissed him.

Their fascination with the mound sent a chill through Piasa's being. Though it did not think the two were immediately dangerous, their interest in its enemy's lair did not bode well. It had waited too long. It was time to investigate and Piasa decided to start with the 'dark one.' It was well to do so since all the 'dark ones' in the area had some kind of affinity with its ancient enemy. Piasa normally did not trouble itself with them since the 'dark ones' tended to neutralize themselves. Any potential for possible mischief seemed to leech out of them as they grew. But not this Conor. This human had potential for harm, Piasa could tell, despite the assurances of Cate and Drake. It needed to touch the boy's mind so it could find him later, and since the boys were in its domain of water, that should be easy.

Conor turned as some huge fish jumped. Didn't really see it, only the spray. And he surely didn't see the forked tongue of Piasa hidden in the water spray, stretching to touch Conor on his forehead, instantly reading the mental footprint. Now, the beast could find him anywhere near the river. It laughed, but the boys heard no sound, just saw bubbles coming from the depths of the river. A hint of concern passed briefly over Conor, but whatever was happening to him was incomplete as yet. All Conor perceived was what he expected to see in a river—fish and water.

The Devourer rolled in the river bottom with pleasure. Piasa could not really read minds—the human thought process was somewhat baffling to it, but since it dwelt in what humans often called the Otherworld, it did understand the realm of dreams. When it touched Conor's mind, it happened upon a dream in the boy's memory that it recognized. As with most dreams, it was pretty much a muddled mess, but logic was never Piasa's strong suit;

images, signs and symbols were and it knew well the reality that this dream came from. What was this boy's connection to it? Perhaps it was best to start there, it thought, and planned to make its nocturnal visit to this intriguing 'dark one' soon. Piasa left them floating in their boat, amused at its power of deception, confident in its ability to triumph.

Piasa chose that night to stalk its prey. It waited till the full moon rose, and then crept like a panther, padding its way up from the river bottom through the woods and into Madoc's Glen. It found Emily O'Rourke's house easily enough and with its knowledge of Conor's mind entered the open bedroom window of the boy as part of the mists of night. Not even the sleeping dog noticed its presence. The somnolent Conor didn't resist the invasion of his sleeping thoughts. Besides, Piasa wouldn't stay long, just enough to push the dream into the direction it wanted it to go. There was a child in that dream and the Devourer of Souls felt the need to know if that child was connected to Conor. If so, it had to get the boy thinking about his origins so that Conor could show Piasa whether or not he truly was a threat. Not only that, Piasa saw its actions as a bone to Cate and the doctor, its way of pushing whatever change was occurring in Conor along just a bit. Like a projectionist readying a film, Piasa readied Conor's entertainment for the night. Looked like it was going to be a night at the horror movies.

BEYOND DREAMS

EMILY LEAPT UP in bed, wondering what woke her. Then she heard the screams and the barking of the dog. In her nightdress, she headed for the stairs. "Lands, but that boy is a lot of work." She muttered it that way because such a critique gave her courage. She couldn't begin to imagine what was wrong.

Opening the door to Conor's bedroom, she turned on the light. Her hand went to her mouth. "Jesus, Mary, and Joseph!" she said, running to Conor's bedside. The bedclothes were strewn on the floor. Conor's eyes were staring sightless at the ceiling and his hands were gripping the mattress. And he was screaming. Sweat was pouring off him; what made Emily hesitate was the dark ribbon of skin snaking its way beneath Conor's chest, across his abdomen, disappearing beneath his shorts only to reappear down his left leg ending at his ankle.

To Emily, it looked like the entire ribbon of skin was moving within itself, pulsating with gold flecks of light. She wasn't sure if that was causing Conor's pain, but the minute she looked at his eyes she knew. Flecked with gold as well, but mist covered with green they were. Emily had seen this before long ago. She knew that alien presence. Without a word, she turned from Conor and walked over to the window, slamming it shut.

She leaned over Conor and grasped his head between her hands. "I see you," she hissed. "You come into my house after all these years and touch one of my loved ones? How dare you! Out of him, now! Brigid, Brendan, Columba and Patrick stand at the bedposts. Apostles Twelve, Michael the Strong, Mary Mild surround us this night. Christ the Healer, touch this lad and make him whole. Drive the demon away as you did in the days you walked among us, over hill, over plain, in the town, in the home. Drive the dark away!" She bent close to Conor's eyes and whispered fiercely, "They are here, powers more potent than you. Leave him."

The screaming ceased abruptly and a mist rose above Conor's head. An echo of raging laughter touched the ears of Emily and then was gone.

"Aunt Emily?" said Conor weakly.

"It's alright; it was just a bad dream."

"Bad dream?" said Conor. "More like 'Nightmare on Elm Street.' It was so real."

"I'm sure it was," said Emily lifting him up and sitting him in a chair. "Put this sheet around you while I change your bed things. They're soaked with your sweat."

Conor whistled low as he saw the lengthened dark line running across his body, but all he said was, "Aunt Emily, this weird skin is hot to the touch."

Emily could see that the ribbon of skin had stopped morphing in motion, quieting to its usual dark color. When she touched it, indeed, it was very hot. "Almost as if it were trying to throw off an infection," she muttered.

"What?" asked Conor.

"Nothing, dear, whatever you saw in your dreams gave you quite a fright, so I'm sure the rise in temperature comes from that. Nightmares do strange things. Now as I take care of your bed, tell me what you remember."

Conor did. "It was like the dream I had the first night in Tinker's Grove. This woman, she was being chased by someone or something. Carrying this baby. They were down by the river; it was winter. She was looking back at whatever was pursuing her, but she should have been looking at the hole in the ice. Something was there, and it reached out and grabbed her and her baby, and it dragged her down, both she and her child, they went under the water. She screamed and screamed until her head went under. That's all I remember, except for one thing.

"I know what dragged her down. I've seen it before, on the first night I was here and not in my dreams. Down by the Indian mound. I saw it in the river there, just for a second that night. In my dream, when I recognized it, it reached for me too and grabbed me saying, 'I'm always with you Conor, even in your dreams.' Then there were shining ones around me, beings I did not recognize. They gave me strength, and there was One, who took me by my hand and pulled me away. And you were there too, Aunt Emily. With them, and then, here holding my head. That's what I saw. That's what I remember. Some dream, huh?"

Emily tried to smile with her chin on a pillow, pulling on a new pillow case. "This is a trying time for you I know, but we must not take dreams lightly. You are very vulnerable now and need to guard yourself. You left your window open. There are things in the night that might try to take advantage of your changing condition, things that can touch your mind when your defenses are down."

"Are you saying that this nightmare ... are you saying that when that thing said it was always with me, it really was with me? Is that what you're saying?" A look of horror crossed Conor's face.

"What I'm saying is that you need to protect yourself. Didn't your mother ever teach you how to do a *Lorica*?"

"A prayer of protection, isn't it, where you ask the saints, angels, Mary and even Christ himself to surround you and protect you from harm?"

"Exactly. Obviously, you at least heard of it, though I can tell from tonight that you don't practice it."

"When I was young, my mother and I always said one at night, but, well, you know, you outgrow those things."

"Really?" said Emily with an arched brow. "Sounds like it might have come in handy tonight."

"Guess I'm just not religious enough."

"It has nothing to do with being religious or pious or whatever. It has everything to do with being commonsense smart. You think all those traditions are just folktales. Let me tell you, they're as serious as the songs you play and sing. And being that we aren't quite sure what's happening to you, we ought to play it safe, don't you think?"

"Yes ma'am," said a contrite Conor.

"Don't 'yes ma'am' me. Just don't be a fool. Now get back in bed. There won't be any more trouble tonight."

"How do you know?"

"Because I shielded you with a *Lorica*—weren't you listening? It won't stop bullets or knives or sticks or stones, but it will banish anything seeking to harm you that tries to invade your mind or soul. You saw it work once. Trust in the good Lord that it will work again. You know lots of people think stuff like this is magic. It worked before because I said it. All you have to do is agree to let it work for you. God will never let you come to harm if you let him in. Goodnight, Conor." She fixed a level gaze on the dog. "Troubles, a little sharper next time. Keep an eye on this boy." With that Emily switched out the light and shut the door on Conor.

"Angels and saints, the Blessed Virgin and Christ himself—well, at least I won't be sleeping alone." He smiled and closed his eyes.

Emily walked slowly down the stairs, care and concern etching her face. Time for tea, she thought, and made her way to the kitchen. But before she turned on the light, her hand paused. She could see the kitchen door was open. The full moon cast a small glow of light on the doorstep.

"Is he safe?" asked a voice.

She looked over to refrigerator and a saw a figure standing in the shadows.

"You!" said Emily. She brushed a wisp of white hair from her face, straightened her glasses, and pulled the nightdress close around her.

"Ah lass, you're as beautiful as the day I first met you." A young man stepped into the moonlight. She could see he was dressed in a homespun shirt and trousers with soft boots. His dark hair, caught in a braid down his back, glowed darkly in the gloom etched by the moonlight.

Emily clicked her tongue. "You'll never change, will you? Always the flatterer, but in the end a breaker of hearts." Her words were stern but there was a twinkle in her eye. Then, her brow furrowed again, "And to answer your question, yes, he's safe. For the moment."

"I was out in the wood. I heard the screams. I heard his voice caught in the grip of that soul sucking dragon. Clearly the time grows near when what must happen to the boy must come to pass. Do you fear it, Emily?"

"Why can't you just go to him and tell him who you are?"

"Do you know who I really am?"

"Of course, you silly thing; you're his father and you ought to tell him."

"But do you know who I really am?" he muttered half to himself as he took a seat at the kitchen table.

The old woman sighed as she put on water to heat for tea. "Only what I've known from the beginning. Sometimes, you know, the burden becomes too great to bear. Sometimes, young man, you speak in riddles even I can't decipher."

"Do you know you've been calling me 'young man' now for many a passing year?"

She held her head up high, as she sat down and took his hand across the table. "I am aware of it," she clipped, "and when you start acting your age, I'll address you by a more appropriate title like 'sir' or perhaps," she paused for a moment, "perhaps even 'your grace.'"

He darted a sharp look at her, "Sometimes, Emily, I'm not sure what you really know, but you were the one, yes definitely, you were the one to take him on this last part of his journey. You know it is for this you remained."

"Aye," she said softly. "Ah, there, I'm talking like you now. Yes, I know I remained for this reason. It's just that, he's so young, and hurting. And with Rory out there messing with his mind ..."

"My younger brother can be a trial," said the visitor with barely concealed anger. "Yet, he is not Conor's greatest danger. It had Conor in his dreams, didn't it?" asked Willie.

"I saw it in his mind with my own eyes," whispered Emily.

The tea kettle whistled a high pitch *screel* and Emily walked over to the stove, poured the water over two cups with tea bags and set a mug in front of the man.

"I think," said Emily, "it only wished to let Conor know that it was there. It was searching for how much the boy knows and perhaps even who the boy really is. It did no lasting damage save for the fright it caused the lad."

"It did not damage, because you drove it out," he said, slapping his hand on the table so hard that the cups jumped. "I tell you lass, you have the fire in you. That was well done. Looks like that faith of yours is good for something. I heard the howling of the beast as it ran for the water. Even the men in their beds throughout the Grove will have felt a chill in their spines at its passing."

A single tear coursed down Emily's cheek. In the dim light, he saw it and touched her face. "Why do you cry, little one?"

"Tell me," said Emily as she struggled to calm her voice. "Tell me, you old rogue, when I die will you remember me? Or will the years dim your memory and will time blur this ancient face of mine?"

He got up from the table and walked around her, putting his arms around her neck and his cheek next to hers. "I could never forget a heart as noble as yours."

A sad smile. "When you remember me, remember me as we first met, when I was young and strong and ... beauti—" she stopped in mid-sentence.

"You were very young when we first met. But I will remember what you grew into, someone who has always been beautiful, always been strong. The years have made it impossible for me to see you otherwise. But why all this talk of death, why now?"

"You see the trees starting to turn," said Emily. "Like their leaves dropping to the ground; I'm not going to see another autumn. The Devourer comes; already he torments Conor's dreams. Somehow, I think I shall meet that old dragon that pursues him and I do not believe I will live through the encounter."

She felt his arms tighten around her. "Don't act so surprised," she said. "I won't be defeated. I just don't think these old bones can make it through such a fight. It will be hard to say goodbye to you though and to Conor; I shall miss our visits. Everything I have ever done these past years since we met, I did for you. And now the boy has come, and I give my heart to him as well."

He spoke softly in her ear. "You are a great lady, as loyal a follower and friend as I have ever had. Someday, when I am released from my task, we shall walk again together."

Emily laughed a gentle laugh. "From the moment I saw you, I think I fell in love with you."

"Ah lass, you know there is only one I can love that way." He straightened up and, laughing, made her look at him. "I cannot help it if my charm provides a promise I cannot keep."

Emily laughed with him. Whatever hurt existed had long passed away to simple regret. "I know you can't be mine, but that's never going to stop me from loving you; I told you that years ago." Her eyes grew thoughtful. "We have much to do yet. The Enemy as made itself known and I fear it has found allies." She told the man known as Willie Archer of Dr. Nicholas Drake, Caithness McNabb and the plans for DIOGENE.

"I understand little of what you said," he muttered, "but that it bodes ill for my son. Caithness McNabb knows me not, but long have I watched her. It's an evil thing to fall in love with a demon. I hear her whispering across the water. She talks to that thing and together they weave webs of darkness and lies, betrayal and death."

"What of the 'dark ones?'" asked Emily. "Do you not care for your own kin?"

He snapped back at her, "They have forsaken their heritage. Long have I sought a reason why they dwindle and diminish as they age. They are like sleepers, drugged by witch-women. Why will they not awake? The only good thing about them is that in their present state they do not catch my Enemy's attention. It cares not for them and sees them as no threat."

He sat back down at the table. "When first I came to this valley so long ago, the thing that was called by the native peoples, Piasa, knew me as a danger. I could not abide such darkness. Yet we were too balanced; neither of us could ultimately defeat the other. I could only prevent it from permanently staining the land with its malice. I even claimed the river as my own and used the water ways for my own ends. I convinced the settlers that eventually came that I was Willie Archer, a rather mysterious trader, tinker and hunter. And when it grew too curious to have me never grow old, I became the mythic protector of this area—not so mythic really, since it has done me good to pain that fell beast. But I have grown soft. In my hollow hill with the remnants of my kind, time flows more slowly. You know that Emily. Not only does it seem that I met you and your sister not so long ago, but it is really true for me. We of the Roan, we of the damned …"

"Stop that!" said Emily, "Stop talking about yourself like that."

"Ah, but we are, lass. That's why we're here. The Lost, the Forsaken. Damned for all time because of who we are, because of what we are." He smiled a sad smile. "Don't look at me like that, though you do shine lovely in your rage. I know what I am, and that I could not have done what you did tonight. You called on powers that long have turned their back to me and my kind. You have the winged Michael, that ranger of the heavens and the shining Brigid of the pure flame, the brave Patrick, conqueror of druids and Columba of the angels, and most important, the Chief of all Chiefs, the King of Heaven himself, the Christ of the shining Light. That is more than I have. Their names, their presence drove the Enemy away. And they did it for you."

"They did it for Conor too." said Emily softly.

"Aye, they might have at that, for though he is changing, he is still more human than not. But when he comes fully into his own, who will protect him then? You? Malachy? Your saints and angels?"

"Malachy thinks you are wrong you know."

"Yes, yes. We've had those discussions. But, Emily, only the humans are redeemed, only they truly live forever. There is no place for me and my kind, though we look like you and act like you."

"Then it's good that time works more slowly for you," snapped Emily. "Because it's taking you long enough to come to your senses. The Lost, the Forsaken. What self-serving piffle is that? How do you know? You live so long, who would tell of anyone who truly knew the truth?"

"All I know," he said, "is that I look up at the night sky and see the beautiful stars and the brilliant moon, I look at the land with its fertile fields and wondrous creatures, I even look at you whom I care for deeply and who is an image of the one I weep for in the grave high on the hill. All I know is that when I look more deeply, I see the cold of the abyss, and no one to welcome me home."

Emily could say nothing to this. But as Willie Archer stood up, she came to him and held him tight, her head barely rising to his chest.

"Well, now," she finally said, "it's a good thing your son has his mother's hope. We'll just have to see, won't we?"

"That is why he is here, Emily, because he is our hope, a bridge between humanity and my kind. He is the hope for the future. Guard him well."

She was left holding empty air, but when she moved to the doorway, she saw in the dim moonlight a white owl on the grass at the edge of her lawn. It hooted softly in the dark and disappeared into the woods.

"Always the showman," she said, with a smile. "Always the great one."

She sat for awhile in the kitchen and finished her tea.

OCTOBER COUNTRY—THE FIGHT

THE WEST FIELD was full of activity. Anyone traveling just a mile or so further down the road could take in the frenetic pace of the final construction of the DIOGENE facilities. That was worth seeing. But here in the West Field, tents were up, the carnival rides were being assembled and all was chaotically approaching readiness for the evening opening of Tinker's Grove's biggest weekend of the year. Here was the place to be.

Owned by Cate McNabb, the West Field was not really barren farmland. Giant oaks dotted the lush grass. Craft tents and display areas, as well as the games and children's courts, popped up under their dark autumn red shade. Only the carnival had the bare field and that was as it should be. A giant Ferris wheel and Tilt-a-Whirl dominated the area. The carnies were assembling the smaller rides around the perimeter.

Always set for the weekend before Halloween and All Saints Day, the October Country Festival was a huge money maker for the community. Craft shows, food and beer tents lured huge numbers of people from the southwest part of the state. Not to mention the music. Traditional Irish music as well as rock for the kids and polka and big band sounds for the older folks drew many. Besides, it came at a good time of the year. The county fairs were over and people had time and currency on their hands. Even the farmers could spare a few days with most of the harvest in. So important was this weekend for the Grove that the Athletic Association had scheduled in a "bye week" for all sports activities.

Conor couldn't believe the number of people. Truly impressed, he thought this backwater town could never attract the crowds, but it did. As the afternoon light faded that Friday, hundreds of people, perhaps several thousand, descended upon Tinker's Grove. Conor walked with Beth through the tent city. Wouldn't be an exaggeration to call it that, he thought. There was a central square lit by a huge bonfire, constantly burning, even during this first afternoon. At each corner of every make-shift street was a six foot high post with a carved jack-o-lantern plopped on top of it. Too cool, thought Conor. "Is it always like this?" he asked Beth

"Every year. And it never rains. At least it never has that I've known of. This is the chance for us to shine. We make a lot of these crafts, though vendors come from around the Midwest. The rent they pay and the crowds keep our little community somewhat solvent throughout the year."

Conor squeezed her hand. He was pumped. Thinking he would only be playing before dozens, he now knew from just a short walk through the growing crowd that he and his little band would draw a fine number of folks.

"Coming tonight to hear us?" he asked.

"Well, Jace is playing. I thought I ought to hear how he sounds." She said it with such a mischievous smile that Conor couldn't even protest.

"Of course, I'm coming to see you," she said laughing.

So she was. At precisely eight p.m. Conor, the Abbot, Jim Warren, Jace, Brother Gerald and Nora Martin, began to play at one of the performance tents. A few people grew into hundreds.

"Guess we're real good," said Conor to the Abbot.

"Seems to be that way," said an obviously pleased Malachy.

"No doubt about it," said Jim Warren, "they liked our first set, but let's see if we can hook them for the evening."

They did. The crowd never diminished. Hour after hour, Conor and the band performed. When he wasn't playing the tin whistle, he was singing, and finding it a grand experience. He loved his duets with Nora Martin. He had to laugh. Every time they sang, he'd look over at Jace and see him wide-eyed looking at them. Grinning, Conor was pretty sure he wasn't the object of Jace's attention. Maybe something was happening. As for himself, well, Conor couldn't help but see that most of the time Beth was in the front row with some of her high school friends, laughing and clapping. Good enough for him.

They gave up the stage about eleven in the evening. Some group was booked after them from midnight till two o'clock but Conor didn't feel like staying around and listening. Taking Beth away from her friends, he said, "Let's check the place out." From tent to tent they went, scoping out the crafts and playing the games.

Thank God for Aunt Emily, thought Conor. Old she might be but she thought enough ahead to kiss him on the cheek this afternoon saying, "Now, I'll be listening, though most of my time has to be spent in the Sodality tent." Stuck some money into his hand. He was about to protest but she said, "Enough. Your mother left a little nest egg for you and that's where this comes from. If you're walking Beth around, you're going to have to buy her this or that. That's what young fellows do. Now get on out of here." She pushed him out the door. Spending money on Beth was an okay thing, he thought. Not bad at all.

Jace found himself alone up on the stage, the last to be clearing away stuff. The Abbot and Brother Gerald had gone over to the Abbey tent to see how the evening went selling monastery wares, and Jim Warren had simply nodded to him and taken off. Jace had hoped Nora might stay around and talk a bit. That would have been fun. But that old biddy of a grandmother had come, pinched face and all, and marched her away just as the last set ended. Geez, let the girl grow up he thought. Then again, as much as he found a little bit of Dort Martin pretty traumatic to take, he couldn't begin to imagine what living with her must be like. He felt new sympathy for Nora.

Left alone, Jace wandered through the tents. Stopping at the Knights of Columbus food kiosk and, dodging the fly strips hanging down, their sticky ribbons twirling in the evening breeze, he got a burger and some fries and shot the bull with some of the men who wanted to relive last week's football game. Fortunately, the Grove had won. Jace had done well, so he basked in the approval of the town's auxiliary coaches. Seeing a couple of his friends a few booths up, he excused himself and went to join them. They had seemed to be heading for the game section. Staffed by the carnies, the games were a ripoff and people seldom won, but who could resist trying to impress the girls and passers-by.

When he got to the rifle range, a few folks were shooting the pellets at targets, but not Jace's friends. They had disappeared. Thinking they had gone behind the tents, he took a little detour down one of the side streets. It was darker there, not so many people about. Still, he couldn't find them. He stopped at the last supply tent bordering the field. Beautiful night. Stars out but you couldn't see them well. The harvest moon, three-quarters full and orange was rising and shining brightly. Looking at it ascend over the field while listening to the sounds behind him, he thought how great the Grove was. Good people, good times. He didn't really want to leave here, even to go on to school.

"Hey guys," said a voice, "look who's back here. The star center of our great football team, and, most importantly, best friend of our favorite freak."

Jace turned to see Fergal McNabb and a fair number of his friends walking toward him.

"What do you want, Fergal?" Jace had nothing against the McNabbs. Fergal seemed to him the best of the lot. But there was an edge to Fergal's voice tonight.

"'What do I want?' he says." Fergal's voice dripped with sarcasm. "I, we, want to know why you keep hanging around the Archer kid. He's trouble. You know it. I know it. All of us have had the experience of Conor's weirdness. Now you play in a band with him."

Fergal paused, bending down to pick up a broken bottle. Tossed it in the air and caught it by the neck. Cocked an eye at Jace. "Guess everybody needs a friend. Hell, I even thought I could be friends with him, but he's just too strange. But he can't have you as a friend Jace. You see, you give him status, you being the big football hero and all. Me and my friends have been talking. The Grove would be a better place without Archer and, fact is, he'd be easier to get rid of if he didn't have you walking in his shadow."

Jace could smell the alcohol in the air. Fergal was always a blowhard when he was drinking. Jace wasn't afraid. He was bigger than most of them. It's just that he didn't like trouble and tried to avoid it whenever possible.

"Fergal," he said softly, "why don't you let me decide who I'm going to be friends with."

"See," said Fergal to his companions. "I told you he'd be unreasonable. Well, if you can't do it for yourself, Jace, at least do it for your sister. Beth deserves better. Saw them walking hand in hand after your little band got done playing. Kissing they were."

That was news to Jace, though it didn't bother him … much.

"You feel okay that she's kissing a freak?"

"That's enough Fergal," said Jace. "Go have yourself another beer."

"Probably will do that," he said, tossing the broken bottle away, "but you didn't answer me yet. You going to hang around Archer or are you going to let him go, fend for himself as it were?"

"Don't have to answer you, Fergal, not you or any of your other friends," said Jace quietly.

From the back of the group came a voice and body pushing it forward. Rafe strode through little crowd. "Didn't I tell you, Fergal, the football star wasn't going to listen anyway, no matter what you said."

"What do you guys really have against Conor anyway?" asked Jace, genuinely surprised at the rising animosity.

It was Rafe who spoke. "He's a 'dark one,' Jace. Never had a problem with the others. Even Oz keeps his place and his distance. But Conor, he's different."

"Basically, it's like this," said Fergal. "The others keep their weirdness tucked inside themselves; on the other hand, weirdness leaks out from him like water from a busted radiator. If you could have seen him a few months ago up at the gravel quarry you'd feel like we do—creeped out. Don't deny it; I bet you have seen some bizarre things around him. He's way strange, maybe not even human, and I'm thinking that maybe none of the 'dark ones' are exactly what they seem."

Jace began to laugh. He really was amused. Everybody in the Grove was peculiar and different in some way; Conor more than most, he had to admit, but so what?

"So here we are at the fair," said Jace, "and a little lynch mob is already forming. Well, Conor's not here. So go away and leave me alone."

"We didn't come for Conor," said Rafe. "We came for you."

"You mean if I didn't listen to you, you'd rough me up or something like that?"

"Something like that," said Rafe and the others muttered in agreement.

For some reason, Jace continued to find all this amusing. It was the prerogative of the big and strong because he had never really been threatened before and didn't think much of this difficulty either. Sizing up the bunch, he began laughing again.

"Don't you laugh," said Fergal.

"Better listen to my brother," said Rafe.

Jace couldn't help himself. He really found the situation funny. Maybe they'd come after him, maybe not, but in the meantime, he laughed.

The sound of mirth carried on the wind through the fields and trees, down to the river and up the White Creek tributary where the water opened to a secret, quiet slough running by the side of a bluff. A cave opened at the water's edge, hidden mostly by brush; a white strand of sand ran twenty yards either side of the hidden opening. A woman was washing there. A very old woman. Blackened teeth. Humming as she washed. Whatever she scrubbed, she held fast underwater, washing, laundering, scouring—her tuneless song leaking through bloodless lips. Until she heard the whisper of laughter on the wind. The laughter of one she knew. Twisting her head up to the sky, she looked at the moon. "Yes," she said, "my Champion stirs. Time for first blood!" The Morrigan thrust herself upright, shed her years and by the time she stood tall at the water's edge she was a maiden again, strong and hardened, a lust for blood in her eyes. "You'll need help my brave one. There are many, perhaps even too many for you."

The leaves swirled on the banks of White Creek as upward the Morrigan leaped. The creatures of the woodland stirred as she flew, a crow winging south in the moonlight, a carrion crow, cawing in the night.

***

Beth and Conor had slowly made their way through all the craft tents, briefly stopping to say hello to Emily, but Conor was intrigued more by the carnies. "Modern day Tinkers," he said to Beth. "They must be a lot like the people of this town once were, back in Ireland."

"They give me the creeps," said Beth. "I mean, they slink around; they're dirty; even their little kids try to pick your pocket."

All of which was true. The carnival life was still difficult, even in the twenty-first century. Conor noticed a distinct difference in the quality of the tents as they entered the space reserved for carnival rides, games, and attractions. Try as the town leaders planned, even they couldn't light up the hint of squalor that appeared in the alleys and byways of this area of the festival.

"Hey look!" said Conor. "It's the freak show area!" Sure enough, there was still room in this world for the Bearded Lady and Snake Girl. Conor had seen a documentary about carnie life a few years back and knew that many of the oddities displayed were not faked—at least not much. Since he had never seen such things close up, he convinced Beth to enter the gallery.

Only a few people were in the tent. Probably because it was late and, frankly, the show was better during the day when there was more light. Some of the strange folk were obviously napping, taking advantage of the lull in spectators. Beth and Conor were surprised to find Oz there, having a look at Snake Girl. Oz was staring intently at the woman whose body had a green pallor, covered with a leathery almost reptilian skin. Conor could see the crude attempt to outline scales to make her appear more the part. Even though her eyes were closed, her tongue kept flicking in and out of her mouth. Conor could see the woman had split her own tongue to mimic that of a serpent. A faint hissing came from her mouth as she breathed.

Both Beth and Conor noticed that Oz was not listening to his own brand of special music. Nothing was in his ears. "Hey Oz," said Conor, not expecting any response.

"Hey back, Conor," said Oz in a normal voice. Beth gripped Conor's hand a little tighter.

"You know my name," said Conor trying to figure out what kind of small talk he ought to use since he and Oz were obviously occupying the same reality, at least for the moment.

The huge man with the childlike face turned his shaved head to Conor and said, "Of course I know your name. Why wouldn't I? I see you've come to see her too. Isn't she beautiful?" His gaze returned to the sleeping Snake Girl.

"Sure," said Conor, "she sure is beautiful."

"I'm glad you can appreciate her," said Oz, "since she is a 'dark one' too."

Beth broke in, "Are you sure, Oz? I mean, how would you know?"

Oz looked at Beth and smiled, "You're real pretty tonight, Beth Michaels. I know because she is lost and forgotten, just like all of us 'dark ones.' Lost and forgotten. I think I love her."

Just then a large bird flew over the tent, letting out a loud rough sound. Oz lifted his face to the ceiling, smiled and said, "She's out again tonight. Must be blood and death around. She always flies right to the scent."

"Conor?" said Beth, a tinge of fear in her voice.

"Yeah, I know," said Conor. "Oz, man, we gotta go now. Wolf Boy and the dwarf siamese twins are calling us over. You take it easy now."

"You get scared over all this, don't you Conor?" said Oz with an easy drawl. "Don't be scared of me; I'm just fine. I know what people say about me, but that's just when the others walk in my soul and talk through my mouth. Can't help that. But you're afraid. Just 'cause things are a little different than you expected. Got a real nice girl there, Conor. A little anchor of normal in your increasingly strange life." Oz broke into a big grin as Conor and Beth backed away.

"You really want to see the dwarves?" asked Beth, glancing over her shoulder to see Oz still following them with his gaze.

"Had enough of this tent, Beth," said Conor, face suddenly grim. "Let's get out of carnie town."

***

Rafe threw the first punch. Made the same mistake Jace's opponents on the football field always made. They thought big and slow, but the football center was fast and huge. Jace darted out of the way. Fergal and his friends rushed him, but even then Jace hadn't stopped laughing. Something was in the wind, making his blood sing. He'd never been in a serious fight before, never had to. Just the sight of him settled most ornery folks down real fast. Jace surprised himself. He could throw a good punch and loved the feel of a busted nose beneath his fist. Arms flailing, he waded into the crowd, thrashing anyone standing before him. He felt their blows on his body. But it didn't matter. Only crushing them did. He had the distinct pleasure of smacking Fergal in the face twice, breaking his nose and blackening an eye. As Fergal fell he took one of the posts that held a lighted pumpkin with him. One McNabb down for the count.

As soon as Jace wasted Fergal, the crowd was on him. He felt himself fall, the worst thing you can do, he thought. Somebody punched him over and over again in the face while he felt a boot in his back and someone else kicking him in the ribs. From far away, he heard the snapping of bones.

It was then that Rafe came back in the fight. Those still standing backed off to let Rafe do his thing. Jace wasn't laughing anymore. Lying on the ground, bloodied and woozy, he could see that Rafe was out to do him serious damage.

"Get the freak out of your life, you crazy dumb ass jock!" screamed Rafe.

Only then did Jace realize he was fighting for Conor. As he looked through Rafe, what he saw was Conor over the past two months, lost and alone, grateful for his friendship. He turned his head, dirt falling from his short blond hair, and looked at the broken-faced jack—o-lantern, burning a shattered grin, not a foot from his face.

"You know," said Jace, slowly getting to his feet. "My daddy always said you were a dumb son of a bitch. Conor's not a freak, but even if he were, I'd still take the freak over the idiot jerk any day. Face it Rafe, your money can't take the stupid out of you."

Enraged, Rafe charged. Jace caught him on the chin with his right fist. It was about all he had left in him, and it was almost enough. Rafe fell like a stone. Jace turned to Fergal just getting up and the rest of his friends. "It's over. Done. Leave me alone and get out of here." A shifting of Fergal's eyes warned Jace. Behind him, Rafe leapt to his feet a knife gleaming in the moonlight. Jace moved swiftly enough to avoid being cut but he felt the air as the knife passed before his face. Rafe was crouched in front of him waiting another opportunity. A scream came from the night air. Down from the sky came a flapping of hard wings. Jace heard them clearly. So did Rafe. As both turned toward the sound, a black cloud of feathers descended upon Rafe. To Jace, it was as if time slowed. He saw the crow perch on his enemy's shoulder and as Rafe turned to look at the bird, the crow screamed at him and jabbed its beak into Rafe's closest eye and pulled. Rafe screamed in pain and Jace saw the bird fly away, a shattered eyeball in its beak. Wounded, Rafe dropped the knife and ran back howling into the fair grounds, bleeding profusely.

Fergal and his friends stood stunned. Jace turned and with a snarl said, "Get out of here, before I make you like him. Go!" he yelled. They fled on Rafe's heels, leaving Jace alone.

Good God, but he hurt. He knew he ought to get some help from one of the medical tents but instead he went into the field over to the edge of some scrub woods and collapsed. His breath was wheezing awfully strange. He could taste blood deep in his mouth.

She came to him, there in the darkness, and as she held Conor not so many weeks before, so she held him. Jace looked up and saw the most beautiful woman he had ever seen.

"My warrior!" she whispered. "Well done! I knew I was not wrong about you. From the first, I saw the champion in you. You stood for him tonight. You defended him tonight even though you only recognized that in the last moments of battle. Blood bonded you are to him now. But you are hurt, worse than you believe, I'm afraid."

"You are the Morrigan aren't you?"

"Some say that," she answered, her hands moving swiftly over his body. "Wounds from battle I can heal. Stay silent. Stay still. Let me do my work. A punctured lung, a damaged kidney, broken ribs, and still they did not defeat you. Oh, yes, I chose well."

As she touched his wounds, Jace felt like lightning was coursing through him. His pains went away and he knew his body was healing.

"This, I will leave," she said pointing to a cut underneath his eye. "All warriors must have scars and this will be but a small one, the first of many you will bear for him. It will remind you of your first battle and of the enemy that still lays in wait for you."

She stood then, tall and beautiful in the moonlight, and Jace saw the leaves begin to swirl around her. As he looked, she was gone, but high in the night sky he heard the call of the crow. He thought of her and what she had done to Rafe. What she had done for him. Saved his life probably.

A few moments later, he saw a figure dimly silhouetted by the last tent. "Jace," said a voice, "Jace, are you out there?"

His heart jumped a bit as he recognized Nora.

"Here," he said weakly. "I'm over here."

She rushed to him and gasped at the blood on his shirt and face.

"No worries," he said. "Looks much worse than what it is."

Nora saw him crack his big, beautiful smile.

"What's still hurting is feeling lots better real fast, now that you're here."

Nora smiled down on him. "Jason Michaels, you don't need to turn your charm on me. Heard you were in a fight, so I came to check it out. Best get you back to Conor and your sister, before they hear about it and start worrying."

"Good idea," said Jace and then thought about what Fergal said concerning Conor and Beth kissing. "Very good idea, let's go." He heaved himself up and leaning just a little, for effect of course, on Nora, he and the girl went back to the fair.

Things were a bit more desperate within the McNabb household. Fergal had called ahead and Cate had taken charge, getting Dr. Drake down to the clinic. Arriving first, he was ready and waiting when Fergal brought Rafe in. Drake could see both were bleeding. Fergal's nose was twisted terribly, but Rafe was moaning and clutching a cloth to his right eye.

"What happened?" asked Drake.

"Fight," said Fergal through a blood clotted nose. "Rafe lost an eye."

Drake raised an eyebrow. "Some fight. Let me see." He was silent for a moment, swabbing the wound; then he said, "Perfectly en-oculated. What weapon did this?"

"It was a bird," said the youngest McNabb, still shaken by the memory.

"What?" said Drake, losing his poise for an instant.

"Long story," said Fergal, blowing out a wad of blood from his ruined nose. "Just help him, will you?"

"Right," said Drake. "But I'm going to need some assistance." He placed a call up to the monastery and asked that Brother Luke be sent down.

Both the monk and Cate arrived at the same time. The sedative that Drake had administered to Rafe was taking effect and the young man was groggy. The added morphine was quickly numbing the pain.

"Good God," said Brother Luke under his breath, looking at the wreck of the two brothers.

Cate said nothing, just walked silently over to Rafe, took in the shattered face and placed her hand on his bloody head.

"Fergal," she said, her voice barely above a whisper, "tell me now how this happened."

"Not till we fix this nose and pack the nostrils," said Brother Luke.

"Don't tell me what to do, monk; he's got a bloody nose; he'll live," she snapped.

"Cate, really," said Drake, "he's right. Be patient a moment; it won't take long."

Brother Luke lived in the Grove where broken noses, like fights, were not rare. In a flash, he had Fergal cleaned up, nose straightened and bleeding stopped. "There you go," he said, "now do as your mother says and tell us what happened."

"I'll ruin the Michaels family," said Cate, continuing to grit her teeth even after Fergal had given the highly slanted version of events at the fair.

"It was a fight, Cate," said Brother Luke.

"Yes," said Cate, "one in which my son lost an eye and my other boy got his nose smashed."

"True," said the monk, "but I can count as well as you. Your sons and their friends against one person? What did you expect the Michaels boy to do?"

"Don't forget the crow," said Fergal.

"Ah, yes," said Brother Luke, "the real culprit in the loss of Rafe's eye, I believe. By the way, how is Jason?"

"Don't know, don't care," said Fergal.

"Well, knowing that would complicate your victim status wouldn't it, Fergal?"

"Don't you dare speak that way to any member of my family," said Cate to the monk.

Brother Luke was not a tall man, but he stood as tall as he could, faced the imperious woman, and said, "Caithness McNabb, I've watched you use your clout and your wealth to throw your weight around. I'm truly sorry for the pain your boys are going through, but it sounds to me they got as good as they gave. To blame anyone else is foolish. I don't fear you. I'd rather not have you as my enemy, but if that's to be, well, I'm told to love my enemies so like as not, you'll notice no difference in my attitude toward you." Looking at Drake finishing up the patching of Rafe's empty eye socket, the monk continued, "My work's done here. Dr. Drake, give me a call when you need me again." He was out the door before anyone could respond.

Conor and Beth ended up having a pretty good time, even though the crowd had thinned greatly. Beth had offered Conor a ride home, and they were just walking towards the exit when she happened to look down a side street and saw her brother being led by the hand by Nora Martin. Conor followed Beth's glance.

"Beth, something's really wrong. He's got blood all over his shirt."

"How can you tell? It's so dark."

"Actually, I can smell it. Bad stuff here, I think."

They both ran to the couple.

"I'm okay, really," said Jace.

"You know, I think he is," said Nora. "Looks far worse than it is."

"Come on," said Conor. "Let's get you to a table. I'll grab you a coke."

Beth had found a cloth and was just about to wipe her brother's face, when Nora took the wet rag and said, "Here, let me do it." Gently she wiped the grime and blood off. The cut under Jace's right eye bled fresh again.

"Just that one cut?" said Conor. "An awful lot of blood for one cut."

"Well, not all the blood you see is mine," said Jace. He told them of the fight, but got real vague toward the end.

"Why would a crow pluck out Rafe's eye?" asked Beth.

Jace was silent.

"Well?" said Beth. Even Conor was beginning to recognize the uncompromising tone that often entered Beth's speech when she'd had enough of delay and indecision.

"I think it was more than a crow," said Jace.

Nora looked at Jace strangely. "Just how much more, exactly? I mean, Jace, you said yourself you heard your own bones snapping, but when I first saw you, well I noticed someone with you. Then I heard a crow cry and by the time I got by your side, you were alone. And despite all the blood, only that one cut. Not a bone broken. In fact, there was a bruise here on your face when I found you. Now it's gone. Who was it with you, Jace? There's only one crow that flies in the dark and comes to the aid of someone in trouble. You were with a woman by the wood Jace. I see that now. And there's only one who heals on the battlefield."

Jace couldn't help himself. "Nora, what the hell are you talking about? There wasn't any battlefield. It was just a fight."

"No it wasn't just a fight," said Nora, her dark eyes distant. "A knife was drawn. Life and death were held in the balance. That's what drew her. The blood and the balance. You know who she was, don't you Jace?"

Jace was silent and Beth spoke up. "I think the better question is, do you know, Nora?"

"I think so. I remember the stories." She smiled for a second. "There's old books in the back of Grandma Dort's store."

"What a surprise," groaned Jace.

"Those books were of old local tales from the 1800's. Stories about a woman who wails and she who drinks the blood of her slaughtered enemies and the maid who is the friend of warriors and guards them in danger." Nora paused for a moment. "From another place, another time, I know, but I thought of her as Jace and I were walking back. You know, the one they call the Morrigan." She looked at their faces when they didn't say anything. "You know what I'm talking about, don't you? You've had dealings with her before."

"I was hurt bad. Worse then I've ever been in football. Yeah, she was there, and touched me. Wherever she touched, I healed. 'I can do this,' she said, 'I can heal a warrior's injuries.' She talked like that, like we were back hundreds of years ago, as if I had a sword in my hand."

"Why did she leave this cut?" said Beth. "Seems a little thing for her to heal."

Jace looked quickly over at Conor. "Had her reasons I guess."

"She is an old thing to awaken now," said Nora, eyes distant once again. "I wonder what it means."

"Don't know and don't care," said Jace. "I'm really tired. Let's go home."

"I've got the car," said Beth, "and I'm dropping Conor off. Why don't you go with Nora?"

The two of them started arguing, Nora paying close attention. Conor got up to throw away Jace's empty cup, when he heard a soft cawing, there in the dark, behind the concession stand. He walked over, curious, and hissed softly when he saw it perching on a fence that surrounded the garbage bin. The crow had blood on its beak. Conor saw the dark stain and smelled the blood. Getting good at this, he thought almost tasting the blood's iron on his tongue. "Got into a fight, I hear," said Conor, a little bit more nonchalantly than he felt. The bird cocked its head and stared at him sideways.

A voice spoke in Conor's mind, "First blood, first battle."

Conor shook his head. "Is that really you?" he said, "the woman thing they call the Morrigan?"

"He fought bravely tonight," said the voice. "He fought for you. He is your Champion and mine." The crow looked past Conor and he followed its gaze. Jace and Beth were still arguing; Nora looking amused by it all.

"Did you heal him?"

The crow cackled softly and a voice entered Conor's mind again. "He may be our Champion but he is also my Warrior. I take care of my own." Conor turned to look at Jace once more and when he turned back, the crow was gone. A single black feather floated into the shadows.

As Conor walked back, he saw Jace take Beth aside. Even though the voices were lowered Conor was able to hear everything and he started to laugh.

"Let's go home," he said to Beth. As Beth said goodbye to Nora, Conor looked at Jace. "Thanks for fighting for me. Never had anyone do that before. Wish I could have been there. I would have stood with you. Hope you know that." Jace nodded. "I'm thankful that witch woman was there," continued Conor, "but I got to tell you, man, the Morrigan has her own agenda. Be careful if you see her again." Conor punched him on the shoulder and turned to go. "By the way," he said, "don't forget that I hear lots better now than I ever did."

"So?" said Jace, a tentative smile on his face.

"Well, I can answer the question, Beth wouldn't." Conor flashed a brilliant smile at Jace. "Of course I kissed her." Before Jace could respond, Conor grabbed Beth's hand and disappeared out the exit.

OCTOBER COUNTRY—THE SONG

"WELL, LOOK AT you," said Jace to Conor the next evening as he and Beth stopped by to pick him up for the festival. "Like a little Irish Traveler, if I ever saw one. The vest is a nice touch, the rolled up, cuffed sleeves on the slightly wrinkled shirt gives you a rough air; but I think it's the cap that does it for me. You're ready to play."

"Pay no attention to him, Conor," said Beth, who did like the way Conor's cropped black hair curled up out of the cap. "As far as I'm concerned, you'll add a bit of class to that band of yours tonight. Sure as won't get any from my brother here. Had to make him take off his raggedy sweatshirt and put something decent on so he wouldn't distract from the music."

Jace lifted his nose at Beth. "Percussion people don't need to look good. That's for the lead singer and tin whistle player *extra ordinaire*."

"Don't forget Nora," said Conor with a smile. "Bet she'll be looking good tonight."

Jace spoke softly, "No I don't think I'll be forgetting her."

Conor looked at Beth, raised an eyebrow and said in his best Irish brogue, "Now would you be looking at him, Beth darlin'; the moon hasn't even risen in the sky but it's plastered all over his face. Crazy he his. All for Nora, now, all for Nora."

Beth laughed and Jace shook his head.

"Well, I know what we'll be doing tonight with the group. We'll be dedicating a song to you and Nora, a special one just for the two of you."

"Get in the car, Conor, we'll be late," said Jace as he moved the car forward. Conor jumped in, Troubles right behind him, anxious not to miss all the excitement.

"Does your Aunt Emily need a ride?" asked Beth.

"Nope," said Conor. "She's been up at the festival all day. Lady just never gets tired."

The sun was swiftly setting as they arrived. Already burning brightly, the bonfire in the tent city square was casting long shadows, dark fingers reaching out to the jack-o-lanterns mounted on the poles. Pushing away a drop of sweat creeping out from under his hat, Conor was grateful for the warm night. If possible, the crowd seemed larger than last evening. Standing in line to ride the rides, the kids had left their parents at the busy craft tents. The food kiosks had done a brisk business all day and they were still jammed with people.

Conor never ate before he played and, at least for tonight, Jace was of the same mind. "Just like a game, Conor," he said. "Too nervous to eat before football and too nervous to eat before we do music."

As they set up their audio system, Beth fixed the chairs on the pavilion. Folks were just starting to come in and grab a seat. It wasn't long before the Abbot and Brother Gerald sauntered in, each in flannel shirts, blue jeans and suspenders.

"Geez," whispered Conor, "they're relaxing a bit more tonight. You know it crossed my mind yesterday, but now I'm sure anyone would think we were a country/western third string band."

"I heard that, boy," said the Abbot sternly. Then he smiled. "Look, it's one of the few times we just get to act our age and play music we love—so give us break."

Jim Warren stepped on stage. Thank God for bankers thought Jace. At least he wasn't wearing anything outlandish—same conservative pants, same white shirt, albeit unbuttoned at the collar. "Hey, has anyone seen Nora?" he asked aloud.

They all shook their heads. Conor pulled Jace aside. "I was wondering if Nora ever said anything to you about her being one of the 'dark ones?' I mean now that you guys are a bit closer and all."

Jace scowled, "Can't just ask her that, Conor. In this town, we don't refer to them publicly as 'dark ones,' because it's just not proper. Besides, most of them will tell you that they don't feel or do anything different from anyone else. I'm sure Nora's the same."

"Well if you ever decide to ask her, let me know, will you?" Conor requested.

Jace nodded and scoped out the growing crowd for any sign of her. He saw her, then, gliding towards the stage through the pavilion with her long dark hair flowing freely. He loved the way she shook her head when she laughed; surprised he had never paid much attention to her before, in that sort of way. Chuckling to himself, he wondered why a person he'd seen most everyday, laughed with, did school projects together, could suddenly change on him and be so much different. Wouldn't have happened if Conor hadn't gotten them together for this little band.

They started their first set at seven and kept capturing the listeners. Even Oz came. Wasn't there last night, but here he was, actually listening to the music, a small smile on his face. Amazing how many people knew the words to the songs. The bar outside the pavilion was doing brisk business and people were raising glasses of Guinness and clapping along with the music.

Conor decided to have some fun well into the first set when he stopped a reel they were playing, turned to the Abbot, Brother Gerald and Jim Warren and said so everyone could here, "We must you know." Obviously in on the deal, all three answered solemnly, "Yes, indeed, we must."

"Ladies and gentleman," said Conor. "An old song, a happy song, a song of true love and one that you know. Sing it now for a special couple whom I'm sure you'll recognize by the time the song is done. Sing with us 'The Black Velvet Band.'"

He played it first on the tin whistle; the accordion, fiddle and pipes joined in. Nora and Jace did nothing, not expecting this song. And then Conor sang,

Her eyes, they shown like the diamonds,
You'd think she was queen of the land,
And her hair hung over her shoulder,
Tied up with a black velvet band.

By this time, Nora and Jace had recovered and joined in and as the song got rolling, Conor called out for Nora to sing the verse, and when the refrain started again, he fell to his knees, held his hands out and sang the refrain to Nora. The crowd clapped and laughed. Nora never stopped playing but she blushed mightily. Conor took the next verse but when it came time for the refrain, he turned to Jace, stuck a mike in his face and said, "Go for it."

Now, Conor knew one thing the rest of the band didn't. He knew Jace actually could sing. Despite Jace's denials, Conor had heard him singing to himself now and then, and after one of the practice sessions actually rehearsed this song with him.

Jace stumbled out of the block but recovered quickly. Conor and the rest of the band made him sing the refrain again. Nora was stunned that such a huge hulk could sing and she just turned and listened. The crowd went wild. They could see why Conor did what he did. The look on Jace's face was too real to be faked. He liked this girl.

So Conor did what he had planned. When the song was done, he handed a rose tied up with black ribbon to Jace and made him walk over and give it to Nora. She kissed Jace on the cheek, and finding that she could play to the crowd, unwound the ribbon from the rose, stuck the thornless flower in her mouth, and tied up her hair with the black velvet band. The crowd cheered again as the Abbot and Brother Gerald fiddled and piped a jig, causing Nora to do a spectacular step dance around a bemused and blushing Jason Michaels.

Conor announced the break.

"I'll kill you for this," said Jason to Conor. "You embarrassed the hell out of me, and probably Nora too."

"Nora, I doubt, but yeah, I think I did that to you. Just too much fun." Conor started laughing and Beth was smiling as she brought the band something to drink during the break.

The evening went like that. Conor made sure every member of the band got a chance to shine, and, since all were fine musicians, the crowd gave each of them a superb reception.

They were on their last set, just after eleven o'clock, when Rory strolled into the pavilion. Conor wasn't even surprised to see him, though he did wonder if the man ever changed his clothes. Same biker gear as that August night, same smirk too; and he certainly didn't come for the music. Sitting in the back, he caused no stir, not for two songs at least. Then Caithness McNabb came in, managing to look regal in her stone washed jeans and blouse. Conor could see the shock of white hair highlighting the black curls. Rory saw her, too, got up and went over to her.

Didn't it look to Conor as if she was crying? Her head rested on Rory's neck and her own shoulders were heaving up and down. Had to be about Rafe, but this emotional greeting between the two was new to Conor. He had no idea that Rory knew Caithness McNabb. They eventually sat down together. Cate's face was a blank slate as she looked to the stage.

By this time in the evening, people were calling out requests. They had just finished singing "Finnegan's Wake" when Rory stood up and said, "Would you do us all a favor and play 'The Banks of the Bann,' you know, the one about Willie Archer, almost your namesake Conor." The crowd chuckled uncomfortably, but Conor smiled.

"Sure enough, Rory, just like I played it for you in Chicago." The band had practiced it because they had always played it before. Conor had found that very odd since it was an obscure song, but he went with it. He was surprised to find that folks joined in with him right away. They all knew the tune and all the words. Thank God, Rory didn't do any dancing this time. Conor was half expecting him to swirl old Cate around like he did that server back at the *DerryAir*. He wasn't biting; Rory just sat there, a smirk on his face. Conor couldn't figure that out until he felt his skin grow warm, specifically, the ribbon of skin winding its way around his body. Nora, the only one of the band who could really see him, was looking at him strangely as were the people in the front rows. He did his usual reel afterwards—his turn to stand out on the instrument and the crowd did nothing as he finished. Conor just looked at them and glanced at Nora. "What's wrong?" he asked. "Why aren't they clapping or doing anything?"

"Your eyes, Conor," she whispered. "My God, your eyes!"

"What about them?"

Beth jumped up from the crowd and began to clap. Rory joined her and that seemed to break the spell. Everybody started clapping and hooting and hollering.

"What about my eyes?" Conor asked Nora again as he waved to the crowd.

"They're glowing, or at least they were, bright gold flecks, and your arm too, that ribbon of skin."

Conor quickly brushed down his rolled up sleeves and buttoned up his shirt. He looked out into the audience and saw Oz staring at him. Flecks of glowing gold were in his eyes as well, as if reflecting dying coals in a fire.

Out of the corner of his eye, he saw Cate approach. Oh no, he thought, she's going to ream out Jace for what happened to Fergal and Rafe last night. But she ignored Jace and walked up the steps to confront Conor. Troubles, silent and laying down at the side of the stage for the whole night, uttered a small growl. Conor stilled him with the wave of a hand.

Her voice was low. "Beautiful job tonight, Conor. Really, you play and sing magnificently. But I didn't come here to compliment you. Oh dear, you missed a button on your shirt, up here by your throat." Her fingers delicately touched the fabric as she whispered, "I saw your eyes. Fey they were. I saw the ribbon of skin become luminescent like a river of gold gleaming softly in the night. I don't know quite what you are yet, Conor Archer, but I know you are trouble. It knows you are trouble as well. You know it," she said as she vaguely stroked his neck, "the one who dwells in the water. The Devourer of Souls, the Underwater Panther, knows of you Conor, and I know you know of it. It told me you saw it. It told me you were to be watched. So I've watched you. One of my sons even tried to befriend you. But you spurned us and caused us great harm. Don't flit your eyes over to your friend Jace. He caused my boys much damage and for that he'll have to pay; but I hold you responsible. You're the real cause. You have come into my life and complicated what was a perfect world for me. And I like things perfect, make no mistake about it." She softly set the last open button on his shirt. "Do not cross me again, for I will be watching. Indeed, now my whole family will be. And Rafe? With one eye he will watch you and bide his time. His eye will never sleep, his gaze never rest, until you pay for what you have done."

"Is there a problem here, Conor, Cate?" asked the Abbot, intrigued by the tenseness radiating from Cate's body.

"No problem, Father Abbot," said Cate, patting Conor on the cheek. "Conor and I were just having an attitude adjustment."

She turned and saw Jace staring at her. She smiled. "Jason Michaels, as a business person and community leader I can appreciate someone who fights for what he believes in. But you better know who you are putting your faith in. I do admire a fighter. However, I'm a mother too, and you fought my sons. Whatever am I to do with you?"

"You're to go home now, Cate," said the Abbot. "Best to let the young ones sort their own disputes out."

"You weary me, Malachy. I'm not in the mood for your preaching tonight."

"The darkness is taking you, Cate," said the Abbot. "Here, take my hand, let's sit down and talk."

Her smile was ice. "Thank you but no. I like the dark. I like the night. When you can't be seen, you're truly free." With that she walked out of the pavilion and disappeared into the crowd.

OCTOBER COUNTRY—THE STORY

"SHE DIDN'T EVEN get on my case; she hit up on you," said a puzzled Jace coming up to Conor. Beth and the Abbot were silent as they watched Caithness McNabb walk away into the crowd.

"I know; she's got some kind of a thing against me," said Conor. "I think if I had to pick enemies, that family would be the worst choice I could make."

"Right you are there," said the Abbot. "This is not good. You'll have to watch yourself, you know. Cate is clever, but her boys won't be subtle. They'll be looking to find you again, Conor. And you, Jace, watch yourself as well."

"Hey, thanks Father Abbot, but I'll be able to take care of myself. I just don't get it though. Why would they jump me last night just because I'm friends with Conor? Why are they getting all spooky on us?"

"Because of me," said Conor. "Because, since I've gotten here, I've become way different, and I scare them. Scare myself too, I think."

"I don't know," said Beth, putting her arm around Conor's waist, "I've told you before, you seem just fine to me."

"But he's waking the old ones," said Nora. She had come up behind them and set down part of the audio system with a thump. "Face it," she continued, "Conor looks like you or me, except for those natural tattoos; but he's brought some changes here to the Grove. You and I, and others, have seen some things or heard about some happenings that should only be in books. None of that occurred till he got here. Or, if they did, people kept silent. Now, people are talking."

"You mean others have seen that witch-woman and that thing that haunts the river?" asked Conor.

"No," said Nora, "they've only heard rumors about that. But they've seen other stuff. Declan Walsh swears that when he was leaving church last Sunday he saw 'things' in among that grove of trees up by the Abbey."

"What things?" asked the Abbot, glancing at Conor.

"Shapes and shadows is all, I guess," said Nora. "He thought they looked mostly human, but dressed like people from days gone by."

"Its okay, Nora," said Conor quietly. "I saw them too, with the Abbot, when I first came here."

"Deck wasn't the only one to see strangeness," said Nora. "Beth, you used to date Tommy Murphy for a while, right?" Beth colored just a bit. "Well, he sat me down this afternoon at the tractor pull. Told me he was out by Muddy Hollow Crossroads one evening a couple of weeks back, and he heard singing. Wasn't any language he recognized, except he said he could feel what it meant. 'It was sad,' he said, 'sad and mournful; about a lost home, and about the sea.' He followed the sound through that one field that arcs up that gentle bluff. Walking through the corn he came closer to whoever was doing the singing. He told me he burst out into a little clearing in the corn and saw a group of men and women, dressed real strange, like in those medieval renaissance fairs they have around Madison and Chicago. They turned their faces to him. They looked at him, but never stopped singing."

"What were they singing, Nora?" asked Jace. "What did Tommy say they were singing?"

"He told me, though I have to tell you Tommy doesn't have a poetic bone in his body. He said they were singing:

We walk o'er this land,
We belong to the sea,
No hope for us save,
The rider of waves,
Home, home, home to the sea,
Carry us safely, home to the sea,
Home, home, home to the sea,
Take us home, prince of the sea,
Let us be free, let us be free.'"

"But that's in English," said Beth.

"Tommy said it wasn't but he understood it clearly," explained Nora. "But the kicker is this. As he stood there, Tommy saw a man come out of the corn field into the … well it was a crop circle as best as Tommy could tell. This man came up, tall, with black hair and flecks of gold in his eyes, a golden circlet around his head and a thick gold collar around his neck. And he sang to them in answer:

Not till my son comes back to me,
Can you go home, home, home to the sea,

He is the hope; he shall save,
Bring you back to ride the waves,
No longer the lost, the forgotten you'll be,
Soon you'll be home, soon you'll be free,
Home, home, home in the sea.'"

Nora paused alone for a moment with her thoughts. Then she said, "You see, Conor, you're a catalyst. Something's happening."

"No offense, Nora, but how come you're taking such an interest? How come you seem to know or recognize so much about what's happening?" Beth's genuinely puzzled expression took the sting out of her words.

"With the exception of Beth and Jace here," said the Abbot, "it seems the 'dark ones', like Nora, are noticing all of this first before everyone else in town."

Conor looked sharply at the Abbot, "You said they didn't remember any of the strange stuff that had been happening to them when they were younger."

"I did," said the Abbot, "but they are obviously receptive in some way to what's been going on."

"What do you mean we don't remember?" said Nora.

Jace took her hand, "I'll explain it to you later. The important thing is that you, Deck, Tommy and who else of the 'dark ones' has seen stuff that hasn't been seen around here for a long time, if ever. That's a good thing. You could be a great help, particularly if the McNabb's get more involved with all this."

"How did Cate know about Piasa?" asked Conor. "I mean, she's just an ordinary person, right?"

"No," said the Abbot. "Hardly ordinary. I've know her all her life and she's always been different. Walks by her own lights, but the only place she ever sees them is in the dark. Her thoughts are wrapped in mist and shadow. Long ago she found the Underwater Panther, the Devourer of Souls, and is in thrall to it."

"That's just a legend," said Nora. "Even the Native Americans had their demons. But they didn't really walk the earth or swim the rivers."

"Really?" asked the Abbot, eyebrow cocked in mock disdain. "Well, Nora Martin, are you so sure about what lives beneath the waters? What about the boaters, the swimmers, and especially the several campers on the sand bars that disappear each year?"

"Accidents," sniffed Nora. "And everybody knows the sandbars shift too swiftly to make it safe to trust them. It's silly to camp on them."

"I suppose you're right," said the Abbot. "But the water sweeps underneath them. Just ask the Riley boys."

"You know they disappeared last summer while they were camping."

"Yes, indeed," said the Abbot. "Disappeared in the night, when the fog crept across the water. Everyone said they drowned, but their bodies were never found. Just their campsite, untouched on a sandbar that was breaking up. Wherever the water goes, Piasa can travel."

Nora just stared at him, not sure what to believe.

"Got to go now," said the Abbot. "I'm up for storytelling tonight by the bonfire. Great ghost stories. Hope you'll come see. Starts in a half hour. Got to figure out what new tale I'm going to tell besides my regular repertoire."

"Sounds like you've got a good start already," said Nora, a skeptical smile on her face after all the talk of ghostly folks and monsters in the water.

The Abbot laughed and left.

"Are we going to hear him?" said Conor.

"Absolutely," said Beth. "All of us. Let's put the instruments and audio in the car and go get good seats."

The four of them managed to get something to eat and still get a great location. The bonfire was crackling cheerfully, and hundreds of people were slowly gathering in the square. A little stage had been set up earlier in front of the fire where the storytellers would hold court.

Most folks who came to the October Country Festival left with great memories of good times and full bellies. Not to mention souvenirs, crafts and other trophies of the festival. But the highlight for the locals was the Saturday evening storytelling. It didn't start till eleven and many of the out-of-towners had left by then. So there was a community flavor and feel to this event. Plus, Grove citizens just wanted a chance to catch their breath and relax themselves before Sunday's last fling.

The guest tale tellers had been around all day doing a few storytelling workshops for the story geeks and holding a few concerts of their own for the crowds. Mary Reading kicked the highlight of the festival off with a rousing screecher of a story called "The Banshee of Loch Iffey." Paul Raintree, a Sauk Indian from Oklahoma, who had made a name for himself recovering old Native American stories, shocked the crowd with a tingling tale of shape-shifting called "The Skinwalker." As good as they were though, they really took a back seat to the local talent.

Conor was impressed when Dickie Bergin, who pulled himself away from the beer tent his bar was hosting, launched into a freaky story about a fur trader from Prairie du Chien who met the ghost of Chief Black Hawk seeking revenge for his dead comrades and their women and children slaughtered by the government just up near Bad Axe River. However, the real prize belonged to Jim Warren, who could not only play music, but capture the imaginations of all the kids who managed to convince their parents to stay for this late evening's entertainment. He told the story of a murder-cursed love triangle that happened down Bagley way. Seems one gentleman killed a rival for a beautiful woman and then terrorized her into marrying him. He then strangled her; but even from death's doorway the hand of justice could reach. The story was called, "Tell Me You Love Me Darling Dear, Tell Me You Love Me, Darling, Darling," and the repetition of that refrain raised the level of suspense till the very end when Jim sent the kids screaming in fright back to their parents. They loved it.

Then came the Abbot's turn. Malachy wasn't in his jeans and flannel shirt anymore. He was dressed in his Benedictine habit with his black cuculla, a black flowing garment that made his silver hair and beard along with a silver crucifix around his neck, shine even more brightly as the flames shimmered off the sheen.

Beth squeezed Conor's arm. "He always ends this session every year. We've handed the tradition down throughout the generations. The Abbot always ends this, whoever he may be."

Everyone quieted to listen to him. As he spoke, even the children settled down on parents' laps. Conor sucked in his breath as he noticed behind the flames a huge harvest moon rising orange, rising late into the October sky like a blazing coal cast from the fire.

Tiny Brother Gerald climbed up to the stage with a bronze bell and mallet. Looking expectantly at the Abbot, he waited for Malachy's nod. The sound of the bell rang clearly three times across the square, vanishing into the night. As the last echo faded, Malachy's voice could be heard beckoning the assembled throng to come with him back to the Ireland of centuries past, to a tiny abandoned village on the southwest coast, down County Kerry way. His words stripped them of the present, took away their possessions and clothing, made them even feel the knot of hunger in their bellies. Into their nostrils, his words forced the stench of rotting vegetation.

"What's that smell, Daddy?" said a small voice near the front of the crowd.

"Hush, child," said the father, "for I smell it, too. It's the potatoes dying, rotting throughout the countryside. We were starving back then, so long ago."

Malachy paused in his tale, hushing the murmuring, reminding everyone that all was quiet in the abandoned village they could see clearly in their memories. Pointing into the dark, where in their minds the sea might have been, he shouted that a ship could be seen, sails billowing in the air, heading west, away from home. No one waved it farewell, for those who would were aboard that ship and only the dead were left to take care of home. On the hill overlooking the grey sea, the rock topped graves watched the ship disappear in the distance. A lonely seal cried out a lament from the water as the waves hid the ship from her dark eyes.

"It's a story about where we came from," whispered Beth to Conor. "He tells it every year."

"Why?" he asked.

"Because, he says, if we forget where we came from we won't be able to see where we're going."

"Now," said the Abbot. "Each of you knows the stories of your families. Pick the one person known well to you who has died and gone to heaven, and tell that story to the person next to you."

"Kind of touchy-feely psycho-babble don't you think?" said Conor feeling just a little uncomfortable.

"It would be," said Beth, "if we'd just have started doing this, but I've heard tell, we've done this every year since the town was founded. My grandmother used to say on this night, 'To remember is to honor.'"

Noticing that the crowd was beginning to do as the Abbot asked, Conor said, "Well tell me about her; tell me about your grandma." Beth did.

In fact, everyone was talking, sharing some story of the peoples of the past. There was quiet laughing as a grandfather would tell the kids some funny tale of a long dead ancestor, and even some shrieks of delighted fright at ghostly happenings, supposedly occurring years ago.

The Abbot let it go on for a while, but then he stopped them. "To remember is to honor, that's what we believe; that's what we say. But I can't let you leave tonight till I tell the tale I've chosen." He reached down to Brother Gerald who handed him his crozier, a magnificently carved staff representing his office. The crozier was topped with an ornate carving of a stag's antlers, interlocked with a carved Celtic cross suspended in the middle, a bright red ruby shining in the transept of that cross.

Malachy raised his arms, staff upraised, as if to embrace the people before him. The evening quiet was broken only by the crackle of the bonfire burning brightly behind him. "I want to tell you a story," he said. "A tale that is as true as it is sad. A tale from which much good will come if those who listen are willing. A tale which can change the world from a place of darkness to a place of light. Listen, my people. Listen to the story of Finola:

"The Grove has always been small as it has always been Irish. A thousand or so souls, give or take a few, have lived here since the mid 1800's, doing what people in small towns always do: farm, mill, gossip, sell a few crafts. Back in 1845, the town was new and fresh. Tinkers we were, travelers from a far land doing what our kind never did—settle. The Indian wars were over and the last of the Indian people were either moving to the reservations or migrating across the Mississippi to lands where whites were as yet a rumor. It

*was in the summer of that year 1845 that a wondrous thing happened;
Finola O'Rourke fell in love. You may ask why such a thing was so wondrous, but I'm sure many of you remember what that's like and you know
that when you are going through it, falling in love is the most wondrous thing
in the world. And so it was with Finola. But not one of the townspeople
knew that she was in love and that in itself was quite amazing since keeping
anything quiet in a town our size is rather difficult.*

*"Yet her love was deep and the man she cared for, if he truly was a man,
was hidden from the town as well. She fell in love on Mid-summer's Day as
she walked along the river that ran by the village. She was out in her favorite
field, Finola was, and stopped by a grove of willows, their long hair still
spring green. Grass grew there on a long low mound, just above a little patch
of sand that lay along the bank of the river. The first of the Indian
Paintbrushes were blooming. She was picking them, along with the wild roses
that grew there. Always she had felt drawn to that place, a place of peace and
joy. She was humming an old Irish ballad; you know the kind, where a
young maid is wooed by a handsome stranger. You can imagine how startled
she was when she discovered she was not alone.*

"Who are you?' she said to a young man lounging underneath a willow.

*"The man smiled a gentle smile that nearly touched the raven hair that
hung down from his head. 'Finola' he said. 'What a beautiful name you
have. I have watched you all spring as you walked by my river.' He stood up,
came over to her and took her hands. 'You are as beautiful as you were destined to be.'*

*"Finola stood transfixed. She could not speak. She looked into his dark
eyes which found a way to reflect the colors of the river—rippled blue where
the sky shone on the water, a hint of green from the willows that bent low, a
touch of brown from the silt at the bottom of the water.*

*"As she looked into his eyes, she fell in love. It sounds impossible to do
such a thing with a complete, and possibly dangerous, stranger; but she was
not afraid. It was as if she had known him always. He bent down to pick a
wild rose and pleated it into her hair. His hands touched her face; their lips
came close. A pause, an embrace, and their clothes became an encumbrance.
His hands were nimble, her fingers fast. Her skin was as warm as the sun-
shine around them; his body as awakened as the new life of spring. They
kissed, and her feet, they fell from her on a sweet bed of sand, and the river
ran, and the willows whispered, and the lovers loved. Later as they lay
together, she turned to him and said, 'I will have your child.'*

"I know,' he said. 'And a great child he shall be, lass.'

*"Please,' she asked, 'won't you tell me your name, so that when my
baby's born I may give him the same? And may we be married, for I believe I
love you as I have never loved before?'*

"'Yes, Finola my love,' he said and looked deep into her eyes. 'My name is Willie Archer, and you must understand, that my home, my habitation lies close to these waters. The river is my life and never for long can I leave here.' Rising, he lifted her to her feet and kissed her full on the lips. 'Farewell my love for I must go, but in nine months I will come for you, after the child is born, and we shall be married. I shall be the King of the River and you the Daughter of Spring, for I love you Finola, and my wife you shall be.'

"'Now,' she whispered. 'Let me be your's now.' But if he heard, he gave no sign. He kissed her again and merely said, 'Till then.' And a great sleep overwhelmed Finola and she slept until evening and went back home.

"For months she did not tell anyone of her pregnancy. But as the young life ripened in her womb, questions were asked. She was truthful. 'Willie Archer is the father; he shall return after my baby is born to marry me.' She was not believed. No one had ever heard that name before. In vain her parents looked for one of the town boys to be the father; then they tried to hunt down anyone by the name of Archer, but no one did they find. Ah, the months they did fly. And in the early spring, when life seeks to throw off the dead cold of winter, a child was born to Finola, a boy with hair black as night and eyes the color of shadow. Finola was doubly happy, for a child was born to her and the one she loved was soon to return.

"That very night of the child's birth, the weather changed. The temperature dropped like the plunge of the hawk on its unsuspecting prey. The old men of the town said a storm was coming; the old women of the town muttered about signs and spells and about birthings of children whose fathers were a mystery. The wind began to howl, and the snow began to fall. Lightning crackled through the sky and thunder boomed. Children threw blankets over their heads and even young adults said their rosaries. The Abbot went over to the Abbey Church and lit every vigil light before the statues there.

"Finola went to the window and looked out over the field that led to the river. Out of the howling wind came a wailing and keening. Finola saw a figure in rags approaching the house. Through the snow it came and stopped at the fence. It was the figure of a woman, bent and old, and from her the wailing came.

"She lifted her hand and pointed her finger at Finola. And as she did her face became clear. It was the face of death, of Finola's face hideously grave-eaten; and the wailing became words, and the words became a curse: 'You are mine and the child is mine; mine is the life that is yours.' And just when the horror seemed too much to bear and Finola felt a scream escaping from her body, from across the field swept a huge white owl with wings like an angel. Its talons struck the wraith's head and its beak tore at the flesh of the banshee. With a shriek of defiance, the hag stumbled off into the snow, and the owl disappeared into the wind.

"For three nights the storm raged. For three nights, the old men of the village remarked as how there had never been a tempest like this; for three nights the women of the village told their husbands that the O'Rourke girl had consorted with a being of darkness and that the storm was God's wrath raised against them; and for three nights the banshee visited Finola and demanded her life and the life of her child saying, 'You are mine and the child is mine; mine is the life that is your's.' But each time the snow-white owl came and Finola did not die and her child was not taken.

"And then one night, the storm stopped. That evening, Finola got up from her bed and walked to the window. The tiny boy-child slept soundly, while outside, a full moon glistened on freshly fallen snow. Her eyes swept the field. What was she searching for? What was she looking at? The owl of course. It was always the snow white owl. It had come out of her dreams into the reality of this night. The bird glided over the snow-clad field toward her, pulling up suddenly, talons ready to grasp the fence post ten yards from her window. 'Finola, I call your name,' it said. 'Come with me and we shall walk by the river, by the river forever shall we walk, you and I.'

"Why should I come with you and walk by the river forever?' she said. And the eyes of the owl looked toward her with love and in a voice as warm as the banshee's was cold the owl spoke, 'You are mine and the child is mine; mine is the life that is yours.' And to her, the words were of giving not possessing, of living not dying, of loving not hating. And so, the woman opened the window and let in the cold as she climbed out with her child. Clothed in only a nightgown, she walked across the snow, her bare feet whispering over the crystals, her hair shining dark in the moonlight, sleeping child clutched to her breast. She walked toward the owl ..."

"No," whispered Conor. "It can't be."

"Conor, what is it?" asked Beth concerned that Conor's eyes were staring wildly.

"My dream, he's telling my dream." And sweat burst from Conor's face. "How would he know my dreams, and how could my dreams be from the past? And the woman, she has my mother's name."

"Conor, it's just a story," said Beth, her arm reaching tentatively around his shoulders.

She could feel him shaking as Malachy continued,

"Finola walked toward the owl and the owl was transformed. Before her stood Willie Archer dressed as he was born.

"'I knew you would come,' smiled Finola.

"'How could I not?' said Willie Archer. 'But, my love, we must go. Too long have I been away from the hollow hill and the river that gives me life.'

"*They walked across the snow; only her tracks were visible. And when they arrived at the mound they saw the banshee crouched by the river. She could not wash her hair. The river was frozen solid. She began to keen her wail again, 'You are mine, and the child is mine, mine is the life that is your's.'*

"*'Enough!' said Willie Archer. 'I have tolerated your twisted plots and morbid intentions for far too long.'*

"*'But she must be mine and he must be mine,' said the hag. 'It is the only chance we have of going home. I will see to it.' She staggered toward Finola, but Willie Archer barred the way. Her claw raked across his cheek. She beat him with her fists and in the swirling blowing snow all Finola could see were dark wings around the face of her love. He rose up into the air, the snowy white owl of the night and fought the Morrigan—for that is who the hag was—he fought her in the wind, in the sky, in the snow, and left his beloved Finola and child alone—there by the river, there by the water where the Devourer of Souls had seen the whole thing.*

"*All of you know of what I speak—Piasa, those who came before us called it—a demon from an ancient time that never slept when the old gods went to the hills and closed their eyes under the earth. It reminds us always that the doorway is never completely closed to that time, to that place, to that Otherworld.*

"*'Piasa snaked through a hole in the ice. Finola heard the movement, but even as she moved away from the river, its claw caught her around her waist. She felt it pierce her, but would not let go of the boy. Dragged across the ice she was, screaming she was, and with her the babe. Nothing and no one heard her. The darkness sucked down her voice.*

"*Around three in the morning, Finola's mother chanced to look in on the baby and saw that the window was open and Finola was gone. She gasped and shut out the cold and looked for the child. Empty was the bed.*

"*'The town mounted a search party. But the wind rose up and blew the snow. There were sounds of men shouting in the night, crying 'Finola, where are you; Finola where have you gone?' It was down by the river they found her nightgown, half in and half out of a bloody hole in the ice. Drowned they said; cut herself trying to crawl out, but still, drowned in her shame. Or so everyone thought.*

"*'The Abbot looked at the crowd in silence and then said, 'You're wondering aren't you? You're wondering if Willie Archer ever came back and saved his love and his little boy. All the Abbots of Stella Maris Abbey have passed this story down. Each of us down through the years has spoken of a man who walks the lands down by the river and the hollow hill, and the witch who wails in the wind. Whispers of a dragon in the water brought each Abbot to bless the river every spring, and every summer they would hear a*

child laughing and see a woman running in the fields at the foot of the bluff.
And I myself have seen the snow white owl in the winter wood, and I've
heard it calling her name in the night; I've heard it calling her name.'"

When Malachy finished he seemed to look directly at Conor. As the applause welled up, Conor stood and repeated over and over with a frightened look in his eye, "The names are the same, but what does it mean; they're the same, they're the same, but what does it mean?"

"Conor," said Beth, anxiously pulling at him to sit down. "He tells it every year. It's all just coincidence."

"No, he said my mother's name. He told my dream and more, but he told it as if it happened over a hundred and fifty years ago!" People were beginning to stare at Conor even as Malachy acknowledged the applause.

The Abbot looked across the crowd and caught Conor's eye. Malachy's face loomed in Conor's vision. "Get away from me!" Conor screamed. And then, his eyes rolled up and he collapsed upon the ground.

"Help him!" cried Beth. "Somebody please help him!"

THE LIVING MEMORY

OF COURSE IT wasn't quite like that. The old man always had to tweak the tale. It was worse. She remembered it like yesterday. She was awake in the snow-drenched winter night, just like her sister. Rustling about to dress the child, Finola couldn't help making a bit of noise, and Deirdre heard. She peered through the doorway, opened just a crack, and saw Finola climb out the window with the baby.

She is so silly, thought the younger girl. Always had been. Going to meet that Willie Archer, she bet, all in the middle of the night. But Deirdre was adventurous too. It took her only a moment to grab a coat and put on some sturdy shoes, and soon she was out in the winter wonderland. Peeking around the corner of the house she saw Finola, baby to her breast, talking with the white owl perched there on the fence post. She couldn't hear but she didn't have to, for suddenly the owl was gone and this most beautiful man was standing there, naked as a new born babe. Well, Deirdre had never seen that before! Couldn't make a sound, so surprised was she. But the vision was gone in a moment for, as the stranger moved toward Finola, the snow swirled round and clothed him in white, all excepting that gold circlet on his forehead and that gold collar around his neck.

Deirdre didn't want to let on she was following so she lagged far behind. That meant she couldn't really figure out what they were saying, and when they came upon the banshee, down by the river, all she heard was a wailing in the wind. She was scared, so scared. This Willie Archer, for she was sure that's who the magical man must be, didn't seem very safe for her sister to be around, or her little nephew.

The wind was picking up again and the snow was blowing when the banshee attacked Willie Archer. Strangest thing Deirdre had ever seen on what was already a very strange night. They met on the icy surface of the river and rose up in mid-air, a huge black crow in the night and a beautiful white owl with flashing snow white wings. Into the darkness they flew, and as soon as they were gone, Deirdre went running to her sister. Finola turned toward her and seemed to see her, but Deirdre was looking behind the mother and child at the beast that rose from a hole in the river ice. She screamed a warning and Finola cast a glance over her shoulder. Claws were on her, big pawlike claws grabbing Finola and the baby, dragging them back to the open river. Now Deirdre was a small lass, but brave. At least that's what she told herself later. She never hesitated. She threw herself onto the river ice and stretched out her hands to her sister. Without a sound, Finola thrust the child into Deirdre's arms as the thing dragged her under water. "Finola, Finola," she called. "Where are you? Where have you gone?" But there was no answer.

Deirdre sat there on the ice, cradling the bleeding child. It had been touched by the monster and lost blood. The boy's face was blue with cold. All the girl could do was call for help.

The light of the moon was blotted out by a shadow hovering over her. "Child," said a voice, "whatever are you doing here?" She looked up to see the face of the Abbot from the *Stella Maris* Monastery.

"He's dead, I think," she said, lifting up the baby, "and my sister is gone, gone into the river."

The Abbot glanced at the river. Knowing he could do nothing for Finola at the moment he turned his attention to the child. Badly gashed, the child let out a gasp for air.

Suddenly, the air was filled with wings and Deirdre saw that the strange man was back. "Where is my son, where is Finola?" he snapped, half feathered thing, half man.

"The child is here," said the Abbot, "but Piasa has taken your bride. Do what you can for her, I will watch over the boy."

Deirdre saw Willie Archer leap high in the air and dive straight into the hole in the ice. She swore that he jumped as a man but entered the water looking like, well, like one of those seals she had seen drawn in her schoolbooks.

"My God," said the Abbot, trying to staunch the flow of blood from the child, "the boy will never make it."

"Can you help him, Father Abbot?" said little Deirdre.

"If the night goes further wrong and he cannot go home with his mother, then we must make him ready to go home to God." The Abbot reached for a handful of snow. He crushed it in his palm and let the drops of water fall onto the boy's head, "I baptize thee, Conor William, in the name of the Father, and of the Son, and of the Holy Spirit."

Just then the ice exploded behind him and from the water leapt a shadowy form, at first, bigger than a man, but as their eyes comprehended the sight, they could see it was Willie Archer with Finola on his back, clinging to his neck. For a moment, thought Deirdre, Willie looked like a fish out of water, flopping on the ice. Then he seemed to get his bearings and stood up, staggering over to the Abbot. "What are you doing to my son?" he cried.

"Trying to keep body and soul alive," said the Abbot. "He is near death, as is Finola."

"Don't you think I know?" said Willie Archer. "I must get them both to the hollow hill; it is their only hope. And they don't need your Christian magic."

"Take them," said the Abbot. "Take them now before it is too late."

Willie cradled the child in his arms, in silence for a moment. Looking at the Abbot he snarled, "Remember, priest, the child is mine."

"Not only yours now, I'm afraid," said the Abbot. "I've baptized him, called him Conor William and so he shall be, made him part of this time and place; and though he will walk in your world, he will never truly belong only to you."

"You had no right."

"Every right, my prince. You are the one who sinned, seducing a woman with lies, loving what you cannot have, disregarding her people and their ways. You wanted this child for your own purposes, reasons which I almost agree with. But his destiny is not simply the one you set for him. The One weaves that web; not even the Morrigan, whose touch you still bear from your earlier meeting, makes the final judgement on this one. Little Conor belongs to humanity as well. Now get you gone, and save your bride and child."

Willie touched his face and looked at the blood remains of his fight with the crow. Amazingly, those were Willie's only wounds; Piasa had not touched him. He looked for a moment like he might strike the Abbot, but then he shook off his anger. He clutched the boy to his chest with one arm and lifted Finola with the other. Part of her shredded night dress fell into the blood pooling where she lay. He leapt from the river to the Indian mound, and Deirdre saw him touch the huge willow tree, its naked branches grasping for the covering snow flakes freshly falling again.
"No!" shouted Deirdre. "You'll not take her away." She ran to Willie, throwing her arms around one of his legs. He paid no attention to her and tried to kick her away. She was tenacious. She caught a foot with the tips of her fingers as he melted away into the ground, there by the willow. Deirdre looked back at the Abbot vainly reaching a hand to stop her. He faded into mist, and she into light. Emily's thoughts we're jolted as Jim Warren drove into Madoc's Glen.

"Almost there," he said. A sound from the back of the car made him turn. Conor moaning again. "I fear for him sometimes."

"As do I," said Emily, "As do I. Stop by my mailbox will you. With all the commotion and the festival, I haven't gotten the past two days mail."

Jim obliged. As he reached to get the letters, he heard Conor say, almost as if in a trance. "D. Emily O'Rourke. And I thought your first name was Emily. What's the D. stand for?" From his resting place in the back seat, he could just make out the sign over the box.

"Never you mind, Conor," said Emily. "Haven't gone by that name in years; don't plan to go by it for years to come. Emily will do me just fine."

JASON GOES FISHING

JACE WAS MAD. For the second day in a row, Conor wouldn't leave his room. Embarrassed or some such thing because of what happened Saturday night. It was bad enough, he thought, that the four of them were only three on the last day of the festival. Had a good enough time, being with Nora and all, but Beth was down in the dumps, moping around because of the absent Conor.

Frankly, he was indeed mad, because the only thing else to do was to go back to the festival grounds and help the men clean up. Hated that idea since a dawn football practice had pretty much drained the energy from him. The Monday after the festival was a holiday from school so the young could help the old pick up after the big weekend. Nope, sure didn't want to do that.

Too nice of a day to stay inside, he thought. Would give anything to do something else.

That's when he saw Walter. Jace had driven from Aunt Emily's place back into town and saw Walter heading for the *DewDrop Inn* for his morning belt of brandy. He slowed the car and rolled down the window.

"Hey Walt," he said, "Don't you have something better to do than that? How about taking me fishing? Maybe go after that huge, imaginary catfish down by White Creek Way."

Walt stopped and looked bleary eyed at Jace. "Nothing imaginary about it, smart mouth," he said. "Taught you everything I know about fishin' and you speak to me like I was, well, like I was a nuthin'."

Jace's face fell. "Geez, Walt, didn't mean to insult you. Just trying to josh you into taking me. Bored out of my mind today; just thought you might like to go—it being so warm and all."

"Well, it just so happens I do. Didn't want to go alone though so I'd be glad of the company. Got to try out my new boat anyway. Go get your stuff and I'll meet you down by the town dock in fifteen."

Things looking up, thought Jace as he drove away. It took him only a few minutes to grab his gear and head back down to the dock. Walt was already waiting for him—the new boat simply the old one freshly painted. Jace stripped down to his t-shirt. Uncommonly warm for this time of the year.

"Old Cat won't even know we're coming," said Jace with a smile. "He probably thought we'd put this gear away for the year."

Walt snorted in agreement and spat in the water. "Bet you're right. Gives us a slight advantage, but never underestimate the Great Cat. The one we're hunting for is well over 120 pounds and has been around for three quarters of a century. He's old; he's wise; and—listen to me carefully here—he's mine."

"Not if I get him first," said Jace.

A cloud of rage suddenly swept over the old man. "He's mine I tell you! Caught him once, years ago, but he was too smart for me. Lost him in the rocks that mark the junction of White Creek with the Wisconsin. All he's done since is nibble on my bait." His face softened, "Almost had him a couple of months ago on a hot August night. But now, you're my luck, Jason Michaels. Yes sirree. You're my luck."

Walt mumbled himself into silence as Jace cast off and started the motor. Jace thought the old man surely was beginning to lose it; crazy mood swings. Slowly they went up the river. After a while, Walt spoke just loud enough to be heard above the buzz of the engine. "Grandma Swift Deer used to tell me what to do if I ever caught the Great Cat. 'Don't let anybody taste him before you do. Skin him, clean him, broil him over an open fire and then eat him with only salt as a seasoning. Give you wisdom, he will. The old ones who swim the river know much. Be the first one to taste the Great Cat and you'll have the wisdom of the land, of the river, and more!' That's what she used to say. And I mean to see her words fulfilled."

Jace knew all about Grandma Swift Deer, Walt's foster mother. Been dead a long time, but you could still buy her post card at Dort's. Wise looking old Indian. Winnebago tribe. All decked out in her fancy Indian regalia.

"Folks hated her," said Walt suddenly, startling Jace out of his reverie. "Just like they hate me. Said she was dirty. Wasn't really. Just poor. She taught me things about the river, about the old ways."

"You part Indian, Walt?" said Jace, just trying to keep the old man talking.

"Nah, you know that. But Grandma Swift Deer said I had the heart of a shaman—always wanting more than what I could see. Didn't believe her, so I ended up making nothing of myself. Nothin'." He spat into the water.

There was no more talking as the boat eased through the water. That was fine by Jace, who was content to marvel at the brilliantly turning trees on the bluffs, glowing orange and golden in the autumn sun. Water and sky, sun and earth, and a fishing pole and a quarry to hunt. Life was good. And for a while, he forgot about Conor and enjoyed the trip.

They anchored the boat right at the junction of the creek and river. Just across the cul-de-sac made by the river bend, Jace could see the Indian mound they had passed. On a spectacular fall day like this, it blended in with the surroundings. If you didn't know it was there, you would never see it for what it really was. No other boats were out; they had this section of the river to themselves.

He caught himself looking up White Creek way, wondering if the fishing was any good.

"Don't even think it," said Walt, taking a drink from a bottle he mysteriously made appear—apparently Dickie Bergin was content to part with his precious alcohol on the chance that Walt wouldn't hang around the bar. "I've told you many times, and anyone else that would listen to me, that no one goes up that way." In fact, it would have been a little difficult. Over the years, trees had fallen and the entrance to the slough was shrouded with deadwood and leafy branches. But still, a little perseverance and one could get through.

"Wasn't thinking of going up there," said Jace a little sullenly. "Just wondering, was all."

Walt topped off his drink with a plug of tobacco against his cheek. "Death waits up there. Don't look at me like I'm telling old wives' tales. It's true. Those that tried, died. Simple as that."

Jace turned his head away and smiled. The old codger was more full of BS than he was of alcohol.

They fished in silence for about an hour when Walt suddenly hissed, "Got something, I think." Sure enough, if his pole didn't bend nearly double.

"Whatever it is," said Jace, "it's big. Do you think it could be the Cat?"

"Oh, I'm a' thinking it is," said Walt letting out a whoop. "I've got you this time you wily fish."

For the next hour, he played with it, reeling it ever so slowly in, keeping it from the rocks and its other hiding places. Jace could see it once in a while surfacing. Silver sides gleamed in the sun, and its mouth gaped wide in fury. Clearly, he needed to steer the boat to a patch of bare shoreline. No way could they haul this behemoth onto the boat. He navigated, Walt continued to fight. The old man was breathing heavily and weakening. Jace offered to help. Walt cut him off. "Waited my whole life for this."

Jace beached the boat and splashed out into the river to help Walt grab the fish. Together they dragged it to the shore.

"It's huge," said Jace. "Nearly two hundred pounds at least!"

"I did it," cackled Walt. "I've caught the Great Cat!" Without another word he took a rock and slammed it over and over against the head of the fish.

"What are you doing?" shouted Jace. "We should take it to town for folks to see!"

"Nothing doing, Jace. I've waited to catch this one for a long time and I'm not going to take the chance of losing his wisdom. I'll be the first to eat this fish and I'll know what he knows. I'll be somebody; I reckon I'll be as smart as Jim Warren and as crafty as that Dickie Bergin. Who knows," he said with a sad smile, "maybe I'll be taken seriously in town."

Jace said nothing as Walt skinned the fish. Walt's drinking over the years had indeed made him a joke to most of the townspeople. Jace felt bad for him; they all just couldn't see beneath the addiction. Broken dreams, thought Jace. But hey, things are looking up for the old man; it really was a mighty fine fish. On Walt's orders he gathered some wood to make a fire and made a spit to roast the huge hunks of fillet that Walt was cutting.

Walt inspected the blaze and how Jace was cooking the fish. "Not hot enough, yet. Keep that blaze going while I rustle up some moss to make a little smoke so's to flavor that fish. I'm thinking too that a little mint might come in handy. There's some not far from here." Walt got up and eased his stiff legs into motion. "No eating the Cat till I get back, you hear?"

"Absolutely," said Jace. "He's all your's, along with all his wisdom." Jace chuckled as he watched the old man go off into the brush. Walt sure was one eccentric guy. For a few minutes he dutifully watched the fish. But the day was warm and the time fishing had made him sleepy so he dozed. Probably his eyes closed only a minute, but boiling sap snapping out of one of the logs jolted him awake. Startled, he nudged the spit holding the fillets just enough to loosen one end and send the spit into the coals.

Without thinking, he reached out and grabbed the fillets instead of the stick and set the whole thing upright again. It was instinct really. The fish was hot and it burned. Putting his hand to his mouth, he licked his fingers, tongue tasting the sweet meat of fresh cooked catfish. He saw that his thumb even had a few crumbs of catfish on it and he stuck that in his mouth, sucking on it a moment. Tasted pretty good. Couldn't wait till Walt came back and they could eat. A tingling shiver began in his gut and spread like lightning down to the tips of fingers and toes. He stared at his hands and made them feel his tingling face.

"Still watching that fish aren't you? Not burning it I hope."

Jace jumped, deaf to Walt's return. Blushing, he stammered, "Sure, sure, it's cooking just fine." The flavor of catfish still clinging to his tongue and filling his nostrils, the curious tingling reaching deep in his body, Jace watched in guilty silence as Walt dug his fingers into a fillet and stuffed his mouth full of fish.

"First taste," he crowed, flecks of white meat flicking out of his mouth as he tried to talk.

Couldn't look at him. Jace just couldn't, knowing now that Walt was truly having seconds, not firsts of that record breaking meal. Shifting his eyes anywhere but where Walt was, Jace noticed movement in the brush not ten yards away. A man stepped out of the thicket, raising a hand in welcome. Jace made to speak, but the stranger shushed him, motioning the boy to follow.

"Be back in a minute," said Jace. Walt never answered, the taste of catfish infusing his being and dreams of wisdom filling his soul.

Walking twenty yards into the brush, Jace came face to face with the stranger from the hollow hill.

"There you have done it," said the stranger. "Walter is going to skin you alive for doing that, skin you faster than he did the Great Cat."

Jace said nothing, just stared at the man he supposed was the Willie Archer of legend. Sure dressed to fit the part: homespun shirt, suspenders, brown trousers and soft boots. From another time.

"I mean it," said the man smiling a little. "You have tasted the Great Cat and now you possess its wisdom."

"No way! I don't feel any different," he lied. "Must be dozens of fish in the river almost this big. Doubt much they all give wisdom." But even as Jace spoke, he knew his words rang hollow. This was Tinker's Grove, the town with the 'dark ones' near an ancient mound of magic. "Besides, that's Walt's fish story, not mine."

"Perhaps, but why is it you can see me?"

"You just came out of the brush!"

"Been here since you landed. No human perceives me unless I will it. Neither of you saw me, until you tasted the fish first. Now you can see me of your own accord. The old man cannot. Walt knows, even if you do not remember your tradition. Your kind and mine brought the legend with us to the New World, though some, like the old Indian woman who fostered Walt, knew the secret as well. In Celtic lands, it is ancient salmon that possess the wisdom. Eat such a fish, and you shall know things, important things that most people will never ken. And you will see what truly is. Like me." The man laughed.

"But Walt—he was to be the first to taste it," said Jace, a sinking feeling growing in his gut.

"He wanted to be, but you were meant for it. It is only a fish now. The wisdom passes once and that is all. Best not to tell Walt about what you just did."

Jace swallowed hard. "Why did you show yourself now?"

"Seeing things a new way may be a fresh experience for you but it is not to me," said Willie Archer. "The river and the land around here are mine to guide and govern. I watch over everyone, and this is hardly the first time I have shadowed you. Humans interest me little, but I have watched you for some reason. Now I know why. A wisdom hunter who didn't even know what he was seeking. But now you pose a problem for me."

"How's that?" asked Jace, slowly recovering his poise. The man didn't seem set on trying to hurt or attack him.

"You are different, now that you've had breakfast," smiled the stranger ruefully. "You will never be of my kind, but you are closer, as kin as you will ever get. You ate of this ancient lord of the river, and you have its power and knowledge. Wisdom and the ability to see more clearly are its gifts to you. That means you will easily perceive me and my kind. I could kill you now—" and the man whipped out a curved knife from his belt and held it under Jace's neck. "But you guard my son. At least that's what the feckless Morrigan tells me."

"Your son?" said Jace. "Conor is your son? For real?"

The man laughed sharply. "I can see the new wisdom moves slowly through your veins. Did you think the story the Abbot told was just a children's tale? Did you think your friend collapsed the other night simply because he was frightened of bad dreams? He knows the truth in his bones, and now you do as well."

"What are you?" said Jace pushing the knife away. "I'm not scared of you and if you wanted to kill me you already would have done so."

"You have seen the land and water around here," said Willie Archer, ignoring Jace's question. "You know most humans in these parts never move away. That is what is unique about this place as opposed to much of the rest of your country.

"When I first came here, I found the mounds empty. Nothing stirred on the bluffs, in the meadows or among the trees. There was no presence except that of the demon in the water. Beautiful but empty were the hills and forests. I still do not know why this part of the New World was so barren of inner life. So I and my kind, strangers in a strange land, filled the hollow hills. We made the land breathe. Surely even you have sensed it. All of you in Tinker's Grove feel this as home. You and your friends, townspeople for generations have been reluctant to leave. Especially those you call the 'dark ones.' They are kept here by the presences, unseen and mostly unfelt, but you have met some of them. There is me and my kind and we are of the Light—or at least we once were. There is the demon you know as Piasa, the legendary evil spirit of the river—here even before my people—and its darkness always seeks to overwhelm and spread. We hold it at bay. And then there is the presence the Abbot and his ilk provide—a different kind of protection than mine, but very useful in times past and present. Finally, there is human evil, such as that dark witch Caithness McNabb and her brood represent. I cannot fight them easily, for they walk in a world strange to me. I tell you now; she has made alliance with this new person in town, this man Drake. He lives and breathes darkness as well."

"I knew it," whispered Jace to himself. "There is something creepy about him." He was silent a moment and then turned to the man. "Why don't you go talk to your son? Why don't you reveal yourself to him? This Rory Nalan—he one of yours? Because he seems to have no trouble talking to your son and making life miserable for him."

Willie Archer's eyes grew bleak. "Rory is my brother and he is ... misguided."

"He's crazy and he sure as hell doesn't walk in the Light."

"Do not judge him harshly. His ways are not familiar to you, but he will not harm the boy. And I cannot speak to Conor. Because not all has happened as it should. That time approaches but is not yet. That is why I need you, his Champion."

"You underestimate him. He'd listen to you."

"No doubt he would, but he would not accept. As you know he is changing, becoming, and he does not want what he will become."

Jace looked at him incredulously. "You must be nuts! What's happening to him is amazing. You could help him through it."

Eyes narrowing, Willie Archer snarled, "Would you want to know you are damned for all time? Would you want to know that you are not human? Would you want to know that all you love and cherish can never be yours because what you thought you were you are not and can never be? You think him human, but Conor is more fragile than you know. Someday, he will be strong, but now he is like a butterfly in a chrysalis. What he needs is to be protected during this time of change. What he needs is you. And to that end, there are things I must show you if you are to stand with him."

"He's no monster," said Jace. "And I don't believe you when you say he's not human. Conor told me what the Abbot said to him, that you and your kind—whatever you really are—might very well be mistaken on that point."

Willie Archer stood over Jace and looked at him severely. "We are similar but so different. It is easy for you to be deceived, or was before your breakfast of this morning. Look at me closely and tell me if I am human."

Jace looked at the tall, well-built man. For a moment, he looked simply like a hunter from a century or so ago, but then Jace noticed the golden circlet on his head. Hadn't seen that before except the night Conor was healed. He sensed the almost animal-like lightness in posture, as if Willie Archer could leap away like a deer, or pounce like a wolf. And there was the slightest shimmer to his body, and Jace guessed if it was night there would be a faint luminescence over Willie Archer's exposed skin, just like that band of skin on Conor that shimmered when the weird things happened to him.

"I wouldn't have been able to see this an hour ago, would I?"

"No, not unless I revealed myself to you as I did the night Conor returned. Trust me, Jason Michaels, if Walt himself were to come upon us now, he would think you speaking only to the wind in the trees for he could not see me," said Willie Archer. "For that I am truly sorry. Knowledge often carries a burden of loneliness. Still, I must ask you, will you stand with Conor? Will you watch over him?"

Jace thrust himself to his feet. "You know I will. I never had a brother. He is like one to me."

"That means little to me who has such a brother as Rory," Willie Archer's laugh was tinged with sadness.

"Then let me say it more bluntly," said Jace. "I told the Morrigan that I would stand for him. I've already done so; I'll continue. Now take my word or leave it."

"That's not enough," he said. He grasped Jason's hand and try as he might, Jace couldn't wrench it free. "Your blood is needed as bond." With that, Willie Archer slashed the knife across Jace's palm.

Jace wanted to yell, but bit his lip as he groaned in pain.

"Do not worry. You won't suffer alone. Your blood bond is with me as well as the Morrigan." Willie Archer sliced his own palm and grasped Jace's hand. Blood mingled and squeezed out through the grip.

Jace went dizzy for a moment and swayed. The voice of Willie Archer was soft. "It is all right, lad. It is just my blood mixing with yours as well as the wisdom from the lord of the river working on you. You cannot become what Conor is; you are not of our kind, but now you shall see more clearly than any man on earth. Come with me."

Willie Archer led Jace toward the bank of White Creek.

"We'll never get through that brush without some tools," said Jace.

"Look more closely," said Willie Archer. "You can comprehend more now, and you can see that what seems to be is often not."

Jace saw the brush was not impenetrable. Small paths led through it that he had never noticed before; and beyond he saw White Creek broaden out to a sun-dappled expanse of water.

"I had no idea the slough was this big."

"No one does. Myself and those with me can hide this place from prying eyes. But I must warn you. We can mold what you see, but unfortunately, I am not the sole proprietor of this body of water. Piasa's lair is here as well. Its evil serves my purpose. No man has gone up this creek in centuries and lived, so firm are the tales of horror."

"Walt said that men have lost their lives here."

"They have, indeed. Piasa has killed several, as have I and my kind."

"You murdered them?" asked Jace.

"No. They were treasure seekers and men of darkness. Their deaths cleansed the web of life. Never forget, Jason Michaels, I will protect what is mine, whether that be the town, the 'dark ones,' the land or the water."

They had walked some ways up the west bank of the creek. Jace was amazed at how secluded it all was, as if an invisible wall shielded it from the rest of the world. Autumn got in though. The trees were beautiful and the birch and locusts were strewing their golden leaves across the slowly moving surface of the slough.

"There it is," whispered Willie Archer. At first, Jace could see nothing out of the ordinary where the man pointed across the water. The hill on the east side was not high but it came rather straight down onto a small sandy white beach. Then he saw that the hillside hid a secret. A tall thin opening and a smaller creek creeping into the shoreline hinted at the presence of a cave.

"We must swim across," said Willie Archer, already wading into the water. Jace followed him. The warm weather couldn't take away the autumn chill that gripped the creek and Jace shivered. The strange man, however, didn't seem bothered in the least.

A few minutes in such cold water wasn't going to cause Jace hypothermia, but it was uncomfortable. He was glad for the warm sun when he got to the other side. He stamped his feet on the beach and clouds of white sand rose into the air.

"It's like powder," he said. "How weird."

Willie Archer only frowned and said, "Come into the cave. There is something I must show you."

A cloying smell assaulted Jace's nose, as if rotten carrion lay near.

"Great place you have here, man," said Jace, stomach turning in protest.

"I share it with the river demon."

"What?" said Jace. "Piasa lives here?"

"The part of it that dwells in this world feeds in this cave. Many centuries ago, I found this place and the Devourer of Souls never has discovered that we share it together. It was the best hiding place for what I am about to show you. Besides, Piasa really does not understand the ways of men or my kind. It feeds on you when necessary, wars on my kind when possible, but it has lived so long that the world of men appears as fleeting as the life of a river fly in the early summer. You are just not that important to it. But Conor is. Already it senses that Conor is more than he seems. Long ago, my companions and I reached a truce with this demon, but Conor's arrival has caused it to doubt. It senses we betray it, and it will not stand for that. And if it discovers that humans are also involved in the protection of Conor, it will exact a terrible price on the town."

They had walked slowly into the cave and Jace noticed a deep channel several yards wide flowed back as far as the outside light would shine.

Willie Archer clapped his hands together and a will-o-the wisp, a ball of light appeared between his palms. He sent it surging forward lighting up the chamber.

Jace let out a low whistle. "Nice trick."

Paying no attention, Willie Archer walked alongside the channel of water. It seemed to butt up against the wall of the cave, far back from the entrance. Boulders and other detritus from the outside, branches and other things were piled there.

"All is not what it seems," said Willie Archer.

"There's something here isn't there?" asked Jace.

"Ah, you see it then?"

"It looks like an old boat; well, bigger than a boat, a small ship behind all this crap."

"Indeed," said Willie Archer. "It is my ship, what brought me and my people here to this place so long ago. She is the *Gwennan Gorn*, and she is my beauty."

"But it's a ruin!"

"No," said Willie Archer with a short laugh. "There is a glamour on her that even your wise eyes cannot pierce. She is as whole as the day we departed on it."

"It almost appears Norse," said Jace with wonder in his voice.

"'Tis a bit, but she is my design really."

"Looks positively medieval."

Willie Archer lifted an eyebrow and gazed steadily at Jace. "A little thick are you not? She has come from a time impossibly far away, but as once I did, so she is yours to captain, though not to possess."

"What?" said Jace. "What are you talking about?"

"When the time is right, you will have to pilot her, lad. In defense of my son. To protect my people. To preserve the land."

"Absolutely nuts," muttered Jace. "Here I am, in a smelly old cave, with a rotted hulk of a boat, and a centuries old guy who is certifiable."

Willie Archer rounded on him and grabbed his collar, lifting Jace off his feet and shaking him as if he weighed no more than a mop.

"You must be a fool if you can taste the wisdom of the land and river and still not understand. I am not showing you this for your wonder; I am showing you this for the purpose of your preparation. When the time for battle comes, when war looms, the *Gwennan Gorn* shall sail again, and you will bring her to aid my son."

"Seriously, man," choked Jace, "who are you really?"

He let go of Jace, and backed away, off to Jace's right—a shadow in the light flowing from the entrance of the cave. For a moment, he stood in silence next to the ruins of the ship, and then dust motes flickered in the air, and a breath of wind whispered around Jace's ears, "My name is Madoc, and as Conor is mine, you are mine, mine is the life that is your's. Look more closely wisdom eater and tell me what you see."

Barely catching the dim outline of the stranger, he tried to pierce the darkness that fogged his sight of the ship and its ancient captain.

"You only see what you expect," whispered the voice, "but you can see more deeply if you wish." Madoc opened his hand and threw motes of light toward the boy.

Jace strained his eyesight, and as he did, sparks of light flew through his vision. Oh man, he thought, last time I had these, a bitchin' migraine was coming right behind.

"A deep breath," said the voice, "and let the Light carry you."

So he took a risk, and sucked down a breath and followed the flecks of light, brilliantly golden. To tell the truth, he didn't even feel his body, and he didn't really care, for he saw what the light illuminated. A ship, and not the ruined hulk he had just seen in the shadows, but a brilliant war-painted long ship with a seal bursting out of carved waves as the prow.

"It's beautiful," he whispered.

"Aye, so it is," said the voice.

Jace turned and saw him then, Willie Archer or Madoc as he called himself, as he was meant to be, a Celtic prince, tall and raven haired with a gold circlet and on his neck a filigreed golden torc. Armbands gleamed beneath the sleeves of his white tunic and leggings, and the crimson cloak was clasped with a knotwork brooch of hammered bronze. Black sealskin boots and leggings completed the look and Jace let out a low whistle.

"You mean, you're the Madoc, like the Madoc of Madoc's Glen?" The vision began to fade in Jace's sight; indeed, the last thing he clearly saw was the fierce face, bone white coming toward him as the darkness descended once more.

Hands like cold steel grasped Jace's neck again. *"Conor is mine."*

"There's only one Madoc I know," shouted Jace. "Some kind of Welsh prince who sailed to America long ago."

"You are mine." The cold hands, felt, not seen, crept up Jace's face, as if an invisible visage was staring at him, that bone white face of a Celtic warrior from centuries past.

"All right, all right," said Jace. "You're Madoc, a prince and not some homespun Tinker."

Jace's head was jerked back. He felt one hand on his chin, the other pulling back his head by his blond hair. *"Little man, mine is the life that is yours."*

WHAT CONOR FOUND OUT

CONOR HEARD JACE come and go. For two days, he had not ventured downstairs. Resisted all pleas from Aunt Emily and even her stern commands. Didn't want to see anyone. Truth to tell, he was embarrassed by his behavior Saturday night. Fainting away like one of those girls down by Navy Pier at a rock venue, overcome with emotion at some drug-wasted rapper hunk. Hated being weak, and that's just what he was.

Sick with some god-forsaken flu, collapses outside of a bus—hi everybody, I'm Conor Archer, see you when I come back to consciousness. Judas Priest, he thought, couldn't even get a break when he walked in the Otherworld. Slapped around by a biker dude who communes with stuff out of legend. Crying in pain, weeping with grief in front of a witch woman who couldn't decide if she was a girl or a grandma. And now, there he was last night passing out, again, in front of every soul in Tinker's Grove, all because some priest tells a story that kicks up memories of a nightmare.

What a man I am, thought Conor. Look tough, play a mean bit of music, almost got friends and a girl who likes me—but, no play here. Freaky ribbon of dark skin—oh, that's right, dark most of the time, but when the weird shit starts happening, what a ribbon of morphing light it becomes. Neon sign saying, "Conor man is changing." What'll it be this time? He who runs on all fours? If the Native Americans—the Winnebagoes, Sauk or Fox were around, or even the earlier ones who made those animal shaped mounds—they'd know old Conor all right. Shapeshifter, skinwalker, the boy who ran with the wild ones.

Cool stuff had happened, no doubt about that. But it hadn't made him stronger, only weaker. He thought about the faces under the water he had seen when Oz had touched him that day after he arrived in Tinker's Grove. Never told Jace and Beth that he didn't just see the strange, almost human faces. He heard their song. *"Home, home, home to the sea; carry us safely, home to the sea."* He didn't tell Beth and Jace that a chill thrill had flashed through him when he heard the song. That was when the mark on his body had really started to grow, and now it moved and twisted around and through him every time he touched the Otherworld. The time would come when the Otherworld would change him completely. That's what really pissed him off. Didn't need this at all. Just wanted to be normal, get back to living life.

"And you," he said to the dog by the side of his bed. "Don't you ever need to go out?" Troubles hadn't left his side in two days. The dog got up and padded over to the bed and rested his head next to Conor's face. A deep sigh came from the dog as the big brown eyes stared into the boy's.

"So you do have to go," said Conor. The dog licked his cheek in response.

Conor got up, pulled on some clothes and went downstairs. The floor boards creaked with his passing. The sun was already high in the sky when he opened the door and let the dog out.

From the corner of his eye, he saw Aunt Emily watching him from the kitchen. Other than to grunt a response from his bed, he hadn't spoken to her in the past two days.

"Come on," she said, not unkindly. "I'll fix you some breakfast."

He padded over to the kitchen table and sat down without a word. He stared at her all the while she fried up some bacon and whisked up some scrambled eggs.

With the plate before him, he picked up a fork.

"Say your prayers first," she clipped. "I may have cooked it but God's given you this good food. Least you could do is thank him for it."

He quickly made the sign of the cross and blessed the food—more out of rote than conviction.

With a mouthful of eggs muffling his speech he said,

"I'm old, aren't I?"

"Old enough to be behaving better than this."

"No, I'm old, aren't I?" His voice was firmer and he tore off a piece of bacon in his mouth. "Really old, I mean. No wonder the town thinks I'm a freak."

"Conor ..."

"Stop it," he said, smacking the fork on the table. "Tell me the truth. I'm old, aren't I?"

"Very," said Aunt Emily, turning again to the stove.

"Like maybe I was born close to when this town was founded. Like maybe I've been through a Civil War and a couple world wars to boot. Like maybe at my next birthday, instead of eighteen candles, you can pack a hundred and fifty, a hundred and seventy-five, maybe two hundred son-of-a-bitching candles on my freaking, white-frosted, chocolate birthday cake!"

"Don't you speak to me like that," said Aunt Emily, but with her voice small and low.

"And why the hell not?" said Conor. "How can all this be?"

"I'm not exactly sure how to describe it."

"Enlighten me. How would you describe it?"

"You are a seventeen year old boy whose life has spanned two centuries."

"Impossible."

"You've already said yourself that it's true."

"There's another thing I know, now," said Conor, spitting the words through his teeth.

Emily was silent.

"There is no Willie Archer, is there?"

"No, there's not."

"That thing out in the mound. He seduced my mother, appeared to her as a figure from a song, something she'd be familiar with, and he did it on purpose for his own ends. Why?"

"He's not a thing. He's your father."

Conor jumped to his feet, tumbling the chair behind him. "He's not human," he shouted. "He is a thing, something that entered my mother and from that coupling came me—demon spawn. Is that what I am? Some kind of alien child, like those stupid sci-fi flicks on TV? Willie Archer, bullshit!"

She turned on him then. Walked over and smacked his face as hard as her hand could fly. It was hard. The imprint of her fingers rose red on the side of his cheek.

He lifted up his fist.

"Go ahead," she whispered, fire in her eyes. "Go ahead and hit an old woman."

He never struck. Realizing what he was about to do, Conor turned and picked up the chair and sat back down at his breakfast. For a long while neither spoke.

"It wasn't like that," she said. "You know it wasn't like that. It truly was more like your dream and the story the Abbot told."

"How would you know?"

"Finola had a younger sister," said the old woman. "The little girl saw everything that long ago night. Even helped rescue you from Piasa. In the commotion, she followed Willie Archer—don't look at me like that; that is his common name around here—she followed Willie Archer into the hollow hill as he and his kind carried you and your mother. Both of you were sorely hurt by the Devourer of Souls, that horrible river demon. While Willie Archer and the people of the hollow hills tried to heal you and your mother, the little girl helped herself to food and drink. She knew she should have been concerned about you and her sister, but never had she tasted anything as delicious as what lay before her—drinks of such sweetness, fruit so full and ripe, and a bread that melted in her mouth.

"She had eaten her fill before the Morrigan stopped her. 'Child,' said the crone, not unkindly, 'what have you done? Out with you now.' And she hustled the little girl up what seemed like stairs, through a dark doorway. The child found herself outside of the mound, standing in the snow. The searchers discovered her shortly thereafter, though they could not make hide nor hair out of what she was saying. They gave Finola and the child up for dead.

"Deirdre, for that was the name of Finola's little sister, seemed never the same again. She told others what she had seen but only the old women of the town even half-believed her tale. Never would they say that in public, but with secret whispers they spread the story and talk of it never really died. Deirdre mentioned it less and less and grew up a normal girl until she was twenty. Then, a marvelous thing happened. Time slowed for her. Others grew old all around her, but Deirdre did not—at least that was how it seemed. She did age though, just more slowly than others."

"Why was that, Aunt Emily?" broke in Conor.

"Ah, lad," she said, "'twas the Otherworld don't you see? She walked through the halls of the hollow hills with the People who dwell there and ate their food and drank their drink, and though she did not stay long, it was long enough to lengthen her days. How she lingered! It was hard at first. She bought Madoc's Glen and built this house, but every generation or so, she had to disappear for a few years. Deirdre didn't relish the thought of being labeled a witch-woman, so she re-invented herself coming back as a distant relative from the far flung O'Rourke clan. Most of the townspeople were deceived, but not all. Some suspected the truth for the old tales never died. There's always been an O'Rourke in charge of Madoc's Glen and that O'Rourke has always been a woman."

Conor looked at her in silence, and then spoke softly. "That woman has always been you, hasn't it? Deirdre Emily O'Rourke."

"Yes, yes it has." Emily looked wistfully out the window and then turned back to Conor, her voice brusque once again. "So you're not the only old one around here."

"But why don't I look old?" he asked, "Like you I mean." His face reddened in embarrassment as he realized what he had said.

Emily just laughed, "Because you've spent little time in this world. During your convalescence and your mother's healing, only a year or two passed in the hollow hill, but decades went by in this world. Only twice did you ever venture out and both times were near calamities for Tinker's Grove. Now you're back. Perhaps you can see why some are just a might bit concerned about you, even the ones who know only wisps of the story as legends heard when they were children."

Again Conor was silent for a long moment. He took a drink of his orange juice and said, "Aunt Emily, are you going to die?"

She smiled a sad smile. "Of course, dear. All things die. Even the people of the hollow hills can die. I am an old woman now, still full of piss and vinegar to be sure, but some day my time will be up. But not till I'm done with you."

Conor looked like he was about to say something, but Emily held up her hand.

"I know what you want to ask, but there are some things only fathers can tell their sons. Let him tell you his story in his own good time. You've waited nearly two hundred years to hear it. A little longer won't hurt you."

Conor pushed himself away from the table. "I need to go out for a walk. Be back in a while."

He took off towards town. When he finally got there, he dropped into Dort Martin's place. To woo the young, the most aggressive entrepeneur in town had started stocking graphic novels in addition to comic books. Even Conor was hooked though he still didn't much care for the lady; to see the painted stories he had to tolerate the busybody.

Browsing the latest *Sandman* tale, he caught Dort looking at him. Their eyes met briefly, but surprisingly to Conor, Dort Martin averted her gaze, making a show of dusting some shelves but all the while coming closer to him.

Without turning her head, she spoke to the old boxed games, flicking a cloth over them, driving the dust to hang in sparkling motes in the few sunbeams that pierced the gloomy interior. "Ought to apologize to you."

"What?" said Conor. "You say something Mrs. Martin?"

"I said," she replied to a 1960's version of *Hi Ho Cherry O* perched on top of a shelf of deteriorating ancient board games, "I ought to apologize to you."

"For what?" asked Conor, puzzled at this new humility from the querelous shopkeeper.

She turned to him, bitter lips parting under sorrowful eyes, "I wanted to apologize for lying to you, about saying that I never knew your mother. What happened a few nights ago, when the Abbot told that story again— landsakes he's told it so many times—what happened to you when you heard it made me see that I can't stop things."

"Stop what?" asked Conor. "What things?"

It was as if she hadn't heard him. "We've got to protect our own, just like I have to protect my Nora."

"You know," whispered Conor, mouth dropping open. "You know about the 'dark ones!' You knew Nora was a 'dark one?'"

"'Course I do," she snapped, her old self again. "Everyone in town knows them, even if they won't say. It's just that Nora's parents wouldn't have anything to do with her—she being strange and everything. They're so modern and all—can't abide the old tales. Oh, don't get me wrong. They put up a good front, telling others she's living with me to help me out and learn the business, but ever since that day when she fell ..."

"What do you mean?" asked Conor. "Did she get hurt?"

Dort gave a short, cynical laugh. "No, that was just the problem. She always liked birds and they liked her. Used to perch on her hand like she was some modern St. Francis of Assisi. It happened when she was about eight. Her mom and dad—that would be my good for nothing son—were raking leaves below her window. She was leaning out. I was walking up the street and saw it all. This beautiful white owl, in the middle of the daytime mind you, flew past and she reached for it, and fell."

"And she didn't get hurt?"

"It was awful, but not in the way you might be expecting. Arms spread out like wings, she simply glided to the ground. Her mother fainted dead away. Her father, useless excuse of a parent that he is, didn't want the embarrassment. Asked me to take her in. So I did. It was the only real strange thing I ever saw Nora do and in the years since, she has forgotten it completely—they all do you know; I've checked. But still, her parents fear her. I thought I was protecting her, but then"—and here she spat out her words in a sorrowful anger—"but then you came along and she started remembering. First I feared you; then I resented you, but that's petty of me, I know. Forgive me for that too. You change things Conor Archer."

"But I don't want to; I just want to fit in."

"Not going to happen, I'm afraid," said Dort. "You're a changer that's what you are. You touch things and they change."

Her wide eyes were starting to spook him a little. "You're saying you did know my mother then?"

She shook her head. "Not well, just for a day or two, really, but I knew her more than most because I saw where she, and you for that matter, came from."

"And where was that?" asked Conor, dreading the answer.

"From the Indian mound, down by the river. One summer's day, I'd walked down from the cemetery, putting some flowers on my own mother's grave. Walked just a ways down the hill overlooking the river. You can see the mound from there, did you know? I looked once—nothing— looked twice and there she was, carrying a child, standing under the huge willow tree on the mound. She started walking through the fields to the path that leads to the Abbey. I cut her off; reached her before she got to the church. 'Help me,' she said. She looked hunted, as if she was running from something or someone. 'Who are you child?' I asked. 'Finola,' she said, 'Finola Archer, I mean O'Rourke.'"

"What did you do?" asked Conor.

Dort smiled a thin bloodless smile. "O'Rourkes have been at Madoc's Glen for generations. They call it that because some Welsh prince was said to have discovered this whole area centuries ago. Misplaced legend I say. That Madoc was supposed to have discovered things farther south. No matter; I wander. Getting back to Finola, Emily would have been her only, albeit distant, living relative. I didn't want to be involved. I knew the other legend from the time of the town's founding. I knew who she might be. Fey girl with a changeling child. Fell in love with the prince from the hollow hills—Willie Archer was the father, she said, just like in the legend.

"But she was lying. Didn't pay no mind to it though, she was so beautiful. A haunting beauty, really. Luminous. Scared me a little. Didn't want to mess with it all. I sent her to Emily. Took her there myself actually. Dropped her at the front door. Emily got rid of her the next morning. Sent her off to Chicago. Went with her actually and stayed there several weeks to get you and your mother settled. And there Finola and you stayed. Until you came back."

"You make it sound like a bad thing that I've come home."

"If I did, then I'm sorry. It's just that I'm like most people here. I like life calm and predictable. Somehow, I don't think you'll be bringing that to us."

"That's enough, Dorothy," said a voice behind Conor. Jim Warren had come into the store; neither knew how long he'd been listening. "Can't you see the boy just wants to fit in?"

Jim Warren looked at Conor and said, "Glad I found you, son. Have some business I want to speak with you about. Let's go over to the bank."

Dort Martin watched the two of them leave, whispering under her breath, "Doesn't matter how hard you try to hide the magic, Jim Warren, this boy has already cast his spell."

"Pay absolutely no attention to her," said Jim as they walked across the street. "Like so many here, she's full of strange stories and old notions that she half believes in. Don't let it all rattle you."

"Like you said, I just want to fit in, get along, feel normal," said Conor.

"Of course you do," said the banker.

He brought Conor in to his office at the bank. As he sat behind the huge cherry wood desk, bare of anything except a pen and pencil set—computers seemed banned from this office—Jim Warren gave every indication that he was now the successful banker and not the folksy musician of a few nights ago. Conor was a little nervous on the other side of the desk.

"Your Aunt Emily has provided you a trust fund—worked out with your mother before her death, so you won't have to worry about making ends meet."

"But my mother had little money."

"True enough for herself, but the O'Rourkes are an old clan here and there will be enough for you for years to come, I suspect."

"But why wouldn't Aunt Emily have sent some money to my mother before this? We barely had anything."

The banker looked at the boy over his glasses. "Had her reasons, no doubt. Have to ask her, I'm afraid. She's a client of mine, too, and I keep confidences very solemnly." He pushed himself to his feet. "Look, Conor, I don't want to rush your grief or stop your questions, but it's best to move on now. Make a life here for yourself. It's not so bad. With DIOGENE kicking into gear, there will be new employment opportunities. You can get yourself a job; go to the university up in LaCrosse or Madison, whatever. So many possibilities."

Jim Warren pulled out a few forms from his desk and asked Conor for his signature to formalize the trust. "You have access to a small amount of these funds without your Aunt's permission. At her death, the trust reverts completely to you."

Conor whistled low when he read of the trust's full worth. He felt an anger growing in him as years of seeing his mother suffer came back to memory.

"Did you know Finola Archer?" he asked.

"Saw her once, a long time ago. Showed up on your Aunt's doorstep claiming to be an O'Rourke. Don't know why Emily believed her; felt sorry for her and her child—that'd be you—I guess."

"Dort Martin has a different take on that story."

"No doubt she does," said Jim Warren, putting his arm around Conor's shoulders, ushering him out of the office. "Gossip, legend and old wives' tales. That's why she's where she belongs, in an old store with old things and memories. Now relax and make this place a home for yourself."

He watched Conor running down the street. Even he could sense the pent up anger in the boy. Didn't do a very good job of convincing him, he thought. Still, it's best he just adapt here. Best for all of us.

Running all the way home, Conor didn't even notice that he wasn't breaking into a sweat. Only his rage made him breathless. He found Aunt Emily out back, snipping some late autumn mums for the dinner table centerpiece.

"You're filthy rich and you never helped her! She could have had the best medical treatment and you didn't do a thing!" His voice echoed off the trees and the barn.

She didn't even look at him, but her voice was soft with resignation. "We had to keep you hidden. Poor people attract no notice."

"So maybe you're right about that, but when she got sick ..."

"Medicine would not have cured her. The doctors called it cancer, I know, but it was not. It was the closest thing to diagnose and because she was poor they didn't probe further. But the disease she died from was not from this world. In fact, it wasn't a disease at all. Look, Conor, I walked in that Indian mound, in the hollow hill but a brief moment and my boon was a life long and lasting. But your mother—she stayed for years of our time in that place, and she grew to see it as her home. So did her body. It adapted to that place. Like the others, she was a 'dark one' but even though they are kin to those who dwell in the hollow hills, their life is in this world and their bodies are weak, like the humans who helped give them life. As much as she loved you and helped you grow, her body longed to return to that place where it had known a stronger more vibrant life, where it knew it belonged. Separated from her husband, her heart ached. Cut off from a stronger source of life, her body languished. The moment she stepped that last time from the Indian mound, she was a dead woman."

"What about me? An early death for me too since I lived as long as she did in that place?"

"I think not, Conor," said Emily. "You are not simply a 'dark one.' When Tinker's Grove was founded, the first 'dark ones' were in their teens. In the blood of those strange children flowed the blood of two worlds, but a choice had to be made. Whatever world they lived in, they became part of. Had they stayed near the ocean where their mothers' wombs carried them, had they lived in the mound that looks over the river; had Willie Archer come for them, they would be like him, dark and beautiful. But they were already past puberty and their destiny was this world, and whatever glory they would have had in the halls of the hollow hills faded among their human caretakers, so they became like them. Your mother was thrust between two worlds and that took its deadly toll. But you, you are different. In your blood two worlds meet, human and something else, but the blood of Willie Archer and those who dwell in the hollow hills is far stronger even than those called the 'dark ones.' You are only one quarter human while the 'dark ones' in this town have, as Drake might say, a diluted gene pool. It's obvious you can walk both worlds. In you, something new is happening and your destiny is not Finola's; nor is it the same as any of the 'dark ones.' What must come, will happen indeed; you must accept it."

"Everybody's giving me advice today. Why don't you and Jim get your stories straight? He wants me to fit in. You want me to change into whatever I'm becoming. Dort Martin fears me like I'm the plague."

"Jim's ever the cautious one," snorted Emily, mostly to herself. "But it's Mrs. Martin who makes the most sense. You are what you are Conor; no use running from it. But you will bring fear as you bring change. Of that there can be no doubt." She turned back to her work.

"You all can say whatever you want, but it doesn't matter. I'm going to decide who I am and what I want to be. Nobody in town, not you, the banker, the Abbot, or anybody from Tinker's Grove or under that Indian mound is going to tell me who I am and what I do. I decide, dammit." He turned on his heel, strode away, stopped and started back. "I decide, do you hear me!" Then he stomped away.

"No you don't," whispered Aunt Emily. "It's too important to be only in your hands. You will be what you were meant to be." She looked at the white mums in her hands, threw them down in disgust and went in to fix dinner.

A FATEFUL AFTERNOON

ENVELOPED IN A cloud of rage, Conor's mind was reeling as he left Aunt Emily. He charged through the house, slamming chairs aside and exited the front door. Just had to get away before he said something else to totally ruin his relationship with the old woman. She'd been nothing but decent to him and here he was, yelling at her for everything that was happening to him. Though she did seem to dole out information in little heaps of crap that never ceased to mess up his life.

Couldn't she just understand that he didn't want all this? He remembered tripping down Michigan Avenue to play at the bar, anonymous, no one paying him no mind. Cecy Carr rumpling his hair as he came in, even old Fintan growling at him—that was normal. This was not. There was an ache in his heart. Being all alone truly sucked.

A soft woof at his side startled him. Troubles seemed to have read his mind and followed him out the door. But Conor didn't answer, just absently patted the dog's head. He heard a car coming up the drive. It was Beth.

"I was hoping to find you better," she said, "but you look terrible."

He stood for a moment in silence gazing at her. She was beautiful, great smile with that blond hair.

"I was saying," said Beth, "that you look as if you swallowed a thunderhead."

The ache in his heart just wouldn't go away. "Been a bad day so far," he managed to choke out.

"Yep, can see that," said Beth. "Get in."

Without another word he slipped into the front seat. As they drove away, Troubles tried to follow. Danger smelled strong in the air though the dog couldn't place its source. He broke out into a run and loped after the car, tracking it as far as the Crossroads. Seeing where it was headed, Troubles bounded down the hill towards the Indian mound. The two young pups needed to be stopped; he who dwelt in the mound would know what to do.

"I'm taking you to my favorite autumn place," she said. "The farmer who owns this field where we're going has a little woods in the middle of all this corn. Nobody goes there but me and if anybody comes, we'll hear them rustling through the corn long before they can disturb us."

She had driven straight to Muddy Hollow Crossroads and then took the quarry road to the left. That led to hill country and sure enough, she hadn't gone more than two miles when the road broke into a vista over a little valley.

"Pretty, huh?" she said glancing at Conor.

"Absolutely!" he said. Didn't remember this place from the Wild Hunt of a couple months back. Rory must have steered clear of it. His heart was hammering still with anger, but at least he wasn't clenching his teeth anymore. How could anyone stay angry with such a valley view of trees in orange, yellow, and red autumn splendor?

"Wait till you see this special spot," said Beth with a mischievous grin. "Just enjoy."

She didn't drive fast, allowing Conor to drink in the brilliant colors and the autumn smell. They both had their windows rolled down, it being so unseasonably warm. She turned into a dirt road that only went a couple of hundred yards.

"There," she said. "Pretty awesome don't you think?"

They were looking through a field of dried corn towards a little hill crowned with huge oaks with deep red-brown leaves and brilliant orange and yellow leafed maples. It was like Paradise, thought Conor. A secret place. No one else could disturb them here. Their place. He felt the tension leech out of him.

"Beth, I've never seen anything this beautiful."

"It looks like this just for a few days in autumn, but it's mine. I found it. Jace doesn't know about it. Was going to take you to it anyway today. Packed some stuff to eat; thought we could spend a little time together."

Conor found himself starting to blush. Had to hand it to her, he thought. In Chicago, the girls could be coy, seductive, whatever, but almost never straightforward and truthful. Beth always spoke her mind. Truth to tell, spending time with her made him feel real normal.

"I'm the one that's going to get mad if you tell me you didn't bring your tin whistle. It's a quarter mile to the hill and I thought you could play us something while we walk through the corn."

Conor got to thinking how this was an awful lot like a forced march and so he handed the basket to Beth and reached into his back pocket and took out his tin whistle. "I always carry this with me. It sends me to heaven when I feel like hell. Now listen."

"What's that?" asked Beth, as they walked through the corn.

"Shhh," said Conor. From the thin metal reed came the haunting notes of an old Irish march. Conor played a few moments, stopped and smiled shyly. "You like it?"

"It's beautiful," said Beth. "What is it?"

"'Brian Boru's March.' He was the greatest Ard Righ—that's high king—of Ireland, at least in historical times. See, I am learning something from Aunt Emily's lessons. Know why I love this music? It's almost as if you can hear his horses and chariots—they did use chariots you know—and see his charioteers hurtling through fields of green." Conor put the whistle to his lips and continued piping their way through the dry corn and up the hill.

Very little brush grew under the trees. It was like entering another world. The early afternoon light made the oaks and maples glow—a last burst of life before the coming winter. There was a little glade in the middle of that hill where the sun dappled the grass with its warmth. Beth set up the blanket and lunch there.

"You came all prepared," said Conor, smiling for the first time that day.

"You bet I did, so sit yourself down and dig in."

He sat, but didn't eat just yet. Looking at her, he said, "Thanks. You don't know what this means. Being here with you is—well, you make the bad go away."

She gave him a brilliant smile and threw him down onto the blanket. They laughed as they ate; Beth just talking nonsense stuff, or at least that's how it seemed to Conor. But gradually she drew out of him the events of the morning. As he talked, he relaxed.

Lying there with Beth, looking up at the brilliant maples overhead was just about the coolest moment he ever had in his life. It was perfect. He had kissed her a few weeks before, coming out of the movie theater in Prairie. Kissed her fast and kind of shyly, because he had thought she would mind. She didn't. Hadn't had the nerve to try that again.

He smiled to himself; he was a little bolder in Chicago and couldn't quite figure out his lack of bravery with Beth. That's when she took his hand, the one that had been wounded. Silently, she brought it to her lips and kissed it, right where the tiny white scars of the bite marks still shone. She didn't say a thing, just held his hand with her eyes closed, held his hand up to her cheek.

He stopped breathing. No one had ever kissed him like that. Sure he'd kissed other girls before Beth. And once, Lori, a college sophomore, bar hopping at the *DerryAir*, had come to him and he and she made out a little after hours—like all of thirty seconds—before Cecy surprised them both and sent Lori home with a scolding, but just winked at Conor. This time was different. Beth was so gentle. And it was just his hand. But it meant more.

She still didn't say anything as she traced the dark ribbon of skin up his arm. He was entranced. All he knew next was that his shirt was off and Beth knelt before him tracing the Otherworld mark around his neck, across his heart, and she stopped, her finger on his belt buckle.

Conor knew he was breathing a bit faster than usual, so to keep from being further embarrassed by his body, he quickly took out the tin whistle and said, "Hey, I've got another one for you, if you want to hear it."

Beth laughed out loud. Looking uncomfortable, Conor grimaced but played anyway. "Ah," said Beth, "it's the *Ballad of Willie Archer.*"

Conor's eyes face flashed a wicked little grin, now that he was in charge of the situation again. He stopped playing and said, "Just reminding you about the guy who preys on pretty maidens and takes their virtue by promising them all sorts of wonderful things." He began to play again, though he was very conscious of her presence. Her eyes were closed, her lips, well, her lips were full. Beautiful. The music trailed off and for a moment he watched her in silence. He knew he loved her, or at least would come to love her. No one had ever listened to him like that before.

She opened her eyes. "You stopped. Why?"

"I—I was just looking at you. You're beautiful."

"Ah, Conor Archer, you are a worthy successor to the hero of your folksong." She laughed, but her free hand rested warmly on his thigh.

She looked into his eyes and said, "I don't know what's going to happen with all this, but my life has gotten way better since you came into it. Your music, your smile—even your weirdness."

He kissed her then, long and hard. And she held him close. He loved her and took her there, in the glade with the falling golden leaves. The ache left his chest as they lay together and all the sorrow slipped away. She filled the emptiness of his heart and, for awhile, they lost their souls in each other's arms there in the forest grass, in the heat of a dying autumn day.

They never saw the white owl glide softly to an oak nearby. Nor the crow close behind. Nor the red fox that crept through the grass and glowered at them. Nor the dog that whimpered at the bottom of the hill. Neither did they see the curl of mist, green with corruption that had traveled far from the riverbed through the fields and stalks of corn, circling and waiting nearly invisible around the hill.

None of those things interfered. All had arrived too late. The fox left in a yip of disgust, the crow a soft caw of disappointment. The dog growled at the mist and chased it as it retreated, a soft cackle of cold reptilian laughter echoing in its wake

Only the owl stayed, and it wept at the short-lived love below it, and the bitterness and darkness of life. They never heard its all too human mournful cry of sorrow, of summer past, of innocence lost, of winter coming.

THE WISDOM OF JACE

JACE WAS SURROUNDED by darkness. Willie Archer's, or should he say Madoc's, sudden departure left the cave black as the night sky. Only a sliver of light from the entrance a hundred yards back kept Jace from being paralyzed with fear. Closed in spaces were bad enough for him, but closed in underground places—he shivered. He would have to pick his way carefully back on the ledge above the channel. He knew the ruined ship—that's what it looked like—again—wouldn't have needed much of a draft, but the water surely would be way over his head. And if it was truly Piasa's lair, well, the water wasn't the safest place to be, he figured.

The mound Dweller, the guy who was now calling himself Madoc, had named the ship *The Gwennan Gorn*. Sounded vaguely Celtic to Jace, but he didn't know what it meant. What little he had actually seen of the ship looked more Norselike, almost like a Viking ship but with a higher hull. Single masted, with a galley for rowing. Probably could have held twenty-five people but trekking across the ocean would have been a hell of a trip. Of course, thought Jace, all of this meant that whoever this stranger was, somehow the name Willie Archer and his bogus history just didn't seem to fit so well any more.

That didn't bother Jace as much as one might think. Tinker's Grove, so full of lore and legend, had filled his mind with stories but also had done something else—opened a place in his heart for possibility. Laugh at the tales all you want, he thought, but when they start coming true, you're not the least surprised. Why? Because you've been watching round the corner all the time for something like this to happen. Whatever had happened to him today, it had suddenly gotten a lot easier to see around the corner.

Jace was tingling with excitement. Wasn't so sure about that wisdom stuff from some ancient catfish lord, but no doubt about it, myth was coming to life. He'd always leaned toward action rather than reflection, but he found himself thinking more lately. Looking over his shoulder, he saw the ship faintly illuminated by the motes of light coming from the far away

mouth of the cave. No one would recognize it for what it was unless someone told them. And yet, was it just a ruin, or something more like what he
had seen when that potential migraine was coming on? Then he caught his
own shadow, looming over the ship, bigger than life and wondered whether
he really had the hero in him. Both the Morrigan and the man he now knew
as Madoc had told him to watch over Conor. Like I'm some bodyguard for
hire, he thought. Except Conor was no wimp. He was big, not as big as Jace
himself, but big enough to handle just about anything that came his way.
What does he need me for? he thought. Yet they want me to watch over
him. He stopped for a moment, the exit of the cave now just a few yards
ahead of him. All this in here is shadow, he thought. What's really real?
When I step out into the light, does everything go back to normal? But if
what's here on the shadows of the cave is true, then reality out there is
going to be way different from now on.

He chuckled to himself, thinking that was about the biggest brain
stretch he had ever done. That's when he felt it—a rumble coming deep
from the channel and vibrating the rock. A chill ran up his spine; somehow,
the black water looked even darker, hiding some deep underground lair.
Piasa's coming out, he thought. As ridiculous as that would have sounded
an hour ago, now his fears seemed prescient. He could sense the thing, and,
indeed, it was coming for the water was beginning to move with the pressure from something approaching underneath. Jace began to move swiftly
towards the light. He burst out on to the powdery beach to the left of the
channel.

Walt saved him. Looking back on it later, Walt saved his sorry ass in
the nick of time, and now he'd never have the chance to thank the old fisherman. "There you are," shouted the old man from across the creek. "Been
looking all over for you! Should've tasted that catfish. Best I've ever had
and, dammit, if I'm not the wisest old feller in the river bottoms." He cackled and took a swig of brandy, dancing a little jig.

For Jace, the moment was surreal. Time slowed and he saw the old
man turning slowly in joy, kicking up a bit of dust from the dying weeds.
Hands held high, one clutching a brandy bottle, the other, the old straw hat
he always wore. Jace couldn't remember any sound at all, and all the color
leeched from the day, leaving just a sepia tone splashing everything with a
somber brown.

An explosion of spray from the channel cut off his sight of Walt as
Piasa shot out of the shadowy cave. The mist of the spray held the monster's shape for a moment, enough for both Jace and Walt to see what it
was. Wings and taloned paws turned Jace's body to ice. He couldn't imagine
what Walt was seeing, being face to face with the thing. The old man

dropped the brandy and his mouth bubbled over with the stuff as he tried to gasp in fear. He turned to run, but he was much too late.

As the spray fell back into the creek, the form of Piasa dissipated, but Jace saw a shimmer in the air crossing the water. And then, Walt's slow motion dash to safety stopped abruptly. He screamed and Jace could see bloody marks appear on the old man's back and buttocks. Clawing the bank, Walt was dragged backwards, screaming, into the water.

Jace fell to his knees, paralyzed on the other side. He did nothing as Piasa, now visible once again in the spray of water, shook its prey back and forth in the stream. Blood was everywhere, and, for the first time, Jace could hear again, but it was horror he heard—the sharp snapping of the old man's bones. Walt, himself, had long gone silent. Suddenly, with a rush, Piasa drug Walt under the water, and slid silently back into the cave.

Impotent tears of rage and fear slid down Jace's face. He picked himself up and started swimming across the creek, caring little for whatever monster came from the darkness now. Retrieving Walt's hat and brandy bottle on the other side, he staggered back to the camp fire. Walt was a harmless old man, thought Jace. Granted, most thought he was a useless drunk, but Jace liked him a lot. Got to know him well over the years. Out on the river, in the boat with Walt was always a peaceful time. And Jace had ruined the one dream that Walt had, of catching the big Cat and getting its wisdom, and the dead man didn't even know that his wish never came true. Left this world happy with an illusory dream that itself died aborning.

He remembered little of the trip back to the town dock. As he was tying up the boat, he felt a shadowed presence behind him. Looking up, he saw the huge hulk of Oz, just standing there, blocking out the afternoon sun. Oz always gave Jace the willies. Made him feel embarrassed, like he was condescending to Oz or something because Oz never seemed quite right. Here, Oz was not even looking straight at him, but gazing out over the water, laughing quietly.

"What's so funny?" asked Jace, growling more than talking.

Oz just kept laughing, amused.

"I mean it, Oz; tell me what's so funny."

Suddenly Oz stopped and slowly turned his dull gaze on Jace. "Looks like Piasa got some Walter." His huge mouth broke into a grin, "Got some Walter! Piasa got some Walter! Told you he would." As he laughed, spittle dribbled from his open mouth.

Jace lost it. Oz outweighed Jace by fifty pounds but the football player had no trouble pushing the man back, grabbing his shirt and shaking him till his head bounced back and forth. "Shut up, dammit all; he was a good man!"

Oz didn't respond. He just let Jace's wrath play out. Even Jace couldn't stay enraged at the blank-faced man who refused to get angry. But with a hissing rage, he yanked out an ear bud and whispered in Oz's ear. "You're not as crazy as you look. I don't know what you 'dark ones' know but I'm going to find out. That monster in the river was supposed to be just a legend; yet now it lives in the daylight, and if you had anything to do with wakening it, I'll kill you myself. Walt was my friend, you hear? Walt was my friend." Jace, wiping tears away with the back of his hand, turned and walked away.

He heard Oz say again, "Piasa's got some Walter." Jace turned again, and saw Oz's face change. His dull eyes brightened with a greenish hue, malice crept over his slack jawed visage and he said, "Going to get some Jace too. Better watch out. Piasa's going to get some Jace."

"Not if I can help it," he muttered, and stomped away.

Needing to get his head clear, Jace drove his car around town for a few minutes and then decided to find Conor and his sister. He knew he should file a report on Walt, but he didn't know what to say yet. Besides, Clyde Warner, the local cop, also doubled as one of the town's garbage collectors and collecting trash was what he was busy doing now anyway.

Jace drove up to Madoc's Glen and found Aunt Emily with the Abbot, standing on the porch. No sign of Beth or Conor.

Both of them smiled at Jace but then their smiles withered like the marsh grass. They stood at the edge of the porch as he approached.

"Something's wrong," said the Abbot.

"Something's different," said Emily.

"He's almost like us," they said together.

"Stop!" said the Abbot as Jace reached the lower step. "What's happened, boy? Tell us quickly."

"Tell us everything," chimed in Emily.

"Walt is dead," said Jace. He told them all he knew. At the mention of the catfish, Emily turned to the Abbot with an arched eyebrow. He said nothing but paled a little. They showed no surprise about either the ship or the being known as Willie Archer/Madoc, and as Jace told the horrific details of Walt's death, their faces softened.

"He was a good man," said Emily, "with many sorrows."

"He was one of us," said the Abbot, "and he should never have perished that way."

"It was my fault," said Jace. Grief overcame him and he sank to his knees on the front porch steps. "I should have tried to save him, but I couldn't move. I couldn't do anything." He dropped his head in shame.

After a moment he whispered, "Exactly, who is this Madoc, and what does he want with us?"

The tip of Emily's cane went under his chin and lifted up his head. He almost gasped. Maybe it was the afternoon light, the shadows being extra long or something, but the two above him looked strangely different than they had a moment ago. Emily looked taller and stronger, like an ancient queen, he thought, and the Abbot, his dark blue eyes held a depth of age and strength he hadn't seen before. He felt his weariness lift and strength pour in to him.

Emily moved her cane and rested it on Jace's shoulder. "You are the Champion you know. Isn't that what the Morrigan said to you? Not that I always agree with the witch woman, but here she was right. Want to be a hero lad? Then learn not be be afraid of being afraid. No shame in that."

"As for Madoc," she continued, "he is older than the fathers of the trees on the surrounding hills, ancient of days and a powerful force here in the land. From across the sea, he came, long ago. For most of my life I have known him. My sister loved him."

"Your sister?" said Jace, incredulously. "Finola was your sister? How the hell does that work?"

Just an enigmatic smile from Aunt Emily. "The two of them gave us Conor, your friend and the one you must protect. Just like he said. The charge is yours."

"You will see things now that you have never seen before. You will understand things that you could not possibly comprehend before this day," said the Abbot. "Wisdom is better than a sword, even though it takes more time to learn to wield. The gift you received today was bought with a life. Treasure it."

"You believe that catfish-wisdom crap?" asked Jace with a skeptical eyebrow.

The Abbot scowled, "And after all you've been through and seen today, you still question? When Tinker's Grove was founded, every last person had come from a land where great bodies of water held the 'salmon of knowledge,' an ancient fish that, it was said, would give a hero wisdom if he would but eat of it. Just because this place is in the good old USA doesn't mean the myth is powerless. I have known the catfish you speak of." The Abbot smiled. "Almost caught him once myself. But he is your prize now, and the gift of that ancient dweller of the waters will see you in good stead."

"What about Oz?" asked Jace. "He knows something. You should have seen the look on his face. I'll kill him if he had anything to do with Walt's death."

"Be careful who you wish to kill," said Emily. "Most living things have a side that feels more comfortable away from the good. Perhaps Oz is more elemental than most. Just be cautious. You may need him."

"Do all the 'dark ones' have secrets?" asked Jace. "Does Nora?"

The Abbot laughed and with his laughter, the air cleared and Jace thought they looked normal again. "No, Jace, she's the real deal I think. But she walks in two worlds, and now so do you. You are more on an equal footing now than you know."

THE UNMASKING OF A RIDDLE

A BRIGHT MOON where his eye should have been. That's all he could see. Hurt like sin; what a bitchin' burn. Out of the Sea of Tranquility—he chuckled to himself; at least he remembered that much from science class— out of the moon's Sea of Tranquility came a bird. A big black bird. Or at least its head, and its wicked cool beak. Can't peck it out again, can you, he thought, and chuckled again. But it did. It slashed at him. Writhing within his dream, he screamed in pain.

Cate wrung out an ice cold wash cloth and placed it on the wound again. Low burning lights cast shadows across her face. She turned to Gordy, "I can't calm him. His fever refuses to break. The socket seeps. Where's Drake?"

"I called him an hour ago. Had to leave a message," said Gordon, glancing briefly without much interest over Rafe's prone figure. Kind of good to see the cruel asshole in a bit of pain.

"Got him, Ma," cried Fergal coming in the front door. "Found him in the clinic. Wouldn't tell me why he didn't answer the call. He's getting stuff out of the car."

Gliding in behind Fergal, Dr. Drake paused to set his bag on the coffee table. Not a wrinkle in his immaculate black suit, just a hint of flashing gold around the onyx cuff links.

"I don't pay you to ignore me, doctor," snapped Cate.

"Trust me," he said, "I'll earn more than your money tonight. I was delayed. Looking for something to help dear Rafe here, thinking about what I have to do to ease his pain." He looked at her with a calculating smile. "Thinking about what it will cost me."

"Why is he getting worse?" asked Fergal. "You pumped him full of antibiotics."

"Because, dear boy," said Drake, shooting a sedative into Rafe's arm, "what ails him is not simply physical."

"It was a bird that attacked him," said Fergal, "just a big, black mother of a bird. Nothing more."

Walking by Fergal, the doctor absently patted his head, "If I start thinking your way, you might as well go out and begin digging Rafe's grave."

"What do you mean?" said Cate, "it was an animal attack; my boys didn't mention anything else strange going on."

Drake began to laugh. "You know, Caithness, sometimes you do surprise me. You loll around the river, communing with your precious river demon, and you think it's the only strange being around these here parts. You ought to look more deeply." Drake laughed again. "Now I'm even starting to talk like the locals."

"What do you know about Piasa?" she hissed. "You've never seen it or spoken to it."

"On the contrary. While I'm not as ... close as you seem to be, I know it quite well. I don't want to bed it; I just want to serve it. You've become complacent about your relationship. You think of Piasa as part of the natural landscape. Well, you're almost right, but not quite. It dwells in many places; the river is just one of its haunts. And, getting back to Fergal's question—close your mouth boy, you look all stupid like that—if an Indian manitou out of legend, such as Piasa, can glide through the waters of the Wisconsin River, why do you think it would be a solitary wonder in this valley? Where it comes from, there are other wonders, some good, some bad. I'm especially partial to the bad, for the marvelous creatures from that Otherworld darkness like to explore this world when they get the chance, and they tend to reward those who help them. But the good can be troublesome. Like whatever took the form of the bird that attacked Rafe."

Rafe groaned and struggled on the sofa.

"And apparently still torments his dreams. Ravens or crows never fly at night. This one did. It had a purpose. It harmed only Rafe and it did so in defense of Jason Michaels. Am I right?"

Fergal nodded.

"Well then."

Cate appraised him with a new look. "How does a doctor, a genetic researcher, know so much about all this?"

"I don't make the mistake that moderns make. Knowledge is power and I take it where I can get it, whether it be from science or from myth and magic."

Gordon smirked, "You said genetic research was the wave of the future—now you're getting religious on us?"

Drake deigned a sarcastic glance his way, "Surely, you didn't think that your little backwater hamlet was that attractive to science? Don't get me wrong, I appreciate the financial backing, but you had more here than a cozy research deal. I am a great geneticist but that is just one of the things I am. Science by itself is not enough to keep me interested; myth tech is."

"What the hell is that?" asked Fergal.

"It's what you are all living, stupid boy," said Drake. "There was a time, centuries ago when magic and science strove together. Magic failed; science triumphed. But both wanted the same thing—to subdue reality to the wishes of men. Science won and got cocky. It forgot that magic and myth were real. Realities that belonged more in their realm simply disappeared from view in the eyes of science. Now, look around you. Monsters out of legend, child prodigies from Tinker lore—you live in the midst of this and you think a little genetic research is going to clear all that up? Well, even in your delusion, you're partly right, but mostly wrong."

"Show us," said Cate.

"What's the matter, Cate? Don't you want your boy healed first?" Drake was scrubbing his hands in the sink.

"He can hurt a little while longer, for his stupidity," said Cate, a hunger in her eyes. "I said, show us."

For the first time that night, Drake was excited. He turned to Cate and said, "Look, the mistake science makes is that it ignores realities magic and myth have always been concerned with. Bringing science and magic back together again makes both stronger. Let me explain. I've examined the blood I took from all the so-called 'dark ones' I've tested and compared the samples to Conor Archer's as well as what I believe to be the 'normal' human population of Tinker's Grove. Over the past few months, enough families have come in to the clinic for me to amass a pretty good genetic map of the town."

"And?" said Cate.

"There are differences. Important ones I think. The differences are on the mitochondrial level. Human beings have two genomes. The first genome is found in the DNA of chromosomes. Most research is concerned with this genome. The less exotic and much smaller genome is found in the DNA of mitochondria. Mitochondria are the energy producers of the body. Terribly small, swimming around in individual cellular material, they may once upon a time have been separate living creatures that got hooked up with humanity and liked the symbiotic relationship so much that over time they became part of us. They replicate independently of the cell, using their own DNA."

"You're boring us, doctor," said Gordon. "Get to the point."

"The point is this:" said Drake sharply. "Each mitochondrion has about 50 genes. Sperm cells don't have many mitochondria, just enough to propel them for their short lives, and those mitochondria, for the most part, are eliminated when the sperm joins the egg; the egg kills them. For the most part. That means that a child's mitochondria are identical to the mother's. Mitochondrial DNA is passed down only through the female line."

"I told you, Ma, that biology was not my strong suit. The good doctor here might as well be speaking Greek." Gordon reached for another drink.

"I said," repeated Drake, "for the most part. That's the essential point. Every once in a while, a male mitochondrion does slip through and end up in the human embryo's DNA. That's exactly what has happened with the 'dark ones.' They have DNA on a mitochondrial level that does not match their mother's. That DNA, small amount as it is, is consistent with every 'dark one.' What's more, I've traced back a few generations. Women with that specific DNA do not pass on the unique mitochondrial material to their children. Only the men seem able to do this. That's probably why there are so few 'dark ones' and why the infected ones seem so random. Even the men with that DNA don't succeed very often in transmitting their peculiar mitochondrial genome."

Gordon shook his head. "The 'dark ones' exhibit their strange gifts only briefly. Why? Why do they go dormant, forgetting what they are?"

"I only have some answers, not all of them. The mitochondria with the rogue DNA have a particular effect on the pineal gland—primitive little thing in the brain that we never have known much about. At least I believe it affects that gland. And yet, I postulate that the genetic answer is not the only factor here. Take Conor Archer for instance; his DNA is also interesting. He has more of this genetic material than the other 'dark ones.'

"Did you know that 'dark ones' never marry one another in Tinker's Grove? It's true. Never. I can't find a single example of offspring between two 'dark ones. Except for Conor Archer. The legends tell of it. Whispers in the night around old womens' rockers here in town. A lass, a 'dark one,' who fell in love with someone strange, presumably another 'dark one,' someone who dwelt by the river."

"Old wives' tales," snapped Cate. "The Conor Archer I know left here as a babe seventeen years ago, carried by that whore Finola Archer who got herself in a bad way with a drifter."

"The stories, Cate, never forget the stories," said Drake drying his hands. "You need to listen a bit more closely to rumors. Finola, the whore of two decades ago, is the same as the first Finola Tinker's Grove ever knew."

"Impossible!" said Gordy, taking a gulp of scotch. "Nobody can live that long."

"I should think that what you all know of the river demon would open your mind to other possibilities," said Drake. "We'd have to get a sample of

Finola Archer's DNA but my hunch is that she was a 'dark one' who for some reason was able to pass on all of her own mitochondrial DNA to her son, giving him a double dose as it were. And if his father is another 'dark one' or something else, well, that may be why Conor can manifest certain abilities at this later stage of adolescence. Rather than diminishing, he is growing in prowess. I need to do some more thinking and experimenting on this, but one thing is clear: the 'dark ones' have something 'other' about them. In other words, they are not fully human. That is somewhat outside the bounds of science and, perhaps, within the realm of myth."

Cate arched her brow. "Coming close to talking nonsense again."

Drake looked at her eagerly. "Not at all. In fact, I'm showing you the way. The genetics answer the 'how.' What I mean is that the 'dark ones' mitochondrial DNA uniqueness rests in that one little gene— that powerhouse gene that gives their bodies the energy to manifest unique abilities. But it only answers the physical manifestations. What the 'dark ones' are and why this powerhouse gene morphs them into something more than human, instead of just superior athletic specimens, remains unanswered. I don't think we'll find the answer simply in science; we'll find it, instead, in myth. The town's ancestral stories are as valuable as lab specimens."

Drake took her hands. "We can tweak the genetic code all we want, try recombinant DNA till we run out of lab samples, but something else is operating here, and until we know what it is, we cannot unlock the secret of the 'dark ones.' But just as Piasa has turned out to be real myth here in these lands, so I think we will find the 'dark ones' to be similar. They came with the Tinkers over the sea. Legends, Cate, of shapeshifters from the sea who took the bodies of women and wooed the menfolk of the land. Beautiful they were and strange. Children were born of that union and traveled here. And only the males of that union could pass on the powers of the People of the Sea. They're called the Roan, and you might have some of them here. Haven't you really ever taken a close look at those tales? What the 'dark ones' relationship truly is to the rest of the townspeople has yet to be discovered, but the stories the Irish tell of men's kinship with strange creatures needs to be examined more closely."

"So the lab is just an expensive front?" said Cate. "Like Gordy says, you used me and my money to set up a useless research facility?"

"That's where you're wrong," said Drake. "The science is essential, but it's just part of the answer. Watch and I'll show you."

From the chain around his neck, he took out the dagger entwined with bone and wood. The red ruby marking the hilt gleamed brightly in that sterile place. Drake gently laid the dagger on Rafe's chest. "I come from an old family from over the sea, and we have many heirlooms. Remember the day you sent me down to the river a couple of months ago, Cate? No doubt you wanted me to meet Piasa. Don't look so surprised. I'm not the only one with ulterior motives."

Drake continued, amused at Cate's embarrassed look. "I did meet the one the Indians called the Underwater Panther, the Devourer of Souls, just as you wished. We renewed an old family acquaintance. Yes, indeed, we really are old friends. This ancient dagger is a link to it. Magic? Perhaps a more primitive time might have called it that, but it's just a communication device to the Otherworld, bound to Piasa from days of old. However the demon first manifested itself here in this land, whether through the conjuring of Native Americans or some other way, it is, in fact, the Worm that dwells at the foundations of the world. I knew that the minute I set eyes upon it. It is everywhere. In every land, in every time and place. There is nowhere it cannot be for it gnaws at the roots of the world. The bone on this dagger is its bone; the wood entwined comes from the roots of the Tree of the World gnawed by the same Worm. My family has always worshiped the beast down through the centuries. It is so powerful! Dear Cate, what the demon won't do for mere love, it will do for adoration. Watch."

Drake stretched out his hand over the dagger, bent low and breathed on the talisman. Tracing his finger counter clockwise over the ruby, he muttered simple words,

> *Out of the darkness, come to me;*
> *Out of the night, crawl to me,*
> *Dragon of earth, Worm of the sea,*
> *Come to me, come to me and heal this boy.*

A psychic shock wave emanated from the house and spread in a circle for hundreds of yards, silencing every living thing with fear. Only one thing did not shrink from its summons. From the river came the mist, just a tendril, but it quickly snaked its way across the lawn into the house. It looked like luminescent green algae, pausing briefly over the dagger and then hovered over Rafe's ruined eye. Only a moment, and then it plunged into the empty socket. A sigh escaped Rafe's lips like steam escaping from a pipe, and he was still. Fergal reached out to touch the mist, but Drake slapped his hand away. It spun over the socket of Rafe's eye for mere moments and then withdrew from the house.

It never made a sound, but all heard its whispering voice in their hearts, "A debt to be paid. Always, a debt to be paid." When the echo died away, they all let out a collective sigh of relief.

"He'll be fine now," said the doctor looking at the wound site scraped clean of corruption. "Of course, as a precaution, we'll have to continue the antibiotics for the physical infection, but Piasa has successfully consumed whatever Otherworld poison that fell bird transmitted to Rafe. Not to worry here."

"It just did that for you?" said Cate, incredulously as a jealous tone crept into her voice. "You just asked it and it did that for you?"

"Of course not," said Drake. "There's always a price; you heard it speak yourselves."

"What do you give a demon that heals your son?"

"Food," laughed Drake. "With this one, it's always about food."

"I've asked much from it over the years, and it has never demanded a price from me."

Drake reached over and gently grabbed her chin. "Why should it when you gave it yourself? Such a beauty you are. That's a gift to feed on for a thousand years."

Cate pulled away.

"Don't worry," said Drake. "This favor was done for me. I'll have to pay the price; I'll have to feed the beast. And I think I know how I'm going to do it so all of us benefit from it. I can't do much more with blood tests. I need ... specimens of the pineal gland. Understanding the biology will help me understand how the magic will work."

"You'll kill the 'dark ones?'" asked Fergal.

"For science," said Drake. Then he laughed. "And for Piasa."

Rafe sighed in contentment. It had come to him again and taken away his pain. "No need for perfect sight," it had whispered to him. "For when I need you, I will be your eyes and ears. Only let me in to stay a little while and I can make you stronger than your wildest dreams."

Rafe smiled in silence.

"There will be things to hurt. We can do that together," said the mist as it withdrew and backed itself down to the river.

A LESSON UNLEARNED

AS THE TENDRIL of mist sunk itself in the pus-filled socket of Rafe's eye, the sun dipped beneath the horizon. Not so far away, Conor watched the sun set between the bluffs from the picnic table out back of Aunt Emily's house. He and Beth had driven up about an hour and half ago to find Jacc, the Abbot and Aunt Emily in some serious conversation on the porch. Jace looked in real pain. Sounded that way, too, as he brought them up to speed on Walt. But Conor could tell something else was bothering him. Jace wouldn't answer many questions about the incident at White Creek. Instead, Jace kept looking at him and Beth kind of funny like, like he suspected something. Probably being paranoid, thought Conor, but Jace was real quiet after sketching out the horrific events up White Creek way. The Abbot seemed in a hurry to get Jace down to the police to file a missing person's report. Beth was worried Jace would be seen to be a suspect, but the Abbot assured her that wouldn't be the case. It wasn't public knowledge, but bad accidents were known to happen around White Creek; the police could probably be convinced.

Aunt Emily still wasn't speaking to him, so he made himself scarce after the twins and the Abbot left. Even Troubles had abandoned him. The dog, usually like glue to his leg, had gotten off somewhere.

He heard the phone ring a little while later. Emily came out shortly thereafter and crisply announced that the Abbot wanted to see her up at the Abbey. Conor should go ahead and eat without her.

All alone, he thought, as the last orange glimmers faded in the night sky. Got cold quick in the autumn, but he didn't feel like going in yet. He felt restless inside, and, surprisingly, a little irritated with Jace. Just didn't like the strange look his friend was giving him, almost like he was jealous or overprotective or something with Beth. Conor spit on the ground. Pisses me off, he thought. Not good enough for his sister. He knew it was unfair to think like that, but that's what he felt. Feeling a little ashamed about not

being more upset about Walt. Didn't really know how close Jace was to
him.

Conor scanned the sky to clear his head of those thoughts. The news
about Walt shook him, but not enough to send away the other thoughts of
the day. He caught himself shaking his head in wonder. What a day! Beth
was just the greatest and though he ought to be feeling guilty about the
afternoon, he wasn't—not in the least. In fact, he was pretty proud of himself. The more he recalled the memory, the more Jace and his bad news
slipped away. Beth was his, and by God, if he didn't love her! What he
loved just as much was the fact that with her this afternoon, he hadn't
sensed a hint of Otherness around. He had gotten used to it, that low hum
of life he could sense underneath all things. Aunt Emily had used some
Celtic word—*neart*—to describe it; the "song of creation" she called what
he had sensed. But now, all was quiet and he was glad. Peaceful evening,
just the few crickets left alive chirping in the brush, and the far off hoot of
an owl.

He forced himself to think a while on Walt. Thought he owed that to
the old man. Said a little prayer for him even. But he couldn't think long on
him without thinking of Piasa, the beast that had greeted his advent into
Tinker's Grove. To hell with demons and other fey stuff. To hell with
shadows and things he had never met before coming to this place.

He remembered Beth's kiss, and her smell. He remembered them
holding each other, and what they did. He smiled.

"So fine you think yourself," said a voice. Conor jumped up off the
picnic table and looked around. Nothing and nobody.

"Struttin' gentleman you are," came the voice again, the brogue waft-
ing on the twilight breeze.

"Get on out here, Rory, wherever you are, so I can see you," said
Conor, pissed beyond belief that Rory should come and spoil what was an
excellent day.

"Yesterday, you could have seen me wherever I walked," said the
voice. "Now, you'll see me when I want you to."

Conor felt a hand gently slap his face. "See what I mean?" said the
voice.

"I fought you even, last time," shouted Conor into the evening twilight. "And I can do it again."

"Think not," said Rory and this time punched Conor in the chest.

Letting out a whoosh of air, Conor sat his butt back down on the picnic table.

"Where are you?" said the boy.

"Right behind you."

Conor swivelled in his seat and there was Rory sitting on the other side of the table like he was waiting for some fried chicken from Aunt Emily's kitchen.

"What do you want?" asked Conor, a little taken aback that Rory had surprised him.

"That's what I should be asking you," said Rory. There was no smirk on his face this evening. Conor could only see the even white tips of Rory's teeth behind his partially open lips. "You stupid idiot," said the biker. "Do you have any idea of what you've done?"

Conor felt himself blushing though there was no way in hell Rory could know anything about what happened between him and Beth that afternoon.

"You bedded that Michaels' girl underneath the oak trees in your secret little hiding place."

"None of your business, you bastard," said Conor, spitting out the words even as his face grew hot with embarrassment.

"Not that I'm in the habit of following the pecadillos of the randy young men around here, but what you did was so unfortunate."

"Why?" said Conor, a little defensive that his voice was rising. "We care about each other; in fact, I think I love her. I've been here long enough to know she's the best thing about this whole place."

"First of all, your God won't look too kindly on this, and secondly, doesn't he say somewhere in your precious Bible that when these things happen, the two shall become one flesh?"

"I'll marry her, you piece of filth," said Conor. "I don't use women."

Rory laughed for the first time, but it was humorless. "I don't care about you boffing the babes who wander into your life; your God knows I've done my share with them. It's the fact that you did it with love. Don't you see, little man, actually loving them, two becoming one flesh as it were, really caring for them—all that means an alliance? And we just can't have that Conor. Our kind cannot abide that. We were not meant to love them or be with them. We were meant to rule them."

"Bet your brother doesn't feel that way. He loved my mother."

"Ah," said Rory, "so he did, but she was a 'dark one.' At least she was kin to the People. I don't deny your point. But your father would say the same as me, just phrase it more gently. Make no mistake, though, he's as worried as I am."

"He knows?"

"He was there."

"Oh, God," moaned Conor. "Who else knows?"

"I'm sure Emily does by now, and the Abbot, since I just got back from whispering it to him as he strolled the Abbey grounds. Troubled he was before that news; now I think I've ruined his evening. Probably is filling in old Emily right this moment. They really ought to know though. Why, even your dog knows. Of course, you missed the mist as well. You were … preoccupied, but since it was a trailing wisp of vapor from the river around that hill with a life of its own, chances are Piasa knows. And if you think I'm unhappy, hard telling what that thing thinks of all this. Might be thinking my kin and the humans are forming an alliance. Your father never let that happen; that's why he sent your mother away when she insisted on dwelling in this world. A fragile peace, but you broke it this afternoon. Congratulations!"

"It's none of your business," said Conor.

"Step back a bit from your surliness, lad," said Rory. "Your Abbot could tell you better than me. It's all about belief and action. Believe in something and you open your heart to its power. It works. Your Aunt Emily is no 'dark one', but she taps into something for her power. Scares the shit out of me, though I think I could take her." He laughed a little. "Feisty little thing. Always has been. But back to my point. You don't want your gift. You've walked away. Already, I've shown you how diminished you are because you do not believe."

"I believe in Beth," said Conor defiantly.

"Oh please," said Rory, "you make my point. You opened your heart to her and she makes you feel all warm and tingly. Fine. You've got whatever power she's got to give. But your lack of faith in yourself and who you are affects both of our worlds. That ribbon of skin on you that moved and glowed with the light of the Otherworld is quiet now. You neither feel nor hear it—that song of creation. It's not your lust that got you into trouble here—it's your love. You put your faith in her and a part of you is dying, just like it does for all the 'dark ones.' They are incomplete, dead to their true kin and damaged goods in the eyes of humans. You think the girl makes you alive, but you are choosing death." Rory put his face up to Conor's and hissed, "And risking death for us all. Piasa will not be quiet, and I fear what it will do."

"You don't get it," shouted Conor, standing up and pushing back the biker. "You showed me the Otherworld, Rory, wonders I couldn't possibly dream of and all it did was spook me. But Beth is real. She anchors me here in the world. I don't deny you offer me cool stuff. I admit it intrigues me as much as it frightens me, but Beth's the real deal. I don't hurt when I'm around her. I'm not scared when I'm around her. And best of all, when I'm with her, I'm not with you, or the father I've barely met, or all the other weird shit that goes on around here. When I'm with her, I'm just fine."

Rory sneered. "For a while you believed. Belief in what I showed you opened you up to a new reality and your body responded. You felt yourself doing things you never thought possible. You touched the Otherworld through your music; that must have been what kept you from withering away like the other 'dark ones,' kept you open as it were." He gave Conor a feral grin. "I just pushed you over the edge. And look what you began to do—your own wonders, starting to make your own legend. Go back now, and you will fade into mediocrity."

They both heard the front door slam. "Emily's back," said Rory. "Best you go in and get something to eat. Going to need your strength in the days to come, when the results of your foolishness today come marching home."

Rory faded into the night and left Conor standing there, good feelings gone, dread the only hunger in the pit of his stomach.

AN UNEXPECTED PASSENGER

JASON HADN'T SAID a word since they left the Abbot at the police station to finish jawing with Clyde Warner, the cop who had taken Jace's statement. No major questions. Of course, Jace simply told him that Walt had gone missing after they had caught that huge catfish. The policeman seemed skeptical at first, but the Abbot started talking and explaining and soon everything seemed just fine. Jace didn't drive directly home. Too many questions. Too many things to say to his sister. So he headed up towards the Abbey.

"Gotta go to the cemetery," he explained to Beth. "You can look out from that hill, see the Indian mound and just make out White Creek. Gotta do that for Walt."

"It's almost dark," said Beth in a low voice. She could sense the tenseness in her brother. She didn't think it was just over Walt's terrible death.

For a while, neither spoke.

"You were with him, weren't you?" he asked.

"What do you mean?" she said, thankful it was indeed dark enough that he couldn't see her blush. "Conor and I went and had a picnic, that's all." She was irritated at her own defensiveness. She punched him lightly on the shoulder. "We're going together. Don't be the jealous brother."

"Don't touch me. I'm telling you, Beth, I'm serious. Were you with him? You know what I mean. I see how you look at him. I saw both your faces just a while ago."

Beth tossed her hair and turned to him, "Listen to me big brother by all of two and a half minutes; I'm your twin and we think a lot alike, but my personal life is not yours. Who the hell do you think you are? Besides, he's your friend, isn't he? Isn't he entitled to a bit more respect from you?"

Jace was breathing hard, biting his tongue to keep from yelling at her. He turned and tried to say something, but the white flash in the front of the windshield caught his eye and he instinctively put on the brakes.

Too late. The thump was crunching and heavy.

"My God, you hit something!"

The headlights shone upon a body dressed in white lying in front of the car. Beth and Jace rushed forward, but already the figure was moving. A hand reached up and lifted back red hair. The Morrigan, her beautiful face beaming at the twins, stood up and smoothed her white dress.

"Can't a girl even cross the road safely?" she purred.

"I didn't see you! I couldn't stop! Are you hurt?" stammered Jace, greatly relieved that she wasn't dead.

"Mind if I hitch a ride?" The Morrigan didn't wait for an answer. She slipped into the back seat.

Shaking, the twins got back in the car.

"Heard you talking, I did," said the Morrigan, laughing lightly. "Voices on the wings of night. Such arguing, such accusation. But tell him, girl. You should, you know. Tell him what it was like."

"I don't know what you're talking about," said Beth.

"I saw you from the sky; I heard your cry."

Beth shook as she listened to the unearthly voice.

"You should have saved your power; it is wasted on him. You can never have Conor Archer."

"Shut up you bitch," snarled Beth. "Shut up. You make it seem dirty and dark."

"Well, it has that potential, foolish child. He is not for you, you know. Cannot have him. And I will not let you." She reached out a beautiful milk white hand to touch Beth's blond hair.

Beth leaned against the door. "Don't touch me."

The Morrigan smiled so brightly that even the night seemed to recede a bit. "Stop the car."

Jace did as he was told.

"Get out, my Champion. The girl goes on alone here. I have business with you."

"No," said Jace. "Say what you have to say in front of us both."

"So brave," said the Morrigan with a light laugh. "What Conor means to the People of the Hollow Hills, to this town, and perhaps to many others was nearly ruined this day by your sister, and by him, though he is a man and barely thinks with the brain he has been given. She enticed him, wooed him, bedded him. Nearly killed him, not with her passion but with her need. Turning him from his road. That cannot be."

The Morrigan got out of the car, opened the driver's door and yanked Jace out with one hand and threw him into the weeds on the side of the road. "I said, 'Get out!' and I meant it."

Dazed, Jace didn't move, but the Morrigan stuck her head in the car and spoke to Beth. "I hope you understand my message."

Beth slapped the woman in her face. "I'm not afraid of you. And I'm not letting what happened this afternoon be turned into some romp in the hay. I love him, and you know something. I think he loves me."

"I have no doubt of that, young lass," said the Morrigan with a taut smile, unaffected by Beth's strike. "But he'll love you to your death. Of that I'm certain."

"Then I'll die. But at least it won't be because some illegal immigrant pagan goddess, far from her real home, tries to manipulate me."

"If you knew me half as well as I know you, you'd understand that I feed on your rage. I am the Morrigan, and death walks with me. When you breathe your last, I'll be there. Now go. I'll send your brother back to you when I am finished with him."

She pulled Beth over to the steering wheel, slammed the door, waiting until the car pulled away.

The Morrigan walked over to Jace who was just standing up. "My Champion," she said and began to laugh. "So jealous of your sister, having someone else to love and care for her. Is that what you need? No ordinary woman for you I think. You are too strong, too determined, and now, well now you are wise, though how much you do not yet know. But the gift you received this afternoon only enhances my attraction to you. Great warrior you shall be. With me by your side. Don't be too angry with Conor. He's a man, like you. And you are all alike. You find us irresistible."

As she spoke she caressed his face and he was mesmerized. She was beautiful, and his breath caught whenever she touched him. Her face swam in his vision, and he felt her kiss him. His mouth opened and pressed against hers. She smelled like fragrant flowers in the night. Falling, he felt himself on the ground. When he opened his eyes, he found her straddling him, unbuttoning his jeans.

His hands reached up and grabbed her arms. He flipped her over on her back. She laughed, until he bent down and kissed her deeply once again. Then he put his massive hand around her throat and squeezed. Her eyes grew wide, not with fear but admiration.

"No doubt you could kill me with a flick of your wrist," he snarled. "No doubt you could make me love you here and now. But you won't. For some reason you need me, and that's the only leverage I have. I don't deny it—you are the most beautiful woman I have ever seen, but I'm scared to death to hold you. You say I have wisdom; so did Willie Archer, or Madoc, or whatever we're calling him now. I don't feel that wise, but I do know something. If I lay with you now, I'm done, I'm finished. I'll just be your creature. And you'll not have me that easily."

He stood up and backed off. Springing to her feet, she reached out and caressed his face again. "You are wise. I would rather have you in thrall to me, but this will do, for I think you find me irresistable, and for a while, that is enough. But mark my words, Jason Michaels, my Champion. You will love me. Either like this," and she kissed him on the forehead, "or you will love me as Walter learned to love me this afternoon."

Her face fell in upon itself in age and ruination. Back bent, milk white skin turned grey and spotted, beautiful nails now just crippled claws. "Yes," she whispered looking into his shocked face, "the last thing he saw in the jaws of Piasa was my eyes in this empty husk of mine, this face of death. And now I go to mourn his passing, to wash the death from his lonely bones."

A rush of air, an explosion of black feathers, a caw in the night and all that was left of the Morrigan was her white dress at Jace's feet.

He bent down and picked it up, his hands gently touching the fabric. For some reason he thought of Nora, and the thought of her tugged at his heart. He felt her voice in his soul calling him home, but it was faint and far away—only a wish and a dream. The dress was in his hands. He brought it up to his nostrils and inhaled.

"That's just the problem," he said to himself. "I know I love the witch woman whether in beauty or in battle, in love or in death. But whatever happens, it will be on my own terms." Dropping the dress to the ground, he began the long walk home, the grieving for Walt forgotten, his heart aching for her arms, his fingers absently touching his lips.

SIGHT AMIDST BLINDNESS

CONOR THOUGHT HE ought to go in and speak to Aunt Emily again to see just how much she knew. He rounded the porch and was about to go up the stairs when he thought of Troubles. Where had that dog gone to? All he'd have to do is reach out and touch the Lab's mind. He'd done that before, many times since that first time in August, when he had chased Rory through the woods. But now he resisted. Hadn't done that in weeks. No more of that. If doing so would come without the price of weirdness, but it didn't. So he called the dog the old fashioned way, shouting out his name.

Opening the door, Conor saw the warm light from inside spread out onto the shadowed porch. He stepped across the threshold and turned back, hearing the sound of running paws—something on all fours. He smiled as he saw the figure of Troubles appear in the evening twilight.

"Come here, boy," he said. He brushed a strand of black hair off his forehead and placed his hands on the door post, standing exactly on the threshold of the door itself. Troubles vanished before his gaze, and he grasped the doorpost as the world shifted.

Something else met his eye. A vista of the river valley, starlit and brightened by a crescent moon. He wasn't flying. It was more like a GPS view of things. Conor could vaguely feel himself straddling the doorway but he couldn't let go. Rory had been wrong. It wasn't so easy to get rid of his gift, no matter how hard he tried. His vision descended, passing over the Indian mound, and settling along the path of White Creek. Slowly he drifted over the waters and more slowly still, until he came upon a little beach by a cave, hidden he suspected, in regular light but very visible to him now. He was intrigued by the beach. The white sand positively glowed in the dark, white as the driven snow. Someone was there. A bent old woman in rags, washing something in the water. She was keening a soft, tuneless song and Conor knew her at once. The Morrigan, in her guise as crone. As soon as he thought her name, she lifted up her head to the sky, but it was him she was looking at. Blackened stumps of teeth broke into a rotten smile of despair. "So glad you've come, boy. So glad you've come to see me at my real work."

Conor wasn't afraid. He had a sense that he was there and not there, that his body was safe in Aunt Emily's house. None the less, he felt a premonition of horror gripping his gut. The stench of evil was everywhere.

"Yes, yes," cackled the old woman, "this is its house, the home of the Underwater Panther, the Devourer of Souls. It eats and I clean the plate. The leftovers must be cleansed." Whatever she was washing in the water was proving difficult to cleanse for her gnarled arms pushed and her broken hands scrubbed so terribly hard.

She resumed her tuneless wail and lowered her head. Conor glanced around. Upon the beach were broken bones, and he had a sinking feeling in the pit of his stomach that they weren't animal remains. The Morrigan lifted a white femur bone into the sky and laughed. "Dust you are and to dust you shall return." She smashed the bone on the ground and used a rock to pulverize it.

That was when Conor nearly vomited. As he realized the truth. That wasn't white sand on the beach. It was bone dust. The dust of Piasa's victims.

Seeming to sense his thoughts, the Morrigan looked up at him again. "I don't take their lives. I just mourn their passing, and wash their bodies clean. I am the Morrigan you see, lover of battle, goddess of war, keeper of the dead."

She reached down into the water and picked up a skull. There were bits of hair on it, dark hair, and with a rush Conor saw he was seeing not something in the past but something yet to come. He had thought it was Walt's bones he was looking at, but this skull was of someone younger, much younger.

"Yes," said the Morrigan. "You are right, Conor my love. Things yet to come. Terrible things. He was so young and had so much to give. Now the Worm that dwells at the roots of the world has him. Its power is great and growing. It knows no life it cannot have if it wills it. It sets its gaze on this little part of the world. You have roused it, Conor. You have brought its rage to the surface again. Everything your father did to quiet this beast has been for nought. Your presence here has awoken it, and the ancient pact is broken. It will hunt again, and before it gets you, it will kill your friends and all who are near."

He could hear her weeping as she washed a spot that would not come clean on the skull. The broken old thing seemed so sad. Conor's heart ached. Until his vision strayed toward the cave. It was then he saw the eyes, deep in the dark. Green and reptilian, full of knowledge that no human had ever known. They grew bigger in his sight, and he knew it was moving toward him. He couldn't breathe and he couldn't break the hold on the door. His arms were paralyzed.

A body crashed into him and he found himself on the floor looking up into the face of Troubles. He buried his face in the dog's fur.

"What is all this nonsense?" said Aunt Emily coming into the hallway. Tsking, she walked by them and shut the door. She turned and looked at Conor getting to his feet, absently scratching the dark skin snaking up his arm. Catching her breath, she stared at his face.

"You saw something," she said. "There in the doorway."

He nodded, tears coming down his face.

"You stood on the threshold of the door and you saw. Oh Conor, did you do that on purpose? You have the Sight. Any in between place can trigger it. Thresholds are thin places. And what did you see, what troubles you so?"

"Death is coming," said Conor. "I brought it, and it's coming, and those who are young are going to die."

CONFESSION—GOOD FOR THE SOUL

CONOR WENT WALKING that Monday night, up towards the Abbey. Took him a while. Nothing on the road. No cars, no animals. Just him and a very subdued dog. Quiet night. For once, he was grateful that Aunt Emily hadn't pressed the issue of Beth. He could tell she knew. Maybe it was the Abbot who told her, like Rory said. But she said nothing to him. Biding her time, no doubt. Waiting to ambush him with guilt.

Not far from the Abbey, he found a white dress lying in the road. Maybe he wasn't the only one who had a little fun today. Stupid ass thought; he kicked himself. Especially where he was going. Troubles snuffled the dress and let out a low growl.

The Abbey Church was open; always it was open. No human was there at that hour, at least not that Conor could see. The thin iron bars that separated the monastic enclosure from the rest of the church were barely visible in the dim light cast from the sanctuary lamp. The gate into the enclosure was locked. Everyone asleep for the night.

Except me, thought Conor as he slid into a pew. He really did like sitting there in the dark alone, but not really alone. The tabernacle glowed a sparkling gold in the candlelight. Always when he came here, he could sense the Presence. No matter what he had done, how he felt, he could always feel the Presence envelope him.

Pulling out his tin whistle he began to play a mournful tune. Loved the way it echoed in the church. He hadn't played long before he saw a cowled figure come out of the hallway the monks used to enter the church.

The Abbot's baritone voice wafted across the cavernous space, "Carry the man who's born to be king, over the sea to Skye."

Conor stopped, "You know the song."

"All about Bonnie Prince Charlie, lad."

Conor grinned ruefully. "Sometimes I feel like him, lost and all alone, with a lot of enemies around."

The Abbot grunted. "You're nothing like him, Conor. He was a feckless fop. Snookered the Highlanders into following him; spent his last years as a dreaming drunk in France. What a waste. So why are you here, lad?"

"Just wanted to, I guess. With all that happened today; you know, Walt and everything."

"Ah, yes, Walt. Truly a tragedy; one among many today, I'm afraid." The Abbot's eyes glinted in the twinkling light.

"What do you mean?"

"Walt wasn't the only one who wanted something he shouldn't have."

Conor was thankful it was too dark for the Abbot to see his embarrassment. "So, Rory was right. You know."

The sadness in the Abbot's voice was palpable. "I know, and I grieve for you Conor."

"Nothing to be grieving for. I love her."

"None the less, it was wrong. Ah, stay silent for a moment. It was wrong not because of the wonder and the pleasure, for surely we were made to be united so. But it was wrong because it was out of time, out of sync, before you could possibly be ready. You cannot love that way before you know who you truly are. There's a selflessness needed, and you don't have that yet. Too young. Too inexperienced. And because your destiny is tied into a very important pattern in the weaving of the world, so much sadness will come from your rashness, I fear."

"What do you know of it? Everybody always telling me who I should be, what I've done right, what I've done wrong. I'm sick of it all."

"And yet you're here."

"Yeah, I am."

"Funny thing about sin," said the Abbot. "It's always more than it looks. Tastes good to the tongue, but often, it's really bitter in the stomach."

"What do you mean?"

"Besides the fact that the God who dwells in the tabernacle you're looking at doesn't like to see love forced too fast?"

"There's more wrong than that?"

"You broke the pact, Conor," said the Abbot. "You broke the peace forged between Piasa and your father long ago."

Conor flared. "What pact, and how could I have known? No one ever tells me anything." His bitter tone hung in the air.

"Like I said," continued the Abbot. "Sin has unintended consequences. Your actions have let loose a great evil on the land. Your father came here centuries ago and found this valley fair and verdant. Only the presence of the water demon marred the landscape and even it, back then, was mostly somnolent. Your father knew what the manifestation of the beast was. He had met it before back in the land he came from. Those pagans who worshipped the ancient forces called a demonic appearance, like Piasa, the Worm that dwelt at the roots of the world. Evil, gnawing, never sated, always hungry. Pops up now and then everywhere, looking different mind you, but always the same Worm. But your father and his people know better. After all, their kind fell with it long ago."

"The story you told me when I got here was true?"

"More or less," said the Abbot. "Words don't always capture the true reality."

"No wonder my father thinks he's damned, if his people fell from heaven during the Great War. That would make Piasa ..."

"At least a manifestation of the one who once was called Light Bearer and now is the Adversary of all that is good and holy and true. But not all who fell with the great angel were damned. Your father's people have been known to humans for ages, called by many different names, but always held to be beautiful and good, terrifying, but not evil. I think our judgement is more correct than your father's."

"So he made a pact with the devil?"

"That the force of evil called Piasa would not infect the land or terrorize its inhabitants for as long as your father and his people dwelt here. Unless ..."

"What? Unless what?" asked Conor.

"Piasa has always feared humans. We are the unknown equation in the balance of the universe. So capable of good, but so prone to evil. It cannot figure us out, and so it feared an alliance between your father's people and humanity. What it feared would come of such a pact I do not know, yet it wrung a crucial concession from your father: No member of your father's community, small as it was, could consort with humans either through illicit liaison or through marriage. A strange concession but one which your father granted immediately. He was not fond of humanity in general."

"What happened?" asked Conor.

"The 'dark ones' happened. Your mother happened," answered the Abbot. "When they came with the Tinkers from over the sea, all changed. Because your father knew they were the offspring of couplings between humans and his kind, he saw their potential. But cut off from any real contact with his people, they withered as they grew. Full of promise that could never become reality. Until he met Finola O'Rourke, a 'dark one' who captured his heart. He lay with her and from that embrace came you, Conor. He knew that such a tryst broke the pact, and so he tried to hide you. Actually, he succeeded, for the attack on you and your mother by Piasa so long ago was not the rage of a double-crossed demon, but simply the anger of a hunter losing its prey. It never knew what you really were, until you came back here. It saw a power in you that no humans have; it wondered and it questioned, and it watched. It was watching this afternoon, and now it suspects strongly what you are. It holds your father accountable for the pact, and the truce appears, in Piasa's black heart, to be weakening and the river demon grows more suspicious. It is nearly convinced of what I, your father, Aunt Emily, and even Rory know already—the pact is irreversibly broken."

"What happens," said Conor, "when Piasa decides to act?"

"All hell breaks loose," said the Abbot. "Literally. This part of the world will be consumed by its hunger and we will all be changed. In thrall to it."

"I did this."

"Yes," said the Abbot, "you did."

"But I didn't know."

"Do you think the Devourer of Souls cares about your will or your knowledge? Your actions broke the truce, and Piasa is gathering its strength, biding its time." The Abbot reached through the iron gating and touched the side of Conor's head. "This happened because you rejected who you are."

"I don't want to be me."

"I know. Few who are young do. But it doesn't change reality. You were born to be more than simply human. You are different even from your father."

"My father," said Conor bitterly, "doesn't even think enough of me to reveal himself."

"He is a great prince of his kind, and has his reasons," said the Abbot.

For a moment, Conor was silent. "There is nothing I or we can do to stop what will happen?"

"I didn't say that. All I'm saying is that Piasa will be unleashed upon us. What happens next will indeed depend on you and others and how all of us react. But make no mistake; the darkness that Piasa represents is rising."

"I've seen something terrible coming. I've seen the 'dark ones' dying." Conor's voice was barely a whisper.

"So gifted," said the Abbot, pity in his voice. "So gifted and cursed with vision. I know what you saw, boy, for I have seen it too."

"Can't you fix this?" said Conor. "You always seem to be able to fix everything."

"There is only, and has ever been or will be, one Savior, Conor. And he tends to work things to the good in the most difficult way possible. No, much suffering is coming. All I can offer you tonight is forgiveness," said the Abbot gently.

Conor bowed his head in silence for a moment, and then began to whisper to the Abbot, kneeling at his feet, the Abbot's hand reaching through the iron barrier to touch the head of the boy.

Conor felt the Abbot's touch and it seemed to him that time ceased for a while. He wept his sorrow and confusion, all the while grateful for the hand of forgiveness on his head.

The Abbot stood straight, face in shadow, lifting his hand silhouetted by the Tabernacle glowing lightly in the dark. "I absolve you from your sins, Conor ..." As the Abbot made the Sign of the Cross, the monk backed away, ethereal in the dim light, no longer the farmer priest who milked cows and plowed fields, but something older, more ancient, and from his hand came power and in Conor's heart spread a growing peace.

NIGHT VISIONS

THE NIGHT CROW flies through the starlit sky, arcing over the tiny town of Tinker's grove. No darkness or structure shrouds her vision. Seeing all as she flies high. There, over the house of Jason and Beth Michaels. The night crow hisses in fury at the sleeping girl, a slight smile turning up her lips, peaceful in her own doom. "Conor," whispers the girl in her sleep. Peck out her eyes, thinks the vengeful bird, and would have had not the night crow spotted her Champion walking up the street to the darkened house.

Her soft cawing laughter was not mockery. The night crow loved her warrior, though gently amused by his own innocence. Should see him again, thinks the soaring bird. Perhaps less intense this time. Age, and much practice, has a way of making a woman too forward and familiar. The night crow laughed at her own wit.

And found herself over Nora Martin's bedroom where the 'dark one' slept soundly, dreaming of holding Jace like she did the night of the fight. My competition, cried out the night crow in a screech of challenge. Foolish girl. Just another weak 'dark one' afraid of who she could become. The night crow cackled to the night sky; she was as successful on love's battlefield as any bloody war she ever invested herself in. This one was not even worthy competition.

Detouring back towards the river; seeing a luminous green tendril snaking out of the water towards the village. Laughing softly to herself she swung down for a better view. The glowing mist stopped its forward progress when it noticed the night crow looking at it intently from a low branch of a dead birch.

"Peeping in windows, tonight?" it croaked softly.

An answering hiss, "I saw the boy today, and the girl. What happened? That was not to be. The bargain."

"Are you so sure he is the one?" croaked the crow.

"The boy smells like the mound dwellers. He did the unthinkable. Now to pay the price."

The night crow was worried. Confrontation was bound to occur, but this was too soon. Conor was not ready yet. "It is not wise to break the truce," she said to the mist.

The tendril took shape as a grasping talon reaching for the crow, but the bird never moved.

"Touch me not," she said, "unless you are sure the truce is broken."

A sibilant hiss and the talon evaporated into the night. But the crow heard the echoing voice. "I am sure, and I will start my revenge small. But revenge it will be. I am Piasa. This is my domain."

The night crow took wing again, soaring into the dark October sky, over fields half harvested. In olden days, the gods would have walked openly on these harvest nights, when everything was ripe to be scythed and bound and taken.

Below her now was the Walsh farm, young Declan Walsh's home, her destination. How sad, she thought as she landed on the oak outside his bedroom window where he slept. The first sacrifice. But she could do nothing. He had to die, so that others might live. It was the way of things, she thought, as she turned on her branch and saw the figures standing in the even darker shadow of the barn, staring at the house.

Oh, she knew them. The tall one, like a cadaver raised from the dead, infested with the new knowledge of this age, yet strangely touched by magic familiar to her. And him, the buffoon who tried to kill her Champion. She could still taste the eye. A thin green mist hovered around them. They stared up at the house, talking softly, unaware of her presence. She could do nothing here. She launched into the dark, clouds now obscuring the night sky.

Turning up towards the Abbey, where presences known and far beyond her constantly hovered over the monks' land, the night crow sees the Abbot and the marked boy. The Abbot she had known for long years; and though he walks a different path, long has she given him her grudging respect. Power must be heeded, she thought. But the boy, destined for a task and journey that could almost break a heart. The luminous ribbon of skin that marked him as one of her own shone not this night. With pity, she remembered binding that hand with cloth she wove from her loom of Life and Death. Clamped the beginning and end of his destiny with her brooch by the waters of the fountain. Gave him some space to come to an understanding of who he was. Now, he had rejected all that. Just a boy after all. Cawing softly in the night, she saw the Abbot's hand raised in absolution. Forgiveness granted, but consequences yet to come. Humans, she rasped in the wild language, so quick to give mercy. Sorrow and anger filled the cries of the night crow as she called out into the dark snapping at the flying locusts that foolishly, blindly, crossed her path.

THE PLOT

DECLAN WALSH AWOKE early as dawn began to lighten the night sky. Had to get going. Might as well get the horrendous day off to an early start. Still no school this Tuesday. Some kind of teacher meeting but that didn't mean he got to take the day off. Going to the back forty of the Walsh farm meant a trek up the bluff to a stand of oak and ash. Cutting down the deadwood and hauling it away would open up a little more pasture land for the constantly increasing herd of beef cattle his father kept amassing. Things were going well on the farm. It was just that Deck didn't feel like spending his day, by himself, chainsawing a bunch of old wood. Always best to work with two, said his father, but Dad was away and with no brothers and sisters, that left the neighbors and Deck just didn't want to bother them.

He liked being alone best, out in the woods. Didn't know why but it was as if he could feel the whole place vibrantly alive. That sense was the only thing that would make this day bearable. Deck wasn't big, but farming had made him strong, so the work would be more tedious than difficult.

Sighing, he snarfed down some cereal, took a jacket in case the strange late October heat broke, put on some work boots and jumped in the truck, chainsaw in the back.

Didn't really need the jacket. The early morning dawn was heavy with damp heat. Weirdest weather for this time of year. More like August than anything. Threatening storms. Distant thunder rumbled through the air.

By the time he got up to the back forty, the leaden skies were just a tad brighter. Made the trees look ghostly, wisps of mist still hanging off the branches. Few had even lost their leaves yet.

Maybe after he felled the wood and stacked it, he could go down to town and bother Jace. Liked the big guy. Jace had always had a soft spot for Deck. When they were little, Deck stuck close to the Michaels boy. Jace kept him from being picked on by the bigger kids. Dark-haired, dark-eyed, Deck was looked on as one of the 'dark ones' but that didn't give him special protection amongst the kids. Oh, they'd fight for him against outsiders, but he was different and that was all they needed to needle him now and then.

Too many had seen the otter thing. Sliding down the river bank with those overgrown water rodents was the coolest thing he'd ever did. Yes, he remembered it. Hardly any of the 'dark ones' remembered their strange habits as a kid, but Deck did. At least he thought so. Of course, it could've been just a memory created in his own mind from hearing those other kids who saw the event tell the story, over and over these past years.

Didn't know how he did it. But they said he just was rolling around with them, swimming with them, chirping like they did. They said his eyes were golden and his smile, as he played with them, feral as a wild child. That would have been tolerable to those who noticed him, but catching fish with his mouth—as many as the patriarch of the brace of otters could catch—that freaked his classmates out. Couldn't do it any more though. Tried, but all wild animals ran from him these days.

No matter. Time to put childish things aside. He surveyed the stand of trees, picking and choosing which ones to cull. Funny, no birds this morning. All was still in the damp air.

He heard a twig snap and whirled around. No one. Laughed to himself. Deck, old man, you're getting as weird as Oz. He'd wondered about him over the years, but Oz was the only 'dark one' that he ever really thought about as strange. The others just blended in with the town. Just like Deck did.

All that changed with Conor Archer though. Deck spit on the wet ground. Conor started people talking. Now, old legends rolled off his father's tongue when they ate together at night. Stories so obscure that Deck had never heard them before. Even hints about where the 'dark ones' came from.

"From the water," said Deck's dad one evening as he washed down supper with a beer. "They came from the sea not long before the Tinkers sailed to these shores. Walked right up the sand into the village. My grandfather said he'd heard they were beautiful. Some of the boys in the town fell for the fey girls right away. Should have been lots of marriages all at once; but there never were. All the sea wives went back among the waves. For a while. Then they came back, with the children. 'Dark ones..' By the time the Tinkers left for here, the sea wives were long gone. Only their young remained, and the Tinker men took them across the sea."

"But what about me?" said Deck, that long ago evening. "They call me a 'dark one.'"

"I know," said his father softly, "but your mother and I are as human as they come. Though there's no telling if some of their blood didn't get mixed in with ours."

He hadn't said that much since before the incident with the otters. Until Conor came, Deck's dad would never speak to him again on the subject. But lately, since Conor Archer came to town, his father seemed closer to him. As if the 'dark ones' legacy was forgiven and forgotten.

That was all right with Deck. Conor comes and stirs it all up again, but maybe that wasn't so bad. Nothing against the guy, thought Deck. Actually like him, especially since Jace spoke up for Conor every chance he could. Jace was Deck's idol; if Jace said the strange guy was good stuff that was good enough for Deck. He thought about Jace taking on Rafe McNabb in that fight a few days back. Deck punched the air with his fist. Always wanted to sock the prick in the mouth. Glad Jace got the chance.

Another twig snapped as Deck reached for the chain saw. He looked around, but still saw nothing. Funny thing about the McNabbs. They were always bossy, rich and power hungry, but now you saw them everywhere—in town, down at the new research center. They were always asking questions, particularly of the 'dark ones.' And they hung out with that creepy Dr. Drake.

Deck hadn't much liked his medical exam in late summer with that weird physician. Oh, the doctor was polite enough, but he poked and prodded Deck like he was looking for something. Took a lot of blood, too. More than was needed, Deck guessed. Hadn't really seen him since football started, except when the doctor was walking or driving with Cate McNabb. The whole town was talking about it, how those two seemed to have a thing going.

Another piece of wood snapped, and as Deck turned he heard the voice. "Saw you punching the air, man. Weren't thinking about taking a swipe at me, were you?" Rafe McNabb stepped from between some trees.

Deck was startled for only an instant. Rafe freaked him for a moment, what with the patch over his right eye. But, after all, in the end it was only Rafe, the blowhard of the McNabb clan.

"Whatcha doing here, Rafe?" said Deck, nodding to the bigger man but turning to grab his chainsaw again. He wasn't in a visiting mood, and he sure as hell didn't like Rafe well enough to start a conversation that he didn't really want.

"Looking for you, actually," said Rafe, sidling up to the truck and leaning against the cab.

"For what?" asked Deck, revving the chainsaw a bit, hoping the one-eyed asshole would leave him alone.

No such luck. "Like you to come with me. Got something to show you."

"Can't," said Deck. "My dad expects this work to get done today."

"Come on," wheedled Rafe. "It won't take long, and then I'll come back and help you."

"No offense, Rafe, but I didn't think the McNabb's soiled themselves with ordinary grunt work. But thanks for offering. Got to do this though. Maybe after I'm done I can look you up."

Rafe got serious, licking his lips in earnest. "No, it's got to be now, hear me? You have to come see now."

Looking at Rafe, Deck could see the big guy was stressed, hands clenching and unclenching. Motivated by something or someone that's for sure. But Deck just didn't have the time. Without a word, he turned from Rafe and began sawing down a wilted oak.

He felt himself being jerked backward, flying through the air. The chainsaw went airborne as well, smacking the ground and falling into silence. Deck hit the dirt a good ten feet from the dead oak he was working on.

"What did you do that for, you son of a bitch!" he said, trying to get to his feet. Rafe helped him all right, putting his meaty hand on Deck's throat and hauling him upright.

"I said you're coming with me," snarled Rafe.

Deck caught a foul smell from Rafe. He knew what it was immediately. It was exactly like the smell in the boa constrictor's terrarium in the biology lab up at high school, right after the snake had sucked down a fresh rat. Decay, offal, death—a distinct and repulsive odor, and Rafe wore it today.

"Let me go," choked Deck. Wasn't much he could do, feet off the ground and all. He struggled to get free but the stronger Rafe and lack of oxygen proved too much for him. His eyes were misting over. Strange. Looking at Rafe's face it seemed different somehow. Greenish almost. And his eye. His one eye had something wrong with it. The pupil wasn't round. It was a slit. Just like the boa constrictors in the biology lab.

Deck felt Rafe throw him to the ground again. Gasping for air, he couldn't move, only hear as the sound of the chainsaw started again.

THE HARVEST

THEY MET AT the entrance road to Madoc's Glen. Conor had jumped out of bed with a scream rising from deep inside him. Just enough sense to stifle it on his lips. What he saw on the threshold last evening, he dreamt about again, only it wasn't skulls and bones on a beach in his dreams, it was a face, a face of someone in terrible pain. He pulled on his clothes and shoes and was out the door in a flash, Troubles right behind. All he knew was that he had to get to Jace and Beth's house. No need though. Jace's car screamed to a stop right at the junction of the road. Both his and Beth's face were white.

"You had it too," said Conor. "The dream."

Silently, they both nodded.

"Somebody's in trouble," said Conor. "I think its—"

"Deck," said Jason.

"Are you sure?" asked Beth. "I mean, I only had this horrific night-mare which I can barely remember, but it had to do with somebody we knew, and it seemed so real. When I woke up, Jace was knocking at my door, spooked out of his mind."

"Not spooked, just real worried. He's in big trouble," said Jace. "I know it."

Conor jumped in the car pulling the dog into the back seat with him. "Come on, let's get to his house and check it out."

Took only a few minutes to get to the farm, but all was quiet. Jace bit his lip, thought for a moment. "He said something yesterday at football practice about having to cut down some wood. It would be a field at the top of that bluff over there."

Beth looked at Conor and her brother. "No other leads. We could try it and hope for the best."

Jace drove like a mad man towards the Walsh property.

When they got to the field, they breathed a sigh of relief. There was Deck's truck all right. Couldn't see him though. They got out of the car and started shouting his name. No answer. Jace found the chainsaw lying by an old dead oak.

Picking it up, he just stared and then choked out, "Guys, there's blood on this. A lot of it."

Beth's scream tore through the wooded pastureland. The boys went running toward her and found her behind the truck, hand over her mouth, retching. Before her was a bloody work boot.

"My God," said Conor. Even his stomach churned. The boot seemed full of blood.

Jace picked it up, but its heaviness surprised him. He dropped it again, and then they saw. A human foot was still inside the boot, severed roughly just above the ankle. They backed up in horror.

"Do you think ..." started Beth.

"Of course it's his," said Jace. "He's got to be around here, somewhere, if he's still alive."

He was nowhere. Only the pickup's tire tracks and the car. Didn't even look like Deck had been dragged. Somebody just up and carried him off.

Troubles put them on the right scent. His low serious woof caught everyone's attention. The dog was standing over some smashed grass, staring down the bluff toward the river.

"The footprints are huge," said Beth.

"Oz, do you think?" said Conor.

Jace bent down and scrutinized the sign. "Not a chance. The prints are big, but Oz's are larger. Whoever this was, and I have a mind I know, moved faster than I've ever seen Oz travel. Oz is capable of carrying somebody, but I've never seen him violent and he sure can't run a chainsaw. Too busy listening to tunes from a different world."

"Rafe, then," said Conor. His guess was confirmed when Jace shook his head.

"Had to be. Though why I just don't know. Rafe McNabb is truly an ass of a man. Deck never harmed a soul, but that wouldn't stop Rafe if Deck was in his sights. Besides, things have happened to Rafe since I got into that fight with him. Seems to have made a mighty fast recovery from his injury. Been seen lurking around town, spying on homes; seems to be homes where kids live who are dark haired and dark eyed. He's getting very strange."

"Even Aunt Emily said something about that," said Conor. "Close one eye on this world, that sight has to go somewhere,' she said. Meaning I think that Rafe is looking into some deep darkness now, and liking what he sees. Sticks awful close to that Dr. Drake. Aunt Emily said she saw them both down by the river a night or so ago. What they were doing she didn't know but they seemed to be headed down White Creek Way."

Suddenly, Troubles howled, muzzle pointed straight up at the leaden sky. Taking off like a shot, he headed, not toward the river where he had been looking, but back down the road, back towards town.

"Come back here," yelled Conor. "Stupid dog! Where the hell does he think he's going? I'll get him back." Conor started jogging down the road, but Beth ran up to him and grabbed his arm.

"We have to find Deck," she said. "He's badly hurt and Rafe won't take him to the monastery infirmary. He'll go to Drake, if anything, or he might just leave Deck out here somewhere."

"Next stop," said Jace, "is Drake's clinic. Hop in the car."

As fast as they went, they saw no sign of Troubles. Conor figured the dog must have taken a short cut, that is, if the Lab had the same idea they did. Conor was boiling inside. He didn't know Deck that well, but if that psychopath McNabb monster was in cahoots with Drake, Deck was in serious jeopardy.

Sure enough, the physician's car was in the parking lot of the clinic and Jace roared his own vehicle right up to the entrance. All three got out and went in. They met Drake and Rafe in the waiting room.

"Can I help you?" said Drake, seemingly not in the least surprised to see them.

Jace ignored him and rushed Rafe, pinning him to the wall. "What did you do to Deck you sub human freak?" Rafe just stared at him with a little smile on his face.

"Gentlemen ... and lady," said Drake with a little bow towards Beth. "Please, this is a place of healing. Actually you three are just the ones a certain friend of yours would like to see. Come, come. Into the examining room."

Bewildered, the three followed the doctor. Rafe watched them, that silly smile still pasted on his lips as he then slipped out the door.

"Hi guys," said a pale Declan Walsh. He was lying on a surgical table, his right foot bandaged. "Got to tell you, that Rafe saved my life. I would have bled to death if he hadn't have brought me here."

"Impossible!" said Beth. "We found ... your foot. It was severed; it was in your boot."

"We have it in the car," said Conor, suspicion tingling the back of his neck.

"You must be mistaken," said Drake. "His foot was cut by the chain saw, but as you can see, I was able to stitch it. Should be good as new in a week or so."

Without a word Jace turned and went to fetch the boot. They had placed it in a plastic bag, but Jace made sure what he thought he saw was still there. He handed it to the doctor. Drake set it on an examining table and opened the bag, drawing out the boot. He took something from around his neck. Conor thought it was a strange kind of knife, almost like a twisted kind of dagger. Drake probed into the boot and then said, "I'm sorry, but there is nothing here but some blood. Are you sure you saw what you thought you saw?" He turned the boot upside down; a few drops of blood dripped out.

"Absolutely," said Beth. "I found it, and it was horrible."

"Sometimes," said Drake with the slightest condescension in his voice, "we see what we fear."

Conor spoke up. "But we all three saw it. Something's not right here."

Drake smiled paternally, "I can see that Declan isn't the only one to be traumatized by this morning's events."

Just then, a howl sounded outside the clinic. A mournful wail that sent a chill up the spines of Jace, Conor and Beth. Conor ran out and brought Troubles inside.

"Can't say what's bothering him," he said as he brought the dog in to see Deck. "He's been worried about you, Deck, maybe seeing you will calm him down."

For several moments, Troubles uttered not a sound. Instead, the dog had stared intently at Deck, never moving. Now a low growl came from the depths of the retriever.

"That animal shouldn't be in here," said the doctor. "Please take him outside." Troubles curled a lip in a snarl toward the doctor.

"Time to go," said Jace. Everything read false to him, but nothing was going to be gained by quizzing anyone further. "Hey Deck," he said, "glad you're okay. You gave us quite a scare. How about we check on you later today up at your place?"

Deck beamed, "You guys are great, but I think I just want to rest. Maybe in a couple of days or so, I'll be up for visitors. Any problem with that?"

"No, of course not," said Beth, just as anxious to get away from the weirdness and unanswered questions.

"Thank you so much for coming to see him," said Drake. "With his father and mother out of town for a few days, you're the closest thing he has to family here. I promise you, I'll be checking up on him."

Drake ushered them out. As they went, a sudden idea flashed in Conor's mind. Thin places, he thought. Thresholds and all that. That's what his second sight needed to manifest itself. He wondered if the doorway to the examining room would work. Didn't really want to try, but, hell, it was for Deck. He strayed to the end of the line and made as if to say something else to his injured friend. Instead, he stood on the threshold of the doorway and looked back.

There was Deck all right, sitting propped up on the examining table, but his eyes were vacant. A twisted black shadow crawled up his torso, opened the boy's mouth and wriggled in. It was as if the lights went on in Deck's eyes, and Conor saw him waving at him and Beth and Jace. He was seeing what had just happened. Shocked, he shook his head and when he looked again, all he saw was cheerful Deck waving goodbye to all his guests. Conor made to leave, and then he heard a whisper.

He turned once more and saw a malevolent grin on Deck's face. "He's in here with us, Conor of the hollow hills, and here he'll stay for a while until we give him to Piasa. Nothing will save him. He is the first sacrifice." Conor shuddered and walked away. Deck's cheerful voice followed, "Sure hope to see all of you again real soon."

DECISIONS

THEY DECIDED TO go to the café for breakfast, tentatively waving goodbye to a beaming Dr. Drake. Conor said nothing until they were safely ensconced in a booth and had ordered.

"It's not him," he said.

"What do you mean?" said Jace.

"I mean, the Deck we all knew isn't there anymore." He described what he had seen and how that thing that crawled into Deck looked just like the creatures that possessed the boys that August night in the quarry.

The café door opened and in walked Rory. He motioned for Conor to move over and sat down with them all.

"Take it you saw your friend." As he spoke, he traced the design of the Celtic knot tatooed on his forearm.

"How'd you know that?" said Beth.

"Haven't had the pleasure yet, but my name's Rory." Small spiked teeth smiled at the girl.

"Haven't heard much good about you," said Beth, disdain in her voice.

"Don't expect you have," he said, glancing at Conor.

"So why are you here?" asked Jace.

"Just wondering what you thought of your friend."

"You know what happened to him, don't you," said Conor. "What are those things?"

For a moment, Rory's face went blank. It was as if he was wiping off the usual sarcastic sneer.

"Changelings," said Rory, a serious note in his voice. "Not exactly, I guess. Failed changelings you might say. Those that don't take a human body when they've quickened get deformed somewhat, become twisted. They're tools in the hands of the more powerful. They were cool to use on your friends, Conor, but I controlled them and they could never do your friends ultimate harm. I never would have let them stay. But this one that has Declan Walsh. Ah, he's a bad one, made more so by the creature that controls him."

"You mean Drake," asked Conor.

"Ah, yes, the great and glorious physician. There's little of Declan Walsh remaining, what with his foot sawed off by that monster Rafe McNabb. Can't believe Cate could have birthed that twisted whelp. You think I'm bad. No, Beth, you were right from the first. He's truly missing a foot, but Drake and the changeling can make you see what they wish." Rory nudged Conor in the ribs.

"Why are you here?" asked Conor.

"To help, if I can. Don't you trust me, lad?"

"I think you have your own reasons that don't always intersect with ours," said Conor.

"Indeed I do, and I've made them clear to you. I want you to become what you were called to be."

"Told you that wasn't going to happen. I don't want what you offer."

Rory's nose wrinkled. "Smell you I do, Conor. And you just used your Sight, didn't you? Don't want to be what you're becoming, but in a pinch, the power's there for the taking and you just go ahead and use it anyway, damn your principles and all."

Conor glared.

Rory looked over at Jace, sniffed and then leaned over the table grabbing Jace's face, forcing him to look into his eyes. "What's different about you that I smell?" said Rory. "There's a peculiar odor of the Otherworld all about this table this morning. The Morrigan has been whispering things around about you, but I didn't believe her until now. But I can smell you. Wisdom permeates your pores; you actually sweat it. How'd you do it? Ambush old Walt in his quest for the great catfish? Let him land it and then kill him for the prize?"

"He was a good man, and I'm not like you," said Jace, twisting Rory's hand off his face.

"We don't even know each other," said Rory, thin lips cocked in a smile. The waitress brought their order and Rory snatched a piece of bacon from Jace's plate, smiling as he ripped the meat in half.

"Conor's said enough about who you are. I mean it; I'm not like you."

"What's he talking about Jace?" said Beth.

He looked sheepishly at his sister and at Conor, and then told them of the other details of Walt's disappearance and the Great Cat that had given him some kind of gift.

"Wisdom or something," said Jace.

"You saw my father?" said Conor incredulously. "And you didn't say a word about it?"

"Conor, things have been happening so fast. Besides," and here he looked at Beth, "you guys gave me something bigger to worry about."

Neither Conor nor Beth said anything, but Rory smirked. "And what does your vaunted wisdom say about all that's happened this morning?"

"That what you say is true; however you dress it in your own concerns," said Jace.

"There you have it, Conor," said Rory. "Your own best friend telling you that I'm a stand up guy. Now go embrace your destiny and kill Drake. He's a danger you know."

"Why don't you take care of it?" said Conor. "You or my father, since you both think you are so damn powerful."

Rory paused and then looked solemn. "Easier said than done, lad. See, both of us, your father and me, are bound by an oath to that river demon. Part of a pact you see. Violate it openly and all hell, literally, will break loose. Although," said Rory, looking pointedly at Conor, "maybe it doesn't matter anymore, now that you know your girlfriend so well. Seems the pact is broken anyway."

Conor blushed with shame. Beth turned red as well.

"Let me out, Rory," whispered Conor, anger seething in his voice.

"Of course, lad," said Rory solicitously, "must be difficult admitting to your best friend that his sister and you are, shall we say, an inseparable item."

Conor couldn't wait to get out of there. He pushed past Rory, but the biker caught his arm. "You've made quite a mess of it," he hissed. "But it's not too late to fix things. Accept who you are, before more go the way of Declan Walsh."

CONOR'S ANGST

HIS FACE STILL burning with shame, he bent down to untie Troubles outside of the café. Conor had seen the look of betrayal on Jace's face. But it's none of his goddamned business either, he thought. If I love her and she loves me, the rest of the world can just leave us the hell alone. Kicking a piece of crumbling sidewalk out in the street, Conor walked rapidly out of town, back towards home.

Troubles woofed gently.

"I know she is his sister," said Conor to the dog. "Don't think I don't know it. Just wasn't thinking about that yesterday. While Walt was dying. While Jace was getting all wisdom oriented. While he was talking to my father. Who won't speak to me." Conor viciously kicked the ground again. "You son of a bitch!" he yelled into the woods. "Why don't you come and talk to me?"

All Conor succeeded in doing was silencing the birds. The dog woofed softly again. Conor knelt down in the dusty road. "Sorry, boy," he said. "I'm upsetting you, I know."

The dog chuffed again, and Conor looked more closely. Yellow gold flecks flickered in the dog's brown eyes. A paw lifted. Conor took it. "What's wrong," he said. "What's up?" He bent forward and placed his hand on the dog's head.

That's when the dark strip on his hand and arm started to get warm. He could feel it move beneath his skin as it snaked its away around his body. Just like yesterday and this morning with the Second Sight. It felt like his body was alive, like his hand was merging with Troubles. He looked again into the dog's eyes as his vision went dark.

But only for a moment. Conor felt his mind shift. He'd felt this before, running in the dark, chasing Rory. Images, not words, filled his mind. He knew enough now to realize that he was seeing as an animal sees, specifically as a chocolate Labrador sees. He was seeing something that Troubles had either witnessed or knew about. The images were kaleidoscopic, jumbled and not logical. There was talking but for a moment, Conor couldn't understand. It took massive effort to actually put sense to the pictures.

Rafe, dragging Deck into the clinic. Drake smiling and patting the McNabb boy on the back. Both of them unceremoniously dumping Deck on a table. A filthy rag used for a tourniquet, a dirty towel to staunch the flow of blood. An IV hooked up. That funny looking knife again from around Drake's neck, plunged into the back of Deck's head. The Walsh kid spasming.

"Don't worry," said Drake to Rafe. "I've got what I need. Material from his pineal gland. I know you don't have a clue what that is, but that rather overlooked and little understood part of the brain is exactly what is going to provide me with the answers on how to walk in two worlds at once."

He smiled at Rafe, "In other words, how to stay human but use all the powers that you've seen the other side has. You know what I'm talking about. Piasa has whispered to you what could be possible. Of course, he wants your soul, but what I offer you is your freedom, his power, and your soul. Oh, you'd have to serve him, but he wouldn't have to possess you in that intimate way of his. Sounds promising, doesn't it?"

Drake continued, "All through the years, my family has served that power. Many went mad. I loved the challenge but feared the result, you see. I became a geneticist not so much to help others as to help me, and those like me who enjoyed serving the dark powers but didn't really feel like being consumed by them. I worship Piasa, Rafe, but I've got to be me. A little bit of science helps tame the wildness of myth and magic. I can control Piasa's influence in this world. I'll serve it better that way. The demon doesn't really understand this time or place or culture. It needs my expertise, and since one can't reason with it, a little genetic manipulation, a little medicine here and there can build the boundaries that keep the Devourer at bay. There now, just what I needed." He scooped the tiny bit of matter out from the incision at the base of Deck's skull. This he treated as gold. Surgical gloves, sterile container. A sloppy makeshift bandage for the back of the boy's head.

"Now," said Drake. "To keep him alive until at least this afternoon. He's pretty far gone. The IV and stimulants will help stabilize his body for a while, but not long enough. He's a dead man walking." Drake laughed at his own joke. "Almost." He was still giggling to himself as he walked over to a closet.

He opened the door. Complete darkness inside. A cold darkness. "Come here little one," he said. "No need to be afraid."

Stretching out his hand into the dark, Drake felt a cold scaly hand on his. "Come out, into the light." And gently he pulled forth the creature.

Wreathed in shadows, it was twisted and misshapen. Rafe stared in awe.

"Looking for a host, Rafe," said Drake. "Looking for so long and never finding one, until now. That's the funny thing about changelings. They belong to the world of the 'dark ones,' the world of the mound dweller and that feral biker. But they're hated in that world too. They are the homeless of the Otherworld. Abandoned, alone. That's why they like the night. That's why they are particularly easy to turn to the one who dwells at the roots of the world. They see that one in Piasa. That's why it was easy to call this little one forth. Problem is they like babies usually. More pliable minds. But beggars can't be choosers and this one has longed for many years and will take anything human right now. Even a dying boy."

"There he is," said Drake, pointing to the unconscious Deck on the table. "Grievously, mortally wounded, but not ready to die yet," said Drake. "He's yours if you want him, my little one," said Drake. "For a while. Then I will give you someone else, more permanent. Does that sound okay to you?"

The creature bobbed whatever passed for its head.

Conor saw Trouble's paws in front of his vision. The dog must have braced itself on an outside wall in order to look into the clinic from a lower window. He heard the dog's nails click on the glass. Suddenly, in his vision came the face of Drake and Rafe.

"Get that damn dog," said the doctor.

"Killed him once," snarled Rafe, "I'll kill him again."

"Conor," came a voice into his mind. "Conor, come back."

He found himself staring again into the dog's face. "Conor, dammit, come back from wherever it is you are."

Turning he saw Beth standing over him. His hand was still cupped on the side of the dog's face, Troubles staring placidly back at him. A wild voice inside his head whispered urgently, "The worlds are merging little master; you will have to choose."

"Where in the world were you?" said Beth shaking Conor and finally getting his attention. "It was like you were frozen, both you guys."

"I saw what Troubles saw at the clinic, before we got there." Conor's face was bleak. "Beth, Drake's trying to make a connection with Piasa. He doesn't want to simply speak to the river demon; he wants powers like Rory, Madoc, the 'dark ones,' even like me."

Beth pulled him upright and put her arms around his neck and kissed him. He let her hold him for a moment but then pushed her away.

"And I've made a mess of it," he said.

"How?" she asked.

"I saw Jace's face. He looks at me as if I betrayed him. He knows, doesn't he?"

Beth blushed. "Yes, he figured it out last night. Conor, it just takes some getting used to for him. He's always protected me, been by me. He's just being a brother."

"And I'm the faithless friend, I think," said Conor, a grimace crossing his face. "I'm disappointing everybody, but it's worse than that. Beth, I think we've changed something here in Tinker's Grove, put the people in danger."

"How do you figure?"

"The Abbot said it; Rory said it. They walk in two different worlds of morality but their judgement was the same. What we did was wrong."

"It wasn't wrong; it was, it was beautiful," she said, blue eyes glistening with tears.

Conor smiled a little. "It was beautiful. At least I thought so. I thought it's what two people do who love each other, but there was something more happening. Somehow what we did, what we did broke something. There was some truce or pact between my father and Piasa. The people who dwell in the Indian mound, whatever they are, came here long ago. They kept to themselves, skirmished with Piasa now and then, but when the Tinkers came with the 'dark ones' Piasa got worried. It saw them as a threat and forced a compromise with Willie Archer or Madoc, I guess his real name is. They could never mingle with the 'dark ones.' But Madoc did. Kept it a secret even, until I came back and made that monster start wondering. The thing spied on us yesterday, along with others. I didn't know we were in such demand as a show. But it watched and it knew what I was. Don't you see, Beth? I'm the one who broke the truce. I've brought down the power of Piasa on this whole place."

He expected Beth to take her tears one step farther and start crying, but when he looked at her face he saw only anger.

"You know, I was never very big on the Armageddon thing. End of the world, end of life as we know it, just seems a bit strong to me. So there was a truce a long time ago. So you came to Tinker's Grove. So you fell in love with me. That scum-sucking water dragon will just have to get used to it."

It was a good speech he thought, till he looked at her face more closely and saw her lower lip quivering. He held her tight then. "I've brought hell to all of us," he said. "And the devil is coming to take his due."

Just then an old F-150 pickup came roaring around the corner. Conor caught only a glimpse of the driver, but he didn't even seem to see them as they jumped out of the way. He was talking, no shouting, something into a cell phone.

Weaving on the road, he kept hitting the dirt shoulder.

"It's Brother Luke," said Conor, "going like the devil's right on his tail."

"He could have killed us," said Beth. "I don't think he even noticed we were here. Something's up in town."

Troubles trotted out to the center of the road. His low whine turned into a growl, but the monk was long gone. The dog started barking, but it was only a warning to the cloud of dust.

DISCOVERY

BROTHER LUKE, SOMETIME physician to the town and Abbey, was driving on auto pilot. He hadn't even noticed the near miss hit and run. He was yelling at Dort Martin over his cell phone.

"You sure it was Deck?" he shouted.

"Of course," she said. "I can see the clinic from here, and not more than two hours ago they—they being Dr. Drake and that McNabb misfit—they brought in Declan Walsh. I could swear the boy was terribly injured."

"Two hours ago?" said Brother Luke. "You said this was an emergency, a matter of life and death. Surely Dr. Drake has stabilized him."

"Wouldn't have troubled you, but the boy just walked out of the clinic with the two of them, got in the car and drove away."

"So maybe he stitched Deck up."

"Well maybe he did, but if so, he's a miracle worker. I could have sworn that boy was missing part of a leg when he was taken in there. Look, just take a look around in the clinic. I don't think it's locked and maybe you can solve that little mystery."

"Dort Martin, you are the biggest busybody in this here entire town," said Brother Luke. "But as long as you drug me down here, I might as well have a look. See, I'm just passing you now. Talk to you later."

He waved at her, staring through her display window, but couldn't find it in his heart to smile. He should be kinder, he knew. Dort Martin was one seriously lonely lady, but her attention to detail, particularly the details of other's lives, continually got her into trouble. This time, her misstep was a beaut.

Getting out of his car, he stared at the empty clinic. One of the few times it was empty these days, he thought. Over the past few months, Dr. Drake had managed to siphon off all the people who used to trek on up to the monastery for medical care. True, the monastery had always provided the service for the town, and there was plenty of business to go around, but Luke found it odd that he now had hours on his hands to deal with. What kind of medical care was this doctor giving them that they flocked to the clinic instead of the monastery? Brother Luke, a Bob Dylan fan, knew that the times they are a-changin.' Always. So maybe the monastery could get out of the health care business, at least a little bit.

He slowly opened the clinic door.

"Hello? Anyone still here?" Even as he spoke, he knew the place was empty. Not knowing how much time he had and feeling like he was related to Dort Martin by blood, Brother Luke stepped through the waiting room into the offices and examining rooms beyond. He scoped things out and, not for the first time, admitted the clinic was beautiful—state of the art. Must have taken a ton of money. Though he knew Drake was wealthy, chances were Caithness McNabb had dipped into her own fortune to make this place a possibility. Just like her, he thought. Like everyone else in the area, he had watched her sink her talons into just about everything in Tinker's Grove. The business alliance with Drake was just another coup for her.

It took him a few more moments to find the room where Deck had been treated. What a disaster! Unlike the rest of the clinic, no one had cleaned up much. Bloody bandages, a used IV bag, all were scattered around the room rather than in the trash. Then he saw it. A sock. Tucked against a wall. He could see it was splashed with blood, and in the shadows it just didn't look right. Pulling on a surgical glove, he bent down to look more closely. Gasping, he pulled it into the light, not just the sock but the ankle and foot it was covering.

"My God," he whispered. "She was right. Then how could he walk?"

He flipped more lights on in the room. What a mess. No self respect-ing doctor would leave a room looking like a biohazard waste dump. Looking carefully now, he saw no thread, surgical tools or scissors. Just a lot of blood pooling from under a dark cloth beneath the table. At least that's what he thought it was.

He bent down to pick it up and gave a low whistle. No cloth. More like skin shed from something vaguely reptilian. Almost transparent, he thought, holding it up to the light. For a moment, he thought it was just his shaking hand that made it ripple, but then the skin took on a life of its own and leapt onto his chest. He screamed and threw himself backward. What-ever it was, it was vainly trying to climb up his body. Brother Luke was no coward, but he hated any cold blooded thing. The monks still talked about the screech he let out when hiking with them on the bluffs and coming across a tranquil timber rattlesnake sunning itself on the trail. That strange memory went at light speed through his mind as he tried to brush the thing off him. Too late. It lifted a scrawny limb upwards to touch his fear- frozen face and then puffed into mist and was gone. Like a shadow of a shadow.

Something terrible happened here, thought the monk. Picking himself up off the floor he shook his head in wonder. Of all the monastic community, he was the most secular, the most down to earth. Being raised in Dubuque, a much bigger city, had done it. Going to med school had finished it. He had never seen a miracle and supposed that if Christ had actually done them, he didn't do them very often and was the last to do a real one.

Abbot Malachy was not above a paternal criticism now and then of Luke's almost agnostic skepticism. Of course, Brother Luke respected the Abbot. But he secretly enjoyed tweaking his superior for the credulous and superstitious sayings and customs the Abbot occasionally touted. Most everything could be explained by science and reason. When he had told the Abbot that, on numerous times, the monk had merely patted him on the head and said, "Most times, yes, but not all."

This was one of those times, just like that summer night a few months ago with the Archer boy. Brother Luke had worked hard to forget that, but no scientific reason was going to explain that away. He knew it in his heart of hearts. And now this.

He ran his hand through his close cropped blond hair. Damn strange. For some reason, he thought of the Abbot again. He whispered to himself, "Oh, Father Abbot, wish you were here to have seen this. Even you won't believe me. Something is terribly wrong."

Shrugging his shoulders in uncomprehending frustration, Brother Luke leaned his forehead against the wall. He was beginning to think like the Abbot—all surreal and stuff like that. It was the last thing he thought. He was pondering the matter right up to the moment he felt a heavy blow to the back of his head and everything turned to night. As the darkness set in his mind he felt himself shouting to the dark, "Help me! For God's sake help me!"

A VISION IN THE WATER

HE HEARD IT on the wind. A faint cry that pierced his heart rather than his ears. Amplified by the flock of sparrows that swirled above the cattle pen behind the monastery. Screaming fear; demanding he do something. Someone or several folks were in a great deal of trouble, the screams a blow to his chest knocking him into the dirt, shutting out the light. He couldn't see, but this time he heard in the dark, "Help me, Father Abbot!"

It was Luke. He'd know that voice anywhere. He searched in the dark. Nothing. Suddenly, he felt himself being shaken, and light gradually returned, the mist cleared and he found Conor looking worriedly at him.

"Father Abbot, are you okay?" he asked. "You're holding your chest. Is it your heart?"

"No, lad, I'm all right," he said, quickly standing up with an ease and vigor that belied his age. "But someone else is not. Something is terribly wrong in town."

"Sure is," said Conor, and he told the Abbot what he had seen.

"Did you happen to run into Brother Luke?" asked the Abbot.

"Nope," said Conor, "it was the other way around. He almost mowed Beth and me down not much more than a half hour ago."

"He's in trouble too, I'm afraid. Look, Conor, I've got to get out of these filthy clothes and vest for Mass. I'd like you to stay and we'll have a look for both Deck and Brother Luke afterwards."

Though he wasn't much in a praying mood, Conor agreed, mostly because he was at a loss as to what else to do. Fortunately, daily Mass at the monastery was pretty short and maybe not too much would happen to Deck and the monk in the meantime.

Conor saw the Abbot motion him to stay in his seat. As soon as the monks and the few elderly townspeople had left after Mass, the Abbot led Conor over to the baptistry. It was in the back of the church, in the center, where everyone could walk by and dip their hand into the waist high circular pool of holy water. The font was large, nearly three feet in diameter. The excess water flowed down the curved bowl into a hidden drain below with a comforting sound.

"Why are we here?" asked Conor.

"We need to look for Deck and Brother Luke."

"Let's go, then!" he said, raising his voice in frustration. "We've wasted so much time already."

"Prayer is never a waste of time," said the Abbot, a severe look on his face. "Besides, I had to gather my own wits about me to figure out what to do. A waste of time would be to go chasing around the countryside looking for those two. They may be together, they may not. Drake and Rafe might be with them. Maybe not. There's a better way to help them. Now be still and watch. Look deeply into this pool of holy water."

The Abbot bent over the font and breathed on the water. Conor could hear him chanting words, and then he put forth his hand and three times cupped the water, letting it fall back into the pool. When the ripples stopped, he said more clearly for Conor to hear, "Luke, my son, here I am. Show yourself to me. I am here."

"Are you doing magic?" whispered Conor, a mixture of wonder and fear in his voice. "I mean, I didn't think you could be messing around with that stuff, being a priest and all."

"Not magic, Conor. Just a talent I have. This is no more magic than what your father can do. Magic is a foreign thing humans use to gain power. Dr. Drake, I'm afraid, is a practitioner. The more I hear, the more I see, the more I'm convinced he long ago sold his soul for the right to dabble with dark powers. What I do here is clean and good. No spells, no calling on a higher power except that of the one God and that only to ask, not to command."

Conor was silent and kept staring at the font. He could see nothing for a moment. The water was dark against the grey granite base. But shadows began to form and he saw a car, driving down a dirt path towards the river.

"Do you see it, lad?" whispered the Abbot.

"Yes, but where is it going?"

"Down by the river near Cate McNabb's estate. The river pools and eddies in the sloughs down there and that path takes you back in that tangled area."

"Is Deck there? Is Brother Luke with him?"

"Shush now. Just watch."

The car stopped as the road began to disappear into the weeds. Conor could see a slow moving branch of the Wisconsin just a few yards away. Drake got out of the front passenger seat and opened the rear door. Declan Walsh smoothly exited, walking on both legs as if nothing whatever was wrong. Rafe went around to the trunk, opened it, and lifted out the unconscious body of Brother Luke.

Conor heard the Abbot hiss in anger, but he could not take his eyes off what he was seeing in the baptismal pool. Rafe unceremoniously dumped the body of the monk by the side of the river.

"It's time," said Drake to Declan Walsh.

"I don't want to leave," said the thing that inhabited Conor's friend.

Drake spoke soothingly, "I know, I know, but he's too severely hurt. Even you can't animate him for much longer. Remember, I promised I'd find you someone better, someone healthier. But you don't have to leave yet. In fact, you cannot until you see the Devourer come to take this lad to itself."

"What about him? Can I go into him?" said the Deck thing pointing at the monk.

"Too old, I'm afraid. You wouldn't take to him. He'd die within minutes and you'd be left to wander again."

"Good God!" said the Abbot, "I know what he's going to do!"

"Can we get there in time?" said Conor.

"Not to save them both," answered the Abbot. "Whatever help we give them, has to be given from here."

Conor listened as Drake and the changeling argued.

Rafe walked over and grasped the changeling by the neck. "You heard the doctor before. There has to be a sacrifice. A life for a life. He had Piasa heal me and now the Devourer must have satisfaction. The Walsh kid will do just fine, and you've done well keeping his body alive. But soon it will be time." Turning to the doctor, Rafe added, "What about the monk? Are we throwing him in for dessert?"

"Yes, I think so," laughed Drake. "A little extra insurance for another time. Come we must prepare."

"We've got to go, now," said Conor. "Before it's too late."

"It's already too late for Deck," said the Abbot sorrowfully.

"What do you mean? He's walking around okay. I know that thing has possessed him, but so what? Do an exorcism or something."

"It's not that simple. You see an illusion only. The changeling has to leave Deck's body not only because they are going to sacrifice Deck but because Deck is mortally wounded. He's dying, Conor, God help him. And they're going to savage him more before he dies."

Drake and Rafe had walked out of the pool's vision, and the Abbot and Conor watched as Deck strolled over to the unconscious Brother Luke.

"Too bad for you," hissed the changeling, nudging the monk with his foot. "You'll be food for the beast as well."

The Abbot reached out his finger and touched the image of Brother Luke rippling in the holy water. "Wake little brother. Wake now, for a dark time is at hand. You must wake and save a soul who is in terrible danger, lost in the clutches of a demon that is sucking away his very life. Wake, Brother Luke and do your greatest healing ever."

Conor watched as the Abbot grew silent, but a great burden fell upon his face. He saw the Abbot's head descend over the image of Brother Luke and heard him whisper something over the water. The words were lost but whatever the Abbot said had a profound effect on Brother Luke. The monk opened his eyes, blinked twice, and in a move that seemed impossible because of his condition he leapt upon the changeling.

"Come out of him, you filth," said Brother Luke. "In the name of Christ, I command you," he said. The thing tried to scream but the monk cuffed him on the side of his face. "Out of him now," said the monk. He traced the sign of the cross on Deck's forehead.

Brother Luke had heard the words of Abbot Malachy. In some way, the Abbot was with him and he felt a new strength throughout his body. Not that he was feeling great. His stomach heaved with nausea after the blow on the head, but he felt curiously detached. He knew what he had to do for Declan Walsh. He wasn't sure the words had that power or whether Deck was just dying and the thing had to exit his body, but whatever, Brother Luke was enormously gratified to see that shadowy, snaky thing crawl out of the mouth of the boy. It didn't even take a second look at the monk as it fled into the weeds by the river.

The physician saw Deck's eyes clear for a moment but then terrible pain cover the boy's gaze. Two terrible wounds were evident in the back of the boy's head and on his leg.

"I know you are hurting, Deck," said the monk, "and I cannot heal your body. I'm not even sure you can understand what I'm saying, but the Abbot says I can't let you be sacrificed to Piasa. Squeeze my hand, man, and know that I'm with you. It's time to let go. I'll walk with you as far as I can. Nothing bad can harm you now."

Deck tried to smile through the pain and he squeezed the monk's hand. Through a mist of tears, Brother Luke saw the light fade from the boy's eyes. "Go with God," said the monk. "Go with God and walk in the true Light."

Brother Luke was amazed that he could follow the diminishing light in Deck's eyes. It was like floating down a dimly lighted cavern. He walked with the soul through a formless place. For a moment, Deck looked at him with fear, but Luke smiled, with more confidence than he himself felt, and said, "Come on, we've taught you about this journey since you were knee high. Don't be afraid. Do you feel your body hurting yet?" asked Brother Luke.

Deck shook his head and said, "I feel an awful lot better. Where are we?"

"Look ahead," pointed the monk. They had exited the cavern and crossed a wasteland that ended abruptly. Before and below them stretched the Wisconsin river basin. "It's my home," said Deck. "And it's beautiful!" Behind them was gray stone, before and to the horizon was a green land with the river winding through it. Trees and fields were in full summer. An eagle called a greeting in the sky.

Ever the skeptic, even the monk was impressed and he found himself saying, "As it was always meant to be. As it is on the new earth." He felt the air grow thick and his steps slow. Deck looked back at him.

"I cannot follow you further, lad," said the monk. "The Abbot speaks to me. He tells me that you are to go home." The monk smiled, "Now don't get all fearful on me. I know you think this is the coolest thing you've ever seen, because I sure do. You know where we are. Even I wouldn't mind staying. Now be at peace and accept this blessing from me, from the Abbot, from all those good folk of Tinker's Grove." Raising his arms, the monk began chanting:

Go home Declan Walsh, this day, to your home of winter,
    to your home of autumn, of spring and of summer.
Go home to this day to your lasting home, to your eternal rest.

Walk now and rest and so fade sorrow.
Walk now and rest and so fade sorrow.
Walk now and rest and so fade sorrow.

Rest now my friend in the arms of the One;
Wait now my friend for those who love you;
Be now at peace my friend for your journey is done;
Walk now and rest and so fade sorrow.

Brother Luke saw Deck walk toward the green fields. Turning for a moment Deck waved to the monk who watched him climbing down the green bluff with ease. Then, Luke's own vision faded, and he opened his eyes on the body of Declan Walsh, crumpled before him. The boy took a few shallow breaths, and was gone.

"What have you done?" shouted Drake. Conor and the Abbot saw Drake appear within their vision again.

The monk was hauled to his feet by Rafe as Drake bent over the boy.

"He's dead. The changeling has fled," said Drake.

"He's beyond your power you sadistic monster," said the monk. "And that shadow demon is gone as well. My Abbot has a message for you. He says you cannot have the children and that what you planned for Declan Walsh is a travesty that will be fought."

Drake stood up and looked in the monk's eyes. "That's what your Abbot says. But what do you say? You don't even believe there is a Piasa. You saw the changeling, but you still think there's some simple scientific explanation for it. You did all this because your Abbot told you. How he did it, I don't know, but I smell a connection here." He came closer to the monk and looked deep into his eyes. "Yes," he said, "your Abbot is there. I sense his presence. You wouldn't have it in you to resist this much if he was not with you even now."

"That's where you're wrong," said Brother Luke, surprised at the calmness of his own voice. "I don't understand what's going on, and yes, I doubt much of what the Abbot thinks of this whole thing. But I know what I see here and I knew I couldn't let that boy face whatever you have planned for him. How you savaged him! What kind of monster are you? Trying to extract something from his brain? Planning to do some mystical voodoo? Oh, I may be too skeptical; I may doubt too much for my own good; but I know evil when I see it, and evil is what you are Dr. Drake. That boy rests in peace, away from the pain you caused and the additional suffering you intended." He spit in Drake's face.

Rafe cuffed him up the side of his head, sending new waves of nausea through the monk's body. Drake just chuckled as he wiped the spittle off.

"Nice speech, but you don't even comprehend what you've gotten yourself into. I can't give Piasa this piece of garbage," and here he kicked Deck's body, "but I can give him you, a feisty little monk. I was going to just throw your unconscious body into the river after the Devourer feasted on Declan, but now, you'll have to do, and you'll have to be wide awake for the experience."

"Have courage, my son," said the Abbot, his own tears mixing with the waters of the font.

Conor saw the monk swing his face toward himself and the Abbot, as if he could see them.

"I don't know how you are doing it, Father Abbot, but its okay. I hear you loud and clear, and I'm ready for anything. I'm not afraid."

"Oh," said Dr. Drake, "you will be. You will be. Rafe, take him to the river."

Rafe easily outweighed Brother Luke and the physician didn't resist as he was marched to the bank of the river. Drake walked before them, striding into the water. He turned and grabbed the black habit of the monk pulling Luke toward himself.

"Give me your hand," he said.

"So where's the Devourer of Souls?" said Brother Luke. "You'd think an educated man like you would worship something besides a muddy river god."

Drake slapped the monk's face. "Don't blaspheme. You're in its element now."

Drake took the monk's hand and with the ornamental dagger sliced his palm. He held the arm out straight as the blood flowed into the water.'

"Ah, I see," said Brother Luke, "my blood for bait."

"Exactly," said Drake. "And once it smells it, Piasa will come."

"It's the middle of the day. I thought its realm lay in the night with the darkness."

"It shows how little you know. Piasa walks between the worlds and neither day nor night, rain nor shine will keep him from his appointed task."

"Sort of like some demonic mailman," said Luke, grinning with contempt at the doctor.

Conor watched all of this with horror. "Can't you do anything?" he begged the Abbot.

"I can ease his pain, and he knows I stand with him giving him strength."

"Well that's not enough," snarled Conor. "Save him."

"He is saved. He's giving his life for you, for me, for Declan. This is his time, his destiny."

"You're just accepting his death?"

"No. What is about to happen is evil itself. But humans cannot do everything, cannot stop death each and every time."

"You yourself said I was more than human. I'll go. I'll save him."

"So now you're ready to accept who you are?" said the Abbot. "Even so, you will not go."

"You can't stop me."

Without removing his finger from the font, the Abbot turned and grasped Conor by the throat. "Little fool. I can only put up with your growing pains so often. Brother Luke dies to give us time. If you go now, there's every chance you will be killed by Piasa. You have yet to develop into who you were meant to be. Now I will let you go, if you promise not to run off."

Choking, Conor nodded.

"There's a good lad. Now focus with me. Brother Luke needs all the strength we can muster for him. His death approaches."

Indeed, Brother Luke was the first to see the ripple in the water coming from the opposite direction of the current. Sniffed my blood, he thought, just like some supernatural shark. The ripple became a wake. Twenty yards from the monk, Piasa emerged. In the daylight, it was almost insubstantial, but the monk could see it manifesting as the Native American manitou—bear snout, bat wings, paws with talons, panther body. He felt no fear. Around him he felt the presence of the Abbot and someone else—the Archer boy. This meant more to him than the monk could ever admit. He was glad of the company.

As the beast approached, Drake went behind the monk and pushed him forward, deeper into the water. Brother Luke held out his arms and didn't even gasp as with one motion Drake gave one last push and drew the dagger across the monk's neck. The blood gushed into the current, but Brother Luke never faltered, nor did his gaze waver. Defiantly, he looked up into the maw of the demon as the bat like wings closed over him.

There was no pain. He knew the loss of blood was what set the grey veil before his eyes, but then his vision cleared and he saw beyond the demonic mist to the bluff across the river. There, on the outcrop, in front of the autumn trees stood a white stag. It turned its head toward the monk and its limpid eyes beckoned him. The monk felt himself lifted toward the peak, and as he grew closer, the stag turned full towards him and he saw between the antlered rack a vision of a land like and unlike the one he knew, a place where it was always summer. "Come home," spoke the stag. "Come to the land of rest."

Conor gagged as Brother Luke's throat was slit and Abbot Malachy used his free arm to hold the boy upright. Conor looked to the end as the waters roiled and the monk's body disappeared beneath the depths.

Drake looked back at Rafe on the bank. "The sacrifice has been accepted. Toss the Walsh carcass into the river. Piasa will take him, if not as sacrifice, then as leftovers."

Conor's last sight as the vision faded on the baptismal pool was of the body of Declan Walsh being dragged beneath the waters.

The Abbot looked at Conor and the boy saw the face of an ancient one staring at him. No more the fatherly uncle, no more the kindly priest. Instead, someone from another time looked down at him and spoke, "You were willing to give your life to save Brother Luke, and for that first sign of selflessness, the choice you made can be made once again. Few have been given a chance to choose their path twice. Do not waste the opportunity."

Conor blinked back tears and saw the Abbot turn from him, making the Sign of the Cross over the baptismal water, all the while whispering, *"Walk now and rest, and so fade sorrow. Walk now and rest, and so fade sorrow."*

CATE AND DRAKE

RAFE MCNABB BURST into his mother's home, and said with a rakish grin on his face, "Sorry to be late for lunch, but the good doctor had work for me to do."

Cate came out of the kitchen, a plate of sandwiches in her hand. She glanced at him cooly before turning her back on him and setting the food on the table.

"You're full of blood," she said.

"Yes ma'am!" Rafe said.

Cate noted the enthusiasm in his voice. Ever since he was a little child he was exuberant whenever he came back from one of his little adventures where several wild creatures would have met their deaths.

"May I stay for lunch?"

Cate looked back at the door and saw a tall shadow in the gloomy light. "I can smell the blood on you as well."

"Well, you know, surgery and all that." Drake moved through the room and stood before her lifting up her chin with his hand. "So much to sacrifice, and so little time."

"Will you be discovered?" she asked.

"Hell no, Ma," interrupted Rafe. "After Piasa is done with them, the river will take the two. Out of sight, out of mind."

"Two?" said Cate. "We had talked about only one."

"An unexpected visitor I'm afraid," said Drake. "Brother Luke. At least I've found a way to eliminate my competition."

"But the Abbot ..." began Cate.

"So what if he discovers a monk missing?" said Drake. "Besides, I found Luke's cell phone. He received and made only one call this morning and that was to Dorothy Martin. She may know something, but we'll cross that bridge. And even if he did get a message to the Abbot, what can he do—tell the authorities? They'll think him mad."

Cate looked severe. "You're a fool if you underestimate the Abbot. He's shrewd and he's been Abbot a long time. God only knows what mischief he can cause. As for Dort Martin, I'll take care of her." She frowned, "Out of those clothes, both of you. These have to be burnt."

"Always planning, aren't you, my love. I think I left a change of clothes here the last time." He bent down and kissed her on the cheek.

"We're business associates, not lovers, Drake. Never forget that."

"Of course, Caithness, my apologies. Never the less, our plan proceeds more swiftly now. Piasa has been appeased for the moment; I have some great bio specimens. Now all I need is to begin testing. Rafe, I was hoping you would let me try some of those tests on you."

"I don't want to be anyone's lab rat."

"Dear," said Cate, "it would only be fair; look at all the pain you put other living things through." She laughed as she ruffled his hair. "I'm just joking. These tests are different than drug tests or experiments on animals. You heard the good doctor the other day. We're trying something new, or old if you'd ever read your history. Science and magic together again, just like the good old days when both were striving for real power. This time, the magic will have the upper hand, but the science will help. Besides, you won't be alone. Fergal will go through the same thing."

Fergal walked out of the kitchen with chips and drinks in his hands. "Won't be any worse than the steroid shots we took when we were in high school for football. Ma was always looking out for us then; she wouldn't let us down now. Right doc? Besides, I want to do what Conor does, what all those timid 'dark ones' could do if they'd only try."

"The tests," said Drake, "always have some element of risk but if successful, you will begin to experience things you never thought possible. You've already given yourself to Piasa. Don't look so surprised, Cate. I can tell when someone has been touched by the Devourer."

He walked over to Rafe and then turned to Fergal. "And it felt good, didn't it boys? To let it into you. You felt its power, and it's a power that just doesn't have to be a visitor in your soul, it can flow through your blood, into your entire being. You will be what the 'dark ones' never developed into. The serum itself will help but alone it can do nothing. No, you have to believe and you have to be touched by the Otherworld. In this case, Piasa is just the one for you.

"Now, hear me carefully. What I took from Declan Walsh will get us started but we will need to harvest more from other 'dark ones.' I can't have the authorities fishing around, and we won't always be as lucky as we were today in getting Declan. We have to have a way to take the ones we need without arousing a reaction from the town or the authorities. Any ideas?"

"Of course," said a voice from upstairs. Gordon McNabb came down with a smirk on his face. Looking at Fergal and Rafe, he said, "While you two are doing the Dr. Jeckyll/Mr. Hyde thing, I'll be helping Mother here with the intimidation of the town. Someone, after all, has to run the business end of things, right Ma? Caithness McNabb Enterprises has spent years consolidating power in this valley. In various ways, shapes and forms, Cate McNabb owns much of it. All she has to do is call in a few favors from the businesspeople and even the local residents. We don't need to trouble them with medieval stories; we can just frighten them where they really care, in their bank accounts."

"What Gordy is trying to say," said Cate, "is that we should be able to buy the town's silence."

"And those we can't, we'll scare to death," said Rafe.

DORT MARTIN GETS A CONSCIENCE

"GRANDMA, WHAT'S WRONG?" said a worried Nora. She had come in the back way to the store and found Dort Martin staring pensively out her display window.

"Bad things," muttered Dort. "Bad things from days gone by, come back to haunt us all."

"Whatever are you talking about?" asked Nora. She put her arms around the older woman, feeling for the first time how frail her grandmother was getting even though she was only seventy years old.

"I called Brother Luke to check on what's happening at the clinic and he's been in there since noon and hasn't come out. And that biker who rode into town the same day Conor Archer came back to us was chatting up your new boy friend a few hours ago, as well."

Nora blushed. It was nearly impossible to keep anything from Dort. Her window gave her a full view of the downtown. To her right she could just see the clinic parking lot a block away and to her left up a half block, Visser's Café. Nora hadn't told her grandmother anything about Jace, but, she supposed, that didn't keep any of the other gossips who had seen them together at the festival from informing her.

"You worry way too much."

"You're right about that," said Dort with a nervous twitch to her mouth. "Worry and never do anything about it. I don't trust that Dr. Drake. Too sneaky for me, and now that one-eyed freakish McNabb boy is his shadow. Do you know why I haven't let Rafe in this store for years? Came in here long ago looking for a big magnifying glass. 'What you want that for?' I asked him. Do you know what he told me? He told me he was going to burn holes in some gophers he had caught. Catch the sunlight and laser the poor little creatures. Sold him the magnifying glass. His money was good, even if he was not. I regret doing that. He had bad blood even back then. That mother of his wouldn't even think of taking him somewhere to have him tested. She just laughed at me when I told her. I wouldn't ever let that son of hers back in here. Made my skin crawl. Just like that biker fellow does."

"His name's Rory," said Nora. "He scares me too. Maybe I ought to take a walk up to the café and see if I can rescue Jace."

"You do that, dear. I'm going to lock up for a little bit and take a walk down to the clinic. I just can't believe that Brother Luke hasn't come back and told me what happened to that Declan Walsh boy. No, I'm not going to tell you now what happened. Get yourself up to the café and let Jace tell you. He was there for part of it."

She watched Nora go. Lovely girl, and with all that Otherworld talent. Dort was like most busybodies. Always a step too slow in actually doing anything about what she saw. Should have helped Nora adjust to who she was, but like everyone else in town, Dort just pretended it didn't exist. Like most of her old store stock that wouldn't sell, inconvenient things didn't just go away. People laughed at her, she knew, because she kept so much of her old inventory. Couldn't throw it away. She just stuck it higher on a shelf or put it in the back room. Just like the town with the 'dark ones.' Who and what they were had always been inconvenient so, if everyone just pretended they were like everyone else, their inconvenient talents would go away. Except they never did. Just can't get rid of the Otherworld like that. Flip a log over and you'll find all sorts of rot, slugs and mold. Flipping it back may cover it up but doesn't get rid of the corruption.

Dort knew other people saw what she saw and never talked about those kinds of things. Kids doing stuff they shouldn't be able to do. Why, she'd seen the O'Leary quadruplets hovering above the sandbox in the school playground one summer morning when they were three years old. A full five feet above the sand! Laughing at each other, having a grand old time. Knew that Meredeth O'Leary saw it too though neither of them ever spoke about it. Too many damn secrets. We just should have up and admitted it all to ourselves a long time ago. That's what Dort was thinking. Little Matty Shaugnessy disappearing four years ago for a week in the woods. The coyotes brought him back, grey down fur on him. Fell off him in a few days, but his eyes remained wild. Now he was a troublesome eighth grader, always causing problems.

What have we become, thought Dort. And now that Dr. Drake taking an overt interest in all the 'dark ones.' Of course she knew. She knew everything. She'd watch the clinic and the families that came were all families who had 'dark ones.' Wouldn't be surprised if he was doing experiments on them. She'd been watching his research lab going up to the south of town. Awfully big place for a small town doctor. What kind of research might interest him? And the town—blissfully, willfully ignorant, not wanting to ask questions. Well, she had had it. No more. She was going to get answers and demand to know what was going on.

Her spine began to stiffen, and Dort Martin felt righteous anger creep into her bloodstream. Felt sort of good. She went into the back room to get her sweater. First stop, the clinic to find out whatever happened to Brother Luke. The Abbey truck was still there.

She came back out into the store proper, and took a little start. Cate McNabb's back was turned to her but no doubt it was herself.

Fortunately, Dort had just a moment to compose her face.

"Cate, I didn't hear you come in. That bell must not be working. How can I help you?"

Caithness McNabb turned and smiled tightly. "Why, Dorothy, I never knew you could see the entire downtown of Tinker's Grove from your display window. No wonder you know everything that goes on here."

Dort pursed her lips but gave no reply.

"Why you can even see the clinic from here. I was wondering, was it you who gave Brother Luke a call to pay Dr. Drake a visit a little while ago?"

Paling a little, Dort said, "Yes, I did. Whatever happened to Declan Walsh looked mighty suspicious to me, and I wanted him to check it out. He's a physician, too, you know; one we've had a lot longer than Dr. Drake."

"Not as skilled, I'm afraid," said Cate. "You know, Dorothy, you really should mind your own business. I know that's a difficult thing for you to do, but poking into areas not your concern could get you into real trouble."

"How is Declan Walsh and what Dr. Drake was doing any more of your concern than mine?"

"Dr. Drake has a business relationship with me. His research involves an investment I have in his company and I'd like him left alone to do what he needs to do."

"What about Declan? Something's not right there."

"Come now, Dorothy. With all due respect, how would you know if anything was right or wrong in the medical field?"

Dort spoke sharply, her temper flaring, "The Walsh boy was sorely hurt; then he comes bounding out."

"Dr. Drake is very skilled."

"Not that skilled, I think," said Dort. "That's why I sent Brother Luke to check it out. He's not come back out of the clinic. His truck is still there, and I'm getting worried."

"Of course you are dear. It must take oodles of energy to worry about what everyone is doing in town."

"I'm going to check on him now," she said, "so if you don't mind, I have to close the store for a few minutes."

Cate laid a cold hand on Dort's wrist. "Let it be, Mrs. Martin. None of this is your concern."

"That's what I've always been told," she hissed back, jerking her arm away as if dry ice had touched it. "For too long I've sat back and let things happen or not in this town. You've really never been a part of us, so I don't know what you know or not, but this town's secrets and our ignoring of them end up hurting people. Now get out of my store; I'm going to check on Brother Luke."

"I'm going to tell you one more time, leave it alone."

"Or what," said Dort. "You'll buy me out? You know this store has been in my family for generations. You can't do a thing to me."

"Are you so sure? How is that lovely grandchild of yours?" said Cate, a small smile creasing her lips.

"Is that a threat?" Dort had never felt her blood boil like this. She didn't know where the courage came from, standing up to this wealthy woman who used her power freely whenever and wherever she wanted.

"Take if for what you wish, but you've been warned."

For a minute both were silent, a quiet but deadly tableaux with a tiny shrew in her fury holding off a huge cat ready to pounce but, for a brief moment, unsure of itself.

Cate broke the impasse. "I'll see myself out," she said. "You have a monk to check up on."

Dort watched her leave, rage still flowing in her veins.

THREATS

DORT MARTIN DIDN'T know it, but her's was the inaugural visit of the McNabb's otherwise very successful attempt to intimidate the town into even more silence than it was accustomed to.

Nora had found Jace at the café by himself. She motioned him into the car and together they drove slowly through the Grove. They absently noticed Gordon McNabb paying a visit to Dickie Bergin outside his tavern and Cate leaving Dort's place and heading into the grocery store. But they didn't question their presence; their minds were still on Rory's words to Jace.

"He just confirmed everything I suspected about Conor and my sister. And now, he's blaming their little one-on-one action for breaking some ancient pact between the mound dwellers and Piasa. I'm so incredibly pissed at Conor and Beth." He pounded the steering wheel with both hands. Nora reached over and grasped Jace's hand, hoping the touch would calm him a bit.

He went on to tell her of what had happened to Walt, of the mysterious meeting with Willie Archer, and even, though he said it somewhat sheepishly, about the humongous catfish and its special qualities. He even told her about last night's meeting with the Morrigan.

"She tried to seduce you?" said Nora. She pulled her hand back from him.

"I didn't do anything!" he exclaimed. "I swear it."

Nora was quiet for a moment and then started laughing. "Of course you didn't," she said. "You're super wise now. You know that if there's a contest between the Morrigan and me, I'll win hands down."

They both started laughing at the incongruity of it all. Nora finally said, "We're talking like we're used to all of this weirdness, like we've known about it all our lives."

"You have, Nora. You just didn't want to admit it. As far as I can see, despite strange powers, magic or whatever, everybody in this story is definitely acting the way they always have. Keeping their own self interest uppermost, striving for power and control, and of course" here he shyly smiled, "a little bit of love mixed up with it all. I've got a hunch that even the Morrigan is being true to her nature."

Nora smiled, an edge back in her voice, "What does she mean, that you are her Champion?"

"Somehow, the more I protect Conor, the more I do her bidding. Fighting for him means fighting for her, and she just seems to love me for it. Kind of freaks me out; like I'm supposed to be some great hero from the past."

Nora was quiet for a moment, then she said, "If we keep going together, you can fish all you want. Maybe you'll catch one that will give you wealth, or fame, or whatever." She punched him lightly in the side.

Jace gave a little laugh. "You're the best thing that's happened to me this fall. It's Conor that's bothering me. I don't want to protect him. I want to punch his lights out. He and Beth, it's like a betrayal."

"O wise one," said Nora. "Think before you throw a punch, okay? That's all I'm asking for the rest of this day. And remember, you don't own them."

They drove out of the downtown in silence and back towards the Michael's house. Jace wasn't quite ready to say goodbye to Nora yet.

Meanwhile, Cate and Gordy were scything through the businesses like grim reapers. They weren't even subtle in their approach. They simply reminded all the business people that, at one time or another, McNabb Enterprises had helped, or substantially supported, their establishments. McNabb Enterprises was now trying to help Dr. Drake establish the DIOGENE company in town, and, in the opinion of McNabb Enterprises, DIOGENE was not getting as much cooperation as it deserved from either the businesses or the people of Tinker's Grove. So the request McNabb Enterprises was making was simply this—whatever the good doctor needed, the town was to provide, no questions asked.

Dickie Bergin was the only one who raised objections to Gordy or Cate. "So what happens if we don't feel like cooperating? Going to come and shut us all down?"

To Gordon's credit, so said his mother later, he didn't even raise his voice. He simply reminded Dickie that the Brothers McNabb could visit the *DewDrop Inn* every night and make it so uncomfortable for the patrons that they'd travel all the way to Prairie du Chien for a drink. "You know how Rafe can get," said Gordy. That shut Dickie up, and no one else had the gumption to question either Cate or Gordy further.

Only Jim Warren, the banker, was left unmolested. Cate did pay him a visit, but she was polite when she asked for his cooperation. He was just as civil to her. He valued her money and promised to do everything he could to make sure the town was a little more enthusiastic about DIOGENE.

"Although, Cate, I think you are wrong. The townspeople have been very supportive of the new clinic. Brother Luke tells me that he gets very few patients from town visiting the monastery anymore."

"I'm sure that's true," said Cate warmly, "but Dr. Drake has informed me that DIOGENE will need help in the upcoming experiments and that the townspeople, apparently, could be of great assistance. DIOGENE will need volunteers; they will be amply compensated."

"I'm sure they will," said Warren. "These experiments, by the way, they wouldn't have anything to do with the so called 'dark ones' would they?"

"Why do you ask?" said Cate.

"You tell me. Seriously, before Conor Archer came here, did you ever give credence to the 'dark one' legends?"

"Conor Archer has nothing to do with this. It was Dr. Drake who piqued my interest in them. As far as the 'dark ones' go, I'll admit that, just like everyone else, I've been thinking about them, wondering if there's more to the rumors than what I've heard over the years."

"Where is this all going to go, Cate?" said Jim Warren, furrowing his brows from behind his desk.

"Jim, that remains to be seen. But I only forecast great things for the Grove. Try and be a bit more optimistic. It's hard for you I know, but just try, this once."

CONOR AND EMILY

CONOR CAME HOME as the afternoon sun was dying, red and gold light through the autumn trees turning sepia. Matched his mood. The dying of the light, he thought. Then he looked up at the porch; Aunt Emily, arm around a handrail, gazing at him with palpable anxiety. Funny how she stood out clearly in the midst of the shadowing day, her white blouse and hair a beacon in the gathering darkness. Tagging along as always with Conor, Troubles woofed a welcome.

"I've been worried about you," said Emily, quietly.

"I suppose you know what happened. You always know what happens."

"Declan Walsh was a good boy. Brother Luke a close friend."

"Looks like I'm the cause of it all. All because of Beth and me." Conor looked up at her face to see how she would react.

"What do you want me to say? What happened between you and Beth is complicated, I know, and you are right, it should not have happened. Can't change that now; can't stop the consequences. But you did not cause the death of those two."

Conor pushed a short strand of hair off his brow. "The Abbot and I saw it all. We looked into the baptismal font and saw it happen, all of it shimmering in the holy water, and couldn't stop it. It was terrible." A sob came from deep in his throat. "Drake slit Brother Luke's throat like he was some sacrifice or something. The Abbot went to tell the monks; I just had to get out of there. I went walking down by White Creek Way. Wanted to say goodbye to Walt."

"You didn't go to the cave did you?" said Emily, a worried frown creasing her brow.

"No. Afraid I don't have the courage to tackle that alone. But I did go to the mound."

There were tears in Conor's eyes. "I shouted for Madoc/Willie Archer, whatever he's calling himself, to appear. But nothing. Why won't he come to me? Even Jace has been able to talk to him in the last two days. Why won't he come to me? I'm supposedly his son, but you'd never know it, would you?"

Emily put her arms around his shoulders. "Whatever he wanted with Jace, it wasn't to give him affection. He had a task for Jace to do. He comes from a different time and place, Conor. When he was young and where he grew up, sons barely knew their fathers. They were fostered out to be raised by the wise."

"You mean like what you and the Abbot are doing for me." Even in his sadness, Conor couldn't suppress a tiny smile.

"If you like," said Emily, ruffling his hair. "Coupled with that is who he is. Part human, more of something else, something wild and wonderful." Her voice misted over with memories.

"So I suppose you agree with the Abbot that we can't go to the state police with all this. I mean we know Drake did it; we know the McNabbs are involved; we know things are going to get worse.

"This is a struggle the police can't help us with. First of all, there are no bodies to be discovered."

"So what?" said Conor incredulously. "We can show them the bone cave."

"Tell me, city boy," said Emily with a glint of mischief in her eye, "do they solve all crimes in Chicago?"

Conor shook his head.

"All murders?"

"I don't know." Conor turned away from her, a sullen tone creeping into his voice.

"Oh I'm not saying they wouldn't poke and prod a bit, but then they would leave us to fend for ourselves, just like they always have. Do you think this is the first time evil has come to Tinker's Grove?"

Conor didn't answer.

Aunt Emily continued, "What's going on here is being fought not just on a physical level but on a spiritual one as well. The townspeople have kept the secret of the 'dark ones.' Now they are coming to the conclusion that Drake has discovered it as well. They took the free medical care, but remember this town's roots. They still have the ingrained suspicion which their Tinker heritage bequeathed them. Nothing in the world's for free. They know that. Why did they let Drake take their blood, examine their bodies, heal their ills? Suspicious, yes, but not sure. They will be more convinced now.

"Even this afternoon, the McNabb's have moved to silence any dissent that might arise, any questions that might be asked. The people aren't sure what that means, but they love their children, all of them, not just the 'dark ones.' They fear what is coming. Then there's you. A mystery they haven't solved yet, but it won't take long for them to see you as, at the very least, the catalyst that has made visible this problem among them. They sense evil not in you, but in the whole situation. They are good people basically, but they've kept secrets for so long that they barely discuss those things among themselves. They will look to the Abbot to be of help, and the woman who lives in Madoc's Glen."

"The dweller in the Glen who has always been named Emily," said Conor.

"Indeed," said Emily, "and the town has kept that secret too, so much so that most folks preserve the fiction that every generation a new O'Rourke woman—whose name always happens to be Emily—takes over the reins and dispenses wisdom and folklore to the town."

"Are they that blind to what is going on?" asked Conor.

"They're people, Conor, and that means things will have to get much worse before they are goaded into action."

"What about me; what will they do about me?"

"I don't know yet," she answered. "Depends, I guess, on whether you are going to accept who you are or run away from it. Either way, I don't expect it will be pleasant in the short run."

"What do you mean?"

"Act on who you are, you are liable to draw the full wrath of Piasa, Drake and the McNabbs—and that's a frightening thought. Walk away and disappear or stay and do nothing; why, you'll be blamed for much of what has gone wrong."

"The Abbot said I had a second chance, but it seems like no choice to me. Now I know what the mound dwellers feel like, damned no matter what I do."

"True. No easy way out now, I fear. But there are always second chances." Suddenly Emily clucked her tongue, "There now, too much talking, almost time to eat. Go build a little fire in the fireplace while I set the table. I have a good stew tonight, and afterwards, we'll have tea and dessert in the den, beside a nice bright fire. Going to be a chill in the air this evening."

Conor did as he was told, though he didn't say much through dinner. Afterwards, before a crackling blaze with a piece of apple pie in his hand— no tea for him, it basically sucked in his view—he began to relax.

"You've been a little harsh on your father, you know," said Emily sitting down in her favorite Queen Anne chair and throwing a shawl around her shoulders.

Conor just couldn't see her as an old woman. Small as she was, she radiated strength. She looked so regal there, lifting up a teacup.

"Let me tell you a story about him."

"You know it first hand?" asked Conor.

"Landsakes, no. It happened two hundred years before I, or you for that matter, was born. Do you remember a Father Marquette from the histories I've been having you read?"

"Yeah, sure," said Conor. "The Jesuit priest who, with Joliet the fur trader, discovered and explored much of the northern Mississippi and Wisconsin valleys somewhere around 1680."

"Right you are; done your homework I see," said Emily affectionately. "Father Marquette met Piasa. In fact, he and his fellow 'blackrobes', that's what the Indians called them, first ran into the glyphs on the rocks above the rivers south of this area—fierce paintings of Piasa. Why, I think you can go somewhere in Illinois now and see what one of those paintings looked like.

"Anyway, Father Marquette was not in the least stunned to see the pictures. It took a lot to shake him. He was reported to have said, 'Well at least we know the inhabitants around here are familiar with the devil; now we shall have to tell them about Christ.'

"He explored all around this area, and, in copies of his journals, which if you are up for it, can be found in our library downtown, he describes the night he met Piasa —and someone else.

"It happened like this. Why in the world he had not yet set up camp, we will never know, but he and four other canoes full of Indians and Frenchmen and a few other Jesuit priests were still out on the water late on an autumn evening. They'd gone up a ways into the Wisconsin and were on their way back when the mist folded in on them. In his own words—I copied them out for you in case the library was not on top of your priority list—this is what he wrote."

She spoke to him then, sonorously, words from another time, long ago:

"Noises could be heard coming from the water, not the banks of the river, but from the water itself. Great gurgling noises and expirations of steam, such as I saw from the great whales when I and my companions set sail from France to cross the great ocean to this land. This foul fog mixed in with the growing mist, and the disruption grew in ferocity. The savages stopped rowing and began a wailing I can barely describe. Such a sound of loss, and of death. My own companions began praying the Psalms aloud and calling to the Virgin to protect us. Only I kept trying to pierce the gloom wondering what doom was upon us.

"Then I saw it. The same beast we had seen earlier painted on the rocks above the various rivers in these areas which we have encountered on our

travels. Huge it was, and lit with a green light as if the corruption of gangrene had suddenly luminesced to display its figure. Clearly it saw us. I had no fear for our souls, for we had Mass earlier in the day, but it came upon the first canoe and smashed it to pieces. I even saw one of the savages caught in the beast's maw. The Devourer, that is what I call it. The Devil in the Water.

"I held high my crucifix and called on the Christ to hear my prayer. That paused the beast for a moment, but then it moved on to the next canoe, toppling it as well and snatching the passengers, eating them before my very eyes.

"Next is a confusing thing for my companions, but not for me. I saw clearly, though they say it was only the rising moon that chased the beast away. The moon clearly rose. I saw it break through the mist. That in itself was strange but in front of the moon, as if it were parting the fog itself, there came a ship, ancient by the look of it, from another time. A leaping seal graced its prow. Standing on the forward deck, one hand on a magnificent sword stood a great man. A white light shone around him. A noble prince I think for he had a circlet of gold around his head, crimson cape blowing in the wind. His sword was unsheathed and pointed at the beast.

"The Devourer must have heard his approach for it turned and roared, a sound that shook the very bluffs around us. It made no attempt to attack that vessel, but disappeared into the waters and was gone. I watched, and I swear to God as my witness, the noble prince held out his sword in salute, sheathed the weapon, bowed and turned his vessel back into the mist and was gone."

The fire crackled loudly after Aunt Emily's tale. Conor stared into the flames, picturing the ship and his father, crown gleaming, sword held high.

"What was the name of his ship?" he asked.

"The *Gwennan Gorn*. It's a Welsh name, just like Madoc."

"How come no one has ever heard of this story? It's not like Father Marquette is unknown."

"You're right, but it's an account that sounds like a legend about a legend. Historians aren't going to place much stock in that. To them, it's just some hallucinations from some very tired explorers."

"You think my father will ever talk to me?" Conor hated the note of expectation in his voice.

"I'd reckon so," said Emily.

"If he wanted to, he could help these people. He could defeat Piasa."

"You're not thinking as he does. He does not care much for the realm of human beings. Long ago, he had to flee the company of humankind. While he tolerated the Tinkers, they being outcasts as well, he's never openly interfered with their way of life. That's why in the minds of many around here, he's simply an old wive's tale, meant to tease the imaginations of children on cold winter's nights. He expects you to bridge the gap."

"What do you mean?"

"Do you think Rory traveled all over, mingling with humans whom he also disdains, just to discover where you were? You have a purpose."

"Oh, I know what Rory wants. He wants to, using your words, 'bridge the gap' by me lording myself over other humans. He told me once that neither he nor Willie—I mean Madoc—care to walk in this world, but that I should. Rory told me I was meant to rule."

"Do you think that's what your father wants?"

"How should I know? Rory seems less than my father, more bitter and hurt perhaps, but he at least doesn't have any problems contacting me. He's probably as bad as Drake. You know, Aunt Emily, this place seemed free of evil, till I came."

She turned her face and looked directly at Conor. "Funny thing about evil. It forces our hand, molds our destiny. Good people who would have lived out their lives quietly now have choices to make when faced with evil. Heroes are made when confronted with utter darkness. I have felt the growing evil for years but only when you came did I know that the confrontation was about to begin. The Morrigan caws with delight over the prospect of the coming battle. She sees the war as her kind always has seen it, a chance to prove the mettle of the warrior or raise songs over the deeds of the dead. Despite her power, she is a simple creature.

"It is true that Madoc and Rory want you to do something, though be careful of taking Rory's version as Madoc's gospel. Rory is elemental, a younger brother of a prince from a time that knew only violence and the satisfying of desire. Madoc is not him. The Abbot and I also want you to do something. Fight this evil, whatever it ultimately wants or intends; you must fight it. That is our desire. Somehow, what your father wishes and what we ask of you merge and mingle the two races that find their existence threatened here in the vicinity of Tinker's Grove. I cannot give you all the answers, for much of what Piasa and Drake, and now I fear Caithness McNabb and her brood desire, is dark to me, though it seems to be unfolding swiftly."

Aunt Emily had sat forward on her chair and she grasped her cane in front of her. Conor was amazed. She didn't look like some wrinkled old crone, but exuded power and authority. She faced him with dark blue eyes unblinking.

"And all this can only happen if I allow whatever transformation is happening in me to complete itself?"

"Yes."

"And if I don't?"

"No doubt about it; the town and those you have come to love will perish, most likely. At the very least, they will be in thrall to a dark power that seeks to absorb who and what they are. It needs to feed, and its hunger will not be sated."

THE HARVEST CONTINUES

THE NEXT DAY, Wednesday, more of the 'dark ones' started disappearing. So everyone figured out later. At first, no one noticed. Only a few had asked about Walt. Some of Deck's friends had trekked up to the farm. They knocked and Mr. Walsh answered. He didn't look too good. Said Dr. Drake had ordered a private ambulance for Deck to take him to Madison to handle some blood infection. That sounded strange to Deck's friends, but stranger still was the presence of Rafe McNabb just behind Mr. Walsh. Like they said, Mr. Walsh didn't look too good. That kept conversation going down at the taverns, at least for the morning.

Then Kimberly Lagan went missing. She was a fifteen year old. Kind of quiet; kept to herself. Kimberly, the tree whisperer. At least that's what her teasing brothers and sisters said. When she was young, she'd walk in the woods, talking to the trees. People thought her strange at first, but noticed that wherever in the woods she walked, the trees grew straighter and larger. Once, said her little brother, who had followed her one evening, he saw white flowers spring up on the woodland floor wherever she walked. Fortunately, thought her family, that strangeness stopped when she reached puberty. Now she was just a shy teenager who faded into the background, barely noticed by anyone.

So no one saw her as she walked to school the morning Fergal McNabb offered her a ride in his car. That had never happened before and Kimberly was more than happy to accept—Fergal was a good looking guy, at least the best that had ever shown interest in her. She picked the wrong time to become more socially outgoing. Fergal didn't take her to school. He took her to DIOGENE.

There Dr. Drake welcomed a confused Kimberly. Assured her that everything was alright and that he had called her parents that very morning to ask for some more tests to go along with the ones he ordered the month before. Since she had already left for school, the doctor asked Fergal to pick her up.

"He's doing a little work for me, and today is gofer day for him, running around, doing some errands." Smiling his most charming smile at Kimberly, Dr. Drake shot her full of enough sedative to fell one of the Walsh's Angus steers.

Her eyes were all ready out of focus when Rafe brought in the unconscious Ronald O'Neill, a big nineteen year old himself, but no match for a sucker punch from Rafe. Ronald had graduated earlier that May from high school and was taking the semester off and babysitting at a summer cabin for one of the Chicago elite in the hills above the Wisconsin River Valley.

Rafe was a little less subtle than Fergal. He simply knocked on the cabin door and when Ron opened up and smiled in recognition, Rafe head butted him, cold-cocking him into unconsciousness. The boy hadn't moved a muscle all during the twenty mile trip back down to the DIOGENE research facility.

No one would miss him for weeks. People stayed clear of Ronald. When he was in fifth grade, the kids were picking on him one fine spring day, bothering him like they sometimes ganged up on other 'dark ones.' Ronald had enough. As best as all the parents could piece things together later that day, Ronald, in a great feat of strength, threw his attackers off him and ran to an oak tree. He pointed up at a bald faced hornet's hive. The children said he buzzed like a thousand bees, but everybody thought they exaggerated. Never the less, without saying a word, he simply pointed at his attackers and like a writhing, curling airborne snake, hundreds of hornets flew from the nest and stung the bejesus out of every one of those kids. Ronald never bothered anyone after that, and, frankly, no one ever bothered him again. Until Rafe came to visit.

"So when do we get to share in the results of your research, Doc?" asked Fergal as he and Rafe heaved the unconscious Ronald onto a gurney.

"Soon, but I hope you understand what will happen."

"You bet, shape-shifting, stuff like that."

"Perhaps. We won't know until we try. Remember, even the 'dark ones' don't actually shape-shift. They seem to absorb or take on characteristics of other forms of nature, even though I suspect they might have progressed farther, perhaps with shape-shifting abilities, if they had accepted what was happening to them. My serum should give you some of their abilities. You'll be stronger, hear better, see farther, but like I said, the serum won't be enough. I can change your DNA, but only a touch of the Otherworld will activate the changes. I suspect that's what happened to Conor. That biker, Rory, has a special interest in the lad and the wound on Conor's hand when he arrived here looked peculiarly like a bite mark. I suspect he's like a 'dark one' and has some sort of a connection with that Indian mound. He or someone like him could have activated Conor's abilities. One of the ways to jump start the boy's latent DNA would be for it to come into contact with DNA from someone from the Otherworld."

"You mean like spit."

"Yes, like saliva. That would have accelerated Conor's physical changes but even that would not be enough. Just like people can deny their own talents in this world, it is possible to refuse Otherworldly talents as well. All one has to do is ignore what's right in front of one's face. Why are some people aware of the spiritual and others not? As much as I despise the Abbot, he and I are more kin than we are to the 'dark ones' who have blinded themselves from a whole new world. Like the abilities needed to play piano, be a rock star, or play football, those of the 'dark ones' atrophy if not used. The potential lasts only for a while and then it goes dormant, perhaps even disappears."

"So Conor gets to shape-shift and I don't." Fergal looked singularly nonplussed. It was hard to tell if Rafe was even listening.

"You, and Rafe and Gordon are human and always will be," said Drake. "Conor is something more, more even than an ordinary 'dark one' if there is such a thing. But with a little help from my research, and a touch of Piasa on your soul, we just might be able to make you and your brothers worthy competitors."

Drake looked down at the comatose Kimberly Lagan. "What I'll inject into you, Fergal, will be the DNA mitochondrial gene sequence peculiar to the 'dark ones.' If this injection is given to a random person, nothing much will happen unless those genes come in contact with the alternate reality I call the Otherworld. Just like sunlight activates photosynthesis or radiation causes the growth of cancer cells, so the environment that is the Otherworld will cause these genes to function."

"By 'Otherworld' you mean the supernatural," said Fergal.

"Not really," said Drake. "The world I'm talking about is actually part of ours, just deeper. I don't know how the physicists would describe it even if they ever attempted to do such a thing. Calling it an alternate dimension doesn't really work since it is in contact with our world. It is basically 'other' than our reality, but 'other' in the sense of being more pervasive, more real as it were."

Drake smiled. "Most moderns have walled that deeper reality off, and so it never touches them. The boundaries of the Otherworld are not physical; they are drawn in the soul. It's a good thing for Piasa, that manifestation of the one I serve. Less good for those of a truly religious mind set. The Abbot spends most of his days trying to get his people in touch with the deeper reality because it is a doorway to his God. But most of them simply don't want to make the effort. My master likes that fine. It can enter our world and feed, or co-opt those whom he wishes as slaves or colleagues, like myself, without most people being any the wiser."

"Colleagues?" snorted Fergal.

"Yes," snapped Drake. "I'm no drone. In this world, the Worm which gnaws at the roots of existence needs people like me. I am his outreach to the masses; I am his viceroy, his extension in this realm of existence. Our family has always been such."

"You," said Drake to Fergal, who for once was giving a lecture almost all of his attention, "have already been touched by Piasa. It has hollowed out a place in your soul; it lives in you. Indeed, it has left part of itself in you, and you are open to it. Once injected with the 'dark ones' DNA, you will experience something none of these strange children in this town have ever fully felt. Piasa's presence will activate that sequence and you will begin to feel a new power within yourself. Exactly what abilities you will have I cannot say. But just like the religious ones here in town," Drake smiled, "you have to take a little bit on faith."

"You mean me and Rafe and Gordon have to get religion," said Fergal contemptuously. "Never had it and never will."

"But you felt Piasa in you, didn't you, Fergal?" said Drake.

"Yes, but that was real, and I liked how I felt."

Drake shook his head, "Simple boy, but you'll do. The only thing the Otherworld needs in order to get a hold on you is for you to let it into your heart. Piasa is from that world. You've let it touch you. Face it Fergal, you're hooked and happy about it."

"So what's the upshot of all this?" asked Fergal. "I mean, suppose this works, what good will come of it?"

"No good for the good, I fear, but for us who serve the Devourer, a richer life," said Drake. "As we proceed and refine the process, the two worlds—the mundane and the Otherworld—will come closer together and possibilities will occur. Piasa will move more freely among new food sources, and you, Fergal, you and your family will get power as the darkness comes."

As Fergal smiled, Drake turned Kimberly over, took out his dagger and prepared to pierce her skull.

"Why not just use a scalpel?" said Fergal.

"Because this dagger is part of the Otherworld, formed from the horn of the Worm and the One Tree of the World. Like a magnet it will search for the richest deposit of Otherworldly DNA material in Kimberly, what makes her a 'dark one.' The best concentration is in her pineal gland. Besides," he smirked with twisted lips, "it saves me the trouble of doing X-rays."

He plunged the knife down twice. Neither the O'Neill boy nor Kimberly ever moved. But in the woods where both once walked, an old hornet's nest fell from an aging oak, and a sighing wind lifted golden leaves from the trees. It was the forest's way of weeping, now that friends were gone.

HANGIN' FROM THE OLD OAK TREE

ALONG ABOUT FRIDAY of that week, it had become abundantly clear to the folks of the Grove that more than a few kids were missing, and parents could not find any trace of them. In most places, the media would have descended and made it a national spectacle, but the people who lived in Tinker's Grove still had the suspicious blood of their ancestors in their veins. More than just a healthy skepticism of the outside world. Instead, their natural inclination in a time of crisis such as this was to pull inward, not talk to strangers, and even less, involve people of authority.

All of which Dr. Drake and the McNabb family had predicted would happen. All of which was very beneficial to their plan. People observed an influx of strangers beginning to show up to work at DIOGENE, a company which created an aura of paranoia by forsaking easily seen barbwire fences with ubiquitous security cams and the occasional dog patrol around the perimeter.

In an atmosphere like that, law enforcement was effectively paralyzed with parents who wouldn't talk and industry that wouldn't give out any public information. What began on Tuesday, with the McNabb boys visiting all the businesses of the town, continued the rest of the week. Entrepreneurs were reminded where their true allegiance lay. Townsfolk, united against the outside world, began to split against each other, frantic parents being chastised by others who didn't want feathers ruffled or authorities notified.

Arguments broke out everywhere, even at the fuel and gruel stop where Beth worked. After an altercation where fists flew, she got Mary Sheehy, the owner, to close early. The October sun was fast losing its heat by the time Conor came by. Folks who had been shouting at each other paused in their anger to glare at the Archer boy.

"Would have picked you up at home," said Beth, hooking his arm and steering him clear of the angry patrons.

"Know that," said Conor, "but it gets a little tense with Aunt Emily these days, people being on edge and all. Besides, it's still a little hard for her to make peace about what happened between you and me."

Beth blushed and shook her blond hair over her shoulder. "I've always been a little nervous around that woman. Just never thought it would be for this reason. So, sinner, want to go for a little ride?"

"Sure," said Conor, hopping into her car.

Low shadows cut across the road as they headed up towards Muddy Hollow Crossroads.

"I can't deal with all these kids disappearing," said Conor. "Especially since I may be a reason for what's happening."

"Me as well," said Beth. "Kim Lagan was a friend of mine, and if those McNabb's or that demented doctor took her there will be major hell to pay. Deck's death hit all of us hard, especially since none of us who know can say anything about it. The police, even the state patrol, can't get anywhere with the people. Town's just closed up tight. No evidence, no crime, and the missing haven't been missing for long enough to goad the authorities into more radical measures."

"You'd think Brother Luke and the mystery of his disappearance was public enough to catch their attention," said Conor.

"I miss him as well, but the monks must know at least some of what the Abbot knows. Maybe that's why the Abbey has stayed so quiet and not rung alarm bells."

"Don't think the Abbot told them. Last I heard, they are just praying for their missing brother. Why are you driving towards the Crossroads?" asked Conor.

"I want to show you something. You knew what they all said about Kim, don't you? About her being the original tree hugger?"

Conor admitted he'd heard some rumor about that.

"We were just kids when it happened, when we came across Fergal and some of his friends up here at the Crossroads, carving their initials into the old oak. Everybody does stuff like that. It's a kid thing. These guys were really going at the tree though, hacking into it for no reason, carving curse words and worse into the wood."

"What did Kim do?"

"She went ballistic, Conor, all eight years and fifty pounds of her. We were just biking towards the crossroads and she saw what they were doing. She shrieked and beat me to the tree. Kim turned into this raving spitfire, kicking, biting and punching every boy she could lay a hand on. Fergal and his friends were older, but they weren't up for that kind of intensity. They booked on their own bikes. They were gone by the time I got to her. She didn't even know I was there. Plastered against that great trunk she was moaning like she was in pain. She ran her hands over every cut and scar those boys had carved into that tree and whatever she touched healed."

"Impressive," said Conor.

"But there's more," she said. "The tree started swaying even though there wasn't any wind. I backed up and found myself standing in the middle of the road. I watched branches bend down around that little girl and caress her. They lifted her up off the ground and cradled her for almost ten minutes. I couldn't even move. And when they let her down again, she walked back to me like she was in a trance. I had to shake her to wake her up. She looked at me, her eyes kind of vacant, and then she looked at the oak and said to me, 'The Tree of the World hurts no more.' That's what she said. Then she shivered and was herself again. She talked all the way back home, but never said another word about what happened at Muddy Hollow Crossroads."

"I suppose you kept that little event secret, like everyone else in the Grove keeps secrets."

"Yes," said Beth, "I told Jace, that's all. Strangeness is a part of the Grove and though we accept it as fact, nobody ever seems to talk about it much."

They could see the Crossroads not far ahead. In the shadows, though, it looked somehow different to Conor. As Beth drove closer, Conor gasped and said, "I think there's someone hanging from the oak tree."

"You've got to be kidding me," said Beth, pulling the car to the side of the road about twenty yards from the oak.

"Seriously. Look, see for yourself."

Conor could see the figure clearly now, swinging slowly beneath a large branch of the oak.

"Can't see anything but the tree, Conor," said Beth.

Conor couldn't speak. He was looking at the corpse. It was a black man, neck broken, face contorted, eyes wide open, but definitely dead.

"I know him," said Conor. "It's Taps Jeffords, music guy. Told you about him, Beth. Couple of months ago, he appears right here, talking to me in broad daylight, though its night for him and he's back in the year 1925. That song I do, 'Down by the River'—he's the one who wrote it, made it famous, and I told him that I saw his death."

"You must have your mojo going again, Conor. Whatever you're seeing is in your mind, not out here; but I'll take your word for it. How was this guy supposed to die?"

"He knew I knew, but I couldn't tell him how. It was too gruesome. He died by hanging in the year 1926, the year after he talked to me under this old oak tree. Lynched right here. Probably the last lynching ever done in these northern parts. Never caught the guys who did it."

A distant laughter caught Conor's ear; he and Beth moved closer to the macabre sight.

"Told you Crossroads were a haunting place," said the corpse.

Conor jumped and Beth shrieked.

"You hear that?" said Conor.

"Just some moaning, there up in the branches," said Beth.

"No, no, he's really talking."

Conor told Beth to stay behind and walked a little closer. For sure, he thought, there was Taps Jeffords' corpse, smiling down on him all beatific like.

"Don't look so surprised," wheezed the man with the broken neck. "After all, I'm the one they hung tonight. Damn Jake McNabb and his hired help. They don't much like black folks but, even more, they hated my helping your Aunt Emily and her sister Finola and you, Conor, lad."

"What?" said Conor.

"Well, I had to help them, you see, or those vigilantes would have done those women and you some powerful harm. Have to say your timing is a little off. Fifteen minutes earlier and maybe my head wouldn't be flopping over this noose, swaying with the wind."

Conor couldn't figure out which creeped him out the most, the scratching of the hangman's rope across the branch or the breathy voice of a man who was supposed to be dead.

"Why did you come back to the Grove?" asked Conor.

"Came for the music. It's All Hallow's Eve on this my hangin' night and I came to hear the monks sing. So beautiful last year, so peaceful and calm. 'Fraid it wasn't that way tonight."

"Conor," said Beth, "you're scaring me. Whoever's talking to you, what's he saying?"

The corpse winked at Conor, "Fine woman you have there Mr. Archer. And while I'm doling out compliments, you're looking different yourself this evening. Last time I saw you, you appeared pretty fearsome."

"I—I wasn't myself," stammered Conor.

"Oh, but you were, you know that. I recognized you right away, didn't I? Seems you aren't taking to being real connected with who you truly are."

"Never mind that," said Conor. "How did you meet my mother?"

"Just don't have any patience, do you boy. Do I look like I'm going anywhere?"

Conor made a move to try to take the man down.

"Leave me be," sighed Taps Jeffords, "I'm already dead. Nothin' you can do to make me more comfortable. Besides, hangin' here is a good sign for people around these parts. Maybe make them ashamed a bit for their inhospitality."

Nobody spoke for a moment. Only the creak of the rope rubbing on the branch was heard; then the corpse began to talk again.

"Started out to be a beautiful day. Came walking up the road past this very tree not twelve hours ago. Walked over to the Abbey and renewed my acquaintance with the Abbot and monks. They invited me to the procession again and I gladly agreed. Gave me a special candle and all that. Met in the crypt chapel at sunset and we began the walk down to the river, singing beautiful songs, Celtic I think. The stars were out early because there was no moon. That song I sang to you last year—"

"It was just a couple of months ago," said Conor.

"Hey, man, I'm hangin' on the Tree of the World here in the middle of the crossroads. Told you last time that everything's different in the thin places, especially in the shade of this tree. Time don't work the usual way. My time is my time; your's is your's. We just got a temporary connection across the years.

"Anyway, as I was saying, that song I sang to you last year made it big in Chicago. The monks were a great inspiration so I thought I might come back and renew the acquaintance. And everything was going right smoothly, until your mama broke into the monk's procession down by the river, near the mound. 'Save me!' she cried. I couldn't see anybody chasing her, and then, from outside the light cast by all those beautiful candles, I saw a shadow. Man-shaped it was."

"My father," whispered Conor.

"No boy, I knew him from last year, but when the shadow stepped into the light I could tell he was like your father."

"Rory."

"Is that what you call him? Well, I got to tell you, son, he was one unpleasant figure. Demanded the monks give him your mama and you. Said something like, 'Madoc's whore deserves to be shared.' Like I said, not a pleasant fellow. That's when the Abbot stepped in. Blocked his way.

"The Abbot turned his head and caught my eye—me the stranger there! He said to me, 'Find the woman and boy and make sure they are all right.' It was then that this Rory swung his fist and clocked the Abbot on the side of the head. I took out after your mama. She had already made a run for it up towards the Crossroads. I looked back and found the Abbot hadn't moved from his spot. Tough old coot. He could take a punch. Last thing I saw he was backing Rory down towards the water's edge with his staff and Rory wasn't giving the old priest any guff. Would sure like to have known what the Abbot said.

"But I had my mission and I finally caught up with you and your mama right here. Asked her if you both were okay and she said you all were.

"Your Aunt Emily came along about then, walking right up this here road. Hugged your mama and said something about sisters sticking together. Hard to believe they were related, your Aunt Emily being a handsome woman and all that, but much older than your mama. Then again, strange things seem to happen quite frequently around these parts." Jeffords began to wheeze and cough for a moment.

"Anyway, the two of them's huggin' and kissin' each other with little you in between. I was right proud that the evening was getting back to peaceful.

"Things would have ended there but who should ride up but Jake McNabb and his thugs. Knew that only later when they introduced themselves as they tightened the noose around my neck. McNabb's a big shot around here I guess. Stopped their horses so fast that a cloud of dust choked us all. You started crying.

"They were drunk. 'What's this we got here?' said Jake. 'A black man and a pretty white woman with a baby and old Miss Emily. Ladies, this here stranger thinking of doing you any harm?'

"'No sir,' I said, answering before the ladies could. Best not to say too much in a dangerous time like that. Your mama spoke right up, 'No harm done here; he's just checking to see if I needed any help.'

"'Well, do you?' leered one of McNabb's men. 'Hey Jake, maybe I could see if she needs any help.'

"'Say,' says this Jake McNabb, 'where do you come from little lady? And who is this boy of your's?'

"Your Aunt Emily spoke right up. 'None of your business Jake. You and your hired help get on out of here. Nothing to see or do here.'

"Jake McNabb gets off his horse and walks over to her. 'I hear things you know, Emily. The river whispers to me. Heard it talking to me tonight. Told me to go to the Crossroads that voice did. Told me I'd find a faerie lady and her changeling child walking the roads on this Halloween night. Told me I ought to do what one does with all fey things.'

"'And what would that be?' said Aunt Emily.

"'Kill 'em!' said Jake with a laugh. 'Kill 'em both. Maybe you too Miss Emily if you get in my way. She's a pretty one though. Shame to do her dead right away, don't you think, boys? Seems to me like we could have some fun.'

"The men got off their horses and I knew right then things weren't going to go well. Should have seen their eyes, Conor. All misty green. They barely looked human. I stood in front of your mama and you. Your Aunt Emily stood right with me—fierce lady that she is. I think she would have clawed their green-glowing eyes out. I told her to run with you and the girl. None of them wanted to go, so I had to yell. 'See here,' I says, 'the Abbot gave me a charge; said I was good enough to protect you all, so get on out of here. Keep that baby safe.' Truth to tell, they wouldn't have gotten very far on their own. I saw Jake McNabb and his boys starting to circle around us, but I had a good size rock in my hand and I planted it right in the middle of the face of one of those leering white boys. You should of seen him bleed!"

The corpse started laughing, a breathy, bubbling, wheezing chuckle. A shiver went up Conor's spine.

"Your mama and her sister took you off down toward your Aunt Emily's place. Don't know what happened to them after that. They seemed to just disappear into the evening. Those men tried to follow but they couldn't find a trace of them. Then, I got kind of preoccupied with my own situation."

"They lynched you," said Conor.

"Sure enough," said Taps.

"My God, I'm sorry."

"Not your fault. Was just my time. Glad it was protecting somebody from harm. Particularly glad I was protecting you and your mama."

"Why's that?"

"'Cause you are special, boy! How many times do I have to tell you that?"

"How can you be so sure?" asked Conor.

"Your father told me," said Taps. "Just a moment before I died, I opened my eyes and saw someone looking up at me. Thought it was an angel at first, but no, it was that same man I saw in the crowd of monks last year, only this time he wasn't dressed as some kind of farmer. He was in one of those ancient costumes—like something Robin Hood would wear— and he had a circlet of gold around his head, and there were tears in his eyes, those wonderful gold-flecked eyes that sparkled warmly in the October night. There was a faint glow around him, a haunting glow for an All Hallow's Eve night.

"'I am too late,' he said. 'But I bid your spirit to stay awhile. There will be no pain.' He said it so gently that I think I wept with him. 'I want to thank you for watching over my wife and son. She is distraught this evening and rightly so. My realm in the Otherworld is not always a peaceful place. Indeed, I was detained, but you have saved her from even greater harm, and saved my son.' Your father stroked the bark of this here old oak. 'It is a good and worthy Tree,' he said. 'To die on this for someone else is the most noble thing one can do.'

"So I've hung around so to speak," said the corpse, laughing again to himself. "Guess I was waiting for you."

"You can't stay here," Conor said. "It's not right."

"'Course it's not right," said the hanged man. "I have to go, but not till I tell you something. I can see things, hangin' here. And I hear things as well. I heard this Tree weep not more than an hour ago. It whispered to me that the one who would heal it of a hurt years from now in your time was dying—just a little child—killed by an emissary of evil. Then this here oak bid me look across the years and see down into your little village. Let me tell you what I see. Four little ones down in the Grove, cute little bugs they are. And the successors of Jake McNabb and his goons have their eyes set on them. Only you can save them Conor. Go now and hurry. Time's a 'wastin.' Touch my hand, boy."

Conor stretched out his right hand. Why the hell am I doing this? He touched the clammy skin and suddenly Taps Jeffords arm jerked and the corpse hand grabbed Conor. He tried to pull away but Taps held him tight and lifted him high.

"Listen to me, Conor Archer. I'm hangin' on the Tree of the World. All who give their lives for others hang here. If you want to be what you were meant to be, you'll be hanging here with me on this Tree. Understand? It's a destiny you can't run away from if you're going to truly be a man."

"Let me go!" shouted Conor. "Now!"

"Can't do it, boy. Not till you promise me that you'll save those children. Save them now."

"Let someone else do it!" said Conor.

"There is no one else," said the corpse.

Behind him, Conor heard Beth scream. He knew she could only see him, levitating off the ground, floating up into the branches of the oak. His arm glowed in the shadows, and visions of snakes and worms writhing free of those trying to catch them danced in his mind. He heard Beth scream even more loudly as the hanging rope squealed against the tree and the corpse hissed like a cobra. Conor felt himself fall to the ground.

"There you did it," said Taps Jeffords, broken neck lolling around the rope. "Slithered right out of my grasp. Knew you could do things like that, but just didn't think you'd do it to me. You're coming back here, boy, here to me. You're coming back to the hangin' tree, here to be with me."

A rasping chuckle broke from the dead man's mouth, a rictus smile that shivered Conor to the bone. He turned and crawled on his hands and knees, out of the shadows, onto the road, into the arms of Beth.

Conor was gasping with fear, and Beth soaked the top of his shirt in seconds with tears.

"You floated," she said. "I saw it and you floated, and then your arm exploded into a mass of snakes, at least it looked something like that."

He could tell her voice was tripping on the edge of an abyss, so he took her by the shoulders, steadied his own voice and said, "I'm okay.

Look. Arm's just fine. No harm done. But I saw Taps Jeffords, that singer from the past I told you about. He's hanging from that branch." Conor pointed but even he couldn't see anyone on any branch any more. "At least he was there. He said there's a problem with four little kids in town. Have any idea who they might be?"

THE FLIGHT OF THE SWANS

BETH SWALLOWED HARD as she and Conor stood up.
"Those four kids have to be the O'Leary quads. They're just four years
old."

"Are they 'dark ones?'" asked Conor.

"Sure look like it. Three boys and a girl, all with black hair and eyes.
When they were born, the Prairie paper did a story on them. They were a
local sensation for a while. Lots of the townsfolk know them well. After all,
the parents needed a ton of help."

"They're the next to be in trouble with Drake and the McNabb's," said
Conor. "In fact, something might be happening now. We've got to get to
them."

They jumped into the car and roared back to town.

"First place to check is the clinic; then we'll go to the DIOGENE
complex if they're not there," said Conor.

As luck would have it, they pulled into the clinic parking lot just as
Drake, Rafe and Fergal, and a dejected looking Mr. O'Leary and the quads
were coming from the opposite direction.

As Beth and Conor climbed out of the car, they also saw Jace and
Nora walking down the hill, Jace carrying his gear from football practice.
Recognizing there was a commotion at the clinic, the two of them broke
into a run. Seeing them as well, the physician tried to hustle the children
faster towards the entrance.

"Dr. Drake, stop!" shouted Conor. "What are you doing with those
kids?"

The man never looked rumpled. In fact, he looked immaculate in his
black suit, holding the finger of one of the quads.

"Conor, Beth," said Drake in his most welcoming voice. "Twice in
one week is quite a surprise, but I'm afraid I have these children to take care
of—a strange illness."

"Take care of them like you took care of Deck and Brother Luke?" shouted Jace as he came to stand next to his sister.

Truth to tell, Conor was pleased to see Jace, though he couldn't be sure the feeling was mutual. Jace had seemed real distant all week long. A pang of guilt washed over Conor; he knew he was the reason.

The four of them were on one side of the parking lot opposite the entrance. Drake was still making his way towards the door. For a moment, they were paralyzed with indecision, unsure whether they wanted to risk getting closer. Rafe and Fergal were looking mighty hostile.

More thuglike than usual thought Beth. She couldn't help seeing a change in them. The more involved they became with Drake, the more animal-like they seemed.

It was Mr. O'Leary who broke the impasse. "Jace, I know you and your friends mean well, but seriously, my kids are in distress and Dr. Drake is going to help them. Really."

"Sir," said Conor, "your children look fine. They're smiling and laughing; you can't believe what this man is telling you. He's out to hurt them."

Drake's own laughter ran clear in the dying light. "Conor, Conor, you are so melodramatic. I'm just going to treat them."

"You've done something to Mr. O'Leary," said Nora. "Playing with the dark powers gives you the ability to cast a spell over the good folk of this town."

"Dark powers? Oh my … I don't know about that," smirked Drake. "Tell me, Mr. O'Leary, do you feel like you are under some kind of spell?"

The father turned his head toward the tall doctor and looked worshipfully at him, "I can't tell you how much this means to me, Dr. Drake, that you are willing to treat my children for free, to make them really well."

"I'm telling you, sir," said Jace. "If you let them go in there, they will never come out the same. You'll lose them forever."

O'Leary just gaped at them, going slack jawed.

"There you see," said Drake in an ominous voice that wafted across the parking lot. "Everything is as it should be. Now go and leave us alone, or I'll have to have my assistants escort you off my property."

A wind blew up from the north, just a gentle breeze at first, and Conor looked up into the sky. The sun had set but a fierce red glow still shone in the western horizon. On the wings of the wind, Conor could hear a faint voice singing and he shivered. Taps Jeffords was singing from the Tree:

O take me there, down by the river,
O take me there, down by the river,
O take me there, down by the river,
Down by the river where the waters flow.

"Leave me alone," whispered Conor.
"What did you say?" asked Beth.
"Nothing," said Conor, but he backed away a little from the group.
The wind was rising and the voice came again,

You're coming back, boy,
Coming here to me,
Here to me on the hangin' tree.
Now be a man,
Do what's right,
Death is stalking youngins tonight.
All who save must come to see;
There's no salvation,
'Cept the hangin' tree.
Nosiree, nothin' to do but hang, hang, hang,
Savin' the world on the hangin' tree

Conor gasped and fell to his knees.

Drake's eyebrow arched in surprise. "Care to come in Conor? Looks to me like you've caught whatever virus is going on around here."

Conor gritted his teeth and spat out, "You'd like that wouldn't you, you morbid freak. You're behind the disappearance of the children of this town and you've cast some spell on nearly everyone so they don't do anything about it."

Drake laughed. "Don't make me so mystical, boy. Magic works in certain ways and it almost never works if people don't know you. Everyone knows me here in town. They trust me now. They listen to every word I say. Very easy to weave a web of deception. Look at the streets. Empty of life. Why does no one run out to help the four of you? It's not that they don't care. They're just not thinking about what's happening here. I can feel their minds, and if a noise or voice captures their attention, I just cloud their vision. Not difficult at all, really. They trust me. They believe in me. That's half of magic's work. Of course, the other half is real power. Want to see how Rafe and Fergal have grown in the past few days? They do as the doctor says, take their medicine, and, my, the benefits are enormous."

Rafe and Fergal leapt across the parking lot. Nora thought their backs bent forward simian-like and their faces took on a cunning akin to predators in the wild.

Beth bent down to Conor. "You've got to do something. My brother can hold those two off, but if Drake gets the quads in the clinic, he'll lock us out and they'll be lost."

Conor was oblivious to her words. All he could see in his mind was the corpse of Taps Jeffords, swinging in the wind. No voices in his ears, just the roaring of the rising wind.

Jace was not paralyzed. He leapt forward in front of the other three and crouched to meet the charging McNabb's. Nora even thought to lend a hand, picking up a rock to chuck at Rafe's last good eye. Over it all, Drake was smiling and leisurely leading the quads to the clinic door. O'Leary himself was shuffling quietly behind.

Against his better judgement, Conor lifted his head. He saw the four little children, obediently following the doctor. The elegant exterior of the physician seemed to him more transparent. Cadaverous, that's what he looks like, thought Conor. Just a corpse in a dead man's suit. In a moment, they would be gone, probably forever lost to the town. He knew he couldn't let that happen, but he had never, except for the Second Sight, consciously tried to use whatever strangeness was in him in a constructive way. He didn't know how.

He reached out his right hand, and saw that the ribbon of skin already was luminescing in the twilight. He looked at the kids and saw in them a fragility, an innocence, that had to be given a chance to live. He thought to himself. If I could only fly to them and take them away, safe under my wings. He found himself whistling, a piercing cry that caught the attention of the children.

They stopped and the one who had hold of Drake's finger pulled her hand away. The four stood looking across the parking lot at Conor.

Drake was annoyed. "Haven't you meddled enough Conor Archer? As important as I think you are, I can still dispense with you. Leave us alone."

But Conor didn't hear him. He looked at the children and saw their eyes. Gold flecks gleaming in the twilight. 'Dark ones' alive! He knew that in an instant. These were young enough to still have power, perhaps old enough to use it. All they needed was a catalyst, someone to show them how. The wind was swirling little dust devils in the parking lot, blowing the hair of the O'Leary quads like feathers shaken from a down pillow. He wasn't sure what power they had, but as he gazed into their eyes he felt their minds, light and free, joyful and soaring, and then he knew. How, he could never figure out later, but he knew what to do.

As the wind howled, he felt a power inside of him growing. He stood up, his hand beckoning to the children. He touched their minds again, and they laughed.

"Conor, Conor, Conor, Conor!" they shouted to him in his mind. "Time to play, time to run, time for fun, time to fly!" They took a step in his direction.

Drake took in the situation. To him, Conor seemed to grow in stature. Like the children, Conor's eyes were flecked with gold but an added luminescence seemed to shine around him. Drake knew Conor had some latent talent, but this was the first time he was seeing it in the flesh. A tingling fear took him and he turned his gaze to Fergal and Rafe who were slugging it out with Jace.

"Back to me," cried Drake to the McNabb's. "Back to me and take the children."

Beth knew she had only a moment and rushed across the parking lot to grab the kids. Drake snarled and took out his dagger and pointed it at Beth. Words foul and dark poured out of his mouth to be swallowed by the roaring wind. But for Beth, it was as if a vice had clamped on her throat. She felt the air squeezed out of her and her body thrown to the ground.

Conor saw none of this. Facing the children he raised his arms beseeching them. "Fly to me and flee from Drake. He seeks to harm you. Fly to me!"

With the exception of the unconscious Beth, they all saw it, and in times afterward both friend and foe still talked about it with awe. Even some townspeople, garnering enough courage to snatch a glance from a window saw. The children jumped with their arms reaching and in the twilight, an explosion of white, wings outstretched, feathers opened wide in the night, a trumpet call of victory as four beautiful white swans ascended into the sky. They flew in a circle above the parking lot and called to Conor. All heard the trumpeting of swans but Conor heard the words embedded in their cry, "You have saved us Conor ab Madoc. Children we were of our beloved father, O'Leary, but creatures of the air now we are. We fly to freedom, saved by you, to meet again one day."

Conor saw Drake enraged, raising his dagger to the circling birds. Hearing the disgusting filth coming out of the mouth of the mage, Conor cried to the swans, "Flee now and preserve your fate. Flee for your father's sake and the people of Tinker's Grove."

Conor had never spoken like that. He felt like some stilted medieval bard at one of those renaissance fairs around Chicagoland in the summertime. But the words were his as was the sentiment. And he feared the words of Drake even if he could not understand them. He could see the cloud of mist they conjured and he feared the pestilence would chase the swans even into the evening sky. He found himself stretching forth his right hand and twisting it, visualizing it around the throat of Dr. Drake. Indeed, the foul doctor immediately stopped speaking and, with his free hand, clawed at his collar. For a moment, Conor enjoyed the sensation of squeezing the life out of the jerk, but then he saw Beth collapsed on the ground and his concentration broke. Drake choked out a command and ordered Fergal and Rafe into the clinic. The door slammed and Nora and Jace rushed to Conor and Beth.

She was unhurt. A little shaken up but no lasting damage.

"What just happened?" said Jace. "Conor did you do that to those kids?"

"I, I don't know," he said. "I think I just helped them do what they had the potential to always do. I opened a gate, gave them an opportunity. At least that's what it felt like."

"And a good thing, too," said Nora. "Drake had bad plans for them, I'm sure."

"What about Mr. O'Leary?" said Beth.

They looked and saw him wandering aimlessly around the side of the clinic. Running to him, they asked if he was all right, but he stared at them blankly, until his eyes fell on Conor.

"You!" he said, his face twisting with hate. "You took my children. I want them back."

"Mr. O'Leary, you saw what happened. I'm not sure exactly how all of this came down," said Conor.

"You made them change. They were my precious dears, and you've taken them away from me. Since my wife died, they are all I've had left, and now they're gone. Dr. Drake said they were seriously ill, and now they're gone and they'll never be well."

Nora touched the stricken father's shoulder. "Mr. O'Leary, Dr. Drake was going to hurt them."

"Never!" said O'Leary throwing off her arm. "He would never hurt them. But you," he spat out his words at Conor, "you are the one who brought change to the Grove. You've made those other children disappear. That's what people are saying, and now I know they are right."

There was no consoling him. They let him go, muttering to himself, weeping at the loss of his children.

"Where did they go, Conor?" asked Nora.

"I don't know," he said. "I don't think I can even get them back."

Jace said nothing. He just looked at Conor, conflict and inner turmoil masking whatever wisdom rested in his heart.

FEAR

THE FOUR STOOD alone in the dark. Even the red sky had gone gray, and night was falling.

"Somebody had to have seen all this. Where are they?" said Beth, looking up the empty street. "Where are all the people?"

"They're there," said Nora. "Behind curtains and locked doors. My grandmother told me what the McNabb's have done. Threats and bribes. Fergal and Rafe may be the muscle, but Gordon McNabb is his mother in spades. He and she have put the real fear in all of them. Over the years, most have become beholden to the McNabb's. My grandmother owes them nothing, but even she is afraid. The night comes every twenty-four hours, and they come in the night now. Caithness McNabb and her eldest. Coupled with whatever Drake does, it serves as well as any spell over the people. The people will do nothing to save themselves or the 'dark ones' in their midst. They're terrified."

The Angelus bell began to ring from the bell tower of the monastery, high on the bluff. Six o'clock.

"Look," said Conor. "There's a light in the tower. It's some huge torch, but it's not burning the steeple. Let's check it out."

"Chill, man," said Jace. "Every year, the fire is lit, just a couple of days before Halloween. Something the ancestors of this village brought with them about chasing away the things that walk in the night at this time of year."

The four looked down the business district, weak street lights casting a mournful light on deserted sidewalks.

"At least there's real light up there," said Beth. "Come on."

They drove up to the monastery and found the Abbot at the door of the church, dressed in his Benedictine habit. He smiled a sad smile at them.

"I've been waiting for you. The darkness is deep down in the town."

"And Drake's been at it again," said Conor. "He's as much admitted to using dark powers against the town."

"And you, Conor," said the Abbot, "what do you admit to? Above the bell tower of this monastery, not twenty minutes ago, in the twilight red sky, four swans flew and trumpeted their cry. I spoke to them, and knew them as well as when I first poured water over their heads at baptism. 'We're free,' they said, and they praised your name, Conor. For the first time, you've chosen to use your gifts, and saved them from a terrible fate."

The Abbot looked at them. "All four of you have destinies entwined. In this little corner of the land, two worlds are meeting and a new creation is occurring. The age old fight of good and evil is fought out even here but with new rules and great wonders. Yet the same is always required, men and women of pure heart and noble spirit. I wonder if you will see the task through."

Conor looked at the Abbot and said, "Why are there torches in the bell tower? Who or what do they burn for?"

"For all those who love the Light," said the Abbot. "Much of what you've seen in our town must strike you as heavy with superstition. But the old ones who came here had a wisdom many moderns have lost. This time of year, the walls between the worlds grow thin. Here in the Grove, where the walls are none too thick, what is on the other side will often walk this land. Much from that world is beautiful, but not everything. The light burning in the church tower serves as a warning. Those who love the dark must beware." He opened the doors of the Abbey Church, and candlelight rushed out. All the monks were in vigil in their choir stalls. A few briefly turned their cowled heads toward the rear of the church, welcoming smiles clearly visible.

"Here the power of good prevails," said the Abbot. "Now look more closely in the surrounding woods."

Conor saw shadows moving amidst the darkened trees. He knew they were from the mound, and he wondered if his father was there.

"Madoc is not," said the Abbot, answering Conor's unspoken question. "But his people are. They cannot help themselves. They, too, are drawn to the Light. They are not children of the night, though they often live as if that nightmare is upon them."

"Rory?" said Conor.

"Oh, he's back there in the shadows, I'm sure," said the Abbot.

"Oz?" said Beth.

"He is not of the People of the Hollow Hills. He is a lost 'dark one' who is kin to them and to us; his way is sundered from them and those in the town. Never the less, he is there too, drawn by the Light."

A soft woof in the dark made Conor turn. Up the road walked Aunt Emily with Troubles at her side. He could hear the tapping of her black-thorn cane.

"Of course, Aunt Emily," said Conor.

"Of course," said the Abbot. "She who has lived long and wisely and made this land her own. She is more of the Light than many of us here."

"What do you want of us?" asked Jace. "What can we possibly do about things we don't even understand?"

"First," said Emily, joining the conversation, "an explanation of what happened just now. I saw swans on the wing and they called to me in human voices. I heard the wind through the trees and whispers came through the falling leaves of an awakening of power. I heard an old friend, dead these many years, neck stretched on the Crossroads Oak speak. What those omens portend makes my blood run cold. Malachy, I thought we had more time."

"So did I, Emily, but events have forced Conor's hand." Turning to the four, he said, "Now tell us quickly what you did."

They spoke, and to everything they said, the Abbot and the old woman simply nodded their heads.

"The time is fast approaching," said Aunt Emily, "when the hints of strangeness and wonder that you all have seen these past months will break open into this world. A battle is coming. Not with armies or tools of technology, but one on one, good against evil, light against dark. There will be no strength in numbers; only your own character, who you are, will see you through. Now, get you into the church."

She looked around at the gathering shadows. "The night has come, the day is spent. This is the time when evil walks more freely than it has for many a year in Tinker's Grove. A little prayer wouldn't hurt a bit." She hustled them inside, leaving the Abbot alone at the doorway. Conor broke away from the group and came back to stand with the Abbot.

"Why won't he speak to me? Why are all his People out there and yet he does not come to me?"

"He is not quite like those he rules. Of noble birth among his own kind, he is haunted by what he did with the human woman Finola, your mother. Many of those he governed argued for closer ties with humans. They thought themselves diminishing and saw humans as their only hope. They wanted, not a partnership, but children. For the People were becoming increasingly barren. Your father argued against that though he himself was a product of such a union. He had watched his own human father's kingdom be ripped apart because of it. Yet, in the end, he was caught in that web by his own love for your mother—a Roan lass, like him, born from the sea she was, a sea wife for a mother, a Tinker for a father. The human blood in Madoc flows thin, and more of the sea than the land flowed in your mother. Long has it been since he walked often in the world of men. Conor, you are Madoc's pride but also his embarrassment—a weakness he once showed to his own People and to the world of men. He is paralyzed into inaction by his love of you and his responsibility for the People."

"He should come to me," said Conor. "I am his son; he is all I have left."

"There you are very wrong. All those behind you in this church care for you very much. The stories have long been told of your coming. You can never be alone. That is where you and your father are very different. Now go. Pray. For yourself and for your friends. You will need all the strength you can gather."

Conor disappeared into the church, leaving the Abbot alone in the night.

He spoke to the shadows. "You are welcome, you know. You always have a place here, even if you have chosen not to use it. Come."

Holding his arms out to the dark, the Abbot waited. Nothing happened. A derisive laugh came out of the woods; a cawing was heard high in the trees. He knew that Rory and the Morrigan would not come. But something moved. Oz. He stumbled towards the Abbot, ear buds plugged into his head. The Abbot shivered. Oz's eyes weren't vacant tonight. One was flecked with gold, the other misty green.

"Always caught between two worlds and two forces," whispered the Abbot. "Come inside, Oz. Come to the Light."

The big man stopped. A moan came from his mouth and he reached for the Abbot, but then, like a puppet on a string he was pulled back into the shadows.

The Abbot's voice grew harsh. "You cannot embrace both the Worm and the Tree, the Darkness and the Light. You must coexist with both, but you must choose one or the other, else the Dark will win. The Dark is rising, it grows in power, and even you of the Otherworld cannot stand against what comes. Together, we may resist and yet win. Come to me."

But nothing answered him. No one came. He was left to shut the door of the Abbey alone.

THE CLOSING OF THE WEB

"YOU'RE A CANCER, Cate," said Jim Warren as he held open the door to his bank to let out the wealthy landowner.

If she was offended, she didn't respond. "Look at that," she said, pointing up the hill towards the Abbey. "Torches on the bell tower. Quaint and old-fashioned, as if they think a little light is going to chase away the darkness." She laughed a dry laugh.

"The Abbot lights those in the hours leading up to All Hallow's Eve, All Saints, and All Souls Days. You know that Cate."

"He may say that," she answered, "but, really, he lights them to drive out the darkness of Samhain."

"Samhain?" said Warren. "Long time since I've heard that word. That's the old Celtic Feast this time of year."

"Why, yes it is, Jim," she smirked, "and you surprise me with your knowledge. The Abbot knows as well as I do, there are things that go bump in the night. Like I've been trying to tell the townspeople. Dark times are coming with the turn of the year. Best to be prepared. Best to have folks like me on their side."

Jim Warren stood by her gazing at the same Abbey tower torches burning in the night. For the past several days, the woman had come to visit him. Trying to intimidate me, he thought. Had to admire the duplicitous bitch. Caithness McNabb had managed to scare the hell out nearly everyone in town.

"Can't just be the fiscal ties you bind them with," he said looking sharply at her. "What's your hold on all these townsfolk? You seem to be feeding off the life in them. Just in the past few days they've all gone dispirited and melancholy." He glanced down the street in both directions. "Look, there's virtually no one around."

"Problem with you, Jim," said Cate in her sweetest voice, "is that you just don't believe in anything. Nothing harder to scare than a man who won't commit to anything or anyone. See, these people believe. They believe in that Abbey up there. They believe in their God. They believe in their Tinker lore. They even believe in their precious children. And that's what gives me power over them. Because everything they believe causes them to believe the opposite as well. Darkness against Light. Piasa against the Divine. Other magic stronger than their faith. A life without a future, rather than their children's grandchildren to look forward to. I'm just painting the dark picture for them and framing it financially or any other way my boys and I can think of doing."

"But why? Cate, the McNabb's have been here almost as long as the town. You're rich and powerful. What more do you want?"

She looked strangely at the banker. "Well, life of course. I want to live. Really live, and not just what passes for life down here in the river valley. Dr. Drake was the catalyst you know. DIOGENE will be the doorway to this area's prosperity, and the key to my family's future. There's new and different times coming, Jim. A darker time, to be sure, but a profitable one. You could be a part
of it."

"You and the Abbot," said Jim, "usually down to earth folk except when you go all mystic and religious on me. I like it better when you talk practical stuff. I agree with you. The company will be a boon to the area. Can't say as I care much for the physician though. Oily son of a bitch."

Only a few people were on the darkened streets. Most furtively walked by the odd couple, avoiding Cate's glance but nodding at Jim as they beat their feet into the *DewDrop Inn* where a cozy light shone out into the street.

Cate laughed. "Dr. Drake has his good points. You don't seem to mind the money he's put into your bank. In fact, I expected more of an outcry from you. Actually, I expected you to be one of my biggest obstacles."

"Why's that?" he said in the most neutral voice he could muster.

"You took care of the Archer boy when he first got here. You're his financial advisor—right? Finola couldn't have had that much, but I bet old Emily has a few coins to pass around. Can't have Conor spending his inheritance too early. Good thing he has you. I've also seen you pretty cozy with the Abbot."

"I try to get along with most folks around here. You know that Cate. I'm a banker. I'm like Wendell Tooms, the undertaker. Everybody is my customer sooner or later."

"I'm not criticizing," she said flipping her black hair behind her shoulder. "I just thought you'd speak up for them more."

Jim Warren laughed softly. "Like I said, I'm a banker. As long as the money is good, I'll take the customers. I'm not the judge of their lives."

"Not even of my life or that of my sons?"

"Not even. I only hope that whatever you're planning doesn't ruin the town. The people are our life's blood. Don't suck them dry."

"I can assure you, I won't."

"Even the 'dark ones' Cate?"

"What?"

"You know what I mean. Everybody's heard about the disappearance of some of them. I think you know more than anyone else about all that strangeness, maybe even know a bit about what's happened to the missing kids."

"Why Jim Warren, I do believe that's the closest a banker can come to threatening one of their clients. You threatening me?"

"Not in the least, but the kids, Cate. Swear to me you've had nothing to do with whatever's happened to them."

"Or what? You'll freeze my assets? Pummel me with an account ledger? Send a bank teller to close off my boys' allowance? Just what can you do, Jim Warren? To act, you'd have to believe in something. I don't think you see the things I see or even that the Abbot is aware of. Kind of blinds you in this situation. Don't worry about the kids. I definitely believe they are the key to the future. So does Dr. Drake. That's what DIOGENE is all about. I'd like it if you would help me make all this a reality." She touched his face with her hand.

Nausea washed over him like a wave but his face never wavered. For a moment, his thoughts replayed a scene from a documentary, about how a black widow spider woos her mate until he copulates with her. Then she poisons him, and sucks him dry. "Glad to hear that, Cate. I'll keep what you said in mind. Here's to a good evening for you." Turning, he walked back into the bank and locked the door.

They had come to him, many of the townspeople. Afraid, checking to see whether the McNabb's could seize their assets. Jim Warren had to admire the planning Cate and Gordon had done over the past few years. Most of the people he saw were deep in hock to the McNabb's. He was surprised he'd never noticed what that power-hungry family was doing. Now with the threats very real, those people in debt to them had few options. Fear was keeping them quiet for the time being. But if the kids kept disappearing, no telling what might happen. Open hostilities between the town and the McNabb's would seem to favor the townsfolk. But, thought Jim Warren, that family had planned ahead this far; it was difficult to assume they had not also planned for that contingency.

Mopping his brow with his handkerchief, Warren felt a chill in his heart. All his life he had been a part of this community. Knew the people, their back stories, even knew the strangeness of some of the kids. But he was a rational man, not given to flights of fancy. That's why he couldn't explain the fear that gripped his soul. As he watched Cate disappear into the night, shadows skittering around her feet, he felt the terror descending on the town. And, for the first time in his life, he didn't think he could do a thing about it. Locking the door of the bank, he headed down the street to see if Dickie Bergin had a single malt scotch hidden somewhere in the bar.

THE PLAN MOVES AHEAD

"YOU CALLED ME back!" snarled Rafe. "I almost had the man who took my eye."

Drake glared at the one-eyed misfit. The doctor had taken both brothers into the examining room and was preparing an injection for each. Perhaps it had been a mistake to even try to turn this McNabb. He was all elemental force and rage. Drake looked over at Fergal, gazing at him with a calmer eye than the cyclops who glared across from him.

"You feel the same?" asked Drake.

"Yeah," said Fergal. "I think we could have taken all of them. I've never felt such strength as when I leapt like an animal—that's what we did wasn't it?—across the parking lot. Like my brother, I could have ripped Jace's throat out. And yet, what Conor did. The swans and all. There's power as well, so I guess a little caution isn't such a bad idea."

Drake was pleased. Not because Fergal was so observant, but that he had kept his head. The serum wasn't useless after all, though it was showing its flaws in other ways. He had been injecting the brothers for a couple of days now with the experimental extract drawn from Declan Walsh and the other 'dark ones.' Normally, he wouldn't have acted so unscientifically, but Conor and his friends were forcing Drake's hand. The doctor had Gordon on a much slower injection plan until he knew what the final result would be. The death of the three heirs to the McNabb fortune all at once, should the experiment go awry, would end whatever relationship existed between him and Cate.

"Listen to me, the both of you," said Drake. "I called you back for precisely the reason Fergal said. There was other power present out there. Frankly, I wasn't expecting it. I only thought Conor had potential, but obviously, he can use whatever talent he has. I couldn't risk losing the both of you. Your transformation is not yet complete."

"Not done being your lab rats yet, Doc?" sneered Rafe.

"The serum works, you fool," snapped Drake. "Even you have to admit you have strength and speed you haven't had before. But those are just the side benefits. The mitochondria within the serum act on your brain as well, specifically in the area of intuitive experience—religious experience if you will. In other words, you become more receptive to realities beyond this dimension."

"The Otherworld you always talk about," said Fergal.

"Exactly," said Drake. "What good is strength, speed, all the powers of the animal kingdom, if such gifts are not directed by those who could teach you how to use your new found enhancements for your benefit and ours?"

Drake took Rafe's arm and prepared to inject the serum into a vein.

Grabbing his wrist, Rafe said, "So what you're telling us is that this stuff basically filets the brain, lays it out, so something like Piasa can go skipping through it."

Sometimes, thought Drake, the oaf was truly inspired. "You put it crudely, Rafe. The serum opens you to hear its voice."

"I've already heard it. So have Fergal and Gordy. Why do we need more?"

"You heard its echo. It can come to you in this world, but it is a visitor here. Without the serum, it could only whisper to you in the night. With the injections, you'll have the power and you'll hear its voice clearly. Like I do."

"You don't take any injections," said Fergal.

"No. There is no need. I told you once before, my family has served Piasa and all it represents for hundreds of years. Long service and sacrifice have attuned our genes."

"Will we hear Piasa better than our mother does?" asked Fergal.

"Jealous, are we?" said Drake, a lopsided grin breaking across his craggy face.

"Jealous of what?" said Cate walking into the room.

"We were talking about the effects of the injections," said Drake. "They wanted the kind of intimacy with Piasa that you seem to have. I told them they would know him even better."

"Don't be too sure about that, Doctor," said Cate with a laugh. "I bring some news. The Michaels girl is pregnant."

Drake's mouth dropped open. "Are you sure?"

"Of course."

"Okay, Ma, when did you take the place of Dort Martin as the town gossip?" asked Fergal.

She walked over to the table and grabbed Fergal's dose of the serum, waiting in the syringe. Turning on her sons, she spat with a flash of anger, "You think you're powerful now. Well it's all true to a degree. You, Rafe, are more of an animal than usual." She patted her middle son's unshaven cheek. "And you, my youngest, your deviousness is increasing moment by moment, like a fox. I'm sure Dr. Drake has told you of your newfound receptivity to Piasa. For that I'm glad. But make no mistake. You will never know it like I know it. The Devourer knows me, do you understand?"

She circled the table and stared at the doctor. "You think you and your family have some hold over this demon. You think that makes you in control. Well the McNabbs have a family with a long history too, and we've always lived near the river. You're not the only one with an 'in' to the Otherworld. Piasa told me the girl is pregnant. It saw her conceive."

"The conception is only days old," said Drake. "How could Piasa possibly be sure?"

"It can smell life," said Cate, "particularly life that might be a threat to it."

"Who's the father?" asked Fergal.

"The Archer boy."

"Piasa told you this?" said Drake. "It actually spoke to you?"

"Our relationship is more complicated than that," said Cate. "But it communicated to me that message, yes."

"Why Caithness McNabb," said Drake, "I thought you only consorted with the river demon because you needed companionship. I didn't think it actually confided in you."

She smiled her lips tightly. "Boys, I know you filled in the doctor here about the spinelessness of your father, but it's clear you didn't tell him of your grandfather Jake, another kind of man entirely.

"I only knew him when he was ancient of days. But in his younger years, he was a mountain of a man, so they say, with Rafe's strength, Fergal's cunning, and Gordon's intelligence. Thank God the genes in the McNabb pool bided their time for a generation. John, Jake's son, my late husband was just a shadow of the old man. You see, Jake knew Piasa and wrote about his relationship with the Devourer in his own journal. They were close, and Jake left instructions on how one might develop such a friendship.

"My husband would have nothing to do with that journal. First in his family to walk away from the river demon, I do believe. But I found it, and I used it, and no one," her voice cracked with tension, "I mean no one will get between me and the one I love. Not my boys. Not you, doctor. And not Conor Archer and his friends."

"The pregnancy gives us opportunity," said Drake to all of them.

"How do you mean?" asked Fergal.

"It's obvious after this afternoon, that Conor and his friends pose a great threat. They know too much and interfere too often." Quickly, he and the boys brought Cate up to speed over what happened in the parking lot.

"I'm telling you," said Drake, "the pregnancy will be our key to destroying them."

"It's too early," said Cate, "she doesn't even know she's pregnant."

"Then we'll just have to tell her," said Drake with a smile. "Leave it to me. Now, dear Cate, give me that serum and let me continue the transformation of your sons."

FATHER AND SON

AFTER EVENING PRAYER, the young folks, Aunt Emily and the Abbot stood on the stairs of the Abbey Church. The golden light shining from inside the church seemed to warm the steps and kept the five from stepping into the shadow of the night.

"Conor, it's time we were home. Walk with me," said Emily.

"I'll come with," said Beth.

"No!" said Jace, a trifle too emphatically. "No. We've got to head back as well. Skipped enough meals to make Mom furious if we don't make it home in time for a late supper. Nora can join us because I know for a fact she's as hungry as I am."

Beth's smile vanished but she didn't argue. "Catch you tomorrow, Conor," she said and walked off with her brother.

"Conor," said Abbot Malachy, "what you did today means that the change Rory initiated is rapidly coming to completion. Ignore it at your peril. You may not like what's happening but power is being bestowed on you."

"I don't like it," said Conor, "but even more, I don't understand it."

"You have never seen these bluffs in spring," said the Abbot with a wave to the surrounding hills invisible in the night. "Sometime in April, the thunderstorms arrive. No one can stop them, not even the hills or the stone in the earth. When the rains come, they melt the snow. The earth protests, sends up fog, turns up mud; but despite itself it begins to bloom. The power descending on you is your thunderstorm. Protest if you must, but it will do you no good. What you were is melting away. What you will become is about to burst into growth. Let it happen, for you are our weapon against the dark."

"To use?" said Conor. "You've waited for me, both of you. You say you're here to help, but you've got plans for me, just as sure as Rory does. I hate being used, whether by some unnamed power or by a priest or by my own kin."

"He's tired, Malachy," said Aunt Emily. "We need to let him be for the night."

"Very well," growled the Abbot. "It is long since I've been seventeen, but try to talk some sense into him anyway." He turned and went into the church, shutting the door behind.

"Walk with me, Conor," said Aunt Emily. Since she gave it as a command, and he knew to his own peril what would happen if he sassed her back, he silently walked by her side, down the Abbey drive.

They didn't speak for many minutes. Emily noticed Conor's head sweeping left and right as if he was searching for something.

"You feel them, too, don't you?" she asked.

"They're following, whatever or whoever was surrounding the Abbey. They're not far behind."

"They won't hurt either of us," said the old woman.

"How can you be so sure?"

"Because they know me, and they know who you are."

"Why don't you ever talk to them?"

"I do, Conor, all the time. Madoc's Glen is a refuge for all who are lost. They come to see me when I garden or when I walk in my own woodland. Even Rory feels free to come, sometimes too free."

"What are they like?"

"Why would you want to know? Your little speech to the Abbot seemed to leave no wiggle room for things that creep in the dark or beauty beyond mortal experience."

"You're mad at me."

"Mad, no; testy, perhaps. I forget how selfish and pig-headed seventeen year olds can be."

For a while, the click of the blackthorn cane was the only sound between the two. Troubles followed silently behind.

Finally, Conor spoke. "Alright, you win. I'll go speak to them. Maybe they'll tell me where I can find that father of mine. I definitely have a few things to say to him."

He left her there with the dog, but she didn't mind. About time, actually, for Madoc to face his own son. Besides, there was nothing in the dark she had not faced before. An October night walk held no fear for her. She thought back to that October long ago, when Jake McNabb had accosted her, Finola and her child. Green were his eyes that glowed in the night. She shivered at the memory long gone. He and his goons would have done the three of them great damage. The smell of river sludge was on them that night, as if they had slid in the muck with Piasa itself. Then like a knight in shining armor came that black singer, Taps Jeffords himself. Who would have thought him a hero? She remembered his voice, singing through the night. Of him coming upon them at the Crossroads, facing down the men, telling Finola and her to run.Run they did. Jake and his men never followed them, but she remembered their laughter echoing through the trees. She hadn't wanted to leave Jeffords there, but getting Finola and the child safe was uppermost in her mind. Jake was bad enough, but what had set Finola's feet flying from the Indian mound was that lecherous Rory who just would not, could not, leave her and her child alone.

Over the years, Emily had pieced Rory's psyche together. He saw the truth in Conor, but twisted it to his own ends. He saw the child as his path to power to supplant his own brother Madoc. Rory had grown weary with Madoc's inaction, unwillingness to assert power in this land. But what motivated Rory wasn't some high and noble feeling for the People; it was lust. He had never forgiven Madoc for taking Finola as his own, and Rory desired her for himself.

Memory was a funny thing. Blowing gently against her cheek, a light evening breeze brought Finola's gasping words back to Emily's mind; words breathed out in a rush as they ran. Of how Rory had tried to take advantage of her, of how Madoc had discovered his brother's treachery, of how they nearly came to blows, there in the mound on the other side of this reality. Of how the Morrigan flew between the brothers and struck at Madoc, giving Rory the chance to escape. Finola ran with Conor and had no intention of coming back. But it was out of the frying pan into the fire, thought Emily. Death stalked her sister in the Otherworld, and even reached out to her in this existence. Jake's dead eyes luminesced in front of Emily—bad memories in the autumn dark.

Finola would not return to the mound. At least not until Emily calmed her down. Sent her back to Madoc that very night. Too early to turn Conor loose in this world. Emily could sense that war was coming, and the war Conor would have to fight would not be with tanks and guns. No. The 1920's were not the time for Conor Archer. She sent Emily back with a hug and kiss after she, herself, rocked Conor into the wee hours of the morning. By that time, all was quiet in and around Tinker's Grove.

Only when the sun rose high did Emily hear what they had done to Taps Jeffords. Hung that poor man on the Crossroads Oak. And now in this present reality, for the second time, the hanged man had spoken to her nephew. Conor was a bit vague over what exactly Jeffords had communicated, but she knew the things that were heard around the Crossroads. Portents, omens, what might be. Enough to scare the pants off even a cocky kid like Conor. Who at that moment was still stalking through the woods. He was heading the long way around the base of the bluff towards the mound at the river bottoms. Up to his left, he could still see torches burning in the Abbey tower. Closer, Conor could hear whatever shadows

had gathered around the Abbey earlier following him through the woodland.

He didn't care. A hunch told him that they were members of Madoc's
little kingdom, curious about what he was up to. He just didn't care.
Though he didn't much like the responsibility being thrust upon him
because of his rapidly developing abilities, he was feeling a little self-
confident knowing that in a pinch, he could make things happen. Feeling
that way until the trail he was on rounded a bend and he ran smack dab into
Rory waiting for him in the middle of the path.

The biker held a torch in his hand. "Nice move, little nephew, earlier
this evening. Told you that your power should be used. I have it on good
authority that you scared the crap out of that prick of a doctor."

Conor had grown tired of the biker's swagger. "You know," he said, "I
always thought that those from days gone by, especially, those from the
Otherworld, were supposed to talk an archaic and elevated language instead
of street talk trash. Can't you make up your mind what reality you want to
walk in, Rory?"

The gold flecks in Rory's eyes flared for just a moment. "Unlike my
brother, I spend time in this world since one day we shall rule it and the
pitiful inhabitants that currently manage its resources. I grew tired of end-
less stories of the past and melancholy feasts in my brother's little piece of
home here in this still amazingly pristine land. I ventured out, am gone
most of the time in fact, and have adequately assessed the nature of the
humans who dwell over the globe. Pitiful. Not fit to rule. Time for a
change.

"Then you were turned loose into the world seventeen years ago, with
that beautiful wench you call your mother. 'Stay away from her,' said my
brother. He tried to kill me once before, and I believe he would have had
me killed if I violated that command ever again. I am no fool, though he
would have had difficulty besting me. Yet I honored his request. He is my
brother, after all. But I watched and waited, and now it is my time."

"You're like Drake," said Conor. "Did you know he uses changelings
like you do?"

"The bodiless ones, the dead souls," said Rory, "are fickle and easily
bent to the will. I used them to prove a point to you; Drake uses them for a
darker purpose."

"Then why don't you stop him?"

"Because twisted though he may be, his goals and mine are similar. We
seek to discover the secrets you possess. We both think you are the hope of
the future. He pursues that hope through science and his form of magic. I,
on the other hand, hope that your courage is greater than my brother's.
Either way, you are unique and capable of being the answer the People

seek. I don't want you in the clutches of the doctor, but frankly, boy, if he can accomplish my goal faster, then I'll let him do it."

"The Morrigan said you weren't evil, but you sure walk and smell like it."

"Do not judge me by what I wear and how I speak. So many disguises. You're discovering for yourself that whether one dresses like the outcasts of this country or wears the mantle of the wolf or eagle, you are still yourself down deep. I'm not so bad, Conor, really. But I want what's best for the People. We need to go home. We need to rise up. We need to rule. Now is our time. And you are our hope."

"Why me?" said Conor. "You've bested me before. You are more powerful than me."

Rory laughed. "Not really, just older and more practiced. What flows in you is the blood of two species, a mating that allows two worlds to meet. It still amazes me that in this little corner of the world such things as 'dark ones' can even be. For thousands of years, my kind consorted with humans but seldom a true conception. Madoc and me, we were the last—at least so we thought. Until one night, on a beach far away, farther away from my time than yours, the sea wives took the Tinker men to bed and voila! What Drake would call an instant hybridization occurred sort of. But the 'dark ones' are like the mules of this world; they never really worked out, never really reached their potential. It was our people's last attempt; never had we tried in such numbers. The attempt failed, and all seemed lost. Until you came along. Maybe my brother is just more potent than the rest of our kind; but you are for real, a true composite of our races. Not a drone; instead, a potent member of the Roan, like your father. You wonder why you are so important to us and to Drake. I can walk the roads of this world, but I cannot produce another Conor Archer. The gods know I've tried. Only my brother succeeded in doing that. And you."

"What do you mean?" said Conor, a sinking feeling in his gut growing stronger.

"Why, little one," smirked Rory. "You thought that your little roll in the hay with that doxy of yours was going to be all about love and romance, didn't you? Well, whatever you thought it was about, you were truly out of your league. I told you there would be consequences. Your precious girl is pregnant."

"How could you know that? Even a pregnancy test wouldn't show that yet."

Rory laughed. "Such a little fool. In the Otherworld where I walk, these things are known immediately. Even your enemies know the result of your coupling. And that makes you even more valuable. A union of two worlds, a possibility of a race of people able to walk between the realm of your father and this world, a people of power."

"That's what this has all been about?" said Conor. "About some frickin' power grab by the realm of faery?"

"No!" said another voice. Out of the woods stepped Madoc. Conor recognized him instantly. He wasn't luminescent as on the night he healed the boy, but rather dressed in medieval gear—soft boots, breeches, a rich white tunic and a dark cloak, maybe crimson, thought Conor, clasped with a Celtic brooch. A golden torque shown round his neck and a golden circlet crowned his head.

"No, that is not what this has been about. I am sorry Conor that you have to hear my brother debase the reasons that motivate our People. I am sorry he distorts the truth about you. His lust for my wife and for the power you represent derange him sometimes. And yet, he is my brother. Though I have tried in the past, and wished to from time to time, I cannot harm him."

"Save your condescension," snarled Rory.

"As you can see," said Madoc to Conor, "we have our family differences. But you, Rory, leave us alone. We will talk again later, you and me."

Rory looked to protest but instead threw his torch down and disappeared into the night.

"The rest of you," said Madoc to the shadows between the trees, "leave my son and me to be alone. We have much to talk about and little time in which to do it."

Madoc picked up the flaming torch and stuck it in a small pile of rocks just off the trail.

"I know you are angry with me," said Madoc to Conor.

Conor just stared, grinding his teeth, wondering what to say first. Finally he spoke, "The whole 'Willie Archer' thing. Was that really necessary? Is that how you seduced my mother?"

A whisper of a smile, a forgotten memory flitted across Madoc's face. "I thought it was then. I had seen her when the Tinkers first came to this place. I loved her immediately. She was one of what you call the 'dark ones' though, like all of them, she had forsaken her powers at a young age and was no longer aware of her uniqueness. She let go of her Otherworld side and embraced her humanity. But still, she was not so different from the People. She used to sing that song about that wastrel Willie Archer, a simple song from her own land when she walked the meadows and woods, exploring this new world she had come to. It was a fancy I know, but I appeared to her as she might expect a stranger to look."

"That was a lie though. You're angels aren't you? Don't your own legends tell of your fall from grace with Lucifer?"

"Yes," said Madoc. "But I've always been a bit skeptical of that. I was not there when we supposedly fell. There was a time when the People had more offspring amongst themselves." Towering sadness washed across his face like an Atlantean wave. "Not any more. I am younger than many. Powers we do have. But we of the People seem to be more tied to earth than to the spirit realm. I have never even seen a real angel; do not know any of the People who have, though I have seen many wonders."

"So what's this business about not being redeemed?"

"It is part of our story. We are a melancholy race, all our joy tinged with sadness. Seldom are there any new additions to our tribe. Though I was not part of it, it seems that fact drove members of my own kind to come up from the ocean to take husbands among the humans, back in the days when the Tinkers lived on the shore of the sea."

"The sea wives!" said Conor.

"Exactly," said Madoc. "They thought that such a mating might begin a new future for the People. No God spoke to them; they felt all alone, there in the sea."

"They lived there?"

"Why yes of course," said Madoc. "Shape shifters we are. All cultures have stories of them. But the Celtic shape-shifters are selchies, the seal people, the People of the Roan—that is the Celtic word for seal. In the lands the Celts ruled, Britain, Ireland, Scotland, Wales, Brittany, we always appeared to the humans in our selchie shape."

"I've seen your people turn into many things but never seals."

"No, and here you will not. Once, when we mingled more openly with the Celts, we ruled most of what is now called Europe. We adapted to the land and the culture of the humans around us. We wore the skin of many things that live. As we were forced to the fringes of the earth, we learned to be at home in the waters and did not mind so much the loss of our lands. And that is why your true home, Conor, is with the sea, with the waters of the Otherworld and the lands that dot its oceans. It is so beautiful." He spread his hands and Conor could see the webbing between the fingers. "It is our mark," he said. "On our hands and feet, even in our human shape, we bear the sign of our ancestry. We are the Roan, no matter where we live."

"Then why do you all think you are lost and damned?"

"Once, so the legends say, we strode the roads of heaven; then we walked the ways of this world. Now we dwell in tiny hills and out of the way places—and in the sea, forced evermore to the fringes of the earth. Fortune has not favored us."

"But you have your own world; you said so yourself."

"The Otherworld, as you call it, is a part of this world and vice versa. They exist intertwined, yet separate, each with its own rules. They were meant to be together I think; perhaps, once, they were. Now they are nearly sundered and many wish to see them together again. Some, like my brother, desire to force the issue so that we may return to the hollow hills and the sea caves across the ocean to wield power once more over the earth. Some, like your Dr. Drake and Caithness McNabb, seek to use the dark powers that dwell in both places to make the merger come to reality and to birth a dark world of magic and malice."

"Why don't you act? Why won't you do anything? The 'dark ones' are part of your world and now they are being slaughtered. Don't you care? By doing nothing, you are killing your own!"

Madoc looked as if to speak, but was silent.

"You are my father, far more powerful than me. I don't even want the burden everybody thinks I should carry."

Madoc spoke. "You are of me, but not me. Of my kind, but not of my world. You judge what you do not understand and call me murderer when I do not interfere.

"I am king of the fallen, lord of the forsaken, guardian of the failed. What mystery I have is fading. What magic I possess speaks nothing to this reality. What you see as wonder is withered glory of what once was, but can never be again.

"You are my son. But we will never walk together. You tread two worlds thanks to the foolish and doomed love I once had. She was beautiful; you know that. But when she left, I could not follow. Where she walked, I could not tread. My home is the hollow hills. Even love cannot break those chains.

"Much heartbreak I see for you, my son. Your love of this girl—ah! Already the same mistake I made is yours, only now, evil waits to exploit that love. I cannot interfere this time; for all my decisions before brought only the death of the one I love and the exile of a son I never have truly known. Much pain still awaits you, for you have not yet come into your full power. For that to happen, grievous hurt must still befall you." He held up Conor's right hand. "A terrible wound Rory gave you, but it pales before what is to come. Will you bear the burden, I wonder. Still, you are my son." His voice dwindled off to a whisper—"Remember the prophecy," he said.

Conor's temper flared, finality in his voice, "You're a coward then; you won't do for me, what everyone else wants me to do—get involved. I'm supposed to buy into your vision for the sake of the People, for the sake of humanity. You can't even help your own flesh and blood."

A sad smile came to the face of Madoc. "Your destiny is your own, my son. I cannot help you in this journey."

"Pathetic," spat Conor. He turned on his heel and walked away from his father. "I don't know what my mother ever saw in you. You are not what I expected. You should have helped, but you are a coward."

"And so I must be," whispered Madoc to his departing son. "For only in this way, do you have a chance of succeeding where once I failed."

THE WORM UNCOILS

DRAKE WALKED ALONE in the dark. He had sent Fergal and Rafe home with Cate. Didn't have the heart to tell her that the serum, while somewhat effective, was having noticeable side effects on the two younger boys. The tumors—such a pity. Already in the lymph glands. Hard to tell if they were malignant, but their existence did not bode well. Gene therapy was hit and miss at best. Truth to tell, he only needed them for a little while longer anyway. But there would be hell to pay with Cate. Loved those boys, she did.

Still, the future was flexible and though the science part was flawed and fallible, there was still the magic side of things. He loved science—it was somewhat predictable, but he adored magic—magic was so much more powerful when it worked right. And magic was in those boys, not just the serum. They had been touched by Piasa. Tumors or not, there was a change occurring in them and the attributes all of them sought were manifesting themselves in them.

Like animals they acted this afternoon, thought Drake with pleasure. Rafe, always a beast, had truly greater strength and speed. Fergal, cunning and wily, could have stalked the friends of Conor Archer and killed them easily. Drake was dispassionate enough to wonder whether they would keep much of their humanity. He hoped so. Not that they were really chimeras. That sort of thing had never worked in science or science fiction. But attributes from other species blended into the human genome—those were real possibilities coming true in Rafe and Fergal, possibilities assisted by medicine but made real by magic.

He thought he'd leave Gordon alone for a while at least, suspending his regimen of serum. If magic failed to prolong the existence of his two brothers, he would need Gordon's voice to calm the rage of Cate.

God, he loved the dark. He felt the shadows wrap him in near invisibility as he walked the streets, up toward the Michaels' house. How to get Beth's attention occupied his thoughts at the moment. He supposed he could have sent Rafe to take her, but he just didn't trust the oaf to leave her unsullied. Not that she was that important but her offspring was. Instead, he had sent Fergal and Rafe off collecting more specimens, confident that they would do their work satisfactorily amongst a now cowed community.

Drake looked at his white hands as he walked. So thin, so fine, so skilled. He possessed the knowledge and ability to take that little bundle of cells from her, to gestate it in his lab. It most likely never would come to term; the artifical womb in his lab, while state of the art, had never gestated a feturs to nine months, but he could know all its secrets before it succumbed. Besides, the lusty little Archer brat could always make another with his true love. The question was should he enlist Beth as an ally, albeit a reluctant one? Or, should he take what he wanted by force? His tongue flicked over his lips, tasting the night air, pondering the decision.

Perhaps a middle way, he thought. The Michaels' house was the last on a dead end street nestled up against one of the bluffs towards the southern outskirts of town. He had walked through the Grove without being seen. Not that there were many passers by. Bending the will of these townspeople had proven quite simple. So as he walked, clothed in black with his silver hair a beacon in the night; he simply willed those who watched to forget his presence. They saw him merely as someone who should be there at the present moment. If questioned, they would not be able to identify him, other than to express a vague feeling that someone else had been near them.

Such little power expended. Almost a parlor trick, he thought. He had no fear standing in front of the Michaels' house; for all intents and purposes, he simply was not there, more like an insubstantial shadow in the dark.

He saw Jace say goodbye to Nora, a long kiss between them. More lovers, he sneered to himself. Patiently, he continued to let the lights wink out in the house one by one. The last one to be extinguished was hers. As he waited for her to sleep, he popped off a cufflink from his right sleeve, lifted the dagger from around his neck and surgically sliced a vein. Wet blood and pain. Exquisite he thought as the coppery smell brushed his nostrils. But there can be no magic without sacrifice and this was a small one.

Blood pooled on the ground before him in a steady drip as he held his arm out, hand pointed at the upstairs window where she rested.

He knew the mist would come, this time swiftly from the river. Thin wisps only. Piasa was giving him only partial attention.

"So you've come," he whispered, "after a fashion. The blood of my family draws you. As it always has. We have always served."

A faint voice touched his mind, "What is it you wish?"

"Lift me up," he said. "Take me to the girl, so that we, you and I, might know what it is she carries and how we should act against her."

No answer but Drake felt his body stiffen and go numb. He knew what was happening and smiled to himself. The river demon was as interested as he was in discovering the secrets of Conor Archer. Entwining his body, the mist caressed his face. "Go," said the voice. "Discover and reveal."

His body never moved, but his consciousness did, soaring above his standing form. Drake turned his gaze to the bedroom window and willed himself within those walls.

Such a girl's room, he thought. Frills and things. Toys and boys, that's all such women cared for at this age. He looked at her sleeping form with contempt. If he scared her on waking, she would scream and rouse that hulk of a brother. There was a problem, he thought. Sensed a knowledge and wisdom in him earlier in the evening that he had caught days before when the boy confronted him about Declan, and with that a scent of the Otherworld. Jason Michaels was not a 'dark one' but he carried their smell now. Why? No time for that worry. Drake loomed over Beth.

She heard a voice speaking and opened her eyes. Sitting up, she looked around and found she was alone, but she was sure she had heard a voice. Then it came again. Her whispered name. Not seeing anything, she wasn't really afraid and that was how Drake liked it.

"Who's there?" she asked.

"Just a friend," whispered Drake.

"Where are you?"

"Right here in front of you."

That scared her. She backed deeper into the blankets and pillows.

"I won't hurt you," he said in a pleasant voice.

"Then show yourself," she demanded.

"As you wish," he agreed.

He decided on the vaguest and most insubstantial form he could muster. Less for her to fear, and less for her to recognize. Besides, in a projection he was not substantial and couldn't physically hurt her if he wanted to. Magic sometimes had its drawbacks.

She saw a shadowy figure form at the foot of her bed. Now she was afraid. She grabbed a rosary from her bedside.

The figure laughed softly. "I'm not sure you even know how to use that, so I doubt if it will offer much protection. In a way, I feel a little like the Angel Gabriel must have felt, for I, too, have come to you with great tidings of joy. Your little dalliance with that Chicago boy has paid off—you are both going to be the proud parents of a child. Congratulations!"

Beth gasped and thought quickly. Impossible for whatever this was in front of her to know. It had been only days and not even modern medicine could identify pregnancy that fast.

"You lie," she said.

"On the contrary," said the figure, "I tell the absolute truth. What science cannot reveal, the Otherworld can, and I assure you, you are pregnant. And that is going to cause you all sorts of problems with your parents, your brother, even your precious Conor."

She recognized the voice now. "Drake," she said, "you're Dr. Drake."

"In a manner of speaking, only," laughed the shade. "I thought a true face to face, after our encounter this afternoon might prove somewhat, confrontational, so I chose this less intrusive way."

"I don't know about being pregnant, but if I was, I know you'd want the child for yourself. You've killed those other 'dark ones.' No doubt you'd think a child from Conor and myself would be a master stroke for whatever genetics scheme you have cooked up."

"Ah," sighed Drake, "it is true about those other children, and I would have had four more tonight if not for you and your friends. They are necessary sacrifices for the cause of science and the Otherworld with which you are beginning to have some experience. But back to the child. You are correct. I have great interest in it, and you are going to give him to me."

"You must be crazy—never!" Beth felt her fear give way to anger. She knew that if he could have harmed her, he already would have. He was negotiating, though for what she could not yet say.

"You're not a doctor are you?" said Beth.

"Of course I am, it is just that I am something other and more than that. Put it this way. I have great faith, both in science and in myth. But make no mistake. Myth is so much more powerful. My family and I have known that for hundreds of years, and what you and Conor have managed to achieve in your lust ..."

"It was not lust," she hissed. "I love him."

"Whatever you call it," said Drake, dismissing her outburst with a wave of an insubstantial arm. "This pregnancy represents a continuation of a breakthrough made years ago when that being that inhabits that Indian mound down by the river lay with Finola Archer and bred your own true love. Now Conor has repeated the miracle and that means that a merger of two worlds is possible. My master, the river demon you call Piasa, initially worried about the power of Conor Archer but now has come to see my wisdom and wishes to seize the opportunity. In a nutshell, the Otherworld wants to break in on our world. There are beings there, my master being the most powerful, that seek dominion here on the earth they once walked but have since been driven from."

"I know about the beings in the Otherworld. In fact I have seen a few of them," said Beth. "If I know about them, then they are already in this world."

"Smart girl," said Drake. "Not a 'dark one' to be sure, but thank God you have some intelligence genes so the genetic gifts to your child will not be all one-sided from Conor. Again, you are correct. Piasa and the others that dwell in that alternate reality have some effect on this world already and can sometimes walk within it. But this world is still alien to them."

"Why would they want to be here? From everything that I have seen, the Otherworld is a far more beautiful place."

"Lovely, yes, perhaps, but so much more limited in many ways. And my master hates loveliness. What he seeks is food, and he is starving in his reality. That is why he seeks more access to this world, rich in suffering and agony, food to feast on for millennia."

"You're demented."

Drake laughed. "Maybe, but I still want your child, and if I get it, I'll let Conor and you live."

"You don't think we'd die for our child?" said an incredulous Beth.

"Yes, I do," said Drake softly. "I never underestimate my opposition."

"Then why should I agree?"

"Because it won't be just you two who will suffer. I'll take them all, your friends, your parents, everyone you know or care about, and I'll make it seem like a plague has come to Tinker's Grove. You know I can do this, and I think you know I will."

"We'll never give you what you want!"

Drake laughed softly and Beth caught a faint whiff of decay on the air. "Courage," he said, "is so noble in the abstract. But I wonder what you will say as you see more death among the villagers. Day by day, hour by hour, I'm going to take their children and there is nothing you will be able to do. I'll take them in secret, when you can't find me. I'll take them in darkest night, when nothing sees in the gloom. I'll take them when I wish for my will shall be done.

"And, little Beth," said Drake as his form leaned over the bed, floating above her as his face crept towards hers, "after they start dying, let's see how you react. Their screams will be in your dreams; you will hear the Morrigan wailing down by the river as she washes the blood out of the stained clothes and scrubs the bones clean of taint. You'll see the blank and devastated faces of their parents as they wonder where their lost children are. Then you will think again of my offer, and you will come to me in your despair."

"You're a monster," she whispered.

She saw his face then, a greenish pale thing looming over her own body. Smiling he bent as if to kiss her, but then, melting as if torched by a flame, his jaw gaped wide and stretching teeth turned into pointed fangs. Like corpse breath, she felt him breathe on her. Stomach heaving, she turned and grabbed the rosary again and threw it in his face. The specter howled and melted away, but his voice remained in her ears. "Come to me in your own good time. I'll be waiting."

Beth was still for a moment, not sure if he was completely gone. Then, she jumped out of bed and ran for the window. He was there, out on the dead end street, like a statue, arm raised, fingers pointing toward her. At his feet a winding green thing like a serpent or salamander, lapping at a dark pool on the ground beneath his arm. The hand fell to his side and the figure refocused on Beth staring out the window. He bowed his head and walked away. The green thing lapped for a few more seconds in silence, lifted up its viper head, hissed at Beth and slithered into the night.

THE ABBOT AND DRAKE

DRAKE ENJOYED HIS walk back down the street. As he turned into the business district, he noted with satisfaction that all was deserted. Only the hum of the street lights could be heard along with some muted laughter from the *DewDrop Inn*. The patrons had a tendency these past weeks of coming early and staying till closing. They all left together. Safety in numbers.

That's why he was surprised to suddenly notice a figure, clothed in black, standing across the street underneath a street light. Only that was not a Gucci suit the figure was wearing. Abbot Malachy was in full dress Benedictine habit—black robe, black cuculla, and a silver pectoral cross shimmering in the light across his chest. Crozier in hand, its curved, twisted antlers framing a Celtic Cross, he simply stared at Drake.

"So you know," said Drake. "I wondered about you, I did."

"I know." said the Abbot. "I know who and what you are."

"Yet, you have never stopped me. Out of fear perhaps? Weakness, maybe?"

The Abbot permitted himself a thin smile. "You are an emissary of evil. You pollute the face of the earth."

"So stop me if you are so convinced of my nasty little ways."

The Abbot said nothing.

"You see," said Drake, breaking the silence, "you are like all the other religious people of the world, so convinced there is evil but when you meet it face to face you are powerless to do anything to stop it."

"I am not powerless."

"Well, yes you truly are. The children are missing; you cry 'Let us pray.' The football player has turned up missing; you cry 'Let us pray.' When one of your own monks hasn't come home, you cry, 'Let us pray.' Hope none of you get a cold. Your prayer does little and Brother Luke doesn't look to be around for a while."

"Already, the seeds of your destruction have been sown. You've tried to co-opt and even harm Conor Archer, but he is the weapon of Light."

"Not such a pure vessel though; just ask his girl friend." Drake smirked at the Abbot.

"You've heard the saying, 'God writes straight with crooked lines.' Conor is young, but his heart is true. I would fear him if I were you."

"Why should I fear him or you for that matter? I still intend to take more children—any age will do, as many as I need. How can you let that happen?"

"You have no inkling of who I am, do you?" said the Abbot.

For a moment, Drake's heart seized a bit with a jolt of fear. It was the Abbot who should be afraid, but strangely was not. Confused, Drake did not answer.

"Long ago I was sent here to watch over the river demon, to keep its power in check. I found it wonderful to meet a race of beings living within abandoned Indian mounds that had the same goal as I—keeping evil within boundaries, keeping a balance. But the balance has tipped over the years. The People of the Hollow Hills diminish; the greed of the McNabb's, the restlessness of Piasa and its own hunger, your coming to our town and yes, even Conor's arrival have set events in motion that threaten that balance between the worlds."

The Abbot continued. "I see that dagger you wear around your neck. I saw it cut the throat of one of my most beloved monks. If I were permitted, I would cut you down now. But I cannot act so openly. You, on the other hand, come from a long line of those who seek to mate with the dark. Your magic tonight stinks to the heavens. I can even smell it here, though God knows what you have actually done."

"So there has been only one Abbot Malachy," said Drake. "How delicious. I haven't seen a nexus of this reality and the Otherworld so strong in decades. And yet, here, in backwater Tinker's Grove, the war goes on. I'm so privileged to be a part of it."

The Abbot began to walk across the street, determination in his gaze. Muttering low guttural sounds, Drake began to chant to build up a wall of protection against the oncoming Abbot. He threw out the spell and the atmosphere crackled in protest at its power.

"Stop this nonsense!" said the Abbot, striding through the unseen barrier and grabbing Drake's arm. He looked quietly into the eyes of the doctor, squeezing and twisting Drake's hand and arm. Drake went to his knees. He pushed a subdued Drake into the dirt of the street and put a sandaled foot on his neck.

"For the sake of your own miserable life, get out of this town," said the Abbot.

"Never!" said Drake, voice muffled in the dust.

"You ought to snap that neck while you have the chance," said a voice behind the Abbot. Turning, Malachy spotted Rory across the street, leaning against the street light, stroking his pointed teeth with a tooth pick.

"Would that I could," said the Abbot, releasing the doctor.

"Your God has too many restrictions on you, I think," said Rory.

"Perhaps," said the Abbot, "but at least I try to keep pointed to the Light. You, on the other hand …"

Rory laughed. "Me? I have no such scruples, but I will not kill him either. He suits my purposes. Look, already, he has disappeared into the shadows."

Rory was right. The Abbot looked back and saw the doctor had vanished. More mischief yet tonight thought the monk.

"You will not succeed either, Rory," said the Abbot. "Less evil in intent, yet your plans I believe will only lead us all to sorrow and woe. You made Conor Archer what he is today; the least you could do is support and help the boy."

"I am, Father Abbot, in my own way. I will not coddle him. My brother and I had a … rather difficult childhood and youth and it only served to make us strong. Conor needs to be tested and if he fails, well, I have waited long and perhaps the opportunity for such a child from the fruit of his love will one day make possible such a meeting of the worlds again."

"So selfish," whispered the Abbot.

"What?" said Rory cupping his ear with an exaggerated gesture.

"I said you were a pig-headed fool."

"That's how I like my abbots," said Rory, "feisty and head strong. Best you get going now and see if you can stop that fool of a physician from bringing the wrath of Piasa on all of us."

Rory turned and strode into the tavern. Shaking his head at the folly of it all, the Abbot headed back towards the monastery.

RISE, MEN OF THE WEST

DICKIE BERGIN HAD been shouting to the bartender when he saw Rory out of the corner of his eye. Dickie always moved liked a bantam chicken so the sight of the owner of the *DewDrop Inn*, frozen in place, jaw open, caught the attention of the patrons and they all looked to the doorway.

"What?" asked Rory, "Can't a lad come in and drink in peace and relative obscurity?" He walked slowly to the bar and asked for a Guinness. "Thank the gods you have this on tap. Few things have been invented in the past thousand years by humans that are worth a tinker's damn but this ale is one of them." He quaffed the pint in four swallows and slammed the glass down demanding a refill. Not a conversation had restarted, not a head had turned back to its business.

Staring at the ceiling for a few moments, the biker lowered his head and took a swallow from the newly poured glass.

"Are you not all a fine bunch of men?" He looked at the gathered crowd, mostly male, fathers and grandfathers and a few older sons watching him intently.

"Seriously," said Rory. "I am impressed. Here you are, celebrating this evening while the youngest of your families have either disappeared or are in danger of doing so. You don't have a clue as to what action you should take, what remedy you should apply for the tragedy emerging around you. Such a worthless rabble."

"I have been told," continued Rory, rolling the Guinness around his mouth like a treasured whisky, "that your ancestors were better men."

"Lots of things have been said about the original settlers here." The voice belonged to Jim Warren, tucked away at the far end of the bar, nursing a single malt.

"Ah, the esteemed banker," said Rory. "And the town's resident historian, so I imagine."

"I know a bit about how this settlement was originally founded. The Tinkers were a strange lot, but their coming to this land was not noticed much. Not when other misfit groups and castaway souls decided the good old USA was the promised land. The Tinkers were just one rag tag group among many."

"So they were, Mr. Warren, so they were," said Rory. "But no documentation," he spat out the words with flecks of Guinness bubbling on his lips, "I say no documentation exists for why they left in the first place."

"It was the famine," said Warren, "all the surviving letters say so."

"Aye, so it was that—'tis true. But not just that-not the real reason really." Rory spread out his arms and circled around the room.

"Come with me lads, just for a moment, beyond the sea, across the years, to a time long gone and a place far away."

He was mesmerizing. He walked through the bar, looking each patron in the eye, and once looked upon, no one took their eyes off the strange biker. Standing still in the middle of the bar, the swagger went out of him, and he seemed to rise taller, speaking as if the ancients themselves were telling their story through him.

There was a night in the old country, not long after an odd group of Tinkers rolled their red and blue and black caravans to settle by the ocean, in the middle of a famine that made their bones stick out and their children scream with the pains of hunger—there was a night when they heard the cries from the sea, haunting cries, sad wails so heartbreaking that even in their own sorrow they wept to hear them on the wind.

The moaning in the night seemed like a forlorn song that went unanswered by the barren cliffs surrounding them all, land where potatoes rotted and hope for food died.

Curious, the Tinker men left their fires and went down to the beach that night to search for those who wailed by the waves. A full moon it was, so they say. Out in the surf, they could see the seals leaping in the moonlight through the shining froth of the water. The cries were coming from them. The men were new to the sea shore, not wise in the ways of those who live near the presence of the seals. Had they been they would have run back to their caravans and stayed close to their fires and smoked their pipes. But they did not know.

Enchanting was the song of the seals. The spouses tried to get their menfolk to come back away from the shore. It was a simpler time then. No worries about spousal abuse or harrassment. The men, enraptured by the siren song, simply beat their women back to the caravans. They would not be denied the sad song they were hearing. Walking to the edge of the sea, they beheld a wondrous sight. The seals leapt from wave to wave, coming towards the shore. Dozens of them heading for land. They disappeared from view for a moment. Then, from the shallows came women, naked they were, with dark raven hair and eyes the color of the blind depths of the ocean. Walking up from the sea. They were singing too, the same song mind you as the seals further out in the breakers.

The sea wives, for that's what they were as truly as I stand before you now, the sea wives walked through the tide up on to the sand. Each had a seal skin tossed over her shoulder and each spread that skin on the white sand there on the shore by the sea. They beckoned the men and those men, your ancestors, went to them. They lay together, human men and the selchies, the women of the Roan. And as each man lay down with a sea wife, the song that was heard, that wailing melody, lost one voice, until the last man took the last sea wife and there was silence on the ocean and on the shore, only the sound of waves meeting the sand was heard. The Tinker men's own spouses looked out the windows of the caravans, but so strange was the sight that no jealousy was felt in their heart, nor anger in their soul. Not then. Not at that moment.

"Now," continued Rory, imperiously holding out his hand for a refill on his glass, "you might think me odd for having said they were manly men and thrice what you piss drinking lackeys are. After all they were beguiled by the sea-wives were they not? But that was not their fault. They were among their betters. As I said, they were new to the sea and did not know the danger. None had ever done what those men did that night, at least not in such numbers. They lay in worship with beings from the Otherworld. As is only appropriate." Rory tipped his fresh glass to all, the silence oppressive in the tavern; anticipation gripping the patrons in the room.

When the men woke in the morning the sea-wives were gone, but their skins remained. No man said a word; they simply rolled up the seal skin and placed each in his own caravan. When their women tried to question them, the words died on their lips so strange were their husbands' faces.

Nine months to the night that this happened, the wailing song was heard again upon the waves, and just as before, the men went to the sea and the sea wives were waiting for them on the shore. In their milk white arms against their milk white breasts they held a child, each with dark hair and dark eyes. The sea wives held out their arms and the men took their children. In exchange, the men gave them back their seal skins. This was the moment of their bravery, little though it was. For the men could have rejected their children and sent the selchies' offspring away, but they did not. They took the 'dark ones' with them and left the sea wives on the sand with their skins. In the morning, the beach was empty, the selchies were gone, but the children remained.

You can imagine the tension in the Tinker community. The human wives of those men were quite suspicious and rightly so. They knew these offspring were different, and when the children began to manifest strange abilities and powers, they did their best to make them conform to the Tinker clan. To their credit, they did not kill the children. But to their everlasting shame, they never allowed them to develop into what they were called to be.

"Shame!" shouted Rory, slamming his glass on the counter, shattering it. "Shame! The men's moment of bravery was gone and all were complicit in hiding the truth about the 'dark ones.' A tragedy really. You were right, Mr. Warren, when you said the Tinkers came here to escape the famine. But that was only part of the reason. Their wives would not let their menfolk remain on the site of their infidelity. Nor would the Tinker women let them wander again in that tiny land. Why? Because anywhere in that land was too close to the sea and too near the waters to escape the songs of the Roan. Anyone who once heard the sea wives sing would be consumed with melancholy intense, mournful longing strong.

"The famine was a convenient excuse to leave, though the hollowness of their bellies was real. America was the fail safe decision and when that little group of Tinkers left to come to this grand continent, you should have seen the sorrow. The solitary ship that picked them up at that very same bay, welcomed wives whose faces turned to the new land across the ocean. But that same ship welcomed grieving husbands who only looked back as they sailed forward, back to the bay where the sea wives played on the waves. They should have been men and stayed, but they fled, thinking that distance would heal the memories. Thus the Tinkers brought the 'dark ones' with them, and the cowardice continued."

His Guinness gone, Rory slammed his fist on the bar. "You cannot run from who you are or what you've done! No wonder you have been haunted by things from your homeland. No wonder the Otherworld seeks you here. A pact was made; a debt incurred. There are consequences to those actions done in your name long ago. Until you accept them, until the debt is paid, doom will stalk this town, and it shall never have peace. Refusing to recognize who you are, your very indecision, has made you powerless and vulnerable to an evil older than time itself. It never hesitates to exploit a weakness. Now your very existence is threatened. So many opportunities. So many chances. All failures."

Rory looked around the tavern in disgust. "Now you drink in Dickie's pub, drowning the truth before you. Because of your cowardice, someone is killing the 'dark ones' among you."

"You don't know that," said Jim Warren. "The children are missing is all."

"Fool!" said Rory. "You know the truth but won't face it. The Otherworld isn't some childhood story to beguile the young. It didn't follow your ancestors here over the sea because of the traditions you hold. The Otherworld is all around you, everywhere. There is goodness and beauty in that land, and I know that well; but evil is there, too. When it touches this world it manifests itself as myth from song and story and nightmares from legend. It molds itself to the culture of the peoples it encounters. Do you think a famine ship could sever those ties, or this land bury them in ancestral memory?"

"Piasa is this land's manifestation of evil. Your forebears knew it by a different name. The People of the Roan—we who watch over you from the mound down by the River ... Don't look at me like that Jim Warren, like I speak some fabulous fairy tale for children. My kind are found in the strangest places, and I tell you we are the only ones to keep this evil at bay. We needed your special children, the 'dark ones,' to strengthen the land against Piasa, to strengthen us in this land. We wanted to bring the worlds together. For years we watched and waited, to no avail. We could have used your assistance, but you were found wanting. Weak men, weak women, you were, stifling such potential. Now there walks among you several who are comfortable with both worlds, but who ultimately love the darkness. They want your children too."

"So let me get this straight," said Jim Warren, "the choice for us was for the children, perhaps for all of us, to be slaves to you, doing your bidding, or for all of us to be food for Piasa?"

Rory smiled his animal grin. "At least, with the Roan, you would be alive, and we would treat you well."

"Let me guess, you saw Conor as the last of your last chances. You wanted Conor to make all this happen? A boy to usher in the Roan to rule?"

"It looks as if in him our dreams may be realized."

"Well," said Jim Warren, standing up and straightening his suit, out of place amidst coveralls and boots. "I don't think I'll be a part of slavery or walk peacefully to my death as fodder for the river demon. You all might be entranced by his fanciful stories, but I am not. Good night to you all."

Jim Warren walked slowly out of the tavern.

"What about the rest of you lads?" said Rory. "Is that how you all feel as well?"

A tired, well-inebriated voice muttered from the middle of the crowd. "He took my children," said the voice. "That boy, Conor Archer, took away my children. He's responsible." Mr. O'Leary's voice grew louder. "He's responsible, I tell you. I don't know about battles between peoples and stuff from legend, seals that turn into women and children from the sea. All I know is that Conor Archer took my children. Flew away they did. And now they are no more."

Dickie Bergin spoke up in his rooster voice. "Don't know about kids flying away, but O'Leary has a point. Things were more peaceful before the Archer kid came to us. If he's responsible in any way, we oughta be doing something about it."

"I tell you, he's your only hope!" shouted Rory as voices began to rise in support of the hapless O'Leary.

"One by one, those kids have disappeared," said an unnamed O'Leary supporter. "Strange things have happened since the Archer kid came back."

"Lives with that witch woman down in Madoc's Glen," said another. "She's a strange bird, too."

"Don't be saying anything bad about Miss Emily," said Dickie, worried now that things were getting out of hand.

Everyone was shouting their opinion. It was clear to Rory that things were spiraling out of control. That became even more evident as people turned their anger towards the biker. A stranger, and outcast, now proclaiming allegiance to whatever haunted the Indian mounds. It was all too much. Rising from their chairs, they turned bloodshot eyes towards Rory. Who laughed at them.

"Look at this lot. If only Conor could see you now. You're sheep I tell you, following wherever your emotions lead you. The land's too good for you; you've lost you're right to rule. I'm telling you this. When everything here at Tinker's Damn Grove is finished, it will not be the humans who reign. Sheep! All of you are sheep."

They didn't really understand what he was saying, except that the insult came through loud and clear. Like as not they would have tried to tear him apart, but Rory leapt up on the bar and snarled at them.

"Watch what your betters can do," he said as he morphed. Dickie told about it for years afterward, though few would believe him, crippled up in a wheel chair, raving about the doings at Tinker's Grove those long years past. He did see the clearest because he was closest. Rory's teeth grew long, biker coat split up the back, spine arched and forcing forearms to the bar, face enlongating into a mouth with canine teeth. With one final cry of "Sheep!" ending in a lupine howl, Rory leapt into the crowd, slashing and howling. Not much damage was done, but it sure stunned the crowd as Rory charged for the entrance. In fear, they shrank back. No one went after him, and by the time he had loped a block away, he resumed human form.

"Told them they were sheep. Should of eaten one of them to make an example." He looked down at the strips of leather still clinging to him. "Now, I've got to get another outfit."

Back at the *DewDrop Inn*, Dickie gave a round of free drinks to the shattered patrons.

"Can't do nothing about him," said O'Leary pointing to where Rory had just departed. "Don't understand who or what he is. But that Archer boy. Got to get rid of him."

"Don't go talking like that O'Leary," said Dickie. "We're not some mindless mob. Best advice is to do nothing. Kids are missing. Let's see what turns up. Let's wait and watch." With that advice, everyone agreed. Few, however, left early. The bar stayed open late. Not a cop drove by to close them down. Tinker's Grove was in siege mode.

SOUL SEARCHING

HOW COULD SHE sleep after that? After that thing said what it said from the bottom of her bed? She was still shivering since she had jumped back under the covers after seeing Drake on her front lawn and that salamander-snake thing lapping up whatever liquid was on the ground.

Angry at her own fear, she threw the blankets back and pulled on her jeans and sweater. Couldn't give in to that madman, but if she didn't, all she loved would be lost. And pregnant? Wondered if it was true, but knew in her heart that Drake wouldn't make that up—too easily checked on. Wondered, too, if Conor knew. Everything was going perfectly; now it all seem threatened.

She loved Conor; damn she did. But right now, she was thinking of Jace, that rock solid hunk of a brother, who would know what to do. Couldn't wake him. He'd be sleeping by now and had been upset enough for the day. Besides, maybe it was best she didn't confide in him. Like as not, he'd go running down to DIOGENE and torch the place before he found Drake and beat up the bastard.

Beth had to smile—Jace was predictably protective. In fact, she remembered what he said just as she was going up to bed tonight. Out of earshot from Nora, he put his arm around her and whispered, "Don't be afraid; whatever happens, I'll be there. We've always been in things together."

Gratified, she had looked him in the eye and asked him not to be too hard on Conor. "I love him Jace," she said. But his expression hardened, even as he kissed her on the brow.

As she walked down the front drive, she paused at the place where Drake had stood. Sure enough, there was still a dark wet spot where the reptilian thing had been drinking. Touching it with her fingers, she smelled the liquid. "Blood," she said, wiping her hand hurriedly on the grass.

She shook her head as she made up her mind. Here it is, she thought, the twenty-first century, and I'm up to my eyeballs in freaks who do genetic experiments, people who look young but are centuries old, shapeshifters and fallen goddesses and angels. But it's the new millennium, and I'm not some 'dark one' hidden for all his or her life. People know me and if I were to suddenly disappear that would matter. Drake won't harm me or the child, if there is one, at least not right away. He needs knowledge and it will take him time to get it. If I let him make the next move, he'll be even more in control. So it's into the belly of the beast to call that doctor's bluff. She thought of Brother Luke as well. He should have been missed but for some reason the Abbot hadn't gone to the authorities. He has his own secrets, she thought.

So she walked. Couldn't really just drive the car down to the DIOGENE plant. Someone would find it abandoned. Drake had expected her to take care of this herself and she didn't want to disappoint.

A light coat was all she wore this warm October night. Only good thing this autumn, besides Conor, was the weather. Little surprised her anymore, so the presence of a crow in the trees, cawing softly from branch to branch didn't freak her out as much as she expected.

"I know you are there," she said. "You might as well walk with me a while."

A rustling in the undergrowth and out stepped a young woman, barefoot, clothed in a sheer white dress. "I wouldn't have thought Conor's whore so brave," said the Morrigan.

"Shut up you judgmental bitch," said Beth. "After what I've seen tonight, there's little you can do to frighten me. You know I love Conor Archer. My thought is that you are simply jealous. How can one live so long and not let go of petty jealousies? Think of all the warriors you have seduced in the past."

Laughing, the Morrigan said in her sweetest voice, "Again, you mistake my affections. Your brother is the object of my feelings and he will be mine. Conor, on the other hand, is my hope and the hope of our race. Your dalliance with him has put everything at risk."

"Leave my brother out of this."

The Morrigan laughed again.

"So," said Beth, "because I love Conor, and you don't approve, you're here this evening to escort me to DIOGENE so the good doctor can do whatever he wants with me and my child?"

"What happened between you and Conor was unexpected, to everyone's plans it seems. You, girl, are the unknown. Don't look so shocked. I've seen your birth and the kind of death you will someday have, but the child is outside the loom upon which I weave. I cannot see what will come of this; but fortunately, neither can the others. Stop here." The Morrigan laid a hand on her shoulder. Beth could see her milk white skin and the beautiful arm and hand. She was thankful the Morrigan had chosen the guise of a young woman. She shivered at the thought of the Morrigan's gnarled claw of death touching her.

Again light laughter. "I see you approve of my form tonight. For now it suits me if it helps you listen. Look, there, in the sky."

Beth looked up at the stars and heard piercing beautiful cries. Four large swans gleaming faintly white in the night flew above them, wheeling high above the lands surrounding Tinker's Grove.

"They'll not go far, even though Conor saved them from a terrible fate," said the Morrigan. "And aren't they beautiful, lass? A testament to what that boy can do if he comes into his power. Are you going to help him or hinder him?"

Beth shook off the Morrigan's hand. "Help him of course. That's why I'm going to see Drake."

"Once you are in there, none of us can assist you. I tried entering once not long ago. All artificial lights and no belief. The ones who work in there have their eyes fixed only on what they call science and, as they say, observable fact. I felt diminished there, weakened, as if my existence would not matter to them. The place sickens me."

"Well, your existence wouldn't matter," said Beth. "What did you expect? Few in the outside world believe in the reality you come from. It's amazing to me how Rory has been able to wander this country. Why didn't he diminish?"

"But he has," said the Morrigan. "His power leeches out, little by little, every trip he takes. He has become little more than what your people call a thug, a bully, a banger, a criminal. We can walk your world, but it is toxic to us over time. It was not always that way. If you could have seen us in our prime, striding the land in our glory, you would have fallen to your knees in worship and despair."

"You hope Conor can bring it all back for you, don't you?" said Beth.

"Yes," answered the Morrigan, "all of it."

"So where does Drake fit in all of this?"

"He is part of our world; his family has always had a strong association with the darker side of our reality, but he has merged it with your world of technology. Strange and powerfully so. Something I have never seen. It, too, is a mystery to me. He is comfortable in both worlds. That makes him dangerous as well. He is a worthy servant of the river demon."

"I have to go see him."

"I know you do dear," said the Morrigan in a raspy voice that caused Beth to turn and look at her. The Morrigan had aged, assuming her crone shape, withered in dusty grey rags. "That's why I want to give you this."

"You only turn that way when death is near," said Beth.

"Indeed, and it is near for you, whether to take you or not I cannot see clearly." She stretched out an aged claw and dropped a wadded strip of cloth into Beth's hand. "Wrap this around your womb," she said, "and if anything terrible is attempted on you in that building, it will protect your child." With that, the crone leapt into the air, and Beth could hear wings bearing her away.

Before her, she saw the lights of DIOGENE. It had been a week since she had last driven by, but much had been done in the meantime. The white buildings covered an acre. No razor wire fences but cams kept intruders out and security notified. She wasn't surprised when the gate automatically opened. She expected to be expected. Quickly, pulling up her blouse, she wrapped the cloth around her waist.

Tinker's Grove was a homey place, thought Beth. The Abbey looked like it had been lifted from a fairy tale castle on the River Shannon. But this, this plant was as sterile as the others were beautiful. It reeked of technological power. Caithness McNabb's dollars were well spent, thought Beth. State of the art stuff here. That's what she was thinking as the door to the main building opened and Dr. Nicholas Drake held out his hand to her.

PANIC

POUNDING ON THE door the next morning, Jace waited, beside himself, for the door to open.

"Jace," said Aunt Emily, sudden concern etched on her face as she saw the distraught boy, "whatever is the matter?"

"Is she here?" he asked. "Is my sister here? Did she come down here late last night? Did she come to see Conor?"

"No, I haven't seen her for awhile."

"Ask Conor for me, please."

"Ask him yourself over breakfast. Come on in."

"I can't," said Jace. "We haven't been talking very well lately. In fact, a lot of it has to do with Beth."

Aunt Emily looked at him silently for a moment, then in a soft voice she said, "You're worried; it's easy to see that. Whatever is between you and Conor isn't bigger than this burden. You need a place to collect your thoughts. Come on in."

Reluctantly, he did so, sitting down at the table. Conor was nowhere to be seen, but Troubles gave him a welcome couple of thumps of his tail on the floor before coming over to be petted.

"She's gone. I got back home, late. Nora and I were out, and when I got back, I stopped to see if she had gone to bed. Her bedroom door was shut; this morning, it was open and she was nowhere to be found."

"Beth is missing?" said Conor walking into the kitchen, his bare feet making no sound.

Jace looked up at him, resentment clouding his face. "Do you know something about this?" he asked. "She didn't tell me anything; did she you?"

"No," said Conor confused. "I don't know where she went."

"Not much of a mystery, here, it seems to me," said the old woman. "Girls do like to be out and about on an autumn morning."

"Yeah," said Conor, "but in a bad time and there's no safe place for her."

"There's more," said Jace. "When I went out into the driveway this morning, I found a pool of very sticky dried blood. Don't know whose it is."

"I'll go with you to look for her," said Conor.

"Thanks but no thanks," said Jace bitterly looking away out the window.

"Jace," said Aunt Emily.

"I don't want his help right now. He knows why."

"Jace," said Conor, "two's better than one. You know I care about her, too."

"Yeah," said Jace, "care maybe a little too much."

Conor flared, "What's that supposed to mean and what's it to you? I thought you were happy I was interested in your sister. Now, you're getting all pissy and protective. What did I do to deserve this?"

Jace threw back his chair and yelled, "You were supposed to treat her with respect, not take advantage of her."

"What do you think happened?" shouted Conor. "Whatever we did, we did because we cared for each other, and frankly it's none of your god-damned business, brother or not."

Jace clenched his fists and might have even struck out at Conor had not Aunt Emily chose that moment to step between the two. "Jason Michaels none of that in my house. And you, Conor, back off yourself. Men always seem to be fighting over women; guess that hasn't changed ever. But anger between two friends like you is just unseemly. Won't feed either of you with that kind of attitude in my kitchen."

"You don't understand," said Jace, clenching his big hands on top of the lace tablecloth. "She and I ... we've been fighting, because she and Conor were ..." He just couldn't go on, slumping back down in the chair, hunched over the table, swallowing sobs of anger and grief.

The story of young love doesn't change much down through the generations, thought Aunt Emily. One gnarled hand closed on Jace's fist. "I know."

"You do? He told you?"

"He did."

"How could he? I mean we were friends and all."

"Didn't mean to hurt you, Jace," said Conor. "Didn't mean for it to happen at all."

Blond hair drifting across his face, Jace just glowered.

Aunt Emily sighed, looking at her nephew. "Best get all the news out now and handle the anger here."

"What do you mean?" asked Jace.

Fixing Conor with a hard stare, she said, "There's always consequences to what we do, Conor. Tell him the whole story."

"What?" said Jace, rising from his chair again. "What does she mean, Conor?"

Couldn't look at him. Hadn't meant to be like a Judas to the best friend he ever had, but the eyes of Jace were so accusing that Conor felt damned to the lowest region of hell. He barely whispered the words, "Beth is pregnant."

How she did it, neither of them ever knew. Such a small thing. But Jace would have killed him on the spot. Conor would have put up no resistance. Even as he moved in to strike, Aunt Emily reached out her arm and placed her hand on the heart of the football player, stilling his movement with the graceful gesture.

"There will be no harm or vengeance done in this home," said Aunt Emily, her voice as regal as a queen. "This is the moment. All hangs in the balance. You were meant to walk together, and if you walk alone it will be but for a little while, for that is all the time that is left before the darkness comes. I can't heal the hurt between you, but if you don't, then all is lost. Promise me that in your search for Beth, you won't destroy each other in the process." She glared hard at the two of them. "Promise!"

Only reluctant nods answered her demand, but it was enough for her.

"Now get yourselves, the both of you, into Jace's car and go look for that girl. See if you can keep your mind on your task rather than trying to imitate the McNabb boys. Now get you gone."

She shooed them out of the house and watched the both of them walk sullenly to the car. Snapping her fingers, she sent Troubles along, padding silently behind. Not going to be much talking on this trip, she thought. Conor's impulsive foolishness was complicating an already dangerous situation. Hope the roll in the hay was worth it for him, for only trouble was going to follow.

A RIFT AMONG FRIENDS

JACE DROVE THROUGH town, both friends silent as they looked at streets ominously empty on the Saturday morning of All Hallow's Eve.

"Jace," said Conor.

"Shut up!" he snarled. "Just shut up will you." He drove aimlessly, half-curious as to why no one was around.

"It's like the whole town is shuttered up and hiding," said Conor, ignoring Jace's outburst.

Jace pulled over to the curb just across from the O'Leary house, its upstairs windows shuttered like frightened eyes.

"Why are we stopping?" asked Conor.

"You know, I ought to kill you," said Jace, white knuckles on the steering wheel. "Didn't mind you dating my sister, but this ... this goes too far. Should have expected it from a Chicago boy—fast mover, little bit more experienced than us country folk in manipulating people."

Conor clenched his jaw but said nothing.

"I mean it, man. You had no call doing that. We all had a good thing going, me and Nora, you and Beth, friends and fun and stuff like that, and you go and change it, making it so serious and all."

"Look at me, Jace. Just for one second, get off your high horse and look at me." Conor turned his head slowly toward Jace and Jace threw himself back against the car door, fear licking at his chest.

Puzzling it out later, he figured it wasn't exactly anything that Conor did, except the boy moved with a liquid smoothness that was unreal. Angry dark brows capped his gold flecked eyes, nostrils flaring with barely concealed rage. Jace saw Conor's tongue flick across his teeth, rather pointed ones he thought. He never noticed that before. Then the hand. Those fine fingers that played a mean tin whistle looked longer and the nails more pointed. Almost as if the hand was about to seize Jace's arm, an eagle's claw grasping its prey. Conor's face seemed to phase for a moment, as if there was some animal force yearning to be free just behind his features.

"Conor!" shouted Jason, clasping Conor's head between his huge hands as if to keep whatever was inside from escaping, "snap out of it!"

Like a balloon deflated, Conor slumped back into his seat, gasping for air. From the back seat, Troubles whined with concern.

"It never stops, dammit—the change never stops. Don't you see, Jace; can't you tell? I mean I have a few issues to deal with here. I never meant to hurt her, much less get her pregnant. Maybe my kind is damned."

"I don't know about that anymore," said Jace. "Human or not, damned or whatever, you're Conor Archer to me and responsible for what happens to my sister. I don't care if you're Piasa incarnate, if my sister is hurt, I'll rip you limb from limb." Clenching his jaw, he stared out the open window. Finally, he sighed and allowed himself a twisted smile. "Can't kill you; couldn't stand the look your Aunt Emily would give me. But I wouldn't hesitate slapping you around, even if you claim to be my friend. Still, you're right; first things first. Let's figure out how to find her."

They drove again, until they saw a woman sitting on the front steps, head in her hands.

"Hey, Mrs. Gillespie," said Jace leaning out the window. "What's wrong?"

She lifted up a tear stained face. "They took her. They took my Sharon."

"Who did?" asked Jace, a sinking feeling in his gut giving him a clue as to who did the deed.

"The McNabb boys. Fergal and Rafe—they looked like ghouls, something from a horror novel—knocked on the door not an hour ago and Sharon answered it. They just grabbed her. She screamed and I came. They said they had to take her away, down to the major clinic at the DIOGENE complex. Said there was something wrong with her. She was frightened out of her mind. I swear I would have taken my husband's shotgun to them both if Gordon hadn't driven up."

"Gordy?" asked Jace, "What did he have to do with it?"

"Oh he was so proper and all. Dressed in a nice suit. Said to me, 'Don't mind my brothers, Mrs. G. They've been out partying all night and look a little worse for wear. But what they said is true. Dr. Drake needs your daughter; he's found something that could be dangerous to her and a few other kids in town. We're picking them all up now. Don't be afraid. I'm sure that he won't keep them long.'"

"That's it?" said Jace. "You just let him take her?"

"'Course not," she said, "but the minute I started protesting Gordon says to me, 'You know that talk my mother had with you and your husband earlier this week?' He was referring to the threat that woman made to re-possess this house. We needed her help once, you see, and she was calling in the favor. Gordon didn't need to say anything more. In fact, I saw him pick a few other children up from some other houses on the street."

"Mrs. Gillespie, how could you give her up just for that threat—I mean it's only a house?" said Jace.

"Don't lecture me, Jason Michaels," she said, finger wagging. "I have a household to think of and besides, tact was never that family's strong suit. They threaten; I respond. Now, I'm sure the doctor means well. He hasn't ever done us any harm. I'm sure that she'll be back. I'm sure I'm just over-reacting. I'm sure ... say, isn't that the Archer boy with you?"

The woman got off the front step and walked closer to the car, point-ing an accusing finger at Conor. "Things were going just fine in this town till you showed up. I don't know what your part is in all of this, but you're involved. I just know it. And if anything happens to my little girl ..."

"Then it will be the McNabb's who'll have to answer for it," said Jace. "We'll let you know if we hear anything." He drove away from the woman, weeping again as she wrung her worried hands together.

"I don't understand it," said Conor. "Enough folks have gone missing to raise a national outcry and it's like a web or something has been put over the whole town, smothering all the news."

"Yeah," said Jace, "And some spider has injected these poor folks with paralyzing venom. They're going to be of no help. Even my Mom and Dad. I talked to them before I came out to your place. You should have heard them. Not a care in the world. They aren't too worried about Beth's disappearance."

"You think the McNabb's have something over them?" asked Conor.

"Not so simple as that," said Jace. "There's more than extortion hap-pening in this town. Weird crap has been coming down on us since you arrived. Of that much, those parents are right. Not saying you're to blame, but when myths and stories start coming true, who's to say what magic has been let loose. My parents weren't threatened by the McNabb's, but it's like they are oblivious to what is happening."

"Didn't think you believed in all that stuff," said Conor, shifting uncomfortably in the car. "Not sure I do either."

"It's not magic like most people think. It's not just spells and stuff like that," said Jace. "It's the magic of another world, maybe a more real world that is pressing in on us."

"I am to blame, you know," said Conor. "I mean, just look at you, Jace. Remember when I started changing after I got here? 'Don't worry,' you said. 'Beth and I will stand by you, even if the others don't.' Now that you're faced with the reality of all this, it's kind of hard to do all that, isn't it?"

Jace was quiet for a while, looking at the houses and lawns, all empty except for the few that had the confused parents gaping vacantly out windows. "I deserved that," he said. "But I'm pissed not because you're different but because I trusted you … and you failed. Shouldn't be that way, I guess. But Beth is my twin sister. We've always looked out for each other, and I should have seen this coming. Strange you may be, but you're a guy none the less and she is really stunning."

"It has nothing to do with her looks, Jace," said Conor. "You're my friend, but she, she understands me. We have something between us, and you know I'd never disrespect her."

"I think you did," said Jace.

"So does the Abbot, so does Aunt Emily, so for that matter, so does Rory."

"Even Rory knows?"

"Don't know how, but all of them knew right away. Just love the idea that my every move is on everyone's radar." He was quiet a moment and then said, "I'll say to you what I said to the Abbot and Aunt Emily—Rory can go to hell for all I care—but I told them I was sorry. I'll say the same to you. Should have known better. Should have understood there would be consequences. Should have thought about your feelings as well. But it wasn't all wrong. What Beth and I have together is real, just should have handled it differently."

"Don't expect forgiveness from me."

"Yeah, I know."

"But I need you now. We gotta find her, and you need to undo the damage you've done."

"And the 'stand by me no matter what stuff,'" said Conor. "What about that?"

"Don't press it this morning, Conor. Don't press it for awhile."

"Look at them," said Conor, "there and there." Pointing to other houses, where mothers and fathers stood gazing from their porches or looking out from windows, lost and tragic emotions washing across their faces. Looking up at the passing car, their eyes registering only memories, hands raised in pleading. Conor's voice sounded far away, using words that were not his. "'A lamentation echoing throughout the desolate streets. Parents, weeping, weeping for their children because they are no more.'"

IN THE BELLY OF THE BEAST

BEEPING, THE MONITORS woke her up once again. She'd been dozing off and on throughout the day. No drugs, in fact, no invasive procedures at all.

He had stretched out his hand to her late last night when she arrived. That gesture, as well as the civilized welcome, was short-lived. Hissing, he drew his hand back and spat, "Whatever thing from the Otherworld you carry or wear, take it off now or I'll call the Brothers McNabb to forcibly remove it from you."

Beth never said a word, but smiled a small, triumphant smile at him. Victories would be few, she thought. This one she ought to savor. "What's the matter?" she asked. "The Morrigan gave me a piece of cloth as a bit of luck to get me through my pregnancy unharmed. Afraid of a goodwill gesture from the hag of the battlefields?"

"Don't fence with me, girl," snapped Drake. "I have little time for any of this, and as important as you are to me, I'm not above making you suffer for any delay you cause."

Reaching behind her, she untied the thin cloth around her waist and offered it to him. Truth to tell, she didn't think it had any power outside of a good luck charm. She was a little amazed when he drew back.

"Throw it into the fire over there." He pointed to a barrel where trash was being burnt. To Beth, it looked incongruous. The only dirty thing in an otherwise pristine landscape, but she did as she was asked. As the flames consumed the relic, she heard a sighing in the wind, a keening echoing off the pristine granite walls of the research facility, and, though she believed it was just her imagination, she thought it was a sad sound, of loss and woe, weeping and sorrow.

But she had no time to think about that. The hand that had reached out to welcome her now grabbed her roughly and hustled her into the DIOGENE complex. As they walked through the halls, Beth was impressed with the state of the art facility. The people who passed them weren't from around Wisconsin. They had an East Coast look to them, but were all uniformly polite and even friendly, offering her a welcoming smile, but noticeably avoiding Drake's gaze. Clearly, he was feared.

He gave her a room. Asked her, rather nicely, to change into a hospital gown. No threats, just an unspoken understanding that he had effectively communicated all she needed to know the previous night—her life was not her own if she wished to preserve those whom she loved. Beth didn't balk, resigned to whatever might come, determined, however, not to let the unknown defeat her.

Some techs came in within the hour and hooked her up to a variety of monitors. Polite, kind even, and they didn't hurt her a bit. For that she was grateful.

Exhausted, she dozed and slept, and when she woke, it was early afternoon. Peeking out of her room, she saw no one. Bored, she decided to explore. Stripping off the adhesive backed monitor leads and switching off the disconnect alarms, she donned a robe on a nearby chair and started down the hall.

Ironic really, she laughed to herself. She truly was a child of the new millennium. A few fluorescent lights, some computers and sophisticated medical technology, and her mind had effectively pushed away the magic and wonder she had encountered the day before. Despite her earlier fears, the antiseptic techno-environment all around her comforted her and gave at least a little security. It was, after all, a medical facility, all about saving lives. So she thought until she came to the end of the hallway. An elevator stared sightlessly at her. Something behind the doors whispered fear in her mind. Thinking of Jace—he would never let a little fear daunt him—she screwed up her courage. Pausing only a second, she pressed the button. Just didn't feel like ceasing her explorations.

Beeping a quiet welcome, the doors opened. No monsters waiting in the brilliant light. Stepping in, she quickly figured out that most of DIOGENE must be underground. Nothing above the ground floor, but four floors beneath her. B4 it is then, she thought. Best to start at the bottom and work her way up.

A smooth and fast trip and when the doors opened again, a similar whitewashed, florescent shrill hallway greeted her. As did the screams.

A familiar chill crept up her spine. No one was being comforted or healed on this floor. She saw no one, but the sounds were coming from a room halfway down the hallway. Double-doors to the right opened soundlessly for her as sensors picked up her movement. Looking something like an animal control facility, the huge room was filled with cells, not to house dogs and cats but obviously bigger things—like people. Or children, she thought, as the first child came into view, looking through the bars at her with tears running down his face.

"Barry!" she cried running to him, reaching through the cage to hold him as best she could. Barry Tully, one of the 'dark ones' of the Grove, barely eight years of age, stared at her hopefully.

"Have you come to take me home?" he asked.

"I, I don't know," she said. "I only just got here myself, and I'm not sure what's going on. I'll find out though and we'll get you home, back to your parents as soon as possible."

A child's scream from a nearby cell caught her attention, and she moved quickly just in time to see Noah Riley's mouth open in horror as a thin shadow moved toward him. He was twelve, and he vainly reached for her through the bars. "It's going to get me!" he cried. And it did. As he pleaded with Beth to save him, the shadow thing climbed onto his back and over his head. It reached long fingers over Noah's face and hooked them into his mouth, pulling the boy's head back. Then, to Beth's horror, it simply crawled in and disappeared down Noah's throat.

Noah's arms fell to his side; he backed up, eyes going vacant for a moment.

"Noah," said Beth. "Noah, can you hear me?"

A small grin came across the boy's face. "Yes, we can," said the child. "Both of us hear you just fine."

Beth stepped clear of the cell as the Noah thing watched her. Cunning had replaced fear in the boy's now gold-flecked eyes.

"What have you done with him?" she said.

"Nothing." The voice twisted Noah's head back and forth, using it like a periscope to take in the view. "He must live, or I won't have a place to stay. But it is good to have a body and a mind to romp in. The things I'll be able to do. The power I'll give him. Ah, we're going to be great friends, right Noah?"

A little cry escaped Noah Riley's lips but the creature's laughter drowned it out. "It will take a while for him to get used to sharing, but all will be well."

She fled past several cages, all with children in them. Some pleaded for help; others laughed with eyes of gold. She saw a little girl staring at her own bloody hand, talking to herself. "That's enough, love," said the girl. "I'm not leaving for nothing, having just got here and all. Just stop your fighting or I'll bite another digit off, you hear me? No reason why we can't share this body together, you and I." The little girl looked up at Beth and laughed at her own words before she took another bite from the hand.

Beth doubled over in pain. Maybe the good doctor had done something to her after all. She fell, rolling to the floor. Sorrow and despair swept over her and tears fled from her eyes. Where was all this coming from? Despite the horror she felt, she knew she was stronger than that. A second wave of sadness and fear crashed into her. Then she understood. The feelings weren't her's. Subtle difference, but still noticeable. She looked around, ready for more magic, but saw nothing but occupied cages. The changelings paid no attention to her, and the unpossessed children quietly whimpered to themselves. Had to come from somewhere else.

Unconsciously, her hand dropped down to her womb and immediately she felt a warmth there, as if something was pressed up against her abdomen, yearning for freedom.

Impossible! She thought. Only a few days pregnant and the cells of the nascent embryo were responding in this way. But she knew it was true. Again, fear swept through her, but it, too, was not her own. A child's fear of the dark, of the unknown. A little one's need to run from the monster under the bed. The magic wasn't out there in the building, it was in her. Something wondrous was happening. Slowly, she climbed to her feet.

"There you are!" cried a voice from down the hall. The tall figure of Drake stood before the only exit. "Taking a bit of a stroll, are we?" he said.

"What have you done to these children?" she said whirling on her feet and dashing towards him. Throwing herself on him, she beat him on the face and chest, but Drake only laughed.

"My darling Beth, these children are experiments for humanity's sake. You surely should have figured that out by now."

"You're letting them be possessed—by those things."

"Not things. Changelings, who long have pined for bodies with which to share their dead lives. Just between you and me, I really could care less about them. Unpredictable and all, you see, but with them in the bodies of the 'dark ones' I can observe whether their Otherworld nature is sufficient to activate the mitochondrial gene each child has from their fathers, the gene that enables them to utilize whatever gifts they have been given. Would you like to know what I've discovered?"

With horror in her eyes, she looked at the doctor. Mage, she thought, he looks like a sorcerer from time gone by but covered with a thin veneer of respectability. "Yeah, tell me everything you freak."

Tsking, he reached forward and slapped her hard across the face. "No need to be rude, dear. Where was I? Oh, yes—it seems that if I surgically remove the pineal gland, not only do I get enough mitochondrial material for my serum to give humans a taste of the Otherworld, but such a procedure also provides a calm and willing body for the changeling, even if the lifespan of its human host won't be that long. On the other hand," he looked expectantly down to the cage that held the girl gnawing on her hand, "if I do not remove the pineal gland and just give the child to the changeling, a battle usually erupts. The changeling always wins, but it can be damaging to the body of the human, as I think you've already witnessed. I suppose I could have spared these some suffering by doing surgery first. But where's the fun in that? Besides, I like to watch. And observe of course. In the end, I need these bodies to function, at least for a while."

Backing away, hands on her hips, Beth was too furious to be frightened at that moment. "You would use these children? You would harm them?"

Drake bent over and kissed her head, whispering, "I would do anything for power and knowledge. Just like I'm going to do anything I like to you to see how this child of your's and Conor's progresses."

"You're going to keep me here for nine months?" said an incredulous Beth.

"Absolutely not!" said Drake. "I've decided to take the child myself, nurse it from an embryo in an incubator of my design. Once I remove the embryo, you are useless to me."

As if sensing the danger it was in, the new life in Beth convulsed her and she fell to the ground.

Drake laughed. "I see you, too, have discovered the little secret of your pregnancy. Come with me, and I'll show you the wonder you and Conor created. Gestation for you will not be nine months. In fact, your days' old pregnancy is far past the cellular stage. Actually, the embryo is developing so quickly that I expect birth in half that time."

Surprised at her own calmness, she said, "Whether or not what you say is true, your taking my child will never happen. I won't let you harm it, and there will be no surgical procedure done on me."

Drake laughed. "I admire your conviction, but you are four floors below ground in my little domain now. Your wishes don't matter to me in the least. I won't hurt you if you cooperate, but resistance will bring unimaginable pain. And, trust me, push me far enough and you will be the next sacrifice to Piasa. This I promise you."

Again, Beth slumped against a wall as Drake looked on. She couldn't believe she actually saw concern in his eyes. He reached out a long arm and grasped her hand, dragging her first and then, as she caught up, walking slowly down the hall.

"Come now," he said, "it really isn't as bad as all that. The pursuit of power and knowledge, especially for the advancement of humanity is a noble and worthy goal. I'm trying to make things better, not worse, for the human race. We've been cut off from our spiritual sides for far too long."

"Right," said Beth. "I've seen how your 'technology' has benefitted the McNabb boys. Your Jeckyll/Hyde serum sure is making them more human.

Did you see what they looked like yesterday at the clinic? I barely recognized them—animals, Drake; they were animals."

"Of course, you're right, you know," said Drake with a sad smile. "They are the first and they have prospered greatly. Already, they are experiencing what touching the Otherworld can bring them. The deformations are unfortunate but easily worked out imperfections over time. Nothing's perfect in the beginning. It's why you cannot get worked up over all these children. They are castoffs, actually. Nature's little experiments trying to put humanity in touch with the Otherworld. Hasn't worked out too well has it? And yet, I don't hear you railing against Nature. But having failed, Nature feels no guilt. It will just try again. And the children—these particular ones—failed in their destiny. They were fresh, newly budded roses from the Otherworld—beauty beyond price—just blooming only to freeze in this reality's cynicism and unimaginative mind set. This world simply couldn't nourish them. To experiment on them, to let them help me, is only justice for lives that are ultimately failures. I'm bringing some good to their miserable existence."

Beth was speechless. Clearly, he believed what he was saying. Reaching the end of the hall, she pulled on his hand to stop as she looked behind her. The wailing cries pursued them. Drake's price of progress she thought. All displayed in a clean, pristine, oh so understandable scientific environment, so it must be all right. She had to get away from here.

"I cannot do anything for them, Beth," said Drake gently. "They must end their lives as hosts for my little changelings. It is the way of things. The strong devour the weak. The future leaves the past behind. The spiritual overtakes and supplants the secular. I'm going to give humanity the chance to walk in a new reality, a stronger reality, a more beautiful reality, and I'm going to show them how to do it."

"Beth," cried Barry from the now distant cage. "Beth, help us!"

But she could do nothing. Like a forest creature in the clutches of a boa constrictor, she was caught. Barely able to breathe herself, she allowed Drake to drag her out of the room and back toward the elevator, back toward her own room, just another prey caught by a superior predator.

"Come," he said, "let's take a look at the little monster you created."

BREAK IN

CONOR COULD BREATHE again. Accelerating out of town, Jace rolled down the windows of the car and let the afternoon autumn air clear the fog in their heads that had built up touring the town. Even the dog began to relax, panting heavily as the breeze struck its face. Though neither of the boys spoke of the town's reaction, they simply couldn't fathom the passivity of the people in the face of the fact of the missing children. Paralysis on the part of the good citizens seemed another strange phenomenon manifesting itself. And, truth to tell, an anxious Conor, tired of roaming the Grove, spinning wheels to no effect in their effort to help Beth, blurted that they needed to get out—something or someone was sucking them into whatever possessed the townsfolk.

Only a quarter of a mile out of the Grove, Jace pulled over shaking his head, "What the hell is wrong with my mind?" he said. "What's going on back there?"

"I don't know," said Conor, "but at least we're headed in the right direction—straight toward DIOGENE. You know she's there and we aren't going to get any help from them."

Turning around, Jace looked at the Grove, just a tiny little town nestled up against the bluffs. All seemed quiet, but he knew that was deceptive. "They weren't doing anything anywhere we went, but it felt like a volcano about to blow."

"That's because something is holding them back, and they're just building rage. It's all going to come out and soon," said Conor. "Now, how are we going to get into DIOGENE?"

"The best way possible," said Jace. "Through the front gate."

"They'll take us for sure."

"Maybe," said Jace. "But chances are the brothers McNabb will try to snatch us sooner or later. I'd rather it be on our own terms. Besides, Drake tries to keep a veneer of civility. We should be okay in the daylight, in the public."

Jace had started driving again and in a mile or so they came to the front gates of the plant. Looked pretty cool really. Nice retention pond out front with a fountain. No barbed wire, just a classy, black, wrought iron fence. But the security cameras were obvious.

Pulling up to the guard house at the gate, Jace gave their names. The guard was a pleasant enough fellow. Drake had chosen to hire outside of the area. He smiled and said, "Oh yes, Dr. Drake said if you stopped by you were to shown right in. Just park over there and go in the front entrance. Sally's the receptionist; she'll help you out."

"How civilized," said Conor. "The bastard is like a spider welcoming us into his lair."

"More like a black mamba stalking prey, sure that all he has to do is strike once and we'll die in an instant," said Jace, "but it's the only option we have."

They got out of the car, went in and found Sally as pleasant as promised.

"Do you have a patient by the name of Beth Michaels?" said Conor. "She would have come in last night or today."

"I'm sorry, sir," smiled the brunette with vacant eyes. "That would be confidential information, but Dr. Drake did say you could wait in room six down the hall. He told me to make yourselves comfortable and look at anything there you wish. He'll check up on you shortly."

The boys walked further into the complex. Lightly staffed, the few who noticed them gave only perfunctory smiles. Evidently, they were not perceived as any kind of threat. A few yards down the wide hallway, taste-fully decorated with abstract but colorful paintings, they found room six. Expecting a small examination station, they were surprised to find a fully functional hospital room with diagnostic equipment everywhere.

"She was here," said Jace, picking up her jacket thrown on a nearby chair.

"Drake wants us to know that," said Conor.

"Look at this," said Jace, pointing to a computer screen on a portable cart.

At first, neither Jace nor Conor could figure out what they were look-ing at; then they knew it was some kind of an ultrasound video.

"Of her womb, I bet," said Jace.

Conor was thankful that Jace was too engrossed with the picture to see him blushing.

Jace pressed a button and the image began to move. A voice recording began to play, and Drake could be heard speaking. "The subject's preg-nancy is unusual. Conception occurred earlier this week and what should be simply a mass of cells is now an embryo presenting advanced development."

"It looks human," continued Drake's voice, "but obviously it cannot be. More proof that Conor Archer is something radically different than we have ever seen before, even more different than the 'dark ones' of this town. I must examine him more fully as well. The subject is irrelevant. As soon as I remove the embryo, she will no longer be of interest. Her DNA is entirely human—she is just a vessel for this extraordinary creature."

"Conor, Jace," said a panicked voice behind them. Turning, they saw Beth staring at them, her arms held by a smiling Drake, her gaze fixated on the ultrasound playing on the monitor before her.

Chuckling, Drake spoke, "Well, Beth, looks like brother and lover know all about the little fella, that little 'bun in the oven' as you folks around here call the result of your spawning."

Twisting in his grasp, Beth broke away from Drake. To Jace's surprise, she fell into Conor's arms. Conor held her tight and found her shaking from her weeping.

"It's alright," he said. "We're here to make it right."

"How chivalrous," said Drake. "But, I, too, am glad you are here. Saves me the trouble of sending Fergal after you. Besides, I prefer you undamaged."

"Conor, something's wrong with the baby," said Beth. "I can feel it."

"I know," said Conor. Lifting his head, he looked at Drake. "We saw your little demonstration on the monitor. It doesn't seem possible. If you've been conducting experiments on her or have hurt Beth or the child in any way, I swear I'll kill you myself."

Drake laughed, "Parental outrage is most commendable, but rest assured I haven't harmed either of them—yet. But for that to continue, I'll need your cooperation."

Jace looked at Beth and whispered, "Are you okay?"

Touching his face, she said, "Yes, but Jace, in the basement, four floors down are all the children, and he's doing things to them. We've got to save them."

"Why did you come here?" asked Conor.

"I had to find out why Drake wanted me. He told me I was pregnant. That's what he's been studying, and now he's found a way to remove the baby without destroying it. He's determined to take the child."

Outraged, Conor looked at the smirking physician, "Don't worry. Jace and I are here to make sure that won't happen. Why didn't you come to me, Beth, when all this happened? He never would have touched you." Holding her tight, he looked at Jace, tension rippling across his face as he glanced at his friend.

"Because it would have been too much of a burden," she said, her face pressing against his chest. "I would have, you know that, but I thought I could handle it on my own, dispose of Drake's threat before it became real, reason with him, make some deal."

"Look at the snake. He'd never negotiate; he'd do what he wanted," said Jace. "You saw what happened to Deck. You know what he did with Brother Luke. And those missing kids. You know we won't find them alive."

"But most are alive!" said Beth. "They're stuck in the lab. He's been experimenting on them. Some are dead—he harvests their pineal gland for some serum. He's using Rafe and Fergal as guinea pigs and, like you said, they're changing, Conor. They scare me to death!"

Conor had been watching Drake walk over to a refrigerator and take out two vials—obviously blood. Silently he poured a little from each on the sterile metal tray by the side of Beth's bed.

"What are you doing?" asked Conor.

"Making sure that you and Jace don't do anything stupid—like try to rescue the children."

"You can't stop us," said Jace.

"As a matter of fact, I can," said the doctor, taking off the arcane dagger around his neck and tracing crude stick figures on the tray with the samples of blood. "I knew you'd come, so I had samples of your blood, Jace and Conor, brought up here to Beth's room."

He laughed softly as he continued tracing.

"Doesn't even look like me," sniffed Jace.

Conor grimaced at the mess the doctor was making, and said to Drake, "I fail to see the point."

Drake looked at him with a condescending eye. "So talented, yet so naïve. You don't even recognize the simplest of magics, do you? Tribal shamans, illiterate peasant women in the Caribbean, even teenagers who haunt occult book stores recognize sympathetic magic when they see it. You see, these two figures are you, not because they physically resemble you but because they are made from your blood. And with this dagger, consecrated as it is to a power far greater than yours, I have power over you—to bind you ..." and here he touched the point of the dagger to each of the figures' arms.

Simultaneously, Jace and Conor felt their arms clamped tight to their body. Try as they would, they couldn't move a muscle.

"Just in case you think you can run ..." Drake touched one leg of each of the figures and Conor and Jace felt their right legs go numb, barely able to support their weight.

"Now, Beth," said Drake, "lest you want them further harmed, get back into bed. More tests are to come." Looking terribly frightened, she climbed back up on the hospital bed, clutching her hospital gown tight around her shoulders.

Drake pressed a button and two security men appeared. Big men, thought Conor, big enough to be a problem for Jace and himself even when all their arms and legs worked.

"Take them down to Basement Level Four. They've been given a sedative that will keep them compliant. Let them wait in one of the empty cells so they can witness the testing of the children."

The men did as they were told; Conor and Jace, unable to move, went along for the ride. They were half carried by the goons.

"Got an idea," said Jace.

"Anything," said Conor.

"The other day, when Walt was killed, I saw your father."

"And you didn't tell me?" said Conor, fury rising in him again.

"Couldn't. Didn't think Madoc would want it. Never mind that now. Besides, it's not like you have been big on sharing secrets lately. He showed me a ship in a cave down White Creek way, and when I first looked, it was nothing more than a ruin. Then he touched my arm, and the ship just shimmered into life. I didn't get it then, but I think I know what he did. When he touched me, he took me into his world, the Otherworld, at least for a moment. What if you did that now, Conor? What if you stepped into the Otherworld? It might break the hold on this magic. At least for you. Maybe it might break it for me too if you held onto me."

"Shut up with that nonsense," said one of the security men. "I tell you, Skip, I gotta get some of whatever the doc shot these guys up with—goofy but in a cool kind of way."

Conor whispered, "I don't think I can. Only time I really tried it was months ago when I—I don't know what I turned into, but I stopped thinking like a human and just let the animal take over."

"Don't do that," cautioned Jace. "Just step into the Otherworld, as you are now, without changing. Maybe do it the way you do the Second Sight stuff. God knows, if you don't, we're dead meat."

Skip laughed, "At least, he's tracking reality with that last comment." They threw the both of them into the elevator and waited for the machine to begin its descent.

Conor really didn't want to try. He was unsure of what would happen. None the less, he agreed with Jace that not much good was going to occur on Basement Level Four. Stepping sideways. That's how he had been told to envision it, so he tried, and, at first, it seemed to him that nothing happened. No great extension of the senses, no smell of a deeper reality, but then he caught the look on Skip's face.

Skip shrieked and dropped Jace to the ground. "Lou, get him off you, now!" Lou took one look at Conor and yelped as well, dropping him and shrinking to the other side of the elevator. Just then, the bell dinged, doors opened, and the security guards went screaming out of the elevator down the hall.

"I look that bad?" said Conor. "Don't feel any different."

Jace allowed himself a deep breath. At least Conor talked like a man, even if he didn't look like one. "Let's just say, I have a pretty good idea of what Taps Jeffords saw under the oak tree the day you first met him."

Conor looked down at himself; all still seemed the same to him. "Hey, I look normal to me."

"That's because in whatever world you're in now, you are revealed as who you truly are, but here in this world, well, let's also just say you've got a lot of pent up rage. You are huge, semi-formed, a ribbon of light wrapped around you." Jace swallowed hard hoping Conor's mind wasn't as beast-like as his body was beginning to look. "Hey, man, at least you scared those guys away."

"Yeah, but you can't move, Jace, and I sure don't feel like dragging you. Here, let me take your hand." As he reached for Jace, the elevator doors closed.

Jason found that his torso could still shudder in horrific anticipation as some vague claw reached out to grab him. Once touched, however, he found himself able to move again, and Conor's true image materialized right through the dark thing.

"I take it from the look on your face, that you've just stepped into the Otherworld with me."

"Yeah, thank God. I like you, at least sometimes, but when you're enchanted or whatever, your look in our world takes a bit of getting used to."

"You were right, though," said Conor. "Going into the Otherworld broke Drake's spell. We've got to get back up there and destroy those samples or else he'll be able to control us whenever he wants. He'll figure out how we got around his magic and either kill us or paralyze us in a way the Otherworld won't be able to help."

ESCAPE FROM DIOGENE

BETH LAY SPEECHLESS in her hospital bed, watching Drake out of the corner of her eye. Humming a tuneless snippet of some strange song, he fastidiously washed his hands, while leaving the bloody stick figures to dry on the silver instrument tray.

"I know," he said, cocking his head over his shoulder, looking at Beth, "I know that you find me slightly strange. Don't blame you really. I'm like a fish out of water, a stranger in a strange land. I feel like that sometimes. Once, it was different, so I'm told. The things that draw me most—chants in the night, blood on the wind, the practice of the Craft—once those were what filled the experience of most people. Even running the hills of Wales when I was but a boy, I could still find the crofter or old biddy woman who could speak of such things with knowledge. They were my teachers, but of a world that had long since passed away. Not completely, mind you. I still saw it around this time of year with your Halloween, our feast of Samhain. Some of our villagers still burned the Wicker Man out by the seashore on ghostly wind tossed nights, but no human ever lost his or her life out there on the sand. We were already past such things then.

"So I had to get myself a modern education, and I did well, but never better than the night my lab partner and I were dissecting cadavers. We had stayed later than the rest of the class and I just wanted to see what would happen. I touched my little dagger—the one you just saw, dear Beth—I just touched it to the stiff, hardened heart of the corpse of a coal miner.

"I've had the dagger since I was a boy—the gift of my grandfather. What a strange man he was, a butcher by trade and so familiar with the blood-smell of things. Gave it to me on my seventh birthday saying, 'Nick, my lad, this blade belongs in the family. I give it in to your care, forever and always.' His wicked black eyes gleamed at me as he took my hand and cut my palm. So sharp was that blade that I felt no pain. Even if I did, I would not have said a thing, for his eyes, black as the darkest night, held my gaze. He spoke to me then,

'The blade that bites, the knife that cuts,
Here is the dagger that calls the dark.
Yours to keep and yours to guard;
Yours to wield when woe is needed.
Blood has sealed; power is passed;
The ancient magic lives again
To bind and maim, to rend and kill,
To open a pathway for the dark,
For the Worm that turns in the dark.'

"For the Worm," he whispered. Drake's mouth hung open in reverie, a bubble of spit perched on his lower lip, like a snow globe of horror memories. Slowly his eyes focused on the present again. "There I go," he laughed, "frightening the children again. So sorry, Beth, now where was I?"

"Yes, indeed, the dagger and the dead heart. So I touched the blade to the decaying organ. And it began to beat, first slowly, then normally. My partner left the room in shock—actually he ran like the coward he was— but I did not. I waited to see what would happen. I actually had to stick the knife into the heart to keep it beating, and after about a minute, the corpse's eyes opened. Guess what? They were green. And they saw me. The mouth opened, and it spoke to me. Oh, I knew it wasn't the voice or the presence of the coal miner. It was the one whose very body helps make up a part of that little knife.

"You ask how I know. My father passed on the heritage, but it was the old women and the crofters I told you about who really initiated me. They saw my interest in what they knew and did. One night—oh, what a night!— they painted my body with blood. 'Worthy of your family's heritage,' they said. 'The blood runs true in him,' they said. 'Tell him whom he serves,' said the oldest hag among them. They whispered it to me then, about the Worm at the roots of the world. 'You'll hear its voice, one day,' they all said. When they left me that night, alone in the sea cave on the rocky beach, blood drying on my naked body, the green mist came to me. Up out of the ocean, colder than the night, it wrapped itself around me. It was the most special night of my life, and I would kill to be touched like that again. That night was when I first heard it speak. Would you like to know what it said?"

Drake drifted over to her bedside and placed his lips next to her ear. Shaking with fright, she listened to his whisper.

"It spoke with my father's voice, *'Blood has sealed; power is passed; open a pathway for the dark, for the Worm that turns in the dark.'*"

Drake stood up, tossed his head as if trying to clear it and said, "And that was that. From that moment on, I've tried to do that—make it live in this world, bring the Otherworld more fully into this world. But few believe in that reality. That does not make it less real, but it does make it more inaccessible. That proves a problem for Piasa. It can only vacation here; it can't live permanently. Only if I open the borders; only if I get traffic from both sides can I begin to permanently break down the barriers that separate the worlds.

"That's where the 'dark ones' come in, Beth, don't you see? They are the bridge, but an unconstructed one. They have a flaw. They are strong enough to manifest some abilities of the Otherworld for a while, and even strong enough to draw forth the Otherworld tenuously around the Grove, but they cannot make the Otherworld a permanent reality here. They can't bring it into visibility. But they are a start. I had thought the ones who dwell in the mound should have been able to affect such a union. But they either refuse to do so, or are powerless to achieve such a thing. I am convinced they are irrelevant.

"Your child, by Conor, however, is a different story. Conor is so much more powerful. Whatever serum I produce from the 'dark ones' will be enhanced much more by someone from as strong a bloodline as your little boy. And since the serum does indeed open a doorway into the Other-world, I'd say that's a promising path to take towards the fulfillment of the goal I set so long ago, there by the cadaver in the lab room at medical school. I can still smell the formaldehyde; even now, the odor has such possibilities."

"So what does that mean for me and my child?" said Beth.

"Yes, you would want to know the practicalities," said Drake. "It says much for your child, but little for you. Frankly, you are rather useless to me. From my research done in the past few days, I now can take the embryo, grow it to viability and raise the child myself, or, if I so desire, produce a product from him that will allow the worlds to merge and meet."

"So your plan is to kill me." A burning rage was silently driving the fear out of Beth's body. "And use my child as a lab rat."

"It is, and you'll agree."

She rose up out of bed. "Don't think so." Moving swiftly she tipped the ultrasound cart over, blocking Drake's way to her. Running she almost made it out the door before his clawlike hand snatched the back of her hospital gown. His strength was prodigious. Turning her around, he lifted and shook her. Neck snapping back and forth, she tried to knee him, missing him by inches as he held her out from him, laughing at her feeble attempts.

Impotent with frustration, Beth was on the verge of giving up, when she caught a shadow on the wall. Someone was coming from the hall. Hoping against hope, she kicked with all her might and this time struck pay

dirt. Drake dropped her and doubled over in pain just as Jace and Conor
rushed into the room.

Conor had found it hard to hold them both in the Otherworld at the
same time. When the elevator doors opened on the ground floor he let go
of Jace, hoping that he had broken the spell cast by Drake's magic. Must
have worked, he thought, since Jace had full movement of his body. Conor,
himself, felt like he was sliding back down to earth. Sounds returned to
normal and the atmosphere didn't have that heightened feel to it. Of
course, he was grateful that Jace kept assuring him he didn't look like a yeti
or Bigfoot, so he was pretty convinced that he was totally and completely
back in this reality. Not much time to think that through for they pounded
up the corridor into Beth's room and saw her give the good doctor a
vicious kick in the groin.

"One for the good guys!" whooped Jace as he picked up his sister and,
with Conor, hustled her down the hallway leaving a winded Drake still
curled up, fetal-like on the floor.

Running, they made it to the car without any hindrance. Sally, the
receptionist, looked up with her gum chewing lips and vacant eyes as they
passed, and reached for a phone. Behind them, from somewhere deep
within the facility, an alarm began to sound. Pursuit would not be far
behind.

Refusing to get into the car, Beth shouted at them both, "Did you see
the kids; did you find them?"

"No," said Jace. "We were on the level you talked about, but the only
thing we heard or saw were two very frightened guards shrieking down the
hall. Conor here put on his best Twilight Zone outfit and gave them an
early Halloween." Jace noticed movement at the facility's entrance. Drake
must have found a few more goons to help him out. Several were running
straight for them. "In the car, now!" shouted Jace.

Stomping on the accelerator, Jace tore through the parking lot.
Troubles stuck his head out of the window and barked fiercely at the gate
guard, who didn't even try to shut the gate but let the car barrel through the
exit. Jace accelerated yelling, "We need to get to town. Get there first,
before he makes another move." Surprisingly, no one followed them. Hard
to figure all that out, thought Conor. He sort of expected a bigger effort to
keep them all hostage. A nagging forboding grew in the pit of his stomach.

"Nora said she'd be at Dort's store," said Jace. "Good a place as any
to hide out for at least a little while." Not hearing any objection, Jace roared
downtown and parked the car on the opposite side of the street from the
store. With Beth between them, Conor and Jace took her inside. Not a soul
was on the street, not a person looked out to see the strange sight.

WHAT DORT DID

COUNTING OUT THE pittance she had taken in that day—not many tourists now that the festival was over—Dort banged the cash register shut with a crash and a gasp as she witnessed a nearly unconscious Beth being dragged into the store between Jace and Conor. Troubles followed silently behind.

"Where's Nora?" said Jace. "Why isn't she here?"

"I am right here," said a voice from the back. Nora appeared, dust all over her from trying to make sense out of the forgotten products in the rear room. "What's the problem?" Seeing Beth, she ran to her friend and helped the boys sit her on a chair behind the counter.

"She's passed out," said Conor, "but I think that's all it is. I didn't see any pills or syringes used or open in her room down there at DIOGENE. God knows what Drake was about to do, though."

"Are they coming?" hissed Dorothy Martin, peering out the blinds of the front window, looking down the street.

"Don't think so," said Jace. "No sign of pursuit when we left, and believe me, if they wanted to, they could have been here by now."

Nora had ransacked the apothecary display and grabbed some smelling salts, grateful for her grandmother's penchant for saving everything. Unstopping the bottle, she sniffed, making a face. Still potent enough. Putting it under Beth's nose was all that the unconscious girl needed to rouse. Opening her eyes, Beth jumped to her feet. "Are we out of there? Are they coming?"

Conor rushed to her side, "You're safe. Hey, sit back down for a second." Turning to Dorothy, he said, "You have any spare clothes around? She can't keep wearing just a hospital gown."

"I'll get her something," said Nora, disappearing into the back room again.

"I knew he was trouble from day one," said Dorothy, mostly to herself as she kept staring out the window. "Got powerful evil in him, he does."

Jace looked at her strangely. "You're right about the doctor, but how do you know that?"

"You think the 'dark ones' or Drake and his ilk are the only magic around here?" said Dorothy. "You think that us normal folks can't be touched now and then with a window to the truth? I'll tell you how I know. First of all, I watch him like a hawk. He skulks with the McNabb's. Looks sincere but his eyes are dead. You hear me, boy? His eyes are dead! He's a corpse walking around. Gives me the creeps. Came in here one day and just stared at me. Didn't say a word. Asked him if I could help him somehow, but he just kept looking at me. His lips were moving though, as if he was talking to someone somewhere else. Then he asked where Nora was."

"You're kidding?" said Jace. "Because she's a 'dark one,' right? What did you say?"

Dort turned from the window, shoulders hunched, looking old. Gently she patted Jace on the cheek. "You're sweet on her, I know, and that's just fine because you are a good man, Jason Michaels. But you already know I would never betray my own granddaughter. I just stared back at Drake. Two can play that game. I stared at him, just like I stare at everyone who comes into this store only to look, never to buy. I stared at him 'til he left."

Conor was holding Beth tight all this time. Jace and Dort were still talking when Nora came back whispering, "Here, let me take her. I'll get her cleaned up with fresh clothes as well." Reluctantly, Conor let go of Beth and allowed Nora to lead her off.

"Can't stay here, Conor Archer," said Dorothy, turning her attention to the boy. "Drake will come for you all. It's only a matter of time."

"We'll have to split up," said Jace. "Got a feeling the Abbot can help. If anyone around here knows how to stop Drake short of shooting the son of a bitch, it will be him."

"I'm not sure shooting him would stop him," said Conor. "He's got enough power to easily flick away anything having to do with modern tech. The more he acts, the more of the Otherworld he brings into this town. Two months ago, the Morrigan was just a story; now she flies the night sky and others see her besides me. Changelings, like the ones Beth saw in Basement Level 4 of DIOGENE, possessing the 'dark ones'—figments of nightmare stories only a few weeks ago. Now they walk the earth. Even the mound Dwellers, just rumors days ago, now seem to be everywhere in the shadows."

Jace's eyes studied the floor, "Have a hunch it's not just Drake that's responsible for all that."

"Of course not," said Conor. "It's me, too. I know that. But I'd like to think I didn't let whatever passes for evil over there break through into this community. Surely Drake has more to do with that."

Dorothy peered out the window again, then spat her words with anger at them. "He needs to die; he's a menace, not just to us but to the world. You have to kill him."

"Hey," said Conor, "let's take a step back here. No one is really talking about killing anyone are they? I mean, we can call the cops, something like that; get the state patrol in here."

Jace laughed, "Conor, man, sometimes you are dumber than cowshit. No one from the outside is going to believe us and anyone coming in from the outside is going to be at risk precisely because they don't believe. This is our problem; we've got to handle it. Drake's gotta go. Has to happen."

"They're coming," hissed Dorothy.

Indeed they were. Several unmarked vans, presumably from DIOGENE, pulled up in the empty parking lot of the clinic, followed by a slowly moving ambulance, warning lights dark. Dorothy could see Fergal and Rafe get out of one van and Drake, himself, exit from the other. Motioning the boys over, Dorothy pointed as Drake threw open the back doors of the vans. From the vehicles poured dozens of children, all 'dark ones.' Conor couldn't believe that Drake had managed to take all of them without the townspeople revolting. Creepy how they just stood there, unnatural, as if a switch was off. Drake had Fergal and Rafe guide them into neat little rows. Observing the work, Drake wiped his hands together and turned up the street.

All three backed quickly away from the window, Dort taking time to pull the blinds shut. "He's coming this way," she hissed. A shadow moved in front of the window, but no one entered the store. Jace risked a peek and saw the back of Drake angling up the main street toward the *DewDrop Inn*.

"Come out!" shouted the doctor from the middle of the street, not at the hidden watchers but at the drinking patrons of the said tavern. Bursting into expansive laughter, he managed to shout between fits of amusement, "Come out my friends, come out. I've got something you just must see."

Out they came, bleary eyed from an afternoon of despair drinking, the men of the town. Not knowing what to expect, they gathered silently on the sidewalk, while Dickie Bergin hung back in the shadows of the tavern's entrance.

"Good news, I think you'll agree, for all of you," said a beaming Drake. "The missing children have been found, and you can thank the McNabb boys for that, all three of them. Gordon has been manning the phones for rumors, tips and news while Rafe and Fergal have been canvassing the surrounding area. Knowing of the effort, I offered Caithness McNabb the services of DIOGENE and for most of the morning and afternoon, that facility has been welcoming the lost back. I would have called earlier, but we felt it best to make sure they were healthy and required no additional medical care."

"Where were they?" shouted one parent.

"Found in the barn at Madoc's Glen," said Drake. "Fergal and Rafe discovered them there and brought them to me."

"That's the witch woman's doing!" shouted a voice.

"Oh, we mustn't jump to conclusions," said Drake. "Emily O'Rourke is not the only one who lives in the house at Madoc's Glen."

"When can we see them?" cried another.

Cell phones flicked open as men called wives and relatives with the news. A stream of people came walking or driving down to Main Street and soon a couple of hundred people were gathering and Drake was forced to stand on the dais of the Iraq War Memorial in order to be seen and heard.

"All your questions will be answered," said Drake, "but first, I am sure you would like to see the children." He dialed a number on his own phone and from just down the street a double file column of children could be seen marching toward the crowd.

"Here they are, my friends, fit and well," said Drake, "including those I had to borrow from you for some very important medical tests. You know I have their best interests at heart; they are the future. They are very dear to me. Thank you so much for your generosity."

A hoarse, half-hearted cheer went up from the crowd and a few mothers dashed forward, running for their children. Over the past few days nearly three dozen kids had either vanished or been snatched in broad daylight, taken for Drake's 'tests.' Less than three dozen were marching forward now. Everyone scanned the approaching assemblage for their loved one; already some were weeping as expected faces failed to appear.

Before the crowd could actually cohere into one emotional response, the children broke ranks and began cavorting up the street and into the crowd, shouting and laughing. At first, it looked like they were ecstatic to be reunited with mothers and fathers. The first clue that smacked Dickie Bergin in the face and let him know that all was not well was the well-placed hand of Tommy Flaherty. Good kid, thought Dickie. Twelve years old and always polite. That's why he couldn't figure out why the lost, now found, waif gave him a crooked smile beneath yellow-flecked eyes and slapped him hard across the face, laughing as he lurched away.

In fact, thought Jace, as he witnessed all this, the movements of the kids looked more like puppets on a string.

"What's wrong with them?" asked Nora as she watched from the window.

"Tell her, Jace," said Conor, "tell her what they were doing with the kids at DIOGENE."

"As always," said Jace, "that doctor lies. He did something to the kids, Nora. Allowed the changelings to possess them. Had them in cages and let the transformation happen. I don't even know if the kids are still there or if the changelings have completely displaced them—listen to me, I sound like that goddamn doctor. Nora, they may be dead, their bodies used by these things from the Otherworld."

"Is this what they were going to do to my granddaughter?" said Dorothy.

Conor looked with pity on the shopkeeper. "He wants the 'dark ones' for some serum he's using to make it easier for humans to contact the Otherworld. He's already using it on Fergal and Rafe and it's changing them. He knows it's not perfect. That's why he took Beth. She's ... she's pregnant by me, and he wants the baby. He thinks our son will be stronger than the 'dark ones.'"

Beth's voice came from behind them. "He wants the baby so that it can provide an even stronger serum. He's willing to kill our child if he has to, but in any event, the baby, like all the rest of the 'dark ones,' is expendable, and only useful for his dreams, his plans."

"Monster!" cried Dorothy, her hand reaching out to touch Nora's shoulder. "I won't let him have you."

"Like I said," said Jace. "Our best chance in the chaos here is to split up. I've got to see the Abbot. Nora you have to stay out of sight."

"I've been thinking about what you said, Jace," said Conor. "I'll take Beth with me. We'll stop at Aunt Emily's and bring her with us. Let's rendezvous at the Crossroads."

"They might come there," said Jace.

"They will find us," said Conor. "It might as well be on turf we're all familiar with."

"Not much of a plan," said Jace. "What do we do when we get there?"

"Don't have everything figured out yet, Jace," said Conor. "But whatever happens isn't going to be decided by the things of this world. The Otherworld is marching home and whatever finale the doctor is planning is going to be waged on that soil. We can't lay out a plan that makes any sense. We'll just have to use our wits and respond to whatever happens."

"Still don't like that plan," said Jace. "But we have no choice."

"No choice at all," said Conor grimly.

Jace nodded and let himself out the front door. No one in the gathering crowd paid the slightest attention to him. He made it to his car, started it without incident and backed it up till he could go up one of the side streets towards the monastery.

Conor saw that Jace went unmolested. "Think we can do it?" he asked Beth. "Just you and me?" The dog whined in protest. "And you," he said, ruffling the Lab's ears. "We've got to make it to Aunt Emily's on foot. Are you up to it?"

Wordlessly, Beth nodded. She was feeling a lot better and the fact that there was a plan, not very well spelled out, but a plan none the less, was settling her down.

"I don't like you young ones doing this," said Dorothy. "Too much can go wrong."

"Right you are," said Beth with a weak smile. "But we have to try something. Drake's causing mischief out there. Who knows where it will lead."

They went out the front door, the entry bells jingling softly. Outside, the chaos was growing. The 'dark ones' mingled freely with the crowd, escaping embracing arms and kisses and causing surprise and wonderment to all present. They really didn't hurt the adults, but their behavior was not that of children. They spat in faces, laughed as they tripped old men and women, pushed and shoved throughout the crowd. Conor and Beth moved slowly on the periphery north towards the road leading to Madoc's Glen.

A voice cried out, "Where's my boy, Dr. Drake? I don't see him anywhere."

Another wept, "She's gone; my daughter is gone. I don't see her here at all."

Still another shouted, "There must be more; my William still is missing."

Then Mr. O'Leary's voice could be heard above the fray, "Dr. Drake, where are my children, my four lovely children? Have you not found them yet? Where have they gone?"

Drake took that moment to garner the town's attention. "My friends," he shouted, "no doubt you are glad to have your children back, but I am fully aware that not all have been found. Mr. O'Leary, for instance, still is missing his four beautiful children. Some are asking how all this could have happened. Some have suspected the McNabb's, or even me as being the ones behind the disappearances. But you know that is false. We have worked tirelessly to find your children, to heal them if they have been hurt, to help them in their need. But Mr. O'Leary has a point. His children have not been found. Tell us, Mr. O'Leary, who took them? Tell us all so that we know."

"It was that Archer boy," said O'Leary with a drunken slur. "That bastard took my little ones and they flew away."

"You're drunk, O'Leary," shouted Dickie Bergin. "Pay no attention to what he says. Conor's a good lad and he took no kids."

"So sure of that are we?" said Drake. "Mr. O'Leary has tippled a few this afternoon; but I happened to be with him when his children disappeared."

Gasps punctured the crowd. This they had not heard before.

"Oh, yes," he continued, "and Conor Archer and his friends were there too. I wouldn't say that he actually kidnapped those children, but he did encourage them to run away. I know. I heard him say it. Now, that's the first good lead we've had to go on in the disappearance of so many young ones. And the fact that the others were discovered in the barn at Madoc's Glen adds further suspicion. What does Emily O'Rourke know, and when did she know it? One can only wonder where the other missing children are. And we can only pray that they are unharmed."

"We knew Conor Archer would be trouble," said a voice from the crowd. "Should never have let him stay. Knew the minute he fell off that bus."

They saw him then. Hard to tell who spied him first, but together a cry went up, "There he is!" just as Conor and Beth reached the northernmost part of the crowd that had spilled all the way to Visser's Café. Troubles spun, growling at the crowd.

"Run!" said Conor to Beth. "They'll be after us in a flash."

But they weren't. For it was then that Dorothy Martin chose to come out of her shop. No one would have noticed her but for the M-80's she threw on the ground. Had a few of those fire cracker explosives from fourth of Julys past. Even she wasn't sure they would go off though the fuses lit just fine. Blow them up and even the crowd would focus on the shrew woman—at least that's what she thought. No damage, but the horrendous noise! In the smoke rising around her she looked like a phantom from hell.

"Listen to me, you drunken fools!" she said. "Don't let this quack beguile you with his innuendo and lies. Conor Archer isn't your enemy. The good doctor is. Look at him, so smug and self-confident, manipulating you. You know no more about Dr. Drake than you do about the Archer boy and you're going to believe an outsider's take on all this? Shame on you!"

Her fist rose high in the air as she marched toward Drake, perched like a buzzard on the war memorial. "You did something to them all. I know it."

"Silence her," said Drake, not speaking to the crowd but to the changeling children. Like marionettes, they stopped cavorting and turned as one, looking at her. The crowd backed away from the shopkeeper and left her standing alone in the middle of the street. Looking around, she felt the first fingers of fear stroking her spine as the children approached.

Saying nothing, they simply looked at her, smirks on their faces with glittering eyes, hands twisted into claws gripping and flexing. Dorothy Martin, who never had been brave in her life, excepting the day she took Nora away from her weak son and feckless daughter-in-law, stood up straight. Not so brave that she couldn't call out for help. She yelled for Dickie, but his eyes were vacant. Couldn't even be sure he could see her. Found the same with Joe Smalley, the postman and Todd Weathers, the feed store owner—staring at her but not really seeing.

"So that's how it's going to be, is it?" she said, not looking at the children but glaring at Drake.

"So it shall be," said Drake, the only adult paying any attention to her.

"You'll taint these young ones' hands with murder? You'll kill me in sight of all those I know and love?"

"My changelings do my bidding; they've taken the children away. And as for the townspeople, I'll have need of them yet, whole and well. They cannot see or remember what shall happen, though the sight would be an impressive lesson for them and for all who oppose me."

A tear coursed down her cheek, not for herself, but for time running out. She wouldn't be able to give Conor and Beth much more of a head start. She prayed that Nora would stay in hiding, there in her store.

Drake snapped his fingers and the changelings closed the circle. At first, the hands just stroked her. Then they pulled her this way and that, scratching and gouging as the blood began to flow. Faces floated in front of her gaze, of children she had known all her life. But she did not know these. Changed they were, whatever humanity remained was fast disappearing.

Guttural sounds and the licking of lips snapped close to her ears as wounds began to be inflicted more deeply on her. God she hated hurting, but the physical pain was nothing to the cry she heard above all.

Nora, calling out her name. Nora, coming to rescue her. Fergal and Rafe, pinning Nora's arms to her side and restraining her. Dorothy Martin could no longer keep silent. With a wail, her frustration broke out, "Oh, get away, Nora! Please, get away."

"Too late!" cried Drake, "for her and you."

Little Noah Riley's face swam into Dorothy's view. He looks so sweet, she thought. Until he grabbed her throat and bared sharp fangs, fangs to cut and slash. No pain as she sank to the ground, though she found it odd that a three-fingered little girl, whose name escaped her, muscled Noah aside, reached out and tore something from Dort's wounded neck. Then Dorothy Martin couldn't breathe, and all went dark.

THE POOKA

WHIRLING THROUGH THE house, Aunt Emily flicked the dustrag at errant motes of dirt that dared sully her home, her own mind a kaleidoscope of jumbled thoughts, her heart a confusion of feelings.

She couldn't get the picture of Jace and Conor out of her mind. Two friends on the cusp of destruction. The bleakness of the hurt in Jace's eyes, made deeper by the wisdom he had touched from another reality; the tormented awareness growing in Conor's gaze as he realized the depth of the consequences his dalliance with Beth was causing.

They were made for each other, not Beth and Conor—that was just a youthful love. She meant those two boys, two friends who, when together, were more than the sum of their parts. They were a new entity, stronger because of their friendship, though too young to know that truth.

Flicking the dustrag caused a skittering of a porcelain bull seal across the coffee table. Aunt Emily paid no mind.

Always liked that Michaels boy. Steadfast heart in that big body, Jace had a stability rare for someone his age. His recent touch with the Otherworld hadn't hurt him either. It would take awhile for the gift he had been given to quicken within him, but Aunt Emily was mighty grateful that he, and not Walt, had been touched with that wonder.

She had the Sight—always had since the Morrigan had escorted her out of the mound so long ago. Saw clearly that together, Conor and Jace made a formidable team—the lines of destiny that radiated from that future burned brightly into the coming years. But apart? Only disaster—that was clear as well.

All was at risk because of Conor. She whipped the dustrag off the plant, a few leaves falling absently to the floor. Stupid boy. Or not so stupid, really. Beth was a treasure, too, and Conor, well Conor was a young man, a lonely young man. What seldom caused a ripple in the world of adolescent transition was an earth shattering event here in Tinker's Grove. Conor's destiny guaranteed that. Laughing ruefully, she shook her head at

the vagaries of human behavior. Love could never be ridiculed, but misplaced youthful infatuation could have such unexpected consequences. In
this case, world-ripping consequences.

Why shouldn't Jace be angry? He saw it as a betrayal of trust. Conor,
only now coming to the realization that his lack of thought might cause him
greater pain than fulfillment. He wasn't all that much different from his
father.

There was nothing she could do. That friendship would either last or
be snapped by the pressure of coming events. If it failed, the odds were just
that much worse for Conor.

Maybe not. The disaster looming in her Sight was not inevitable. Perhaps she could nudge it aside a bit. Perhaps a little meddling by the old lady
of Madoc's Glen might be in order. Perhaps a cup of tea with the other
matron of the area, Caithness McNabb. Always good to keep one's enemies
close, she thought. Besides, if events turned out well, she might put a crimp
in the plans of that cunning, crafty, cruel woman who threatened her
nephew and the people of the Grove.

Gripping her blackthorn cane, tossing the dustrag aside, resolution
gleaming in her eyes, Aunt Emily went out to do battle with the McNabb
heiress. Never met anyone she couldn't handle once she put her mind to it.

Walked she did. And a far way it was. But it didn't matter. For as she
walked, she talked to the unseen around her. The ordinary folk who might
have observed her would have thought her mad, but she talked anyway. To
the mound Dwellers that tracked her every move. To the Morrigan who
flew above her. To the Dryads and Naiads who inhabited the woodlands
and streams, she talked. And they responded. Mostly in ways she felt in her
heart, but sometimes physically. She passed the Crossroads without incident. The tree was filled only with colored leaves. But as she went down-
ward toward the river, toward the McNabb place, even the trees tried to
hinder her. Along the road, roots sprouted, trying to trip her, and once,
under a canopy of aspens, branches reached down to restrain her, but
always her cane came up and she resisted.

"I must go," she said, "even if it is to my death. Caithness McNabb is
a servant of darkness, and if there is any chance to turn her to the Light, I
shall try." She spun in the road. "Hear me clearly; do not hinder me. I do
the will of Madoc ab Gwynedd and the Lord of All. I shall not be stopped,
even if it is to my death I go."

The last part of her journey—up the driveway of the McNabb estate—
was uneventful. Unseen presences slipped away, and she realized she was all
alone. Indeed, no one seemed at home. She came to the house, ringing the
bell, and no one answered. Not one to take no for an answer, she opened
the door and went inside. Nothing of interest in the house, with the

exception of bandages, extraordinary amounts of bandages, and she could only assume they were for the progeny of Cate—Conor had been specific about what was happening to at least two of the boys. Who would have guessed that the obscenity of genetic manipulation would be visited upon Tinker's Grove?

She walked the lawn and thought of the river, but at three o'clock in the afternoon she doubted Cate would be communing with the river demon. So she angled towards the stables, also quiet, but ominously so. Deceptively still. She went in and saw the sunbeams dancing off the stalls, all empty of horses. Then she saw the last one—a darkness there where no light shone.

Coming closer, she knew something was in there, unilluminated by the late fall sunlight that fell freely into the rest of the stables from gabled windows high above.

As she walked nearer, she saw vapor steaming from the last stall and she knew it was occupied. Never one to be afraid, she strode boldly forward and looked into the darkness. Nothing she saw but the vapor.

And then a voice. "Deirdre, it has been so long."

"Who knows my true name?" she snapped.

"One who has been deprived of your presence for so many years," said the voice.

"Show yourself," she demanded.

"As you wish," said the voice.

To her eyes, a vast shadowy bulk approached toward the front of the stall. Involuntarily she stepped back. Then she saw. A black horse, with yellow eyes, came into view, vapor from the stallion's nostrils rising in the autumn afternoon. Even in the shadows, the shape of the horse shifted almost imperceptibly as if an unseen puppeteer manipulated the sleek flesh.

"O my God," said Aunt Emily, "she's gone and called up a Pooka."

The horse whinnied and neighed, laughing at the woman. "How I have missed you!" it said. "When you were a little girl, I saw you for a moment, there in the hollow hill, and your courage and ferocity amazed me. Trying to protect your sister and her child. Willing to walk among the People and taste of their food and drink. And you survived. Special you are. Touched by destiny. None of that has diminished over the years. How fine you look."

"Do not flatter me, creature of the dark," said Emily. "I cannot believe that Cate would have called you forth."

"She did not," said the Pooka. "I was a gift from the river demon itself. She will have need of me before the day is out."

"Does she truly know you, what you are capable of?" said Aunt Emily.

"Does not matter. Where she wishes to go, I will carry her, protect her where necessary, destroy her enemies. Do you like my form?" asked the Pooka, prancing in the stall.

"It matters not what form you take. You have eyes from hell, and they reveal your soul and your intent. I won't let you harm my nephew."

"The shapeshifter?" said the Pooka. "He and I have more in common than you know."

"You are nothing like him," said Aunt Emily. "The Light burns brightly in him; he has not sold his soul to the darkness."

"Always the romantic," said the Pooka. "If you only had a smidgen of darkness in you, I would carry you wherever you wanted to go throughout the world. Caithness, however, puts you to shame. Such thoughts in her mind; such darkness in her heart. Piasa has trained her well."

"You know I can stop you," said Aunt Emily. "You know I can still the heart that beats in the body you have formed."

"You can try," said the Pooka, its horse lips curling in a sneer, vapor snorting through its nostrils. "But I think you'll have a difficult time. It has been long since you walked in the Otherworld; perhaps whatever magic inherent in you has diminished."

"Do you really want to find out?" said Emily, a small smile on her lips.

"Do your best old woman, but I fear your time is failing. I know not of your nephew, except what Cate has spoken to me about and what Piasa has said. Do you know that the river demon fears the youth? Truly he must be wondrous, for nothing has shaken the Devourer for centuries as much as the coming of this boy. I long to meet him."

"Touch him and you shall die," said the old woman, her teeth setting on edge, determination in her eyes.

"You think you can kill me?" said the amused Pooka.

"Absolutely, and I am ashamed that I haven't done it already."

Aunt Emily faced the black stallion and raised her blackthorn cane. From her lips came an incantation, with the cadence of the ancient druids, a hint of magic from an older time, but set in the context of a prayer:

> "Michael, Gabriel, Raphael, Uriel,
> Angels of earth, water, fire and air,
> Shield my soul with the shade of your wings,
> Shield my soul here and in heaven,
> From foes upon earth,
> From foes beneath earth,
> From foes in concealment;
> Protect and encircle

My soul 'neath your wings,
Oh my soul 'neath the shade of your wings!"

Each word she spoke was like a hammer smash against a nail. Every sentence, a vise tightening. As she spoke, the Pooka backed away. Its huge body began to shrink and shift. The demon that took the form of a stallion could no longer sustain the charade and fell to the floor of the stall in the muck and the mire, a withered, leathery thing flopping in the dung. Its hold on this world was failing and it was becoming transparent.

The voice of the woman carried throughout the stable, and as she spoke, the light grew brighter. She smiled as she saw the Pooka diminish and allowed herself a brief moment of respite, a time to savor the destruction of such evil. Bad mistake. She had defeated but not conquered. She lacked the word of completion, and, before she spoke it, she felt another behind her. No longer young her reflexes could not respond fast enough. The blow was painful, but before she could cry out, the darkness overtook her and she knew no more. She hadn't been out long when she woke, trussed up like a slain deer ready to be thrown on the back of a truck. The sun was still shining, the late afternoon shadows lengthening in the stable. Propped up across from the same paddock where the Pooka had been stabled. Where the demon still was, in full glory, again a black stallion. Flashing sulphurous eyes, gloating at her.

"Awake, I see," said the Pooka. "All for naught, all that energy and effort. Should have taken me when you could. The arrival of my mistress was most fortuitous, wouldn't you say?"

Aunt Emily only glared as Caithness McNabb came into view. Even through a splitting headache, she could see that Cate looked resplendent in her black riding gear. A black cape loosely tied at the neck cascaded down to the floor of the stable.

"So sorry Ms. O'Rourke," said Cate with a small smile. "I simply couldn't let you extinguish my special helper this evening."

"Do you know what you have done?" asked Aunt Emily. "Consorting with a being such as this is a grave danger."

Cate laughed. "I've consorted with Piasa, who is many times greater and more dangerous even than this magnificent beast."

"My God," said Aunt Emily, "I thought I could come and reason with you, but clearly, if you think you can harness a Pooka and control Piasa, you are deranged."

"Watch your mouth, old woman," snapped Cate. "You almost destroyed an essential part of my plan, and had you done so, we would not be talking now. I kept you alive, however, for my own purposes. I can't afford to have one of Tinker's Grove's finest citizens suffer an untimely death, with all the disappearances that have been happening. Yet, vex me too much, and I'll find a way to explain away your unfortunate demise."

"You'll kill me anyway. I've seen too much."

"True, but after tonight, I think much of that will be water over the dam."

"What do you mean?"

"Your nephew and his friend have been up to no good today. Mucking around DIOGENE. We have the situation well in hand. And even now he and his girlfriend, pregnant girlfriend that is, are fleeing from that complex. The watchers in the woods allied to Piasa tell me they flee to the Crossroads. The Pooka and I will intercept them there. Then we shall see what happens. If your nephew is reasonable, he should be fine, at least for now. If not, well, it is All Hallow's Eve, and in my view, Tinker's Grove has long been without a sacrifice on the Feast of Samhain."

"You are insane," said a horrified Aunt Emily.

"Not at all. I love the dark, and you think, you believe, that is insanity. I cannot expect much more from you; you simply cannot understand what Piasa is offering—to me, to you and to this community."

"Slavery?"

"Hardly," said Cate.

She approached the trussed old woman, looking down on her with something akin to pity. "The Devourer is so ancient—the knowledge it has shown me. It could be yours as well. Next to it, you, and he who inhabits the mound, are but youthful neophytes in the Otherworld."

Aunt Emily said nothing as she blew a wisp of white hair off her brow. Cate bent down and touched the loose strand, whispering, "It can give you back your youth. You've lived long but will not last forever. What it has promised me, it can give to you. It respects your power, if not your wisdom. Come, join me. Help me convince Conor; help me show him that together we can do much for the Grove and even beyond."

The old woman began to laugh. "You are tempting me, Caithness Mcnabb? You who murdered your husband, the only decent McNabb in generations? And you believe the lies of the Worm that haunts the waters and gnaws at the roots of the Tree of Life? It promised you immortality? Undying death would be a better comparison. It may have some attraction for you, that much I'll admit, but you are but a tool in its age old plan, a mere beachhead into this world. When it chooses it will cast you aside."

Cate flew to her feet. "How dare you! What I offer is a fair deal. But why should I be surprised? You've always kept your own counsel." She turned to leave and paused.

"Kill her now," hissed the Pooka, a noxious vapor escaping from the nostrils of the stallion.

"No," said Cate, "but she shall pay for her insolence." Swiftly turning, she brought down the riding crop on the old woman's face. The crack was terrible, and immediately a bloody welt appeared diagonally, streaking from her temple to her cheekbone. She never uttered a sound.

"There," said Cate, "old and scarred, and soon to die. Rest tight here, Emily. I'll be back soon, with your nephew's head hanging from my saddle. Oh, and just in case you try another prayer to hurt my pet ..." Cate ripped off a piece of duct tape and slapped it over Emily's mouth.

Through a bloody mist, Aunt Emily saw the vile heiress vault into the already saddled stallion. She turned the Pooka toward the battered woman and the stallion reared in defiance. Then, almost gently, the horse bent low and brushed its lips against the old woman's forehead. As she swooned from the noxious breath, she saw them gallop through the stable out into the gathering night. An appointment at the Crossroads.

All was quiet now. Her back hurt more than her face. Truth was she was getting old. Really didn't fear dying, though it was a might inconvenient at this particular time. Especially when Conor needed her help. The bonds were tight though, and her own craft seemed insufficient to the challenge. No ordinary rope would have kept her restrained. Cate planned for everything; perhaps even expected her visit.

At a loss, she began to feel the first twinges of panic deep in her gut. A rare feeling for her indeed. But this was the night. Of that she was sure. All things were coming together. The restlessness of the town; Drake's acceleration of his plans for DIOGENE, Conor's awakening powers. And here she was helpless.

Then she heard it. The easily recognizable sound of a motorcycle coming slowly up the drive. She saw him dismount, a shadow within shadows just outside the stables. He stood there, silently looking into the barn. With his sight, she knew he could see her clearly, though she was tucked far back into the building. But the dark was taking her again as her eyes closed once more on this world.

Sputtering, she came to consciousness, the leering face of Rory bent over her, sponging her brow.

"Ah, lass, an unexpected turn of fate, me being the doctor and all to you, the one who lost a fight." He laughed as she tried to struggle upright. "Now, now, patience. You've been bound tight in rope twined with hair from that stallion, that Pooka that I saw rushing through the woods with the devil itself on its back."

"That would be Cate," said Aunt Emily. "She's gone and got herself a pet."

Rory let out a low whistle. "Brave, even for her. Won't come to any good I expect. Chancy things, those Pookas. Don't like them myself. Did I ever tell you that my brother and I killed one once, back when we were lads. It was haunting the countryside and homesteads of our land. Black as the night and in horse form as well, though some said it shapeshifted now and then into a wolf, but when we tracked it, a stallion it was, fierce with glowing eyes. Ah, you should have seen my brother then. Brave, deadly. The Pooka had done a mischievous thing and circled back while I was tracking it. First thing I know it was rearing over me. Hoofed me in my temple— good thing I have a thick skull. Knocked me senseless and was about to devour me. Don't look so horrified Deirdre, you know they eat flesh, and it certainly was about to devour me. Then Madoc was there, my elder brother whose footsteps I worshiped then. God, but I loved him when he was strong. He had his sword, but it wouldn't do any good against a Pooka. Could have killed its form but the demon would have survived. No. You know what he did? He had taken an iron horseshoe from a nearby homestead, sharpened the ends himself. He had carried it all night. The pain it must have caused him. But with a cry from the depths of hell he was upon the stallion and with his bare hands he drove the horseshoe into the chest of the Pooka. You should have heard the screams. Like all of us of the Otherworld, Pookas hate iron, but they are especially susceptible to it if it touches them. This was driven into its black heart. Burst into flame it did, right there on the moor. The fire shot high into the air; the screams of the dying demon were atrocious, and I loved my brother then, like I've never loved him before or since. His hands were blackened. It took a long time for them to heal, but he did it for me, Deirdre, back when he thought I was worth saving."

"Can you untie me or not, or do you insist on jabbering away the evening?" At any other time, she would have been entranced by this revelation, but time was wasting and concern for her nephew was making her own heart race.

Rory looked offended, but took a black knife from his pocket and cut the bonds. Emily rubbed her hands and arms back to feeling.

"I don't mean to be ungrateful, Rory, but I'm vexed enough as it is and time is wasting. Something terrible is about to happen."

"Aye, with that I agree. I'm heading for the town. Rumor has it that changelings are massing there. No good coming from that either, I afraid."

A scream tore through the night, and, like stargazers watching a meteor arc across the heavens, the heads of those two scanned the skies and the woodland until both sets of eyes gazed towards Muddy Hollow Crossroads, two miles away.

"Get on my bike," said Rory. "I'll take you there."

"Never!" said the shocked old woman.

Gently, he touched her face, swelling from the blow Cate had given her. "Ah, lass, I am a rogue, that much is true. But your love for that boy, that nephew of yours, does you proud. Come, I'll take you to him."

Still, she hestitated and Rory's voice hardened.

"Unless you've learned to fly, you'll never make it in time. Now get on." He pulled her to the motorcycle, climbed on and beckoned to her.

She had to get to Conor. There was no other way. Distastefully she clambered on. The minute her arms went around Rory's waist, he fired up the engine and they were off, Rory's laughter riding the wind; Aunt Emily's pursed lips already betraying her preparation for whatever she might find at the Crossroads.

FLIGHT TO THE CROSSROADS

"FOR GOD'S SAKE, Beth, we've got to run." He took her by the hand and pulled her along the road, Troubles bouncing at her side trying his best to keep her alert.

"It's no good, Conor; I'm just so tired. Maybe Drake did slip me something; it's like I have no energy"

Troubles whined in concern. He nuzzled the exhausted girl's hand as she absently petted him.

"We can't stay here on the road," said Conor. "Drake's goons, Fergal and Rafe, will be on to us soon."

"They're busy with the crowd in town; they won't be sure which direction we went."

"Seen those boys lately?" asked Conor. "More animals than men. They'll sniff us out faster than we can travel."

"Then what's the point?" said Beth, sinking to the ground. "We're as good as done for." He tried to rouse her, but she had passed out.

Holding her unconscious body, he turned to Troubles. "What did Drake do to her?" The dog woofed in concern. The last of the glowing red sunset winked out in the west. Moonrise was imminent, but at this moment, the darkness was almost complete.

"Remember how you carried me a couple of months back? No way you could do that unless the Morrigan changed you. You were bigger; had to be to carry me. My hunch is that she made you step into the Otherworld, or surrounded you with it or something like that. It seems to me you might be more real there, larger if you'd like. Else how could you have carried me? You know how to do that, boy?"

Troubles woofed in seeming agreement again and assumed a Sphinx pose—the 'sending thoughts' position that Conor had seen before when the dog wanted to pass information to him. Tentatively, Conor stretched out a hand and touched the side of the Labrador's face. Instantly, he saw— images of that long ago night when Conor collapsed after the first fight with Rory in the woods—the Morrigan weaving her hands to cast a spell. The fabric of the atmosphere ripped and expanded, enveloping Troubles, and, to Conor's amazement, the dog simply grew to the size of a small horse. Through the dog's mind, he saw the Morrigan set Conor onto the dog's back and sent the beast home.

"I can't cast spells, Troubles," said Conor. "I don't know how and I'm not sure I would if I could."

The dog whimpered. Obviously, Conor wasn't getting the right message. Conor touched the dog's head again, and this time the rift torn by the Morrigan jumped out more clearly.

"Okay," said Conor, voice becoming a bit more excited. "She did it with a spell, but the Abbot and Madoc …" he bit his cheek in thought, "they do it differently. They both told me once to 'see the mountain behind the mountain.' Whenever I tried to do that before I started changing. When I see things as they really are, I'm able to make them truly become present in this reality. Like those little kids. I looked inside them and saw they could fly. I just pushed that thought at them. Maybe what everyone else sees as magic is just the ability to bring two worlds together and make visible what has been invisible.

"Don't you see, Troubles? In this world, you're just a dog. That's how people see you, but you got a taste of the Otherworld when you were a puppy; you were made a part of that place when Madoc saved your life. What you truly are is a much more magnificent animal—still a dog, mind you, but what a dog was always meant to be, sort of the idea of a dog made into flesh and blood. Most people never see that in you, but when you are touched by the Otherworld—well, you become something special. All I have to do is make that happen again—make you be who you really are."

Troubles woofed. Taking that as a yes, Conor raised his arms, noticing the ribbon of skin faintly glowing again, running like a river down the course of his body. Pointing a finger from his outstretched arm, he turned in a circle clockwise. Aunt Emily had taught him this, after she was done chastising him for not knowing how to create a *lorica*—the Celtic prayer of protection.

"Prayer isn't just a state of mind, and it involves the physical as well as the spiritual. Going to protect something? Then draw the boundaries. By the way, as you change, you'll find your other powers work the same. Not just in your mind, lad—get them to work out here." He remembered her smacking her cane against the Crossroads Oak where that lesson, not so long ago, leeched into his brain.

Arm throbbing, faintly rippling with light as he cast the circle, he pressed his sight against the darkness as if it were something solid. If he had to explain it to someone he knew he felt as if the world slipped, the skin on reality sliding back. As the circle completed, a sound like a thunderclap rocketed across the river valley, the smell of ozone signaling something monumental had just happened.

"Hey Troubles," he whispered, "wherever we are is different from where we've been." The dog was silent.

For a moment, Conor was transfixed with the scene around him. On second thought, it wasn't as if he was in a different place. It was still early evening, though the shadows were deeper. He was still in woodland, though the trees looked much larger. Why he still could make out their shape in the dark was a mystery to him. It was still the countryside around Tinker's Grove, just bigger. He could hear the water from some nearby stream, but it sounded livelier, fresher. It was the same place only more real. And then he looked at the dog. Still sitting sphinxlike, Troubles was, well huge, thought Conor with his head easily reaching Conor's chest. The dog was laughing at him with incredibly intelligent eyes.

"You can speak to me?" asked Conor, touching the dog's face.

No words, but images again, only these were brighter and easier to understand. Pictures of a dog and boy over the past months, waves of friendship washing over him, deep solidarity, images of an unconscious Beth placed on Troubles' back.

"Geez, Beth!" said Conor, turning to where he had placed her on the ground. As she moaned, he set her quickly on the dog. He was grateful that she was regaining consciousness. Explaining to her what he had done, not sure she truly understood, he begged her to hold on tightly. Whispering to Troubles, he said, "We've got to run. Just make sure she doesn't fall off." Far behind him, he heard a feral howl as if the hounds of hell were after the three of them. "Now go!"

THE JACE RACE

CHILDREN, CAVORTING LIKE sprites or wraiths. What a Halloween parade. But what really freaked out Jace as he was leaving were the parents, just standing on the sidewalk, watching the grotesque panoply. Stunned into paralysis. Shocked at what their little ones had turned into.

He looked ahead of him and saw the torches on the Abbey tower burning brightly again this night. The monks would be beginning the vigil for All Hallow's. Jace had gone to it once or twice before. The monks gathered in the Abbey crypt to sing psalms over their dead brethren. He remembered it was kind of spooky, but rather cool as well. Maybe there would be help there.

Tearing up the road to the Abbey, he found all was quiet on the grounds except for the cawing of a crow.

He saw her then; beautiful she was, waiting for him outside the Abbey entrance.

"I thought you couldn't stand on holy ground," said Jace to the Morrigan, looking at her bare feet showing under her simple white dress.

"Believe me, my Champion, it hurts a little, but the pain is nothing compared to the joy this moment brings me, as I look upon you …" She licked her lips, "and as I gaze down upon your little village."

"You like what's happening down in the town?" said Jace incredulously.

"I live on chaos and, frankly, I smell blood in the air tonight."

"You are so dark," he said with a shake of his head. "I never know whether you are friend or foe, dark or light."

"Poor boy," she said, moving forward and stroking his hair. She was so beautiful, he couldn't even move. Why he let her touch him, he did not know. She whispered, "I am from such a different time and concepts of good and evil mean slightly different things to me. But if you question whether I want children to die, or Piasa to rise up, or the dark to win, ease your mind. The Light must rule. Even I know that. But the excitement, the blood, the death—these are what I live for. Tonight, though, I live for you as well, my Champion, for you must go to Conor and save him."

"Save him?" said Jace. "I'd sooner break a two by four over his head for what he did to my sister. She'd be ok now, instead of spun up in Drake's plan, if Conor had just left her alone."

"This is wisdom talking?" said the Morrigan. The Morrigan began to walk around him, her head jutting forward like a bird with each step. "Your friend has offended you and you cannot see beyond his misstep? You know what he represents. You know how vulnerable he is. You swore to protect him." She looked him up and down, as a vulture surveys its prey, looking for the most vulnerable place to gorge. "Your anger means nothing to me now. Better to focus your rage on those who seek to destroy him."

"I can't," said Jace. "Not after what he's done."

"Then all will be lost," said the Morrigan, "I will feast on the dead, and it will be a bitter taste to me."

"True wisdom," continued the Morrigan, "is selfless. The stories the bards have told of me and my warriors always focus on death and carnage, but those who served me in my need, brutal though they were, gave of themselves for a greater good. That is often forgotten. The Hound of Ulster, Finn McCool, Brian Boru—names out of legend, heroes from another time. You are of their lineage, Jason Michaels." Her hand stroked his cheek as he clenched his jaw. She cooed softly at him, "You were right to come here. The Abbot has information you need. But you are wrong to abandon Conor to his fate."

"I'm not abandoning him; I told him I'd meet him at the Crossroads."

"Unless your heart is united with his, you cannot help him, even when you see him again."

No sooner had she said these words than a thunderclap boomed across the valley. Both looked up at the stars and the sky, blood red moon rising over the land.

"There's no storm, no lightning," said Jace.

"On this night, the worlds meet," said the Morrigan. "Someone has just forced open a door and the Otherworld has intruded. Only desperation from a power this world has not yet seen could have caused such a ripping of the fabric of space like this. Quickly now, my Champion, do what you must in the Abbey and then, go find Conor. Save him, and meet your destiny. But before you leave, I have a gift for you—a kiss, for strength." She pressed her mouth on his and he felt himself hold her tight; she moved her mouth to his neck and lightly nipped him with her teeth. Caressing his chest, she kissed his heart, pushing away from him. For a moment, he was left breathless, and then he ran.

Leaving her there, he dashed through the church, pausing only to genuflect before the tabernacle and whisper a little prayer begging forgiveness for the rush, meaning no disrespect, and he vanished into a side door that led to a stairwell down to the crypt.

Already, he could hear the monks chanting, and when he burst into the crypt he saw dozens of them, dressed in their black cucullas or cowls, censors swinging from one arm, candles held in the other hand as they sang:

Holy, Holy, Holy, Lord God of hosts!

Only lit by candlelight, the underground chapel still shone with a beautiful glow.

Heaven and earth are full of your glory!

Quartzite crystals embedded in the vaulted ceiling sparkled and threw back the light so even the shadows seemed muted and harmless. The monks were ranged on either side of the center aisle where lay the abbots of the monastery in their stone cold tombs and various reliquaries of martyrs and saints collected from around the world.

The glorious company of apostles praise you.
The noble fellowship of prophets praise you.
The white robed army of martyrs praise you.

The smoke from the incense cast a cloud of otherworldliness about the place, the odor of the burning incense allaying any thought of death's doom and decay. The monks sang of hope and eternal life, their voices pushing into the shadows the fearful thoughts of one's own end. The peace present in the crypt struck Jace like a force and he ground his feet to a halt.

Silent for a moment, then his face hardened and he shouted to the monks, "Quiet! Quiet! All of you!" The chanting ceased and wondering faces turned toward him. "Don't you know what's happening down in the village? Aren't you going to do anything?"

Abbot Malachy, dressed in a gold embroidered white cope, matching miter on his head with his crozier, the shepherd's staff, in his right hand, moved from the far end of the crypt towards Jace. The crozier glittered as it moved, a silver Celtic cross suspended between carved antlers, a glowing ruby burning in the transept of the holy symbol.

The silent eyes of monks followed their spiritual father as he walked down the center of the crypt chapel. Silently, he passed the tombs of the former Abbots until he stood before Jace.

In a quiet voice he said, "Yes. Yes, I know what is happening in Tinker's Grove tonight. Death and evil walk the streets."

"And all you do is pray," said Jason, spitting out the words in disgust.

"It is not so bad a weapon," said the Abbot, wryly, "considering that Drake and the McNabbs are sprinkling evil wherever they go. Got any better ideas, son?"

"Yeah," said Jason, "You. Conor's told me a bit about his conversations with you, and I've done a little digging myself. You always know more than most and say little of what you do understand. You act when necessary, but I always have the hunch you could do more if you wanted. You look the same to me now as you did when I was a kid. I wonder if your brother monks have noticed the same. I think you could stop all this. I think you could help us. I think you could have found those lost kids and my sister when Drake held her at DIOGENE if you would have even dared to try."

"But I need proof, don't I?" said Jace, pushing past the Abbot. "All of you," he said looking at the monks, "you think I'm crazy, but I'm not. He's not who you think he is. Look at these tombs. You see them more than I and we all think the former Abbots are laid to rest here because each tomb says *Abbas*, and each tomb has a number: Abbot I, Abbot II, Abbot III and so on. You think the bodies of your sainted leaders of times past lie in peace here resting silently. But it's all a sham. The one who could stop all this, he's been living a lie, and getting you to do the same. Isn't that right Abbot Malachy?"

The Abbot simply looked at Jace in silence, an unreadable expression on his face. Jace snorted in disgust.

"Let me show all of you," he said.

He went to the first tomb. Couldn't understand why he had never noticed the odd history of the Abbots—now it seemed so clear to him, as if a veil had been lifted from his mind. How could anyone not see the strangeness all over this town? It was like a spell cast just over the valley, not enough to really damage people, but just enough to make them forget the inconsistences, the anomalies. Not thinking of the heavy stone lid, he easily shoved it aside. The kiss of the Morrigan was a strength giver all right. Empty. The tomb was empty. Even the monks gasped. Jace repeated it again, going up the aisle, flipping off the stone lids from the abbatial sarcophagi. All were empty.

After the last one, he turned to the stunned monks. "Don't you see? There's only ever been one Abbot Malachy. This one," he said pointing down the aisle at the silent Abbot. "He's lied to you."

"Lying is a strong word, Jace," said the Abbot. "It presumes malice and deception for private gain. Nothing could be further from the truth regarding me. But you are not entirely mistaken. Every twenty years or so, the current Abbot Malachy dies to the world, and a new one takes his place. It has never been hard to do, for though the look of shock on my monks is genuine and real at this moment, each time I 'die' I gather them together and explain why I am here and what I must do. Then with their permission, I take away their memory of that event, and life goes on with a 'new' Abbot, named Malachy. Life goes on, Jace, as it always has here at *Stella Maris* Abbey, high above Tinker's Grove. Watch now, and learn."

The Abbot walked slowly down each side of the crypt touching the monks one by one on their forehead, murmuring something Jace could not hear as he traced the Sign of the Cross upon them. After his passing, each monk slumped a little and wiped a hand over his own brow, and then recognition dawned in their eyes. They showed no surprise or anger as forgotten memories and promises made came back in to their consciousness.

"I would have done this at the conclusion of Vespers this evening," said the Abbot, "because for the first time in many decades, we go down by the river tonight, to the mound, to sing of the oneness of the worlds and of a time to come when all shall be in harmony again. Surely you remember what the Scriptures say, '*All creation groans aloud, waiting for its redemption from the Son of God.*' It is our hope that what we do here might hasten that day. And," said the Abbot, "try to forestall any mischief Piasa has planned for this night. I fear something terrible shall happen."

"Worse than what's happening in the town?" said Jace. "Aren't you going to do anything to help those people?"

"Much is happening tonight, and I am not God," said the Abbot. "I have my part to play, as do you. You came here this evening for answers and for help. You have had both, but not what you wish. The Morrigan has called you her Champion, and so you are. You have a task to do for the People of the Hollow Hills and the 'dark ones' and for Conor. But you are my Champion as well. It is not just the ones I mentioned who have a stake in this outcome. As she has given you gifts, so let me give you my own. First of all, forgiveness for your anger. Let go your hatred of Conor, for you can never save him if rage gets in your way. Second, the gift of Wisdom from the Otherworld is truly precious, but crippled without its consort." The Abbot breathed on him. "Receive the Insight of Solomon, the partner of the Wisdom you received, and act accordingly. It will open doors hidden to you, find answers that you seek, and enable you to choose between two goods when only one can be had. Lastly, remember that the coming struggle is a battle not fought entirely on this plane of existence. The Otherworld is involved and for that you need a more ancient weapon. Go back to the first sarcophagus and take what is in there."

Jace walked slowly up the aisle, monks watching expectantly, and reached into the tomb. It wasn't completely empty. A cloth covered object lay nestled on one side of the tomb. Picking it up, he unwrapped the heirloom and gasped at its beauty. It was a Celtic sword, scrolled iron guard pointed toward the blade, leather wrapped grip leading to an iron pommel, center set with a brilliant ruby.

"It is the Sword of Light, and for ages it has been mine," said Abbot Malachy taking the sword from Jace's hands, "a weapon from another time and a task I once was given." He lightly rested the blade on the shoulders of the young man, and as the metal touched Jace, blue runes flared along the edge of the blade, making the sword seem somehow alive. The Abbot said, "Take this sword into your care. The deeds you do with it will make it yours and bind it to yourself. We shall see what the night brings."

"I'm not a swordsman," said Jace. "I don't know how to use this thing."

For the first time, the Abbot allowed himself a huge smile. "You'll be surprised what you can do this evening. All the skill you need has already been given to you by the wisdom you devoured and that which I have just breathed into you. Besides, you are a football player are you not, bashing and crashing your opponents with no hesitation? This is not a weapon for fencing; no prancing or mincing courtier steps for you. The sword is meant for business—so swing away as you need. You will find you shall have no problem. It is All Hallow's Eve tonight, and though much evil has already occurred, much that is wondrous shall come to pass."

"As for me and the monks of the Abbey, well, you heard the thunderclap did you not? It echoed even in this chamber. Conor has torn a rift between the worlds. A little desperately, hence the noise. They come together now, the worlds do, and the future is sealed. He is in danger and you best see to his safety. My monks and I have business with Madoc. Piasa seeks to enter this world in a way not attempted for many a year. The river demon must be bound. I fear that not all can be saved this night."

The Abbot looked with sad affection upon Jace. "I am so sorry all this had to fall upon you. From the day I baptized you, when you were but a squalling infant, I have watched you grow. Your life has been one of peace and joy. No more. I grieve for that fact. But Conor must not be alone. Much sadness and sorrow awaits. If I could lift the burden I would, but even those dedicated to the Light cannot lift all grief or pain from a person. A great doom lies upon you. How it will resolve itself I sincerely do not know. But I trust in your strength, in your new-found wisdom, in your goodness. Let us pray that it will be enough. Now go, the time grows short and much needs to be done ere the coming of dawn."

The singing resumed behind Jace as he climbed the crypt stairs, the Abbot blessing his departure. Gazing in awe at the sword, Jace stepped back out into the night. He wasn't sure, but Conor and his sister must have reached the Crossroads by now. Throwing the sword into his car, he peeled out of the Abbey driveway and headed toward Muddy Hollow.

TO THE CROSSROADS

RUNNING SILENT FOR a while, Conor had a few minutes to assess what happened. Probably rent a tear in the fabric of space and this alternate reality; maybe just pushed his own world aside like a less real fog or mist. Nonetheless, he thought, this Otherworld is following me like the eye of a hurricane. If people looked, would they see that horrendous monster that Jace and Taps glimpsed along with a dog the size of a small horse loping beside the transformed Conor, a beautiful unconscious girl on the canine's back? Sort of Beauty and the Beasts, thought the boy.

Conor noticed that he did not seem to have changed—at least not physically, at least not to himself. Yet, it was clear he was running easily with the dog and was not tired. More strength, more energy. Maybe if he hadn't been so afraid of the transformation inside him, he could control all this better to get them out of danger. "To Aunt Emily's, Troubles," he shouted. "We've got to get ourselves away from town."

As they ran, Conor could hear others running through the woodland, not far from him. Fast enough to follow, but not fast enough to overtake. Whatever lived in the Otherworld had no lock on bravery and courage. It seemed like whenever he needed a little bit of their help or support, they just watched and waited—or followed a safe distance behind. A testing maybe, to see if he was really the one, or maybe whatever greatness they once possessed had degenerated into cowardice.

They sped past the house at Madoc's Glen. No point in stopping. All dark. Wondering where Aunt Emily was, Conor hoped she was okay. He was determined to take a path he found in the woods that would shortcut the way to the Crossroads. No danger among these trees, yet his unseen followers tagged along.

Breaking out into the main road, he saw Muddy Hollow Crossroads from afar. A huge blood red moon hung just above the oak tree, now even more enormous in this enhanced reality; its leaves moving slightly in the autumn breeze. He called for Troubles to stop, and as the dog did so, the animal seemed to shrink back to normal size. Beth slipped to the ground, off the dog's back. Conor heard a soft pop all around him as the ordinary world slid back in place. Everything seemed normal again. No heightened senses; indeed, the night seemed flat to him. The richness of the Otherworld had fled, leaving just a tree lit by an October moon. He was thinking that he needed to get a better handle on controlling his travel between two worlds. Slipping sideways was okay, but he guessed it could get him into trouble.

Like now. Before him lay the Crossroads and the giant oak, looking normal but still huge, looming over the road. The full moon lit the area with a blood red glow, but someone had gone to the trouble of firing torches, four of them at the four corners of the crossroads. No doubt, thought Conor, it was the person who sat on the black horse, staring at him.

Caithness McNabb. He could see her pale face, the shadows tossed by the dancing flames seeming to draw back the Otherworld around her. Such a mystery she was. Dressed in black, she wore a flowing cape that cascaded down her stallion mount. For a moment, surprise washed across her features, and he knew that to her, he and Troubles and Beth had just popped into her reality. She masked the surprise quickly.

"Nice trick, Conor," said Cate. "You can walk the worlds now, somewhat, though not perfectly. If you could, I doubt you would have picked this spot to become visible. See, I've been waiting for you. I knew you'd come this way. My sons guarded the southern flank when you sprung Beth and there really weren't many other ways to go than by the Crossroads. Except if you decided to hide in the town, and based on what's been happening down there this evening, I knew that was an unlikely possibility.

"Of course, you could have taken refuge at the mound, but you're still not sure about he who dwells there, and I know you fear what swims in the river. Listen on the wind; you can hear the monks singing down by the mound, down by the river, trying to pray the darkness away. Don't think they will succeed tonight. The Feast of Samhain, All Hallow's Eve to you, just about the only celebration we have in common. A time of sacrifice when the old ones walked the land, blood sacrifice. Great isn't it, that the good old times have come again? Like I said, you're just not proficient enough to walk the worlds at will; no doubt, this night helps you a bit, the walls between the worlds being so thin. So I was right to simply wait and intercept you here."

Conor was picking up a rapidly recovering Beth off the ground when he said, "What is it you and your family want with me? What do you want with Beth?"

"Well," said Cate with an exaggerated sigh, "if it was up to me, I'd as soon have killed you the day I met you. You were trouble from the get go.

A faded memory come to life. Got the townspeople all talking. Looking too closely into stories out of time, out of song. Even got the river demon shaking just a bit. You were just a bit too soon for all of us. Me, I like things very orderly. But I had a new business to run—DIOGENE, so I bided my time. My mistake. Always, you interfered."

"I've done nothing to you!" protested Conor.

"Just by being you, you've done much damage. I'm not even sure what you are, but Dr. Drake, my CEO and resident brain trust, assures me you are dangerous. Piasa tells me you are dangerous, and wherever you have been you have caused suffering to my sons and if there's one thing I won't stomach it is an affront to my family. You need to be disposed of."

"All right, you can have me," said Conor, "but let Beth go; she's done nothing."

Beth shook herself free from Conor and faced Cate. "I'm not letting you hurt him."

Cate laughed. "So loyal, but so useless. Frankly, you're not in the picture Beth, but your child is."

"Child?" said Conor looking at Beth and then fixing his gaze on Cate. "What do you know about that?"

Cate laughed. "I know she bears your child, Conor, so don't pretend ignorance. Even I can see that whatever grows in her womb is important to this world's science and the Otherworld's need. May even cement this new company's reputation in the world of genetic research. Surely it will please the one I serve."

Cate moved her black stallion forward a few steps. "Enough discussion. We'll wait here for my boys and Dr. Drake, and then, we'll finish this."

"We've got to run again," said Conor in a low voice. "Think you're up to it?"

"Yeah," said Beth. "I'm okay, but where?"

"Anywhere but here." Turning to the dog, Conor shouted, "Troubles clear a path, now!"

Conor tried to step sideways again; anything to give Troubles an additional advantage, but he found he couldn't concentrate. Every time he tried to enter the deeper reality, his attention riveted on the stallion. Something was wrong with the horse. Its eyes were sulphurous, betraying an alien intelligence. It was as if the image of this magnificent animal was superimposed on something darker and very evil. Maybe it had distracted him on purpose, but he saw it rise on its hind legs and then it was too late to shift. Troubles was already bounding forward.

But it was not a dog the size of a horse that charged Cate McNabb—it was just Troubles the Labrador, noble and brave but with only the strength and speed of this reality. As the dog leapt for the throat of the woman, his body was no match for the flying hooves of a stallion who, to Conor's sight, now obviously belonged in the Otherworld. The dog fell to the ground unmoving. Cate smiled, black cloak billowing, having no trouble holding her mount, and shouted, "Too late, Conor Archer, my boys have arrived!"

From down the road, they came. Loping nearly on all fours, Rafe and Fergal raced towards the Crossroads. Beth screamed, and she and Conor began to run, but were easily cut off by Cate and the Pooka she rode. Last hope was to find some refuge under the oak, so Conor turned and dragged Beth under its branches.

Rafe and Fergal, more cautious now, were laughing to themselves as they approached the couple, circling like wolves cornering their prey.

"I don't want them hurt, yet," said Cate. "Bind them so they can't run."

To Conor, the pair of brothers looked almost sub-human. The greenish cast to their eyes certainly helped with that picture, but it was their brutishness and heavy boned body structure that lent them a simian appearance. Tumors could be seen on their faces, arms, some leaking a vile green fluid. Conor guessed there wouldn't be much FDA testing of whatever serum Drake was using. Just a few too many side effects. He was calming himself down now, keeping his eyes away from that damnable horse, and thought that if he could just shift into the Otherworld, he too might possess their strength. Maybe he could still save her.

"Ma, the Archer brat is doing something. I feel him pressing against me." Fergal looked anxiously at Cate, even though he was at least a yard away from where the two cowered against the tree.

"Thought he might try that," she said, jumping down from her mount. From a little pouch she pulled a flask. "Hold them tight."

Rafe rushed forward, grabbing Beth while Fergal leapt on Conor pinning him against the oak with his body. Conor could smell foul breath and turned his head away even as he struggled to shift, to change, to do something. Hard to focus when a person's afraid, but he tried and indeed was succeeding. Just as before, he felt the atmosphere part, but then, the bubbling liquid forced down his throat brought him back to the present moment.

"Sorry, Conor," sneered Cate, "but Dr. Drake said you were manifesting powers and suggested a sedative might keep you from concentrating on what you were doing. Works almost instantly. Looks like he was right."

Conor's vision blurred and the last thing he saw was Rafe putting his lips on Beth, nuzzling her neck as she screamed. Somewhere down the road, a motorcycle roared towards the Crossroads. Then all went dark.

HANGIN' ON THE CROSSROADS TREE

HER SCREAMS BROUGHT him back to consciousness. How long he had been out, he didn't know, but he was tied to the tree and in the light from the torches he saw Fergal sitting crosslegged close beside him. Somewhere out in the dark, Beth screamed again.

"Ma let Rafe have a go at her," said Fergal with a smile. "Hope you don't mind, Conor. Rafe and I have had a thing about her for years. Never thought we had much of a chance with Beth. Since we'll not be needing her as such, didn't think it would do any harm to let Rafe see what she was like. I'm next," he said beginning to laugh. "Don't mind being second since she's a strong girl and all. Think I'll take a look see as to how the little woman is doing." Fergal disappeared into the dark.

Tears rolled down Conor's face and he screamed his defiance. No sign of Cate; it looked as if they were simply in the animal hands of her goonish offspring. Then he heard hooves again as Cate approached from the south. She towered over him.

"Drake is coming. Best get this over with." She turned to the woods where Beth's screams had stopped. "Boys, you come on out now. Play time is over. Bring the girl with you."

They came from the woods, dragging Beth's body, each by an arm. She was barely clothed and even in the dim light Conor could see she was covered in blood.

"O my God," he whispered. "Beth!" he screamed. "What have you done to her?" He lifted his face up to the pitiless moon and shouted for help again. No one came. Then he heard a truck moving slowly up from the town. It was an ambulance. Not the monastery's but DIOGENE's. Drake stepped out of the driver's seat and surveyed the scene. Uttering curses at Rafe and Fergal, he ran to Beth looking for a pulse.

"Fools!" he cried. "I needed her alive."

"Not her," said Cate cooly. "You need her child, that little embryo in her and you've got the technology in the truck to take it from her. Like you told me once, all good things demand sacrifice and my boys needed a little sustenance—they've worked hard for you. Besides, she still breathes. But from the looks of my boys, they won't have much more time in this world to enjoy themselves. I trusted you, Drake, and you've poisoned my own flesh and blood. Why shouldn't your little experiment also go awry?" Her mount stamped its hooves in silent fury.

"Ice cold bitch!" snapped Drake. "I gave your sons power beyond any they could experience, and just because they are a little misshapen doesn't mean they're going to die. My magic can preserve them, even if my medicine can't."

"So you say, doctor, and for your sake, you better be right. Because if they die, I'm afraid you will too, without enjoying the fruits of your research. Blood is thicker than money or profit. I can always find someone else to run DIOGENE, now that I own most of it."

"If the child of Conor and Beth has the potential I think it has, I won't need DIOGENE." His voice softened as he stood over Beth's body. "But I will need you, Cate." He walked over to her and she looked down upon him.

"Never," he said, "have I found anyone with as close a rapport to the one I serve. You could be of so much help to me."

She struck him in the face with her riding crop. "That's for what you've made my boys look like."

He touched the welt on his cheek. "I suppose I deserve that. Not for what I did to Fergal and Rafe—they wanted what I offered, what Piasa offered; they knew the risks. I'm sorry I didn't inform you first. But I needed them, too, Cate. Otherwise, how could I have gotten the children? How could I have done the first round of experiments? How could I have given the first sacrifices to the one you truly love?"

Her face softened a little. "It does appreciate what you've done. It is pleased. So should I be. So I am." She leapt down from the Pooka and touched his cheek. Malicious madness glittered in her eyes. "All better now. Let's take care of business here."

Walking over to where Conor wept, tied to the oak, they stood there looking at him. He lifted up his head and saw, through the murk of the sedative, their pale faces observing him dispassionately.

"Conor," said Drake, "nothing personal really. You're just on the wrong side. But your child won't be. I am going to cut it from Beth's womb, and nurture it, grow it in my lab. You'll always have a son, even if you won't be around to see him grow. I thought once of preserving you, but you're a wild card, too powerful to control I think. I'll do better molding your son."

Drake gestured to Fergal, "Go into the ambulance. On the floor you'll find a silver hammer and an iron railroad spike. Bring them to me."

Doing as he was told, Fergal loped over to the vehicle. Drake turned his attention back to Conor. "In olden days, people would protect themselves from folks like you with iron. They thought that Otherworld beings were hurt by the metal. Old superstition mostly, as you already instinctively realize, since you've handled iron all your life with no harm. Of course, the closer you get to realizing your potential, the more uncomfortable the touch of this metal will be to you. But not deadly. As you come closer to the Otherworld, iron increasingly will become taboo. It will never be kryptonite to you, but it will be unpleasant. I'll show you how this is so in a moment.

"Look upon this ancient oak. On this tree you will die, Conor Archer. It sits on a crossroads and its roots reach down to the base of the world where the dark things live and try to gnaw at it. Fitting you should die here. They tell me the last person to die on this spot was a musician, too, a long time ago. Maybe you'll hear the whispers of a funeral dirge as you breathe your last."

Drake took the hammer and spike from Fergal, and motioning to the brothers, he had them untie Conor and lift him up on the trunk of the tree. Easily they lifted him till his feet were a yard above the ground. He made them fasten the boy to the trunk with the rope once again.

"O dear," said Drake, watching Conor sag forward, "now he's taller than I am. Caithness, help me out will you."

She smiled and vaulted onto her stallion, rode the black horse over to the tree, and grabbed the hammer. The Pooka bent its head to sniff Conor's face.

He opened his eyes to stare at the demon. Nauseous breath touched hotly on his face and he felt his stomach heave. In his mind, he heard the Pooka laughing at him.

Cate placed the iron spike on Conor's right wrist, just below where the dark streak began to journey up his arm. Stretching out his arm a little farther she was able to reach the first of the low branches. Surprisingly, it took her only three swings of the hammer to drive the nail in tightly, though Conor's screams drowned out the sound of silver on iron.

"Why not the other hand?" grunted Rafe.

Drake laughed. "Because he'll pick at the nail with his free hand and flail around. It causes more pain, and the one we serve likes pain as well as blood."

They backed up to look at their handiwork. "Not bad," said Drake, "though I almost neglected the most important element. I need to seal the sacrifice." Carefully taking off the dagger around his neck, he kissed its surface and walked towards Conor.

The boy stared at the twisted dagger. Dark wood, white bone, wrapped together. An evil thing he thought. Drake came to him and looked up at his face. Humming softly, the doctor cut off the boy's shirt and then began to draw a circle six times counterclockwise around the boy's abdomen. Just enough pressure to raise a red welt. Then in a sing song voice he chanted softly

Tree and snake,
Wood and bone,
Now you are pinned inside their home,
There to bleed, there to die,
On the Tree of Life this night,
Food for the demon's jaws that bite.
Blood shall drip,
Pain shall flow,
And this world will come to know
A greater lord
Than the silent god
Shall be loosed on earth to trod.
Dead shall be beauty,
Gone shall be truth,
Ripped apart by dragon's tooth.
Hear my call,
Heed my cry,
Comes the time for you to die.
Breathe your last,
Let go life,
Bring to pass a world of strife.
This my curse,
This my spell,
On Samhain night, the touch of hell.

Watching in horror, Conor screamed as Drake shoved the twisted dagger into him, piercing just beneath his rib cage. He felt the point exit his back and go into the tree. Writhing in pain, he nearly passed out, but heard clearly the dispassionate comments of Cate and Drake.

"You see, Cate, this one was special to Piasa. Perhaps it will come and visit, to touch the corpse and take it itself. The dagger I'll retrieve later. I've made sure no one will pass this way tonight. He'll take a while dying."

Cate smiled tightly, "At least we're done with him. Now get the girl and let's get out of here."

JACE TO THE RESCUE

EVEN WITH THE windows closed and the engine revving, Jace heard Conor's anguished scream. Echoing in his head, it pierced to his very bone. Unearthly. He was just rounding the bend, when the macabre sight hit him squarely in the face.

Odd, to say the least, was the presence of the ambulance on the side of the Crossroads, but that barely registered in Jace's vision. Gasping in horror, he focused on the figure of Conor crucified on the old oak tree. Desperately, Conor was trying to pull out the spike that pinned his right hand to one of the branches of the oak. Blood sprayed in the night, black drops illuminated by the flaming torches.

A riderless black horse stood not far from Conor. Movement catching his eye, Jace's gaze shifted to Cate McNabb and Dr. Drake, bending over something lying on the ground.

He was amazed to hear himself speak with a calm voice, "What you all looking at, Mrs. McNabb, Dr. Drake?"

Both jumped at the sound of Jace's voice, and as they turned, Jace saw a blond head, bloodied and bent.

His voice felt disembodied, calm while the rest of him tensed, sword in hand. "Is that my sister, lying there?"

"Why Jason," said Drake smoothly. "We certainly weren't expecting you this evening, but I'm glad you're here. Loose ends you know, and now I won't have to go searching for you. Yes, yes, I'm afraid it's your sister. She still breathes but not for long. A little accident it seems. All we can do is try to save the child."

Surreal. Jace shook his head in incomprehension. Everything seemed in slow motion. "What's wrong with her? What happened?"

"Just like Conor," said Cate, "unknowing and out of the loop. Unable to see the bigger picture. She's pregnant, Jace, and if we can't save her, at least let us attempt to save the child. Pregnant for just a few days, yet her child is ... much more advanced than the simple cellular structure it should be. Have to figure out why Jace. Have to try to save this child, no matter what the cost." Her tongue flicked to lick her thin lips. "Don't think there's much we'll be able to do for Beth, though, now that my boys are done with her."

"Boys?" said Jace, not understanding. "What do you mean?"

"My boys, idiot," said Cate. "The ones behind you."

He had only a moment to look over his shoulder, seeing two figures hurtling at him. "Back!" he cried, brandishing the sword. "Back before I kill you!"

Fergal and Rafe skidded to a stop, warily circling their new prey. Drake and Cate were lifting Beth's bloody body and carrying it toward the ambulance.

"No!" cried Jace, running towards the pair.

He was tackled by Fergal. Turning to face the youngest of the McNabbs, Jace gasped at Fergal's face. Pasty white, with tumors, some larger than others, bloating his features.

Not waiting to argue, Jace punched him with his free hand. Fergal rolled off, but as Jace tried to sit up, he found his sword arm pinned to the ground. Rafe sneered down at him.

"Found yourself a little sharpie toy, huh?" Rafe spat out the words through bloated canker stricken lips. Kicking the blade away, he hauled Jace to his feet.

Staring at the empty socket of Rafe's eye, seeping some kind of greenish pus, Jace managed a grin, "Ought to get something to cover that thing. Girls don't like holes in the head ... especially leaky ones."

With a roar, Rafe threw Jace to the ground. Which Jace was hoping for. Swinging his legs underneath Rafe's feet, he knocked him into the dirt. Jace scrabbled on all fours, reaching for the sword. Grasping it, he swung blindly catching Fergal who was coming up from the rear. Fergal grunted at the blow, but Jace had only hit him with the flat of the blade.

Can't believe it, thought Jace. That Abbot promised I'd be able to use this thing. Wanted to run that pissant through. Needing some space, he rushed towards the oak, turning around just in time to see the ambulance pulling away; the black horse and its rider close behind. Cate had left her brood to fight him alone.

"Beth!" he cried to the departing ambulance. "Jesus Christ, Beth, what have they done to you?"

"She was sweet, wasn't she Fergal?" said Rafe, giggling a little. "Actually, I think she loved me, there at the end."

"Nah, Rafe," said his little brother, "she distinctly whispered in my ear that I was the best. Then she said, 'Whatever you do, don't tell Jace what happened.' But you are right, she was just great." He turned his green eyes to Jace. "Hope I didn't hurt the kid."

Jace wanted to run. He had to save Beth, if he could. Just then, the carrion crow cawed in the night, and he remembered the Morrigan's words. He was Conor's Champion. Supposed to save the one person who had betrayed him the most.

"Jace," whispered Conor from the tree.

He turned and saw that he was not six feet from his best friend. The blood was flowing freely over Conor's body; but his eyes were bright, though full of pain.

"Conor, geez, they ran you through." He stared at the dagger piercing the boy. Tears began to course down his face.

"I trusted you!" said Jace. "I trusted you and it's all gone to hell."

"I'm so sorry," said Conor, "but whatever is between us you have to put it aside. Got to try to save her. Leave me."

"I'm charged to protect you, though God knows why I choose to do so."

"Go!" said Conor, "Leave me on this tree." He began to laugh a little. "Besides, I have these two freaks to keep me company."

Jace waved his sword to keep the brothers back. "I have to stay, you son of a bitch. And don't you know, Conor. I've never used this weapon before. Don't think I'll be much of a champion."

"Please," pleaded Conor, "go save her. She's your sister and she carries my child."

"I know," said Jace, swinging again at Rafe and Fergal. "The only good thing to come out of all this."

"Cool man," said Fergal, "all this talk about friendship and love. Shouldn't have betrayed your best friend, Conor. Should have had a bit more discipline."

"Aw shut up, Fergal," said Rafe. "Conor's as good as dead, but I want this one. I mean I really want this one. He took my eye. And it was on the best side of my face."

Jace couldn't believe what he was seeing. Even as they taunted him, they changed before his own eyes. No more talking as they resumed a four point stance. Their faces elongated and whatever beasts they thought they were becoming were things that Jace had never before seen or imagined. He could tell they could not speak anymore, and he guessed that the time for any reasoning was over.

Without waiting for a charge, he stepped forward and aimed a blow at Fergal. Too quick, the feral beast danced out of the way. Jace pursued but didn't watch his back. Rafe jumped him. Much heavier, Rafe pinned him to the ground. This is it, thought Jace. Should never have even half believed that witch. I'm no warrior.

Just then, he heard a howling. Managing to turn his head, he saw Troubles, running towards them. Looked like the dog was hurt badly though, favoring a front leg. Hadn't even known the Labrador was around. Troubles leapt onto Rafe and the two rolled off Jace, the dog worrying the neck of Rafe, the morphing man screaming incoherently as he tried to shift his attention back to Jace.

Rafe was just too big. Jace knew the dog would only slow Rafe down, but he took the opportunity, grabbing his sword and looking for Fergal. Needn't have worried. Fergal was charging him and Jace had only a moment to swing the blade. It cut cleanly into Fergal's neck, severing his head and shutting off the guttural unintelligible vitriol pouring from his mouth. Blood spurted everywhere as the head landed in the dirt. Jace immediately vomited.

Wiping his sleeve on his mouth, he heard Troubles yelp behind him. Heaving himself to his feet, he went to help the dog, but he was too late. Jace looked on in horror as Rafe took the dog's head and snapped his neck.

Conor screamed behind him at the sight, and Jace lost control. He could never piece together the next moments clearly but three things stood out as moments in what happened next.

Rafe threw off the body of the dog and ran on all fours towards Jace. Jace remembered raising the sword, point high by his own ear. The man thing was roaring; Jace felt himself screaming as the point rushed down and caught Rafe in the chest as he leapt. They both hit the dirt, Rafe on top of him, but the McNabb boy lay still.

Green pus mixed with blood dripped on Jace's face. If he could have, he would have vomited again. Pushing Rafe's body off himself, Jace looked around. Nothing moved. Fergal's headless corpse lay not far away. Troubles' body grotesquely twisted.

A groan from Conor made Jace look at the Crossroads Oak. Conor lifted his head, despair graven in his face.

"Jace, it's all gone to hell."

"Don't say that, Conor, not yet."

"Don't want to, but I think it's true. Don't even know where they've taken Beth."

"Here, let me get you down."

"No!" Conor spat out the words with blood flecked saliva. "No, you've got to try to help Beth on the chance that it's not too late."

"She's badly hurt, Conor. It may already be too late. But it's not too late for you."

Jace moved toward the tree, dragging his sword behind him. Thinking he might be able to pry the nail from the tree with his blade, instead, he stood transfixed at the sight of the twisted dagger; the evil blade plunged deeply beneath Conor's rib cage. He reached for it but jerked his hand back as the tree itself suddenly gave a great screeching of wood. Jace was sure branches were falling from the trunk but as he stepped back he saw they were only sweeping down to cover Conor's body.

"Conor!" he shouted. "Conor, can you hear me?" Jace tried to push the branches aside, but they were as dense and impenetrable as a stone wall.

"I'm still here," said Conor gasping, "though it looks like the tree has other thoughts than you saving me. I told you, I'm not going anywhere. Get Beth and get her now!"

"I'll come back for you, Conor. I will. I promise." Jace backed away from the tree, glowing orange, lit by the torches on the Crossroads.

"Don't," Jace whispered, "don't die on me, man. Please." He ran to his car and tore off down the road, following wherever the ambulance and that horse from hell went.

AUNT EMILY'S RIDE

LAUGHING INTO THE wind, she was amazed at the incongruity of life. Old arms wrapped around Rory's otherworldly physique. Wasn't often that an old lady could go biking with a near immortal. There was a time though, she remembered, when he sought her, wooed her and ended up almost as disappointed as when Finola slipped through his grasp.

They rocketed up the McNabb road, heading for the Crossroads. She was aware, as was Rory, that the elementals from the Otherworld as well as other denizens from that place were following, both curious and anxious about what was happening. Seldom did they walk in this world, but it was All Hallow's Eve and the walls between the worlds were thin this evening.

She loved the autumn; must be because she was finally getting old. The twilight autumn trees held so many secrets and they whispered to her to come and join them. Soon, she thought, soon. My bones will merge with the earth and I shall be free.

It had been a long time. Mortals were not meant to live forever. Finola knew that better than she. Rory knew it not at all. He had wanted Finola for himself and when that didn't happen, well, he lost not only a potential lover but a brother as well. The sundering of that friendship had ripped their little section of the Otherworld apart and only a needful truce to keep Piasa at bay had kept the brothers from coming to blows. Yet the rift between the brothers along with Rory's inability to have either of the O'Rourke girls had twisted the biker. What goodness remained was seldom seen.

Looking back at her, Rory laughed a fresh clean laugh there in the evening. For a moment, he was a young prince again, not seeing the age on the face of his Deirdre, but recalling the young girl she once was, back when there was hope, back before bitterness and cynicism set in.

She smiled back at him, her grey hair flowing in the wind. For a moment, the past was gone, and they laughed together. Guilt crept up her spine, but she banished it. They could only reach Conor and the others so quickly. What would happen would happen, and she would be ready. After all, she had prayed and trained and planned for this very time. But it was good to see Rory as himself again.

The moment passed. Before them loomed the hill upon which lay the Crossroads and Drake had left something for them there. Splotches of darkness, blacker than the encroaching darkness, alien to the landscape, strategically positioned at the base of the hill, there to deny them entry. Meant for Drake's foes, since ordinary people would never have seen this otherworldly barrier.

Rory slowed. "What are they?" he asked, genuinely puzzled.

"Hard to tell," she answered, "but I think I'm going to need my blackthorn cane."

"I'll be your chariot driver, my lady," he chuckled. "Whatever they are, we are going through."

Holding on with one hand to his waist, she raised the cane level with her chest, as if it she were about to begin an ancient joust.

"*Fiat lux!*" she cried, "Let there be light!" From the piece of wood she grasped burst forth a radiant light as Rory slowly went forward.

Black shadowy talons reached out to grasp the two, but always the light thrust them back. She thought she had cowed all of them, but out of the corner of her eye, a rushing shadow took aim, not at Rory, but at her and, with sudden physical presence, swept her off the bike. She rolled in the bracken unhurt, still clutching the blackthorn cane.

He stopped for her, but she motioned him onward. "You must go. Head for the river. The Abbot should be there by now. He seeks alliance with the Roan. You will be needed. I will deal with whatever waits at the Crossroads."

"You are not that powerful," he said softly.

"Perhaps not," she said with a small smile. "If it is my time, well then, that comes to all mortals. Go with God, you old rascal."

Smiling an even softer smile, he said, "I'll go, not with your God, but with your love. I've lost all three now, Finola, you, and my brother. All things turn to the dark." Bleakness covered his face as he turned from her, mounting his motorcycle.

She had not time for his regret. A last shadow lunged at her. Pointing the blackthorn at its heart, she sent a ray of light into its midst, an echoing wail vanishing with the shards of shadow.

She looked at the hill. Not too far to walk up. A scream from the top. As fast as she could she made her way as Rory spun out of sight toward the river.

A MEETING OF WORLDS

THE ABBOT PERMITTED Prior John Riley, himself a 'dark one,' to lead the All Hallow's Eve Procession down to the river, though whatever dreams of other worlds and possibilities once drifted through that man's sleep were now buried far in his unconscious. Malachy couldn't think of a duller man to hold that post in the past century. Yet, when these processions were yearly, it was always the Prior's place to lead the monks down to the mound.

The Abbot allowed himself a small sigh as he passed through the cemetery with the rest of the monks. He paused for a moment at Finola's grave, thankful that it was undisturbed. For three nights after her funeral, he had posted a monk at vigil at the grave, just in case Madoc came and attempted the unthinkable. Finola's time in the Otherworld would have allowed Madoc at least a chance to resuscitate her, but that time was past. Her soul had long departed her body to rest with the Lord. Hurriedly, he made the Sign of the Cross over the grave and moved on.

The procession always took the pasture path down to the river and he had made sure that the novices had cleared a wide swath last week. Strange, for so many years he had absolutely insisted on the All Hallow's Eve Procession. It seemed necessary for he and Madoc to keep the demon bound to its own world, at least mostly. The procession contained ritual—binding prayers that kept back the evil present in the dark waters. There were and could be no negotiations with the Devourer. Even in the Otherworld, it was an inscrutable enemy. Many guessed its true origins, but only the Abbot and Madoc really knew. Madoc was here by happenstance, having stumbled across this thin place between the worlds so long ago. Seeing a need over eight hundred years before when he first arrived, he held the demon in abeyance, but its power steadily grew until others became aware. And so Abbot Malachy was sent, though he was new to that name and vocation.

He remembered coming shortly after the Tinkers did and authorizing the building of the monastery. Where the funds came for that building project remained his own secret; no religious order in Ireland or America had the money to build such an edifice. Yet, he had succeeded. Not of Madoc's kind, yet he had an affinity with the prince. Malachy laughed to himself. In other ages, people had called him 'He Who Walks The Worlds' and they were not far from the mark. He guessed that was the best title for him—a walker of the worlds. But he was just a man, a man given extraordinary powers and responsibility, but a man none the less.

Once, long ago, he had stopped the All Hallow's Eve Processions because the danger seemed to be receding. Even the events of 1926, when Taps Jeffords was hung from the Crossroads Oak, terrible though they were, seemed isolated and without the direct intervention of Piasa. They weren't repeated the next year or the year after, so when the Great Depression occurred and sorrow gripped the country, he felt he could discontinue the procession, meant to be a visible reminder to an invisible demon that the powers of good still held sway. Piasa truly had evaporated into mist and legend.

Marveling at the beauty of this night, the Abbot allowed himself a brief moment of enjoyment. The full moon had left its blood red glow behind and now shone harsh and pale upon the landscape. He could see all the way down to the river where the moon cast a silvery reflection on the waters. Even the willow trees on the mound were clearly highlighted.

Chanting filled the air. The schola master had put the monks through their paces learning an old Gaelic chant, similar to its Gregorian cousin but harsher and more elemental. Malachy felt the power surging through the atmosphere as the song penetrated the river valley and he listened to his monks, singing of protection and power, binding and losing, shields raised, evil dispersed, elements surrounding, earth responding, the world's powers raised against the onslaught of evil.

Taps Jeffords had tried to capture the message of that ancient chant, remembered the Abbot, but the musician succeeded only in part. He comprehended the optimism of the chant and the conviction of its power to give life. But the raising of earthly elements and powers, keened in a language almost vanished from the world, had gone over his head. The Abbot allowed himself a silent chuckle. African-American melodies and Celtic harmonies—proving once and for all that music cuts across all cultural boundaries. None the less, Taps Jeffords was himself an embodiment of Light and did so much that night long ago to protect Finola and Conor. Saved their lives when others were too far away. And it was a good song he wrote. With regret, the Abbot said a silent prayer for his soul; no one deserved such a fate, but his death for them spoke of the nobility of the singer's heart.

He saw the first of his monks reach the mound and begin to range round the raised earth, painstakingly shaped centuries ago in the shape of an owl. As they outlined the figure, the mound grew in mystery and power. Anyone from up the hill by the cemetery would have easily recognized what the raised earthen outline was meant to represent. Malachy wondered whether the ancients who originally built the mound ever lit it like this on their holy nights. He hoped so, because the illumination of the mound showed forth the power of the land intersecting with the heavens. Shaking his head at a sight that never ceased to amaze him, he let himself be over-taken by the music. The chanting never stopped. Walking like an ancient druid baptized into a deeper mystery, he carried his antlered crozier with its ruby-fired Celtic cross into the assembly—a power from earth and heaven settling over the crowd.

Parting to let the Abbot through, the monks then closed the ring around the mound. As the Abbot moved to the large willow tree in the center of the hollow hill, the chanting changed, growing louder and more insistent.

With words that even Madoc would comprehend, the monks beseeched not only the saints and the elements and powers of this world, but all those who were friends of the One, whether dwellers of the air and water, or inhabitants of the hollow hills, denizens of the Otherworld to respond in kind and come this night to bind the dark and let loose the Light.

In a crescendo of sound, little different from the ancient Druids with the exception of its focus on the dying and rising God, the chant reached its zenith, abruptly coming to a stop. The resulting silence was deafening.

It lasted but a moment. A breeze ruffled the golden leaves of both willow trees and shafts of light were seen rising from the ground, insub-stantial as mist. Figures were walking there upon the mound, faint at first, but growing in substance, beings of light. Conor, had he seen them, would have been reminded of the firefolk his mother always talked about when she told him stories as a child. Noble they looked and fair they seemed to the assembled monks. Not a few of the brothers quailed with fear, but the Abbot stood unafraid, sad only because it had been so long since he had convened members of the Otherworld to join in the All-Hallows Eve celebration..

Madoc was the last to appear, but there was no doubt in the assembled throng, of this world and the other, as to who he was. Princely in bearing, noble in figure, golden torc around his neck and golden circlet binding his long dark hair, crimson cloak flung over his shoulder, clasped with Celtic brooch.

Standing together, the two surveyed the throng. Beautiful to behold, the crowd numbered only dozens, not hundreds.

"We are far too few," said the Abbot.

"As has always been the case," answered Madoc.

"You have heard what is happening in the town?" asked the Abbot.

"Indeed, the Morrigan was here not long ago with the news. I must say she did not seem as sad as she should."

"She is what she is," said the Abbot. "Any word on Conor?"

"No, I sent the Morrigan to find him, but you heard the thunder as I did—he is coming to his doom."

"You should be by his side," said the Abbot, already regretting the reproachful tone in his voice.

"Aye, so I should, but I am not what I once was and I fear my direction will not be the clear path he needs. He is conflicted over me. You and Deirdre, she who is known to the world as Emily O'Rourke, have done well fostering him."

"But I am not his father. Your absence grates on Conor."

"I will not be the first father resented by his son," said Madoc with a sad smile.

"No, but the stakes are considerably higher in this situation."

"You think Piasa will make its move tonight?"

"I have no doubt," said the Abbot. "Always, the demon has exploited weakness. The McNabbs and their greed were its first entry into this world in centuries and now its anchor in this time and place. Then comes that scheming physician …"

"More devious than you know," said Madoc. "I have seen him, and I know him.He is a powerful mage, as were his kin. From Gwynedd they came, and when I knew that blighted brood they were deep in dark magic. A tainted Druid faction they led. A shame their seed never died out."

"Never the less, he is here, and he awakes the Devourer in ways I did not think possible. Its reach now frequently extends within the town and the manifestations of the Otherworld, so open, so visible, are causing the townspeople much fear and consternation."

"You seek to raise a barrier this eve?" asked Madoc.

"Yes, as once we always did on this night, but strengthened I think to dissuade the demon's presence."

"Perhaps it is too late."

"Perhaps," said the Abbot, "but we must try."

They stood back to back then, Madoc ab Gwynedd of the People of the Roan and Abbot Malachy of *Stella Maris* Abbey and both began respective chants, circling sunwise and pausing at each of the four points of the compass, they chanted:

Abbot: In this fateful hour,
Madoc: We place all heaven with its power:
Abbot: Creator's arms to shield in strife,
Madoc: Shining sun to strike with brightness,
Abbot: Touch of the Spirit to grace the head,
Madoc: Gleaming snow to cleanse with whiteness,
Abbot: Cross of Christ to redeem our life,
Madoc: Burning fire to consume the chaff,
Abbot: Eyes to see where heaven's hosts tread,
Madoc: Flashing lightning to strike with wrath,
Abbot: Angels' words on my lips to start,
Madoc: Swift winds to blow upon your path,
Abbot: God's power in my hands to banish weakness,
Madoc: Rolling sea to moan with its deepness,
Abbot: A home for God in the depths of my heart,
Madoc: Sharp rocks to break with their steepness,
Abbot: Quiet soul to welcome God's peacefulness,
Madoc: Tortured earth to cry with your starkness,
Abbot: All these we place, by the Almighty One's help and grace,
Madoc: Between ourselves and the powers of darkness.

For a moment, nothing happened. Everything was silent as all monks held candles around the perimeter and the People of the Roan stood illuminated in eldritch light in the center of the mound.

Then, as if the Aurora Borealis, the very Northern Lights themselves were come down to earth, a shimmering curtain of light expanded from the Abbot and the Prince, flowing outward around the mound. "And now to seal it," said the Abbot.

"Brother!" shouted a voice from the field beyond. "Why can I not enter through the barrier?" said Rory mockingly, looking sleek in biker leathers. No one had heard him drive down through the bracken on his motorcycle.

"Why, indeed?" answered Madoc. "The good may pass; the evil may not. What mischief have you done this night?"

"So now you sit in judgement on me? I have been here and there, roaming the town and the valley from one side of the river to the other, but the dark of this night is not my doing."

"Then," said the Abbot, "in your innocence you should be able to enter."

"But I can't!" snarled Rory. "Once again, you meddle in our business. Leave us alone. Things were simpler before your kind came along."

"That may be," said Madoc, "but hold your tongue little brother, because without the monks of *Stella Maris* Abbey and the Abbot who serves them, all would have been lost years ago."

"Do you think," said Rory, "that your little show tonight will be enough to keep Piasa within its own realm? Have you such little respect for what the good doctor and darling Cate with her brood have accomplished? For months now, they've opened the passageways, making it easier. You've seen the Devourer's presence far beyond the river, and if you were to walk into town right now you'd sense it near. You know its smell don't you? Like rotting barge flies in the hot June sun. The streets of the town are awash in its stench tonight."

"And what did you do to stop its presence?" challenged the Abbot.

"Nothing. I did nothing," said Rory. "And there's a reason for it, wouldn't you like to know? If letting the Devourer walk this land would make Conor accept his destiny, I'd go into the river and escort it on a royal tour of the lands all around. Don't you see, Conor has to accept who he is. If I can scare him into his true self, so be it. If I can coerce him into it, all the better. If the land and its people must die to make it happen, I will help it be so. Whatever I have to do, I will, for our time is now."

"Our time is past, my brother," said Madoc. "Long ago, we walked into the hollow hills. Once I thought as you did but no more."

"Listen to the both of you," said the Abbot. "One speaks defeat, the other madness. Your kind thinks itself superior to humans, but what little wisdom you show now begs that question. You, Rory, would dance with the devil if he gave you what you wished; and you, Madoc, I cannot say for sure what lies in store for your people, but you are here, in this place, in this time for a purpose. How can you let your own son be without his father in his time of need?"

"I should have killed you, Madoc, the last time we fought." said Rory.

"Aye, so you should have," answered the prince, "for it is only in that way that you can ever bend me to your will. And as for you Malachy, though I have great respect for you, I do not see you as a judge of my people or a questioner of our motives."

"Fools, both of you!" said the Abbot. "While you dither, evil rises. Look to the river!"

A cauldron of bubbles burst in the middle of the channel as it swirled into a whirlpool. A greenish light burned from the depths as a sigh of fear ran through the monks.

"Courage!" called the Abbot. "The barrier will hold around the mound."

From the depths of the water a shapeless mist was rising, two points of baleful green light surveying the crowd.

Rory was laughing, but louder than his own laughter came the insane cackle of many voices from the hills, high above the flood plain.

"They come!" said Rory, "The children of tomorrow. Piasa's brood and my mischief makers. The Tinkers are bringing the future to the river."

They had little chance to comprehend what was happening. Above the din, came a piercing scream that sliced the night with terror.

"Conor!" shouted the Abbot. "Madoc, you must go! He needs you desperately."

"Don't worry about a thing here," said Rory cheerfully. "We've got it well under control."

"Go," said the Abbot to Madoc, "Rory can only be a nuisance. The barrier will hold against Piasa. Whatever it intends with the changelings, my monks and your people will deal with the matter. Now go and find your son."

Madoc hesitated only a moment and then ran for the barrier, slipping through easily. The Abbot looked at him and sent a blessing his way,

Madoc who has charge of Conor,
Put round about that boy,
The embracing love you have for him.
Drive from him temptation and danger,
Surround him in this time of confusion and weakness,
And in his waking, walking and sleeping,
Keep safe his life, guard him always.

Running parallel to the hill towards the Crossroads, Madoc's passing caused consternation among his own kind and the monks. Few could give him much notice for long, for something was rising from the river as a wave of dark things crested over the monastery hill and made their way down towards the water.

Piasa took its time, rising from the bubbling whirlpool, looking distinctly more and more solid and of this world. Huge leathered bat wings flipped spray high into the air. Its scaled body stood upright in the midst of the vortex, no doubt standing on solid river bottom while its scorpion tale waved high above it. Massive front legs, a cross between paws and talons reached toward the crowd on the mound. Only its face was indistinct, shadowed by antlered rack. Some said it had the snout of a bear or panther, others that it was almost human in form. All agreed the face of the demon kept changing. The monks saw flashes of Brother Luke's visage and of Declan Walsh along with some of the other missing children. Despair gripped the hearts of those who looked too deeply. Yet the demon was silent as it swept its gaze over the mound and swung its piercing sight to the monastery hill, taking in the commotion washing down the hillside like a wave.

The changelings were leaping and spinning and cavorting down the bluff. Only by a stretch of great imagination could the Abbot see in them the children they once had been before their possession. They were grotesque under the light of the moon. Shadows themselves, they cast even longer shadows down the hillside. Screeching and howling, the din grew louder as they recognized Piasa's presence in the river.

What most disturbed the Abbot was the silent crowd that followed them. Townspeople with downcast eyes as if the inevitable had dulled their wits and taken away their love for their children.

THE PASSING

DRIVING AS FAST as possible down the winding road, Drake prayed to every dark power possible to preserve that child in that dying girl's womb. He could take it from her now, but with just himself and no surgical staff, it would be risky. He had stabilized Beth, but she was critical. Wouldn't last the hour. In the rearview mirror, he spotted Cate following on the Pooka. Amazing how fast that fell beast could run. Turning his eyes forward again, he gasped as he slammed on the brakes. Someone was standing in the middle of the road.

As the ambulance skidded to a stop, the lights from the vehicle illuminated the figure. Drake hissed in anger. Madoc. Had to be. Not many others wear cloak and torc, tunic and boots this far from some Halloween party. Wondering how solid the Otherworld really was, Drake revved the engine.

"What's going on?" shouted Cate riding up behind him, the truck blocking her view. "Why have you stopped?"

He didn't answer. Instead, he shifted into gear and prepared to ram the prince. Then he saw the light, a ball of fire forming in the hand of Madoc. The barbarian never threw it; the flaming globe simply floated forward, first slowly, then picking up speed. Before Drake could step on the accelerator, the fireball exploded into the grill of the ambulance, flared then vanished, along with all the electrical energy powering the vehicle. With a cough echoing off the encroaching trees, the engine died.

Drake hustled out of the vehicle and ran back to Cate. "Madoc is here," he said. The sound of another car approaching caught their attention.

Jace drew up in a shower of gravel. Jumping out, brandishing a sword, he yelled, "Where is she, Drake? Show me my sister."

"Where is my son?" said another voice, as Madoc stepped around the ambulance and confronted the humans.

Cate looked down from the height of her mount and smiled, "Dead, I believe. Isn't that right, Jace? You were the last one to leave."

"Don't listen to her," shouted the boy. "I just left Conor; he's alive. But, Madoc, Beth is dying. Help her please. She's got to be in there."

"Whatever will you do, princeling?" said Cate. "Here you have your enemies where you want them, but take us now and, in the time spent, you'll lose your little grandchild and your son. Take on the dark, and your future dies, even if you happen to win this particular battle. By all means, let's end it here."

"What are you saying?" said Drake. "We can't fight him and just leave Beth's child—it's everything we've been working for."

"Patience, doctor. We're not the only ones in a bind. Can't you feel it? The Devourer has made its presence known in this land. Already, its spell has infected the town. Much is already in our grasp. If Madoc grabs the child, finds some way to preserve its life that is no setback for us. We know he will take good care of it. But if he tries to attack, he may win, he may kill one or both of us, even the Pooka, but, in the meantime, the child will die and he will ultimately lose. We hold the better hand here. Isn't that right, Madoc?"

"Madoc, please!" pleaded Jace. "She's dying."

Suffused with barely channeled rage, Madoc spat out his words. "So much of the land has been poisoned. So much of what was good here is gone. She speaks the truth. Get you from my sight Caithness McNabb and you, druid spawn. But go now, for the door that leads to your safety closes even as we speak."

"Go to the river, doctor," said Cate. "Your presence is needed there now. The fool monks are attempting to hinder the Devourer's advent."

"You better be right about this, Cate. And you better hope he has the power to save that child." With a hiss, Drake disappeared into the brush, heading towards the river.

Steam snorted from the Pooka's nostrils as Cate spoke. "My mount wishes to make a closer acquaintance, Madoc, but as for me I'm glad I finally met you. Now that the worlds are to be joined, we shall be seeing much more of each other. I hope you will consider joining us. This world is ripe for the taking. Piasa would have a place for you."

"There is no home in darkness. There is no love in evil as you will soon discover," said Madoc.

Jace was already ripping open the doors of the ambulance. "Madoc, please; she needs you now!"

"Help the dying bitch," sneered Cate. "I need to go back and finish what I started. I was so sure your son was dead. Never count on the heavy hand where a woman's touch is needed." She wheeled the Pooka around and with a laugh, galloped back up toward the Crossroads.

Madoc reached for her, but then his arm fell to his side, failure graven in his face. Sighing, he leapt into the ambulance, finding Jace bent over his sister. No electricity; none of the machines were working.

"She's not breathing!" screamed Jace in panic.

"Patience, Champion," said Madoc, bending over the girl's body.

Madoc stretched out his arms over her, breathing upon her. For a moment, Jace thought the air itself was glimmering, but his attention turned immediately to his sister. Shallow breaths and then coughing. Beth opened her eyes, her gaze taking in the strange man standing before her. "Who are you?" she asked.

Madoc smiled, "Just a friend, little one."

"You saved her!" said Jace.

"No," said Madoc, "and she knows that as well. I have given her a little of my life's energy to help us do what must be done. She must pass on; her time here is done."

"No!" wailed Jace, sword clattering to the floor of the ambulance.

"Jason," said Beth, "listen to me. I'm not in pain and I'm thinking clearly—I kind of like this Otherworldly energy." She smiled a weak smile. "But I know I'm dying. Something's broken inside. I heard Drake say there was nothing he could do. He only hoped to keep me alive long enough to take the child. Listen to me, Jace, what happened between Conor and me ..."

"Don't talk; it's okay."

"I love him, Jace, and I know you care for him—even in your anger. For me, if not for yourself, stand by him. This man called you 'Champion.' Watch over Conor, for me. And the child." She turned to Madoc. "Can you really save the baby?"

Madoc looked at her with warm eyes, stroking her blond hair. "Yes, little one, but not in the way you think. I can save the child and preserve its identity and life force in the Otherworld. A purely human child could not endure what must be done, but Conor is its father as well. I can preserve the child's existence, but as I do, you will release your hold on this world. Are you brave enough for the journey? Are you trusting enough to let me care for your offspring?"

"But won't Conor ..."

"No, not for a while. First he must survive this night, and that is not certain. If he does, his destiny is elsewhere, but when the time is right, he shall be reunited with the fruit of this union. He must never know until then that the child lives."

"Absolutely not!" said Jace. "You're not going to manipulate a whole new generation."

"It must be so. More is at stake here than Conor's happiness, your wishes, or Beth's desires."

"Let it be, Jace. He has the power to do as he wants. We have to trust him."

Jace bent swiftly and picked up the sword. Slowly, he approached Madoc and placed the tip of the blade at the base of the selchie's throat. "I may not be of the People or the Roan as you call them; but I have a sword of power and the wisdom of both worlds. I am not so easily turned aside."

"The Abbot has gifted you with a great weapon—little do you know of the battles that blade has won—but you are so young, and strong as you are for a mortal, you might find me more than a match. Use your wisdom now and help me do what is necessary to save this child."

For a moment, Jace tensed, about to strike, but then he let the blade drop, shoulders slumping in despair. He felt Madoc's hand on his shoulder. "Come now, a most difficult task awaits."

Madoc instructed Jace to hold Beth's hand. "You must lead her to the Summer Country."

"What?" asked Jace.

"What you mortals call 'heaven.'"

"How can I do that?"

"Walk with her as far as you can; there will be others to take her hand when you can go no further."

Tears coursed down his face. "I don't want you to go, Beth."

"I know," she wept. "But I have to; I have to."

While they were speaking, Madoc stretched his hands over the girl's womb. He could sense the life present there. Thankfully, as swiftly as the child was developing it was still in embryonic form, its body still malleable and able to be formed into the shape that would guarantee its survival.

"What I must do now will frighten you both, but stay strong. As I lift the child from you Beth, you shall die. It will be painless but inevitable. Farewell, brave one; we shall watch over your offspring."

Madoc looked upon them, an Otherworldly prince. To Jace, he seemed the most noble person he had ever met. To Beth, he looked almost angelic and, indeed, his body became as motes of light swirling in the darkened ambulance. His features vanished, only his form could be seen as he lifted high his hands and then plunged them into her womb. She gave a little gasp of wonder, not of pain, as she saw him lift a blue light from her, formless but pulsing with life. A voice penetrated the light.

"This is your child, your son, Beth and the child of my son, Conor. I have changed his form in order to preserve his life in the Otherworld. He will be nourished and raised in the Light, and be a hero of great deeds. But that is for the future. As for you, little one, rest in that knowledge. Because of your courage and love, your son lives and will weep at the gentle bravery that has come from your care. From the suffering you have had to endure some good has touched this night. Sleep now and rest and so fade sorrow."

Madoc and the blue light he carried faded from sight and Jace was left alone with his sister, looking distinctly pale, her breaths shallow and faint.

Tears fell from his face. "Don't go. Don't go."

She smiled up at him, "It'll be okay. Just look at my eyes."

He did, and saw, and walked with her a ways in the dark, squeezing her hand. She touched him back as he saw light twinkling in the depths of her gaze.

"Time to let go," she said.

"I know. I love you, little sister."

"Love you too, big brother. Tell Conor that I will love him always. Tell him I'm so glad I gave him my heart. Take care of him, Jace. You'll need to be his strength, his friend."

He wept then as she fell silent, his cheek pressed against her dead face, his arms holding her shattered body.

CONOR ON THE HANGIN' TREE

THE BRANCHES CAME down and enveloped Conor a yard or so in front of his face, effectively cocooning him from Jace and the carnage at the Crossroads. Shouting for Jace to go and help Beth, he breathed a silent prayer that Jace would be in time, not sure whether Jace even heard his last cry.

All was silent. Conor slumped forward, causing him to yelp as the nail tore into the flesh of his wrist, the dagger ripping more deeply into his gut. "I'm all alone. I'm dying all alone," he whispered to himself. A faint echo of a song drifted from higher branches:

> *"All who save must come to see;*
> *There's no salvation,*
> *'Cept the hangin' tree.*
> *Nosiree, nothin' to do but hang, hang, hang,*
> *Savin' the world on the hangin' tree."*

For a moment, all was quiet, but no matter how he tried, he could not force the pain away, shape-shift, or anything. Taking several deep breaths, once more he tried, and felt the branch of the oak tree moving against his cheek. Rather forcefully, he idly thought, as if it had a mind of its own. Pressing against his face, filling his mouth with autumn leaves which even in the night were golden to his sight. Then he knew. The tree was pushing his face to the left, as if it wanted him to look. Why, thought Conor. No one is here to help me, and he didn't feel like talking to Taps Jeffords, if the musician should attempt to put in another appearance. But he could not help himself. Inexorably, his face turned and he allowed the branch to move his head. And he looked.

Taking a sharp intake of breath, he realized that what he saw was not of his time. Not far from the tree was a ruined stone wall. Just over the wall several standing stones. None of those in southwest Wisconsin, thought

Conor, and these looked to be smaller cousins of the ones in Stonehenge. Whatever he was seeing was long ago and far away. The far away part he had figured out but it was the torches burning between the standing stones and the stone altar before them that convinced him the past had come back to haunt him.

On the altar lay a young man, tied fast to the four corners. Half naked, he was dressed in breeches and soft leather boots. What little he wore was rich clothing. His face was turned from Conor and he seemed to be gazing out and through the stones to the darkness beyond. It was night, a moon as full as in Conor's time blazed down with cold silver upon the scene.

"Where are you?" shouted the stranger. "Come back and finish this, you coward. Where are you?"

Conor never could figure out why he spoke, but he found himself saying, "I am here." His voice rasped so quietly that the rustling leaves of the oak drowned him out. "I am here," he said again. Barely a sound on the whispering wind. Licking his lips, speaking through his pain, he croaked more loudly, "I am here."

And the figure turned, eyes wide with wonder. Conor knew if the stranger could have moved, he would have leapt off the altar not with fear, but with an urgency, so taut did his muscles strain against his bonds.

"Who speaks?" asked the stranger. "Who speaks from the Tree of the World?"

Recognition dawned in Conor's eyes. He knew this man. Younger surely, but still the same. Drawing on all his energy, he spoke again. "Father! My father!"

The stranger's eyes narrowed. This was no easily frightened man. "I am but twenty and have known many a woman, but I have sired no son, surely none as old as you sound. I am Madoc. Show yourself."

Conor managed a strangled chuckle. "I can no more move than you can, but your son I truly am and in years to come you will claim me as your own."

Madoc's eyes swept the shadows, finally settling on a darkness suspended from the branches of the oak. Now that he could actually see the figure hanging on the tree, the young man's breathing returned to normal. Shrewdly, he looked at Conor, "Much is possible for one who sees the Tree of the World. Doubtless I have been given this vision because it is my doom soon to die, but I know nothing of what you speak. Have you been sent by the Druid?"

"A druid tied you up? He is trying to sacrifice you?"

"Yes. It is the Feast of Samhain and he seeks to sacrifice me, and my own father, King Owain agrees."

"Your own father wants to kill you?"

A cynical laugh. "Obviously, you do not know Owain ab Gwynedd. He has scarcely met any maiden that he hasn't ravished, human or not; that makes for too many sons, and my brother and I are two too many to love."

"Meaning what?"

"He wants my brother and me dead. The Druid has convinced him that we seek to overthrow his rule. The King has two dozen sons, all of them human except for my brother and me. On two occasions he had a dalliance with the seal-folk, the People of the Roan. Bewitching they were, he said. Beguiled him on the beach not far from here, always when he returned from a military foray. He told me how it happened. A summer's night, warm. Himself alone by the ocean, and them standing in the shallows singing a haunting song of blue waves rippling, deep currents running—the song of the sea. Seaweed in their hair, but the one who chose him, her body warm and inviting. He could not help himself, he said. Nine months later on a cold winter's day, he walked the shore again and twice a bundle in the sand, first myself then two years later, my brother. Honor bound him to raise us, he said. But not to love us. He always kept his distance. As did the rest of the family. Fey we were. An uncertainty in his very regimented world. Never good to keep the Otherworld close. So he thought. Now civil war is come to Gwynedd, and my brother and I are the scapegoats. Our deaths will be a sign to those who seek to overthrow my father that rebellion will not be tolerated. And as another prize, the death of his by-blows will sever any connection with the Roan. Humans are hard enough to rule and conquer; he doesn't need the mischief the People can cause."

"Why all this?" asked Conor. "Why not just kill you and be done with it?"

The young man laughed. "My kind is not so easy to kill. We of the Otherworld do not just roll over and die with a spear point in our back or a sword thrust to our gut. It takes a powerful magic to end our lives."

A rustling in the dark caused conversation to cease. A dark-headed youth, younger than the one to be sacrificed could be seen rushing between the standing stones.

"Rory," said Conor.

The figure stopped and gaped. "Who said that?" He looked wildly around. "Again I say, speak now." Drawing his knife he spun around.

"Peace, little brother," said Madoc. "Look across the wall. Tell me what you see."

Rory peered into the darkness and Conor saw the familiar features. But they were less pinched and cynical. He could hardly believe the innocence he saw on Rory's face. The younger man had not been touched by tragedy. At least not yet.

"There's something there, brother. A tree, dark and looming, and … something hanging on its trunk. I can barely see."

"The Tree of the World," said Madoc. "It has many secrets, and this night, it says it has my son."

Rory laughed aloud. "Not mocking your virility, brother, but even you can't make a boy grow into manhood in minutes. Whoever hangs there is as old as we are."

"True, but before we chat further, unloose my bonds before that devil of a Druid reappears."

Rory was about to cut him free when a noise down the path announced the return of the Druid and his apprentices.

"No time," hissed Madoc. "Hide yourself and await any opportunity. And you who hang on the Tree, if you can do anything to help do so. Now is the time for magic, for the Druid is strong in the ways of darkness."

Again, crippling pain sent new waves of nausea through Conor's vision. He could barely keep himself conscious. But he had not seen the last of the night's surprises. Dressed in ratty grey robes, an emaciated old man with a staff limped up the path towards the standing stones, assisted by two young men in equally filthy clothing. Stone knives glinted dully from the belts around the young men's waists, but what drew Conor's gaze was the small dagger around the elder Druid's neck. Just like Drake's. Indeed, the old man even bore a resemblance to the doctor.

In a voice like dead leaves whispering over grave stones, the Druid spoke, "Madoc ab Owain ab Gwynedd, your sacrifice will please the old gods and settle this war once for all. You will give your father peace and your blood will enrich the land."

Madoc spat at the face of the Druid. "I expected no love from my father, never having been the object of his affections, but you who saw to my education all these years, who claimed friendship with me, have betrayed me, and you will do the same to my brother."

It seemed to Conor that genuine sadness flickered in the eyes of the Druid. "We are what we were born to be. I serve the king and in this time of change when the old religion is fading away and those who serve the Christ gain strength, I take any opportunity to show the people that the old ways still live, are still strong. The people know what you and your brother are. They fear the sea and those who dwell in it. Your deaths will ease their fear and the peace that comes to the land will strengthen my power and the power of the old ways to bring stability."

"I beg you not to do this," said Madoc. "I do not fear death, but neither mine nor my brother's will stop this civil war. And sundering the Roan from those who dwell on land will further separate the Otherworld from the world of men. Is that what you want?"

"Who knows what truly will happen? Important as you are, even your deaths will not cause that much change. Magic will keep the worlds in touch with one another."

"Use your power," said Conor.

The Druid started and looked for the speaker.

"Use your power, Madoc," said Conor in what he hoped was a shout.

"Whoever speaks, listen to me," said the Druid. It was obvious to Conor that the old man could not pierce the darkness with his vision and apprehend either the Tree or his own aching body. The priest continued, "This one has no power, for I have taken it away. The draught he and his brother earlier drank at the feast was drugged. An ancient recipe, I might add, but very effective for dulling the Roan's ability to shape shift and use the strength the Otherworld gives."

"I tell you, Druid," rasped Conor, "look over the wall and into the dark and still say you can complete this sacrifice tonight."

The Druid looked; it seemed to him and his companions that the darkness parted and in the skittering shadows cast by the torches, a tree could be seen and something else. He and his companions hissed at what they saw. "Whatever you are," said the Druid, "you have not yet come into your full power or you would have used it already. A beast you appear, but that is not your true form. A creature of the Otherworld, yes, but something more, though not yet quickened, I believe. I fear you not." With that dismissal, the Druid turned away and raised his own dagger to plunge it into Madoc.

Rory screamed and leapt from the shadows but not quickly enough. The Druid's two apprentices had been waiting for just such an ambush and quickly pinned him against one of the standing stones.

"Your time will come in a moment, second bastard son of the King," said the Druid. Swiveling his head back to Madoc, his uplifted arm plunged down with the dagger, point poised to pierce the young man's heart.

In a rage full of sadness and grief, Conor roared his anger into the night. With his free hand, he wrenched out the dagger that pinned him to the tree and threw it with all his might. Truly it flew, but it did not strike the Druid. Instead, it flew to its double and twisted around it till both daggers were one. The Druid looked up in astonishment as the merged blade took on a life of its own, rolling in his withered hand. Trying to drop it, the Druid backed away, but the dagger seemed glued to his fingers, bending it toward the Druid, himself. Slowly it seemed, inexorable it was, but the dagger's point turned from Madoc to the heart of the Druid. A brief pause as it hovered above the priest. Then, faster than sight, the old man's arm moved and the dagger plunged into the Druid's chest. He screamed in pain and, in echo, a laughter was heard dwindling away in the dark. Falling dead at the base of the altar, he moved no more.

Rory took his chance. Feeling the grip on his arms loosen, he kicked out with his legs and broke the hold. Nothing to fear from the apprentices. Too stunned at the death of the Druid priest, they simply turned and ran.

"Well, done!" shouted Rory to the figure now slumping forward, held aloft still by his iron pierced hand and the rope around his waist. "Well done!" He rushed to free Madoc, who, when free, silently stood and walked to the wall.

"We must help him," said Rory, reaching over the stone to grab Conor's arm.

"Do not touch him," said Madoc. "We are from different times and who knows what will happen. We could destroy him and he us."

"Nonetheless," continued the prince, "I echo my brother's joy. You have saved me, you who claim to be my son. And it grieves me that I cannot ease your pain."

Conor gave a weak laugh. "That's your problem in my time as well. For everything that you are, all the power that you have, you do little to help your own flesh and blood."

Madoc's hands tightened on the stone wall. "I have killed men for lesser insults. Only your deed and my reverence for the Tree of the World spare your life tonight."

"Be careful," said Rory, "he could be of use to us."

"You boys sure have an ego," said Conor. "You are as insufferable in the twelfth century as you are in my own. With all your power, you bring disaster and death not only in your own time, but in mine as well."

"If you truly are who you say my son, then you are of the People, and you have the power to save yourself. The Druid spoke rightly though. You have not yet come into your own; you are not fully Roan."

"I can shapeshift," said Conor. "I just can't do it every time. I can walk in the Otherworld, just not always."

A small smile crept over Madoc's lips. "Bold words and brave deeds I think for someone who has not had a mentor in the ways of our People. It is not just a matter of becoming another living thing. It is a matter of learning the land, what it is made of, what beings live on it, above it and below it. Feeling its heart, knowing its soul. The underlying energy of a place, *neart* is what it is called. In this place, in this time, I walk by the shore of the sea and in moments I can dance on the waves, a selchie among the seal folk, almost indistinguishable from them except that I am more than them. But in another land, away from the sea, I might be something else. Perhaps you have not felt the land in which you live and listened to what it is calling you to be. Let its power flow in you."

Conor simply stared.

"I know this seems not much of a gift, especially to one who has saved our lives. But think on it. You face a danger in your own time. Much evil. It has tried to do to you what was nearly done to Rory and me. It is no stronger in your time than in mine. And yet, you defeated evil here tonight. Surely, you can do it in your own."

"I am not strong enough."

Madoc laughed. "Of course you are not. None of us is. But let the land speak through you and you will find the strength."

Rory said, "There is one thing more. I nearly forgot it in all this tonight. The hermit in the woods, you know him Madoc, the Christian priest that lives not far from here. He saw me today and told me something that made no sense at the time. Now it does. I thought he was raving—you know his reputation. He came up to me on the forest path and said, 'In the dark of this day you will meet someone who will need your aid. Say to him, *He who wields the thunder, he who captures the light, will hold the serpent at bay, and defeat the demon of night.*' I have little time for Christian priests, especially mad ones, but perhaps his words were meant for you, future son of my brother."

"Take them, and what I said," spoke Madoc to Conor. "It is all we can give you now, for soldiers are coming and we must flee to the sea. My father will pursue us all the more once he sees his Druid dead. He will follow us wherever the chase leads."

"Go then," said Conor, bitterness spat with the words.

"My son," said Madoc "for I believe what you say, it appears you have as little love for me as I for my own father. May that change in time to come. I am not all I should be, but what I am is true. Rely on my strength, trust in my blood, and do me honor in your time and place."

Conor said nothing and Madoc and Rory merged into shadows, denying him more vision. He was left alone with his pain hanging on the Tree of the World.

From far away, it seemed, he heard a beautiful voice:

Tree of life, release this shield,
Conor Archer to me yield,
With grateful thanks when worlds collide,
Be still O Ancient One, in peace abide.

Suddenly, the branches parted, drawing Conor's gaze and he saw the Morrigan standing there, in his own time and place. Her white shift was spattered with something dark as her red hair followed her head in a swoon like a keen.

Through a blood mist he saw her come, walking toward him, all in white, stained with blood. Beautiful as the moon with pallor dead and ghostly. She was carrying a human skull with reverential care.

"What is it you want now?" he said, moored to the Tree by sticking wounds and fatigue.

Turning the skull around, she offered it to him. He could see the back of the skull had been shattered and scooped out, as if the facial plate was more a mask than once the house of a human mind. "Look through the eyes of the dead," she said. "Tell me what you see."

As she held the skull out, she licked the fingers of her free hand, wet with some dark substance. Beyond, were the corpses of Fergal and Rafe, looking rather mauled. With a sob, he recognized the body of Troubles lying close by.

"You did not touch my dog," snarled Conor.

"Nay, young, one," said the Morrigan. "I never feast on the most noble of heroes."

Still, thought Conor, she was looking rather longingly on the blood that still flowed from his own hand and side.

"Who once looked through that face?" asked Conor in a whisper.

"One who almost was wise. One who paid the price and died. One who might have the answer that you seek."

She had no difficulty reaching into the branches and with a flick of her fingers she drew the iron nail out of the tree and back through his hand. He screamed in agony again as the nail smoked in the Morrigan's grasp. Distastefully, she threw it to the ground as Conor slumped forward, held only by the rope tied around the Tree of the World.

With one hand lifting up his head, she gently held out the skull. Again she said, "Look through the eyes of the dead; tell me what you see."

Groaning, his freed hand shaking and bleeding profusely, he took the skull and held it up to his face. Gently, she pressed it tight. He had not the energy to resist.

THE FIGHT AT THE CROSSROADS

THEY ARRIVED AT the same moment, Aunt Emily, huffing and puffing up the hill, fresh from zapping the shadows that Drake had used to surround the Crossroads; and Caithness McNabb, looking all high and mighty on her spectral stallion with the sulfurous eyes.

Both surveyed the carnage before them. Both took in the fallen bodies of the McNabb boys and the dead dog fallen near. Cate shed not a tear over her boys as Emily bent down and stroked Troubles' fur, a grim anger sweeping across her features. Their eyes fell on the Crossroads Oak at the same moment, both seeing the Morrigan hold the hollowed out skull to Conor's face, his crumpled bleeding body hanging on the trunk of the tree. She turned her head to behold the other two women and began to laugh.

Enraged, Cate McNabb urged the Pooka to charge the pair. She had enough of the boy that just would not die and was not going to allow even the Morrigan to interfere. Aunt Emily saw the look of death on the face of McNabb clan's matriarch and strode forward to meet her charge.

Of course, Conor neither saw nor heard any of this. As the Morrigan touched the bony face plate to his skin, he felt the world recede and himself meld with the remains of the dead.

"Tell me what you see," whispered the Morrigan from shadows beyond his vision.

As the skull burrowed more deeply into his face, he looked through the shattered eye sockets and saw the banks of White Creek.

"I see the place where you wash the bones of the dead," he whispered. "I see the place where Walt died. It is his face I wear, through his eyes I see, isn't it?"

"Yes," said the Morrigan. "Do not be afraid. What will happen will happen. Watch and learn."

He saw that fateful afternoon just days ago. He watched his best friend Jace stumble out of the cave onto the bone dust beach, face transfixed with joy. Whatever happened in there had transformed his friend. Jace looked at him—no, not him, Walt—and waved. Conor heard Walt's voice exulting over the catch of the great Cat, of wisdom received, and sorrow struck his heart, because he knew Walter had just missed that gift. Fate, or something or someone else, had gifted wisdom to Jace instead. And that was Walt's death sentence.

Conor saw Piasa erupt from the cave entrance, the Underwater Panther unleashed. It rushed towards Walt and then time slowed. The boy saw what Walt saw in those last seconds before the dragon snatched the old man. Not the beast; that was a sight dreadful enough. There, on the bank, not more than five feet from them stood an old Indian woman. Conor knew at once it was Grandma Swift Deer, the last Winnebago native in those parts, Walt's foster mom and his teacher of the lore of the Wisconsin and Mississippi River Valleys. Dressed just like she was in the dog-eared post card sold in Dort Martin's shop, Conor thought, wrapped in a beaded blanket, her grey hair tied in beaded locks. Wrinkles as deep as the river valleys coursed through her features and her eyes burnt with a tribal wisdom of centuries.

Her toothless face looked with pity on her foster grandson, but then her head snapped to the side. Clearly, she was aware of Conor. "You!" she said, "your coming has cost this man his life."

"I didn't mean for it to be this way," he stuttered. "I didn't ask for this."

"We never ask for our fate," answered the Indian woman, spitting a gob of tobacco from her lips. "But you have not accepted yours. And because of that, this world and one other hangs in balance and people die."

"I want none of this," said Conor, feeling the pain of his wounds, despairing about the dead all around his body at the base of the Tree of the World.

"Your wish will be granted if you persist." She waved a frail arm. "None of this will be, for it will all be destroyed because of your cowardice. Is not the death of this man enough? And wait, I see not far from here the deaths of others you know and love—the one you bound your heart to—is her death not enough?"

"She's dead?"

Conor gasped. "Beth is dead?"

"Her spirit whispers in the wind. The claw of the Devourer has reached far and snatched her away from you—because you will not decide."

His hands reached up to throw off the mask, but it only burrowed further in. He looked to see the Indian woman, her face inches from his own. Smelling her tobacco breath, he tried to turn away. Her withered hand held his face fast.

"Those who love you tried to tell you—the Christian priest, the old woman, the crow who speaks, the one who dwells in the mound—you have power to unite the worlds, but only if you accept it."

"What do you know?" said Conor. "You're a Native American, the one who dwells in the mound is a Celtic prince, and I'm supposed to be a shapeshifter from a race that thinks itself doomed. I don't even belong here."

"Foolish boy," said Grandma Swift Deer. "The People of the Roan are known by many different names in different lands. They are few, but powerful. The shapes they take are rooted in the lands they walk, the waters they swim, and the tales the people of those lands tell. When the one who dwells in the mound manifests himself in power he does not appear as a seal or a whale here where the two great rivers meet." The old woman starting laughing and coughing at the same time, amused at her own humor. "Those beasts would not fit well in the waters here. I saw what he would look like in his own homeland, once in a National Geographic my Walter showed me. No, the selchic prince never was a seal here." Her dark eyes flashed. "But I have seen him as a wolf who runs in the night, and a bear who shambles in the autumn leaves, and a white owl that flies at dusk. He has no trouble being of the land—a prince he is, yet he humbled himself to be one of us, for he has lived with us a long time. Too long perhaps, for his power is fading. So the land now looks to you."

"I cannot defeat Piasa," said Conor. "I do not know how."

"Fortunately for you, boy, you do not need to know, you simply need to be. You have not yet come fully into your own, but you have enough strength to fight this battle, with the help of your friends."

"How?"

"Look into the folds of my blanket. What is embroidered on it?"

Conor looked at the intricate pattern and immediately saw the figure of Piasa, rising from what could only be the rippling waves of the river. It was stretching out its wings and reaching out its claws to something hovering in the air, another dragon perhaps? But on closer inspection, Conor could see it was a man-like bird with huge wings and talons and a staff in one hand from which shot forth bolts of lightning.

"Yes," said Grandma Swift Deer, "the Thunderbird, the one creature from the Otherworld that can stand before Piasa."

"You want me to become that?" said Conor, his voice rasping with incredulity.

"You are that," said the old Indian woman. "At any one time or place, there is only one Thunderbird. Here in this land, the struggle of good against evil is always the struggle of Thunderbird against Piasa. That is the shape this battle takes and that is the shape you must take if you are to save the worlds, if you are to save the land, if you are to save yourself."

"I can't."

"You must, or all is lost. Here now, I must go, for my Walter calls for me in his last agony."

"Are you dead?" asked Conor.

The old woman gave a sad, toothless smile. "Of course, but your own faith tells you that death is but a doorway. Right now, that doorway must open for Walter, for the Great Spirit who watches over us all will not let this evil take ultimate triumph over this man. Piasa will be the cause of his death in this world, but I am here to take him to the next, just like I have always been there for him."

Behind Conor, Walter's screams could be heard as time resumed and Piasa gripped the old man in its talons and ripped with its jaws.

"Don't let him suffer," pleaded Conor.

"It is part of our lives," said Grandma Swift Deer, "but it shall not be forever." She moved out of his sight, cooing in her own language, trying to comfort the dying man.

Conor gasped as pain returned to him. The skull mask was suffocating him and he reached to fling it off. This time he was successful; the mask popped off with little effort and he found himself looking up at a laughing Morrigan. "We have visitors," she said. Aunt Emily strode forward to meet the charging horse. Cate reined in the beast not four paces in front of her.

Cate laughed in mockery. "You were going to take us on with your little cane? You are getting senile, Emily."

Aunt Emily stood there in her jeans and flannel shirt, silver hair tied back in a bun, clutching the walking stick. "You of all people, Cate, should know better. You ride a Pooka, you consort with Piasa, you dabble in the dark arts with Drake and you really think I'm that stupid? I've lived a long time, several lifetimes in fact, and my knowledge is deep. Long have the Abbot and I prepared for this day. We have kept weapons hidden, ancient things of power, knowing that this was the place the Worm would try to make a beachhead into this world. That time has come at last. The sword that Jason Michaels carries now, the one that dispatched your worthless sons, is a weapon of the Light, long used in times just such as these, wielded by champions of great courage. And this cane, as you so disparagingly call it, is not what it seems. Behold, the Spear of Destiny, lost for ages, found decades ago, and placed into my care. It has helped hold the truce between Piasa and us, but now, in time of war, it comes to defeat the dark."

The blackthorn cane was changing. Conor could see that clearly. It was growing in size and changing in color. Silver it was now, with a definable spear tip at its end. Emily seemed to have no trouble wielding it as she pointed it at the Pooka.

"I told you before, creature of the dark, get you gone before I destroy you."

The Pooka snorted, a grating voice seeping across the Crossroads clearing, "You tried earlier to kill me, but it didn't work."

"Too gentle then," she said. "It is one of my weaknesses. No such mistake now."

Cate snarled in fury and raised her whip to strike Emily. As she snapped the leather, the thong wrapped around Emily's left hand. The Pooka reared and leapt forward to crush the old woman under its hooves.

To Conor, everything seemed in slow motion. He watched the slight figure of his aunt twine her hand around the whip and rip Caithness McNabb from her mount, leaving her lying in the middle of the road, while at the same time, Emily planted her feet firmly, crouched beneath the spear and then leapt upward as the Pooka came crashing down upon her.

The stallion from the Otherworld was huge and sparks flew from its hooves. Baring its teeth and screaming defiance, it bellowed the stench of sulphur everywhere, but even the Pooka could not escape the power of the spear. Like a knife through butter, the spear pierced the breastplate of the horse and the demon within howled an unearthly wail.

From the corner of his eye, Conor saw Drake appear from down the road and come rushing towards Cate, dragging her free from the battle.

The Pooka thrashed in its death throes as Emily held on, immovable there by the Crossroads.

"Quick!" hissed Cate. "Use the dagger and kill that bitch."

"The dagger's in Conor's gut."

She looked more carefully, watching Conor's struggles. "No more," she said. "It's gone. Look at him. Soon he'll be free of the Tree."

"It's not important," said Drake, arm around her shoulder, hustling her into the brush. "I had to come back for you. Do you have anything that Piasa has given you?"

She looked suspiciously at him. "Why?"

"These talismans have power but even without their power they are channels. The dagger was important because it once was part of Piasa and the Tree. But I can call for help and use Piasa's power if you have anything of his to help channel that force."

Reaching into her pocket she lifted out a black obsidian irregular disk.

"Ah," said Drake, "a scale from its hide. It will work perfectly."

The death screams of the Pooka ripped through the Crossroads as Aunt Emily held firmly to the spear.

"Behold the Warrior Woman, as in the old days when we strove with men in the battles of the past!" said the Morrigan, as she cradled Conor in her lap.

"Help her," he said. "She's an old woman; she can't fight that thing."

"Do not underestimate her love for you, Chosen One," said the Morrigan. "She will not be defeated."

Indeed, the impaled stallion could not free itself and its form began to change. A viscous thing of the dark, it morphed into several hideous incarnations, each an undefined nightmare, but still she held fast the spear.

"Why won't you just die?" she shouted into the maw of the demon.

The Pooka laughed in the midst of its pain. "I have no doubt you have killed me in this world. Let me repay the favor and take you with me."

With one last swipe of its hoof, it tried to trample the woman, but instead of rearing backward, Emily pressed forward, driving the spear still more deeply.

The Pooka screamed again and then was gone in a flash of flame. Only a searing smell of sulfur remained. Emily dropped the spear and fell to her knees.

"Well done!" shouted the Morrigan. "Who would have thought the tiny girl of long ago could defeat such a powerful force of evil."

Conor had the feeling the Morrigan would have cheered the Pooka if it had won the battle, so much had the battle lust come upon her during the fight.

No one noticed Drake and Cate. With the obsidian scale from Piasa, Drake began to channel a word of power that called the Devourer to him. Drake could tell the Dragon was irate with being disturbed, but the green tendrils came from the river anyway and Drake spoke to the Worm and made his needs known.

Like huge, tendril fingers, the fog wrapped round Drake and the McNabb matriarch, pulling them back towards the river. Even Piasa sensed the need for haste and stealth. Not even the Morrigan saw the escape.

Aunt Emily roused herself from the dust and walked over to where Conor, tied to the Tree, had slumped into unconsciousness.

"Away from him, creature of battle," she said to the Morrigan. "You usurp my place."

The womanly version of the Morrigan smiled sweetly, "As you wish, Deirdre, though I think it would be unwise to have me go far. He is sorely hurt and likely to die should I leave his side." The Morrigan reached out and with a fingernail slashed the rope that bound Conor.

Aunt Emily cradled Conor in her arms, rocking him back and forth, oblivious to the blood pouring from his wounds.

"What have you done, child? What in the world have you done?"

"Just tried to figure out what the right thing to do was, Aunt Emily," whispered Conor, regaining consciousness. "Just tried to figure out the right thing to do."

"Did you find what you sought? Was it worth this price?"

"No," said Conor. "Aunt Emily, Beth is gone."

"Hush now, we cannot be sure. Morrigan, can you heal him?"

"That remains to be seen," said the Morrigan. Neither Emily nor Conor had seen her change once again into her crone shape. Her gnarled hands reached out to touch the boy.

"I can heal these death wounds," said the Morrigan. "You know that is so, Deirdre. But there is another price."

"With you, there always is," said Aunt Emily.

"His wounds come from the Otherworld, and so should his healing. But since these are wounds of death, his will is involved, his cooperation is needed, his consent required." Her scratchy voice wheedled like an old gypsy woman's bargaining pitch.

"What do you want of me?" said Conor. He could barely see the two of them looking at him. I'm fading, he thought, just fading away. Maybe that would be a good thing.

"Accept your destiny, child," said the crone, not ungently. "Accept who you are, and I can take away death."

"Oh, Conor," said Aunt Emily, "you know I can't stand this ... this witch woman, but she has a point. On that, everyone who cares for you agrees. You must become something different, or else you will surely die. And the choice is yours alone."

"If I choose, will it bring Beth back?"

The Morrigan cocked her withered head to one side and cackled. "No, it will not. She is gone as the old Indian woman told you. Nothing you do will bring her back. Her fate has been woven as a dark thread into the loom of life and death."

A tear crept down Conor's cheek. "How did I mess all this up?"

Aunt Emily hugged him to her breast. "By being young, Conor. By being a boy. By being human. And whatever evil was there rested not in malice but in the mistakes of youth. Don't be too hard on yourself. Evil itself had choices and decisions to make in all of this. I think you could not have prevented her death."

"What good could come out of my choosing to accept whatever destiny I have, whatever change is coming over me?"

Again the Morrigan cackled. "Much can happen. Much will. All things will be possible. Battle will be assured. Blood will flow. You will make me happy. But, in answer to your question, choose rightly and many more will live, both in this reality and in the Otherworld."

Conor was silent for a moment, and in the faintest voice he then said, "I choose to change."

She paused in her seemingly insane cackle. "Do you understand what this means?" asked the Morrigan. "You saw what you must become in order to defeat Piasa? You know that even making that choice will not let you assume your full power. You remember the rune: to come fully into your own, thrice you must be pierced. This was only the second time, painful as it was; many wounds you have received. You will need help from the Champion, from the priest, and even"—here she affectionately touched the strands of silver on Aunt Emily's head—"even from this ancient warrior."

"What of my father?"

"What of him?" snapped the Morrigan. "I spoke not of him. His power wanes. Perhaps he may help; perhaps he may not. You saw the power you must draw from the land; you know what form you must take. Will you do so?"

"Yes!" said Conor, putting more force into the words than he truly felt.

"Then," said the Morrigan, "I can heal you."

She began to unwrap the gray shroud around her body.

"That is the cloth of death," said Aunt Emily.

"Only to those whose time has come. In this case," scratched the Morrigan, "it is the healing garment of life. Away from him and let it do its work."

Emily stood up and backed away. As the Morrigan threw the cloth into the air, she disappeared with the cry of a crow and the cloth floated down like a gossamer silk upon the dying body of Conor Archer. Slick with blood, he reached out a hand to grasp it but it molded itself around his form.

The cloth was almost translucent. As through a silvery grey curtain of rain, he could see the outside world. It was then he knew he was truly dying. And it didn't feel so bad. Peace was never a bad thing, and walking away from all of this would be a great relief. But he had just promised the strangest woman from a pagan time and place that he would fight. For what, he did not know. For whom, he was not sure. All those who had already died? And Beth, whom he knew was gone from him? If he let go now, perhaps he could see her again. He was on the brink of reneging his pledge to the Morrigan when, through that same cloth, he saw a figure approaching, far away at first, coming out of the woods.

It was the stag, the White Stag, looking whole and young. My God, it has the warmest eyes, thought Conor. It came up to him and nuzzled his cheek, touched his wounded hand and blew warmth on the terrible wound beneath his chest. The pain vanished.

Conor knew him. Just as those throughout the ages knew whom they met when the White Stag appeared.

"Please," said the boy, "who am I? Who do I belong to?"

The face of the Stag, its huge rack looming over him bent down in front of the boy and once again the animal breathed on him. Conor saw in a flash of light, vast oceans where swam a People who danced on the waves. He perceived a huge fist of rock, furthest outpost of Europe, jutting from the sea into the sky, and he knew that where that rock was, where those waters were, was his true home.

"You want me to go there?" he asked, but the beast never answered, only touched the boy's face again. Conor saw the river valley and bluffs he lived in now, a darkness over them, and he knew what was being asked.

"I am of the Roan, the People of the Sea, a selchie in the water but a man on the land. The faces Oz showed me last summer, the seals in the depths, my people. The 'dark ones,' able to change shape almost and become familiars of the beasts here, they show me the way. I am lost here but called to do something, what the Indian Woman said and asked, but I don't know how. You must help me, please."

The White Stag bent down its head even further and Conor grasped the rack with his hand. The Stag pulled the boy forward and as Conor rose the grey garment dissolved into him. He felt his body absorb the Morrigan's cloth and as it did, new strength flowed through him, his wounds closed and healed. He gasped in wonder as his wounds vanished, leaving only a terrible ache in his heart. He looked deep into the eyes of the fantastic beast and saw sorrow and grief there as well. Then he knew that wound in his heart would not be taken away. The beast lowered its head and moved closer embracing Conor's body with its antlers and resting its head on his pounding heart. Conor felt power surge through his body, a courage tangible taking away the paralysis of grief, focusing his whole being on what was being asked of him. Groaning in wonder, he stood even taller as the Stag backed away and bounded into the forest. Even Aunt Emily had her mouth wide open in awe. At her gasp, he turned to face her, blood soaked, but obviously healthy.

"Did you see him? Did you see the White Stag, Aunt Emily?"

"No, son," she said. "You simply rose up and stand here now healthy and whole."

His relief was short-lived as he took in the carnage surrounding him.

"Look at what's happened!" he cried, walking over to the bodies of the McNabb boys. "Where's Troubles? His body was just here." Sobs began to wrack his bones as he fell to his knees, remembering the dog leaping to save him and Jace.

"We cannot grieve the valiant, yet," said Aunt Emily putting her arms around him. "If his body was here, it is not now. Remember, Madoc made him a part of the Otherworld. It will be hard to destroy such a noble soul as his."

"Here," she said, gently smoothing his hair. "I need to give you something, a wondrous thing for the trials to come." She handed him the Spear of Destiny, and as he touched it, the spear changed, not into a black-thorn cane, but into a six foot oaken walking staff. "It has many disguises. For you, and for the journey you will soon take; providing you survive the night, it will travel with you in this form. However, I fear you will need its power yet this evening, and when that moment comes, it will be the Spear of Destiny again, ready to serve you and the powers of Light."

THE FLIGHT OF THE MORRIGAN

SHE FLEW HIGH after draping the gossamer cloth over the body of the dying boy. Beheld Piasa rising from the river and the demon children swarming by the shore. Saw the Abbot extending a protective envelope around his monks and any of the People within his reach. Watched as Rory rejected the monk's offer and strode toward the riverbank. Glimpsed Oz lumbering down the hill from the Abbey, the unpredictable force in the chaos below. She chanced a look back to see Conor rising up from his death bed, renewed. Sighing, she thought there still might be a chance. But not without the Champion.

The carrion crow cast her sight wide till she spied the ambulance down the hill from the Crossroads. Quickly she flew and as she alighted, took the form of the maiden, dressed in the black of battle, mourning and death.

Looking into the darkness of the vehicle, she saw and heard a sobbing Jace cradling the head of his dead sister. For a moment, even the Morrigan was touched by grief. But not for long. Keening and wailing and all the accoutrements of mourning were for after the fight, not for the middle of the fray.

Wrenching him back with her free hand, she then swung and slapped him in the face. "What are you doing?"

He looked at her, not even recognizing who she was. "My sister. She's my sister."

"And she is dead," said the Morrigan. "You want to avenge her; you want to make her death mean anything, then put aside your insignificant feelings. There is a battle by the river that will decide the fate of worlds and you are to be a part of it, not sniveling in the back of one of this age's accursed vehicles."

Fury rushed through Jace's body. Seeming to grow in size he moved toward the Morrigan and with one swift motion reached behind him and unsheathed his sword.

"I should kill you now," he said quietly.

Softly laughing she said, "Many have tried, many have wished, many have plotted, but none succeed. I am the Morrigan, woven into the fabric of both worlds." Her voice was soothing as she gently pushed his blade aside. "What I am made of lives within you Jason Michaels, and who you are is needed now. You promised to be my Champion, you promised to be Conor's, you even promised Madoc to be the same. Now do your duty. What happens on the riverbank is swiftly coming to its conclusion. What Madoc gave you is needed now. I can take you to it quickly by secret ways, but we must run now."

He looked back at Beth's lifeless body and sobbed.

Speaking softly, the Morrigan touched his shoulder, "The evil that killed her is growing in power. Do not let the dark succeed."

He turned to her then, blue eyes flashing. "Take me to the ship; tell me what to do."

She made to leave, but he grasped her arm. "What is this sword?" he asked. "The Abbot gave it to me this evening and said it is a weapon of great power."

"He speaks the truth. It is one of the three sentinels that stand against the dark, only needing a worthy wielder to make it work."

"I can barely swing the thing," said Jace.

The Morrigan laughed, "Precisely because you see it as a thing. Let it become a part of you. Swordplay is rare in this age, but once all who carried a blade knew that the weapon was an extension of oneself. More true in this case. The blade becomes part of you, this Sword of Light. Accept who you are, and it will help you accomplish your goal. Now come; we waste time."

She grasped his hand and it seemed they flew through the woodland, down paths he didn't know existed and into hollows as dark as caves. They splashed across swamp land coming to the banks of White Creek. Without a thought, he and the maiden swam across the dark waters and found themselves facing the cave where Madoc had shown him the ship. He stood before the entrance.

"Do you really think I can make it work?"

But as he turned and looked, he found he was alone. The Morrigan was gone.

THE BATTLE AT THE RIVER

AS PIASA ROSE from the river, true chaos erupted in the little valley. The Abbot surveyed the deteriorating situation. Once again, his monks had taken up the Celtic chant and the People of the mound joined them. They weren't believers, but they were enraptured with beautiful music that held real power. One takes help from wherever, thought the Abbot. Not only did the music calm his brethren, it seemed to strengthen the barrier the Abbot had placed around the mound.

If only he could extend it to the villagers. They truly must be under some spell that Drake and the changelings had caused. Even in the bright moonlight, Malachy could see the blankness on the faces of mothers and fathers who should have been in the middle of the melee of children, yanking their own flesh and blood back to themselves. Such was not to be. The adults stood as a group, back a bit in the meadow, silently watching the changelings cavort on the banks of the river.

The possessed children seemed thrilled with the emergence of Piasa, though the demon gave no hint that it even recognized their presence. Bowing, jumping, even slashing themselves with broken clam shells, the little monsters wouldn't give up the effort to make the Devourer aware of their worship.

No doubt about it, thought the Abbot. The town was emptied of life. All were present here. Funny how world changing events are often barely noticed. If Piasa was allowed to truly enter this reality and set up an abode—it was bad enough that the demon occasionally manifested itself here down through the ages, terrifying the Winnebago tribe and serving as fodder for the nightmares of children for hundreds of years. But if the Devourer's intentions were to create a tangible bridge between the worlds, physically existing in this one in a way not possible before, then doom was definitely upon this age of the world.

The Abbot sighed, wincing at the despair he was beginning to feel. Conor was the hope. He, too, carried within him the ability to unite the worlds. Both worlds were dying. This world, corrupted by unbelief and humanity's inability to understand its place in the cosmos, and the Otherworld, separated from humanity which it once inspired and ennobled—now that greater world was evaporating as myths and legends were no longer needed and its very existence was doubted by humanity. But Conor could have begun the process to unite the two, to give a new lease on life to this world and enervate the Otherworld, allowing its strengths to give depth and life to the physical universe once again. He could have done it through the path of Light.

Piasa wished to unite the worlds through darkness. With Conor's reluctance to even accept who he was, Piasa certainly seemed to have the upper hand. Which was why, thought the Abbot, the beast was allowing itself this moment to savor its impending triumph.

Two things caught Malachy's attention. First was Oz, trundling down the hill, still listening to his own kind of music. Second was Rory, strutting forward to pitch words with the river demon.

"So you scaly motherfucker," said Rory, his cocky brogue showing every bit of self confidence, "you finally decided to put in a real appearance here in our beautiful valley. Understand why Madoc and I made this our home for centuries? To keep you out. Nice of you to leave us undisturbed until now. No doubt you think the truce has been broken since old Conor came around. I must confess, he had you worried didn't he? Such an insignificant boy to trouble such an ageless devil like you—I am surprised. All my fault really. Went around my brother's back, I did. Recruited Conor at my own expense and effort. Oh I realize he is my brother's by-blow with that Tinker wench but I could turn him for my purposes. I set him at odds with you. Didn't want you to know that he was my plan to make the People rise again. I know, I know, you wanted this place for your own, but so did I. We were worshiped once by humanity—you just managed to freak them all out and scare them half to death over the ages. To each his own I guess, but I sort of liked the worship. You just sucked up the power. So I suppose I am your enemy and the one responsible for pushing you to the limit. How about taking vengeance on me, and leave these poor folks alone?"

A rumble came from the beast in the river.

The Abbot laughed a little to himself. Rory was the supreme nonconformist. A little too much on the dark side for the Abbot's taste, yet he was grateful that Rory was stalling for time. Didn't know why. Hard to fathom where all this would lead.

A non-human scream was heard from beyond the bluffs—something dying that did not belong of this world. Piasa's head tilted upward, listening. Then it moved. Standing upright in the water, it raised its front talons and uttered something in a language foreign even to the Abbot. At once, green vapor coalesced around the claws and shot forward, up the hill and over the bluff.

The Tinker folk did not notice, engulfed in their grief stricken trance, and the changelings, always hungry for a show, continued clapping their hands in celebration. The monk's chanting faltered for a second, but carried on. Having rushed up and over the bluff, the vapor swirled, reversing direction and became opaque as it returned to the beast. Things were entwined in the foggy slime's tendrils, and before the mist disappeared, it deposited two forms on the shore.

Immediately, the Abbot recognized Drake and Cate McNabb, looking a little worse for the wear. Drake's eyes gleamed as he took in the situation, but Cate had eyes only for Piasa, and, at the moment, it only had eyes for her. Communing in some way from the look of ecstasy on the woman's face. Again, the Abbot was grateful for the delay of whatever was coming. He used the time to pray for a strengthening of his own barrier, unsure whether it could withstand the onslaught of Piasa and the changelings, perhaps even the villagers.

Into the night cried a voice, one the Abbot knew well. "Piasa!" it shouted. "Piasa, I have come!" As the Abbot looked up the bluff, there on a rocky outcrop stepped forward Conor Archer, bloodied, leaning on an oak staff.

"Now comes the time," whispered the Abbot.

Conor, himself, was appalled at what he saw. The figure of Piasa was alarming enough, but the changelings had built fires everywhere, lighting the scene below with an almost infernal glow. Like some body snatched zombies out of a horror film, nearly every denizen of Tinker's Grove stood mesmerized off in the meadow. Only the Abbot and his monks and a few of the mound Dwellers seemed safe enough, a faint luminescence surrounding them, Conor hoping that protective bubble had more strength than visibly evidenced.

I am not strong enough, he thought. No way, no how. The tingling began anyway. He knew it would. Was kind of surprised it was so slow in coming after he accepted whatever was supposed to be his destiny. Pretty cool being saved by the Morrigan's cloth and the White Stag. One minute, he was dying, bleeding to death, guts ripped apart and the next he was just damn fine. Hadn't a clue what he was supposed to do, so he sent Aunt Emily down another way to join the Abbot, if she could do that safely, while he reconnoitered the scene from the bluff. Just after he yelled Piasa's name, the uncomfortable tingling started again.

He looked at his hand on the oaken staff. Sure enough, the ribbon of skin was glowing and moving. Shining even through the blood on his neck and chest. And energy. Great energy flowing through him.

The Abbot saw it too. The ribbon of light on the bluff. "O God," he prayed, "not just the power, but the reason for using it as well—give him that or he won't be successful."

Conor surveyed the scene. I don't believe in half this stuff, but it's here whether I want it or not. Ghosts and visions and legends telling me to feel the land and what it needs to be delivered. I'm supposed to love a people I don't even much care for since they hate me anyway and see me as the source of all the bad things that have been happening. Even if I'm not the root of all the problems, I'm the catalyst.

He knew that evil was trying to make an inroad here at this place, at this time. He knew that Piasa was a manifestation of the evil that all religions and cultures have known through the ages. He knew that somehow the Crossroads Oak was part of the Tree of Life that gave this world its power and vitality and that since time began evil had gnawed at its roots and that once in a while someone had to come to make sure that evil got knocked back a step. He knew the big war had been won a long time ago. He grew up in a belief system that held that fact central. But he also knew that even losers seldom give up. He had been told evil was a big loser. Wasn't very sure about that, given the record of woe in the world, because evil always seemed to come back for another try, and if it was not resisted, good people, good creatures, and good land suffered. Even here in Tinker's Grove, an out of the way place, but central in the warfare that played out in the universe and world behind it.

He was supposed to fix all that. He wasn't sure how, until Piasa looked at him. Conor had called him out, and the beast had spotted him on the outcrop of the bluff. Howdy, you piece of pig shit, thought the boy. First time they had met eye to eye. Conor saw the malice, age old evil with lots of experience. For a moment, consciousness of his insignificance threatened to force him to retreat. Then he saw the strangest sight and heard the oddest sound—white swans flying and crying out to him. The voice of the wild children telling him to hold fast and stand strong. They circled above him, singing encouragement, begging him to listen to the others who pleaded for his help.

Suddenly, his body was wracked with pain again, not from Piasa, but from a cry deeper than the noise in the valley, more rich and varied than the malice from the demon. It rose up from the dirt and rocks around him. The land, Conor thought. The land is weeping. The cry of the very stones, the earth in the fields, the trees in the forest, even the waters demanded deliverance and the wailing of the elements fell like body blows upon the boy on the bluff. He felt himself being drawn into the cry, a pain of the ages as he found himself raising his arms as if in benediction upon the land and the river before him.

No words filled his mind, but meaning was imparted in his heart. The land beseeched him for release from bondage; the waters cried for union, the very world that gave him birth pled for banishment of evil and a uniting with a greater world long sundered from the only one Conor had ever known.

He saw the Abbot turn toward him, raising his crozier high. The moon caught the antlered staff and illuminated the ruby shining in the center of the Celtic cross that hung suspended between the rack. Body pounded by a wordless wail, horror gripping his heart as possessed children screamed in worship of the rising demon, sadness growing for the impotent townspeople, and then the voice he had heard so long ago, of a nameless biker man in a bar shouting to him the same words he spoke at the edge of another river, "Welcome to my world, lad—welcome to the family!" Rory, silhouetted by Piasa, laughing as he watched Conor change before his eyes.

All Conor could see were his hands stretched out before him, webbed and illuminated by light now pulsing on every inch of his skin—like he was on fire. Even the staff he grasped in his left hand seemed to shine with light. Bolts of pain shot through him as he morphed. His back split open and a cool breeze shot above him. He turned and saw rising, wings, beautiful wings, of iridescent color. Even in the lesser light of the moon, they were dazzling, unfolding under the night sky.

He had no time to admire the wonder as his head began to change, and then his mind. Feeling his human thoughts recede, he felt his face elongate into a raptor's visage, head crowned with the same iridescent feathers. At the same time, the webbed hands stretched into talons of fierce strength. He wasn't even surprised as he saw the claw of his left hand clasping, not a wooden oak staff, but a silver shining spear. Almost dispassionately, he saw the last vestige of his clothing fall away as the transformation completed the rest of his body, legs growing unknown muscles to flex the even larger talons now gripping the rock of the bluff.

Somewhere in the back of his mind, he felt the land sigh and whisper, "Thunderbird." That's what I am, he thought, and knew in his mind's eye that he had morphed into Piasa's worst nightmare, the savior of the native people who once walked the shores of this river, the only one who could truly, decisively, protect them from the Underwater Panther.

Everything that had been said to him now made sense: the Abbot's instruction to see the mountain behind the mountain, the Morrigan's cry to accept the fact that his body was listening to the land as it tried to change and adapt, even if he was not, and Rory—damn him to hell, and his insufferable, superior air demanding that Conor admit that he was different—and Aunt Emily's words of love and acceptance, she who would love him no matter what he became since he was her sister's son.

In his mind's eye, Conor saw again the image of the old Winnebago woman, Grandma Swift Deer, talking about Piasa with its age old struggle against the Thunderbird. He opened his mouth to shout to the Abbot, "I understand!" But what came from the depths of his being was a thunderous inhuman cry.

The land and the river spoke through the rage building up in Conor. He wanted to hold on to who he thought he was, but the pressing power, the potency of earth and water crushed in on him, becoming part of him. Amazed at the energy he felt coursing through his being, he whispered, "I accept,"—the same words he had spoken before and this time he actually meant it. No longer caring what those below heard, the Thunderbird cried out, "I am of the People, I am of the Roan, tied to the land, tied to the sea, fallen to the earth long ago, exiled but not abandoned, forgotten but not destroyed."

The moment he spoke the words, first in his mind, then uttered out loud, he felt his consciousness relax. It wasn't as if he lost control, but he let the power in him take hold. Above him, lightning flashed and thunder rolled without a cloud in the evening sky, and he knew. It wasn't a disturbance in the atmosphere, it was worlds coming together, two worlds colliding there in the valley, as good and evil struggled once more. He cried the inhuman shout again, and with golden raptor eyes, looked upon what he had become.

Then, the Thunderbird crouched, and sprang into the air, feathers flashing in the moonlight, as he cried and swept up over the valley, preparing to descend upon Piasa.

All in the valley had fallen to the ground, even the People of the Hollow Hills could not stand with the earth quaking. And as everyone slowly rose, they saw a shimmering in the air as the bluffs grew higher and the river expanded while the whole valley grew deeper and richer as the Otherworld manifested itself and worlds merged.

The Abbot observed all this with great wonder. Even he had never seen such a thing. He had walked the Otherworld of course, long ago, but never had that land manifested itself so completely in this reality. The world of Tinker's Grove was transformed. What a difference it made.

The whole valley itself looked like Paradise. Even in the night, with the moon much closer, shining brightly, and the stars beaming more brilliantly, it was possible now to see clearly. The ones who changed most were the People of the Hollow Hills and the changelings. To the Abbot, the People had always seemed almost translucent, faded nobility from another time and place. Not now. They were clearly taller, stronger, more beautiful than any human the Abbot had ever seen. No longer did the changelings look like the children they possessed. Their incarnate evil had pushed the human children's forms into the background. Pointed ears and twisted bodies, human in shape but alien in likeness, their activity had not stopped.

All this happened in a moment, as Conor launched himself into the sky.

THE RAISING OF THE
GWENNAN GORN

SEARCHING THE SKIES for the departing Morrigan couldn't hold Jace's attention, but the heralding cries of four white swans sounding above him focused his thought. Flying low, they circled Jace as he stood before the cave and then winged their way towards the main channel of the Wisconsin River.

God knows they'll have something to cry about when they reach that valley, thought Jace. Letting out a whoosh of breath, he stepped into the darkness of the cavern.

He couldn't begin to imagine how he was ever going to see in that inky blackness. Hugging the right side of the cave wall, he gingerly walked, trying to avoid the channel of black water to his left. Fifteen yards in, he could go no further. It was pitch black.

Jace shouted to the dark, "How am I supposed to find this ship, this *Gwennan Gorn*?" But as soon as he said the name, a faint golden light began to grow in the distance. At least bright enough for him to see. Walking again, faster now, he turned a corner and there it was. Just as he had remembered it—an old hulk of a ship, faintly Viking style but hybrid built, not as sleek as a real Norseman would have designed it but still carrying a decaying majesty. Leaning against the side of the cave wall, faintly luminescent, the ship gave out an expectation of waiting, like an abandoned house with a gaping hole where the door had once been. As if an invitation had been given, but the kind of welcome still undecided.

It'll never float, thought Jace. The hull was breached, ancient oaken planks stove in below the water line. How could he possibly use it tonight to help his friends? That's when he heard the distant thunderclap and felt the earth begin to shake. Instead of the roof of the cave falling, Jace saw it expand, growing higher, the underground river channel widening beneath. Where once there was bare rock wall, now another cave appeared sloping away from the water deep into the side of the bluff. The ship itself had moved. In the midst of its ruined luminiscence, it seemed to shake itself aright, scattering motes of light. A broken, split, decayed mast became whole; rotten planks sealed themselves; from the prow of the leaping seal, the ship began to glow in brilliant color like a newly dyed barbarian tartan. Its fifty feet of length now floated quietly in the channel.

Jace reached up to touch the prow. He stroked the smooth wood and heard the faraway echo of music. It was coming from the newly opened passage, sloping away in the distance into the solid rock of the bluff. For a moment, he couldn't understand the words—Celtic they seemed to him. Then his mind clicked into gear—translating the song for him, or maybe he just became able to understand. Couldn't really figure out why, maybe it was that otherworldly Wisdom again, but no matter. It was men who were singing, and he knew who they were. Far away the song seemed, but he knew it was Madoc's men, notes of single-minded rage echoing in the cavern, and they were marching to war.

Jace didn't wait long. Light grew more brilliant as the People of the Hollow Hills came closer. Then he saw them. Tall they were, and golden eyed. That's how they appeared to Jace as they stepped out into the main cavern, carrying torches and weapons. Virtually no armor, but that didn't matter. Somehow, the golden bands around muscled arms and silver torcs around their necks, along with their brightly colored tunics, made them look invincible. Of course, it didn't hurt to have various swords of bronze, types of long bows and light spears to complete the picture. At least thirty of them, he thought, and they looked inhuman in their martial beauty— bodies ready for battle, eyes glinting in anticipation of war. Jace wanted to dismiss this anachronism, a war band out of place in this new millennium. Still, they were his help and he wasn't about to complain.

When the last warrior stepped from the cave, they silenced their song, forming two ranks facing Jace, silently measuring the boy before them.

Stepping forward, a tall warrior, silver torc flashing in torch light, reached out his arm and with his hand grasped Jace's chin.

"Small in stature, barely bearded, dressed like a peasant—surely Madoc jests over this, this boy being the Champion." A mocking laughter whispered through the ranks.

Jace, too, laughed about it later, but at the moment, he thought the freak from the Otherworld reminded him of that asshole of a captain from Pike's Point football team, who a couple of weeks earlier, had ridiculed Jace at the coin toss, mocked him as the pissant center of a candy-ass football team. Jace hated the loss of face then and he didn't much like it now so he did the same thing to the warrior as he did to the opposing captain at the game. He landed him flat on his back with a shoulder block that took the warrior by surprise. At the game, he waited for the first play to knock some sense into the captain, but here, he just barreled into the huge man. Not much Wisdom in it, thought Jace, but a whole lot of brawn—felt good too. Clean, righteous, violence rather than that evil crap that had been going down for days.

The warrior blinked in the flickering light as Jace stood over him, hands clenched. The mocking laughter turned from Jace and wafted over the fallen man.

"Here's to the boy, Gwydion!" shouted one of the other men. "Lots of pluck in the peasant even if he is just a human."

Gwydion snarled and made to leap up but Jace was having none of it. He reached back and pulled his sword—blue runes flickering on its gleaming metal blade. Before Gwydion could even rise, the point touched his throat.

A hissing could be heard—Jace wondered if it was some new weapon when Gwydion spoke. "If you do not mind, lad, moving the sword the iron in it makes me uncomfortable."

Jace saw the wisp of smoke then, rising from the warrior and traced the hiss to the point of his sword, burning the neck of Gwydion. His anger vanished and he stepped back in horror.

"Man, I'm sorry! Didn't mean to hurt you. Didn't know this stuff was poison to you."

A wry smile twisting on his face, Gwydion accepted Jace's offered hand and pulled himself upright. "Unless you thrust that blade into me, it cannot kill us despite what the legends say, but that we don't like it and would rather not be around the accursed iron—well, 'tis true."

"Look," said Jace, "I don't have much time. Conor's in trouble and Madoc told me that I'd have to use this ship sooner or later when danger came. I'm thinking sooner."

"Indeed, lad," said Gwydion, "the time is now and that is why we are here, warriors of the Roan—to man this ship, to sail it once more."

"To carry you to your doom!" said a voice from the back of the crowd. The warriors parted and Jace saw Madoc standing tall.

Madoc gently cuffed the side of Gwydion's head as he passed the soldier and stood before Jace. "Now is the time, young one; now is the hour, O Champion. Now you must earn the respect of my men and save my son."

"Save him yourself," spat Jason, who was thoroughly miffed by all the portentous posturing of the prince. "He's your son."

"I cannot ... intervene," said Madoc sadly. "Though centuries separate our times, I too was young once and felt betrayal and loss, as you have had to experience. My son has harmed you. This I know. And yet, the great who walk among the fields of the earth must know that personal considerations can never ultimately force one from the destined path. He is still your friend, even in your anger. My time to intervene in this earth's history is waning. You heard the thunder; you saw the ship revive. My son has joined the worlds together, if but for a brief time. Only when the worlds are one again in perpetuity will I be able to claim the power I should have."

"Did you fall from heaven?" asked Jace, unable to keep himself from questioning.

"Nay, none whom you see before you are that old. But all of us come from those that did, and we are as forsaken by God, as they. The Morrigan, however, pestilential crow that she is, she remembers what it was like and she has told us around the fires of centuries past when fresh from the sea we crawled on the ground. She filled our minds with tales of past glories and what we could someday yet be. That is what I seek, O Champion. I am not striving for heaven. At least not yet. I am simply looking to reunite worlds, so that I can be ..."

"What?" said Jace, "The ruler, the once and future king, the puppet master of some new world order?"

"No," said Madoc, "not king, just myself."

"And that, boy," said Gwydion, "would be more than any king or ruler. We of the Roan would walk freely again, aboveground on land rather than the sea, and we would show the humans how to truly live."

"Or enslave them," whispered Jace.

"Come, Madoc," said Gwydion, "we do not need him. Let us sail, let us do battle with Piasa. It is a war long overdue."

"No," said Madoc, "we do need him." Turning to Jace, he said, "Please, save my son; we can talk later, but now he needs your protection, and only you can accomplish that task tonight. We are merely here to help you on your way."

Staring at the prince in silence, Jace then reluctantly nodded his head and Madoc turned to his men. Some unspoken command leapt between them for as one, they jumped for the ship and in moments had manned the oars.

"I will take the helm, young Champion," said Madoc. "Your place is on the prow."

Jace stepped forward and jumped up the side of the vessel. For the first time he took a good look at the leaping seal arising from the front of the ship. It's back arched and there, in the middle of the carved body was a place to stand on top of the seal, places where feet should be planted. Gingerly, Jace stepped onto the markings and instantly felt his hold solidify. Some magic was at work, he supposed. Couldn't fall off if I tried, he thought.

Madoc looked up at him. "Do not worry Jason Michaels. On this most sad of nights for you, joy is coming. Watch, and learn, and rejoice, for the *Gwennan Gorn* goes to war again!"

With a thump the oars extended and on either side of the ship descended into the water, the warriors pulling in unison. Majestically, she began to move. The channel had definitely widened, thought Jace. Once in the middle of the waters, the shoreline on either side was at least fifty yards away. The ship sent out more light now, its source unknown to Jace. It was bright enough to see several yards ahead. They should have reached the entrance to the cave long before, but everything seemed larger, more immense. Just as Jace was beginning to wonder where they even were, the cave opening appeared ahead, much greater in size but still recognizable. With only the sound of the oars, the *Gwennan Gorn* slipped into White Creek, now, a major body of water, rather than simply a back water slough.

Once out into the night, the Roan began singing some elemental war song. Jace felt a litt in his soul that felt strangely embarrassing. He risked a glance behind him and found Gwydion manning first chair and grinning up at him.

"The battle lust, lad. That's what you are feeling. It comes upon you. As good as a woman, in its own way."

Jace was grateful it was night so the warrior could not see him blush. Gwydion had spoken truly. Jace felt a twisting in his gut, almost a lust akin to what he felt when the Morrigan had kissed him earlier in the evening. Guilty, he thought he should have visions of Nora in his mind, but the upcoming battle drew him like the mysterious Morrigan. He wanted the fight, like he wanted her. His eye caught several other warriors raising the sail, cream colored and thick with a leaping seal surrounded by a rune covered circle. Lifting the sail, a breeze filled the canvas, the men stopping their song long enough to cheer heartily. Even Madoc was grinning. Gwydion rose and threw his blue cloak across the shoulders of Jace. "This is not a place for peasant garb, Champion. Wear this *brioch* with honor as the warrior you are called to be."

"A long time since last we sailed," shouted Madoc, "but a worthy time to journey again. Too long have the stories been silent about the magnificent lady, the *Gwennan Gorn*. Too long has she been still. Only the One knows what this night shall hold, not the crow that flies above, nor the barrow prince hidden in the mound, nor his brother the one who walks the twilight bound. It may be that the Worm shall drag us down, destroy us, deny us, to the great deeps carry us, until each one of us, in despair drowns. If that is the doom of the Roan, so be it, for better to sail this night, than let that foul thing have its way with the children of men who know little of wisdom, less of true evil, but do not deserve this fate. Look my friends upon the prow; we carry the Champion of Men and of Roan. Upon the seal argent he stands, carrying the Sword of Light, a weapon both friend and foe to us, but tonight an ally in the struggle dark. The union of men and Roan, sundered through the ages, brought together for a brief time tonight, to defeat a common enemy, the Devourer of Souls who gnaws at the roots of the Tree of the World. Without the Champion we fail, with him, a chance at success. But all is poised on a breath of the wind, for the coming of the one who is both Roan and man—my son—whom many of you wanted killed in his crib so long ago. But he lives for this day, our day, the day of destiny when our exile shall begin to come to an end. Champion, hear; if he dies we are sorely doomed. Protect him for his task, guard him from evil and we will be the arms and force that give you the time to complete your task. Sail men, put on the roar of battle, let the beast hear you coming, for the *Gwennan Gorn* goes to war once again!"

Jace understood little of all that, but it was like electricity to his body. The thump of the oars turning, the splash of them churning the water, the matching song of the warriors filled his heart with fire. He turned and saw Madoc at the tiller, crimson cloak flying in the wind, eyes wild and free, pointing at him and smiling with joy. It was as if power shuddered through Jace, and with the Roan behind him singing and shouting, he felt strength rising within him. Billowing his cloak, a fresh breeze struck his face, filling his lungs. No trouble holding the sword high. As the metal caught the cold white light of the moon, he felt the boat shift as if it was rising a little. Good thing too, for before him rose an immense barrier. In his world, the barrier between White Creek and the Wisconsin was a formidable mass of twisted detritus and shattered trees, but here, it looked like a walled oak fortress.

"Pay the wall no mind!" shouted Madoc. "She is a warship and can easily pass."

So Jace waited, not breathing as the ship pressed on with great speed. In concert, the oars lifted to the skies, and then, the ship hit the wall with tremendous force. No vessel made of wood in Jace's world could have withstood that impact, but the *Gwennan Gorn* sliced through the mass of trees and brush that blocked the way. Like ice breaking, the barrier shook, and Jace found himself dodging branches thrown up into the air. The ship never slowed in speed, and the song of the warriors never faltered, but grew louder. In a shower of light, the vessel burst through the barrier and Jace's eyes were bombarded with a kaleidoscope of images. Fires burning on the banks. Demons cavorting on the shore. Abbot Malachy and some of the Roan stood with the rest of the monks enshrouded by white light on the Indian mound, the Abbot's crozier held high. Jace had no doubt that was the power that pushed the dark away. But what grabbed his vision and froze it was the immense thing in the river. Roiling in white foam, the waters themselves had transformed the placid Wisconsin into a powerful force of nature.

Simply put, the river was huge, and Piasa looked right at home. Like a southwestern Wisconsin Godzilla thought Jace. He noticed, too, the antlered, morphing face; but to him the Devourer, while physical in nature, also was emitting something more. As if on coming close to it, another doorway, not to the Otherworld, was opening, and it led down, down under the hills beneath the earth to places where no living thing should ever go. It was repulsive, dangerous and deadly, thought Jace. And we've got to fight it.

As his stomach turned in horror, he heard a piercing cry from the sky. Dark as it was, he could see the figure aloft clearly. A winged man/bird thing, he thought. Flying high and iridescent in the moonlight. Piasa saw it too, for its attention had turned from the riverbank to the skies.

For a moment the Thunderbird, for even Jace now could see what the form was, had paused aloft, wings outspread, hovering in the air. Then with a cry of righteous rage, it screamed out a challenge and plummeted from the sky towards Piasa.

The Devourer of Souls raged back and rose again from the water, this time on two thick reptilian legs. Front paws outstretched like a grizzly bear, ready to grasp and tear, and snout morphing from panther to tiger, bear to lion, it waited to snatch the plummeting figure in its maw.

"Conor," whispered Jace. "The thing in the air has to be Conor." Where the scream came from, Jace never knew, but he uttered such a cry that the warriors in the ship answered immediately with rage of their own. Madoc turned the ship towards Piasa and it glided swiftly toward the beast.

Jace swung toward Piasa as he stood on the prow and now the Devourer risked a moment to meet its new pursuer. Green eyes of malice pierced the boy's heart and for a moment he quailed. But his feet were secure, the sword was strong, and something in his heart felt like singing and he gave himself to the battle lust, opened wide his arms and said, "Come on you mean motherfucker, take on somebody your own size, not some Chicago kid who isn't sure if he's man or beast." He shook the sword in the air. "This is the Sword of Light and it seeks to bite the dark. Come to me, Devourer of Souls."

And Piasa came.

AT LAST TO FLY

"GET UP!" SAID the voice. "Get up now."

Nora raised a tear-stained face to the speaker above her. My God, she thought, another one of those McNabb cretins. After Rafe and Fergal had forced her to watch the murder of her grandmother, they loped off with the other changelings, though where to she did not know. Nora had cradled the bloody body of Dorothy Martin, sightless eyes staring up into the night. Now, she had to stare into the face of Gordy, smirking at her.

"Not a good idea to mess with my mother and Dr. Drake, is it?" he asked. Kicking the dusty ground with a booted foot, he began to laugh.

"Won't be so funny once the state patrol arrives," said Nora, hoping against hope she was right.

"Won't be coming," he answered. "Had them detour traffic around Tinker's Grove for a couple of days. Told them DIOGENE needed to replace some water mains down by the plant. Nothing can come from the south and nothing from the north either. Tinker's Grove is in a world of its own."

"Got it all figured out, don't you Gordy," said Nora, gently laying her grandmother's head to the ground. "You've called up the Otherworld and think you have everything in control, that you can manipulate things in that reality like you do here."

"Seems to be working out okay so far, don't you think?"

"Maybe, maybe not," she answered, looking more carefully at him. "You look normal, not like your brothers. Why is that? Didn't you do a deal with the demon like they did?"

"Sure did," said Gordy, "but unlike them, I'm a patient man. Drake wanted to rush whatever plans Piasa had. Thought I'd see what the results would be with my brothers before he pushed ahead with me."

"They're freaks you know; mutants who don't have much time to live."

"You're a freak as well, of nature if not science," snapped Gordy. "Though you might be right—they're not my little brothers anymore. But the power they have. Even I can feel it. Watch me, Nora."

Gordon stuck out his hand and held it before his face. Nora thought herself silly thinking that there was no webbing between the fingers. Whatever power Gordy had was bought by dealing with the devil, not by genetics, heritage or destiny. But her thoughts were shattered as she watched his fingers grow and the nails sharpen.

"I can control it pretty well, darling," he said. "I've decided that I won't let the change control me like it does my brothers. Don't mind being beholden to Piasa, but I like to keep my free will if you know what I mean."

Nora saw the facial features of Gordon sharpen. She wasn't sure what he would become if he let the change happen, but the predatory look in his eyes made her certain that few would stand much of a chance facing him once the transformation was complete.

Then he was back to normal, talking gently to her.

"Nora, Nora, Nora, I really am sorry about your grandmother. But it doesn't have to be that way with you. The town's never going to be the same after tonight. Join me, won't you? I can help you be everything you once thought of becoming."

"What's going to happen, Gordy? What's tomorrow going to look like here in Tinker's Grove?"

"Power is what is going to happen, for me, for my family, and for anyone to whom I choose to give it. Two worlds are coming together and the bottom line is this. For that to happen, Piasa must be released into this world, not as a phantom or a myth, or a thing that once in a while can snatch a meal from a credulous human. No. The worlds must be fused so that it can walk this land in all its fullness. It needs to feed, you see.

"The Otherworld is dying. So Piasa whispers in my mind. Without a connection with this world, the spectacular wonders of that one fade and die. In some way, the Otherworld needs us to exist. I guess it is supposed to be part of this reality, but we wretched moderns have pretty much severed the connection. Like a body split in two, like a man separated from his soul, the whole begins to die. Even our own world fades.

"Don't quite understand it all myself, but look at the facts. Those beings in the Indian mounds—they can't do much here; they are dwindling. You 'dark ones' sprout like spring flowers and wither by summer's end—you can't seem to exist well here either. Science doesn't have any explanation for you. Even your genetic abnormality is but an odd piece in the puzzle of your existence.

"But Piasa is offering a chance for all of us to become something else and claim both worlds for our own. It's a risk, I know. A toss of the dice.

Piasa is evil; Drake isn't much better, but my mother has navigated these waters without harm. Rich, powerful land owner, and now she wants more too. I say we take it Nora. There's always a price." He started chuckling, "I mean look at my brothers—they'll never woo the girls now. 'Course they can take whatever they want."

"This world won't let you do it. It will fight you."

"Doubt it, Nora. Know why? Because the evil of the Otherworld already walks here. Piasa and what it represents has ways of infiltrating this world. Been here a long time. Look at what's happening. Civilization itself is shattering and becoming less cohesive. Technology grows, morality shrinks, violence looms, peace flees. That's how it's been lately. Just because Piasa wants a more incarnate presence doesn't mean people are going to freak out. It will be more of the same, just a bit more intense. And by the time folks realize what's really happening, well, it will be too late."

He grabbed her arm. "So come with me now to the river. That's where things are happening. Look toward the edge of town."

Thinking it was a growing fog, she saw instead that it was a shimmer and warping of the atmosphere, as if something was creeping through the town and changing it.

"What is it?" she asked.

"The Otherworld," said Gordon, "come to bring us to our true home."

"I'm not going with you."

"Not an option," he said, grinning and pulling her up the street.

A shot rang out and a cloud of dust exploded just a foot before Gordon McNabb. His jaw dropped in shock. Out of the shadows, right by the bank, stepped Jim Warren. The banker looked especially haggard, hands gripped on the stock of the rifle as if it was his only hold on reality.

"You stop right there, McNabb. You and your kinfolk have done enough damage for the night. Let the girl go."

"And if I don't?" said Gordy.

"Then I'll kill you where you stand." He looked past Gordon at the body of Dort Martin. "Don't think I'll feel real bad if another body lies down in this street."

Gordon let go of Nora and raised his hands. "Let's not get hasty, Jim. There's plenty for you too, after tonight. I know; Piasa has told me."

"Don't want to hear about it. Far as I'm concerned all that stuff is myth."

"Well what about what you saw tonight? Even a skeptic like you ought to put aside your disbelief."

"I saw a town lose its mind this evening," said Jim Warren. "I've watched it lose its soul the past few days. I've seen you and your family and that Drake fellow do your best to make all that happen. I can't make things better, but I can stop you from hurting this girl who's never done anything wrong to you."

"I'm taking her, Jim. She's essential to the plan."

Warren raised the rifle. "I'll see you dead, Gordy. Make no mistake about it."

Gordy laughed and turned away from Jim reaching for Nora. The girl shrank back and would have run, but the gun cracked again. Gordy screamed in the night.

"You son of a bitch; you shot out my knee!"

"Thought I was a better aim," said Warren. "I had pointed toward your motherless heart."

The young man writhed on the ground as Nora ran past him to Jim.

"You all right?" he asked.

"Fine, but those creatures—they killed my grandmother and then they and all the townsfolk took off toward the river. I've got to get there."

"No," said Jim, "she'd want you to stay with me. Let me lock this poor excuse for a man in my vault and I'll take you home. You'll be safe there."

She didn't know what else to do. On the verge of accepting his offer, she suddenly heard cries in the night. The fluting of the swans—she recognized it from the day before. O'Leary's children were coming back.

"What in the sam hell is this?" said Jim, looking up at the sky and seeing four birds wheeling just above the buildings of downtown Tinker's Grove, their white wings flashing in the moonlight.

They landed in front of the two. The swans turned as one and hissed at the spasming figure Gordon McNabb, in his own little world of pain.

"What are these?" said Jim.

"You know who and what they are," said Nora. Reaching out a tentative hand, she touched his arm, "But you don't want to believe."

The birds moved closer and began to shepherd the two away from Gordon and towards the approaching disruption that was slowly making its way down the street from the outskirts of town.

"I have to go with them," she said.

Jim Warren's face looked bleak. "I just don't understand. Everything that I thought was true is changed."

Nora smiled and touched his face. "Not everything, Mr. Warren. There's still goodness here, and courage. You're a rock, even if you don't see what's really happening. Lock Gordon up, and wait; hopefully Conor and Jace can make things okay."

With that she walked with the swans. Their waddling gait sped up and they became less awkward as they approached flight. Nora laughed as she ran with them. She remembered a program where humans raised swans from chicks and taught them to migrate. They used ultra-light planes to lead them on their migratory routes. She thought of that as she ran with them and as they took flight, they kept up with her, voicing their song by her side. Faster and faster she ran, and still the swans flew by her side. Never had she run so swiftly. They sounded as one and then lifted higher into the sky, just as they passed into the morphing mist. For a moment, Nora was disoriented as everything expanded and the air became richer. She expected the swans to disappear from her sight. Only Nora was not left behind. She stayed by them. For a moment she thought she was running, keeping up the pace, but then she looked down and saw the ground receding. Opening her mouth to scream, what came out instead was the beautiful trumpet of a white swan flying with her compatriots on that All Hallow's Eve.

Jim Warren saw it all. Couldn't deny what his sight confirmed, but he didn't have to process it either. Turning to Gordon, he saw the young man trying to change as well.

"If those hands get any longer, and those nails any more pointy, and if your filthy teeth begin to fang out from under your lips, I'll shoot your head off. Do you comprehend what I'm saying?"

Gordy nodded, falling back into the street.

"Get up. I want you more acquainted with my vault."

THE BATTLE BEGINS

TO THE ABBOT, everything happened at once. He saw the Thunderbird reach the apogee of its flight. Out the corner of his eye, he glimpsed a bedraggled Emily O'Rourke finally make it to the mound. From the sky behind him came the haunting cry of swans and suddenly feathers were everywhere as five huge birds landed, one of them instantly transforming into Nora Martin. But he had no time to even gasp for a booming and snapping came from the river. Just up White Creek way, the Abbot could see that the huge barrier of fallen trees and brush that effectively hid that slough, now a big river in itself, was splitting asunder. Crashing merrily through it came the *Gwennan Gorn*. Astonished, Malachy beheld Jason Michaels perched on the prow, blue cloak flying, arms stretched wide and in one of them, the gleaming Sword of Light. He was laughing and the Abbot thought the boy had lost his mind. More than simply smashing through the barrier, a warlike chant rose from the ship as the oars, spread like wings, now dipped back into the river as Madoc and his warriors sang themselves into the main channel of the Wisconsin.

Piasa turned to face the ship, ignoring the plummeting Thunderbird. With seconds before ship, beast and bird collided, Malachy let the glowing dome of protection around the remaining Roan and his monks die. Pointing the top of the antlered crozier at the battle in the river, he sent a ruby red beam of light at the Devourer, hoping to lend a distraction to aid the Thunderbird and the fast approaching ship. The Abbot was no longer worried about an attack from the changelings or even Drake or Cate. All eyes were feasting on the scene in the river.

With a thunderous collision the *Gwennan Gorn* slammed into Piasa with little effect for the beast barely budged. But then down swung Jace's sword and it bit deep into what passed as flesh for the Devourer. Piasa lifted its horned head and screamed. Afterwards, all said, the features on the morphing face resolved themselves for a moment into something almost human, a noble visage ruined with gore and marks of violence. The coalescing was momentary for the Thunderbird, spear thrust out before itself, reached the nadir of its dive and hit Piasa in the neck, embedding the spear deep within.

Another raging scream tore through the night, ripping at the hearts of all who heard. The changelings began running in circles clapping their ears with their elongated claw-like hands. Tears were running down the faces of Drake and Cate. The Abbot watched as Cate reached out a pathetic hand at the beast, her lover sorely wounded.

The Thunderbird dug its talons more firmly into Piasa's back, seeking leverage to force the spear even more deeply. Without effect, the Devourer vainly reached around trying to grasp the Thunderbird in its own claws; but every time Piasa came close, its adversary beat wings and lifted out of reach, only to plummet and grasp again.

Half the warriors had deserted the oars and rushed to assist Jace, who hadn't ceased slashing the belly of the beast. New wounds to attend to, Piasa swept its gaze down at the ship and its eyes rested on the human, the source of the pain in its gut. For all its immensity, Piasa could move like a panther and swiftly reached for the boy. Gwydion saw the movement and threw himself between. A horrendous claw grasped, lifting him upward and the chieftain found himself looking into Piasa's maw.

Madoc turned the tiller hard, yelling for his men to push his ship free. The remaining oarsmen acted as one, a mighty fist turning the ship and giving Jace another chance at the armored monster's underbelly thinking that maybe, like the dragons in children's tales, Piasa had a weak spot.

Ignoring the ship, Piasa concentrated on its captive. Putrid breath fell on Gwydion's face, and then a voice spoke, a sibilant hiss easily heard by Jace through the battle noise, "Gwydion, son of Siobhan, whom I knew well in a time long past—this is your doom for opposing me." The serpent tongue stretched out and touched the chest of the warrior, withdrew, and then fast as lightning whipped back out of the monster's mouth and punched a hole twice as big as a man's hand in the center of the warrior's body. Gwydion screamed, blood everywhere dropping into the river as motes of light. As his body dissolved like a sunbeam shaken apart by a cloud there in the grasp of the beast, the screams echoed more softly on the hills, as, with a snarl, Piasa turned once again to Jace.

The Thunderbird itself shrieked in rage and yanked the spear from the monster's flesh, this time hovering and aiming for the eye. It thrust true and the spear buried itself in the Devourer's orb. A shudder shook the beast and instead of flailing or screaming it came to a standstill. The Thunderbird, one claw on the spear, flapped its iridescent wings, hovering in front of the beast. Jace paused, arm ready for another thrust of his own sword.

Piasa slowly turned its face to glare at the Thunderbird with its one remaining good eye. The collective breath of all those who watched released in a horrified gasp as the beast began to laugh—at least that's what it sounded like.

Then, fast as a snake, Piasa leapt out of the water, snatching the Thunderbird in mid-air, and dove, reaching out and sweeping Jace as well into the depths. All three disappeared between the waves, leaving the *Gwennan Gorn* floating alone.

CHAOS ON SHORE

"NO!" CRIED THE Abbot, as chaos burst out on shore. Changelings laughed with glee and Drake and Cate got to their feet daring to hope that Piasa might yet be victorious.

"Do something!" said Emily.

"Look!" said the Abbot. "Piasa rises from the depths."

Indeed, the Devourer's back appeared as the beast humped along the water, aiming for the opposite shore.

Emily hissed her concern, "Now, Malachy, while there is still a chance the boys are alive."

Malachy did not answer, though his gaze swept the quiescent ship, the only movement being Madoc's scramble to assemble and account for his surviving warriors.

"Those boys are on their own?" questioned Emily. "Unacceptable, Malachy!"

"But true, none the less. You knew this might happen. This conflict was meant to be. Exactly how it was to play out was never fully revealed to us."

"But they're boys!" said Emily, heartbroken.

"Boys with much power," said Malachy. "Have a little faith, Emily. The One who created them, redeemed them, watched over them since birth, will surely not abandon them now. Besides, we have more immediate pressing problems. Look."

Indeed, Drake had turned from the river and began to take charge of the changelings. While the monks and Madoc's people seeking refuge on the mound could not hear his incantation, they felt its power to bind and command reaching out even to them, blanketing them with despair and hopelessness. The only ones not affected seemed to be the silent villagers standing coma-like on the rolling hillside meadow.

Rory, no longer hindered by the barrier now fallen, ran to the mound and berated all present.

"Well done! You've let the beast get its hands on our only hope. You were supposed to empower Conor, not give him over to his mortal enemy. And my brother …" Here, Rory turned a contemptuous glance at the ship floating silently in the middle of the channel. "Useless as always, totally unable to effect any real change for the Roan."

"Rory, please," said the Abbot, "can you not feel it in the air? Whatever has happened is not over. More is to come and I fear it will not be for good."

A howling reached their ears. Between the mound and the townspeople stood Oz, alone, face turned towards the river now emptied of Piasa and Thunderbird. Arms slack at his sides, ear buds useless around his neck, the strange man wordlessly continued to moan. Neither the changelings, villagers, monks nor the remnants of Madoc's people moved toward him. For a moment, they were mesmerized by the sound of loss and woe emanating from his body. Then, as if an invisible hand was slapping the face of Oz, the man child's head jerked back and forth. The howling ceased, his eyes cleared and he looked across the waters to the farther shore.

"Oz!" cried the Abbot. "Can you hear me?"

Slowly, Oz turned toward the Abbot. An intelligence shown in his eyes that the Abbot had never seen. But whatever looked out from that face that had known only confusion and ambiguity before was human no longer. It tried to work Oz's mouth, but the sounds that came from him did not match the attempts at human speech. It was as if the words were being expelled with only a half-hearted attempt to match Oz's mouth to the words spoken.

"I took all of the she wolf's three,
Took the children whose bodies you see;
Mine are they whom I bind to me.
Water and mist, to blood and bone,
Life from the worlds drains to my own.
Monsters from myth, the stories known,
Vessels through which my evil is sown.
From heaven's heights my body thrown,
I am the Worm that gnaws the world's bone,
Snatching the bird that against me has flown.
Death shall come and life shall flee,
Now that the one upon the Tree,
Is fallen, fallen, fallen as me,
Mine are they whom I bind to me."

"Piasa!" said Emily. "It speaks through him! But, Conor wounded it."

"Not badly enough," said the Abbot. "But possessing Oz …"

The Abbot turned to those on the mound. "Beware, a power is present here that seeks only to destroy. Do not listen, do not look, do not witness. Only pay enough attention to protect yourself or others. The Liar, the Devourer, this Worm is older than the bowels of the earth that shelters it."

The thing in Oz laughed. "You are not my first concern, Malachy. I go to him now, the one you call 'your hope,' but leave you with something to keep you busy." The body of Oz jerked forward and walked down to the shoreline. "My little changelings," it said, "time for you to feast." The Oz thing shambled over to where Drake and Cate stood. "Druid," said the voice, "give them the power to finish these fools. And you, dearest Cate, I saw your tears and know your love. Do not despair, you shall be with me and the sacrifice of your two sons shall not be forgotten."

Cate fell to her knees and kissed Oz's hand. Drake took to his knees as well, lowering his eyes from the fierce intelligence that gleamed from Oz's gaze.

The water in front of Oz began to bubble and steam and the thing inside of Oz began to laugh. "Oh, Father Abbot," it said, "remember this one? Such an easy thing to replicate, walking on water."

Oz shuffled onto the water and immediately a steaming, bubbling path shot forward to the other side as upon that road Oz now walked, leaving chaos in his wake, blanketed by a rising vapor from the river.

The fog moved quickly onto shore, and the Abbot divined the purpose behind it.

"Come to me now!" he shouted. "All you townspeople come to the mound!"

He uttered the prayer again to raise the barrier, but no one in the meadow moved. Their gazes were fixed on their once children whose shadows could still be seen in the gathering gloom moving closer to their parents.

"They are not yours!" cried the Abbot. "They are not themselves. Come to me before it is too late."

But they did not come. And the fog fell upon them all.

PIASA'S LAIR

JACE KNEW THE sword was keeping him from drowning. How, he wasn't exactly sure, but he felt the power of the blade flowing through his body. So the fact that Piasa held him firmly in its claw, deep in the embrace of the river, and the strange sensation of rushing water past his face frightened him less than he would have expected. He just hoped to God that whatever remained of Conor in that Thunderbird costume had the sense to keep hold of that spear, a weapon surely akin to his blade.

Though he couldn't see anything, he knew they were moving swiftly. Wondered where, but was more amazed that the thing holding him hadn't crushed the life out of him by now. Maybe it couldn't because of the sword. Whatever. He saw faint light above him and realized that their direction had changed. The surface couldn't be far away, lit by the harvest moon. Wishful thinking, probably, but he was already needing a breath of fresh air.

Piasa broke the water's surface with a furious speed and Jace watched its bat wings flare and lift all three of them into the air. Not far it turned out. Jace recognized the shore opposite the mound, even if it was in its Otherworldly phase. Almost gently, Piasa set the two of them down on the sand, not far from the entrance to White Creek. With a strange sigh, Piasa collapsed on its side.

"We killed the son of a bitch!" whooped Jace, getting up and running to the prone figure of Conor. The Thunderbird guise was already melting off of him as he changed back to the person Jace knew so well. But he didn't move, and as the Thunderbird wings withdrew into Conor's body, Jace was struck by how fragile he looked. Really like a bird, thought Jace, and then realizing Conor was laying there without a stitch of clothing on, he unclasped Gwydion's cloak and threw it over Conor.

The boy didn't even know Jace was there. As he came back to consciousness, he remembered everything, the power, the flight, the fight. He knew he had hurt Piasa, yet he had been so much more than himself when he did it. Lifting up his head, he stared at the Devourer, its ruined eye leaking fluid into the sand. The face of the beast still swirled beneath a twisted rack of antlers in all its morphing splendor. Watching the patterns there, Conor saw pictures in those swirling shapes that he almost recognized. He should have felt elated, but a terrible tiredness suffused his body. Accepting who he was and what he had just done seemed only to bring more pain, more mountains to climb.

Then he heard Jace beside him. "Conor, can you hear me?"

"Yeah," croaked Conor, swinging his gaze to look at his friend. "What a fight, huh? And Jace, where did you learn to swing a sword like that?"

"From the same school that gave you flying lessons," said Jace. He reached down to lift up Conor. But before he could complete the task, they both heard a splashing behind them. For a moment, they couldn't make out what they were looking at. It seemed as if an arrow of mist and steam had driven itself across the water. A shape was there moving towards the shore, moving with a stumbling and shambling gait. As it stepped on the sand, they both recognized Oz. How he did it, they couldn't figure out, but Conor remembered that there was more in that strange man than met the eye.

"Jace," said Conor. "What's he doing here?"

"Don't know," said Jace, "but don't let go of your spear." His own hand tightened on the sword.

"Evening Oz," said Conor.

The figure before them laughed and a most cultured voice spoke, "He is not here tonight, but I am, Conor Archer. And I must say, you have done great damage to my incarnate body." The speaker who wore Oz's form ran a hand over the fallen figure of Piasa. "It served me well, though, in this land. I could watch and wait, observe and plan. Piasa had its limits however. Tell me Conor, when you were the Thunderbird, how clearly did you think?"

Despite his misgivings, Conor felt himself compelled to answer, "Well, I knew I was myself, but the thoughts I had, they were …"

"Primitive? Bestial? My sentiments exactly. I loved the predatory nature, the lust to destroy in Piasa, but such an incarnation made me so basely violent. Still, like I said, it had its uses."

"Who are you?" asked Jace.

Disdain crept over Oz's face. "That hurt you know, Jason Michaels. Your blow. The sword cut deeply, as did your spear, Conor. But I can forgive you both."

"And we should care? Why?" asked Jace.

"Because you are mine now. Not that I don't grant you the victory in some small way here, but you still are mine and will willingly be so."

"I won't serve you, whatever or whoever you are," said Conor, pulling himself upright with the spear.

"Yes, you will, once I show you what you have now become of your own free will. Why, even your friend here, the one you call Champion, can watch and affirm that I speak truth."

Oz reached out with a hand and touched the morphing face of what seemed to be the dead Piasa. "The face of this Manitou was what drew me to it in the first place. Always changing, never the same. Like the Crossroads Tree, it is a liminal place. Forgive me Jace, I speak too technically; you are a jock after all—I mean it is a threshold space, a thin place, a portal to other destinations. And a powerful one. It can take us wherever we desire. Come with me for a moment. Don't you want to see who you are?"

"I want to know what you are up to," said Conor. "What's your plan?"

"Plan?" said the thing in Oz's flesh. It laughed. "I really have no plan except to devour. Another thing I loved about Piasa—it let me feast on bodies and souls—with abandon. But I digress. I own the worlds you brought together this night, Conor, and indeed, I am not unhappy that you did so, for I too wish to see the Otherworld and this reality be as one. Easier for me. Yet you did it out of a sense of justice and compassion, and I think even out of love for wonder and beauty. Can't have that. Any union of the worlds must be on my terms, and they are terms of fear and conquest, domination and power. These are my worlds; they represent my domain. And as a good citizen of both, you Conor, belong to me, alive, of course, because of your obvious talent, but to me none the less. I want you, Conor, of your own free will if possible, but you in the end. That is my plan. Take my hand and see."

The voice had become more seductive and even Jace felt lulled by its power. Conor, despite himself, felt his right arm raising. The ribbon of skin was luminescing again, moving like a serpent underneath the surface of his body. He distrusted the thing in Oz, but everyone else had been making claims on him, why not see what this one wanted. And so, over Jace's objections—and he felt them concretely as Jace's fingers bit into his other arm—he grasped the free hand of Oz.

The world turned dark and spinning; vertigo gripped them. To Jace and Conor, it felt like they were falling. Definitely felt like they were landing as they smashed into a rocky ground, dimly lit by a faint light on the horizon. It took them only a moment to see they were on a plateau beneath a peak, a mountain surrounded not by a river, but by a huge ocean.

Oz lay beside them, blood flowing from a cracked skull. Jace ripped apart his shirt for a bandage to staunch the flow as Oz opened his eyes and spoke in his own voice, "Jace, we are far from home. Not in Kansas anymore?"

"No, bud," said Jace, a soft laugh coming from his throat as Oz made his little joke. The same thing he always said when in a strange or unfamiliar situation. "We're far away, but don't worry, we'll be okay."

Conor looked closely at Oz's face. "Whatever was in there is gone now, and we're stranded." They took a moment to reconnoiter their position. It seemed to be a small island, very mountainous. And they were on a flat rocky outcropping close to the highest peak on that land.

"Why did that thing take us here?" mused Jace.

"If we're really here," said Conor.

"Oh, I think we are," said Jace. "The blood on Oz's face is very real."

A furtive scratching caught their attention. Something was moving behind a boulder close to the face of the mountain.

"Show yourself," said Jace brandishing his sword.

Around the rock, she came, dressed in a flowing black dress, her lustrous black hair falling to her waist, her face radiant in the dawning light. For a moment, both thought it was the Morrigan, but then Conor leapt to his feet.

"Mom!" he shouted. Now that they looked more closely, without a doubt it was Finola. The minute Conor saw her, the sorrow welled up in his throat. A year of miserable sickness and of watching her die flickered through his memory and tears he had barely shed burst from his eyes, clouding his vision as he beheld her return. He made to run at her, but Jace caught him from behind and held him.

"Let me go!" shouted Conor.

"Not a chance," said Jace. "You don't know if it's really her."

Conor twisted out of his grasp and made to run again. Catching his arm, Jace spun him around and swung his right fist. It connected solidly with Conor's jaw, and he went down in a groggy heap.

"Boys, no need for that," cooed the woman. "I have come to give both of you the knowledge you seek. Conor, have I ever lied to you?"

Conor moaned and made to crawl.

"She's not Finola," said Jace. "She's something else. Remember what brought us here."

"Pay no attention to what he says, my son," said Finola. "Soon all will be made clear to both of you, even to Oz."

"But you died!" said Conor.

"I am one of the 'dark ones'. How could I really die?"

"Conor, I'm telling you she's lying. And stay where you are or I'll punch you again, dammit."

Finola laughed, and her laughter was sweet there in the dim dawn.

"Look to the skies," she said "and you will see what happened long ago. The heavens will give you the answers you seek."

Conor staggered to his feet. Seeing that he was keeping a distance from the woman, Jace let Conor be for a moment. Everyone there on the rocky outcrop lifted their head, even a groggy Oz, sending their gaze sweeping upward. It began with points of light in the darkling sky, with the first gleams of the rosy red sun sending bloody swaths across the silver glass sea. A wind picked up, licking the waves and shooting up the side of the mountainous island with great speed. Lifting in the breeze, Finola's hair wreathed her wraithlike body as her arms beckoned to the heavens and what descended from them. Like meteors they fell, first just a few, but then thousands of fiery streams streaking across the horizon, bright fire blazing and then smashing into the ocean. A sad keening cry followed the shooting stars as they passed through the atmosphere.

"Beautiful, is it not, in a melancholy way?" said Finola above the billowing breeze. "It happened so long ago, but I never tire of seeing it. To be back here, where it began. Look closely, my son. To the east are islands green and fair. Here, only water. Such a sad defeat, such a magnificent fall they had. Even vanquished, they were so proud. Watch closely and heed me now. The fire folk fall not only on the sea, but on the islands to the east as well. Those in the ocean become the Roan, the shapeshifters, the selchies. Those on land become the People of the Hollow Hills. All of the same race, all of the same kind, all fallen, all damned."

"They fell with the angels?" said Conor.

Sweet laughter echoed off the mountain peak. "No my son, that fall was much more spectacular. But they were allies to those greater beings of light and as damned as those who sought the throne of God. Damned they are still. Never forget it."

"Then its true," said Conor, slumping to his knees.

"Don't listen to her," said Jace. "She's lying."

"How do you know?"

"Because she's not your mother. Take a good look at her."

Indeed, the dawning light was growing brighter and Conor could see his mother's face. For a moment, it looked out of focus, but as he concentrated, he knew something was terribly wrong. Her right side had been hidden in shadow, but now he could see she had no eye. A viscous liquid dripped down her cheek. On her black dress, right by her rib cage, a dampness spread.

"She's hurt!" cried Conor.

"She's Piasa; the wounds are in the same place as on that corpse lying by the Wisconsin River," said Jace. "Just another disguise."

"No! You lie!" said Conor refusing to believe his sight.

"Do I need to knock even more sense into you?" Jace felt his anger getting the better of him. The two looked to come to blows again, but somehow Oz maneuvered around the two and grasped them both by their necks.

"Time to go," he said, in his toneless voice.

The woman moved closer, almost spiderlike in her movements. "Conor, don't leave me again!"

Conor sobbed. When he was the Thunderbird, it had seemed so simple; when he thought of the high destiny charted for him by Rory, the Abbot, Aunt Emily, it all had seemed so clear as he stood up on the bluff looking at the forces of Light and Darkness gathered in the river valley. When he thought of his earlier decision to accept the changes happening in him, he remembered the relief he felt as he gave in to the warring emotions and physical changes in his body—but now, the doubts were back. Mom was here and a chance for things to go back the way they were. Even if she wasn't who she said she was, wasn't there a chance, a chance to turn back time?

"Of course," said the woman, divining his thoughts. "We can go back to the way we were. You will always be special, Conor Archer, but you cannot belong to the Light when you come from the dark. You cannot be redeemed if you are damned already. I show you all this to convince you. But condemned or not, there is much still to enjoy. Bring the worlds together under my command, and much power will be yours and a chance for us to be together."

His head swam. Of course this wasn't his mother, but whatever it was, it promised peace. Madoc was so sure he was of the unredeemed; why shouldn't his son also be, despite what the Abbot said. The world Conor was familiar with didn't have much use for religion anymore; it wouldn't sit in judgment on him, all it cared about was prosperity. He didn't really know that much about the Otherworld, but what he had seen had been impressive enough—enough to satisfy him.

Finola walked closer to the three and reached to touch Conor's face. "Mom," he said again.

"My son," she said and began to embrace him. A gasp tore through her throat and her remaining good eye bulged large as Jace's sword pierced her midsection. He pushed her away as he withdrew the blade.

She fell to the ground and gasped again, "You call him friend? You call him Champion? Because of him, I die in front of you again. Kill him Conor. Kill him now, for he has surely killed your mother."

Jace let the sword fall to the ground. Shaking off Oz's grasp, he opened his arms and looked at Conor. For a moment, rage enveloped Conor, but then he saw his friend almost inviting a fatal thrust. A friend who felt sorely betrayed, the brother of the person he had loved and lost. A sob escaped Conor's chest, "No," he said to the woman. "I'm the only one here who has killed a loved one. You are not my mother, and I am not your son." With that he took the spear and drove it into the false Finola's neck. A look of pure hatred flashed across her face as her screams like sea spume were dashed upon the rock and her figure dissolved into the ground.

"What now?" sighed Conor.

"We don't belong here," said Jace, picking up his sword. "It's not our time, not our place. Grab Oz's hand. Can't lose him. Whatever's going to happen is already coming from the horizon."

Rushing toward them came a wall of shadow, as if the very world they were in was collapsing around them. Yet instead of being buffeted by wind or smashed by falling rocks from the mountain peak above them, they merely felt the shadow touch, then their vision darkened, and the sense of falling hit them again. With a not very gentle thud, they landed again on the sandy shore by the body of Piasa. New wounds were on its monstrous flesh; and where its morphing face had once been, now only slime remained. As they watched, the body collapsed upon itself and sunk into the sand.

"The stench is awful," said Jace.

"Yeah, but to me it smelled like that when it was alive. Come here and help me with Oz."

Unconscious, and oozing blood from his temple again, Oz's face looked almost childlike in repose. His breathing shallow, he didn't respond to any of Conor's or Jace's attempts to rouse him. They cradled him together, there in the filth slimed sand, and it was there that Madoc found them as the *Gwennan Gorn* slipped silently up to shore, its golden light casting a warming hue on the three travelers.

"My son," said Madoc. "We must go. Much mischief occurs on yonder shore."

"Nothing you could do anything about, I suppose," said Conor bitterly.

"It is your moment now, and your people who are in need. I care enough for my own. Come, time enough if we prevail, for father and son to fight later." Sending a few of his men splashing to shore to carry the unconscious Oz, Madoc reached out his hand to help Conor and Jace board the ship. Reluctantly, both accepted his offer of assistance and within moments, the *Gwennan Gorn* was rowed out to the main channel, making its way to the farther shore.

FROM THE RIVER TO THE SEA

COULDN'T SEE A thing. Conor tried, but no go. Fog was just too thick. Wrapped in the blue cloak, he was warm enough but felt useless as the ship glided through the waters. The Wisconsin River, big enough in the best of times was huge now that two worlds had merged. The River behind the river. Conor laughed ruefully to himself; this was what the Wisconsin really was: huge, vast, powerful. He could only imagine what the nearby Mississippi looked like. The Otherworld was a magnification of everything he had ever known.

Keeping his distance, Jace was. Conor was too tired to be guilty anymore. Besides, his damn face still hurt. Jace wouldn't have minded very much knocking some sense into him when he saved Conor's life. Maybe the big guy would never forgive him.

Think, think, think, thought Conor. He was beginning to hear the screams from the farther shore much more clearly now. The Abbot must not be able to hold the changelings back; and Conor had a feeling that Madoc's People were not going to do much.

So passive with so much power. What was with them? Rory always pressing him; even Madoc in his own way demanding that Conor 'meet his destiny' whatever that truly meant. It was as if the Roan were paralyzed. The answer had to lie in what he had seen in Piasa's vision. The Roan, falling from the sky—the Lost, the Forsaken. Just like the angels that rebelled. Yet not. Madoc wasn't allied with Piasa. He was his sworn enemy. Nor, was he an independent source of evil; clearly he embraced the good, just in a despairing sort of way. They longed to go back to wherever they came from; so why couldn't they? Or wouldn't they? And why did they seem to need him so much?

A piercing woman's scream cut through the fog. The rowing warriors woofed in unison their anger, and redoubled their pace. But Conor couldn't wait, nor could he stay preoccupied with his thoughts. His whole body felt on edge. Indeed, he held out his webbed right hand; and again the ribbon of light rippled through his skin, from his webbed hand and around the rest of his body. Almost of its own volition, his body began to move. The cloak fell off as he began to run on the deck, past the warriors, past Jace, toward the prow and the carved seal. He reached it in two leaps and launched into the air. Already, feathers flashed through his body and wings sprung from his shoulders. A collective, awestruck sigh rose from the boat as the Thunderbird ascended once again.

But only for a moment. Flashing brightly in the moonlit mist, a silver cord slipped round the Thunderbird's neck, tightened and then pulled the morphing Conor to the ground. Taken by surprise, the Thunderbird had no time to react and it plummeted dozens of feet, splashing half in the water, crashing half on shore. And Conor was himself again, dazed, looking at the cord around his neck and listening to Rory laugh in the fog.

"Got you again, little nephew," he said. "Though it was a splendid display out there. You truly are coming into your own. We've come a long way, you and I, since that evening at the pub when we shared a glass or two. Now, don't be looking at me like that, all critical and such. Here, put these on." Rory tossed a pair of pants and a t-shirt to Conor.

"Somehow, we who shape shift for a living always have to have an extra change of clothing; otherwise, you'll lose a bit of your dignity there in your birthday suit."

"What do you want?" snarled Conor.

"I want you exactly where you are right now. Look around, can't you tell what's happening?"

Conor looked and saw Madoc and shipmates frozen on board, Jace reaching out to him but stopped in mid-grasp.

"Threshold," said Conor. "Land and water—an in-between place. This is the Second Sight again."

"So it is, so it is," laughed Rory. "And before you ask, I'm with you because I was holding on to you through my little silver cord when you fell. I get to sneak a peek, and I think it will be worth looking."

To Conor, the mist seemed the same but, hearing a noise, he turned, thinking to run smack dab into a changeling, but instead saw through the fog to the lonely island again and witness the star fall of the Roan from the heavens. But just briefly. Back then, to the valley where there were birds in the sky; swans driving back the mist, filling his vision for a moment with winged delight, lifting his sight to a beach with sea water lapping. Blinking away the sight of the swans, he beheld a view of a place far away, clear ocean in front of him, caught in a bay, breakers crashing in the distance. Before him stood ghosts, specters rising from the water they seemed, women they were, beautiful, holding their hands out to him saying, "We will come to you, O noble prince, if you but call us with tears and song.

Sing and weep, sing and weep, and we shall come." It was all he saw and heard. He turned to Rory with his mouth agape, and saw the biker shrugging his shoulders.

"It's a vision boy; figure it out. I know no more than you."

"Sing and weep?" said Conor. "That's how I'll get help? What does it mean?"

"It means," said a voice in the mist, "that one must weep seven tears to call the sea wives of the Roan and they are far away. I think, little one, brave as you have been and ... remarkable in deed ... you do not have the years of sorrow in you to weep strongly enough."

The Morrigan appeared from the fog, shrouded in black, her beautiful, young, porcelain face framed by her red hair and punctuated by her blood-red lips. "But I have the years and I have the sorrow. Let me weep for you."

"But what do I sing?" asked Conor.

"The Song of the Land," said another voice, and stepping out of the mist came Taps Jeffords, strutting in perfect health. Seemed to be humming to himself—that song he wrote long ago. Hummed and sang a few bars— "There's a place I know, down by the River ..." Then he caught Conor looking at him strangely.

"It's the Second Sight, boy; of course I'm going to be looking my best. Got tired of scaring you, like I was some kind of bogeyman."

"But you were hanging on the Tree."

"So were you and you're looking none the worse for wear. Besides, those of us who've had that happen need to stick together, not be scared of one another."

Taps cupped Conor's chin affectionately in his hand and rumpled his hair. "Looking less beastly, too, I might add. Coming to grips with a few things, I don't doubt, but you ain't finished yet—you're not complete. I can tell that. Like this lady says, not enough years of sorrow in you little man; but, my lands, what you will be when your suffering is done. The things you shall do. But I'm off my topic. You was talking about singing."

"Right. What song do I need? How should I know?"

"But you do know," said Taps. "You've heard the Song of the Land. Sounds a bit like the song I wrote. Sounds more like the music of yonder monks from whom I took the inspiration for that song. Just listen all around you, then play that tune, such as it is. This ain't no Celtic ditty or some Chicago bluesy-gospel tune. It's the Song of the Land, what keeps the whole place going. Until I came to visit here so long ago, I never really heard it clearly. Then, in this valley, the echoes filled my soul. Man, I could write music then. But now, this night, you joined the worlds. Can't you hear the tune thrumming underneath and overhead? Conor you've done something that even your father hasn't been able to do. And I think it's got him, frankly all of us, just a little afraid if we have to admit it. With the tears of that pretty lady over there and your music, who knows what might happen?"

"But I don't even have my tin whistle, and I'm sure not going to hum it; that would be so lame."

Taps smirked but then held out a small case. "Got a gift for you that fits the occasion right well. I was hanging on that tree for a long time. Had some time to kill, you might say. So's I just took one of its branches and whittled me a little flute, or like you call it, a whistle. Made from the Tree of the World. I want you to have it. The original whistles were made of bone. The Tree of the World is the bones of the earth, its very substance and structure."

Conor took the case and opened it and there it was. Simple, beautiful, shiny and gleaming as if there was a coat of varnish on it—just one single carving.

"It's beautiful," said Conor, "but it's not going to be able to sound the right way."

"No, that's the true beauty," said Taps. "It will sound better. Whatever music you play, it will sound out perfectly as it is supposed to. It's the Tree of the World, man! The Song of the Land has its roots with the Tree! I don't doubt that if you play the right something, more than beauty will occur—things will happen!"

"Conor," said the Morrigan.

Rory hissed, "Enough chatting, all of you!"

"Listen to the lady," said Taps. "Listen to the surly one as well," he said, hitching his thumb to where Rory stood, silver cord still in his hand, loosely holding the loop around Conor's neck. "It's time for you to leave this window of vision, and I can't go with you. For where you go I have already been long gone. Peace, my little friend—though that's not a gift I need to give you. Already deep down, there is a center in you now that wasn't there before. Acceptance of who you are does that. Now be. Be what you are supposed to be. And remember me once in a while, down by the river, where the waters flow."

The musician smiled, white teeth shining out of his dark face and Conor smiled back. Only joy here, not even mystery or terror anymore. Humming again, Taps turned and disappeared into the mist.

Conor stepped forward just to touch him once more, but the moment he did, reality slid and the Second Sight was gone. Only chaos remained.

The screams started again. Behind him, Madoc and Jace and the warriors were shouting. "Where did you come from, Rory?" shouted Madoc. "What mischief now?"

"None, older brother," said the biker, walking over to Conor and slipping off the cord. "Just had to do your duty again and help your son figure out the next move."

Suffused with anger, Madoc's face contorted and he made to leap off the boat and tackle his brother.

"Stop it, both of you!" said Conor. "Listen!"

The Abbot's voice rose above the chaos, "To the townspeople, brothers! The changelings look to kill them! Should that happen, more than they will die, for the children will see and hear and never recover from what they are being forced to do!"

Conor's mind reeled with the vision he had just seen, but he had enough sense to know who he needed now. Into the fog he cried, "Nora, I know you are there. Come to me with the swans."

Uncanny how fast she moved. Before him a blanket of mist, and then, in the white fog, things whiter. Four swans stood before him and Nora. "I am here," she said.

"Nora!" cried Jace. "You're okay!"

She nodded and smiled. "Don't worry, Jace; I've got the best protection this night can offer. Kids who can fly and who taught me to do the same."

"You're kidding," he said, lightly jumping onto the shore.

"Don't touch me yet," she smiled. "Just watch." And in front of Conor and the man she loved, she morphed, almost faster than sight, and became the fifth swan standing before them.

"What's happening here?" said Jace. Quickly, Conor told him of what he saw in his Second Sight.

"You know what I want you to do," said Conor, turning once again to the swans.

"Yes," came Nora's voice in his mind. "I saw what you saw in your vision. How, I don't know, but we can do it. Stand back."

With that, the five swans rose in unison. By the sound of their cries, Conor could tell they were circling above the river and then they rushed forward, past the shore and the mound, towards the meadow. Pass after pass they made and wherever they flew, the mist was shredded. The moon shone more clearly through ragged wisps of that deadly fog and vision quickly improved. But what Conor, Jace, Madoc and the warriors saw caused each to gasp in horror. The changelings had massed as one. In fact, they were like a single cloud of black smoke. Individual limbs and faces could be seen here and there, but the shadowy shapes moved as one.

Conor looked around and there, not too far from the river on a little knoll stood Drake with Cate collapsed at his feet. Gone was the bruised and bedraggled wreck of a physician Conor had seen from the sky as the

Thunderbird. Drake stood tall and menacing, suffused with new power. Hands twisting in some obscene sign language, a guttural chant gurgled from his mouth, spittle flying. He was incanting something, and the changelings were responding. They had already reached the first of the townspeople. Bones littered the ground where the changeling shadow had passed. Conor saw an arm reach out from that dark cloud and snatch Mr. O'Leary from the townspeople's phalanx. He was unaware and did not resist, but in a moment a scream pierced that shadow as the changelings did their work.

"Soul-ripping," said Rory. "That's what they are doing."

"You controlled them before. Stop them," said Conor.

"Aye, I did, but that was then. They were weaker, as was Drake. You can see the death of Piasa has not diminished the good doctor's power, only enhanced it. The Devourer is not truly gone. Its evil always finds another vacuum to fill. What Drake is doing is not only destroying their bodies, but reaving their souls as well, feeding them to these dark things, a hell even worse than the fall our ancestors once faced."

"The fire folk from heaven," said Conor. "I watched them fall."

"And a terrible thing was that. And sad," said Rory.

Conor looked quickly at the biker and saw grief graven on his face. Nice to know some things still moved that otherworldly cynic.

"If it was up to you," said the Morrigan, "we'd all be reminiscing this night away. But living things are dying and I must be with them. The changelings are not the only ones who need to feed. Seven tears and a song to sing for your vision to manifest itself. Do you want the tears or not, Conor?"

"Do what you must do," said Conor, "though I don't see how any of this helps."

"Tell them, Champion," said the enigmatic beauty to Jace. "Use your wisdom and tell them what happens."

Jace's face went blank for a moment and then he said, "I don't know how I know this, but there's something ... something here inside my head about 'tears of sorrow' calling those who fell from the sky to the sea. Whenever the Celts needed the Roan, that's how it was done. Salt from tears mixed with the salt from the sea. Seven's the perfect number—a sort of mystic shout of 'hey, we need you.' Only tears from powerful sorrow will work. And Conor, we're not that strong. Only the Morrigan knows that kind of grief."

"Let's just skewer that son of a bitch over there," said Conor pointing to Drake, getting tired again of all this mystic crap. "Maybe then we can break his hold on the kids and we won't even need the seawives or whatever they are."

"Fool of a cub," said Rory. "You'll never get close enough to him. See the glamour around him? Similar in effect to the one that earlier wrapped the Abbot and the mound with protection; but its source is evil, from the Worm that gnaws at the roots of the world."

"But we killed it," said Conor.

"Just this manifestation of it," said Rory. "Besides, look how evil fills the vacuum. Do you remember Drake that tall, that powerful, that confident?"

"Silence!" said the Morrigan. "Conor Archer, you who can unite the worlds and hear the music of the spheres, play your song, and let us see if we cannot call the Roan from across the sea. All waters in the Otherworld are connected, so perhaps they can come to us through passages unknown before."

She bent to the river and flipped her flowing hair over her head. As it fell in front of her face, the color leached out of it and it became deathly white. Her porcelain skin wrinkled and the toothless crone began to wail. Not that many truly heard, for the din by the river was growing. Those townspeople caught in the changelings grasp came to full consciousness and began to shriek, bodies wracked, souls ripped and riven.

Conor saw the Abbot look over at him, a terrible sadness washing over his face. With a cry, Malachy urged his monks forward. All the brothers ran to the villagers and began pulling them away, slipping and sliding over the marshy meadow back towards the mound. But Madoc's people did not move, either on the mound or on the boat. Clearly, thought Conor, they do not think of this fight as their own. Caught in some ancient, self-pitying paralysis.

Bringing up the whistle carved from the Tree of the World, he began to play. First it was Taps' old tune; then Conor changed it to the Celtic chant it was taken from. Nothing happened. Even the Morrigan seemed to be wailing incoherently to no effect.

Conor turned again and saw the Abbot looking at him. They weren't that far apart, but the noise was too loud to communicate verbally. He saw the priest mouthing something, but he couldn't make out the words. The Abbot's finger came up pointing to his ear and then Conor could read his lips, "Listen," the Abbot was saying. The 'power pervading everything,' thought Conor. The 'mountain behind the mountain.' Maybe others had perceived it with sight or intellect. Maybe some great saints had felt it in their souls. But Conor had a hunch that he had always felt closest to it when he played his music.

For moment, the fierce face of Fintan Carr rose in his mind. He saw his old boss pointing to the plaque above the *DerryAir Pub* in Chicago. 'Hear what this says, boy, and take it to heart—*Who knows where I go when I hear Celtic music, and we are left a little while alone?*—Understand, Conor, and play your tunes, piping the people to another world. Do that and your music will be alive.' Conor shook his head at the memory. Maybe that power was manifesting itself now in the Song of the Land. Because he could hear it, thrumming deeply all around him, deeper than the chaos in his midst. He felt it more than perceived it with his ears, but there was logic to it, rhythm in it, and most of all, just plain common sense to it. A simple tune really, and one that he could definitely play.

Blowing the whistle, Conor made the song come alive in the midst of death and violence. And the moment he sounded the melody, he knew he performed it truly. Suddenly the Morrigan herself began to speak in the same cadence as the song, swinging her head to the beat of the music, white hair floating and swirling on the waters of the muddy Wisconsin River. In a beautiful voice that belied the wreck of her body, she sang:

Seven tears to call the Roan,
Seven tears from sorrows grown,
Seven tears to mark the ones,
Who died in battles beneath the sun,
Beneath the moon, that evil won.
One for the woman who bore the child,
One for the healer of sickness wild,
One for the grief of the children mild,
One for the warrior in an effort to save,
One for the old man searching wisdom's cave,
One for the girl whose love she gave,
And one for the dying brave yet to come.
Hear me, you who are fallen from grace,
Come to save those in this place,
Come to rescue the little ones,
Born from your wombs, touched by men's sons,
Save your children's children now.

Haunting was the chant, and Conor, himself, felt drawn into the cadence. He had played well, but as a neophyte, just discovering how the music was put together. Now he repeated the song, playing swifter, with more abandon. Watching the Morrigan, Conor saw tears of fire falling from her face, lightly hissing on the water. Seven there were. Let the Morrigan's chant be heard, he thought, through the hills and the valleys, the stream and the river, for all waters flow to the glassy sea, where dwell the Roan, the ones we need. Song and chant came together—Conor could not even feel his fingers playing the whistle anymore. All was music and a strange, sad beauty, and without shouting or the screech of tortured instrument, words and notes blended more loudly till they drowned out the screams and the chaos around.

Conor risked a look through the desolation and saw that Madoc was looking at him strangely. Abbot and monks had turned and even the shapeless shadow of changelings had ceased its depredations on the towns-people. Drake's hands were still twisting, as if weaving a spell of bondage towards Conor, but the druid's magic had no effect. There was an older power at work here.

Tears began to run down the face of Jace and the others as the music soared in melancholy beauty and longing, a sadness and a sorrow of want-ing too great to bear, too heavy to grieve and yet hope there, a beautiful possibility of salvation. Conor's own face was wet with tears and, yet, he could not stop playing. From out in the middle of the channel, a splashing could be heard, and dark shapes could now be seen, dozens of them.

A moaning sounded and Conor looked towards the ship. Oz was get-ting to his feet, holding his head. No tears on his face, just an awareness that Conor had seldom seen. Not the evil cunning he had witnessed on the mountain, but an ancient understanding. Stretching out his arm, Oz pointed at Conor and said in a rasping voice, "What you saw when you touched me long ago, waits for you in the waters. Go to them now, while there is still time. Run for the water, rider of the waves, and bring the help that is needed."

Conor let the fluted whistle drop from his hand. He knew of what Oz spoke. The summer when he first met the odd man. Oz had touched his face and Conor felt like he was drowning, before he saw them. Brown faces in the deeps around him, strange they were but with human eyes. He remembered the wonder, but more than that he now knew what they were. He ran to the water's edge and never stopped; began swimming when his feet no longer touched the bottom.

His webbed hands and feet aided his powerful strokes, and he found himself soon in the middle of the channel, dark shapes leaping around him. He reached out to touch and then found himself pinned between two of the shapes that took him down, underneath the water. Too surprised to morph or shape shift, he swallowed water and began to panic. To his amazement, faces appeared before him. Furred they were but with human eyes. My God, he thought, they're seals. Into his mind came unearthly thoughts that seemed to say, "Sorrow and song have called us here; music and weeping have pulled us from our homes; a grieving sadness that shakes the world must be answered. What do you want rider of the waves, prince of the sea?"

I must be drowning by now, he thought. But the faces were insistent and he found himself throwing thoughts at the swimmers around him. "Save the children, they're yours you know. From time past when you came ashore—these are yours and are in danger now. Save them from the dark."

Two seals lifted him up and bore him to the surface. All turned toward shore and sped for land. A sea wave rose there in the channel, brought with the visitors through ways unknown, and Conor rose from the depths and sped toward the shore, born on the waves by the Roan. Conor rode the seals, with water flaring to the right and left. Wonder was on the faces of his father and Jace. Rory's face was twisted with triumph. The Abbot raised his arms laughing for joy as the bells from the Abbey above tolled midnight, ushering in the Feast of All Saints. The swans called loudly from the sky. Yards from shore, the seals dove, but Conor leapt from their backs and seemed to run on the remaining water to the land. He turned and looked as from the waters rose the sea-wives, wrapped in foam, carrying with them the scent of salt-spray and sea breeze. In answer to his call, the Roan had come.

HOME TO THE SEA

THE MUSIC WAS to die for, thought Jace. But then it stopped. Conor inexplicably ran to the water and threw himself in. Swifter than Jace thought possible, Conor stroked out towards the middle of the channel where whatever was coming cavorted on, in and under the waters. Then Conor disappeared. Seemed like an eternity but when he emerged he rode the backs of huge otters—then Jace corrected himself—seals. Damned if Conor hadn't pulled it off and opened some sort of portal to wherever these creatures, called by the music and the Morrigan, came from.

For a second it almost looked like Conor walked the last few yards on water as the seals dipped below the surface, but Jace didn't have time to think about it. For right behind Conor, rising from the river, were women clothed only in the froth of the sea. Pale with long dark hair, they keened the song, starting the melody once again. In their arms, each held some sort of bundle. In unison, they each unrolled something dark and spotted. Skins, thought Jace. They are the skins of the Roan seawives, shed in order to become human.

Conor shared Jace's wonder, and, for a moment, he looked baffled at what to do next, but hearing the song of the seawives, he found the whistle that Taps Jeffords had given him and began to play that same melody again, only this time he directed it to where the seawives were gazing as the Morrigan sang, towards the changelings.

Drake was controlling them, transferring his own rage at the towns-people to the demonic things that controlled their children. Like some puppet master, the physician used the words he spoke as strings to control and send the changelings to destroy the hapless villagers. But he faltered in his task as Conor's music took hold. To Jace it looked like the physician was distracted, or that the music itself was raising an invisible wall between Drake and the shadows.

Clearly, a battle was being waged on a field Jace couldn't really under-stand. Just as bright in his mind was the fact that in some way Drake was wrestling with that song played by Conor and sung by the seawives. He could feel the energy building all around him, and just when he thought the very atmosphere couldn't get more tense, the Abbot sent a flare of light straight at Drake. It burst against whatever field of protection surrounded the druid, dazing him and forcing him, for a moment at least, to drop whatever field was protecting him and Cate. In that moment, Rory bent down, picked up a stone and hurled it at the mage. It struck true and felled Drake where he stood.

The shadowy ball of changelings ceased advancing on the townspeople. Without a coherent mind directing them, they were bereft of any purpose but to feed. But the music continued, wrapping itself around them, through any gap that appeared, until they found themselves surrounded by song. Despite their clawlike hands clapping around their ears, they listened. As one they turned, forgetting the townspeople, held against their will by the music, and they came slowly to the shore where waited the seawives, arms outstretched, seal skins unfolded.

When the black ball of shadow reached the water, it dissolved and dozens of changelings, like ants on the back of a migrating queen, flowed apart and each moved to one of the seawives whose keening never ceased. The women in the water never smiled. In fact, thought Jace, their faces were cold and hard, their eyes hungry as the changelings crept forward. As each one approached a seawife, the woman would bend down and enfold the changeling in the seal skin. For what seemed a long time to Jace, this ritual was played out until every last one was bound within a skin.

Then the Morrigan, crone shaped and crooked, went weaving in and out of the seawives ranks splashing in the shallows, a mad woman in an ecstasy of joy. Her voice, no longer beautiful, became an old woman's cackle, a sing-song banter as she began a new, more sinister song:

"Twist and bend,
Rip and rend,
Split the shadow from the light.
Tear and bite,
Separate spite,
Snatch the children from the night.
In my grasp,
Free shadows fast,
Hold the Roan to your sea breasts tight."

She chanted and clucked between the ranks of the seawives, importuning them, though they stood silent in the flowing river. Yet they heard, for as she sang, they clasped their seal skin bundles tightly to themselves.

But not tightly enough. As the Morrigan chanted and shrieked her command, from the tiny fold at the top of each skin came a claw, black as night, inhuman in its grotesquerie.

The Morrigan harvested each changeling she found, plucking them from the seawives' bundles and holding them all by her left hand. Whatever happened to them inside the seal skin, something had sapped their energy. Like a dance of death, she dragged them along, through the shallows to the shore, past the mound and into the swampland behind. No longer looking remotely human, the otherworldly dance of death pranced behind her unwillingly, the changlings' hands grasping toward the freedom of the river. The Morrigan glanced back at her parade of followers, a gap-toothed smile crossing her wrinkled visage. For her captive guests, the river was no longer an option.

As the changelings disappeared into the dark and the bracken, the seawives ceased their keening and all was quiet. Until the otherworldly screams started, from beings not human but able to be harmed, able to be killed, able to be consumed by the thing that haunts the battle field and sometimes wears the guise of a woman, old or young.

When the death cries finally ceased, the women in the water bent gently down and upon the river unwrapped their bundles. The skins floated serenely and on top of them, curled in a deep sleep, lay the children of the town, the 'dark ones' whole and healthy.

One by one, the swans landed upon the water. Swimming majestically between the seawives, they pushed the little rafts to shore. Nora resumed her human form and went to Jace and Conor. Helped by the Abbot and some of the monks, they all lifted the children from the skins and laid them on the sand.

The seawives turned to Madoc, standing tall by the tiller of his ship. For the first time, one of them spoke out loud. "Well met, Madoc, gone these many years from the sea, your true home. Your son has brought the worlds together so that we might meet again. Will you return with us while you can?"

A sadness gripped Madoc's face, a countenance melancholy but relieved as well. "I cannot, for I read my fate as remaining in this land for a while. But my People, the Roan who chose exile with me, they have longed for this day, and as you say, my son has provided the opportunity. Let them go with you back to the sea, back to the waves, back to the home and the People they love."

A murmuring grew on the ship and from those still on the mound, a groan of protest and understated outrage. A warrior stood up at one of the oar locks. "We followed you long ago, Madoc, you and your brother. How can we leave you now? How can we abandon you who saved our lives from your foster father? Neither the One who dwells above, nor any other human being or creature, has cared for us but you—we are the Lost, the Forsaken, without you we are nothing."

Tears glistened in the moonlight on Madoc's cheeks. "I am touched by your love and your loyalty. All of you. But this must be. For a moment, the worlds are together, perhaps for all time. Yet we cannot be sure. Take this moment now. Go, and someday soon, I and my brother, who is as bound as me to this fate, will follow."

Nothing else was said. Madoc leapt to the shallows and came and stood by his son, Rory just paces away and silent. The Roan gathered around Madoc and knelt in silence before him. He walked among them, laying his hands upon their heads, a benediction from the lord to the ones he ruled. A private moment, out of place and out of time. Jace and Conor shifted nervously. Even the Abbot felt the awkwardness, but the intrusion could not be helped. The seawives were leaving, and the chance for the People of the Hollow Hills to return to their true home was swiftly fading. The Roan moved to the ship, and once boarded, the warriors prepared to row. As the vessel moved out, the seawives followed till they wrapped their skins around their shoulders and began to swim.

Jace never noticed the moment of transformation. One moment they were majestic women swimming effortlessly in the slowly moving river, next, they frolicked in the water, seals once again. The *Gwennan Gorn* gleamed in the night but as it receded it also faded as the river joined the waters of the world and the Roan returned to their homes.

AN EVIL STRIKE

"WE MUST GET them to their parents, those that still have them," said the Abbot. There was no time to mourn the passing of Madoc's people. Children were in need. Everyone who was able, even Madoc and Rory, lent a hand, lifting up the somnolent children, carrying them into the meadow where a bemused and confused group of parents stood, not comprehending a thing of what had happened. Only that their children were being returned, whole and well. In that, they rejoiced. But some of the little ones were clearly orphaned now. No mothers or fathers waited for them. Monks carried the little ones up the path to the monastery, as the other villagers led their families home. The fallen, for a moment, were left behind.

"Beth," said Conor, choking back a sob. "I've got to go get her."

"You'll see her soon," said the Abbot, also holding out a hand to restrain Jace from leaping up the hill to the abandoned ambulance. "I've already sent someone to take her body to the Abbey Church."

A chuckling behind them caused the three to turn. Drake had risen to his feet and was wiping blood from his eyes. "You think you've won, Malachy, but you have not. The girl's dead, and with her, the future her child represented. You all think that the death of Piasa is some great feat accomplished here, to be told in bard's tales or maybe a snap documentary news feature. Wrong!" he said. "Wrong, wrong, wrong! The worlds aren't joined forever."

Rory ran past the three and delivered a well-placed punch to Drake's face. For the second time, the man fell. Rory turned back and started laughing. "Been wanting to do that for a while; much better than a rock. I think I broke his nose."

Conor shouted, "Rory, behind you!"

Making a remarkable recovery, Drake vaulted to his feet and leapt upon Rory's back, arm round his neck, as if to choke him.

Still, Rory laughed. "The parasite just won't stay down."

"No, I won't, you otherworldly freak. Passed down from generations is the story of your kind. You should have been wiped out centuries ago, particularly the line you and your brother represent. I cannot get both of you this time, but I have you now."

Rory reached back to peel the druid off, but Drake was too quick. Holding his right hand high, he brought it sweeping across Rory's neck. The gesture didn't even break the exasperated smile on the biker's face, and yet, Conor caught the bemused look in Rory's eyes. He reached out a hand to Conor, trying to speak. A small rivulet of blood appeared on his neck.

Drake let go and Rory fell to his knees. Though no words were spoken, Conor heard the biker speak distinctly in his mind: "Ah, the treachery of the truly wicked; and I fell for his ruse. My time is short, lad. I'm only sorry that I won't get to see what you make of yourself. You've done well, better than I hoped. Someone waits for you across the sea to take my place. Once I am gone." His eyes began to roll up as he staggered. A whisper in Conor's mind, "Now, I'll finally get to see what hell looks like."

Rory tried to laugh out loud, but a gaping wound appeared in his neck, and he fell backwards, his blood gushing upon the sand.

"No!" cried Conor, rushing forward. Madoc caught him in his arms before he had gone two steps. "Fool of a boy! That's what Drake wants—for you to come near. Look at what he holds."

Conor glimpsed what looked like a sharp, dark rock in Drake's hand. "Some kind of scale? From the hide of Piasa! But how could it kill Rory?"

"We can die, Conor, if the weapon is right and the hand is sure. You saw that in your vision on the Tree when the ancestor of the scum who stands before you tried to kill Rory and me. It takes a weapon of the Otherworld, touched by evil, but it can be done. And it has. Look now, for the last time, upon my brother."

Motes of light were swirling around Rory's body, covering him with a luminescence that grew brighter and brighter. When the light finally dimmed, only blood remained on the ground; the body was gone.

From the slough behind the mound splashed the Morrigan. Forward she came, bent and bloodied as well from feasting on the rogue changelings who hadn't possessed bodies of children.

"Who has died?" she croaked. "I smell powerful blood."

"My brother," said Madoc, "Prince of Gwynnedd and of the Roan."

She crept forward and sniffed the blood pool, stretching out her tongue to touch the remaining liquid. "Rory," she whispered. "A brave departure you have made." She stood up straight and walked over to where Drake stood, the hand with Piasa's scale still upraised.

"You think to destroy me as well?" said the Morrigan. "Some have tried; all have failed."

"Enough of this!" cried the Abbot, walking forward. The Abbot smashed his crozier over the shoulder of Drake, causing him to drop the scale.

He pinned him down to the ground saying, "You're stronger than just a few days ago, but I handled your grandfather, generations removed, and you can't possibly be worse than him."

Behind the Abbot came a hissing of breath. "You were the priest, back in Gwynedd. The one who saved us," said Madoc, recognition suddenly dawning. "How could I not have known?"

"I was ragged and wild then, just new to that kind of life," said the Abbot. "I was not who I am now. Then, I was a walker of worlds, sent to watch over the likes of you and your brother and all those blended beings that result from the coupling of the Roan and humans."

For the third time Drake rose, right arm broken, hanging limp by his side. His eyes were green and the voice that spoke from his mouth was not his. "For the moment, you have won. An alliance of men, the old gods and the Roan. But not forever. Look to your back, and I shall be there. Look in the corner and see my shadow. Wake from a nightmare and feel my touch on your neck. I shall be there. For I gnaw at the roots of the world. Hear me well, Conor Archer. Your attempt to unite the worlds does not succeed, for you are not yet at full strength. And I have time. No matter where you flee, I will be there. Remember what you saw on the mountain in the sea. Falling angels, the ancestors of the Roan. They are damned."

Looking around, Drake gestured to Madoc. "Your father cannot offer you any future. Already in his heart, he hears the screams of his brother in torment for the crime of his forebears and for his many sins. Madoc's fate will be no different, even if he lives long. Think hard on this, Conor before you finally decide, before …"

The shot rang out and echoed over the hills. A huge hole appeared in Drake's back and chest. Drake's body jerked and convulsed. Even the Morrigan, standing before him, was splattered with gore.

A voice rang out. "I just couldn't listen to that son of a bitch jabber on like that any more."

They all looked to see Jim Warren, shotgun in hand, casually reloading. "Now you all listen to me. Lots of strange goings on tonight. Lots of weird stuff. But I've got a town to put back together and I'm going to leave you all to handle this, whatever this was or is. I'm taking Cate with me because I've locked up her last son in my bank and somebody's got to take care of her; might as well be Gordy. I don't expect to hear a thing about any of this tomorrow. Just help get us back to normal."

As if his words had the power to command the elements, a huge thunderclap sounded in response. Everyone felt the earth tilting for a moment, and most saw the strangest thing. It was as if a transparent slide of the world slid off and began to harden; only like a photograph, it could not capture the reality that lay just behind and beyond. It was a smaller view, bounded more tightly. Conor saw the river shrink. Emily the hills lower. Jace and Nora felt the air grow heavier. Madoc and the Abbot saw the worlds separate once again and the wonder vanish.

But Jim Warren saw nothing. He walked over to where Cate lay and lifted her up. "Come on, Caithness. Your boy will be happy to see you." She followed him meekly up the hill as they watched, a shadow of the river slowly streaming by them.

WHERE THE WATERS FLOW

ONLY JACE AND Nora, the Abbot and Emily, Madoc and Conor were left by the mound, the Morrigan having slipped away once again. All stood in silence, watching Jim take Cate McNabb up the hill back towards town.

"What will you do?" said the Abbot to Madoc.

The prince had drawn into himself. Eyes cold, voice distant, he said, "My fate was written long ago, as was my brother's. I thought we should die together, but such was not to be. Nonetheless, my doom has not changed. Until the prophecy is fulfilled:

> *"Three times pierced,*
> *Three times wounded,*
> *Thrice to bring the king to birth,*
> *Once, comes the Otherworld,*
> *Twice, the pains of Change,*
> *Thrice pierced, a Kingdom gained.*
> *So says the crow that flies above,*
> *So says the barrow prince hidden in the mound ..."*

"*So says he who walks the twilight bound,*" finished the Abbot. "I know what it says, Madoc, and it says nothing about your exile."

"The prophecy was spoken by the Morrigan long ago as a hope for us—that some time would finally come when the exile our forebears caused would be ended." Madoc walked over to Conor and put his hand on his son's shoulder. "You have done well, but you have not done all. You have accepted who you are, but you are not yet all you will someday be. Until that time, we have but a reprieve. My people may return, but I may not— insurance as it were."

"And if I don't succeed?" asked Conor. "Will your people have to return here?"

"No," said Madoc. "They will die, and all those like them across the sea. Our being here in this land is the result of another terrible mistake my brother and I made. One that happened after the vision you saw on the Tree. Had we but listened," and here Madoc turned to the Abbot, "things would have been different; but we did not and were forced to take a terrible journey to this land. It is not so bad, really. I have grown to love it deeply, but I miss my home, and there are barriers to my return. Indeed, until tonight, I dared not hope that I would ever return. I should have perished with Rory, yet I did not."

"Even you cannot read all the folds in the fabric of time," said the Abbot.

"Apparently not," said Madoc ruefully. "Yet, I do know that nothing changes for me until my son succeeds or fails."

Walking up to Madoc, Emily put her hand into his. "Can you not walk with Conor? Can you not give him any assistance?"

He touched Conor's cheek even as he squeezed the old woman's hand. "I cannot. And I would not if I could. He must walk this road alone."

Madoc turned and strode swiftly to the mound. Underneath the huge willow tree, he turned to face the company. He lifted a hand in farewell and then amidst swirling motes of light, he disappeared, back into the mound, now bereft of the People.

"Emily," said the Abbot, "take Conor and get him ready. There is little time. What needs to be done must be done tonight. Jace, Nora, go to the Abbey, you'll find the funeral director there along with your parents, Jace. They believe Beth has died in a single car crash. Make them believe it."

"Wait," said Conor, "ready for what? I'm not going anywhere but the Abbey."

"I'm afraid that's not possible," said the Abbot. "Jim Warren was absolutely right. Much has happened here that must be forgotten. The townspeople will remember little, but only if their routine goes on. The other deaths of the parents need to be explained, and I can do that, but only if things look relatively normal tomorrow. If you are here, Conor, that will not be possible. Their suspicion of you will clear their minds of any illusions I might cast tonight. No, you must go."

"Besides," said Jace, "you've caused enough damage tonight."

"Jace," said Conor, but couldn't say anymore as Nora and his friend turned away. In anguish, he watched them trudge up the hill toward the Abbey.

"Conor," said Emily, "he will come to see more clearly. Already, he knows Beth's death is not your fault. He's just struggling to make sense out of everything."

"But it is my fault. And now, I've not only lost the one person I really loved, I've lost my best friend as well." His face bleak, he let Emily lead him up another path towards Madoc's Glen. The Abbot was left standing amid the blood-soaked ruins. He took his crozier and touched the body of Drake lying twisted on the grass. There was a sharp flash of light, and nothing was left but some ashes, blowing in the night wind.

PLACES TO GO

SHE LET HIM fall on his bed fully dressed in the clothes Rory had given him. Within moments, he was fast asleep. Wasn't much to get ready, really. Before she had taken off for Cate's house, she had already packed his things, pretty sure that this night would be the crucial one. Hadn't been wrong. Rocking, she watched over him as he slept. She moved the chair closer to the bed and took his right hand. Grateful that the ribbon of skin was quiet, she gently squeezed his palm. In his sleep, he tightened his grip, and until the dawn, she would not let him go.

Eyes opened to the setting moon, its failing light falling through the window. Dawn wasn't far off. He felt chilled and realized he was still dressed. Must have just collapsed on the bed. Felt the touch of a hand upon his and saw Aunt Emily, fast asleep, holding him. Movement wakened her.

"Lands sake," she said, "I shouldn't have slept this long. Get up, Conor, times a'wastin.' We're due to meet the Abbot in—she checked the mantle clock in the bedroom—in forty-five minutes. Time for you to get a shower and get dressed." She hustled him out of bed, turned on the hot water and went downstairs to make a quick breakfast.

The mist lay heavy across the land as they retraced their steps from the night before. Down to the river they went, Conor with a full backpack and the Spear of Destiny, now disguised as just a walking stick, in his hand. Aunt Emily led the way. As they crossed the meadow, the two saw the Abbot in his Benedictine habit and cuculla, leaning on his crozier. Even Conor thought he looked otherworldly, like an ancient wizard rising above the mist. The antlered crozier with the Celtic Cross hanging from the points caught Conor's attention.

"Curious about my staff?" said the Abbot, welcoming them.

"It reminds me of something I've seen," said Conor, suddenly uncomfortable about saying anything more.

"Indeed," said the Abbot, who paused for a moment and then continued down a different path of conversation. "I've been busy since you left.

I've procured Walt's boat—have to get rid of that anyway—and we'll use it to get to where we must go."

He reached into a deep pocket and brought out two envelopes. "Here are funds to see you to your destination. And here is all the information, including the confirmation number, for your flight to Shannon, Ireland."

"Ireland!" said Conor. "Why there? Why so far?"

"The next stage of your journey lies there, from the Emerald Isle even to the highlands of Scotland," said Aunt Emily. "There will be people to help you and things you will need to do."

"You can't stay here, Conor," said the Abbot. "We've been through this. I've done what I can to cloud the minds of the townspeople, but, in fact, there will be those who will remember fairly clearly what happened down here by the river, people like Caithness McNabb, and once brought up to speed, Gordon, her son. DIOGENE still exists and the 'dark ones' will still be in danger. Come back as soon as you can, but in the meantime, travel safely. We'll go with you for the first part of the journey."

The three of them got into the boat and pushed off. The Wisconsin gently took them in its grasp and sent them floating down towards the Mississippi. The tiny motor hummed, adding a few horsepower to increase the speed.

"We'll go south to Cassville, where you can pick up the bus again, which will take you to O'Hare to catch your flight. Cassville's far enough away, yet close enough to make swiftly by boat," said the Abbot, standing up now and looking ahead. The mist was thinning, now all three could see through the light fog to the bluffs on each side, their summits touched with the rosy red finger of dawn.

"It's beautiful," said Conor.

"Aye, that it is," said Abbot Malachy. "Look," he said, "we're being watched." He pointed with his crozier.

Conor looked up the bluff and saw standing on a promontory the figure of an old Indian woman and an immense white stag. The woman raised her hand in greeting and the buck bowed its head in recognition.

"You know them?" said Conor.

"Both of us do," said Emily. "They guard the land and its secrets and more, I believe."

A soft, hooting cry was heard and all three looked up to see a white owl floating above them, calling mournfully.

"He misses you already," said the Abbot.

"I'll never understand him," said Conor.

"Perhaps not, but do not judge him too harshly. He carries a burden you do not know."

"Must be pretty bad to keep him exiled here," said Conor.

"It was a long time ago, Malachy," said Emily.

"That it was, but though the sin is forgiven, the consequences remain. He has work to do here, and with Conor gone, will be one of the few bulwarks against the rising tide of evil."

"You expect things to get worse?" asked Conor.

"Absolutely. As out of the way as Tinker's Grove is, you saw for yourself how it acted as a magnet for Drake and how those disposed to the dark, like Cate and her brood, snapped up the opportunity to seize power. These things are happening in our out of the way part of the world. Imagine the world over. What sort of darkness is leeching out into the Light in other communities?"

"And I'm supposed to fight all that?"

"Not alone," said Emily, "but you will bear the greater burden."

Before them, the Wisconsin opened wider and ahead could be seen the mighty Mississippi.

"We'll hug the shore line, but we'll still make excellent time," said the Abbot.

"I've never been down this way before," Conor said, astounded at how awesome the confluence looked. Even in this world, the rivers were huge. He wondered how much more immense and impressive the joining of the rivers would look in the Otherworld.

"A new journey for you, Conor Archer," said Aunt Emily. She smiled at him affectionately. "Now pipe us a tune."

Conor reached back and pulled out the whistle and began playing. Aunt Emily and the Abbot had surprisingly good voices as they sang:

"Speed, bonnie boat,
Like a bird on the wing,
Over the sea to Skye,
Carry the man,
Who is born to be King,
Over the sea to Skye ..."

It seemed to Conor, as he played, that the boat sailed truer and faster. Taps Jeffords had said there was power in the instrument, made as it was from the Tree of the World. Unlike the Spear, which was destructive, this was a power of creation; he could do positive things with it. Sailing along with the rising sun to his left, Conor wondered which he would be, a creator or a destroyer.

EPILOGUE

THE SUN HAD risen and melted the mist. Another warm day, this Feast of All Saints. Jace walked slowly down the Abbey path towards the river. Didn't take him long. He had spent most of the night consoling his parents over the loss of Beth. They didn't even ask the most basic questions. He wondered how the Abbot did it, confusing their minds to the real truth they couldn't possibly handle.

Reaching the Indian mound, he sat underneath the large willow. Peaceful, much more so than last night, he thought. Conor should be long gone by now. The Abbot had told him that Conor was off to Ireland, to finish his training or some such thing. Not that Jace was going to get all hot and bothered about it. Just as happy to see him gone. He knew it was unfair to keep blaming Conor for Beth's death, but it was convenient. Staying mad put the grief to the side, for another day, another time. He couldn't cry for her, not yet.

A girl's giggle startled him out of his doze. Came from over there, in that copse of aspen, he thought. The Morrigan again. Could she never leave him alone? Then he heard her run away, through the weeds and leaves, but she had left something behind. Something very much alive. He could sense it, and it seemed familiar to him. A low chuffing noise reached his ears, and he smiled.

"Don't know how you did it, but you might as well stop hiding and get on out here. Right now."

Guess he would have expected him to leap into his arms, but it didn't happen. Instead, the dog stepped out from the copse of trees and looked at him. Huge. It was huge. Same Labrador shape, same chocolate color, but at least half again the size of the Troubles he knew.

"Come here," he called. The dog moved slowly forward and lay down with his huge head in Jace's lap.

"You're supposed to be dead," he said. "I saw you die last night; dead as a doornail. But you've never been ordinary, have you?"

Dark brown eyes looked somberly up at him.

"No," said another voice, "he is not ordinary, not anymore. Touched by the Otherworld once when young, and then again last night. I took him, for we need him, all of us." The Morrigan in her guise as a beautiful warrior woman strode up the hill and sat herself down by Jace and the dog.

"He fought valiantly," said Jace. The dog whined in pleasure. "But he shouldn't be here. He needs to be by Conor's side. That boy is going to need him."

"Then send him, if you dare. That would mean you care for your once friend still."

"I do care for him," said Jace. "And I regret my words. But even if I saw him now, I couldn't say the right thing. It's not the time. But I don't wish him ill." Turning to Troubles, Jace said, "You should go. Go to Conor. You know the ways of the Otherworld that you can travel in order to find him. You don't belong by my side; you belong by his. Find him, watch over him, protect him and guide him, because I can't. At least not yet. Will you do that for me?"

Into Jace's head came a sound. At first, it seemed to be all raspy growls and whines, but to Jace they formed words, and as he listened they became clearer. "I will," said the dog, "until the time when we can watch over him together, I will guard him alone. I give my word; I give my faithfulness."

"He talks!" exclaimed Jace.

"All living things speak," said the Morrigan, "and you have the wisdom now to hear them, though you are not one of us."

"Go," said Jace. "Find my friend, and keep him from harm."

The dog stood up and licked the face of Jace, then turned and leapt into the river, swimming strongly into the channel. Then he dove, looking for the entry into the waters of the world where all things are connected and all paths lead.

"Thanks," said Jace.

"For what, Champion?" said the Morrigan.

"For keeping Troubles alive. You should have seen him last night. I wouldn't have been able to triumph if it hadn't been for him."

"He deserves to live," said the Morrigan. "As do you. You are so full of sadness, so full of despair. Even in your victory you grieve. How can I still your sorrow?"

"I loved her so much," said Jace. "She was my little sister, and she's gone for good."

"In your grief, your wisdom fades," said the Morrigan. "She lives, you know; she walks in the Summer Country."

"But it will never be the same."

"All things change, and in this world, all things must one day die."

"That sucks."

"It does."

"What can I do?" asked Jace. "I don't even feel like going on."

"You can do nothing until you grieve, my Champion."

"I haven't even shed a tear for her."

"That I can help you with. Here, let me hold you."

He allowed her to cradle him as if he was a child. Her lustrous hair fell round them both and he heard her start keening softly, of battles won and lives lost, of light gained and warriors fallen, of love found and love lost, of family ties and war ravages, of kinfolk sharing and death cleaving. And Jace began to weep, there on the mound, underneath the large willow tree with its golden autumn leaves.

SOURCES

At the *DerryAir.* "Gaelic Music" Selected Poetry of Jessica Powers (London: Sheed and Ward, 1991), p. 77.

Much of the poetry in the novel reflects the style and vocabulary of the Celtic Peoples of Ireland and Scotland. For more on this, check out Alexander Carmichael's translations of the prayers of these people in *Carmina Gaedelica*, available in many different editions.

The legend of Madoc ab Gwynedd is ancient and vague. A Welsh prince, son of Owain Gwynedd, he is believed to have traveled to America in the Middle Ages, sailed its rivers and left a people there, some of whom intermarried with Native Americans. Legends of a tribe of light skinned Native Americans with blue eyes also abound.

And of course—the selchies. The novel describes them as per legend and myth. Anyone who travels Ireland and Scotland, along the coastline, cannot fail but see the seals with their almost human eyes. Curiously attracted to humans, the stories and tales were bound to arise of selchie men and women who came on land to converse and sometimes marry the humans they encountered.

About the Author

E. R. Barr spent his youth wandering around "Conor Country" known better as the southwest corner of the state of Wisconsin. The Mississippi and Wisconsin Rivers and the lands around them, dotted with Indian mounds and filled with stories and legends, fueled his imagination. Not till he started traveling world-wide did he truly begin to see connections between Ireland, Scotland, Wales and the lands where he was born. His forebears came from those ancient nations and settled there in Wisconsin. Always wondering why, he kept searching for answers. A writer on all things Celtic, a follower of Lewis and Tolkien, and a popular speaker on these issues, E. R. Barr makes his home in northwest Illinois. This is his first novel. Find out more about him and Conor's world by checking out the following website:

www.erbarr.com

CPSIA information can be obtained at www.ICGtesting.com
Printed in the USA
LVOW07s2219200114

370261LV00002B/126/P